UNBOUND

SONGS OF CHAOS BOOK TWO

MICHAEL R. MILLER

Contents

From The Author

Thank you for checking out my books – wherever in the world you may be! Whilst this isn't the place to thank everyone who has helped to make this book possible, here I can thank you, the reader, upfront. Without you, there would be no series.

In the past I have asked my US readers to forgive the use of British English. This time around I ask my UK readers to forgive the use of US English. Unfortunately, Amazon only allows one edition per language to be uploaded.

In saying this, I am Scottish and so the odd mistake may still be present in the text as I attempted to write in US English. A botched spelling perhaps or a phrase not often used across the pond. Hopefully this does not affect anyone's enjoyment of the book!

Without further ado, I hope you enjoy Unbound!

P.S. To chat to me and like minded readers join my Discord server here https://discord.gg/C7zEJXgFSc

P.P.S - You can grab two FREE epic fantasy novellas from my worlds by signing up to my mailing list here https://www.michaelrmiller.co.uk/signup

Storm

Reaving River

Northern Tear

Skipta

SKARL EMPIRE

Smidgar

Roaring
Fjord

Groef

Claw
Point

Upsar

FORNHEIM

Brekka

FJARRHAF

Bitter
Bay

Vardguard

Sk
Spe

Stroef

Sunset Sea

Haldask River

Port
Bolca

RISALIA

Drakburg

Red

Wismar

The Crag

WITHERING
WOODS

Toll Pass

Red Rush

Azure Fl

Midbell

Sidastra

FEORLEN

Range

Sable
Spire

Mort Morass

Howling Hills

Versand River

BRENIN

Ruins
Aldus

Laone

The Stretched S

SE

Scalding Sea

JADE

LAKARA

Songs of Chaos

WHITE WILDERNESS

Dead Lands

FALLOW
FRONTIER

White
tch

ine

rost Fangs

Windshear
Hold

Oak Hall

COEDHEN

Grim Gorge

Brown Wash

Bright Wash

FAE FOREST

IRA

Red Rock

Loch Awe

Ruins of
Freiz

DISPUTED
LANDS

The Serpentine

caer
tress

eat Chasm

MITHRAS

Alamut

Squall
Rock

ING SANDS

Negine
Sahra

AHAR

een Way

The Caged
Sea

ngkor

Prologue – Seven Days and Seven Nights

Osric Agravain watched Sidastra burn. At his jailor's behest, he sat upon the scourge risen dragon, hovering at a safe distance from the battle. Osric fought back the only way he could, attempting to defy Sovereign enough that the dragon had to exert some of his will to maintain a grip on him as a helmsman clutches the wheel in a storm.

With an effort, Osric managed to tilt his head down, gazing longingly into the black abyss below.

Let me fall. Let me die.

"You do not wish to die," the charming voice suggested. And Osric remained where he was, a sudden instinct for self-preservation reasserting itself.

He had tried so hard to fight Sovereign back in the throne room when his niece had lunged at him with fire blazing. All he had been able to do was get a few brief words out to the boy, and only because Sovereign had lost focus for a moment, angered and infuriated by the child and his dragon. Osric could feel Sovereign brooding on the scrawny white dragon. Never had he been as fixated on anything in all the miserable years Osric had served him.

Silver lightning flashed, followed by the distant boom of the Storm Lord's power. Osric felt Sovereign's hunger for the white dragon grow ravenous, as though this hatchling were to be his first meal in months. As quickly as it rose, it vanished, replaced by an equally powerful wroth.

The storm dragon was dead. The utter black clouds of his magic dissipated, allowing moonlight to shine through.

Hope kindled in Osric. Had his niece somehow achieved the impossible? Then Sovereign's presence re-entered his mind in full, and Osric's ember of hope guttered out. It was rare for Sovereign to take control of him completely. Such total domination required increased use of the dragon's core. Yet this was the decisive moment in his plans. The fall of Sidastra would mark the beginning of the end. Much of Sovereign's will and strength had been spent on handling the swarm and other matters leading to this moment. Sovereign could not afford to fail.

So it was that Osric Agravain, that once proud warrior, awarded the Gunvaldr's Horns by order of Empress Skadi, and the so-called 'Hero of Feorlen', now curled up inside his own mind.

Afraid. Helpless. Pathetic.

Sovereign took control of his faculties. Osric watched on as though from afar as his body leaned over the scourge dragon's neck, bracing himself. Given the dragon's rage, Osric thought Sovereign would enter the battle himself through Osric, risking an arrow or ballista bolt after all. As Sovereign's will solidified inside Osric, his tether to the queen of the swarm weakened. Without restraint, the queen surged forward. The ghouls and bugs were careless without Sovereign's guidance, running headlong into any trap or defense set against them. Not that it would matter if Sovereign decided to risk himself – well, Osric – in the fray. Talia would stand no chance against him.

His last wish was not to kill Talia himself. Killing one family member had been ruinous enough for his soul.

Just as it seemed they would descend toward the city, there came numerous dragon roars. Much closer. Disembodied as Osric now felt, he could still feel his heart pound.

More dragons were out there. Were they scourge risen, like the beast he rode? Osric couldn't say for certain either way. Sovereign kept his thoughts and plans hidden from him.

Then he felt it, a power greater than any he had felt in his magical senses since bonding with Sovereign. Through his bond, Osric felt fear for the first time.

With a sudden rush of wind, a dragon flew perilously close by. An emerald drake swerved around, flew toward them, its jaws open and green power gathering.

Sovereign's grip on him loosened. The dragon's presence retreated across their twisted bond and Osric came slamming back into control of his own body. The emerald came on, intending to kill the scourge dragon he sat upon.

Osric had no choice. He could not recall the last time he had had a choice. He reviled magic. Magic had placed him in chains, yet if he was going to survive, he required it now. He pulled magic across the bond and channeled Sovereign's mystic motes into a swirling black ball in his hand. It was the first ability Osric had ever learned to use.

Fear.

When the dark power hit the emerald, the dragon cried out in alarm, beholding waking nightmares. It writhed, clawing at its own face as it began to fall through the night, no longer a threat.

Yet the blazing power was still out there along with many other cores: cores dense with power, rich with age and experience. Hundreds of lesser ones besides.

It wasn't the dragon riders. It was an entire Wild Flight.

"Retreat," the charming voice instructed. "Fly to Windshear. Meet me there."

Osric then desired to do this. Flying to Windshear Hold seemed like the exact thing he ought to be doing. A part of him knew it wasn't his idea. Years ago, that part of him had been stronger, more vocal in voicing alternative proposals to the charming voice. Yet now, after so much, after the voice had given him so many solid, sensible ideas, it was almost impossible to argue against it.

The scourge dragon he rode had the same good idea, for it dived, speeding away from the approaching emeralds, and turned to the east.

And so Osric Agravain flew to Windshear Hold. He did not stop for food or rest; his body, as strong as any Lord of the Order, did not require immediate sustenance. The dead dragon needed nothing.

Seven days and seven nights. Over the mountains of the Red Range, over the border between Brenin and Risalia, over the Free City of Athra and east across the fertile plains of the horse masters. Farther still over the disputed lands, turning north to glide over the vastness of the Fae Forest and the city of Coedhen built within its branches. Farther north and east, and still farther, until the winds carried a bite out of the frozen White Wilderness.

Windshear Hold. Once the reigning seat of the dragon riders, in the days before the Fall of Aldunei. It arose from the northeastern fringe of the Fae Forest on a plateau of jagged bedrock. Five towers were connected by five walls, laid out in a perfect pentagon, each one gargantuan in size, palatial at a dragon scale, yet now worn beyond hope of returning to their former glory. Windshear was bleak as the sky and rock surrounding it, a place to breed hard fighters back when scourge incursions were an annual threat.

Sovereign held it these days.

The scourge risen dragon flew into the largest nest of the mystic tower, the only one of the five to receive repairs under Sovereign's stewardship. Osric dismounted, relieved to finally be off the wretched thing.

Three figures wearing cloaks of dragon skin rushed to meet him, bearing platters of food and wine.

"Your magnificence," a female cultist wearing the skin of an ice drake said. "We were told to expect your arrival. The Shroud are at your service." They all bowed to him. Osric dearly wished to spit in their faces and call them Wyrm Cloaks, but that clever, knowing voice at the back of his mind had warned him that would not be wise. They were friends. Allies.

Osric grunted by way of reply to the members of the Shroud and inspected the food they had brought. Two whole chickens, an oval loaf of flame-crusted bread, a pot of steaming beans, and a flagon of wine. Not enough to account for seven days and nights of fasting, but he wasn't a man to complain. He didn't need the charming voice for that.

He tore into the chicken where he stood, knowing the hunger was there, though not feeling the pain of it as a mere man would. He devoured the bird without pleasure, then reached for the flagon of wine and drained half of it in one long pull. It was watered down. Not that a single flagon would have had any effect on him. As he reached for the loaf, the female cultist spoke again.

"We hope the nourishment is to your satisfaction."

"Most so," he found himself saying. "Prepare this nest for Sovereign. He will join me soon."

The cultists all turned to each other, white smiles flashing in delight.

Osric grimaced. He looked inside to the bond with Sovereign. It pulsed as a black hole. Sovereign had closed the connection so Osric could not register the dragon's whereabouts or intentions. Yet during his long journey from Sidastra, Osric had been able to gain glimpses of Sovereign's core and could be sure of one thing.

The battle had weakened him.

Direct possession of Osric and other forces over such a distance had severely drained Sovereign's magic. His core would need tending to, and for that he required Osric.

Another long, strained silence fell as Osric methodically chewed his food and drank the last of the wine. Yearning for his bed, he left the cultists and made for his chambers within the mystic spire.

He would sleep while he could. Sovereign would have him Cleanse and Forge night and day once he arrived. A part of him knew the right thing to do would be to plunge a dagger into his heart, but after failing time and again to accomplish this, when the charming voice had grown cruel and harsh, Osric no longer tried.

His chamber was bare, minimalist and, despite its location near the top of the spire, surprisingly small. Perhaps they had been the quarters of a Lord before the luxuries and indulgences of the modern Order had become the norm. The only personal effects in the room were the iron brackets hammered into the wall to hang his axes and the stand that held his gray cloak. He hung his axes and then caught himself looking to his old cloak for a longing moment before averting his unworthy eyes.

Osric stripped down and got into the cold bed without further thought. Sleep came quickly these days when he was allowed it. Usually, he relished this. When he slept, the connection to Sovereign was weaker. In dreams his mind was free, although he dreaded what his dreams might show him this night.

As darkness took hold, Osric saw his brother Godric before him, tall and proud as ever, only this time he did not back away from Osric but charged at him.

"Was I not enough?" Godric demanded of him. A sword appeared in Godric's hands and he slashed, forcing Osric onto the back foot. Godric drove at him, yelling, "My daughter too?"

"She's not dead," Osric tried to tell him, but his words fell on deaf ears. Somehow his axes were in his hands, and he defended himself against Godric's assault. He parried, then used his momentum to carry him forward under Godric's guard and plant one axe in his brother's chest.

Godric looked at him with the same lost, pleading eyes he had on that day. The greatest military triumph of his career, simultaneously the best and worst day of Osric's life. Usually this was where the nightmare ended, but this time Talia now appeared before him. Loathing burned in her eyes.

"You'll pay for this, uncle."

"I know," said Osric. "I know."

ONE

The Bound

Osric awoke before dawn, as he always did. At once he threw off the covers, letting the cold air bite his skin and wake him. He got out of bed and began doing squats. Interspersed, he dropped and did pushups. Three hundred of each, without a break. With his enhanced body this only caused a light burn, but Osric would not break his habits.

In the same vein, he shaved his face clean of any prickle of hair. He enjoyed the steel brushing against his skin, bringing death so close to the throat but never pressing it in. The way each pass turned his face from rough to smooth, from mess to order. Hot water wasn't needed anymore, not now his skin was tough as hide. When he had finished, he felt one last time for any spots he might have missed. Finding nothing, he placed the razor down, satisfied. A new day truly began with a clean face.

Next, he dressed, cladding himself in warm wools, from trousers to tunic. Unfussy, unflattering clothes. No cloak. The wind in the mountain fortress made cloaks a liability. Moreover, he would wear none other than his gray cloak, the shroud of his free company. The last time he'd worn it had been when he'd traversed the mountains of the Spine on what he'd thought would be his final journey.

After all he'd done, he had made a mockery of it.

At least what he wore was his choice to make. His decision, without interference from Sovereign. For that, the plain wool might well have been fine silks from Ahar.

Armor was unnecessary here at Sovereign's stronghold. Besides, given his toughened skin, it would take something beyond common steel and strength to pierce him. Nor did he need to fear the razor-sharp scythe of a flayer's arm unless Sovereign turned his minions upon him. The riders of Falcaer wore expertly crafted brigandine armor, steel plates bound by tough leather which married protection and movement into one. Lacking a set for himself or anyone with the skill to make it, Osric opted for warmth over cumbersome and unnecessary mail or plate.

Finally, his axes. He took them down from the wall and tested their edge with a finger before honing the blades with a sharpening stone. Every morning he sharpened them. The sound of the stone scraping across the metal was music to him.

Once ready, Osric descended the mystic spire and strode out into the great inner yard of Windshear Hold. Wind battered against the walls of the old keep. A cloudless sky allowed the red dawn to bathe the fortress in ominous light. All was tinged crimson, from the potted grounds of the yard to the roofs of the western storehouses and ancient washer rooms, to the distant forges and workshops by the southeastern walls.

Osric went to stand upon the stone dais on the south side of the yard, where Paragons and Lords would have spoken to gathered riders below. Currently, none of the other occupants of Windshear Hold had mustered for the day.

Osric was early. He was always early.

He stood at ease. Out here, he could at least be alone with his thoughts.

What happens now? he asked himself. If Osric were in Sovereign's place, he would discard him. The benefits Osric offered had been voided by his unmasking in Sidastra. As the dragon had gone to pains to extract him from the throne room and bring him here, he clearly did not intend to dispose of Osric. At least, not right away. Perhaps after he had Cleansed and Forged Sovereign's core back to something resembling its former strength?

Yes, that seemed the likely outcome. Doubtless Sovereign would dispatch him as easily as a common ghoul. But Osric was used to that. People dismissed soldiers the moment they were done using them. And Osric had been a soldier since he'd been a child wrestling with his brother.

As the morning wore on, cloaked members of the Shroud began filing out of the mystic tower and from the great storehouse by the western wall. The storehouse was the nexus of many servant walk-ways and passages under the walls and yard, allowing them to move about without being seen by superiors. Though such hierarchies were blurred here, habits remained.

Four wild dragons emerged from nesting spaces within the mystic tower to join the cultists assembling in the yard. Two blue ice drakes, a black storm dragon, and one red fire drake. Osric knew there were more sworn into Sovereign's service out in the world; there were more dragon riders like Silas Silverstrike too. Doubtless on missions for their new master.

Falcaer must suspect, Osric thought. *Surely too many have turned to go unnoticed.*

There was still strength in the Order, and Sovereign had suffered a blow. Should the Order descend in force upon Windshear Hold, they would take it at a stroke.

As he pondered this, a knot of thorns untangled at his sternum and beat painfully. Sovereign re-opened their connection, and unfiltered thoughts and emotions rushed across from the dragon.

Anger. Impatience. The Elders. A touch of fear. Anger. The white dragon. Hatred.

Osric tried to close himself off from the sudden influx. It was unlike Sovereign to allow such an easy flow over their bond. He was ever sealed off, allowing Osric snippets here and there, and then only by accident when his anger flared or when his attention was focused elsewhere. Now the dragon's mind raced. He seemed flustered and unsure in a way Osric had never known him to be.

If only Falcaer knew, Osric thought grimly.

To the distant north, the dark outline of a great dragon beating its wings came into view. With the connection re-opened, Osric's magical senses came back to him. He could feel the cores of the four dragons in the courtyard, each somewhat weaker than a dragon paired with an Ascendant rider. Truly, the wild dragons developed slower than their kin in the Order.

An air of palpable excitement and anticipation piqued in the yard. It could be felt even though all had gone as still as the grave.

In what seemed no time at all, Sovereign glided over the dilapidated northern walls of Windshear Hold. One of his great wings clipped the fire tower in what Osric suspected was deliberate malice. Fire was ever celebrated as the mightiest type of magic. Old stone and timber crashed down out of sight.

Sovereign's dive steepened so that he landed at the heart of the gathering with a hard impact. Mystics could come in many colors. Sovereign was the sort of red Osric associated with gut wounds on the battlefield; dark, near black-red blood hailing the most long and painful of deaths. The bone ridges along his back were a dirty ivory. They ran down to the end of his tail, which was near twenty feet of lean muscle. While his scales shone with health, the sinew of his wings had the tattered yellow quality of old paper, which perhaps indicated old age or a deep sickness. Yet there was no mistaking from his eyes that he was fully aware, fully present, his mind as sharp as his sword-like talons. There you could see the hatred writhing moment to moment as he looked upon the humans in the yard. In those eyes brown as old, gnarled oak, marbled from bloodshot veins, there could be no mistake. Whenever Osric looked into them, he knew that Sovereign hated Osric more than he, despite all his trying, could ever return to the dragon in kind.

"Hello, worm," Sovereign said in greeting.

Osric said nothing. There had been a time when he spoke back, but the fight had been beaten out of him.

The cultists bowed in every which way, some down on their hands and knees, others bent standing at the waist like unsupported marionettes. Several senior ones raced to greet Sovereign, near tripping over themselves in their haste to bow and bleat and offer him food.

"Even this one's own flesh, if desired," one cultist offered.

It is not your flesh he would take but your mind, Osric thought.

Sovereign ignored them.

"*Loyal friends,*" Sovereign said, casting his thoughts only to Osric and the dragons present, "*we suffered a setback. No matter. The bulk of our enemies remain ignorant of us. Our work continues.*"

So ended Sovereign's rousing speech. He beckoned the four dragons forward. Each lowered their neck flat to the ground before him. Osric heard nothing of what passed between them. After some time, the dragons took flight, each heading in a different direction on their own mission. Then, at last, Sovereign focused his baleful gaze upon Osric again.

"*Are you ready?*" Sovereign asked.

"*Of course,*" Osric replied over their bond.

With pleasantries over, Sovereign took off to make the short journey into the lowest and largest of the dragon nests built into the mystic tower. The cultists remained none the wiser as to what was going on.

"Members of the Shroud," Osric called with a practiced battlefield volume. "I shall be tending to the master's core. You know your orders during this time. Dismissed."

They hurried back to the mystic tower like eager puppies. Osric looked on in disgust. Not an ounce of discipline between them. They lacked equipment and proper drilling. He would have to have a word with the Speaker when she arrived.

For now, he had more pressing duties. He found Sovereign inside the second-floor nest, the only one large enough to house him. If there had once been stalls for multiple dragons, they had rotted over time or else been torn down. Although exposed to the elements on one side, the nest was sheltered from the wind and warm enough that Osric unfastened the collar of his tunic. He sat before the dragon.

"How bad is it?"

"*See for yourself,*" Sovereign said, and then he widened the bond.

The last time Osric had seen the core, it had been countless black steel chains, massive in size and wrapped around thick, ornately carved pillars in a great columned hall.

The difference now was stark. Never had he seen Sovereign's core in such a sorry state. In what now seemed an empty cavern, a rusted chain lay sprawled across the ground. The air was a thick malaise of dust, the ground piled with rubble as though an earthquake had wrought destruction.

As he lingered upon the core, he heard Sovereign's dragon song. Dark, cold, an intense monophonic sound that did not change but remained steadfast and single-minded. A single shrill note ran behind the rest of the somber melody, like a long-drawn-out scream. Hairs prickled on the back of Osric's neck.

A fleeting thought crossed his mind. Was Sovereign weak enough that he might now break free?

Sovereign, of course, anticipated this would cross his mind.

"*Go on then, worm. Do whatever you have the courage to try.*"

Osric's silence spoke volumes.

Sovereign blew out a long exhale of smoke. "*That's what I thought.*"

"Any of the Shroud would be willing to serve you. Why not one of them?"

"*Their devotion is… unsuitable.*"

The dragon bond thumped painfully at that, and Osric fought back a wince. The connection to Sovereign was an ache he hadn't missed. Such a thing formed from coercion and loathing did not sit comfortably in his soul.

"*Your determination is but one of the reasons I selected you,*" Sovereign continued. "*You know the techniques now, and you do them well.*"

Do the job and do it well, Osric thought. The mantra he had sworn by since leaving Sidastra as a younger man. His personal oath.

Sovereign carried on and, as he often did, he tried to coat his poisoned words in honey. "*Anyone might be forced to Cleanse and Forge, but I value your other talents, General.*"

He could refuse. He could just refuse, stand up and walk away. What was the worst that could happen to him now? Death? He had no true life to miss.

"You won't refuse," said the charming voice. *"You don't have it in you to refuse an order from a superior."*

These little nudges were all it took. Even now, he was a soldier following orders through and through.

Do the job and do it well.

"After the strength of your core returns, what do you intend?"

Whatever it was, Osric would ensure the best possible path toward achieving that goal.

"The contingency plan is already underway," Sovereign said.

"You might have told me. Perhaps I could have assisted—"

"Your use is not in controlling the scourge. Your little kingdom was fortunate, but another blow to the western lands will topple the region or else distract the Order long enough for our other task."

"You will strike at Feorlen again?"

"Feorlen, Brenin, Risalia, any of them will do. With luck it will be your wretched homeland."

"Luck?" Osric said with disgust. "Better not to rely on it. Has your grip on the scourge faltered? Your core is weak."

Sovereign glared down at him. *"All the more reason why you will Cleanse and Forge day and night."*

Osric inclined his head and let the matter slide. Sovereign had never revealed how he held sway over the scourge and clearly wasn't going to change that policy.

"What is this other task you speak of?"

"We will gather defective dragon eggs and hatch them here. Those hatchlings worthy of my tutelage shall join me."

Osric nodded. "This is because of the white dragon?"

"Ash holds a power never seen before," Sovereign said. It was a remark of the begrudging respect Sovereign had for the young dragon that he used his name. *"His notes were of the moon and stars. His light is destructive to the scourge."*

"Surely one dragon cannot make such a difference?"

"Not at their current rank, but if they should be allowed to grow in power—"

"You fear needlessly," Osric said. "The Paragons will not accept a blind dragon and a role breaker into their ranks. The pair will go untrained."

"There is a greater worry than the Paragons. The Life Elder may take them under his guidance. Worse, the Elder must now know that such eggs hold greater potential than we ever considered."

"Assuming this Elder didn't kill Ash himself."

"Other flights might have, but not this one. Of the Elders, the Life Elder is the one who most regrets the scourge. Ash is the first real counter weapon to arise. The Elder will not discard eggs from his flight again. I am certain of it. In time there may be many lunar dragons roaming this world."

Osric saw Sovereign's dilemma in this. Before the white dragon and the Emerald Flight's involvement, Sovereign could have attempted incursion after incursion until he succeeded in his plans to wipe humanity out. Now, given time, more dragons could appear with lunar powers or other types either from a willing Order or under the wings of the Life Elder. Unless the other Wild Flights of fire, ice, mystic, and storm could be swayed to his cause, Sovereign would lose in the long term.

He had resources. Riders and some wild dragons who he had brought into the fold quietly over the long years. And he had the scourge itself. Presently, the one thing he lacked was time.

"If you are to succeed, then we must escalate quickly," Osric said. "Taking eggs is only a short-term solution. You cannot take them all."

"Little can be achieved before I recover. While I am here, we will gather as many eggs as we can."

"And what if the Life Elder himself comes for you?"

"He has been cowardly and cautious until now. He will not act alone. As for the others..." For the first time, Sovereign appeared to consider. The sides of his mouth twitched. *"They created the scourge to rid the world of your kind. They will understand my purpose."*

Osric had doubts about that. If Sovereign was so confident that the other Elders would support him, why hadn't he sought their aid or approval? His grip on the scourge was real but not total. Wild dragons still fought the bugs and the blight still infected them just as much as any human, plant, or animal.

Yet having seen Sovereign's depleted core, Osric worried events may have slipped out of the dragon's control. Still sitting cross-legged on the floor, Osric placed his hands upon his knees, as though bracing himself.

"Be truthful with me now. If I am to advise you and carry out your objectives, I must know. How strong is your hold over the scourge?"

Sovereign lowered his snout to look Osric right in the eye. The bond widened and Sovereign's presence rushed across it, filling Osric's mind, pushing him out. The next thing Osric knew, he was on his feet, holding one of his axes against his own throat.

"I have control where it matters."

He let go. Osric came rushing back into control of his body and placed the axe through the leather loop on his belt. An easy act of domination was not an answer to his question, but Osric knew the dragon well enough to know that such a display meant he was concerned. He still held control of the scourge, however he had achieved it, but it must be slipping.

Sitting back down, Osric moved onto the next issue he foresaw. "What of the riders? My niece was alive at the end of the battle. She will have rejoined their ranks and will be telling anyone who listens about me."

"The riders could present a problem," Sovereign conceded. The flares and ridges along his body bristled. *"It all depends on the timing and whether the Paragons have the spine to act. We have our agents across the order halls. For now, we wait and listen. Should the opportunities arise, we will turn more and destabilize where we can."*

Osric nodded. The old plan had involved much the same, using the backdrop of a fallen Feorlen and the enormous swarm that would have risen in its wake as the perfect time to wreak havoc on the Order both from within and without. So long as the riders of Falcaer remained numerous, strong, and united, Sovereign would not succeed. Feorlen's loss alone may not have destroyed the world, but in dealing with an out-of-control incursion, the Order would have been crippled for a generation. Then they would have been open to further turncloaks, or else a direct assault.

"I have asked this before, and I feel compelled to ask again—"

"*I will not reveal the dragons or riders in my service,*" Sovereign said. "*You may yet prove of use in the field. Were you to be captured, and I too weak, too distant or too distracted to guide the knife into your heart—*"

"Failing to tell me about Silas did not help."

Sovereign's nostrils flared. He bared his teeth. "*You would be wise not to question my judgment. Not when you failed me!*"

Osric became gripped in a sudden, torturous pain. His chest felt as though claws raked through his soul and flesh. It ended as abruptly as it came on. This time he flinched. Gulped. Despite needing to maintain a level head for Cleansing and Forging, his right hand trembled, curling in and out of a fist.

"The situation on the ground changed," Osric said through gritted teeth. "I had to adapt. I couldn't just kill the boy."

"*That is not the failure I speak of, kin-slayer.*"

Osric saw again, as if a phantom were before him, his brother collapsing at his feet, his eyes going cold.

"You forced me to do that."

Sovereign croaked a laugh. A little more smoke escaped his nostrils.

"Have I amused you?"

"*You are so like the others that came before you. You tell yourself I force you to do things. If that makes it easier, so be it.*"

"Who would willingly kill their own brother?"

"*Who indeed, Osric Agravain?*"

Lies. All of it lies. Sovereign couldn't help but torment him at every turn. Their bond was one of hate, after all. Osric waved the ghost of his brother away as though it were really smoke in the air before him. Then he fought to center himself for the meditations ahead. With his left hand, he held the right one steady. Once calm, he shifted to sit cross-legged and closed his eyes.

Sovereign growled in satisfaction. "*Begin.*"

TWO

Good Hunting

The young buck lowered its head over the mushrooms on the forest floor. At a safe distance, Holt's heart thumped embarrassingly hard. Those mushrooms had been a good find. He wanted to eat them, but he knew deer favored them. And they needed the bait. Indeed, they may have learned that lesson from this very buck four days ago.

He recognized its scent and salivated at the thought of its sweet meat upon his tongue and the warmth of its blood in his stomach—

No. No, those were Ash's feelings.

Holt didn't shake his head to clear it for fear of making a sudden movement. Instead, he focused on his breathing, as though he were Cleansing. This allowed him to observe Ash's sensations flit across their bond without consuming him.

Ash sat uncannily still. Pressed against the ground with his wings tucked in hard to his sides and his tail wrapped up underneath him, he appeared less than half his true size.

Across the moonlit glade, the deer jerked its head up.

Fear surged from Ash. The buck would bolt. Holt felt it come on like a fierce gale. He tried to observe the sensation rather than bathe in it, but found his mental defensives swept aside. It had become an increasing issue the more desperate Ash became.

The buck decided nothing was out there after all and settled back into its meal.

Feeling relief wash through him, Holt spoke across the dragon bond so as not to utter a sound. *"We'll get it. Remember, rise and make one smooth shot."*

Clumsily chasing after the buck last time had proved even an Ascendant with an enhanced body could not outrun such an animal in full flight. Nor could Ash chase it any quicker on the ground. Flying gave them the edge in terms of speed, but diving through the canopy had proved more dangerous to themselves than their prey.

"This one can't escape," Ash said, his voice a plea rather than curt.

A curling knot of pain from Ash's empty stomach reached Holt. He fought back the desire to wince.

"I'll try too," Holt said. He began prepping a Lunar Shock, drawing on power from Ash's core and sending motes of magic down his left arm.

"On three. One."

He gathered the lunar motes in his palm.

"Two."

The beginnings of his Lunar Shock formed. A flash of bright light in otherwise dark woodland. Ash summoned white light to gather at his own mouth. Holt knew their mistake at once, yet everything carried on as though to mock him.

The buck twisted its head toward him. Its tail rose. Its body went taut.

"Three."

Ash rose and unleashed a beam of white light. The buck sprang into a run, swerving away from Ash's attack and bounding off between the trees at a pace to shame a flayer of the scourge. Holt's own Lunar Shock flew uselessly off to the right as the deer disappeared in a matter of seconds. He could still hardly believe the buck's speed, but then again, only the quickest deer which had outrun dragons and flayers would have survived in past generations. Holt's appreciation for the skills of huntsmen swelled.

Ash groaned and flopped to the ground, limbs splayed, defeated by a deer where a Storm Lord, a Scourge Queen and a band of dragon-killing cultists had not succeeded.

Holt didn't feel like poking fun. Ash hadn't eaten properly in five days, which would have put anyone on edge, never mind a still ravenous young dragon. Even his own supplies from Sidastra were beginning to run thinner than he had planned for. He'd eaten too much on their first days, enjoying the adventure with his dragon without thinking heavily about the coming days. Without Brode's guiding hand, their inexperience showed.

Holt walked up to Ash and attempted to sit down. The attempt failed because Brode's enormous sword caught against the ground. He hung it from his waist because he could barely draw it from his back, but, dangling from his hip, its size was cumbersome. For now, he unbuckled the belt and put the scabbard down.

Taking up a cross-legged position by Ash's head, Holt began to stroke the dragon down his long neck. "Next time. We'll get him next time."

"You said that before," Ash said glumly. He blew air through his nose, throwing up leaves and small twigs. *"How are we going to do all the things we set out for if we can't even catch our dinner?"*

"We'll figure out a way," Holt said. "Just as we'll figure out the rest. We've got to," he added somewhat lamely.

Still, he was right. They would just have to figure things out or else starve in the short term and face terrible doom in the long run. Giving up wasn't an option in either scenario.

There had always been one option so far as feeding Ash was concerned, one Holt had hoped to avoid if they could help it.

"If we leave the forest and travel east, we'll probably come across a farm sooner or later."

"You want us to steal?"

"If it comes to it," Holt said, though he felt a squirm in his conscience all the same. "Besides," he said, brightening, "Talia gave us some money. I can leave coins behind. So it wouldn't exactly be stealing. But if it ever came to it, I'd do it, coins or no. Wouldn't you?"

Ash huffed again through his nostrils. *"To eat, yes."*

Holt nodded and stroked the dragon's neck again. "There isn't much I wouldn't do for you. Nicking a sheep would be the light end of things."

"Same, boy. But if we can't manage this on our own—"

"We'll figure it out," Holt insisted. "You'll feel better once we've found you something to eat. Take it as a compliment. All the wildlife is terrified of you." He stood, determined to keep them moving rather than sitting and wallowing.

The key to the box of Brode's ashes tinkled on the chain around his neck. Absentmindedly he touched it, not wishing to let his own worries about their quests rise high enough to pass across to Ash.

Right now, Holt had to be the strong one.

He strapped Brode's sword back on, then moved to collect his pack from several trees behind. Backtracking, he trudged past Ash and carried on to where the deer had been eating those good mushrooms. To his delight, some of the patch remained untouched. He set his pack down again, took out a linen wrap that had once held oatcakes and began to pick the mushrooms.

Knowing how hungry Ash was, Holt suppressed his own enthu-siasm at the find. Morel mushrooms were ugly things – cone-shaped and yellow-brown with pitted wavy flesh – yet tasted incredible when cooked. Few types of mushrooms were as meaty.

Ash padded over to his side while he worked. Holt turned the last of the morels over in his hand, then flicked it over to Ash in desperation.

"Give it a go."

Ash sniffed warily at the mushroom, gave it a tentative lick, groaned, then ate it. He groaned louder in displeasure and wrung his head, spitting, as though Holt had fed him poison.

Disappointed, Holt secured the bundled morels into his pack then shouldered it. At least its weight felt like nothing to him.

He started walking east.

"I know we don't want to resort to stealing a sheep, but to be on the safe side we should make for the edge of the forest. I think that will take us into Brenin. Or maybe Risalia. One of the two."

Holt's sense of geography was poor to say the least. A lifetime spent in one town had hardly prepared him for such a trip. The maps they had were useful on a large scale but day to day it was impossible to tell exactly where they were.

After parting from Talia and Pyra, they had flown east toward the mountains of the Red Range. They had enjoyed a few days at higher elevations, flying over mountaintops and soaring carefree through the valleys that Feorlen, Risalia, and Brenin frequently fought over. Yet it was east they had to go, and so they descended from the Red Range into the unnamed sprawling woodland which hugged the eastern side of the mountains.

Unlike the Withering Woods in Feorlen, these wildlands seemed untouched by the blight. As spring headed toward summer, the warmer, longer days made this almost a pleasant place to be. Quiet. Isolated. Just he and Ash together, briefly relieved of the immense burdens placed upon them.

In the eyes of the Order, they were little better than rogues, and he was a banished, nameless, roleless sixteen-year-old to everyone else. Out here, in these woods, they might as well be kings. Holt might have lingered in these hinterlands between the three kingdoms for longer were it not for Ash's current plight.

Ash walked slowly beside him, his breath labored and his tail dragging behind him. Fresh worry and guilt rose in Holt, and something Brode once told him came to mind. No one is truly free, not even a rider. Everyone has their duties, their responsibilities, their loved ones. To be truly free meant to be alone from everyone and everything; to be truly free would mean Holt would not be with Ash, and he would rather die than face that reality.

"Perhaps I should have asked Brode to teach me archery rather than swordcraft," Holt mused. "I could hunt better then. Bright light is a bit of a giveaway."

Ash said nothing.

Their footsteps tread soft on the earth, the stillness of the night broken only by the occasional hoot of a distant owl or the rustle of leaves.

To fill the silence, Holt began voicing his thoughts. "How do you think we'll know when we've found Erdra's grave? Brode only made mention of 'some forsaken hill along the road east of Athra', which isn't much to go on."

"If we do find it, I might hear the notes of her song," Ash said. *"They live still in the sword."*

Holt looked at the giant green scabbard at his waist. The Life Elder and even the mysterious Rake had said something similar about hearing echoes of a dragon song from Brode. A part of Brode's dragon, Erdra, had gone into forging this blade and into Brode, lingering after all this time. Dragon songs were still mysterious to Holt. He could not sense them as dragons could and only occasionally heard Ash's own song.

"I'll take your word for it," Holt said.

"If we ever find the place," Ash said rather darkly. *"Just like if we can find another Wild Flight, with even fewer directions to go on. How are we going to do that?"*

Holt understood that Ash's mood emanated from his empty stomach, but the dragon had a point. They had set out in a rush of emotion, high from victory and purpose bestowed on them by the Life Elder. Now the true extent and vagueness of the task at hand had settled in, Holt worried that the whole thing was laughable.

"We'll find a way."

Ash growled. *"I do not understand why the Life Elder could not have come with us, if finding his brothers and sisters is so important."*

Holt considered his response. What could he say?

"Do you remember what Rake said, about adversity making us stronger?"

"I do."

"Well, maybe that's what this is. Rake could have helped us, but if he had, our bond wouldn't have grown as fast as it did, and I wouldn't have been an Ascendant for the battle. So maybe... maybe it's something like that," he added anti-climactically. "I'm sure the Life Elder did it for a good reason."

"The Elders also created the scourge," Ash said. *"They can make mistakes and their mistakes will be all the greater for their power."*

This knocked Holt's optimism. He was trying to stay bright and strong for Ash, but he doubted the dragon would rally until he was fed.

"The Life Elder also said his brothers and sisters parted ways in bad blood after their greatest mistake," Holt said. "They want nothing to do with each other, especially since it was the Life Elder and the Mystic Elder who pushed toward the creation of the scourge. If we're going to convince them of anything, we'll need to be as strong as we can. We know what most dragons are like."

"That is true," Ash said, sullen as ever. *"Except,"* he added on a lighter note, *"except for Master Rake?"*

"He's definitely not like the others," Holt said, but that was all he was willing to commit to for now. Rake had saved their lives, and his decision to send Brode's body to the Life Elder had helped spur the Elder to bring his emerald dragons to Sidastra. However, Rake clearly had his own goals and motives. And, like them, he stood apart from the Order. From everything. "But we should still be cautious. Just because we're outsiders doesn't mean we can blindly trust everyone else who is."

"You sound like Talia now."

"I'll take that as a compliment. It wouldn't hurt to consider what Talia would do from time to time."

Holt yawned, a tiredness creeping upon him. He realized he hadn't slept in almost two days, Cleansing and Forging Ash's core at nights. While his rider body could take it, it would be unwise to push himself too often. Back at the Crag, the riders had kept a strict daily routine, which included sleep.

He yawned again, longer this time. And after walking for an indeterminate amount of time, his vision began to drift in and out of focus. He blinked fiercely and kept going until Ash padded out into his path to stop him.

"You need rest, boy."

"I'm fine," Holt said thickly through another yawn. "We need to find you—"

"We won't tonight," said Ash. *"It's like you said, everything here is too afraid of me to come close. We'll have to leave the woods, but not tonight."*

"I should Cleanse your core," Holt said groggily. He put his pack down, unstrapped his sword belt, and sat cross-legged again. When he closed his eyes and reached over the bond to tap Ash's core, white light seared harshly in his inner eye. Then it faded, blotting out he felt himself falling deeper and deeper into a soothing darkness...

Something jostled him. Holt opened his eyes with a snap and a gasp. Ash's snout was right in front of him.

"You're too tired. One night's work won't matter."

Holt swayed forward and placed an arm over the dragon. "Every night counts."

'Help the others.' His father's parting wish played over in his mind.

"We have to be strong, Ash."

"And we will be. In time. Sleep, Holt."

Holt nodded and turned bleary-eyed to search for his sleeping roll. He unstrapped it from the top of his pack and yanked it unceremoniously over a patch of reasonably dry, flat earth. It scrunched up at the end, but before Holt could smooth it out Ash delicately took the end of the fabric between his teeth and pulled it out flat for him.

"Thanks," Holt said, getting into his cold bed fully clothed. "Couldn't do this without you," he mumbled. Ash curled up beside him, their bond beating gentle and warm as, at last, he fell to sleep.

Holt awoke in a painful blaze of sound and light. Something thumped the ground nearby and sunlight beat down on him through a gap in the branches. Was that why he felt so hot? He scrambled out of his sleeping roll, kicking it free before realizing the heat was coming from inside him. The dragon bond pounded.

For a second, Holt thought they were under attack, but then he saw Ash not far off, hunched down, tail sweeping back and forth across the ground. Happiness spiked across the bond with each hard beat.

Though Holt's mouth was dry, he felt a touch of something warm and coppery upon it. Fighting Ash's sensations away, Holt got up and approached. A rabbit's foot poked out from under Ash's right talon. This seemed to be a spare, for he was still in the middle of devouring another rabbit.

"How did you find them?" Holt asked.

"They came out of a tunnel," Ash said. His teeth crunched through bone even as he spoke telepathically to Holt. The sound was more off-putting than Holt had been prepared for. He had always prepared meat for Ash before now. Never had he seen Ash so... bestial.

"Do you want me to cook the second—"

"No," Ash said, sounding firm as he swallowed.

"Alright then," Holt said, turning away from the savagery. He rubbed at his eyes. The sun seemed to be approaching its apex; it was nearly midday. He'd overslept by a long way. With a good portion of the morning already gone, they would have to get moving soon to make the most of the daylight for traveling. Then he could Cleanse and Forge tonight to make up for yesterday. The only other option was to sleep much earlier tonight to try and reset his sleep pattern, but he didn't like the idea of missing two nights of meditation in a row.

Another loud crack came from behind as Ash ate. Holt felt a little sick and tried to suppress it so Ash wouldn't feel it. At least he had found something to eat, and so easily in the end.

"Nice to have a little bit of luck," Holt said, risking turning around as the sound of chewing subsided. He found Ash licking his talons, his feet, and his scales to clean the blood from them. Then Holt spotted the entrance to the rabbit warren. A hole underneath a gnarled tree. It struck him as odd that the rabbits would emerge at all, especially with Ash present. "Could you sense them below us last night?"

"I only heard them as they were heading up the tunnel. Their hearts beat as fast as their paws. They must have been running in fright. When they saw me, they froze, and their hearts stopped straight away."

"You scared them to death?"

"I think so." Ash bared his razor teeth for a moment as he licked them clean. Holt tried to imagine how Ash must look to a smaller animal, large and milk white, with eyes hidden behind a ragged strip of dark cloth. Holt judged that to be the most menacing thing about him, trying to look at it objectively. There was something alien in not seeing another creature's eyes – in not being able to see their true feelings or intentions.

Yet to Holt, Ash would always be the tiny hatchling who had curled up on his lap, who had been frightened and needed him. And Holt knew that as large as Ash was to other animals, for a dragon he was on the runty side. Their short food supplies had not helped with the dragon's weight. He looked scraggy as ever.

Ash finished cleaning himself and seemed to sense Holt was staring at him. *"Are you hungry, boy? I should have saved one of them."*

"Don't be silly. You needed them both. You really needed a dozen."

Ash got up on his four legs then and, in the wake of his meal, stretched luxuriously. From tail to snout, he must have been close to twenty feet long, but about a good half of that length was his tail. He shook as though ridding himself of water, then settled again. Not being fully stretched out, he seemed to shrink back to what Holt considered his 'normal' size.

Just as it seemed Ash might say something, he suddenly braced himself, wings arcing and tail swishing threateningly across the ground.

Holt's hand went to the hilt of Brode's sword. "What is it?"

"He's near," Ash said. He bounded off without another word, heading east as fast as the forest floor would allow him.

"Who's near?" Holt asked, sending the question telepathically. In response, he received an impression of the young buck they had been ineptly hunting. *"Dammit, Ash,"* Holt said. *"You'll scare him off again."*

Scrambling, Holt tidied up his sleeping roll, strapped it onto his pack, hoisted it over his shoulder, and ran after Ash. Out of sight, Ash roared. Holt had learned to read what his roars meant. This one was of anger but tinged with irritation. He must have scared the deer off again and small wonder.

The moment Holt caught up, he could tell something was wrong. Ash prowled back and forth as though readying himself for a territorial duel. Some way off was the deer alright, though it lay flat on its side. Dead. An arrow protruded from its flank.

"A hunter?" Holt said needlessly. "Where?"

"He's hiding behind that tree with the flowers in front of it. I could have heard his heartbeat from Sidastra."

"You'll have scared him half to death as well," Holt said, finding the tree with the flowers before it and marveling again at Ash's sense of smell and hearing.

"Hello?" he called out. "This dragon's name is Ash. He's not a wild dragon. He won't hurt you."

"He took our kill, boy."

"And we'll get it," Holt said so only Ash would hear. He didn't like Ash's implication. A bit of hunger and hunting definitely brought out the 'dragon' in him.

"Hello there?" he called again. If it came to it, he'd run over. The hunter wouldn't be able to outrun him, but he'd rather it not come to that. He was sure the man would understand him, at least.

A common tongue persisted in the provinces of the ancient Aldunei Republic even after its collapse. Whether they were in Brenin or Risalia, they were still well within the Republic's old boundaries.

"He's coming," Ash said.

Sure enough, from out behind the tree with the flowers in front of it stepped a tall, lean man holding a large hunting bow above his head in surrender.

"Be nice," Holt said as he stepped forward to meet the hunter.

"So long as he's nice," said Ash.

"A foul mood doesn't suit you," Holt told him, and then they reached the fallen deer which lay between themselves and the hunter.

"Mr. Hunter," he began, adopting his polite servant tone, "my name is Holt Cook. This is my dragon, Ash. We mean you no harm."

"Euh, a cook?" the hunter said in a nasally voice. His face was fear and confusion both. He looked from Holt to Ash, back to Holt, and then to the deer. Any number of things must have raced through his mind as to why he had found a cook so far from a kitchen with a dragon in tow.

"That's right," Holt said, extending his hand for the man to shake. "And I'd like to buy your kill from you."

"Buy it?" the hunter said, still in mild shock. Then everything seemed to fall into place. He took stock of Holt, the giant sword at his waist, the large white dragon. Going bug-eyed, he inclined his head in a bob of courtesy. "Oh, no, Honored Rider, I could not, no. The deer, it is yours."

It took Holt a second to wrap his head around the way the man spoke. Although it was the common tongue, the man's accent was far removed from anything he had heard in Feorlen. Well, far from anything he had heard in western Feorlen and specifically the Crag. There had been a rider apiece from Brenin and Risalia at the Crag, though he had had little to do with them and couldn't say for sure which voice belonged to which region.

The hunter stepped back to observe the respectful ten feet Holt used to employ. "It is yours. Take it."

"You should be paid," Holt said again. He rummaged for the bag of coins Talia had given him. The bag jingled as he pulled out ten silver pieces, much to the astonishment of the huntsman, as though worried Holt were playing some trick on him. "Dragon riders are to pay for their wares now."

It only struck him as he said it that such a law had been passed in Feorlen by King Leofric, Talia's deceased brother, but perhaps not in this land.

Fresh confusion split the huntsman's face. "I'm sorry? I do not understand..."

"Which kingdom are we in?"

"Brenin."

Holt searched his mind for the name of the King of Brenin, but it eluded him. Much about Brenin eluded him, other than knowing it was where Talia's mother was from – and he knew that only because she had told him. Talia's uncle, her mother's brother, was the king in these lands, but that knowledge did him little good.

Perhaps in light of Holt's clear ignorance, the hunter relaxed, the balance of knowledge and power shifting ever so slightly. "You are not from Sable Spire?"

Sable Spire? That rang a bell. It was the Order Hall in Brenin.

Holt considered whether to lie, then decided there was no point and opted for the direct truth.

"No. I'm not part of the dragon riders here. I'm from Feorlen."

The hunter nodded, his eyes widening in newfound understanding. "Ah, yes, your voice... euh, but you said your name is Cook?"

"It was—it is," he corrected. "Listen, in Feorlen, the riders must pay at least cost for anything they take. So please, Mr. Hunter," he added, handing out the coins, "take it."

The huntsman stepped forward and hastily counted the coins by dabbing a finger over each one. The coins were stamped with the face of Godric Agravain. Holt hoped they would be of worth to the man here in Brenin. They must have been, for he pushed three slightly aside and took the remaining seven.

"Thank you, Honored Rider. Enjoy, enjoy," he said, bowing again and sweeping backward.

Ash growled then. The hunter froze and Holt turned sharply upon his dragon, fearing he was about to do something stupid. But the growl morphed into a loving rumble, much more like his usual self. Mr. Hunter's eyes seemed to pop in amazement and Holt guessed Ash was speaking to him. This suspicion was confirmed when the huntsman raised a shaking hand and Ash stepped lightly forward, pressing his snout into the man's palm.

The huntsman let out a laugh of relief and wonder. He looked at Holt again. "A strange place, Feorlen. Very strange." Then, seeming much more cheerful and no longer afraid, he shouldered his bow and took his leave, seven silver coins richer for the encounter.

Ash padded back over.

"What did you say to him?" Holt asked.

"I thanked him for doing what we could not. That I was hungry, and that he had helped me."

Holt gave him a playful shove. "You love anyone who feeds you."

Feeling significantly better than he had in days, Holt set about getting out the equipment he would need for the job at hand. Knives, salt to preserve the spare meat, his pan, the remainder of his butter, and the wonderful morel mushrooms.

For the rest of that day, at least, the road ahead seemed a lot less bleak.

THREE

New Threats

"Arms up, Your Majesty."

Talia raised her arms, and the blacksmith wrapped twine under her armpits to take the measure of her chest. She wore a black gambeson, which would act as a layer between her and the planned brigandine armor, so the measurement would be accurate.

They were in her office within the palace. A run-down room, in truth, with old furniture and tattered azure rugs and drapes.

"Take a deep breath in for me, if you please," said the smith. Talia did so. Her lungs expanded, and she felt the smith's twine give another inch.

The smith murmured the measurement to himself, noted it on his sheet of parchment, then returned and placed the twine at the base of her neck, running it down to her belly button to measure the 'trunk' of the armor.

"Would her Majesty not prefer a suit of plate instead?"

"It must be brigandine," Talia said. "That is the armor of the riders. Our bodies are too strong and flexible for full plate. That's why we wear no armor on our legs."

"As you say, Your Majesty. And arms down, if you please."

He measured her from neck to shoulder, from shoulder to elbow, and from elbow to wrist, as well as the circumference of her tensed biceps.

"Feet together, now."

She placed her feet together, and the smith took a measurement of her waist. After taking the measurements of her back, he gathered his notes.

"When can I expect it?" Talia asked.

"I shall need at least three weeks, Your Majesty. Rest assured it will be my sole focus."

"Thank you, Mr. Smith. I most look forward to seeing your work."

He bowed and retreated out of the room.

Standing alone in the office, she thought it too large a space for just one person. Perhaps because her desk was smaller than the over-sized drinks table at the center of the room. Glass bottles containing various levels of liquid were squashed onto three shelves. She had forgotten how fond her father had been of his drink. The place had been even more disheveled and in need of cleaning when she had first entered it. Leofric had worked in here too, her councilors told her, leaving the state of the place a poor indictment on his brief reign.

Pleased to have finally commissioned a new set of rider armor, Talia returned to her desk in higher spirits than she had been of late. The feeling vanished the moment she sat down and stared at the stack of papers. She swore the pile had grown, despite the fact no one else other than the smith had entered. Setting the stack on fire crossed her mind. That would have been Pyra's solution. Yet, while cathartic, burning the reports would not be a queenly act. Better to tackle the papers and attempt to bring some order to the chaos.

Talia reached for the next sheet. A strand of her long red hair fell across her eyes, and she brushed it back behind her ear as she began to read.

This news came from the port city of Bolca to the north. According to the report, trade from the Bitter Bay had not been impacted by the incursion. However, an estimated six hundred and seventy citizens had found passage out of Feorlen during the incursion, seeking safety on ships bound for Skarl territory, for Fornheim, and even for Risalia.

Six hundred people slipping out of the kingdom under Ealdor Odilo's nose was a problem, even if he skipped over it breezily. Perhaps she could take him aside when he arrived for the coronation and ask him to explain in person. Or would that be too aggressive?

Back at the Crag, Master Mirk, Commander Denna, and other senior riders were blunt in pointing out her errors. Alas, the court of the realm was a far cry from the Crag. She had little concept of how she should proceed on such matters with her Ealdors, whom she needed on her side.

She would have to do something though. The Master of Roles was drowning in a flood of census reports from Sidastra and its environs alone. The little Talia had gleaned so far had been bleak. The loss of six hundred people from the north would come as ill news with so many roles to be refilled or reallocated in the wake of the incursion.

Setting the report onto her 'read' pile, Talia sat upright and stretched, feeling a taut tension in her body. Her rider's blade lay propped up against the desk, its crimson scabbard and hilt striking against the blue décor of the room. She yearned for a proper sparring session. No one in the city could give her a worthy match, never mind train her.

Her bond with Pyra – beating dully in a manner that disapproved of her inactivity – picked up suddenly.

"Something wrong, girl?" Talia asked over their bond.

"Nothing," Pyra said. *"I'm going to see the emeralds."*

Again? Talia thought. She could hardly blame Pyra. With her rider stuck inside trying to be a queen, no missions to go on, and no senior rider to train them, Pyra had little else to do.

Talia got the impression Pyra was already halfway across the lake. Speaking across the distance was already a strain.

"I'll see you after sundown to Cleanse and Forge," Talia managed to say before the distance between them grew too great.

Pyra did not answer. She must have flown out of range.

Talia slumped in her chair, then she shook her head, rallied, and got back to the task at hand. After two more papers, a bustle arose outside her office, a common occurrence here at the heart of the

palace. Talia ignored it as she might when meditating. With her training, it was easy to focus instead on the grain of the paper between her
fingers, the musty smell of the old wood and fabrics, and even on the
burning sting of alcohol wafting from the center of the room.

It was only when the door swung in without so much as a knock
that Talia took notice. She was halfway to her feet to reprimand the
intruder when she froze.

"Mother?"

Felice Agravain, formerly Felice Valois, stood in the doorway.
Though just shy of her fortieth year, Felice still held an arresting quality
in which youthful looks had matured into a stately, dignified beauty.
Her hair mirrored Talia's own color, though it was shorter and ornately
braided. She wore a surcoat – opened at the top in a tasteful fashion –
and a trailing skirt, both made of silk and both the perfect green to
complement her hair. She also carried an old, compact wooden box.

"Talia, my darling," her mother said, her Brenin accent diluted due
to prolonged absence from her native land.

Talia abandoned any sense of restraint and leaped over her desk
from a standing start. Landing halfway across the room, she bounded
in Ascendant-powered strides to meet her mother. Felice let out a cry
of shock and delight, unable to return Talia's embrace as she clutched
the box now wedged between them.

"Someone might have told me you had arrived!"

"I wanted to surprise you," Felice said. "Oh, that's a bit hard,
sweetling."

"Sorry," Talia said, letting go. Her mother breathed a sigh of relief.
"How are you? Was anyone hurt at Beordan? I've just read a report
from Bolca that said the scourge didn't harry the north badly. Is
there—"

But Felice raised a hand to interrupt her. She then curtsied and
said in a stiff, formal voice, "Your Majesty."

"Mother," Talia said, half exasperated. "You don't need to—"

"Perhaps you might first invite me to sit?" Felice said. "You haven't
forgotten your etiquette, have you?"

Caught off guard, Talia muttered, "Er, no. Please, mother, won't you sit with me?" She waved toward the numerous sofas, loungers, and plush stools surrounding the drinks table. As an afterthought, she added, "Would you care for a drink?"

"A brandy wouldn't go amiss," Felice said. "Godric had one I liked kept in stock. I can find it." She set the box down upon the tabletop and began rummaging among the bottles below. Emblazoned in gold upon the box was the royal sigil of Feorlen: two crossed swords encircled by a crown.

Talia spun the box around to face her. She had a hunch about what would be inside and her stomach squirmed at the thought of it. A crown would make it all too real.

Felice pulled out a bottle, found a glass, and poured herself two fingers' worth of the dark amber liquid.

"Won't you join me?"

"It won't have an effect on me," Talia said. "Not unless I drank the whole bottle and then some."

"I didn't realize the only point of drink was to get drunk." She took a hearty sip of her brandy. "Your Ealdors may take offense if you don't drink with them."

Talia pursed her lips. Minutes after their reunion, her mother was already on her case.

"Riders generally don't drink," Talia said. "We need to keep a clear head."

Felice swirled her glass.

"For our meditations," Talia continued, "never mind if we have to fight."

"You're not a rider anymore," Felice said in a calculated manner. Her eyes flicked toward Talia's sword then back to Talia and roved her attire, a practiced movement of her eyes, quick and clean.

Talia braced herself for some comment. She wore the informal rider garb she had been given upon returning to the city, thoroughly cleaned and repaired after the battle. A moss-green quilted doublet under a layer of leather armor. Her trousers matched her doublet and dived into knee-high leather boots. Rider attire, but hardly the fashion of a noble woman, or indeed a queen.

Yet Felice said nothing and returned to her brandy. Deciding to take her mother's advice on board, Talia rummaged for some red wine and poured herself a small glass. The bottle had been amongst the drier reds, but it smelled overly sweet to her.

Talia drank and fought back the desire to wince. It would hardly do not only to abstain from drinking with her Ealdors but then to shudder like a child at the taste of it. Before it had been her youthful palate that had discouraged her, now she suspected it was Pyra's preference for heat and spice over sweet or sour.

She set the wine down. "I'm not truly a rider anymore, you're right. But I am one at heart. Saving the city has dispelled any notions that the dragon riders aren't necessary. My only regret is that I couldn't be there for you and Leofric when you needed me most. If I had, perhaps he—"

She stopped herself. Even if she had received Leofric's letter in time and come before his death, it would have made no difference. Alone, she would have proved no obstacle to Osric—no, to Sovereign's plans. The dragon was to blame. She had to bear that mind.

She had been clenching and unclenching her fists and only noticed this when her mother's eyes were drawn to her hands. Talia flattened them across her knees and tried to find a positive note.

"I don't know what you've been told, mother, but Leofric did not lose his mind in his final days. In fact, were it not for him, I would never have uncovered the truth." Talia explained as much as she knew about what had occurred in the lead-up to Leofric's death. When she reached the part about Deorwin Steward returning as a prisoner of war with a ghost orb containing evidence of the true events at the Toll Pass, Felice interrupted her.

"Deorwin brought this?" she asked, flustered. "Where is he now? I must speak with him."

"No one knows," Talia said. "After he left Sidastra he disappeared and was last seen heading south. Into hiding, most like, if he thought

Osric would be a danger to him. I hope he returns. A steward of his experience would be invaluable."

"That is assuming Osric did not have him killed and buried in the wilds," Felice said. Her face darkened. "He and your father had their difficulties, but I never would have thought, never..."

She seemed to run up against some unbidden, unpleasant thought.

"I don't think Uncle Osric was in his right mind," Talia said in a consoling voice. "He was being controlled by a powerful dragon."

Felice gave her a sharp look. "Controlled? How?"

"By magic. A mystic dragon might be capable of it as their powers are drawn from thought. I don't know when exactly this started, but anything he said or did in recent years likely wasn't really him."

"He seemed the same Osric to me," Felice said darkly. She delayed speaking further by finishing her brandy, then set the tumbler down near Talia's barely touched wine.

"I wasn't aware you and father had issues with Uncle Osric," Talia said, unsure where this was going. Osric had been a brilliant warrior, tough, loyal, the sort of man you wanted around in a crisis.

"Well, we did not air our dirty linen in front of you and *Leofric*," Felice said, her words catching at the mention of her son's name. "You two always looked up to him. You most of all," she added with a wan smile. "In simpler times, I would never have admitted this, but it was better for everyone when Osric was away. Better for him too, I think."

"I thought everyone admired him," Talia said. "The Hero of Feorlen." The title stuck in her throat as she spoke it. It had been bestowed for his supposed grand victory in the Toll Pass. The same battle in which he had let his own brother die. Yet, even before that war, she had often heard his name spoken with a sort of awe.

"We got on just fine when he wasn't around," Felice said. "And we'll do just fine now he's gone again." It was clear from her tone that she wished no further discussion on the matter, that she considered the topic of Osric Agravain a closed matter.

Talia felt wrong-footed on the subject. Holt had said the real Osric had reached out to him during a conversation with Sovereign and that he had asked for Talia's forgiveness. She had been ready to give it, but

Felice's blunt revelation gave her pause. Her mother seemed pleased to be rid of him.

Feeling it would be better to change the subject, Talia placed a hand upon the box with the royal seal. "My crown?"

Felice took up the change in conversation enthusiastically. She nodded. "Yes! I crossed paths with a jeweler on my way here and insisted I bring it. Put it on."

Talia undid the latch and opened it. Inside, surrounded by velvet and silk, was her father's crown. *My crown,* she reminded herself.

Golden and glistening from sapphires and rubies, with an ermine border at the base, it only seemed real to her now she held it. With exaggerated delicacy, Talia placed it on her head. As the crown settled, it became tight. A metal band compressing her skull.

Felice's radiant expression fell. "Is something wrong?"

Talia whipped the crown off. "Not the best fit."

"We can have it adjusted again," Felice said brightly. "I'll summon the jewelers right away—"

Talia was about to tell her she had more important issues to attend to when she seized up. Her dragon bond pounded and Pyra reentered telepathy range at speed.

"What's wrong, girl?" Talia asked, blinking back the headache that rose as she struggled to communicate across the distance. Forgetting all else, she staggered to her desk and reached for her scabbard.

"Talia?" Felice said, startled, but Pyra's voice drowned out her mother's next words.

"Emeralds have returned from a mission to the chasm. Many injured. Others did not return at all. The Life Elder wants to speak with us at once."

What did that mean? Had whatever attacked the emeralds followed them back to the city? Had the remnants of the swarm reformed and launched another attack?

Somewhere across Lake Luriel, Pyra roared. It reached Talia here in the palace as a dull tremble.

"I'll come down at once," Talia said.

"There's no time. Stay where you are."

Talia strapped on her sword and spun around. For a split second she was surprised to find her mother in the room. "I'm sorry," she said, half-dazed. "I must go. Pyra needs me. The Life Elder needs me."

"Who?" Felice said, completely lost. "Talia, what's wrong?"

"There's been trouble at the chasm."

"Chasm?" Felice said, then she caught up. "A scourge chasm? Are we under attack?"

"I don't know."

"Pyra, did scourge forces follow the emeralds back to the city?"

"No. Head to your balcony."

Pyra rapidly closed the distance between them with each second. Speaking to her felt much easier than it had only moments ago. At least the immediate fear of an attack could be set aside.

"Summon the High Council in case I have need of them," Talia called out as she stepped onto the balcony.

Outside, she faced south over the island rings of the city, toward where the great lake stretched further south to the horizon.

Pyra dove down from the west and came to hover before the balcony.

"Let's go."

Talia jumped, landed on Pyra, and gripped into position. Pyra banked right and made for the western shore.

Up here, the extent of the damage done to the city was stark. The fires had blazed hottest in the West Quarter, leaving no wood untouched and the stones charred black. Deep ash piles remained. Three outer islands, one north, one east and one south, which had been used as traps during the battle, lay in similar ruin: each a black reminder of the price of victory. Reconstruction would take a great deal of time.

Upon reaching the west bank, the Elder was impossible to miss, so large that he would not have been comfortable inside the throne room of the palace. His scales shimmered and changed with each move-ment, as though his body were a landscape of grassy hillsides in the breeze. A spine of dark bone ridges ran down his back and tail in stark contrast to his luminous body.

The Elder moved between emeralds sprawled on the earth, each in some form of distress. Legs broken, wings ripped, wounds seeping blood or worse.

"*To me, daughters of fire,*" the West Warden said. One of the chief lieutenants of the Life Elder, the Warden was as mighty as a Lord of the Order. Talia spotted him some way from the Elder, his scales the color of shadowy ferns.

When they landed, Talia got down from Pyra, then sank to one knee.

"Honored Warden, Pyra tells me there has been trouble at the chasm."

"*The enemy came upon us in numbers I did not anticipate,*" said the Warden. "*Beneath the earth, their presence is hard to detect. I am ashamed I led members of my flight to their doom.*"

"*Then we shall return with you,*" Pyra assured the Warden, "*and make the enemy pay.*"

Talia felt heat rise within her as Pyra's fire crossed the dragon bond.

"*Patience,*" Talia told her. "*We can't make a promise we can't keep.*"

Pyra snorted and clawed at the earth.

The Warden's gaze remained fixated on the injured emeralds. The Life Elder pressed his snout into each one with a delicacy Talia thought impossible for such a large creature. Green power danced like leaves caught in the wind, and then each emerald lay down and slept in peace. When he had finished, the Elder came to greet them.

Talia bent one knee again. Pyra lowered her neck to the ground, as did the West Warden.

"*Daughters of fire,*" the Elder said, his voice as sweet sounding as a kindly old man, yet simultaneously as strong, immovable, and ancient as the ground on which they stood. "*Rise, younglings.*"

Talia raised her head and met the Elder's eyes. They had radiated the freshness and hope of spring when she'd first looked into them, but now the season had changed and his eyes had changed with it, glowing now with the lushness of summer, of trees in full bloom and untamed grasslands.

Talia let loose a held breath. This was an Elder. An actual Elder dragon. She had flown beside him at the end of the battle, but her exhaustion had numbed her to the reality of it. His power dwarfed every dragon in the vicinity, such that she could not register their cores against his. Pyra's core, a bonfire in her mind's eye, stood as a candle on a distant mountaintop compared to the Life Elder.

When Talia spoke, her voice trembled with awe. "Honored Elder, I am grieved to hear of your losses. If there is anything that Pyra and I might do to assist you and your flight, you need only name it."

"The scourge still plagues this land. And yet you linger in this city. Why?"

Talia felt embarrassed.

"My duties demand my presence here for now, Honored Elder. Rest assured that sealing the scourge chasm and removing the last of the swarm from my kingdom is my topmost concern. Had I known you intended to send emeralds to the chasm, I would have sent forces to assist them."

Talia thought it a mark of the West Warden's shame that he did not rise to tell her that dragons needed no help from children.

"I do not wish the chasm to be sealed," the Elder said. *"Not yet."*

Talia could not help but look at Pyra for her reaction. The dragon's amber eyes widened.

"Honored Elder, I do not understand."

"The chasm troubles me. I sensed a presence beneath the earth, deeper than deep, neither living nor dead. I cannot grasp it. The squadron I sent to the woods were to scout the area, yet it seems the scourge are regrouping there in great numbers. Once closer, my Warden could sense what I felt from afar. Something is down there."

Talia gulped. "Something that... isn't the scourge?"

"We cannot say. The land weeps from the damage of the blight. Fear has seeped into root and stem, into soil, worm, and bird. I intend to lead my flight in force to secure the chasm, but we are too large to enter the tunnels from which the enemy arise."

Talia's heart skipped a beat. "You wish for Pyra and me to venture down into the tunnels at the chasm?"

"You and whatever forces you deem fit."

Pyra's excitement was palpable across the bond. *"We relish this chance to prove ourselves, Honored Elder."*

A low rumble gathered in the Elder's chest. *"This is not some test to be passed. It is what must be done."*

"But, Honored Elder," Talia began, fighting to steady her breath and voice, "such chasms are always sealed in the wake of incursions. To do otherwise is too great a risk."

This finally got a rise from the West Warden. *"Do you question my Elder's judgment?"*

"No—" Talia began, but the Elder himself interjected.

"Settle. Warden, do not let your shame and guilt rule you."

The Warden rumbled, then lowered himself further until he lay completely flat against the ground.

"Knowledge is what we need," said the Elder. *"Too long has the enemy gone unchecked. Gathering in the dark. Growing unseen. We must know more, and we must take the fight to them."*

"Pyra and I are only at the rank of Ascendant, Honored Elder. Our powers are limited. You might be better served sending emissaries to Falcaer Fortress to beg for their aid."

"Until Sovereign and his followers are unmasked or brought under the talon, I trust only those of my flight who have remained loyal to me, you daughters of fire, and Holt and Ash, sons of night."

You do not trust other dragons and riders, yet you sent Holt and Ash out into the world alone? Talia did not understand this. Yet if the Elder would not seek assistance from Falcaer, no aid would come. She did not place much faith in the Order answering her own calls this soon. If this task needed to be done, then she and Pyra had to do it.

"Very well," Talia said, her voice higher than usual. "I will do all that I can."

The Elder hummed.

"I shall take the best part of my flight to the chasm tonight. The rest shall depart abroad to rendezvous with emeralds still in the east, north, and south. If there are other recent chasms, we must find them. Go now, child. You have your new role. Fulfill it well."

FOUR

Shady Dealings

For what felt like the hundredth time that night, Holt reached for the handle of Brode's sword. He had resolved to master wearing and drawing it from his back, as a dragon rider should. Although Holt had been around riders his whole life, he had never stopped to consider why they wore their swords this way, nor the special technique and equipment they used to enable them to do so.

The hilt poked out above his right shoulder. It had taken him an embarrassing amount of practice to realize what he had to do when drawing in this manner. As his arm reached the point where it would lock out and be impossible to continue forward, Holt shifted the draw to his right. This allowed the blade to come free from the upper portion of the scabbard, where there was an opening on the left side. After freeing the blade, he could fully extend his arm.

His issue was speed. If he tried to draw to the right too soon, the blade would catch in the scabbard. Too vigorous and he would pull himself forward and fall. Comical though that might be for Ash, it would not be a wise move in combat. On top of that, Holt was not the most confident with a sword in the first place.

This time, he managed a smooth albeit slow extraction of the broad green blade, ending with his arm extended down. He allowed himself a small smile.

Ash returned from drinking at the river they were following. Now out in the open, moonlight made his scales glisten as though absorbing the cold silver rays, and lunar motes shot through the orbit of his core like so many falling stars.

Ash stopped, cocked his head, and flicked his tail. *"You've been doing that for ages,"* he said in a tone that suggested he was rolling his eyes.

"And I'll keep at it until I get it right. Won't do us much good in a fight if I fumble drawing my sword."

Ash sniggered. *"You can draw it fine from your waist."*

"I can, but I'd need to be about a foot taller to use Brode's like that. You must have heard the scabbard scraping along the ground."

"It's an option until you get better."

Holt grumbled and brought Brode's blade up to hold it in both hands. It really was absurdly wide and thick, and even its tip was unusual, as though someone had taken a neat diagonal slice off the top to leave a slanted edge. Rider blades were forged by new Ascendants at Falcaer Fortress. A piece of the rider, their dragon and their magic type went into each creation. Brode's dragon Erdra had been an emerald with an affinity for the earth. Something about the sturdiness of the design did make Holt think of rock and stone.

He sighed, a little annoyed at his lack of progress, but he'd had enough for one night. So, for what felt like the hundredth time that evening, Holt attempted to sheathe Brode's blade. Putting it back into the scabbard was actually harder than getting it out. He carefully brought the blade behind his head, lowered it further than felt instinctual and then gingerly felt for the opening of the scabbard. He just missed, tapping steel against wood. A few more bungled attempts led to him reaching back to help guide the sword into the scabbard. Once he managed that it would slide in easy enough, but it was far from a smooth process.

At least he was getting better at drawing it, which was the pertinent element when it came to a fight. Until he mastered it, he would still have his normal sword that hung from his waist.

However, to be comfortable while Cleansing and Forging, he unstrapped both and laid them beside his backpack. Their remaining venison lay in a sack beside it. They must have stripped seventy pounds of meat from the buck, which Ash carried on his back during the day.

Holt inhaled a strong waft of raw meat from the sack. Much was preserved with salt, but he had left some fresh. He pulled out a hunk of the fresh stuff and checked it for spoilage. The flesh was damp to the touch but not yet slimy. Good. It still smelled gamey. Also good.

"Have a whiff of this?" he said, throwing the meat over to Ash. His superior nose would pick up any foulness.

Ash inhaled long and slow and shuddered in anticipation. He scooped it up and began chomping.

"Well, that settles that."

Ash swallowed and sniffed eagerly.

"I'll give you one more piece. I want to do a simple test, but after tonight we've got to ration it out. The moon is waxing. Won't be long until the full moon, and I want to take every advantage we can during that time. I also want to test different ways of cooking to see if that makes any difference, so try not to eat it all raw."

Ash snorted at this imposition but stretched out his wings and tail to expose as much of his body to the moonlight as he could. Now he had eaten some venison, the volume of lunar motes drawn toward him saw a marked increase. The next thing would be to compare the lunar flow after Ash ate cooked meat.

As Holt busied himself creating a fire, he brooded over the rider perks he and Ash were missing out on. When riders traveled, they could stop at any village, town, city, or even a farmstead if needed and be welcomed. Even if they weren't truly welcomed, who would refuse them? The logistics of food supplies for a dragon over days, never mind weeks, didn't need to be considered. Riders could expect top treatment wherever they visited. Yet he and Ash had to stick to the wild and fend entirely for themselves.

"I suppose at some point I could slip into a town by myself and buy supplies," he mused aloud. "When we really need it… Talia's coin won't last forever."

As the fire finally caught and sparked to life, Holt sighed and rubbed his hands over it. Only now, as the flames sent waves of heat over him, did he realize how much he had missed a fire. The crackle of the wood was a comfort, so too the smell of smoke and ash.

"Come and lift your wings around it like Pyra does," Holt said. "It will block some of the light."

As Ash adjusted his position, Holt extracted dry oat cakes and hard cheese from his pack and rammed some into his mouth. While he chewed, he opened the meat sack and brought out another portion of the unspoiled fresh meat. He cooked it simply by holding it over the fire on a skewer, not wishing to sully the test with different ingredients. The moment it was ready he passed it to Ash, who obliged by scoffing it.

Ash smacked his lips as it went down. *"That was better."*

Holt wasn't surprised. Dragons preferred their meat to be cooked, often in exacting ways. Brode had called them fussy, claiming the dragons in the Order had grown pampered. Yet Holt wondered if there was more to it. If the correct meat helped to pull raw motes toward the core, then surely other ingredients could improve upon this. If so, that would explain why the dragons preferred some tastes to others.

Talia had admitted that most riders in the Order didn't examine their dragon's core at mealtimes and rarely Forged at the same time. She had explained this was to give some balance to their lives. Even they could not train or work every minute of the day.

Yet Holt needed every advantage he could get. If cooking the venison in a certain way attracted more lunar motes to Ash or made Forging them easier, then it would be worth the trouble of finding out.

For tonight, the test was simple. Observe if cooked meat pulled in more motes than raw meat. Judging from the near blinding surge of new motes swarming into the core's orbit, his assumption was correct. Cooked over raw. No surprise there, but it would be worth checking again when the moon had fully waned to see if there was a difference when their source of power became low. Assuming they found more fresh venison, of course.

He took out his father's recipe book, a sealed pot of ink, and a quill. He hadn't opened it since they'd left Sidastra. The ease with which he had just reached for this family relic took him aback. It had been hard even looking at it for a while. Now he traced the soft leather cover with a finger, running over the gold embossed cook pot beneath a flying dragon, before opening it up to the small, mostly empty section for 'deer'. Using the first available space, Holt wrote in his first entry to confirm his findings. His letters weren't as neat as the previous author's, looking larger and childish by comparison.

Still, he was pleased to be contributing to the family book. With his exploration of a unique dragon type and his additional insight from being a rider himself, he reckoned he would have a lot to add over the coming years.

He closed it with a *thunk*. "Well, that's something done at least."

Ash growled softly. *"You're too hard on yourself. We have many nights ahead of us."*

Holt gave a wan smile and nodded. "I'd just like to feel like we're making progress. We don't even know where we're going. Not really."

East. East was vague.

While putting the recipe book away, he brought out one of their maps. This one covered the lands between the southern tip of the mountain range known as the Spine and the Stretched Sea. A clean slice of the center of the world, encompassing Feorlen on the western peninsula and Brenin to the east. East of Brenin, across the River Versand, were the lands controlled by the Free City of Athra. East of Athra was where they needed to go. A large swathe of land there was marked as the 'Disputed Lands'.

Perhaps there they would find respite from Holt's fear of their discovery. Did the riders patrol those Disputed Lands as well? In truth, he had no idea.

The immediate issue was crossing northern Brenin. Holt's eyes were pulled down to the center of the kingdom, where Sable Spire stood. The Order Hall of Brenin would have been ideally placed were it not in a large swamp called the Mort Morass. The maker of the map had colored the tower black, making it foreboding even on parchment. They had also drawn in other useful markers. A green skull sat above the Morass, which, according to the key, marked it as an area with high scourge activity.

A dark tower in the middle of a scourge swamp. Holt had no desire to visit it, either as a guest or worse if he and Ash were caught. It would only take one of the riders of Brenin to fly close enough to sense them. Could their luck hold for long enough to make it across the kingdom unseen? He dearly wished to know what technique Rake used to veil his core – that would allow them to roam freely.

After the full moon waned, Holt would risk flying under the cover of total darkness. That way, they might reach the Disputed Lands quicker. Until then, it would be walking by day, Forging by night. In any case, Ash could not carry Holt, all their equipment, supplies and seventy extra pounds of venison. He was young and lean and, by all accounts, weedy for a dragon.

Baby steps, he thought, remembering what Brode had tried to impress upon him. *First, we must get through Brenin. Then we'll figure out the next part.*

Reluctantly, Holt put out their fire and their warmth before turning determinedly to his meditation. As he settled, his focus turned entirely to the bond. The white ball of the core swirled amid a rainstorm of light. With so many motes there, the pressure he applied from his side of the bond swept the motes forward in a snowball effect. His delight faded as he discovered such large clumps required extreme pressure to hammer into the core. After a concerted effort, the first clump sunk in; the core flared for a second, then resettled a fraction larger than before.

Holt eased off, coming back to reality with care. Once done, he blinked and rubbed at his eyes. They hurt as if he had truly been staring at strong light.

"This isn't going to be easy."

"I wish there was something I could do to help."

"Might be there is, but for now this is all I know how to do. Just have to keep at it."

Holt wasn't averse to hard work. He'd sworn he would get stronger. And he'd sworn he would not come across someone in need of their magic again and let them down.

He closed his eyes and carried on.

The following days became a repetitive cycle. Traveling by day, Cleansing and Forging by night. Experimenting with Ash's food. Holt hardly slept.

Each day that went by without incident only put him more on edge, as though he were dodging invisible blows. He reflected again how ambitious the Life Elder had been in sending them off on this journey alone and about whether they would be able to live up to the task.

When not on the move, Holt continued his sword practice, getting better at drawing Brode's sword from his back and becoming more focused in his meditations. Well over a week of increasing lunar activity and vigilant effort on his part was starting to take effect.

Ash's core had grown by half its previous size. Granted, it had been small to begin with, but Holt was satisfied to see progress. The ball of white light looked that bit grander against its inky void.

One morning, drawing close to a road, Ash heard the trundling wheels, voices, and footfalls of a trading caravan. Not long after, he heard another group approaching the road from the other side, this one heavily armed. A fight broke out.

"*Bandits,*" Ash announced. "*We should help.*"

Holt bit his lip. "It was bad enough we spoke to that hunter."

Thinking back, revealing themselves so readily had been bold. Word might already be spreading of a young rider from Feorlen who was paying for wares. Moreover, he did not like the thought of killing humans. Riders fought the scourge. Turning his Ascendant strength and magic onto regular humans felt like an abuse of power.

Moving on would be the sensible course, given their need for secrecy.

But screams for help pulled on his heart strings.

Holt clenched his jaw. "Okay. But no killing."

Ash bounded ahead without another word. Holt tore after him, apprehensive as to what he would find.

The bandits had taken the guards with ruthless efficiency. Six lay dead, another two were on their knees with their hands behind their heads. The robbers were in the middle of lining up the merchants when he and Ash arrived.

Ash caught the first bandit unawares, throwing him onto his back and pressing a talon upon the man's chest. The bandit squirmed but could do little.

Holt gathered light in his left palm as a warning. "Put down your weapons."

The bandits looked at each other and then to the biggest one there, presumably the leader. A giant of a man, six foot five at least with savagely unkempt hair and beard. Had he been a knight once? He bore a kite shield, a longsword and wore plate steel vambraces which were dented and stained. If he had been a knight, he had fallen far. His eyes bulged, all bloodshot and full of madness.

He charged at Holt.

Holt still did not want to hurt him. He darted aside and kicked the back of the bandit's knee. The man crumpled.

Holt heard weapons dropping before he even turned to face the others.

"That's better. No running either. You know I'll catch you."

Ash growled to emphasize the point. The bandit beneath his talon stopped squirming. As the ruffians began crying for mercy and forgiveness, the merchants rushed to bind their hands and legs, then tied them up to one another.

An older merchant sidled over to Holt. He'd suffered a cut to his temple but otherwise looked unharmed. A large silver coin embossed with a set of scales hung from a silk chain around his neck.

"Honored Rider, let me convey my utmost gratitude."

"That's quite alright, Mr. Merchant," Holt said. "You may repay me by informing the local bailiff of these men and by keeping my presence well out of it. If anyone asks, you can say a rider helped you, but give them no details of me or my dragon."

The merchant gave him a rather grave but knowing look. He nodded sagely and hastened to say, "Naturally, sir, naturally. Do you wish to inspect the cargo before you depart?"

"Why would I do that?"

A little sweat glistened on the merchant's brow, and he hastened to dab it with a handkerchief. "I – well… if you'll take my word that the egg is secure. I just thought that the Honored Orvel may wish to know—"

"Did you say the 'egg' is secure?"

"I did, sir."

"A dragon egg?"

The merchant gave a small nod.

Ash growled. *"He's afraid,"* Ash told Holt over their bond. *"His heart is racing."*

"If he's got a dragon egg, he ought to be afraid."

Holt stepped closer, wondering what on earth he had stumbled upon. "Why do you have a dragon egg?"

The merchant gulped. "Your master, Honored Orvel, provided it before we left Sable Spire. We were to take it to the town of Gironde just north of here and await his buyer. Is that… is that not why he sent you to guard us?"

Ash padded closer. *"He does not lie."*

The dragon's ability to hear a heartbeat was useful in more ways than one.

Holt did not doubt the truth of the merchant's words. It would be an absurd lie to tell, without believing Holt to also be in on this scheme – whatever it was.

Holt looked from this merchant to the others. Each one of them shrunk back as though fearing they would suffer the same as the bandits. Everything about this was unsavory. Eggs weren't moved around by merchant caravans. Holt had never known one to leave the

Crag in all his years there. If the riders from Sable Spire had a need to move one, they would surely do so themselves and not by this slower, more secretive means.

"Show me," Holt said.

Gingerly, the merchant took Holt to the largest wagon, big enough for a man to live in. Inside, the smell of herbs and spices, along with strong cheese, was potent. Buried at the back was a great strongbox which the merchant opened, revealing a stony gray dragon egg. It was very small. Smaller than Ash's egg had been when he had first saved it.

Holt picked it up. Cold stone to the touch. No one protested as he brought it outside to hold before Ash.

"*Can you sense anything from it?*" he asked privately over their bond.

"*I think I am too young to sense any life that may lie within.*"

Ash must have gleaned this from his blood memories.

Holt continued to hold the egg under Ash's nose, playing for time. "*What do you think? Should we take it with us?*"

"*It might bring this other rider after us.*"

"*True enough, but I have a bad feeling about this. It doesn't seem right.*"

Despite his gut instinct, Holt's heart and his head collided once more. Taking the egg with them seemed the right move. Yet it would almost certainly send this Orvel after them. And if the egg hatched, then they would be weighed down by another hatchling. It had been hard enough feeding just Ash. They had a mission. An important mission. There was just no logical reason to take it.

Holt spun to face the merchant. "I shall take charge of the egg now. Master Orvel wants it taken to a new location."

No one would believe him. He had clearly not known of the egg in the first place. But none of the merchants were prepared to argue with a rider either.

The sweat at the older merchant's neck sparkled. His skin might have been freshly oiled.

"Of course, Honored Rider. Of course."

Ash rumbled beside him and swished his tail. "*You did the right thing.*"

Holt nodded, more to reassure himself. Then he considered the stores of food the merchants had. Would it be akin to robbery to ask them for supplies? They wouldn't refuse him, nor did they seem the most honest in the first place to be dealing with contraband eggs. And yet, Holt could hardly blame them either. For as much as they were wary of Holt, they would have been unable to refuse this other rider – Orvel – as well.

Tucking the egg under one arm, he pulled his coin purse off his belt and shook it once to clink the money within.

"I'd like to make a few purchases."

The merchants were as shocked as the hunter had been, yet they fell over backward to assist him once they understood he was serious.

"We have excellent prices, sir," the lead merchant babbled. "No better in Brenin!"

Holt secured three loaves of bread along with butter which was 'added in for free'. He was endlessly grateful to have access to butter again. He also bought a string of onions and garlic and refilled his supply of salt. It did not end there. Desperate to please him, the merchant offered him salted pork and a pick of early season raspberries, all at half price. Or so he said.

"Half price, you say?" Holt said in a level tone. "Prices in Brenin must be high indeed if that is half." A real rider, born from nobility, might not have known the price of bread, salt meat, and fruits, but he did. The merchant fell further in Holt's estimations. Still, he wouldn't rob the man blind. "I'll pay you fifteen silver and forty coppers for the lot. That's a fair price and you know it."

The merchant accepted the coins with a nervous laugh. "A generous offer, Honored Rider." He bobbed and bowed so low that his medallion scraped the ground.

With the egg and their new supplies secure, Holt and Ash extricated themselves from the caravan and continued their journey east. They spent the rest of that day in silence, each caught up in their own thoughts.

Holt puzzled over why a rider would smuggle an egg out from an Order Hall. The merchant had spoken of a 'buyer' for the egg, so he ruled out the possibility that Orvel was trying to save the egg from being destroyed. It spoke of something nefarious, and Holt's admiration of the Order took another knock.

By the time they stopped for the night, Holt felt starving. However, his first task was to feed Ash. He had already tested cooking the deer with some of the rosemary, marjoram, and savory that he'd brought from Sidastra. None seemed to make a marked difference to the activity of lunar motes. Tonight, he had butter to test.

As he sat holding the pan over the fire, he realized just how much longer it took to heat the metal over a naked flame without Talia and Pyra there to speed things along. A pang ran through him at the thought of them. No doubt Pyra would have had a few choice words for the merchants smuggling a dragon egg. She would have left them with singed cloaks too.

The egg lay by his pack now, its dull stone made orange by the glow of the fire.

Why do I make life harder for myself?

Eventually, the pan was hot enough to cook on. Holt searched the venison sack and noticed there was a piece that looked darker than the others. Worried it had spoiled, he took it out. It was harder and drier than the other portions, though still soft enough to give way when he pressed into it.

"Does this smell okay?" he asked Ash.

Ash sniffed. His senses were so good he didn't need to come closer. *"Nothing is rotting, though that piece smells more intense than the others."*

"It's starting to dry out." Holt turned it over in his hands. "I seem to have cut this a lot thinner than the others. Did I salt it?"

Ash sniffed again. *"You did, not so much as the other salted steaks though."*

Holt sniffed it himself but could not have picked up salt from it if he tried. In happier times, Ash would have made the perfect cook's assistant.

"Might be if I left it out for a few days on a rack it would turn to jerky, though it's too big a slice for that really." He caught himself before he mumbled on. "Let's use it before it goes off."

He threw a knob of butter into the pan, letting it melt before adding in the meat. A nutty, fatty aroma soon made his mouth water.

"Here you go," he said, setting the pan down for Ash. He sat cross-legged, ready to observe Ash's core, and fought to stifle a yawn. Something struck him as strange. Ash hadn't pounced on his meal. "Do you not like the smell of it?"

A gargled, light rumble shook in Ash's throat. He lowered his snout and pushed the venison across the ground toward Holt.

"You have it, boy."

"But it's for you," Holt said, confused. "If you don't like it, I can try something else."

"It smells tasty, but I'd still like you to have it."

"I don't need it. You do for your core."

Ash shook his head. *"I'll make it for one night. You've been too hard on yourself. You've hardly slept, and you haven't had a hot meal in a long time."*

"Ash," Holt said, a little exasperated, "it's almost the full moon. This is the best time we'll get to Forge. It's too important—"

"You're more important. You spend all your time taking care of me. Now I'm trying to take care of you. We had a hard day. This land is full of strange people. Forget Forging for one night and rest. Or I'll pin you down."

Holt gasped a laugh. Now he considered it, his eyes did feel tired and sore, in a way he hadn't felt since becoming an Ascendant. If his new enhanced body was getting worn out, then he probably did need a break. Ash was going to force him to have one regardless. He could feel the dragon's worry over the bond.

"Alright, Ash. I'll rest."

Ash fluttered his wings and swished his tail merrily.

"Shall we share this piece then?" Holt cut the venison in the pan in half and speared one chunk of it for himself. As he bit into the hot meat, his mouth melted under the intensity of the gamey flavor. Weeks of hard biscuit, cheese, and other dried goods left much to be desired.

Ash began to eat his half of the meal, and the dragon's pleasure flared over the bond, amplifying the taste in Holt's own mouth. The dragon bond turned from warm to red hot. It burned as though they were in battle. Then a new source of white light appeared, coming from Holt's own skin.

A faint white light pulsed from the ends of his trousers, from the nape of his neck, from the ends of his sleeves. His hands became webbed in veins of moonlight, although the lines clustered and balled up at his palm. The backs of his hands were dim by comparison, with only a few faint lines running there.

"What's happening?" Ash asked.

"I'm not sure," Holt said. He jumped to his feet and drew upon light from Ash's core as a test, sending the core-forged motes down to his left palm as if to charge a Lunar Shock. The new white veins grew thicker, and energy visibly flowed through them as his power gathered.

"I think," Holt began, a little unsure, "I think my mote channels have become visible."

Smiling now at this strange but exciting discovery, Holt took off his jerkin, rolled up the sleeves of his shirt, then gathered and regathered power at his palms, watching the light run down his arms and wrists.

The process felt smoother, his control more nuanced than usual.

Magic rushed to his limbs, giving him a sense of stability. His enhanced body felt taut again, the tiredness banished.

It had started when he ate the venison. Was this the result of adding butter? Surely it could not be so simple? He had to note it down. No sooner had he opened the recipe book than the brightness of his mote channels faded.

"I'll make more. Hold on."

Holt placed the pan back on the fire. In his good mood, he decided to prepare what amounted to a small feast for himself. He sliced up an onion then finely chopped a clove of garlic. Over the garlic he sprinkled salt then pressed down with the flat of his knife, dragging garlic over the coarse salt until it became a paste. Once the pan was hot, he threw in more butter and then the onion, letting the pieces caramelize. He added thick slices of bread to one side of the pan, keeping the now sizzling onions to one side. As the bread began to turn crisp and golden, he added a final pinch of butter and the garlic paste, turning the bread over to coat it in the garlic butter on all sides. The aroma alone would have been enough to revive his strength.

He was so eager to eat that he near burned his fingers picking the bread out from the pan. It was too hot for his mouth as well, but he didn't care. Chewing fast, he scooped some of the onions out on the flat of his knife and laid it over the next chunk of bread. The sweet onions cut perfectly across the garlic butter.

Ash had not been wrong. Hot food was doing wonders for his spirits. Alongside a new discovery with magic, he briefly forgot about the dragon egg, about their difficult mission, about everything.

He cooked two more pieces of venison. One for each of them. With high hopes that a larger piece would produce the mote channel effect for longer, Holt wolfed it down. Ash ate his. Holt stood, braced himself.

And nothing happened.

"Come on," Holt said.

His mote channels did not oblige his request.

"Maybe it was just that piece."

Holt considered it. Riders must have eaten the same meal as their dragon countless times in the past. Brode or Talia would have mentioned it, wouldn't they? He tried to think if he had ever seen Talia eat beef alongside Pyra but couldn't remember.

He stared at Ash, searching for the answer. The mote channels had become visible after he ate the meat.

No, he thought in realization. *It was after Ash started eating too. Not just the same type of meat, but the same piece. We shared the same food.*

Sharing the same meal seemed more along the right lines. Sharing seemed connected to the bond, but was the use of butter really the deciding factor? Something in his gut made him doubt he had all the answers. Yet having already used three portions of their limited venison in one night, he wouldn't waste more just to satisfy his curiosity. There would be other nights to test the theory. Besides, he had no idea what visible mote channels might mean. Yes, he had found manipulating the magic in his body easier, but that could have been coincidence.

Time would tell.

He explained this to Ash as he noted down all his suspicions in the recipe book under a new heading he titled 'sharing meals'. He re-read his notes on the matter three times to make sure he had it all down, then rummaged in his pack for the raspberries he'd bought from the merchants. A bit of sweetness seemed the right way to round off the evening.

With a full stomach for the first time in weeks, Holt sighed deeply. He felt warm and tired, and so he moved over to sit beside Ash and rest his head on the dragon's leg.

"I'm more worried after today. The sooner we're out of Brenin, the better."

"Then let us fly away."

"After the full moon. I'm not sure it would be wise to linger longer, even if it means dropping some of our supplies."

"I look forward to it." A rumble rose in Ash's throat that persisted as their bond glowed. Ash brought a wing around to lay over Holt like a blanket. *"Sleep, boy. Rest well."*

Holt didn't fight it. In Ash's warm embrace, he drifted off peacefully, and for once his mind did not spin around matters of cores, Sable Spire, Wyrm Cloaks, Elders, Sovereign, or the endless road ahead of them.

FIVE

Old Threats

The walls of the tunnel closed in around her. Talia drew on fire from Pyra's core, channeled the motes to her palm and held them there to light her way. But the light revealed nothing. Where was Pyra? She called out to her dragon, but it was her uncle who answered.

"There's my little soldier," Osric said. It sounded as though he were standing right in front of her. Talia groped ahead in the darkness and fell. Down and down she went until she hit a cold floor. She rose to find her father, her brother, and Osric waiting.

"Come," Osric said, "they need help."

Talia tried to move, but her feet had welded to the floor. "I can't."

The whites of Osric's eyes went pitch black. *"Help them,"* he said in his dragonish voice, then he plunged a knife into her father's back.

Talia screamed. She heaved at her restraints but could not break free. Leofric, pale as ever, reached out a hand to her.

"Help them," Osric said, then he plunged the knife into Leofric. The moment Leofric hit the ground, Osric's eyes returned to normal. He dropped his knife and looked at her.

"Help me," he said, sounding like her uncle once more. "Help me," he begged with open hands.

Talia had lost her voice. She couldn't breathe. Her own hands turned brown and sticky from dried blood. Before she could answer, Osric's eyes turned dark again. He grinned, showing dragon teeth, and lunged, his jaw wide—

Talia woke, sat bolt upright in her bed, and breathed hard. The sheets were singed from where she had gripped them. She checked on her bond. Pyra was still asleep out in the grounds.

Sleep eluded her. Rising, she cooled her face at the basin then donned her robe. Her feet took her down into the coolness of the crypts beneath the palace, to where her brother and father lay in tombs beside each other. She lingered at Leofric's tomb and drew fire into her palm for real to see his face better. The masons had captured his likeness well. His fine, slim features, the frailty but the kindness too.

"I'm not built for this. I liked the simplicity of the Order where problems were faced head-on." She lay a hand on the cold stone. "At least you can rest. I hope you are."

Feeling tired again, she returned to her room and drifted off.

All too soon, the morning light and knocking servants woke her. Her head felt clouded as though she were sick, something she hadn't felt since becoming an Ascendant. Chalking it up to several nights of disturbed sleep, she readied herself to meet her High Council.

When that meeting came, it felt like a blur. Her clouded head still plagued her as each Master and Mistress brought endless questions and issues to her attention.

"I'm hearing problem after problem, yet few solutions. You cannot expect me to make decisions on all matters."

"Your father wished to have the final say on most issues," said Ida, the Mistress of Embassy. Though wizened in appearance and soft in voice, her eyes and mind had not dulled one bit with age.

"I am not my father, nor am I Leofric. My own priorities are clear."

Ealdor Geoff Horndown of the East Weald and Master of State motioned to speak. Horndown was often the largest man in the room, and this was no exception amongst the council. His height, broadness, and dark hair and beard made him seem part man and part black bear.

"Your Majesty," he began, "this proposal to make an expedition into a scourge tunnel seems absurd to me." Horndown also rarely minced his words. "The risk to your life alone. Block the chasm, I say. There are still pockets of the swarm left to mop up across the realm, never mind this counter-assault."

"It is a reconnaissance mission," Talia said. "The Life Elder believes there is information on the enemy we can learn. Pyra and I are best placed to make those findings."

Lady Elvina, the Mistress of Coin, cleared her throat with a delicate cough. Alabaster skin, an immaculate white gown, and hair like liquid gold made it effortless for Elvina to attract the council's attention. Even the stewards, coteries, and scribes at the edges of the room looked at her attentively, some with barely concealed desire.

"Would Your Majesty not call upon Falcaer Fortress to undertake this mission?"

"The Life Elder does not think it wise," Talia said. "We cannot know which riders and wild dragons can be trusted. Not when they might be allied with Sovereign like Silverstrike and Clesh."

She scanned her councilors' faces. Each had grown better at hiding their skepticism where an evil dragon overlord of the scourge was concerned. Some bit their lips, others pursed theirs.

"Look," she said, scrambling for purchase. "Paragon Adaskar is not known for being lenient with oath breakers. Incursions, they say, are like lightning. They do not strike twice. The Paragons may use this as an excuse to delay the reestablishment of an Order Hall here. We will have to learn to cope with that until they relent."

She had thought about an offering of goodwill, of gathering the blades of the fallen riders of the Crag and sending them to hang in the halls of Falcaer with their names and deeds. Those at the Crag might be recovered, but Silas had ambushed most of the riders in some unknown location. The only sword she possessed presently was Silas' own, kept in the royal armory. Sending Silas' sword alone seemed an insult to those he had killed.

"Your Majesty," the Mistress of Embassy said in the most concilia-tory tone in her arsenal. "I agree with Ealdor Horndown. Such an expedition does not seem worth the risk. We still await the reaction of foreign powers to your ascension. Risalia could use this as an excuse to stir up fresh hostilities."

"I won't have us quivering over what Risalia might do. We beat them before."

"We are weak now," said the Master of State. "Our supply lines hang by a thread."

"The treasury reels from the incursion," said the Mistress of Coin. "Gold is needed for reconstruction, to resettle those displaced by the summons."

"And Risalia may not act alone," warned the Mistress of Embassy. "Athra might join them."

"How likely is that?" Talia asked, feeling this might be fear-mongering on the Mistress' part. "What would a Free City have to gain from such a war?"

"It is not a matter of gaining but of maintaining," said the Mistress. "Mithras is wealthy. Coedhen is rich in resources and learning. But the horse lords of Athra dominate with an unmatched military. A dragon rider threatens to change that. They will move against us, not least to make it clear that the old laws still stand. Mithras and Coedhen will fall lockstep in behind them if pushed, mark my words."

"If that should happen, we would face the world alone," said the Master of Roles. "The Province of Fornheim often looks to the Skarl Empire for guidance, yet if there is easy plunder, they are likely to join Risalia and any Free City coalition. Your uncle, King Roland, could not possibly allow Brenin to stand with us against such overwhelming odds."

Talia ran her hands down her face.

"Need I remind this council that you chose me? Were these issues not considered?"

The Master of Roles found his voice. "The council did what we thought best for the stability of the realm. The possibility of renewed conflict with Risalia was weighed against an inevitable civil war for the crown. Faced with such a choice, would you have had us choose differently?"

Talia flushed. She felt suddenly young and childish, the very thing she feared they thought of her.

"No," she said. "I would not have seen my home fall into that sort of bloodshed."

The Master of Roles inclined his head. "Then it is our duty now to minimize any further harm to the realm."

"But what would you have me do?" Talia asked. "If being a rider is the problem, then I fear there is nothing we can do about Risalia, Athra, and all the rest."

There was one solution, of course. One Talia found so horrifying she did not even let herself think about it.

The Mistress of Embassy leaned forward, sensing victory. "For now, I urge you to do nothing that might cause more offense to the ambassadors here in Sidastra. We must await their reactions and which powers denounce or accept your investiture. Your coronation will be the telling moment."

"I concur," said the Master of State. "It would be a damned thing if you took troops to the scourge chasm, only for Risalia to cross the border and catch us with our trousers down. Besides," he added, with an air of having found the winning argument, "if it's troops you want, then a Master or Mistress of War is required."

"In an emergency, the monarch can assume direct military control," Talia said.

"That would be improper," said the Master of Roles. "Emergency powers are intended for war. We're not at war."

"We're *always* at war with the scourge," Talia said. A pinch of fire flitted across her dragon bond, warming her blood and laying the groundwork for the anger to follow. She breathed deep, fighting Pyra's rage. She lost that fight and slammed her fist onto the table. "Other humans are not the main threat to this kingdom. The scourge and the dragon who controls them should be our only concern."

She drew a deep breath in through her nose and exhaled. A trace amount of smoke blew out of her nostrils, causing the old Master of Roles to pull back. Even Elvina's perfect features broke into surprise at that.

Do they think me unhinged?

Talia did not speak until certain her voice would not betray her. "This is the most valuable opportunity any realm has ever had to combat the scourge. A Wild Flight and their Elder will support us in this. Ending the scourge for good could begin right here in Feorlen. There are no other riders to venture into the depths. You made me banish Holt and Ash, remember?"

The Master of Roles, the eldest of the council, raised his chin defiantly. "The council did what we thought best for the stability of the realm," he repeated, solemnly. "Transgressors cannot be allowed to walk free. Others may follow suit. Chaos lies down that road."

"Chaos may well consume us all unless we act now. Councilors, my will on this cannot be swayed. I want an expedition ready to march with all haste."

The Master of Roles lowered his gaze to the table and pressed on. "Very well, but Your Majesty will not hold those official emergency powers until after your coronation. Surely you will consent to wait for that."

Talia considered it and decided not to push the point. Already she overreached, grasping for powers, the very thing feared about riders wearing crowns.

"I can wait for that," she said through gritted teeth.

The High Council relaxed, then tensed again as Ealdor Horndown leaned over the table. Talia braced herself for what she knew would come.

Horndown clasped his hands together. "Has Your Majesty given any further thought to the matter of a marriage?"

Between this and fighting for her expedition, Talia had felt caught between the stinger and the juggernaut. She had considered many things before accepting the crown, but one thing that had slipped her mind had been the expectation of a marriage. As a rider, she had sworn such things away. *'I shall take no love and rule no lands.'* She'd broken one part of that oath already and wasn't eager to break the other. Moreover, having prepared to join the Order for years, that area of life had never been at the forefront of her mind.

Besides, who would want a temper-ridden girl anyway?

"I'm sure the kingdom will survive without me marrying for a time."

"It would display a true break from the Order," said the Mistress of Embassy. "It could be vital in improving your image with key ambassadors."

"And an heir will help stabilize confidence within the kingdom," Horndown said. "Not least, it will make your death in battle, should that occur, less disastrous. Without an heir, Feorlen might be plunged into the very chaos we sought to avoid."

Talia felt a heat rise in her neck that, for once, had nothing to do with Pyra.

"Drefan Harroway is of an appropriate age," offered the Mistress of Coin.

Talia supposed a twenty-six-year-old was appropriate, if not her notion of ideal. A nine-year gap seemed like a chasm. In the reverse, it would be like her marrying an eight-year-old. However, Talia had her doubts about the Mistress of Coin's suggestion.

"Drefan Harroway is also your cousin, Lady Elvina." The Mistress of Coin smiled sweetly but did not deny it. "Besides," Talia continued, "House Harroway remains under investigation. Their use of dragon blood greatly upset my dragon. Any ties to Wyrm Cloaks must be found and rooted out."

It was a delaying tactic, nothing more. She knew she could only stall the issue, but she intended to stall it for as long as possible.

Talia stood, signaling the meeting was adjourned. "My Ealdors, I feel we have little more to discuss on these matters. Once my coronation is over, I intend to make for the scourge chasm for the good not just of Feorlen but of all life. I know my duties. It led me to accept the throne, and I know this must be done."

Each High Council member hastened to their feet, giving small bows from the neck. "Your Majesty," they said in unison.

Talia left the council chambers and headed for her office. A fire burned in her chest as Pyra's eagerness for news crossed the bond.

"Did the robed ones agree to fight?" Pyra asked.

"They are cautious, girl. They don't understand the will of an Elder like we do, and they see a greater threat from Risalia and other foreign powers."

"Make them listen. You are their superior."

"This isn't like the Order. I'm not a Flight Commander who can expect obedience on every matter."

Even at this distance between them, Pyra's disappointment lurched over the bond. That hurt more than any wound.

"I've agreed to wait until after my coronation. Then I will have emergency powers to call upon."

"There's no time to waste." A roar tore through the palace grounds, and the windowpanes in the hallway reverberated from Pyra's bellows. Her frustration pounded into Talia across the bond as if Pyra's tail had slammed into her.

Heat roiled inside her. She itched for training. She itched for a fight. All this sitting around gave Sovereign time to regroup and scheme.

This politicking had not been what she wanted. Leofric had prepared himself for this, not her.

Her pace down the hallway slowed as she fought to control her spiraling thoughts.

She should have gone with Holt and Ash. They were off to find the Wild Flights and stop Sovereign. That was more important. She should never have taken the crown – never broken her oath.

The heat became too much. Talia turned and punched a suit of armor, causing a mighty clang that rang down the hallway. She extracted her fist from the dented metal and noticed with horror that Elvina was standing outside the council chamber at the end of the hall, looking right at her. Talia's anger cooled as though she'd been doused with cold water. She moved away at an Ascendant's pace, heading for her office where her mother would doubtless be waiting to probe her for information.

When Talia entered, Felice set her brandy down and the wave of questions began. Talia mechanically shuffled to one of the chairs, slumped into it, then clutched her head, unable to take anymore.

"Just stop," she implored. "Can't you – can't you just be my mother for a while and nothing else? It's just you and me left."

Felice's expression softened. Then she looked ashamed. She sat down beside Talia and tentatively opened her arms. Talia's first instinct was to jump to her feet again and say 'I'm fine' but, somehow, she let herself sink into her mother's embrace.

How long had it been since she had been held by a parent?

Felice stroked her hair. "You're right. If you'd flown off to Falcaer, I don't know what I would have done."

Heat prickled behind Talia's eyes. But she did not let the tears fall. Forcing them back, she sat back upright and edged out of her mother's arms. *What would Commander Denna say if she saw me like this?*

"You're warm," Felice said.

Talia knew she ran a little hot these days. An inevitable side effect of bonding with a fire dragon.

"Don't worry. I can't get ill with an Ascendant's body."

"I see," Felice mumbled, though it was plain she didn't understand. "You are capable, Talia. I know that. I'm afraid I can't help being both your mother and the former queen."

"Just as I can't help being a rider."

"Of course." Her tone suggested she admitted defeat on that point.

"I thought you wanted me to be a rider."

"I did. You know how much I fought for it. But now... I know what the council will be telling you. The dangers are clear. I'm... I'm afraid of what might happen."

Talia got to her feet again. She found it easier to suppress anxieties while upright.

"I'll value any advice you wish to give me, but I'll be blunt with you as I can't always be with my Ealdors. Fussing over what other powers may think of my investiture may prove a distraction. I was part of the Order. And both as a rider and as queen, I know that the true danger out there doesn't come from the snide comments of ambassadors or even the blades of Risalia. What we just faced was a purposeful incursion, directed by a dragon of immense power with a rogue rider and Wyrm Cloaks as his allies."

Feeling a sense of urgency come over her, she began pacing. Her mother had to understand this. Even if the others did not, she at least had to.

Felice looked both impressed and concerned at the same time. "And what does this-this dragon want?"

"To kill us all," Talia said, a little out of hand. She thought about all Holt had told her of the foundation of the scourge and his own mission that the Life Elder had imparted. Holt had told her with the Elder's permission. How much should she reveal to others in turn?

"What has Feorlen done to him?" Felice asked.

"We were just a weak and small first target, I think. That or, since he already controlled Osric, he could do the most damage here."

"Euh, I see," Felice said, her Brenin accent coming out thicker, as it did when she was angry or worried. "Still, Talia, I would not do anything to antagonize Archduke Conrad while we are fragile. He might use you as an excuse to go to war again."

She can't grapple with the true threat, Talia thought. *Sovereign is amorphous, magic, distant, and unknown. Risalia is steel on the border.*

Out of the corner of her eye, she glimpsed the stack of papers on her desk. Her heart sank. *So much to do, and yet none of it may matter when the true fight comes.*

She had to be Feorlen's instructor now, training her nation, making it ready for the battles ahead. Sovereign seemed the type to hold a grudge, and if his plans to annihilate humanity were true, then a direct confrontation would be inevitable.

Talia had to forge Feorlen into something stronger, as she Forged Pyra's core. Therein lay her second great worry. How were she and Pyra to advance without a mentor of their own?

Her head throbbed again. She clutched it.

"Please, mother, I'll need your help to ensure my Ealdors understand."

Felice's mouth had been ajar during Talia's outburst. After a momentary pause, she closed it, cleared her throat, and smoothed down her gown.

"It may take me some time," Felice said slowly. "What you say sounds so... so terrible. But I am here for you, Talia, as I tried to be here for Leofric." Felice smiled, then cocked her head as though seeing Talia again for the first time.

"What?" Talia asked.

"I forgot for a moment that you are only seventeen. It seems cruel that this should fall onto you. You're not my little girl anymore." She stood with the sort of serene grace only earned through a lifetime of courtly practice and, for a moment, Talia thought she would try to hug her again. Then Felice picked up a box that Talia hadn't even noticed. Her crown.

"I had it adjusted," Felice said.

Talia took the box and opened it. There lay the crown in all its glory. She tried it on.

"It fits perfectly."

"Good," said her mother. "One less thing to worry about. Allow me one piece of advice for now. If you do not wish to drink what's here," she made a motion toward the old drinks cabinet, "then remove it. Replace it with what *you* want instead. A tea trolley, if you so desire, but take the initiative."

Talia needed a second to catch up. The advice seemed so out of place with the issues she faced. "I don't see why that's relevant?"

"Make your Ealdors take your lead on even these small things. It will help. Leofric did not make his mark," she added with a sad shake of her head.

"He did come to the throne in dire circumstances."

"Even so," Felice said, determined. "Oh, don't mistake me, your brother would have been, was in fact, a more considerate and careful ruler than Godric ever was. But ruling is about more than being considerate, thoughtful, and efficient. Make yourself into a queen who inspires, Talia. You'll need to win Feorlen completely and friends from elsewhere too if what you say is true, no?"

Talia bit her lip then nodded. There was wisdom in that.

"Thank you, mother. I appreciate the advice."

Talia removed the crown and placed it back in the box. Felice took it and curtsied.

"Your Majesty," Felice said. Then she left.

Feeling a little better, Talia returned to her desk. She drank in her father's old office with a new view. *No, my office,* she reminded herself. On this matter, her mother was right. Much was out of her control or loomed uncertain, but this small thing she could achieve, and that was something.

Grabbing a blank sheet of paper, Talia began writing instructions for the Master of the Royal Household. She had a few ideas in mind.

SIX

Powered by the Moon

The moon shone bright, a full silver orb in the night's sky. The scourge had picked the wrong time to come across Holt Cook.

Wielding Brode's sword, he cut through two ghouls with ease. In the dark it was hard to tell how many were coming, and soon he heard enemies on all sides. Surrounded, Holt drew upon Ash's core and funneled the magic down the mote channels in his legs to charge his Consecration ability. On his next step, he pushed the magic out of his heel and into the earth. A web of crisscrossing white light cracked the ground, racing out in a ten-foot radius around him.

The benefits were threefold. First, the pale glow provided light to see by, revealing the diseased, gray-skinned corpses caught between human and insect. Second, the lunar-infused ground slowed the ghouls and emitted fiery flakes of light to burn them every few seconds. Last but far from the least, Holt felt stronger upon such ground.

Under the full moon, Ash's scales shimmered silver. White light flashed with each step he took, every strike he made with talon or tail, as though lunar power burst from the seams upon impact. Some of that power trailed from his mouth as white smoke. Even carrying their supplies and the dragon egg upon his back, his ferocity wasn't hindered.

Holt didn't have to fear for Ash in this fight.

He focused on making quick and efficient work of the ghouls. Talia and Brode had urged him to keep his use of magic to a minimum to maintain the integrity of the bond in battle, using sword skill to defeat foes wherever possible. Upon Consecrated ground, facing only ghouls and wielding Brode's sword, this wasn't an issue. His strokes were broad and lacked finesse, but they didn't need to be graceful. Dragon-steel cut with ease, even through those with hardened carapaces over their skin.

With the dragon bond wide open, running hot in combat, and Ash's dragon song ringing in his mind, Holt felt elated.

And then the ground shook, and a shriek higher and shriller than a dying horse cut above the gargled cries of the ghouls.

A flayer hurtled out of the night. Flayers might once have been mantises, with wedge-shaped heads, bright overlarge eyes, mandible mouths, and scythe-like arms. They moved fast and this flayer was no exception, running on lithe legs toward Ash. Holt was about to help Ash when a juggernaut stampeded onto his Consecrated ground. The lunar power barely slowed this hulking beetle, and it lowered its hammerhead to ram him.

Holt gathered light for a Lunar Shock and released it. The attack sparked off the juggernaut's heavy hide. It roared, more angered than wounded, and kept on coming. Holt pivoted too late. An explosion of pain rang at his midriff.

Knocked to the earth, Holt gasped for air. He cursed himself for not moving first before attacking. Panic had cost him and would have shattered half his bones were it not for his enhanced body. He rolled aside, and a ghoul stabbed down where he had been moments before. On his way to his feet, he cut upward, splitting the ghoul open, before twisting to find the juggernaut.

It had run off the Consecrated ground and stood stamping in the half-light just beyond the boundaries of the ability. Smoke rose from where Holt's Shock had hit its shoulder, and its red eyes were trained onto him. As the light in the ground began to dim, the juggernaut snorted and braced for another charge. Holt hastened to place another Consecration to slow the beetle down. The juggernaut charged as fresh white light zigzagged across the earth. It stepped onto the lunar ground, roared, thrashed about, then veered off course.

Holt stepped aside this time and brought Brode's sword down in an overhead strike, emptying his lungs as he yelled with the effort. He intended to sever one of its legs but missed, cutting into the heavily armored abdomen instead. Even dragon-steel struggled at the thickest portion of this exoskeleton. Black blood ran from the wound, stinking of rot, but the beetle carried on, trampling a ghoul in its path.

Out of sight, the flayer's cries turned into a gargled splutter, and Holt felt a surge across the bond. Ash had won his battle.

The juggernaut remained to be dealt with. Holt readied another Lunar Shock. At the same time, he attempted something he had never tried before; he sent power down his right arm and pushed it into Brode's sword. Talia channeled fire through her sword to make for powerful blows, and Holt hoped his next strike would hit harder in turn.

His Shock gathered perfectly, but Brode's sword proved resistant to his magic, as if he were pushing a heavy load uphill. The juggernaut charged again. Holt released his Shock. The beetle lowered its hammerhead and absorbed the brunt of the damage. Brode's sword shone with a web of light, though the light was pale as watered milk and winked feebly. It fizzled out before Holt could bring it to bear against the juggernaut. This time he managed to cut into one of the creature's front legs. He did not quite sever the limb, but the beetle stumbled and collapsed upon its own weight.

Before Holt could finish it, a flash of light forced him to shield his eyes. The juggernaut bellowed a death cry. As the light subsided, Holt blinked and found Ash running to his side. The beetle lay slumped. White smoke billowed from its side. The same lunar vapor trailed from Ash's mouth.

Quick as it began, the noise of battle ceased.

"Is that them all?" Holt asked.

"All the ones nearby."

"You can hear more?"

"Faintly." He turned abruptly and stretched out his snout to point the direction. *"That way."*

Holt had no idea which direction that was. He was not apt at telling the point of the compass using the stars alone, and the fight had got him all turned around.

Before a decision could be made, he had to regain his composure. Slowing his breath, he cleaned Brode's sword on a patch of grass. Fumbling, he managed to sheathe the blade onto his back after only three failed attempts. An improvement. As he finished, the light from his second Consecration petered out, leaving the grass and earth burnt in silver and purple.

Holt drew lunar motes to his left palm to create a torch of soft white light. He had no fear of running out of motes, at least. With the moon full, there was an endless supply of the raw stuff hurtling through the orbit of Ash's core. He could barely risk a glance over the dragon bond, lest their brightness hurt him.

Using raw motes to power a Shock or a Consecration would make the ability weak, if it had any impact at all. Raw motes were weak compared to those that were refined and made dense inside the core. However, to create a light source, the raw motes worked well, meaning he did not have to waste core-forged magic to do so. Drawing on raw motes still strained the bond, of course. Any magic pulled across it taxed the connection, yet he'd be able to keep this up much longer than drawing directly from the core.

The bond itself was still in good shape. Its edges remained solid, and its burn was pleasant, far from the searing fire it would become as it neared fraying. As an Ascendant, Holt could draw up to half of the core before the bond frayed. He risked a glance at the core and judged it had barely drained during the skirmish. His hard work Forging was paying off, giving both him and Ash a larger pool of power to draw from.

He checked Ash for injuries. "Are you hurt?"

"Just a scratch from the flayer."

Holt found it. The flayer had cut into Ash's hide between his neck and wing joint but not deep enough to draw blood. A portion of Ash's pain crossed the bond, but as the dragon wasn't complaining, Holt wouldn't make a fuss over it.

"We need to get as far away as possible!"

"But, boy, there could be people out there that need us."

"What if Sovereign was controlling those bugs? What if he knows where we are now?"

"He does not know everything. He did not know who we were until he met us through Osric."

"Good point, but there is always a chance."

"What does it matter? Will you never fight the scourge again because of him?"

"No, of course not," he conceded. Trying to push the thought of Sovereign from his mind, he looked at the issue more logically. "The scourge are drawn to the greatest population. Just the two of us alone could not have drawn them. Those must have been stragglers from the larger swarm you can hear, which means there must be a town or village nearby."

Ash clawed at the ground. He puffed light-vapor from his nostrils, then nodded. *"Agreed."*

Holt nodded back, feeling grim. Leaving the scourge roaming free did not sit well with him, but they would be fools to engage any sizable swarm alone. Riders from Sable Spire would arrive sooner rather than later to deal with the threat, and he and Ash could not afford to be caught when that happened.

They really ought to burn these bodies as well, but even if they had the time, he wasn't sure he could build a fire large enough out here on his own. Another disadvantage to not having Talia and Pyra with them.

Ash growled and nudged him. *"Come on, boy. We must go."*

"Lead the way," Holt said, determined.

They moved with haste. Holt maintained his torch of raw lunar light while Ash stayed ahead, his snout twisting this way and that as he picked up sounds and smells to follow. Soon they were bounding over the low stone wall of a farmstead. Such a find meant a town or village could not be more than a day's journey away.

"There is battle ahead," Ash cried, and his pace picked up, tearing through a copse. Between the dark branches, Holt glimpsed orange light. Sure enough, when they burst through the thicket, he saw the silhouette of roofs above a palisade wall. Fires lined the wall, though they were the red flames of the defenders, not the black of the scourge.

Ash skidded to a halt. *"I sense no other cores."*

That was all Holt needed to hear. Either they helped or else allowed a village to fall.

"We should fly."

Wasting no time, he cut down their equipment from Ash's back, pulled out his old satchel with his father's book in it and flung it over his shoulder. Next, he dug out the box with Brode's ashes and placed them inside the satchel alongside the cookbook. Pots and pans could be replaced, but neither of these could.

The egg. The egg was a problem. Without time to weigh up where it would be safest, Holt squeezed it into his satchel too, which now bulged. At least the weight meant little to him.

He then ripped open the venison sack and pulled out the last of the meat.

Holding it under Ash's nose, he said, "The smell of this, the wind on our skins."

Ash nodded, and then Holt turned all his focus onto those senses while simultaneously opening the dragon bond. Meat filled his nose; the air was chill at his face and neck; across the bond he gained an impression of how Ash perceived these things until their senses blurred.

Holt spoke the first line. "My eyes for your eyes."

The connection strengthened.

"Your skin for my skin," Ash said, lifting one front leg for Holt to touch.

"My world for your world," they said together.

As the sense-sharing technique snapped into full effect, Holt's world transformed. He heard the distant battle as though he were in it; the screeching of the scourge, the cries of the defenders, the heavy boom of a juggernaut hitting wood, and the twang of bowstrings.

He dropped the meat on the ground for Ash, and as the dragon wolfed it down, Holt jumped onto his back. Across the bond the volume of lunar motes grew so great that the core was lost in a sea of light.

"Just like at Sidastra," Holt called. "Let's go!"

Ash roared and took off, using Holt's eyes and the fires of battle to see by.

Holt's first concern was for stingers, the mutated wasps that menaced the air. He saw one scuttle along the top of the town's meager defenses. Another two rose out from the town itself, heading to face the oncoming threat. Their wings moved in a blur, so fast it was as though they had no wings at all.

As the buzzing grew louder, Holt brought both palms together for a charged Lunar Shock. It cost him twice the magic for not quite twice the effect, but he wanted the stingers dealt with as quickly as possible. If he and Ash could take control of the sky, then they could bombard the swarm with impunity.

Ash stayed low, feinting so that the first stinger came at them from above. Holt tilted up, held on until the last second, then blasted the nightmarish wasp with his charged attack. The Shock blew through the creature's pinched waist, cutting it clean in two.

Seconds later, Ash slammed into the other stinger. They rose in the air while their claws and teeth raked at each other. Holt held onto one of the ridges on Ash's back and pressed his legs in as tight as he could. Increased strength, agility, and sense of balance allowed him to stay on, but it was dizzying.

Ash twisted violently to one side, throwing the stinger off with bleeding wounds for its trouble. Holt cursed and just held on. The third stinger swooped in from behind. Ash needed no warning. He pivoted mid-air and blasted their enemy clean through with his breath attack; a silver beam of power, so thick and bright it appeared solid.

Bits of stinger, shell, black gore, and silver vapor rained to the earth. Ash's beam of lunar light dissipated around twenty feet out.

With the third stinger dead, the sky was clear.

"Don't hold back now," Holt said across their bond.

Ash dove, pulling up to fly low over the swarm, and drew his lunar beams through the packed ranks, shearing through ghoul and flayer alike as he dragged it out for seconds at a time.

After several passes, the scourge entered a state of complete disarray. Whichever bug down there was leading this swarm had most likely been seared by Ash's magic in the blink of an eye. Using the raw motes to bulk out each attack, Ash had not yet drained a third of his core.

On one pass closer to the wall, Holt caught sight of the few soldiers there. He had expected cheers and cries of thanks. Instead, they were screaming at him and pointing down. Wood rent and cracked. Juggernauts still rammed the gate.

The juggernauts were covered from above by the gatehouse itself. As one, Holt and Ash decided to land behind the creatures. Without hesitating, Ash unleashed his fury at them. His beam of light blew through the first bug, but whether Ash had put too much power into the attack or whether he had misjudged its range, it carried on, through the bug and into the very gate they were trying to protect.

"Stop!" Holt shouted too late.

Ash's beam blew a small hole into the gate, leaving the wood around the hole purpled like a black eye. Now weakened, the second juggernaut smashed through and into the town.

The scourge surged toward the breach. Those that had been fleeing turned and headed to rejoin the fight.

"Block the gate," Holt cried. He canceled their sense-sharing now they were back on solid ground, leaped from Ash, hit the earth, and laid down a Consecration. Together they held the enemy at bay. Only when a death cry bellowed from behind did Holt remember the juggernaut that had broken into the town.

He sprinted through the broken gate to find the bug half-buried under the rubble of a collapsed building. A dozen soldiers surrounded the beast, stark-faced. Crushed and pulped bodies were left in the juggernaut's wake. A small hand stuck out from amidst the rubble.

The elation of the fight, of the thumping, burning dragon bond, began to wane. Holt knew the town would likely have fallen had he and Ash not arrived. All the same, they could have prevented this. Their error had led to needless extra deaths.

Outside Ash roared, delighted with their victory. Holt felt his joy cross the bond only to be buffeted by his own hard reality check. Lesson one of the dragon riders had reared its ugly head again. And now it was over, Holt began to see other losses. The damage wrought by the stingers which had entered unchecked, the soldiers fallen from the walls, the corpses lying along the streets with blood pooling beneath them.

"Are you okay?" Ash asked.

"Just taking it in." A few of the braver soldiers were heading his way now. *"Take a breather and then we can start curing those of the blight that we can."*

As in Sidastra, it took Holt some time to convince the people that his magic would not harm them. The blight here was as fresh as it could be. Only in a few had it taken hold such that his powers were still not strong enough to banish the sickness.

One was a middle-aged man with a full head of hair, yet the green of the blight marbled his face. As he wheezed, a trickle of bloody puss ran from his mouth.

"Pleaaaase, Honored Rider."

The weakness of the man's voice caught Holt off guard. Hearing such a lifeless rasp brought him back to the quarantine isle in Sidastra when he'd held his father between his arms. This man might be someone's father too. Holt couldn't have guessed at his role-name, and no one was in a hurry to enter the building full of blight to tell him. The world contracted to himself, this dying man, and the flashes of light he produced in vain to save him.

Not again. Not again!

"Boy, it's too late."

Ash was outside. The hurt in the dragon's voice mirrored Holt's own pain. Through the bond, he could tell Ash was fixated upon the juggernaut he had carelessly allowed into the town, upon the tears and heaving breaths of those trying to clear the rubble.

Holt looked the man in the eye, and as he said, "I'm sorry," his voice cracked. "I'm sorry," he repeated, trying to convey this to the others in the sick house as he laid the man down and backed away.

The man reached out an arm. *"Pleaaase."*

How cruel, Holt thought, to have seen others cured, only to be left alone, to die alone, because he carried death in his veins. Such was the nature of the blight.

Holt found Ash sitting outside with his head slumped low to the earth. The townsfolk were giving them a wide berth, a mixture of respect, of fear, and maybe, for some, of anger at their blunder.

"We did our best," Holt said, stroking Ash's neck.

"We could have done better. I could have done better."

"Just learn. That's all we can do."

All the same, he clenched one fist. All his Forging had helped them tonight. Even after the battle and curing fifteen people of the blight, Ash's core had about a fifth of its power left. Their bond had only started to tremble as Holt reached his last patient.

Still, the timing had been lucky. It was a full moon. Could they have managed this alone if the moon had been new and not yet visible in the night sky? Holt did not think so. They had blown a lot of their magical stores on Ash's aerial assault. Quick, brutal, and effective though it had been, if there had been more scourge or if they had made more mistakes, the core would have depleted well before the battle was over.

As the night wore on, Holt aided in gathering the scourge corpses outside the walls to be burned. Ash sniffed out Holt's scent to retrieve their equipment and supplies. They learned that this place was called Dinan, a small settlement unused to fearing the scourge. The garrison commander had fallen atop the walls, and so it had fallen to the bailiff to provide leadership to the survivors. When he made offerings of thanks to Holt, all he asked for was some new rope so he could tie their equipment back onto Ash.

As dawn broke, there was little more they could do and there was little sense in staying, despite the hospitality offered. Every second they lingered endangered themselves and perhaps the townsfolk by association.

He led Ash outside. Pyres consumed the scourge, and the air grew thick with the smell of burning wood, smoke, and ash, mixed with the acrid leavings of the enemy. Holt secured their gear onto Ash's back, then climbed up himself. Without a large supply of meat, the weight was now no more than when they had left Sidastra. And as for trying to remain discreet, well, they had blown that. Holt's wish was now to get as far away as possible. Even Forging could wait until that was achieved.

The rising sun gave them a clear line to the east.

"We fly until we cross the Versand."

They flew all that day. As the afternoon waned, their bond cooled from the burn of battle and an ache settled in, like a muscle overworked from a day's training.

With the sun at their backs, a welcoming sight speared the horizon. A great river, near five leagues wide, its dark waters marbled by the fading light. And then entered a most unwelcome presence. Another core, another dragon, drew close in behind them.

Holt threw a glance over his shoulder and saw their pursuers. There was little they could do. As the dragon and rider closed the distance, Holt sensed their power. This was a Champion.

Though it seemed futile, they kept flying until they reached the water. They were halfway over the border when the Champion and their dragon overtook and then cut across their path.

Ash came to a halt. The Champion's dragon returned to hover before them, its verdant scales marking it as an emerald. The rider's features were hazy at this distance, but their blade was long, fine, and leaf green.

"*Back you go,*" the dragon said, her voice confident as a cat toying with a mouse.

With little choice, Ash turned and flew back to the Brenin side of the river. He landed on the bank and the emerald dragon landed beside them. The rider seemed an old man in appearance, as gray and white as Brode had been, though he retained a brightness in his eyes and the smooth complexion of one with access to a dragon's core. Where Brode had had short hair and stubble, this man had flowing locks and a thick snowy beard. He wore brigandine armor the same bright green as his dragon.

"Who are you?" Holt asked, dreading the answer, knowing the answer.

"Orvel, and this is my dragon Gea. I am placing you under arrest, rogue."

SEVEN

High and Low

Holt searched desperately for a way out. He and Ash were facing a Champion rider and his dragon. As if they weren't already outclassed, he and Ash were still weak from defending the town of Dinan. Yet as Holt inspected the power of Orvel, he thought the man weaker than the two Champions he had met near Sidastra.

"The emerald is tired," Ash said. *"Her heart races, her wings ache."*

"You can tell that?" Holt asked.

As they spoke privately, Orvel jumped down from his dragon, Gea. "Descend and surrender your sword to me," he said, his accent marking him as a man of Brenin.

"I don't think so," Holt said, playing for time.

"Could we make enough light to blind them for a bit?" Holt asked Ash. It was about all he could hope to do. Orvel might well chase them across the border into Athran territory, but they would only find out one way.

"You seem to misunderstand the power difference between us," Orvel said. At once, Holt felt a roving presence over his bond with Ash. "A strong bond for such a young Ascendant. Has that made you overconfident?" In his left hand, he held his leaf-shaped blade and pointed it toward Holt. "Get down and surrender."

Holt did as instructed. As he landed, he adjusted his satchel. The egg still lay within the bag.

"What am I under arrest for?" Holt said, feigning innocence.

Orvel stroked his beard once, as though sizing Holt up. "A white dragon and a young male rider. A Feorlen accent, if I'm not mistaken. You'll be the rogue wanted by Falcaer Fortress, but you also have something of mine. Hand the egg over – and before you think to pretend otherwise, my merchant friends described you perfectly."

"Right down to the blindfold over the weakling," Gea said.

Ash snapped his teeth at her. *"I have the blessing of the Life Elder himself. Your words wither in the air around me."*

"They lie as easily as they breathe. And each of his flawed breaths disgusts me."

"Now, now," Orvel said, "this blind dragon and his rider did us a favor, Gea. We owe them thanks for saving our friends upon the road. Now, hand it over."

Feeling there was little use in protesting, Holt brought out the egg. "I might be a rogue in your eyes, but we both know you weren't supposed to give this to a group of slippery merchants. I don't think your superiors would be happy to hear of it."

Orvel said nothing. Gea flexed her talons.

"If you let us go, no one need find out."

Orvel took several measured steps forward. This close, Holt could see a flatness in his gray eyes. The man was neither cruel nor charitable, neither insane nor intelligently fixated. There was a detached quality to him that unnerved Holt more. It was impossible to predict what he would do.

"And why should my superiors believe the word of a rogue rider who is implicated in the death of Silas Silverstrike?"

"Silas betrayed everyone!"

"So you say," said Orvel, his voice level. "You overestimate your bargaining power, but I shall grant you one chance. Hand over the egg, and I'll let you go."

Holt clutched the egg tighter. "And then you'll sell it? No way."

Gea growled and advanced to join her rider.

"She thinks we should just kill you both and throw the egg into the river," Orvel said. "It's defective, after all. I don't know why anyone would place such value on it."

Gea gnashed her teeth and growled again.

"You know, I think she's right," said Orvel. "Much cleaner this wa—"

Orvel ceased talking, looking stricken, and cast his gaze toward the west. Gea turned her attention in that direction as well, falling silent.

"There's another rider coming," Ash said.

Holt felt it a second later. Another Champion had just entered the range of his detection, this one stronger than Orvel.

Their would-be captor rounded on them, raised his green blade, and cut through the weak points of his armor on his upper right arm. Blood welled.

"It appears you attacked me, rogue."

He moved in.

Holt had a split second to think. The dragon bond still ached from their recent battle and their prolonged sense-sharing while flying. Ash's core was a little below a fifth of its strength. Holt raised his free hand, pulled hard on the magic. Power flowed unchecked. In his panic Holt drew on too much, expelling the brightest burst of light he could. Not a Shock, just raw light without restraint. Their bond blazed to a screaming heat, then frayed.

Orvel halted mere feet from him, yelling and throwing one arm across his face to shield his eyes.

Holt pivoted and jumped onto Ash's back.

"Fly!"

There was no time to share senses. Ash just had to take off. It was their only chance.

Roaring, Ash bent his legs then froze.

"Something has me."

Holt looked down. Roots and vines curled around Ash's feet, trapping him. Ripples in the earth ran back to Gea's talons. Beneath her, the earth shimmered as though in a heat haze. Nearby bushes, trees, and even grass swayed and groaned. Grass retreated into the soil, and in its wake fresh vines lashed up to bind Ash and heave him down.

As Ash fell, Holt lost balance, and the dragon egg slipped from his grasp. He groped in the air but missed it and was thrown from Ash's back. The egg hit the earth and rolled toward Orvel, who had recovered enough from the light to brandish his sword and advance again. His bloodshot, watery eyes held anger now. He thrust clumsily. Holt dodged.

Gripping the hilt of Brode's blade, Holt drew it out for the first time in combat. Despite all his training, the hundreds upon hundreds of draws, it could not have prepared him to do it for real. He fumbled at the last moment, leaving his sword arm wide and awkward. It would have cost him his life had a cold wind not whipped between them followed by a shard of ice which struck Orvel's hands. The ice shattered upon impact, causing Orvel to howl in pain and drop his weapon.

A third dragon bellowed, and a rider in pale blue brigandine dropped from the air to land between Holt and Orvel. The other Champion had arrived.

Her power was great. She crashed into Holt's magical senses like a boulder into a calm pond. Her bond and the power behind it were an order of magnitude stronger than Orvel and Gea. Yet where Silas and Orvel both looked older, she did not look a day past her mid-thirties—though she may well have been much older than she appeared. Long braided blonde hair, streaked with white, fell to the middle of her back. Although she was shorter than Holt, she so clearly dominated the scene that she might have been a giant.

Before Holt could say anything, blocks of ice formed around his feet, shins, and calves, holding him in place. His feet seared from extreme cold. Gea's vines still bound Ash on the ground. He lay flat, branches, roots, and vines constraining his snout so he couldn't summon magic for a breath attack.

The ice Champion only had eyes for Orvel. She lowered her sword toward him; cobalt blue, long and triangular, the blade narrowed to its tip like an icicle.

Orvel fell to one knee.

"What's the meaning of this?" she demanded. "Why did you

abandon me during your watch?"

Orvel raised his head, blinking hard and fast. A tear fell from the water pooling in his eyes, and Holt wondered just how bright a light he had cast.

"Gea and I wished to fly to the region's defense and defeat the scourge alone, Master Ethel." Orvel spoke carefully, yet he could not hide the resentful bite in his words. "To repent for insisting we patrol the northwest territories instead."

"And you thought it appropriate to sneak off in the night?" Ethel said.

The ice dragon landed then. It touched down behind Gea, and Holt shivered as its aura swept over them. The chill from this dragon was far stronger than even that from Mirk's dragon, Biter.

Orvel threw a glance over his shoulder to acknowledge the dragon's presence before continuing. "We wished to earn your praise, Master Ethel. To prove ourselves after our error."

"Then you failed," Ethel said. "The people of Dinan told me a boy and a white dragon saved them. You were nowhere to be seen."

Unless Holt was mistaken, her accent was of Feorlen too. Noble, of course. Perhaps she had been from the southern coast once but time away had diluted her tongue.

"I heard the same tale," Orvel said. "Though as I arrived not long after they had left, I decided to give chase. Rogues should be brought to justice, after all. This Ascendant is one of the Feorlen traitors!"

"We're not—" Holt began.

Ethel rounded on him. "Did I give you permission to spea…" Her words died in her throat as she stared aghast at the sword in his hand. Her voice turned hoarse. "Where did you get that?"

"The sword?" Holt asked. He winced from the pain of the ice around his leg, gritted his teeth, and said, "I got it from my mentor. Well, not exactly, but—"

Ethel moved at a Champion's speed to stand inches from him. "It belonged to an old friend of mine."

Behind her, still on his knees, Orvel grinned. "You killed your own master and took his sword?"

"What? No. Never. Brode was..." Holt hesitated. What was Brode to him, really? He hadn't known him for long and yet it had felt as though he'd known him for years by the end. "Brode was our guide. Our first teacher. A grumpy big brother and our old neighbor all at once." He looked imploringly at Ethel. "Please, you must believe me. I'd never harm Brode. He died defending me and my dragon Ash and our friends Talia and Pyra from Silas Silverstrike."

"So you *are* one of the rogues from Feorlen?" Ethel asked.

"I suppose I am."

"And did you really kill Silas and Clesh?"

"Well, Ash and I killed Clesh," Holt said. "Ash can take the credit there for tricking him. It was Talia who defeated Silas in a duel."

"She... defeated him in a duel," Ethel said, matter of fact.

"It was after we killed Clesh. He'd lost most of his powers and was half-mad with grief at the time."

"And how did a fresh-faced Ascendant and a blind dragon manage to kill one of the most powerful dragons in the Order?"

Holt's teeth began to chatter. "Let me out of this ice, and I'll gladly tell you. I can tell you of your friend's attempts to sell a dragon egg too."

"Liar!" Orvel called. "Master Ethel, do not listen to this traitor. He attacked me." And he displayed his arm for her. "All to protect his contraband." He stood and walked the few paces to where the dragon egg lay. Holt's heart gave a painful beat.

"You see," Orvel said, handing the egg over to his superior. "This must be one of the eggs that went missing from the Spire."

One of the eggs? Holt thought in alarm.

Ethel studied the egg with narrowed eyes while her dragon stalked around the group, snorting blue smoke and ensuring they were chilled and uncomfortable.

"You have any ideas?" Holt asked Ash.

"This Ethel knew Master Brode. If we can get her to trust us—"

"But how?" Holt said.

"I believe you're right, Orvel," Ethel said. "Notes from the flight song of Sable Spire can be heard upon the shell. Weakly. It is one of the defective eggs." Her narrowed eyes turned upon Holt again. "What reason would a rogue have with a worthless egg?"

"It isn't worthless," Holt said. "Ash was considered defective too, but he's as powerful as any dragon. Maybe more so," he added pointedly to the emerald and ice drakes present. "Or how else do you explain how a, how did you put it, a fresh-faced Ascendant and a blind dragon defended Dinan on our own?"

He allowed a moment for the dragons and Champions to consider this before soldiering on. "For all we know, another dragon like Ash might hatch from that egg. As to why I have it, I took it from a group of merchants who claimed Orvel gave it to them. They outright told me, thinking he had sent me to guard them on the road. They were heading to a town called Gironde. You could fly back and ask them for yourself, Honored Ethel."

He gave her a small bow as a courtesy. "As to why someone else may want an egg like this, well, there is an enemy out there who knows of Ash and me, and he might desire to hatch a special dragon of his own."

The words tumbled out of Holt. Yet, hearing them out loud, he had a foreboding feeling they were true. All the riders of Falcaer believed he and Ash were traitors, or at least rogues. Only one other person out there – well, one dragon – could know of the potential hidden powers in unusual dragon eggs.

"An enemy?" said Ethel. "And who might that be?"

"His name is Sovereign. He's a powerful mystic dragon controlling the scourge."

Gea and Ethel's dragon both laughed with a dark, derisive rumble.

"Such tall tales," Orvel said.

Holt met his bloodshot eyes. Had Orvel known what he had been getting into? Or had he been trying to sell an egg for his own dubious reasons? Holt hoped for the latter, hoped that his theory was wrong. The idea of more riders helping Sovereign seemed to freeze him to the bone.

A moment later, he realized this new drop in temperature had come from Ethel herself. She had raised her hand toward the laughing dragons. "Quiet." The air grew even colder. It even smelled cold, chill, and clean, as though winter had arrived on the west bank of the Versand. Holt's breath steamed upon the air.

"The boy tells me one thing, Orvel, and you another."

"You can't believe this nonsense? A dragon controlling the scourge – it's preposterous!"

"As preposterous an idea as two Ascendants turning traitor to kill Silas Silverstrike," Holt asked, "only to stay and defeat an incursion while all the riders of the Crag perished around us? You tell me which is more unbelievable."

Orvel changed tack. "Master Ethel, let us bring the boy and his dragon back to Sable Spire. There he can be interrogated at length."

Ethel gave the barest of nods, yet her eyes found Brode's sword once more. "Where were you going, Ascendant?"

"We were traveling east," Holt said. "East of Athra. We're hoping to find the gravesite of Master Brode's dragon so we can bury his ashes alongside her."

"You have his ashes with you?"

"Yes, in a lockbox amongst my equipment." He looked at Ash, still bound by Gea's power. "Please let Ash go and I can get the box for you, if you like."

Ethel sniffed hard, then gave another curt nod. The ice encasing Holt's legs melted away.

Gea, however, did not release Ash.

"You heard your superior," said Ethel's dragon, his voice surprisingly high and crisp for such a large male. He snarled, and Gea finally relented.

Ash got back onto his feet, shaking the vines free. He stretched and groaned from relief. Holt took a step or two, unsteady for a moment on numb legs, before running to Ash's side. He ran a hand down the dragon's neck.

"You alright, Ash?"

"I've felt worse." He snaked his head around and pushed gently into Holt's own. Holt reached up to give his snout a hug. *"It's not over yet,"* Ash continued. *"Show her Master Brode's remains."*

Holt searched in his pack for the lockbox. The fight had reduced his remaining loaf from the merchants to crumbs. Thankfully, Brode's sturdy container was intact. Holt presented it to Ethel with both hands before retreating ten paces as a servant might and kept his head bowed. Better to be respectful.

"I can open the box if you wish, Honored Ethel," Holt said to his toes.

"There is no need."

Ethel ran one hand over the box, her eyes shut. After four passes, she opened her eyes and looked at Holt in a newfound light.

"It really is him."

Her dragon gave a deep, mournful growl, expressing the grief Ethel hid so well.

"I'm telling the truth," Holt said.

Orvel looked horrified but did nothing.

When Ethel spoke next, her words were a little choked. "He never spoke about what happened on that mission."

"His dragon, Erdra, fought so hard her core drained. The blight got in her, and Brode... Brode said she asked him to kill her before it took hold."

Even Gea emitted a low moan at this thought and moved to wrap a wing around Orvel.

"There were rumors of it," Ethel said. "High command knew, I'm sure, but it never officially came out. How awful. To break a bond in such a way..." She winced at the thought of it, then handed Brode's box back to him. "I believe you."

"Master Ethel," Orvel said, stunned. "The boy is a convincing liar but—"

"And yet his story, wild as it seems, has detail. You speak vaguely. Rather than convince me with truth, you only condemn the boy and his dragon. I assume you were about to kill them before I arrived?"

"I intended to arrest them and bring them alive to Sable Spire."

"He lies," Ash said. "You cannot deceive my ears. Your heart races with every word you utter."

Ethel turned on her charge. "Champion Orvel, you will get a

chance to prove your story. I think a trip to Gironde might be just the thing. I'll speak with these merchants. If they've moved on, I'm sure the bailiff can point us in the right direction. I do hope they were loyal to you."

Orvel's features returned to their blank, near-emotionless state again. "Gea and I were out fighting the scourge, defending the living, doing our duties while you were still in pigtails."

"When I was a young girl you were a Low Champion, and that you have remained while I've advanced to High Champion. Is that why you're so resentful, Orvel? Do you know why the Flight Commander changed the pairings? He feared you and Hasten were no longer singularly focused on your duties."

"And how will he react when he learns you let the rogue go?"

Holt held his breath. For a moment, he feared Ethel would cut some deal with him over it. A code of silence and call it all quits.

"Then I'll explain myself," Ethel said, "and trust the Commander remembers why he placed his faith in me." She extended her hand. "Surrender your sword."

Orvel's cheek twitched. He raised his sword and remained tensed like a cat ready to strike. Gea gave a throaty rumble and nudged him gently. Words might have passed between them. Orvel looked to his dragon desperately but then hung his head and handed his blade over. That done, he fell to his knees again, and Gea lowered her head to the ground.

"I willingly submit myself to you, Master Ethel."

Ethel's dragon snorted in satisfaction and the sheer cold in the air began to subside. Though the sun was beginning to set, Holt felt its faint heat upon his skin again. He breathed on his hands and rubbed them, trying not to dwell on their near chance with death.

We must become stronger, he thought. *Stronger. Faster.*

"No rash moves," Ethel told Orvel, then she returned her attention to Holt. "What's your name, boy?"

"Holt." He left out the Cook this time.

"You are a rogue from the Order, Holt," Ethel said. "I really ought to bring you in as well. Why didn't you join when my fellow Champions demanded it of you?"

Holt hesitated. "The Life Elder himself set a task for me. I could not follow his will by joining the Order but, if I'm honest, I did not wish to join either. Not after all Ash and I had gone through. Not knowing how we would be treated as part of your ranks. We're better off on our own."

"Champions Sigfrid and Maria reported the presence of a Wild Flight in Feorlen."

Ethel's dragon approached Ash then, looking at him with wide eyes. *"An Elder spoke to you, youngling? What was it like?"*

"Overwhelming and calming all at once," Ash said. *"His song is so mighty and rich, yet its notes are almost one with all the world around him. He is life, and life is him."*

Holt only recalled the fresh grief from holding Brode's body while his father's death mingled with fatigue and desperation. He had not heard the Elder's song.

The dragons appeared to enter a discussion of their own, heads bobbing and tails moving.

"You might not believe everything that's happened to us," Holt said.

"I have so far," Ethel said.

And so, Holt did tell her, as brief as he could make it, of all the events of the short, brutal incursion of Feorlen and his role in it. He told her of the task the Life Elder had given him and Ash to find the Wild Flights and convince them to join the fight against Sovereign, although he omitted the part about the Elders creating the scourge.

Orvel remained on his knees, still and silent as the grave.

When he was finished, Ethel stared into the semi-distance, weighing up his words. At last, she looked at her dragon, and their eyes met. Holt guessed that words were exchanged in private, then she turned back to him.

"I hope I haven't been wrong about you. If I am, if you've somehow deceived me, know that if we ever meet again, I'll encase you in ice and haul you back to Falcaer myself."

"You won't have to."

"Then I shall let you go."

Holt breathed easy again. "Thank you, Honored Ethel." He bowed low.

"You really were a servant, weren't you?" she said, amazed.

"I was, and a part of me will always be a Cook. Before we go, I must admit that Ash and I weren't sure exactly where to go. We know it's east of Athra but no more than that. If you know anything of Brode's last mission with Erdra, we'd be grateful to hear it."

"I believe it was a settlement in the northern disputed lands, bordering the Fae Forest. A remote place called Red Rock. The name reflects the environment. You'll know it when you see it."

"Thank you, Honored Ethel," Holt said. He prepared to leave, repacking his gear and Brode's ashes, then got onto Ash's back. Just as he considered beginning the sense-sharing process, he remembered the poor egg that had caused all this trouble. Ethel still held it under one arm. He looked at it and said, "Don't let them destroy it."

Ethel pressed her lips into a thin line. Her dragon grunted and thumped his tail against the ground.

"It's the way things are done," she said. "I will think on all you've told me. Yet if what you say is true, then we need order now more than ever. It is not the time for rash actions. Reckless emotion is what got Erdra killed all those years ago. Brode should have known better."

"Change doesn't need to be reckless," Holt said.

Ethel remained unmoved. "Yet so often it is. Go now, Holt Cook. Before I *change* my mind."

With that final warning, Holt and Ash blended their senses. The bond was frayed and so the sharing was garbled and caused them both a headache, but they fought through it, flying over the Versand to leave Brenin and enter the realm of the Free City of Athra.

Their thoughts now turned to Red Rock, and more than ever since leaving Sidastra, they also returned to Sovereign. Holt and Ash were to gather allies against him, but they feared now that they might not make enough progress before the enemy made his next move.

EIGHT

A Poisoned Gift

Talia stood sentinel at the base of the steps to the throne, unmoving as only a rider with an enhanced body could. Green satin robes draped her from head to toe. They were trimmed in silver and bore the royal sigil: two crossed swords encircled by a crown. Beneath, she still wore her hardened rider leathers. Her mother had questioned what some would think if they glimpsed her armor beneath the robes of state, yet with Pyra sitting at the base of the throne, Talia felt the damage was already done. She had a dragon, and everyone would have to get used to that.

You want me to make my mark, mother? This will be it.

Her mother sat on her left-hand side, where family and key members of the household had the privilege of a chair and cushion from which to witness the proceedings. Everyone else, be they Ealdor or guilded merchant, military or civilian, would stand before her in the hall.

The great doors at the end of the throne room were open, a symbolic gesture that the ceremony was for all. Talia hoped fresh air would run in a through draft from the shattered stained-glass window above the throne and toward the open doors to cool the hall. However, it was an uncommonly hot and still day. With the hall so packed with people, both standing on the floor and squeezed up in the galleries overhead, the usual cool stones seemed to trap the heat. The air stifled.

Talia was no stranger to heat, but her mouth had never felt so dry. After today, there would be no going back. She would forever be an oath breaker. A chaos bringer.

"You aren't nervous, are you?" Pyra asked.

"No," Talia said reflexively. She didn't want Pyra to think poorly of her in this moment, not when she had been the one to change their lives so radically. *"I'm just impatient for it to be over."*

"I found our own initiation tiresome. All I wanted to do was begin training with you, but Master Denna just droned on and on."

Talia smiled. *"I remember. Everything felt so exciting and so sure. The road ahead was mapped and plotted. We had a routine, small goals to work toward. And then everything fell apart. How I wish we could go back to those early days. Just being together."*

"I would rather look to our future. Think of all we might achieve, as no rider and dragon have done before. Our song shall be unique. Our song shall be great."

The bond flared and widened, and Talia heard Pyra's dragon song in her mind, so loud that it drowned out all noise from the throne room. It exploded into a rampaging pace, the notes rough and coarse. Her heart quickened, her fingers twitched – an urge for battle and for action came upon her.

The music faded all too soon, as the dragon song so often did. Hearing it was an infrequent luxury. With it gone, the mundane, slow world of the throne room returned.

As the last stragglers were herded in at the back of the hall, Talia spared a moment to check upon the ambassadors and their entourages.

The Athrans wore the formal senatorial attire of the city. Velvet riding jackets over a white shirt, the sleeves of which were rolled up from the wrist to display stiff, oversized cuffs. Cream woolen breeches and high black boots gave the impression they could hop on a horse at a moment's notice. The ambassador had the honor of wearing a simple horseshoe ring of woven hay upon his head. This was a lesser imitation of the true civic crown worn by the archon of the city.

The ambassadors from Coedhen and Mithras each had a version of their own civic crowns; a ring of spruce leaves for Coedhen and a laurel wreath for the Mithrans. Apart from this link to their Alduneian past, the rest of their attires held nothing in common.

The Coedhens dressed as woodsmen might, in brown leathers and green cloth. Most striking was their great hooded traveling cloaks and prominent vambraces. Much as the Athrans seemed ready to ride, the people from Coedhen in the Fae Forest seemed ready to spring out from behind cover with a drawn bow.

The Mithrans wore short, tight-fitting doublets. Their trousers were also cut in tight to their legs, giving them the appearance of having been stretched upon the rack.

Behind them, the Risalians stood regimented in decorative black hose and black brocade tunics with white buttons. Behind them were representatives from the Province of Fornheim. The Margraves of Fornheim were historically reactionary and defensive. They rarely, if ever, made the first move.

No representatives were present from Ahar, but those lands were distant, and word of her ascension may not even have reached the Shah yet. The same held true for the peoples south across the Stretched Sea, though they always seemed a world apart and uninterested in the goings-on in the lands of the old republic.

The Skarls were absent too, as they had been for decades.

At last, she caught the eye of the Master of State, who gave her a curt nod. It was time.

Trumpets blared. Drums were beaten. Pyra added a long roar to signal the start of the ceremony, causing many in the hall to cover their ears or cower.

When the fanfare subsided, the Master of State strode out to be front and center. Heeled shoes added another three inches to Horndown's impressive height, meaning even those at the back of the hall would see him. Today his beard and hair had been combed and oiled to a glowing shine. His robes, like all the High Council members, were pale blue and unadorned.

"People of Feorlen," he called, "and most honored and welcome guests, today a new age begins in our lands. I call now upon each Ealdor of the realm to submit fealty on behalf of their families and the people of their lands and holdings. May these oaths be binding and may pain befall any chaos bringer who should break them."

They came one by one, each flanked by aides or guards carrying an offering to her. Some gifts were practical, others ornate. Their house sigils were prominently featured on their garb, but the Master of State announced each Ealdor as they approached, lest Talia's memory betray her.

Ealdor Odilo of Port Bolca brought her pelts and furs acquired through trade with the Province of Fornheim across the vast Bitter Bay.

"I also grant the gift of naming our first new ship built in Her Majesty's honor."

Talia thanked him, though if he hoped this would make her forget about the citizens he let flee during the incursion, he was mistaken.

When it came time for Ealdor Ebru to kneel before her, Talia honored her with a kiss on her brow. This drew mutterings from the crowd. Talia was not supposed to express favoritism, but the Ebru family had sheltered her, Pyra, Brode, Holt, and Ash after the battle outside of Midbell. Lady Ebru conferred her gift – a dazzling silver windchime – then swore her fealty and moved on.

A young man approached whom she had never met, but the blue hawk of House Harroway gave him away. That and the Twinblades of the house who flanked their new Ealdor, their every movement made in unison.

Drefan Harroway had a jaunt in his step. He halted at the servant's range from her, smiling. He was handsome, she had to admit, though he might have benefitted from a little roughness around the edges. Something about him seemed too well kept, and his smile verged too close to smug for her liking. What made him so pleased with himself?

Had Elvina overstepped and suggested that Talia was open to a marriage?

Pyra growled at the Twinblades. *"What are they doing here?"*

"Do nothing, girl," Talia told her.

"Ealdor Harroway," she said, her voice loud enough to carry but flattened to reveal no emotion. "Are you willing to swear fealty to the crown and to my person?"

He knelt before her, maintaining eye contact all the way. "I do so swear my loyalty to the crown and pledge my service to you. My house and name have suffered blows, both to our reputation and in the loss of my good father. I hope I can fill the void he left, both in my lands and however my queen thinks fit to use me."

She bid him rise, and when he did, his smile grew wolfish. "Your Majesty is gracious. May I present my gift to you." He stepped aside as the Twinblades marched forward. Both fell to one knee. Were it not for the different styles of their dirty blond hair – one long, the other short and wild – it would have been impossible to tell them apart.

"We seek the forgiveness of our queen," said Eadwulf, the long-haired of the two.

"We did not know of the substance we were given," Eadwald said.

"Our honor was besmirched through lies," said Eadwulf.

"But only we can be held responsible for our actions—"

"And so, we offer our service to you, our queen—"

"In payment of our folly," Eadwald ended solemnly.

In fluid movements, the twins unstrapped their sword belts and held their sheathed swords up to her.

Talia checked for the reaction of her High Councilors. The Mistress of Embassy looked wide-eyed at the Master of State who, for once, seemed lost for words.

Pyra understood the significance of Harroway's move. She growled from deep in her chest. Talia could feel her pained restraint, and that need for restraint only made the dragon angrier. That anger rose in Talia too. She gulped the feeling back down as though it were rising vomit, and she tasted a hint of smoke at the back of her throat. She wanted to claw that smug smile off Harroway's face.

I don't have claws, she reminded herself. That was Pyra's desire.

Nonetheless, Talia very much wished to slap him. Harroway's play had been so neat he might have tied a ribbon on it. By offering the twins to her publicly, she could hardly refuse – not at her own coronation, where she was supposed to accept any gift graciously. To refuse would be yet another severe break with tradition. At best, it would make her look petty.

The Twinblades were a central part of the investigation into House Harroway's use of dragon blood. Accepting them into her personal service would be an effective declaration of forgiveness to the entire house. Continuing the investigations would be rendered moot at best or, at worst, make Talia seem a real fool for bringing men into her service who turned out to be connected to Wyrm Cloaks.

Caught between the juggernaut and the flayer, she thought bitterly.

She forced her lips into a polite smile, even as the heat rising within her made her dizzy. Fire was not supposed to be contained like this.

"I humbly accept your offer, Eadwald and Eadwulf. Rise now. Your skills in swordcraft will be needed against the challenges ahead."

Wishing to get this over, Talia continued accepting offers of fealty from her remaining Ealdors. The members of her High Council came last. Collectively they presented her with a ceremonial sword as a symbol of her promise to defend the land and with a scepter to symbolize her right to rule. It was then her turn to grant some powers back.

The Master of Roles was so old he could not have knelt and risen again without pain, so he alone of the High Council remained standing and inclined his neck as she dubbed him. She tapped him once on each shoulder with the scepter and once again with the sword.

"To you, Ealdor Hubbard, I confer the office of Master of Roles, with the duty to ensure all in my realm have a position to fulfill, that our homes are guarded, our streets cleaned, our roads maintained, and our bellies kept full, and above all to maintain order against the chaos that would destroy us."

"I do so swear," he said.

She dubbed and swore in each High Councilor until, at last, it was over. The final step had come. A steward from the royal household approached, holding the crown upon a velvet pillow. Its rubies and sapphires shone bright, the gold had been polished, and the white ermine at the base had been cleaned spotless.

The audience seemed to draw a collective breath as the Master of State picked up the crown. Her own breaths came short and shallow. Everything felt disembodied. She repeated the words the Master of State asked her to affirm, but she did not consciously do this.

I made the right choice. This is my duty. I made the right choice.

Horndown stepped behind Talia. He was so tall there was no need for her to sit or lower herself. He finished speaking, and then she felt the weight upon her head. It was done. She was Queen of Feorlen.

I must walk up to the throne, she thought, remembering at the last moment.

Talia took the first step on the looming stairs. About halfway up, a commotion from the crowd caused her to turn.

The foreign dignitaries shuffled as the black-clad Risalians filed out one by one into the central aisle. Their ambassador did not have the courage to look at Talia, and instead he addressed the crowd.

"You make this oath breaker your queen? The Archduke of Risalia does not accept, nor should any realm which still believes in order."

He turned and stormed off down the aisle, leaving his associates to hurry after him.

Guards at the edge of the hall looked to Talia for orders. She signaled that they were to do nothing. Though provocative, that had been no declaration of war. Seizing the ambassador by force would be all the Archduke needed to throw his army into the Toll Pass.

Yet Talia was fast losing the capacity to contain Pyra's fire. Motes from her core crossed the bond. Talia raced to channel them evenly through her mote channels to absorb them without causing any physical manifestations to appear.

Down below, Pyra's growling rose to a full snarl. Smoke billowed from her nostrils and her amber eyes were lit with fury.

"Do nothing," Talia told her again. *"They are baiting you."*

Still, it was all Talia could do not to have the Risalians intercepted at the door. Knowing that realm would be hostile to her rule was one thing, but to use her coronation as a stage for their grievance added insult.

"If anyone else has an issue with my reign," Talia called, "let them leave now, be they Feorlen or otherwise. The doors are open, after all."

She returned to her climb up the stairs. When she turned again to survey the hall, fifteen feet above the floor, she was pleased to find the crowd still intact. Lifting her robes, she took her seat in the great high-backed chair.

Another round of trumpets blared, drums beat, and Pyra roared.

"Long live the queen!" boomed the Master of State.

The crowd was half drowned out by Pyra's second roar.

Talia was about to breathe more easily when the ambassador from Athra stepped out from the crowd. He moved to the center of the aisle, but unlike his Risalian counterpart, he said nothing. Over the din of Pyra, he wouldn't have been heard. Instead, without any bow or courtesy, he turned his back on her and strode up the aisle. The rest of the Athrans followed his lead.

Their departure sent a wave of unease throughout the crowd. People fell silent when they saw them or else attempted to stand on tiptoe to see what was happening. The chanting for Talia's long life faltered, and half the trumpeters ceased playing. Most of the Feorlens in the hall were of high enough station to know who had just left. And what a blow that was to their new queen.

Talia might have been able to contain her anger – Pyra's anger. The moment the Athran ambassador had stepped out, she had begun to breathe as she would for Cleansing, focusing solely on the cool intake of air at the tip of her nose, allowing all else to wash over her. She cycled the fire through her mote channels, keeping it flowing without letting it build up in one place. Had she closed her eyes, she might have been able to maintain it.

But then she caught the look of despair on the Mistress of Embassy's face and then the smirk on Harroway's. The dam burst.

Talia tried to push the power back across the bond, but a fresh wave crossed unchecked from Pyra's side. The resultant internal clash made her feel as though she'd been plunged into scalding water.

She gasped. Her neck grew red and sweaty as blood and magic rushed to her head. After the moment passed, she sagged in relief.

Her nostrils twitched. Smoke.

Her mother rushed to the base of the throne's steps, pointing and shouting, but it was Pyra's voice that got through to her.

"Your crown!"

Talia raised her hand and ran her fingers through naked flames. The ermine lining at the base of the crown had caught fire. Talia calmly lifted the crown from her head, safe in the knowledge that such small flames would not affect her.

She sat there, holding her burning crown in one hand, and only then noticed the scorched wood from where her hands had gripped the throne. Things could only have gone worse if Pyra had eaten Harroway alive.

She let out an exasperated laugh. All her worrying, all the carefully rehearsed words and lines, none of it could cover who she really was. She had brought Pyra to the ceremony to make it clear she had no shame in being a rider, and yet in every other way she had tried to cover it up.

Clarity came to her then in what she could only describe as her own moment of madness. She wondered, as she stood, if this had been how Holt had felt when he decided to save Ash's egg.

Talia Agravain, Ascendant of Fire, placed the still burning crown back onto her head, then leaped from the elevated throne. Her green robes billowed beneath her and fanned out as she landed with cat-like grace.

She grabbed fistfuls of her satin robes and channeled motes to her hands. The silk ignited and spread fast. Her hardened leathers beneath would not burn easily. Talia raised her arms, and any who looked upon her would have seen their young queen inside a cone of fire. Unburnt. Unharmed. A queen wrought in flames.

The hall fell silent.

NINE

A Worm's Work

It had been two years since Osric Cleansed Sovereign's core. In that time, the volume of incompatible motes had become a choking dust in the air of the great hall. Prior to bonding with Sovereign, Osric had not fully grasped why the dragons of the Order were more powerful than their wild counterparts. Given the mess of Sovereign's core, the benefits of having a rider tend to it were plain.

Osric's initial efforts were rusty, but after several days of labor his efficiency returned. Unfortunately, no matter how good he became, the technique remained an exercise in slow torture. He despised each breath. Drawing the dust across the bond, into his soul, then into his mote channels to raise and expel it felt like rubbing grit into a wound.

Magic did not suit him. He'd ever been wary of its use. Chaotic, it always seemed to him, a force of the natural world spawned from primal furies of fire, of bitter winters, of raging storms that battered and broke homes. Humanity's brittle order seemed ill defended by the very forces which daily sought its destruction.

Osric felt safest in routine, in discipline, in the unquestioning role of a soldier. A true soldier was the antithesis of the scourge and even, he thought at times, of the riders themselves. Magic created the ills of the world. One did not put out a fire with more fire.

He raised another jagged lump of impurities to the back of his throat before heaving to expel it. The cluster was big enough that he physically felt the energy leave his body. He pictured the purple-black light trailing from him like smoke from a tallow candle.

After recovering for a few breaths, he looked at the core again and drew in another cloud of impurities.

On it went. Each day he could Cleanse longer than the last. When he returned to his chambers it was only to sleep, rise with the dawn, shave his face, perform his exercises, and linger for a moment upon his gray cloak and the true soldier he used to be.

Such a plain garment, but for a time it had been the symbol of the finest free company in the world. Guards to the Archon of Athra, the men who held the eastern Mithran Commonwealth when the riders were slow to respond, and the bane of the desert tribes plaguing the Shah of Ahar. While wearing the cloak, he had achieved his greatest triumphs and suffered his worst heartbreaks. Without it on, he felt lesser, naked, as though the cloak were a shield around his body, mind, and soul.

Sovereign sensed his lingering thoughts. *"What sort of general holds so much fear over a piece of cloth?"*

Fear? Osric thought, taken aback. *Not fear. It's shame.*

Or was the shame caused by the fear? Either way, he could not bring himself to touch the fabric, never mind fasten it over his shoulders.

Those days were over. His life had collapsed into Windshear Hold, into the great hatchery of the mystic tower, and into the bond-scape hall of dark chains.

As his efforts to Cleanse Sovereign's core bore fruit, he began to switch his efforts to Forging. Pieces of rubble were lifted in this manner to rebuild the huge pillars. New links formed on the black chains. The cultists also fulfilled their role. In the rooms adjacent to, below, or above the hatchery, they read, wrote, played cards or dice with each other. Any activity which generated thoughts and thus extra mystic motes in the vicinity.

"A stale feast," Sovereign remarked when first tasting these motes. *"Yet even dry meat can build a body."*

Though the dragon's core was still a shadow of its former power, Osric couldn't help but be impressed with how fast Sovereign was recovering. Cultivating a core the size and strength of Sovereign's was a feat few dragons ever managed. Not until he had sensed the power of the Elder of the Emerald Flight had he felt a core comparable to Sovereign's at the height of his powers. A strength that had taken generations of time to gather would surely take years at least to gather again, even if Osric sat here day and night.

"Will you consume some of their minds to aid the process?" Osric asked.

He hoped the answer would be no. Sovereign could, when focused and at his most hateful, reduce a mind to raw mystic energy and draw that energy into himself. A large injection of mystic energy which would be absorbed in time or else Forged by Osric. It always disturbed Osric to see this effect, of reducing a thinking, breathing, living person to something worse than dead.

"Not now," Sovereign said. *"That takes power in itself to achieve, and the cloaked scum are still useful to me."*

And so Osric worked, and the chains wrapped around thick new columns. Osric performed his task expertly, but the mystic motes swept forward with ease, requiring the merest push from Osric's end. Dragons naturally gathered power into their core, yet the rate at which Sovereign did could not be normal. No doubt this played a great part in how he had become so formidable. Osric and the riders who had come before him were mere catalysts to this already rapid process.

Day in, day out, this unwavering routine marched on until he entered a flow so smooth and efficient that he did not break for food or rest. *Do the job and do it well.* For seven days and seven nights, Osric had flown from Sidastra to Windshear Hold. For nine days and nine nights, he Cleansed and Forged Sovereign's core.

Throughout the nine days and nights, Sovereign sat there, brooding and silent. At last, on the morning of the tenth day, he stirred again.

"Rise, worm," he commanded.

Osric opened his eyes, then squinted against the light pouring in from the opening of the hatchery. He rolled his shoulders and cricked his neck. Even for a Lord's body, such extended stillness led to stiffness and lethargy.

"What are my orders?"

"Your body needs sustenance. Eat. I sense loyal drakes will return soon."

Osric made his way to the mess hall. Upon entering the ancient great hall of the mystic riders, he discovered that the word mess had never been so apt. The long tables were positioned haphazardly. One was upturned. What would have been the table for the Mystic Lords and Paragon at the top of the hall had a leg missing. Bones and spillages soiled the floor.

Feasting halls in the outlands of the Skarl Empire were cleaner than this.

There were even members of the Shroud present, eating and chatting. They laughed at some private joke. Laughed while their environment was filthy.

"Members of the Shroud," Osric barked. They all looked at him in their own time, some apparently unsure who had just spoken. None stood.

What rabble does Sovereign rely on?

"Stand," he ordered.

They did, though few stood straight or looked directly at him.

"This," Osric called, walking into the hall toward them, "is an unacceptable condition for a military barracks. Who is the most senior here?"

It had been years since Osric had been around the Shroud for a prolonged time. Their numbers changed rapidly given their line of work, as did their strongholds, even more so now Sovereign engaged them in increasingly dangerous missions.

The cultists looked between themselves, uncertain. Osric noticed then how young they all were. None of them even wore the infamous dragonhide cloaks, which gave them their less favorable name of Wyrm Cloaks. Instead, they each wore traveling cloaks dyed different colors to imitate the dragonhide worn by the most devout and experienced members. Given this, none of them could be of officer rank.

The bravest of them, a pale-skinned boy with short black hair, spoke up. "We don't have officers." His accent was of the Province of Fornheim, a watered-down version of the Skarl tongue and part blended with the Risalian as well.

Osric narrowed his eyes. His cheek twitched. Before leaving for his Feorlen mission, Osric had been assured by the Speaker that a proper chain of command would be installed. Though disparate and distant from each other, each chapter of the Shroud ought to have its own commander, lieutenants, and devoted foot soldiers mapped out.

Osric drew up before the pale boy so that the insubordinate pup would feel his breath upon his face. "What's your name, soldier?"

The boy had the sense to look to his toes. "Gunsten."

"Address me properly, Gunsten."

He gulped. "Uh... I am sorry, Honored Rider—"

"No. I am no rider. I did not swear the oath. You shall address me as General, as sir, or, if you must, as *magnificence,* though only in the name of the dragon I am bonded to. Is that clear?" He looked at the others. "Well?"

"Yes, sir," they told him.

All except Gunsten.

Osric stared him down.

"We joined to serve the honored Sovereign in bringing chaos," Gunsten said. "Sweet chaos. Freeing. Fair. In chaos, there are no rules or lords to decide our every waking moment. In chaos, we are all equal."

In death, we might be.

He grabbed the boy by the scruff of his cloak, taking fistfuls of the blue cloth. Osric lifted him bodily into the air. The boy wheezed, clutched at his throat, and flailed his legs.

"Do you think yourself equal to me, Gunsten?"

He spluttered. "No... your mag-nifi-cence."

Osric dropped him. Gunsten crumpled into a ball upon the ground, hacking and coughing.

"You are young and unbloodied," Osric began, "so I advise you learn this lesson now, before you learn it painfully later. Whether it is order or chaos you are in, there will always be those stronger than you, smarter than you, better loved than you. You will never be equal to some. Not even if you try your best every day of your insignificant lives. Yet so long as you are under *my* command, you will do *your* best." He swept his gaze across each young face. "You will have discipline. You will have order. You will work hard if you wish to see Sovereign's plans fulfilled. Am I clear?"

"Yes, sir!" they said again, even Gunsten this time as he picked himself off the floor.

"Stand straight," Osric ordered. "Shoulders back, eyes forward, hands by your sides when at attention."

They hastened to comply.

"Good. Now we will improve the standards in this mess hall."

He set them to work. Soon the long tables were neatly ordered, the floor swept clear, wooden bowls stacked where they had otherwise been left to fester. The broken table of the Lords and Paragon was taken away and replaced with a smaller one, which was all they needed now. There were no Lords and no Paragon in the mystic tower. Only Osric.

Satisfied for the moment, Osric called for the cultists to be at ease, then returned to his original search for food. The cooks always had a broth bubbling away for those who ate at odd hours, and unless better food was brought to him, Osric always ate what his men ate. The cultists were a poor imitation of his Gray Cloaks, but they were all he had now.

He filled a bucket-sized bowl with the broth, picked up four hard bread rolls, then returned to the hall and took his place alone at the high table. Machine-like, he consumed his food in silence while other cultists sat in huddled packs, talking in low voices.

He finished, wiped his mouth, stood, and took his dishes to the kitchen to stack them with the others. Sovereign reached out to him then.

"To the inner yard. I shall meet you there."

Osric exited in haste. Out in the yard, Sovereign already stood in wait, his focus on the west. Rarely was the mystic dragon so anxious to receive his followers. Even the mighty dragon Clesh and his rider Silas had had to wait upon Sovereign's pleasure. Other members of the Shroud were there too, prostrating themselves on the ground behind Sovereign. Crates of straw and soft linings sat off to one side.

In time, two dragons came into view. One ice and one fire. The ice drake arrived first, delicately placing an egg upon the ground before landing. The fire drake did the same. Both dragons stepped back and pressed their necks low to the ground.

Sovereign loomed over the two eggs before bending his huge neck down to sniff each in turn. His delight rushed over the bond. For normal riders, this was likely a joyous feeling. For Osric, it caused the knot of pain in his chest to tighten, as though the ends of the rope were being pulled over sandpaper. The perverse part was that some of the joy did reach him, meaning he felt happy in this pain.

"You have done well," Sovereign said to the dragons, allowing Osric to hear.

The ice drake raised its head. *"The riders of Skyspear take their spares to ridges of the Frost Fangs to freeze."*

Osric tensed. Skyspear was the Order Hall in the Province of Fornheim. Sovereign risked much in brushing so close to the Order.

The ice dragon continued. *"As long as I do not remove too many at once to be noticed, it should prove to be a steady supply."*

Sovereign rumbled with approval. His attention turned to the fire drake.

"If you will it, your magnificence, I would try again," she said. *"Though it could be dangerous to risk your servant at Falcaer twice."*

From Falcaer? Osric thought in alarm. Running the risk of drawing Skyspear's attention was rash enough. For an asset at Falcaer itself to smuggle out an egg seemed a needless risk. Sovereign should have counted himself lucky to have retained eyes and ears within the headquarters of the Order.

His talons tighten around them, and they don't even realize.

"*There is no need,*" Sovereign said. "*We still await the return of other agents, including some of the cloaked scum. Worm?*"

Osric stepped forward. "What are my orders?"

"*Take these eggs inside. See that they are kept warm and place them together. Heat and the presence of other eggs and dragons may rekindle the hatchlings within.*"

Without question, Osric whistled for the cultists to bring two of the crates over. He placed an egg inside each one, then escorted the cultists as they carried the crates into the mystic tower.

After passing the nest Sovereign used, the next was a middling-sized one several floors up. They entered it and were met with the detritus of generations of birds who had made use of it.

"Clean this place," Osric instructed as they placed the crates side by side. "Open the others and prepare them as well. Sovereign would have these eggs hatch as soon as possible. Set up braziers and start fires."

These cultists were more seasoned than the ones he'd found in the mess hall and wore dragonhide cloaks. They bowed and said, "Yes, General," before setting about their work.

Osric spared a moment to inspect the eggs. He picked one up. Dragon eggs were ordinarily uniform, like smooth, stony chicken eggs. This one was melon-shaped with a rippled shell. The other seemed normal at first glance, but then Osric turned it over to find a strange, gnarled lump on one side.

It would be a miracle, he judged, if either of them had survived the journey. These were supposed to be, in the dragons' eyes, weak, defective eggs, after all.

Over the course of the next week, whenever Osric was not Cleansing or Forging, he collected more eggs from drakes loyal to Sovereign. They came from old emerald nests in the Fae Forest and from the leavings of Order Halls such as Alamut in Ahar and the island fastness of Squall Rock in the Stretched Sea.

Another of the nests higher up the mystic spire had to be reopened, cleaned, and prepared as the twelfth egg arrived.

Alas, the first team of cultists to arrive did not come bearing the gift of dragon eggs. Osric met them in the western storehouse, where he found three of them looking bedraggled, their cloaks dirty and their faces flushed red and sweating from the ascent. The only way in or out of Windshear by foot was a long and winding servant stairway built into the bedrock of the fortress. Their empty hands said it all. Sovereign's presence crossed the bond so he could view the cultists through Osric's own eyes.

The oldest of them wore a dragonhide cloak the color of burnt orange. He must have seen something of the dragon behind Osric's eyes, for he fell to Osric's feet and said, "Forgive us, your magnificence, we came so close."

Just like in the throne room of Sidastra, Sovereign spoke through Osric, warping his voice as he did so.

"Explain."

The cultist's face ran through a series of pained expressions as he searched for the right words.

"The arrangements were made. Our contact knew of a disillusioned rider from Sable Spire. They had the egg in their possession, but another rider interfered."

A drop of fear crossed the dragon bond.

"Did this rider of Sable Spire get cold feet?" Sovereign asked through Osric.

"No, your magnificence," the cultist said. "But the egg was taken. They say by a young rider with a white dragon."

The drop of fear turned into a surge of fury.

"A white dragon?" Sovereign snarled. "Were you discovered?"

"No. When we learned of this, we fled Brenin as fast as we could."

"This is why you only work with those already in my service," Sovereign said. "One mistake and Falcaer might fly in force against us."

"Your magnificence, I prostrate myself, I beg your forgive—"

"Enough," Sovereign said, and then he left Osric, retreating across the bond.

"*Punish him,*" the charming voice said.

The dragon's ire was Osric's own. This fool may well have started a chain of events that could lead to active efforts from the riders to investigate their own ranks. Was this Brenin rider being questioned even now? Worst of all, the very worst insult was that the boy and the blind dragon had once again proved themselves a nuisance.

Osric's hand twitched.

"Make an example of failure," the sweet voice told him.

It had an excellent point.

Osric assessed the most efficient method of doling out this punishment. The cultist's orange cloak protected his body from most slashing attacks, including Osric's axes. Being only plain steel they would struggle to part dragonhide, even with his strength. His armor covered the man's neck as well, where the cloak wrapped around to fasten at the front.

"Rise," Osric told the cultist. The man rose, shaking. Once upright, Osric reached for his throat. He took it in his right hand and squeezed. Hard.

The other two cultists beat a hasty retreat, backing away and raising their own cloaks to shield behind. For all the good it would do them if Osric went for them next.

He squeezed harder, looking into the man's bulging eyes as the air escaped his mouth in a rattling whistle. Muscle and vertebrae buckled. The crack rang like split stone.

The dragon chuckled. *"Brutal as ever, worm."*

Osric dropped the man. His hand felt stiff. A little blood wet his skin and a drop rolled over the back of his hand, covering the tattoo there in a red trail. The blood seemed to burn where it besmirched the inked honor of Gunvaldr's Horns, though that, he was sure, was only in his mind. Empress Skadi of the Skarls had bestowed the symbol upon him for saving her life. How many lives had he taken rather than saved since then?

Yet in the afterglow of the killing, he found such thoughts did not trouble him. A tension left him like poison drawn from a wound. In the past he would have held back; he would have exhausted himself in finding restraint, which would only have made it worse. But now, what was the point in that?

"Take his cloak," Osric commanded. "Then dispose of him."

As the two survivors set about stripping their comrade, Osric cast the dead man one last look. His neck had crumpled much like Godric's chest. His axe would have been the better way to do this. Quick and clean. The way he had ended that traitor in the first Risalian War.

He reflected that he hadn't used his axes on Godric either – he would have been a fool to inflict axe wounds on him. He'd picked a mace for the job, lifting it out of the hands of a dead Risalian as he sped ahead of his men. That had been the weapon he'd planted into Godric's chest, cracking ribs with the blow. That had been the weapon he'd pointed to in rage when the rest of his men had caught up. His axes had remained clean.

The stiffness in his hand ceased as he curled it slowly into a bloody fist.

TEN

Handling Heat

"I believe you have outdone yourself, Mr. Smith," Talia said, admiring her new brigandine. The pieces comprised of heavy leather lined internally with small sheets of steel riveted to the fabric. A final layer of crimson linen completed Talia's set.

The blacksmith beamed. "Would Your Majesty care to try it on?"

She already wore her black gambeson, which would act as both padding and further protection. The thick quilted tunic was tough enough on its own to withstand blunt attacks and stop all but the most razor-sharp of strikes. She belted the gambeson in at her waist, then reached for the chest piece of brigandine with childlike eagerness.

The harness could be put on like a coat. Talia slipped her arms through the sleeve openings and fastened the armor at the front with a series of buckles. Another reason riders favored brigandine was the ability to attach it singlehanded if necessary. Today, Talia allowed the smith's apprentices to help her. They tightened the shoulder straps to secure the harness to a snug fit, then fastened on the pauldrons and her vambraces.

With the armor on, Talia now matched the renovations to her office. Scarlet drapes and crimson rugs had replaced the old blue ones.

Her father's drinks cabinet had also been removed. In its place was a trolley laden with a bounty of spiced snacks, from olives stuffed with peppers to raw chilies.

Her mother sat cross-legged on one of the freshly upholstered chairs, the linen now stitched in yellow and orange flames. She sipped at a cup of Talia's unique batch of nairn root tea and made a pained expression.

Talia stretched and twisted. The armor moved with her and felt even better than her old set had.

"What do you think, mother?"

"It doesn't seem very sturdy," Felice said.

The blacksmith's face dropped, but Talia hastened to answer for him. "It's more flexible than full plate. My speed and strength are my real advantages. This is more a precaution in case some ghoul or flayer happens to get a lucky swipe in."

Her mother did not look wholly relieved to hear it.

"If I make it to the rank of Lord," Talia went on, "then my own skin will toughen like dragon hide. I wouldn't even need this then."

Although how she would ever manage that given her current situation, she had no idea.

The blacksmith made another bow. "Is there anything else I might assist you with, Your Royal Maj—"

"You can call me Talia."

Who needed the grandeur of 'Majesty' when you were an enhanced human, with the powers of fire and a dragon to call upon? Nor was she a rider, so 'Honored Rider' would not do either.

She was Talia.

Felice wrinkled her nose at the instruction but said nothing.

"As you will, Your Royal... Talia," the smith said. With that, he and his apprentices retreated out of the room. Talia caught a glimpse of the backs of the Twinblades standing guard before the door shut, leaving her and her mother alone.

"Don't you like the tea?" Talia asked.

Felice took another sip, winced, and sniffed at the drink. "Nairn root usually has a sweetness to it, no?"

"The roots are normally softened by boiling them in sugar and cinnamon." Talia hadn't known this before discussing her needs with the cook in the palace kitchens.

Felice almost choked on her next sip. Her eyes began to water.

Talia moved in to take the tea from her. "You don't need to drink it like this. Here, I've got sweeteners for those I wish to take mercy on." Under the tabletop were several lidded dishes. Talia took two out. One contained honey, the other dark brown sugar.

Felice dolloped honey into the drink and dabbed at her eyes with a silk handcloth she had produced seemingly from nowhere.

"Your father's whisky burned less than this. Do you intend to set your councilors and guests on fire with it?"

"Not quite," Talia said. She poured herself some of the unsweetened tea. "But this is what I prefer. So, I'll take the lead, and my good Ealdors can be on the back foot as opposed to me refusing to drink or pretending I like wretched cakes." She took a long drink of the tea. The heat felt good as it ran down her throat, the untampered spice even more so. It had the fiery taste of ginger, only intensified to what Talia knew would be unpalatable levels for anyone other than herself. Well, perhaps other fire riders.

"You've moved quickly on all of this," Felice said. "Nothing rattles you for long, not even when everything goes wrong like at the coronation." She laughed. "I would have died had that happened to me."

Talia put on a brave smile. She had always tried to be tough and strong, largely because her brother had been sickly, and in seeking the Order she wished to give no one any reason to speak out against her desires. Especially her father. Looking back, she ought to have thought longer on his misgivings. Look at the situation they had ended up in because of it. Osric, however, had always been encouraging. 'My little soldier,' he called her.

For a moment, she considered telling her mother that she still woke from nightmares and how the future frightened her. Yet, seeing how her mother beamed at her, Talia did not have the heart to shatter the illusion.

What faith will anyone have in a weeping rider? Or a weak queen?

She opted instead to change the topic.

"Have you any word from Uncle Roland?" Since the coronation, Brenin – the one realm Talia had hoped to count upon – had been ominously silent. "He has not responded to any of my own letters."

"Nor mine," said Felice.

"Does that not trouble you? Mother, we might have to prepare for the possibility—"

A knock came at the door.

"Yes?" Talia called.

The Twinblades entered.

"The Master of Roles is without," said Eadwald.

"He is due at this hour," Eadwulf said.

"That he is," said Talia. "Please see him in."

Felice stood, curtsied, and left. High Council business was not hers to be part of. Talia thought it a pointless convention. She would discuss any issue she wished with her mother. Talia almost asked her to stay but restrained herself. Enough had changed. Some scraps of the order they all knew should remain.

The Master of Roles entered, his steps slow and deliberate and his expression determined. Talia rose but did not move to help him. Commander Denna had often impressed upon them, 'Do not help those who can help themselves.' There was dignity in overcoming struggle. A student should struggle until they mastered an ability, a sword form, or a meditation technique.

If someone else always picked her back up, she would learn only to fall.

Trailing in the Master of Roles' wake were two stewards, each holding a stack of books, parchments, ink pots, and quills.

The Master stooped his shoulders and neck to Talia before taking his seat. His stewards stood behind him. Talia opted not to subject the old man to her spicey traps. As Queen, the onus was on her. If she did not drink, he would not have to. If she did not offer him food, he would not ask for it.

"Your Majesty."

"Ealdor Hubbard, last time we spoke, I made it clear you can call me Talia. I'd honestly prefer it."

"Forgive me, Your Majesty," he said with a slight wheeze. "But that would not be proper."

Talia blinked. Frail of body he might be, but his grip on protocol and tradition was iron.

He turned to his stewards. "Glasses." One of the stewards presented him with a pair of half-moon spectacles. He perched them on the tip of his nose, then clicked his fingers. Two sheets of parchment entered his hand. "This is a summary of my first reallocations for royal assent and an updated incursion death toll."

Talia frowned as she took the parchments. Seeing the death toll rise with each visit of the Master was most unpleasant. At least the number rose a little less each time. She turned her attention to the reallocations. As she read, he summarized.

"As you can see, I haven't taken sweeping measures yet. I won't have a firm grasp of the impact upon the whole kingdom for some time. For now, the losses from Port Bolca have been noted, but I await the role-names of those who fled from Ealdor Odilo. The destruction of the Crag has been noted too, of course. Two hundred and sixteen of the survivors remain in Sidastra. Given the damage incurred by the capital, many of them can stay and be integrated into the city's infrastructure."

Those poor people, Talia thought. Many she knew, if not by name then by face. Many she had ignored too, as she had ignored Holt once. It gave her a horrible sense of disconnect and of squirming guilt. Still, she could sympathize with having one's life uprooted and moved in such a painful and dramatic fashion: told now to ply their trade on a street they'd never seen before, for people they did not know. Yet in the wake of an incursion, people tended to count themselves fortunate to be alive.

A steward placed a heavy book beside Hubbard with a dull thud.

"The census records for the capital," the Master said, waving a hand over the great tome. "It is Your Majesty's right to inspect the work."

Talia thought she ought to, but then she had so much else to do, and truthfully the tome looked like tedious reading.

"Has the Master of Roles and his service thoroughly checked the details?"

"Thoroughly."

"Then the Queen will trust him."

"I am most gratified by your trust, Majesty. However, it would be proper for you to be made aware of one significant adjustment. We suffered a high loss in the number of Ferrymen. Of those families, six had children aged sixteen or over who could inherit the role. The rest will need to be replaced soon to maintain vital haulage and transport capacity, especially while the population is swollen with people from the summons."

Talia nodded along. Summons were used across the world and were designed to gather populations into fortified cities to draw the swarm for a decisive confrontation. In theory, a full third of every town, village, and hamlet in Feorlen should have evacuated to Sidastra. It caused a mess post-incursion, but it was the only sure way to lure a swarm to where the living had the advantage. And better a mess than a bloody mess.

The Master carried on.

"The destruction of the West Quarter has left many without their place of occupation, however Innkeeps are one of the less vital roles, and I intend to re-allocate five to make up the shortfall in Ferrymen. They will be trained by those who know the city's waterways best. This will take time, of course, but they'll be posted to the easiest routes. Does Your Majesty assent?"

"I do," Talia said. She took the parchment to her desk, signed it, poured red wax onto it and stamped it with the royal seal. She handed it back to the stewards.

"What of our armies?"

"The incursion was ill-timed so soon after the war with Risalia. The ranks had already been refilled, but I can't say if we'll have the spare hands to do so again. Your uncle's betrayal kept the western garrisons in their barracks, so they at least should be intact. Some might be redistributed to the east if required. However, Majesty, such matters are most properly dealt with by the Master or Mistress of War."

"I understand," Talia said. She admired his tenacity at pushing the matter with her. "Though I am troubled that no candidate put forward by the council is willing to support my expedition. I cannot in good conscience appoint anyone who does not share my concerns."

"As you will." He braced his knees then stood slowly, placing a hand on the back of his chair for support once upright. He paused in his departure and seemed to work up to something. "May I speak freely, Your Majesty?"

"Of course. I'd rather you speak freely than behind my back."

He inclined his head. "This grieves me to say, but I think, on this matter, you are wrong. The clarity of your wishes is admirable, but it is a failing not to give way to wise counsel."

"I am my father's daughter. When I set my mind on something, I mean to have it."

"More your uncle's niece, I think," he said. "Your father was a determined man, true enough, but he would compromise on almost anything if it hurried matters along. Osric, well, he had focus too and no mistake. But with your uncle, his way was the only way a thing would be done. No exceptions."

Talia shifted her gaze from the Master of Roles to a point over his shoulder. Comparing her to Osric made her more uncomfortable than she cared to admit.

"Alas," he continued, "I have said all I can on the matter. Majesty," he added with another dip of his head. With his assistants in tow, he shuffled off.

Talia was left with her thoughts circling once again around her uncle. First her mother, now the venerable old Master of Roles. How many others were happy to see the back of him? How many others harbored secret misgivings? Or had she really been shielded from his true nature all these years? Her family had its skeletons. Rumors of her grandmother were still whispered furtively. Even so, where Osric was concerned, there was a world between rubbing people the wrong way and the acts he had later taken.

That was Sovereign. All Sovereign, she told herself. Though perhaps it would do her good to dig a little deeper. He was still out there and bound to Sovereign. Defeating the dragon would mean either saving Osric first or killing him in the process. Could he even be saved at this point? Talia had no concept of how Sovereign's powers worked. A darker question presented itself to her for the first time.

Should he be saved?

Caught up in her thoughts, Talia returned to her tea to find it cold. She reached to her bond and pulled in a tendril of flame from the bonfire core. It was harder than it should have been. Pyra was only out in the grounds, but even accounting for the distance between them, Talia felt more resistance than she expected. Already, she was getting rusty. The rigor of her old training had buckled under the weight of the crown.

She felt guilty for this too. With the emeralds gone, Pyra had been left on her own most days. Getting this expedition to the scourge chasm underway would be vital, not just for the mission itself but for being with her dragon, like she was supposed to be.

A loud voice rang outside her office.

"I know I'm early, you dolt." The voice of Ida, the Mistress of Embassy, was unmistakable. "It's urgent. And learn to talk in complete sentences the pair of you!"

The door burst open, and the Mistress of Embassy stormed inside, drawing to a sudden halt and bowing as an afterthought.

"Talia," she began, having no issue with using her name alone. "It's a disaster. A disaster!"

"Go on," Talia said. "Is it Risalia? Have they declared war?"

"No, no," Ida said. She shoved a crumpled piece of parchment into Talia's hands. "It's Athra."

Talia braced herself and read.

The letter from the Athran ambassador was short and to the point. They could not endorse the ascension of a rider to the head of any state. As Feorlen had so flagrantly disregarded ancient laws regarding relations with the dragon riders, Athra would be withdrawing their embassy and placing trade sanctions on the kingdom until Talia abdicated.

"Well," Talia said, "we anticipated resistance from Athra."

"But so soon?" Ida moaned. She looked despondent at Talia's new assortment of snacks. "I could have used a drink," she barked.

Talia breathed steadily. Athra's rejection came at a sore time. A portion of Feorlen's grain supply relied on trade from the fertile plains controlled by Athra. At least it wasn't war.

"What are our options?" Talia asked.

"Few," Ida said. "I doubt even a hasty marriage will help now. That was always a long shot at best."

Talia felt glad for that assessment, and simultaneously guilty that she found relief in what was a terrible situation for her people.

"We need formal alliances to buttress ourselves," Talia said. "I think it's time to push my uncle into making a decision on where Brenin stands."

Ida groaned. For once, the fight seemed to have deflated out of the old woman. Alliances meant enemies. Alliances meant war was expected.

"I fear that is our only course."

"Queen Felice should lead a diplomatic mission," Talia said. "If she can't convince her own brother to stand with us, I doubt anyone else will."

"There will be a price," the Mistress of Embassy said. "Brenin is a strong kingdom, but your uncle is not a gallant man to come hurrying to our rescue nor a bullish ruler to look for a fight like your father." The moment she said it, her eyes widened in alarm. "My apologies, Your Majes—"

"It's fine. Speak your mind, Ida. I know my father was not perfect. Nor Leofric. Nor myself. In the Order, my mentors were eager to reassure me of my shortcomings on a daily basis. It is how we advance. King Roland will need something, you say? What?"

"That will be for Queen Felice to determine."

Talia nodded. "Can I trust you to make the arrangements?"

"Of course. If that is all?" The Mistress made to leave but turned back. "The royal smiths did an excellent job with your new armor."

Talia smiled. Was this a reluctant sign of acceptance for what she intended to do? Of what sort of queen she would be?

"Thank you. I'm sure it will serve me well."

"I dearly hope that it does, Your Majesty."

As the Mistress left, Talia called, "Eadwulf, Eadwald."

The twins entered. Without their striking blue Harroway tabards, they seemed plain in their mail and leather. If she kept them around, she would have to garb them in some crimson.

"I have need of the Master of State. Bring Ealdor Horndown to me. He is past due delivering me an expedition. Accept no excuses from him, understood?"

"At once, my queen," they said together.

Half an hour later, there came another knock at her door. *That was fast,* Talia thought. *The Twins are as efficient as riders.*

Yet the man who entered was not who she had been expecting.

"Harroway? I don't recall asking for you."

"You didn't, Your Majesty."

As before, Drefan Harroway's clothes were crisp, clean, and impeccable. His hair was well-groomed, his face shaven. All the discipline of the soldier but lacking the beaten brow of the veteran.

"I shall not waste my words. I've come to offer you my service as Master of War."

Talia gave an exasperated laugh. "You're serious? After your stunt at my coronation?"

"Stunt?" Harroway said. "Whatever do you mean?" He moved to hover over one of the comfy chairs at the heart of the room. He didn't have the temerity to sit without permission, but he was altogether too pleased with himself.

"I thought we weren't wasting words?" Talia said. "That stunt you pulled with your family's two guard dogs. Good fighters, though. Assuming there are no ties to Wyrm Cloaks to worry about, they'll make a perfect start to my Queen's Guard."

"I am sure there is nothing to worry about," Harroway said. "Investigations have been dropped, after all."

Talia glowered. He was close to getting banished from court back to his estate.

"If you had nothing to hide, why not let the investigation run its course?"

"A drill sergeant inspecting his troops will always find some error if he looks hard enough. Besides, I value my privacy and that of my family."

"Above the security of the realm?"

"My queen," he said, much more serious. "I give you my word as one of your soldiers, of the head of one of Feorlen's longest-living houses and its sworn defenders, that my family, and my father, had no knowledge of the crimes of your uncle. I hoped his sacrifice in defense of this city would prove that."

He gave his word. How much worth was there in words? Little more than in the air they traveled upon. And yet, at other times, more valuable than if they were written onto gold.

Talia motioned to the chair. "Sit." He did, and she took up the chair opposite, leaving the table between them. "Would you like some refreshment, Drefan?" She waved a hand over the food, then picked up a nut dusted with a purple-red spice. It might have been cayenne. Holt would have known the nuances. Talia only cared that it was hot.

Next, she picked up a long, thin red chili and bit into it raw. The heat burst in her mouth, a warm pleasure that seemed to reach down to her soul.

Harroway eyed the bowl warily, then he picked out a green chili. Talia grinned as he bit into the end of it. Rapid chewing quickly slowed, and his face grew redder with each movement of his jaw.

"Good, isn't it?" Talia said.

"If you say so," he said, beginning to sweat. To his credit, he took another bite, and then another until he had consumed the whole chili.

"What am I to do with you, Ealdor Harroway?"

"Two things," he said between sucking in cooling breaths of air.

"Two? I thought you wanted to be Master of War?"

"I do, and you should appoint me, but unless cousin Elvina's information is wrong, there might be some other role I may fulfill. But she's never wrong."

He was good. The casual reminder of his ties to the Mistress of Coin. Now Talia considered it, she thought she could see a strain of familial good looks between them.

"Elvina is a little behind on this one," Talia said with relish.

"Alas, no wedding bells?"

"Given our current situation, a foreign alliance will be more valuable."

"True. If you could find one." Despite the bad news, he leaned back and crossed his legs. "A shame. I would have made a good King Consort. Master of War it is then."

"You seem under the impression that I will accept."

"You will. No one else is willing to undertake this wild expedition to the scourge chasm."

"I intend to lead the expedition myself."

"And what experience do you have for that?"

"Fighting the scourge? I'm a rider. It's all we're trained to do."

He leaned forward, serious now. "I do not doubt your abilities to combat the bugs, but this is another art altogether. Leading and commanding thousands of soldiers. Chain of command. Tactics. Setting up encampments. Maintaining supply lines."

"And you're willing to do this? Do you agree that I am right?"

"No. I don't agree, Your Majesty. If you accept me, know that I will be nothing but honest with you on that. As far as I'm concerned, you should never have become queen."

The sheer brashness of it left her speechless.

"You would have preferred civil war?" Talia said, eventually.

"I would never have allowed you to join the riders in the first place if I had had any say. My father rightly objected. We agreed it was your own father's biggest mistake in indulging it."

"Indulging?" The heat rose within her now. Worst of all was the fact that he had a point.

Perhaps misinterpreting the source of her renewed anger,

Harroway added, "I did admire your father greatly for taking the Toll Pass, of course. Feorlen will never be more than a scrubby kingdom at the edge of the old republic unless we prove ourselves. Risalia knows that now."

"The Free City of Athra may well join them," Talia said. "Possibly Mithras and Coedhen too."

"That would be something," said Harroway, a glint in his eye. "To face down the armies of the world and triumph. With a fire rider at our disposal, what could go wrong?"

So, it's glory he wants.

Pyra sought greatness for herself and Talia. Could she criticize Harroway for wanting the same?

From what Talia had read of his career thus far, his ambition and talent were clear. At the age of fourteen, he had disguised himself to hide his age and won a tourney hosted by the Horndowns, beating grown men in the joust. At sixteen, he served in the border garrisons of the Red Range. During the war, his father gave him command of Fort Dittan, which guarded a narrow, perilous passage from Risalia into northern Feorlen. An important command. The sally he led broke the Risalian siege there and earned him the Mark of Valor. During the incursion, he had also repelled an offshoot of the swarm attacking his family's holdings. An accomplished record for a young soldier.

Yet for someone who wanted the position of Master of War, he was making an excellent case against himself.

"I know this expedition is unorthodox," Talia said. "I know it will have dangers we can't possibly know about going into it. But don't you agree that the scourge is the greatest threat of all? In the face of death itself, who cares what Risalia does?"

"As someone who bled in the war, who lost friends and loved ones during that war, I care."

"I lost my father."

"You did," he said, and he had the grace to look ashamed for his lack of tact. His demeanor softened. "And I lost mine to the bugs. Fighting the scourge is a noble cause, but I urge you not to confuse your role as rider and queen."

Talia strained to keep her patience. "What will it take? An Elder dragon has urged me to this task. This is unheard of. There must be a reason."

"There must be a compelling reason why it's never been done before."

"This could give us insight on the enemy. Surely as a soldier you value that?"

"It's not a matter of reconnaissance, it's..."

He froze, and Talia at last gleaned it from his eyes.

"You're afraid."

She felt ridiculous for not realizing this before. Everyone must be terrified by the idea of venturing down a scourge chasm, deep into the dark. Fear above all was what drove their objection.

Harroway puffed his chest.

"Aren't you afraid?" he asked, the veneer beginning to break.

"No," she lied. "I'm a rider."

He snorted, ran his hands down his face, then took a long deep breath. "Make me your Master of War. I swear I will support your expedition. Allow me to garrison the Red Range as needed, and I will spare every sword I can for your mission. I won't hamstring you. If you're determined to march good men and women to such a cursed place, then it should at least be done right."

At last. At long last. She had her man.

Talia rose and extended her hand. "Then it seems we have an agreement, Master of War."

ELEVEN

Red Rock

Ethel told them they would know the right place when they found it. She had not been wrong. After days of flying east, they turned north, traversing what seemed endless plains. Little civilization lay out in these Disputed Lands, or at least, little had been marked upon the maps. On and on the landscape stretched until the flat lands broke in the most dramatic fashion.

Yellow, burnt orange, and mud-red pillars rose sheer and sudden to the north like a dawn of stone. These pillars erupted from a network of narrow, rugged canyons, walled on all sides by high cliffs as though a mesa had been hewn out to create a labyrinth. Further north, the land dropped steeply to the edge of the Fae Forest.

Neither Holt nor Ash had any doubt that the town of Red Rock would be here. Drawing closer, they spotted smoke rising from an inner canyon, and Ash began to hear the bustle of life below. Their bond flared as they swept over the inhabited areas to announce their arrival.

Through sense-sharing, Holt heard an echo of what Ash heard; the clatter and thunk of work, the calls of people to one another, the baying of livestock. This took him aback. In the past, Holt's hearing had improved while sense-sharing with Ash, but this was altogether different. These additional sounds were muffled to him, and each time he tried to focus on them they slipped away until he only heard what his human ears could register.

The effect was dizzying, and Holt was glad they would land and break the sense-sharing soon. They dove into the widest and most occupied canyon. People below scattered to make way as they landed.

Holt broke the sense-sharing and got down. He marveled at the place, a shanty town of dark wood, where the dwellings were half carved into shelves of rock. Holt reckoned they were in some sort of town center or market. Stalls and carts of goods surrounded a thin spire of stone more golden than yellow. Someone had adorned the golden spire with dragon wings fashioned out of green cloth. The dry air had a haze of red dust to it, heavy with the smells of grilling lamb and charcoal smoke, though this could not mask an underlying odor of waste and grime.

The smell of lamb made his mouth water and roiled his empty stomach. Their meager food reserves had run out two days ago. Despite the still frail state of their bond, Ash's hunger pounded over it.

Holt made a beeline for the closest of the grills, reaching for the coin pouch at his waist. Skewered lamb sizzled sweetly. A large droplet of fat fell onto the hot coals, throwing up a bout of flame.

The owner of the stall looked around, evidently horrified that Holt had come to his outlet. Holt shoved a handful of coppers into his hand, then promised there would be silver for anyone who could supply Ash with a good portion of meat.

As he tore into the first seared chunk of lamb, Holt paid more attention to the people watching him. They wore rough spun clothes and favored shawls, all of which were coated in the same red dust which lingered heavily in the air.

Holt asked if this place was Red Rock. It was. He asked if there might be anyone who remembered another rider with an emerald dragon. One person did, they said. An elderly woman with the dragon amulet.

A few brave souls approached, who Holt assumed to be guards. Under their shawls, they wore the basic protection of half helms and boiled leather, though their shields were not uniform in size. Instead of swords they wielded spears. Bewildered but sensing there was no harm from these people, Holt followed the guards through narrower, winding passages to another enclave of tottering structures. Rudimentary ballistae guarded the sky here. Unlike the buildings in the market canyon, the wood here had been afforded the luxury of patchy paintwork, giving a rough yet lively feel to the place. A small crowd followed him and Ash but kept their distance.

Holt was directed to a building at ground level which looked more like a grand shed than a home.

"I won't be long," Holt said.

"Take your time. These people are anxious about our arrival but are not afraid of us. They whisper, fearing the scourge must be on its way."

Holt felt a bit guilty for that. A rider's arrival often heralded woe.

"There are no scourge coming," he called to the onlookers. "My dragon and I are here on business of our own. Have no fear."

Eager now, he faced the door. He knocked.

A sinewy old woman answered. Though thin, she seemed healthy for her age and her hair retained its brown color. Otherwise she wore clothes as plain and rough as everyone else in Red Rock, except for a pendant around her neck. Even this simple adornment looked little more than a smooth green stone.

"A rider, is it?" He noted that she did not use the honorific title. "What can an old woman do for you?"

"I've come seeking information on a rider who once came here. His name was Brode."

"For Honored Brode? Yes. Yes, come in." She beckoned him inside.

Holt entered, and the woman indicated he should sit at her table. The table was but a large rock at knee height with a flat, smoothed top as muddy red as the stone underfoot. Sheepskin rugs were arranged around it.

"Tea?" she asked. Holt nodded, then sat quietly, feeling the strain of their flight from Ethel and Orvel weigh upon him. Due to near-

constant sense-sharing, their bond had not fully recovered since fraying. It might not have been the best time for prolonged use of the
sense-sharing technique. Even now he had canceled the effect, Holt
still heard the chatter of people gathered around Ash, smelled the dirt
and sweat on their skin, felt them pushing through the air and
sending ripples to his scales—

No, not scales. I don't have scales.

These sensations were Ash's, yet he sensed them, distant and light
as far echoes like phantom pain from a missing limb. It might be wise
not to blend their senses for a while.

The old woman returned and placed a small steaming bowl before
him. It had a heavy, earthy smell. At first, he thought she had served
him soup, but then she sat down and began to drink directly from the
bowl as if it were a cup.

Holt followed. He almost gagged on the first sip – the tea was so
bitter and had such a strong metallic undercurrent he was reminded
horribly of blood. Yet even as he swallowed, the back of his throat
tingled, and his thirst was quenched as though he'd drunk a flagon of
water.

Something of his surprise must have shown on his face, for the
woman said, "It's the spring water. Made rich by the stones, folk say."

"It's rather... intense," Holt said.

"You get used to it." She took another sip. "What business do you
have regarding Honored Brode? That was such a long time ago."

"I've come to find the resting place of his dragon so I can bury his
ashes alongside her."

Her face fell. "I did fear when I noticed his sword upon your back."

"You recall his sword?"

"I recall it all," she insisted. "I'm the last of those who can recall it.
Everyone else has passed now or were too young then to remember.
The fear. The shrieking of those monsters. The way the very rock and
earth trembled as that noble dragon spent her power to keep us safe.
She died so we could live, even though we were only bastards and
outcasts."

Holt allowed himself a small smile. Brode's ability to grumble had been core-forged most of the time, yet he understood now why Brode would have fought so hard here. Brode had been half an outcast himself. A bastard of Athra, the ill-begotten son of a senator of that city. If this was a place for lost souls, that might explain its strangeness.

"You were fortunate that it was Brode who came here during that incursion," Holt said. "He helped me as well."

"The other one left."

"Silas. He's dead too." He decided to leave the details out.

"I can't say I'm saddened to hear it. He didn't think our lives were worth his time. But then some think chaos bringers deserve the scourge, don't they?" She eyed him warily.

"They do. But I've seen enough of late to know not all chaos bringers deserve their fate, and not all who uphold order deserve its protection." That had come out more bitter than he'd intended. Was that truly what he thought now? Perhaps it was the exhaustion speaking. He drank some more of the coppery tea, hoping it would revive him.

It didn't.

The old woman eyed him intensely. "You must have seen some terrible things to think of your fellow riders like that."

"I'm not a rider. Even Brode trained me reluctantly. Before this, I was a cook. Holt Cook."

"Holt Cook," she said, understanding and acceptance dawning on her face. "My name is Fiona. I had no role name."

Having shared these understandings with one another, Holt felt the guardedness of Fiona dissipate. A kinship of sorts existed here, impossible to pin down, an unspoken mixture of respect and condolences for hardships suffered.

"Do you know where Erdra was buried?" he asked bluntly.

She nodded. "I walked with the men as they laid logs one after the other to roll her body to the burial grounds. But Honored Brode did not wish her to lie with the rest. He took her further south to a small hill on its lonesome."

Some forsaken hill on the road east from Athra, Holt thought.

"Could you take me there?" he asked.

"Were it for anyone else, I wouldn't suffer such a journey with these old bones. But for Honored Brode, yes. I should like to pay my respects." With evident effort, she got to her feet and disappeared into a back room behind a loose curtain. She emerged wearing a green shawl and a determined expression.

When they left her house, they took only a few steps before she grew unsteady on her feet. Holt offered her an arm, and she looped her thin, bony arm through his. Ash padded up to join them, and together they made their way slowly through Red Rock.

As word spread, the crowd following them swelled. Fiona's children, grandchildren, and great-grandchildren came running to offer her a wagon to take her down. She refused. She said that she would make the trip on foot as her tribute. A small sufferance compared to what Brode had suffered.

It took the best part of that day to reach the site. Atop the lonely hill rose a lonely pillar of red stone, looming over oak and hornbeam trees. And at the bottom of that hill lay a cairn of stones.

Holt brought out Brode's box of ashes and was about to approach the cairn when Fiona stopped him. She took off her pendant and handed it to him.

"Erdra made this stone for me," she said, "out of a common pebble. I tried to give it back to Brode as a keepsake, but he wouldn't have it. Said it had been made for me. I say put it back now."

Her family uttered protests, but she shook her head and handed it to Holt.

"They think that stone has kept me alive for so long. Well, I say her magic has bought me enough good years. Give it back to her, I say. It's all I have to give."

Holt accepted it. The stone was leaf green, pearl smooth, and diamond bright. Small wonder Fiona's family thought it magical, but Holt could not sense any power in it. He placed it around his neck, then climbed to the top of the cairn.

He moved the top layers of stone, enough to make a small well, before he scattered Brode's ashes to sink down between the nooks and crannies. No wind blew them away. He placed Fiona's pendant at the top, under the last stone. Then he was left standing at the top of the cairn, facing the quiet crowd below.

Some words seemed expected of him.

"My role-name is Cook. My father was a Cook, and his father, and all their fathers. I wasn't supposed to be a rider, and the truth is I'm not really one. I've sworn no oaths. I'm as much an outcast from them as I am from my home. Brode claimed he cared about such things, but when it came to it, he cared about helping others more. About doing the right thing, even if that was the hard choice. Even if that cost him everything." His voice began to waver now. "He was a good man. He was one of us. And I hope he can rest now."

He climbed down from the cairn and went to Ash. They took comfort in each other and stood vigil as the folk of Red Rock returned home one by one.

It had not been nearly as hard as laying his father upon the pyre. Yet, far out here in lands alien to him, Holt felt more astray than ever. Delivering Brode to Erdra's side had been a beacon to them since leaving Sidastra. Now the daunting task of finding the Wild Flights lay ahead, and he did not have a clue where to begin.

"I feel we're lost," he said quietly, so that only Ash could hear. His optimism had been checked by the hard reality of an antagonistic Champion. They weren't prepared to take on the world.

"*We just need to rest, boy. We flew hard.*"

Holt checked on their bond. Its edges were still torn. What light he saw of Ash's core flickered feebly. Magical impurities had grown thick from the lack of Cleansing, the core as hazy as the dusty air of Red Rock. Perhaps they ought to stay here for a time, if the people would let them. They would be welcomed here, just two more outcasts who had nowhere else to go.

"Do you mind if we stay here a little longer?" Holt asked. "By the cairn, I mean. I'm so tired."

"*Of course,*" Ash said. Even damaged, a soothing warmth passed over their bond. "*We did all we could for Master Brode. He would be happy to know we brought him here.*"

Ash sat down and wrapped his tail around Holt. More warmth passed over the bond. It felt like placing aching muscles into a hot bath, and Holt sunk into the feeling, pushing all else from his mind – all worry, all grief. The world faded just as it did when he meditated, and for the first time in weeks, Holt heard Ash's dragon song.

It had altered a great deal since the Withering Woods. The sad flute-like tune had morphed into something purposeful. Fluttering notes over a simple melody. It put Holt in mind of those tranquil moments felt in night's dwindling hours: of stillness, the lone hoot of an owl, the anticipated draw of breath for the day to come.

So at peace did he become listening to Ash's song that twilight fell without him realizing it. By the time he did, all the townsfolk from Red Rock were gone.

He decided then that he and Ash should stay for a while, recover, and grow their strength before heading back into the wilds. Orvel would not be the last enemy they'd face, and next time they couldn't count on luck to save them.

Absentmindedly, he reached for the hilt of Brode's sword and drew it flawlessly this time. *Typical,* he thought. The broad green blade still felt wrong in his hand, like wearing ill-fitting clothes. It had not been designed for him, yet he tried to wield it as if it were his. Perhaps it too deserved, like Erdra's magic stone, to be laid alongside her and Brode.

He climbed the cairn once more and rearranged the stones to form a crevice in which the blade might stand. He set the broad sword in place and was about to begin piling rocks back around it when a voice called out from higher up on the lonely hill.

"Do something this foolish again and I'll take your head off myself. It's clear you aren't using it, and I abhor waste."

Holt twisted around so fast he cricked his neck. Ash sprung up, growling, wings and tail shaking.

Silhouetted above them stood a tall figure, seven feet tall, wielding a great polearm with a glassy orange blade. The figure's face was obscured by a hooded traveling cloak, although a tail swished out beneath the rim of the material. Large blue eyes glowed in the darkness.

"Rake?" Holt asked.

"Take back the sword, Master Cook. I have need of your service – and trust me, you're going to want a rider's blade."

TWELVE

New Embers and Dark Flames

The cone-shaped egg shook in its crate. A tiny talon punctured the shell, then another, until, in fits and starts, a turquoise hatchling broke free and took its first breath. Its second breath did not come easy, and it hacked and spluttered as it struggled to open its airways.

Osric looked upon the creature in pity. When the hacking didn't stop, he gently lifted the baby from its crate to examine it. Down on one knee, he pried the baby's mouth open. So far as he could tell, there were no shell fragments or fluid blocking its throat. If its lungs were malformed or some other issue prevented it from drawing breath, there would be nothing he could do. He returned the hatchling to its crate and wiped his hands clean of the stickiness from handling the baby.

Another shell cracked. It was the egg with the great lump on one side. This hatchling emerged easier, smashing its way free. Already it was large, double the size of the other hatchling. Its scales were a pale, ginger red and appeared stretched in places. It stood on swollen feet and its neck and body bulged as well, possibly from inflammation.

Neither hatchling offered an auspicious start.

Sovereign wanted strength. New powers. New magics.

Eighteen eggs had been gathered in total. Those hatching had been amongst the first to arrive. They kept about five eggs to each hatchery to provide enough space for the babies to grow. When not Forging, Cleansing, eating, or sleeping, Osric attended to the eggs, checking they were warm and their straw fresh. Grunt work for a general, but Sovereign trusted no human to be around the eggs in case they hatched and bonded with one of the cultists. If they were to have riders, it would be on Sovereign's terms.

Osric inspected the remaining three eggs in this hatchery. Two remained stiff and unmoving. Only one gave the slightest of trembles. It was unusually round, closer to a ball than an egg.

Something heavy smacked against the side of a crate. The swollen hatchling beat its tail against the wood. Already it splintered and buckled under the blows. Osric raised his brow, and his initial impression of the pale ginger dragon changed.

"He'll like you."

Out of sight, the turquoise dragon continued to cough.

Osric returned to the hatchery door, ordered the cultists outside to bring back meat and fresh dry straw for the dragons, then returned to check on the last of the hatching eggs. The trembling of the spherical egg had picked up in tempo.

When the shell gave way, the dragon that emerged had two colors. Its front half was gray, while its hindquarters and tail were a striking green. Other than its color, this hybrid dragon seemed the most normal of the trio. It croaked a soft cry and craned its neck up at Osric.

He stepped away from its crate, not wishing for the babies to grow more attached to him than could be helped. Both the hybrid and the muscled ginger started yammering. Their cries were high and concerned.

At the same time, the hacking of the turquoise drake intensified.

Osric returned to its crate, but even as he peered in, the hatchling coughed dark blood and lay still. A weight slid through him, from chest to toes. He had witnessed endless death in his career, but watching a creature be born into pain, know only suffering, and then wither within minutes unlocked sorrow even in his stone heart.

A knock came at the hatchery door. Meat for the dragons.

Osric realized he was gripping the side of the crate and let go. Sighing, he turned his back on the turquoise hatchling. When he returned, he carried a bucket of chopped rabbit and dropped a few pieces into the crates of the muscled ginger and the hybrid dragon.

As the dragons ate, he scooped out the broken eggshells and the damp straw, replacing it with dry hay. He picked up the crate with the dead hatchling and handed it to the cultists at the door.

"Bury it outside the walls."

Finally, he picked up one of the eggs yet to hatch. It felt heavier than the others had. Perhaps with magic he could have detected life inside it, but Sovereign had their bond closed over and Osric felt no desire to reopen it.

He brought the cold, heavy egg before Sovereign.

"Are you able to sense life in it?"

Sovereign rumbled and lowered himself until his snout hovered just above the tip of the egg. He sniffed, then snorted.

"*Matriarchs have an intuition for this,*" Sovereign said. "*Though I sense nothing in it. Do you recall where this one came from?*"

"From Squall Rock."

"*It may have petrified on the longer journey,*" Sovereign said. "*Or it may have been stone cold the day it was sung into creation.*"

"Two of the five in the first hatchery were like this," Osric said. "Three hatched, though one died shortly after."

"*I expected there to be losses. And of those that survive, not all will be suitable. Go to the others.*"

Osric did, checking in on the hatcheries one by one. Only one more egg hatched that day, a navy dragon whose eyes cycled between many colors. Of the eighteen eggs gathered, four had hatched. One had died. One had been confirmed as stone. Time would tell for the remaining thirteen.

On his way back to Sovereign, Osric passed a group of cultists carrying buckets of blood. Their resident blood alchemist had been hard at work since fresh drakes arrived to pledge their allegiance to Sovereign. Osric did his best to avoid that laboratory if he could help it. As with many aspects of Sovereign's command, he was surprised that he allowed the shroud to continue their practice of drinking dragon blood. Osric supposed that this blood was given willingly now and not taken from those they 'freed' from the Order.

Days passed. More Forging. More Cleansing. Osric checked in on the hatcheries twice daily, both to check on the progress of the unhatched eggs and to tend to the hatchlings. Another egg hatched, while two more were confirmed as stone.

Their steady supply of eggs also dried up. The easy pickings were gone. Risks had been taken and would not be taken lightly again. The ice dragon who plundered the leavings of Skyspear from the Frost Fangs had been sent again to retrieve what he could.

Fresh hope arrived in the form of a fire rider from Alamut, the Order Hall of Ahar. Osric met her out in the yard. She had a broader face than those he recalled during his time in those lands, but this only made her more striking. Moon-shaped eyebrows, full lips, and dark hair cut short before the base of her neck. Under one arm she carried a dragon egg. Her fully grown dragon stood behind her, red as hot coals.

At first, she did not register Osric as he approached.

"Welcome to Windshear Hold, Champion Dahaka," Osric said. Sovereign had informed him of the newcomers' names. "And to you, Zahak," he added, addressing the dragon.

Both rider and dragon blinked at him, bewildered. Dahaka squinted, as if trying to recall his name.

"Do I know you?"

"I shouldn't think so," Osric said. He had led his Gray Cloaks in the desert borderlands of Ahar for almost two years, but he'd never had direct dealings with the riders of Alamut. "I am Osric Agravain. I come on behalf of Sovereign."

Her gaze shifted back over his shoulder to the door of the mystic tower. "I would speak to Sovereign or his rider. No one lesser."

Her dragon puffed smoke in agreement.

Osric nodded, then, as though unwrapping a bleeding wound, he reopened the bond to Sovereign.

The fire dragon pressed his neck to the ground at once. The rider looked horrified, then fell to one knee and raised the dragon egg to him in offering.

"Forgive me, Master. I did not sense your power."

"The power is not mine," Osric said. He took the egg from her all the same.

"Let me feel how Zahak has grown in strength," Sovereign demanded.

Grimacing, Osric used what magic was needed to reach out and inspect the core of the dragon. It felt like needles pierced him all over. Next, he checked the power of Dahaka and Zahak's soul bond. The pair were clearly powerful Champions. As Osric understood it, the riders used three distinct tiers to help convey the gap in power between a fresh Champion and one pushing at the boundaries of Lord. Low, High, and Exalted. In his estimation, Dahaka was an Exalted Champion of Fire.

Sovereign's satisfaction pulsed across the dragon bond. Osric wasn't sure if that felt better or worse than the pain of the magic.

"I will accept their fealty. Send them to me."

"Sovereign offers you audience."

Dahaka bowed even lower. "Thank you, Master Agravain." She gave him the title as though he were her direct superior in the Order. He had never understood why riders knelt to each other. Soldiers did not kneel before their officers. They knelt for kings, empresses, and archons, but it was out of deference to the position, not strictly to the person.

"On your feet," Osric said. "Reserve your bows for Sovereign. While before me, you will stand at attention, for you are a soldier in his army now."

Dahaka stood and snapped to attention far better than any of the Shroud did. She looked upon him a new light and understanding dawned on her face.

"May I speak freely?"

Osric nodded.

"Are you the same Agravain who led that mercenary company? I believe I saw you at a banquet the Shah once hosted."

Osric recalled, as if from a dream, the lavish feasting hall, swaying dancers, platters of fruit, steam billowing from dishes of saffron rice and enough laughter to drown out a battle. He was surprised he could recall that much of the feast given who had attended it with him. Had he even taken his eyes from her for one moment that night?

"That was years ago," Osric said. "And another life."

Not far off, two dragons, one ice and one storm, growled deep in brief pain. They stood surrounded by members of the Shroud. Both dragons had small cuts on their flanks, and the cultists held buckets up to catch the dripping blood. More fuel for the blood alchemist's work.

Osric gritted his teeth. Drinking dragon blood held all the appeal of magic to him. There was no denying its potency, yet the Shroud had increasingly come to rely on it and, Osric was certain, were increasingly being changed by it. Those who drank it were temporarily not in their right minds. The blood of another, stronger being no doubt imparted a piece of that creature as it coursed through their veins.

"Is something wrong, Master Agravain?"

Osric snapped his attention back to her. "You'll find Sovereign in the hatchery on the second floor," he said, motioning to the mystic tower. "You're dismissed, Champion Dahaka, Zahak," he added, with a curt nod to the dragon. He swept back to the mystic tower and took the stairs, winding many levels until he arrived at the fourth hatchery.

At the higher levels, the nests grew smaller. This one could only house four babies in truth. He placed the latest egg in with the others yet to hatch. One new egg seemed a poor replacement for those they had lost.

Over the coming days, Dahaka began to share in the duties of tending to the hatchlings. With a soul bond of her own, she could not bond with another. Another benefit of her and Zahak's arrival was that an additional dragon might speed the remaining eggs on their way. And it was perhaps because of this, three days after they arrived, that two more hatched. One seemed healthy. Osric suspected the other was deaf on one side. Dahaka shook the hatchling as though expecting to hear a rattle before she placed it back down.

"What use does Sovereign have with ill or broken hatchlings?" Dahaka asked. "I had one chance to raid the hatchery of Alamut before I left. I could have taken a strong, wholesome egg."

"These eggs may hold a powerful new type. One already hatched in Feorlen to the west. A lunar dragon."

"Lunar?" she said, as though the idea were absurd.

Osric didn't feel it warranted a reply. Small talk, even on the business at hand, held little interest for him. He replaced the new hatchling's straw bedding and fed it a bit of cured ham.

"Do I make you uncomfortable?" Dahaka asked.

Osric looked at her, then quickly looked away again. Perhaps she did. Was it because her face reminded him, even faintly, of Esfir? Like looking on the face of a distant relation. No, he considered. More than that. Truth was, he had never been comfortable in the company of women. It was why he had trudged into the snows of the north to become a berserker in a Skarl warband. It was why he'd invited only men into his Gray Cloaks.

"I prefer to work in silence."

She shrugged and left it at that. Now she wasn't looking at him, he felt he could risk a glance in her direction. He wondered privately what had driven her here. The Speaker of the Shroud was a crazed woman, as in love with the idea of a desolate world as Sovereign was. Did Dahaka feel the same? She did not seem fanatical. He wondered, but he did not ask. If she wished to tell him, so be it. Otherwise, it was not his business to know why. She had come. She and her dragon had sworn fealty to Sovereign. And once one had joined him in service, they did not leave.

Osric knew. Osric had tried. Osric had failed.

The next day bore no new hatchlings, but three more eggs were confirmed to be stone. Only six eggs remained. Six chances.

"*I want more,*" Sovereign demanded of Osric when he returned to Cleanse and Forge.

"You have more riders in your service, do you not? Have them bring more." He wondered not for the first time how Sovereign even communicated with his agents halfway across the world. The same way, Osric assumed, that Sovereign influenced the scourge. A secret the dragon kept guarded.

"I cannot risk more from them in the near future."

"Then send more drakes to the Frost Fangs. One large raid should carry plenty away. It's unlikely the riders from Skyspear will even notice. Isn't that the beauty of it? No one cares about these eggs."

"That area lies close to Drakburg as well," Sovereign said. Osric knew Drakburg to be the Order Hall of Risalia. *"A large group of wild dragons flying near their territory will arouse suspicion."*

"Then send one at a time."

Sovereign growled. *"I need more than that."*

Osric pondered the issue. "I once heard of rumors that wild dragons inhabited the black valleys east of the Fae Forest. The area some call the Grim Gorge. Is that true?"

Sovereign growled and turned his snout. For the first time, Osric thought the dragon had hesitated in his answer.

"It's been centuries since I flew that far east."

"Here at Windshear, we're not so far away," Osric said. "One successful raid might double the eggs we have. By your leave, I would lead this raid for you."

Osric considered it a matter of course. He often closed over his bond due to his hatred of it. That would keep him cloaked from the dragons of the valley, allowing him and a team of the Shroud to get in close. And Sovereign had no need to fear betrayal from him. Such days of resistance were long gone.

Sovereign growled and flashed a few teeth. *"Then lead it you shall."*

He evidently thought the same way as Osric. Still, the speed at which he accepted the plan took Osric aback.

"Such a raid would bring the risk of retaliation and discovery," Osric said. The more experienced, zealous cultists would die to defend Sovereign's whereabouts, but a precautionary vial of poison for each of them would not go amiss.

"I need more," Sovereign said, drawing each word out. *"I have no intention of lingering here longer than needs be. And as I consider it, of all the flights to steal from, my own is the most vulnerable."*

So, the rumors were true. Mystic dragons did inhabit those valleys.

"I shall ready a force to leave at daybreak," Osric said.

"Not so hasty, worm. We must await the return of—" Sovereign broke off in a rare grunt of strained pain. He scrunched his eyes shut and half turned his snout to the opening of the hatchery, as though he were about to turn and leave.

"What's the matter?" Osric asked. No response. "Can I assist you with it?" A snarl from the dragon but nothing more. "Is it the scourge?"

"You don't need to know," the charming voice told him.

Osric reconsidered. He didn't need that information right now.

Sovereign righted himself and returned to glowering at Osric. *"We shall await the return of the Speaker,"* he said, finishing his train of thought. *"She is to bring the means to prepare you, and in your absence, she can direct her followers. In the meantime…"*

Sovereign did not need to finish.

Osric returned to sitting cross-legged on the hatchery floor and began to work on Sovereign's core. He would await the return of the Speaker.

THIRTEEN

A Mad Scheme

Holt had a barrage of questions for Rake, but the half-dragon waved them away and sat cross-legged as though he were about to meditate.

"I'd rather hear your story first," Rake said. "You can begin from when we parted in Feorlen and continue until this very moment. I want it all. Every detail you might think boring I promise you I shall relish."

And so Holt told him. When he reached the part about his father, he found it didn't hurt so much in the telling. Already it was easier to recite that dreadful day without his voice choking. Rake barely moved or said a word until he reached the part where he and Ash managed to surprise Clesh and shoot him with a ballista bolt.

"Storm clouds covered the roof of the palace," Holt said. "I could barely see. It was all down to Ash."

"Intriguing. Sense-sharing is so often a discarded feature of the bond. I wonder if..." He trailed off, looking pensive, before saying, "Carry on."

Holt felt a bit put out. He'd hoped Rake would have had higher praise for their achievement. Nevertheless, he continued with the story of the Battle of Sidastra, of how Talia slew Silas in single combat, and how the Life Elder and the Emerald Flight arrived to secure the victory. How, despite all he and Ash had done, they were banished. And how the Life Elder gave them a quest to find the other Wild Flights and convince them, somehow, to join the battle to end the scourge once and for all.

"A big task for such a little person," Rake said. "Well, that is quite a tale. And where is the fiery Miss Agravain now?"

"She was crowned queen."

"Was she indeed? I shall have to return to Feorlen one day and remind her she owes me a favor."

"I'm not sure how well that will go," Holt said. "She didn't trust you very much."

Rake gasped in mock horror and placed a hand over his heart. "How will I ever hold my head high?" He grinned, a smile of many sharp incisors. "Few enough trust creatures like us, Holt. Those uncategorizable. That is why you were sent away and why not even your friend would stand up for you."

"She did," Holt protested. "Talia didn't want us to go."

"Grief was in her heart when she told us," Ash said.

"There is always a way to achieve what you want," Rake said. "Always. Now, I do believe there is a little more to your tale."

"We traveled east, spending time in the Red Range and the woods east of the mountains before entering Brenin."

He then went through their trials in that kingdom, telling Rake about Orvel and the stolen dragon egg. Rake nodded throughout, unreactive even to their most perilous moments.

"Were it not for Ethel, we'd probably be dead," Holt said. "She knew Brode and that he and Erdra had fought at Red Rock. But how did you know to find us here?"

"The Life Elder did not take every member of his flight to Feorlen. I had need to speak with the East Warden. He's not as accommodating as the West Warden, and that's saying something, but I had it out of him in the end. You were heading east of Athra to a gravesite of your mentor's dragon. East of Athra is a lot of ground, but I recalled, as did the emeralds, how a smaller secondary swarm had risen on the borderlands of the Fae Forest during the last great incursion. That helped to narrow down my search area, though it took me a full week before I picked up the old notes that lead me here. Truth be told, I was beginning to worry you weren't coming."

"Well, we're here now," said Holt. "And we're ready to help you. Whatever you need."

"We'd be honored, Master Rake," Ash said.

Rake chuckled, which was a strange hybrid of human and rumbling dragon laughter. "You might not be so enthusiastic once I tell you what it is I need. But first, let me fill you in on my own adventures since we parted. With the name of Sovereign as a starting point, I ventured east to consult with my own Elder."

Holt's heart skipped a beat. "You know where the Mystic Elder is?"

"She tries to elude me, but I always find her in the end," Rake said.

"Can you take us to her?"

"Perhaps. Though I will be less inclined if you continue to forget your manners and so rudely interrupt my story. Where was I?" he said, over dramatically. "Ah yes, I sought my Elder, but she refused an audience with me. Yet, outcast as I am, I still have friends here and there. A few mystics told me in private of similar disappearances of their kin, of drakes departing north. I went to investigate and found a lot of activity around the old fortress of Windshear Hold. Do you know of it?"

Holt thought it sounded familiar but shook his head.

"It was the first headquarters of the dragon riders. Before they relocated to Falcaer. When I arrived, many drakes patrolled the air. And there were cloaked humans coming and going. I believe they were Wyrm Cloaks. Were it not for my veiled core, I'd never have been able to linger and learn as long as I did. Not long after I began to watch, one of the cores I sensed inside the fortress began to swell with power. An efficiency I've never seen before."

"Do you think that was Sovereign?"

"I couldn't be sure. Before the power swell, I could not have picked the core out from any wild dragon. Yet I stayed and watched, and when the opportunity arose, I pounced upon a group of cultists. I exerted a little pressure on them—"

Holt couldn't say he felt sorry for Wyrm Cloaks.

"—and they confirmed Sovereign was at the fortress, babbling and praising him over and over. And now our adventures share a step on the road, for I too liberated a dragon egg from them."

Holt looked to Ash. That unspoken fear of what destination the poor egg in Brenin had been destined for sank through him like ice.

"Was it an egg like Ash's?" Holt asked. "One dragons would consider… different?" He refused to use the word 'defective'.

Rake inclined his head. "It was, though this one was cold as true stone. A friend of mine confirmed no living dragon remained inside it, and we buried it. But," he said, his tone growing darker, "that was only one egg. As clumsy as the Wyrm Cloaks might be, I fear many more will reach Windshear Hold. And not all of them will be stone."

It was Ash who responded first. *"We cannot let him hatch them."*

"I quite agree," Rake said. "Given he learned of Ash during your brief encounter with him, I'd say he's hoping to hatch more lunar dragons or perhaps other types hitherto unknown. That we cannot allow."

"How are we supposed to do that?" Holt asked.

Rake brought his polearm into his lap and thumbed the glassy orange blade. "Oh, I thought storming the fortress and killing Sovereign would do the trick."

Holt did not think he could have uttered a word if any had sprung to mind. Ash too had been stupefied. His jaw hung open and his forked tongue lolled out.

When neither of them answered, Rake frowned.

"I had hoped for a more enthusiastic response. Perhaps I didn't make the situation clear?"

"You made it clear as a bright moon, Master Rake," Ash said, *"yet this is a great burden. Sovereign's power is immense. We felt only a piece of it before and it was almost impossible to resist him. How can you be so certain that you can defeat him?"*

"I obtained a good feel for his core in my reconnaissance. It is regaining strength rapidly, but it's akin to refilling a lake one bucket at a time. If we move fast enough, I might have a chance. It may be the best chance we'll ever get, and I intend to take it."

Holt finally stammered through a response to this madness. "I'd love nothing more than to help you defeat Sovereign. That's half the reason we've been sent to find the Elders in the first place, but what assistance can we be when we're still of a low rank and power?"

"I wasn't planning on throwing an Ascendant against the forces of Sovereign," Rake said. "I'll do my best to train you in what time we have."

"Why?" Holt said, suspicious now. This all seemed both too dangerous and too beneficial at the same time. "What's in this for you, Rake? You don't seem the type to do something out of charity."

Rake clutched his chest again in an exaggerated manner. "Once again, my feelings, Master Cook. You wound me."

"That's not an answer."

Blue ridges along Rake's head and back flared, the way a human might raise their eyebrows. "Isn't it enough that a dragon of tremendous power is up to villainy, and we really ought to do something about it? We won't be charging full-tilt into battle alone. For such a mission as this, I'm putting together a team. You merely have the privilege of being the first members."

"What do you think?" Holt asked Ash over their bond.

"We did want to find Master Rake," Ash said. *"We need a teacher, and he's the best we're going to get. Besides, he knows where at least one Elder is. He can take us there."*

That's an excellent point, Holt thought.

"If we agree," Holt began, "would you take us to see the Mystic Elder? Perhaps she can be convinced to aid us in attacking Sovereign."

Rake flexed his talons, deep in thought. "If you will assist me first in recruiting our next member. I have a friend who I'd like to accompany us. He lives not too far from here, but I require your help in convincing him. Will you help me with that, Holt?"

That doesn't sound so bad.

"Of course," Holt said.

Rake proffered one of his huge hands. "Then it's a deal."

Holt took his hand to shake it, then Rake pulled him in close, rose, and swept his tail to take Holt's legs out from under him. Rake lowered the glassy orange blade of his polearm to Holt's throat.

Ash roared and scrambled upright, but he would have been too late. Compared to Rake, their every movement seemed sluggish.

"We'll have to improve those reflexes," Rake said. He withdrew the weapon. "Take some rest now and eat something, will you? The pair of you look like half-starved scarecrows."

With Rake guarding over them, Holt slept deeper than he had in weeks. Yet as soon as they woke, they were on the move again.

"Keep up, Master Cook," Rake said. There was a jaunt in his step as he passed between the border trees of the Fae Forest.

"You still haven't explained where we're going."

"I think you'll find that I did."

"You said, 'we're going to see an old friend of mine', but not who they are or where they are."

"Or when we shall be home for supper?" Rake chuckled. "You sound like a fretting mother, Holt Cook. Where's your sense of adventure?" With that, he bounded off through the trees. His strides were enormous.

Ash followed, fresh and eager. *"Come on. We must not fall behind."* Although the dragon's eagerness soon hit a snag in navigating the dense woodland.

Rake did not slow down though and was ever in danger of slipping out of sight into the undergrowth.

"Wait!" Holt called. "We're not as fast as you!"

"What's that?" Rake called back. "I can't hear you. You'll need to catch up." Then he disappeared into the forest.

Holt huffed in indignation.

Ash sniffed the air with wide nostrils and raised his ears to pick up every slight sound.

The dragon hit his tail against the earth and trunks as he moved, creating a mental image of the world through sound.

Somewhere ahead came a crack of wood, then another and another.

"I think Master Rake is using his weapon to make noise for me," Ash said. *"I have more information to hear by now."*

"Where did he go?" Holt asked.

"This way."

Holt followed, glad for Ash's increased senses. He would have struggled to locate the half-dragon. Rake kept his core veiled so Holt could not even track his power. This seemed like some game or test, but Holt would play it. Being with Rake was their best chance to rank quickly and gain the strength they needed to complete their quest. That is, if they survived Rake's own mission.

Deeper in the forest, the character of the woods became clearer. Where the Withering Woods were unpleasant due to sickness and decay, the Fae Forest seemed to suffer from the opposite problem. An overabundance of life.

Where trees fell, two more sprung in their wake. Moss begot fungi which begot flowers and weeds that Holt had never seen before; all of them bright with colors of every sort. There was a dampness underfoot but not in the air, which held the sharp fragrance of a rich woodland: of sweet flowers, and of other stark aromas of wild herbs. All of it trapped under the thick roof of the forest, which blocked the moon and stars as night descended.

A pitch blackness took over the world and barely a lunar mote shot by the orbit of Ash's core.

Holt stopped, shut his eyes for thirty-second intervals, then opened them. He still struggled to see his own hands in front of his face. Ash followed Rake by sound or smell, but Holt had nothing to go on and even lost sight of Ash.

"Slow down Ash," he called. "I can't see. I'll need to stick right beside you, even if it slows us down."

"You should try to see as I see."

"My ears aren't good enough for that."

"Then share in my ears. I see through your eyes when we fly."

Holt considered it. He had experienced something like that when they had flown into Red Rock. In theory, it might work.

"Is Rake still moving on without us?"

"He's stopped somewhere. Still tapping."

"Alright. Let's try this. Bear with me." He felt around in the dark until he found what he assumed to be a piece of damp bark. He picked it up and they began to blend senses, smelling the earthiness of the wet wood together. Their senses were already melding before they said the words and touched skin to scale to aid the technique along. Even before it completed, Holt began to hear Rake's *tap tap tap* in the distance. It was so soft to him, like hearing water drip into a basin, yet it was there.

As the sense-sharing completed, that faint tapping grew in volume until it sounded as though Rake were clicking his fingers nearby. For Holt, the world remained dark and elusive. Other sounds also filtered through which he had not heard before – small creatures rustling in the undergrowth. He could smell a whiff of them too, something of the fur and the oil on that fur.

He reached out again with one hand to feel the world around him. The bark of a nearby tree felt rougher than usual, and as he took a step forward, he could feel the give of the earth more than before.

Yet the new clarity did not last long. His own senses were not shut off, and so the input from Ash came to him as if on a delay, echoing after Ash heard or smelled the thing first.

Holt had taken no more than three steps before the disorientation got to him. He reached out for Ash again and steadied himself with one hand on his dragon's side.

"I've said it before but it's beyond impressive how you move so well in darkness."

"It's not dark to me," Ash said. *"I see the black night now our eyes are one, but when I'm not seeing through you, I don't see darkness. It's just... nothing."*

Holt thought that sounded like a cold way to live. No light, no color. He was thankful he could offer Ash glimpses of the world.

He closed his eyes, hoping that would help him rely on his other senses. He strained, trying to separate the sounds he heard with his own ears from those Ash heard. An impression formed of a root sticking out of the ground, but he could not discern if that was the work of his own mind or something else passed over from Ash. When he stepped and tripped over the root, the worst part was he could not tell in what way he had been wrong. All was confusion and reverberating noise.

He got back to his feet and listened again. If he concentrated hard enough, he could hear Rake beating a distant tree to the northwest, but he knew he had no hope of navigating there like this.

He cut the sense-sharing, his head sore from the experience this time.

"I think you'll have to give me a lift."

Ash rumbled and licked his hand. *"My pleasure."*

They continued chasing Rake through the forest for another few hours before he let them catch him. Holt saw him as a pair of sapphire eyes floating in the dark. Rake might have been leaning against a tree waiting for them.

"You gave up easily, Master Cook."

"What do you mean? We're here, aren't we?"

"I mean in your attempt to see in the dark. You suffered it for all of five minutes I'd say."

Holt would have asked how he knew that, but as Rake seemed to take pleasure in withholding information, he decided not to further his enjoyment.

"Doing something under pressure for the first time is hard."

"You don't know what pressure is yet," said Rake. "But you will." He shifted, and his cloak rustled against the forest floor. "I've taken the liberty of building a small fire here. Sit with me."

Rake lowered himself, then struck flint. Sparks flew, and in the momentary light, Holt saw that Rake was not hitting flint with steel but rather striking his own talon-like nails across the stone. The result was the same. More sparks flew until the kindling caught. He blew out a long breath to stoke the flames and bring them to life.

Holt sighed in relief at the warm light and got down from Ash.

"Let's give you a rest," he said, taking their pack and supplies off

Ash's back. Pots and pans jangled as he set the equipment down. Ash stretched, then curled up and rested his snout upon his talons.

Throughout this, Rake sat cross-legged by fire. His polearm lay on the ground by his side, however the flint he had used to start the fire was nowhere to be seen.

Does he have pockets in the lining of that great cloak?

Feeling somewhat at a loss, Holt asked, "Would you like some food? We don't have much with us but—"

"I am well satiated for now," Rake said. "These days I eat little."

That struck at Holt's curiosity too much for him to resist.

"Dragons eat a lot. Don't you have to as well because you're, well... because—"

"Spit it out."

"Because you're half a dragon."

"Perhaps I have half a dragon's appetite? In the beginning I was ravenous, though cravings diminish after three hundred years. Even for wild dragons."

"I assume lamb is your favorite? Being a mystic and all?"

"After a fashion. Before I *changed,* I was rather fond of a slow-cooked stew, I think. Where you could still taste the wine in the sauce. But it's been so long."

"Maybe one night I'll be able to make that for you."

Rake laughed his rumbling laugh. "That's a thought, but we won't have time for such things, I assure you. Nor do I envision much of a chance to enter a winery. I'm quite conspicuous in case you hadn't noticed."

"I'm not so conspicuous," Holt said. "I'm used to blending right into the background. If there is ever the chance, I'd like to cook that dish for you all the same."

Rake smiled, not his usual grin but something genuine. "You've a kind heart, Master Cook. Doubtless why Ash is with us now."

Holt still had half a hundred burning questions and many lesser ones besides. He tried a few. Who would be joining them on this mission? How could he and Ash advance in rank quick enough to be of use? What was the Mystic Elder like? Would she be willing to join the Life Elder in his new war on the scourge?

Rake nimbly evaded them as fast as Holt threw them out.

"Stop dodging my questions."

"You do have so many of them." Rake raised one finger. "We'll have time ahead for every small detail. For now, you may ask me one thing and I promise I shall answer."

Holt bit his lip. What were the most pressing issues? He knew Rake was a half-dragon and he'd confirmed back when they first met that he'd been in the Order once. He clearly wasn't on Sovereign's side, but he wasn't fully trusted or accepted by wild dragons either.

"Any help, Ash?" he asked over their bond.

"What do you desire, Master Rake?" Ash asked.

Rake took a few moments before answering. "I desire but *one* thing. To undo what happened to me."

"How can it be undone?" Holt asked.

"That's another question," Rake said, "but as I do not have an answer to surrender to you, I'll allow it. Because if I knew the answer to that most important of questions, I'd have done it. Now," he said in a more business-like manner, "we shall spend the night here and await my friend at dawn. Let us Cleanse, be at peace, and recover some strength."

Understanding that he would get nothing more from the half-dragon tonight, Holt did as he was bid and began to sink into the process of Cleansing Ash's core.

"We can trust Master Rake," Ash said low over their bond. *"I am sure of it."*

"I really hope you're right, Ash."

FOURTEEN

The Apothecary

Holt spent the remainder of that night in the woods Cleansing alongside Rake in silence. Their fire burned low, then guttered out. Rake sat still throughout, save for the strands of pale orange and purple light which peeled away from his shoulders.

As the first rays of dawn crept through the canopy, fending off the utter darkness of the Fae Forest, a dull thud came from the ground. It beat again, coming from underneath Ash.

Holt scrambled upright, picked up the scabbard with Brode's sword and drew it.

"Ash, wake up!"

He searched his magical senses and felt a solid orb of power down below, though beyond that he could not say. The ground dampened his senses.

Ash woke with a start as the banging grew louder. Then, in a great boom of effort, the ground beneath Ash burst upward, knocking Ash over and throwing soil in all directions. It was in fact a great trap door of gnarled roots.

"Oops," Rake said, though he seemed otherwise unconcerned. "I forgot exactly where he placed his front door."

Holt's mind tried to process this but failed, so he ended up spurting out stupidly, "Front door?"

Ash growled, rolled to his feet, and shook the dirt from himself.

Rake moved to the hole in the ground and called down. "Aberanth? Don't fret. It's just me and a couple of guests."

A voice answered telepathically. *"Guests, hmmph? That implies they were invited."*

"Don't be sour," Rake said. "You need company from time to time or you'll grow even madder down there."

"Bah, you're one to talk, Rake. I already told you I wasn't interested in your crazed plan. Good day!"

The trap door began to swing shut, seemingly of its own accord. Rake caught it in one hand. Braced on one knee, he held it open.

"Hmmph," Aberanth huffed again. *"I won't thank you for bringing others to my home either. Go. Be gone!"*

The trap door shook, desperate to close, yet Rake held firm.

"You're going to want to meet my companions," he said.

"I don't think I do."

"One of them is a lunar dragon."

"For goodness sake, Rake, leave now or… lunar? Did you say lunar?"

The trap door ceased shaking.

"That's right," Rake said. "Come here Ash. Stick your snout down there for old Aberanth to see you."

"Old? I'm younger than you, you shriveled old snake, you, you—" He gasped as Ash stuck his head down into the hole in the ground. *"Whiter than any I have seen before. Albino, are you? I can't tell so well in the half-dark. A blindfold! You're blind? Gracious, who let you hatch?"*

"I did," Holt said proudly. He sheathed Brode's sword, then strode over to the hole in the ground. Leaning in over Ash, he saw a pair of yellow eyes blinking back at him in the dark. Now the ground no longer interfered, he could make out that the dragon's core was not leagues beyond an Ascendant's power.

"Hello," Holt said to the eyes. "My name is Holt, and this is Ash."

"Hello," Aberanth said, as though he'd forgotten how to say the

word. His yellow eyes flicked over to Rake. *"Very clever, Rake. Very clever. I can't imagine where you found them, but it won't work! I shan't come."*

"I am truly sorry to hear that," Rake said. "Might you at least invite us in for a moment? We've been running through the woods all night and you usually have something vitalizing brewing down there."

"Oh, very well. If it will let me see the back of you sooner, come on down." The dragon's eyes disappeared as he turned in the dark, grumbling back down the underground passage.

"In you jump, Holt," Rake said with a nod of his head. "Ash, you'll have to wait here I'm afraid. You won't fit."

Ash slumped to the ground and snorted.

"You'll have an important job," Rake said. He placed his polearm down beside Ash. "Guard this for me."

Holt felt bad, but he jumped in as Rake bid. Once in the tunnel, he could just about stand upright and so he wondered how Aberanth fit in the tunnel as a dragon. Rake came down a moment later, and he had to stoop to move.

The tunnel wound farther underground before leveling out and weaving this way and that. The initial darkness soon gave way to pale blue and green light. Drawing closer to the source, Holt discovered they were fat insects whose bodies glowed. His first instinct made him draw back.

"What are those things?"

It took Rake a moment to understand what had caused the alarm. "These? They're just fireflies."

They clung to the roots and rock like torches in sconces and seemed content to remain there. Still, any bugs this close to Holt reignited foundational fears.

"Not all insects are the scourge," Rake said. "Aberanth has bred these a little different, but they're still harmless. Come on."

Holt did. Now he was getting used to them, the firefly light was beautiful. From farther down the tunnel there came more light, muted yellows and oranges emanating from many branching veins of the deepest sort of roots, so that the underground world was as welcoming as any homely hearth. Before long, the passage widened and a larger room became visible. Rake placed a hand in front of Holt to stop him entering.

"Don't touch anything."

"I won't," Holt said, slightly concerned.

Rake smiled, then passed through. Holt followed and his jaw dropped in awe.

His first thought was that he had entered an apothecary's store deep underground. Pots and cauldrons bubbled with bright mixtures; mortars, pestles, and other equipment lay neatly upon great tabletops that seemed to grow out of the walls. Crates of glass vials and bowls sat near the door.

Yet the real marvel was the huge trunk of a beech tree at the center of the cave, branching off into a canopy of earth that formed the ceiling. Many of its descending branches wove through the walls, emanating that same soft light as the tunnel passage. In places, roots and vines also sprouted out from the walls to hold vials and other equipment like so many fine fingers.

Rake could stand comfortably within the grove and Holt found the place airy for something so deep underground, though an unmistakable scent of strong alcohol lingered over everything. Taken by surprise, he did not at first notice where Aberanth had gone. A fully grown dragon would still have struggled to maneuver in here.

Holt searched, then found him half hidden by the trunk of the central tree. He was the smallest dragon Holt had ever seen, perhaps the size Ash had been when they had arrived at Fort Kennet, which was about the size of a small pony. His scales were a muddy color, more brown than green, and his wings were akin to the bark of the astonishing beech tree. Like all dragons he had ridges down his back and tail, though they were stunted, rounder, and smooth at their tops.

"Forgive the mess," Aberanth said.

"This is amazing," Holt said. He took a measured step inside, then, recalling what Rake had said, he stood awkwardly in the middle of an aisle between two workbenches, trying to stay away from everything.

"About that refreshment?" Rake asked.

"Yes, yes," Aberanth said testily. *"The cauldron with the orange infusion should serve."*

Rake rubbed his hands eagerly, then found a cup and scooped some of the liquid out. He drank, and steam vented from his ears and nostrils. Rake gave a roar of delight.

"I'm afraid it would boil your human insides," Aberanth said to Holt. He padded around the trunk and approached him slowly, head cocked and sniffing furtively. Holt noticed then how the dragon's eyes were too big for his head, gazing wide and inquisitively at him. *"That sword doesn't belong to you."*

"It belonged to my last master," Holt said.

"And now you follow Rake?" Aberanth shook his head. *"A blind dragon. A sword that isn't yours. And yes, I can hear notes of a different sort from you. They remind me of the stars. Hmmph,"* he added, though less cross than before. He stepped closer, like a shy cat. *"May I inspect your soul bond?"*

"Oh, yes, you may."

A quick presence swept over his soul, experienced and precise like the hands of a physician. Aberanth's eyes widened further.

"As pure a bond as I've ever felt." He snaked his head around and narrowed his eyes at Rake. *"Now I understand."*

Rake smiled, shrugged, and moved off as though one of the experiments across the grove had him enraptured.

Aberanth returned to studying Holt with eyes much too large for his small body. *"Fascinating. Quite fascinating. A new type of dragon? What does the magic entail? But no,"* he said, quick and terse, and shrugged away from Holt as though he were a temptress. *"I won't be party to it, Rake. You ask too much."*

"Remind me," Rake drawled, "who brings you all this human equipment when you are in need? A flock of geese? A horde of squirrels?"

"Don't try to guilt me. I've sheltered you plenty of times during the storms you bring upon yourself, but I won't abandon my laboratory, my mushroom farms, and all my research to go galivanting into danger!"

"Why do you work underground?" Holt asked.

"My emerald brothers and sisters do not appreciate my approach. They see

only cold calculation in such learning compared to the songs of the living world. A small ridiculous dragon they think of me. Dullards I call them."

"Dragons can be cruel. Ash and I found that out the hard way. I'm sorry you went through that too."

"Yes, well, these things happen," Aberanth said sheepishly.

"What are you researching?"

"Everything I can. How things work, and how they might be changed. I noted you humans are ever tinkering with the world, often to great effect."

"Aberanth has been doing fine work on the energy flow of mote channels," Rake said. "It could prove useful in fending off whatever mind tricks Sovereign throws at us."

"I told you before, it's still experimental. I have no way of knowing what effect the elixirs will have in the long term, never mind in a combat situation."

This did not seem to be going well. Holt was still at a loss as to how his presence would make any difference in persuading Aberanth to join the mission. The odds of success had not been tipped with the inclusion of an Ascendant.

"I'd have thought a bit of field testing would help you straighten out any kinks in the formula," Rake said, tapping a vial of pus yellow liquid.

"Keep your talons off my work," Aberanth snapped. *"Or you'll likely lose them."* He held up his front right foot, where the talon on his middle toe was missing.

"So you won't help us?" Rake asked. "The intention is to kill the dragon who controls the scourge."

"That is mere conjecture. You have no evidence for that."

"We spoke with him," Holt said. "Ash and I, that is. He tried to get us to join him. He said the scourge would fulfill its purpose."

"Well, I am working on a solution for that too!" Aberanth declared, delighted. *"Even if there is some mad dragon controlling the scourge, it won't do him any good if I can find a serum that combats the blight."*

Holt stared wide-eyed at the little brown dragon. "You can do that?"

"Well, not yet," Aberanth admitted. He moved to one side of his grove, where a long workbench supported a series of large vials

containing leaves suspended in a clear liquid. Each leaf suffered from a different severity of the blight, ranging from little to black.

"*These things take time, don't you know,*" Aberanth said.

"Meaning you've got nowhere," Rake said.

Aberanth blustered in a dragon manner, all growls and squirming wings. "*I'm attempting something no one else has ever done. Hmmph. How long do you think it took humans to invent their steel?*"

"Why are you working on this on your own?" Holt asked. "Even if other emeralds think your methods are strange, surely the Elder would want to see the scourge weakened."

Even as he said it, Holt could well imagine why the Elder frowned on any further experimentation with the scourge. That was how it had all begun in the first place.

Aberanth scoffed. "*Oh, child. If only everyone would listen to logic and not their feelings, we could be a damn sight better off. Fundamentally the blight is a sickness. Sicknesses can be combated if the body has the strength to do so. Riders and dragons can throw the sickness off, even when injured. It's a simple matter of power levels. Pit a Warden against a hatchling and the outcome is certain. But face two Wardens against each other, ha-har, now we have a real fight on our hands!*"

Holt looked to Rake. The half-dragon met his gaze and returned it with a wink.

Aberanth barreled on to the end of his rant. "*Either we must find a way to weaken the blight, which I don't foresee, or we must find a method to help patients fight it off.*"

"What about those already dead?" Holt asked.

"*Ah,*" Aberanth said, "*well, that can't be helped. Dead patients rarely can be, hmmph.*"

"Nor even the living sometimes," Holt said. His father and the blight-stricken souls of Dinan resurfaced painfully to him. "The blight is strong, Aberanth. It may even have grown in strength of late. What you're trying to do sounds difficult."

"*Yes, it is proving rather elusive... but I am making headway, and running off to get killed along with Rake in a fool's errand won't help. My work is too important.*"

Rake sighed dramatically. "Oh well, Holt. I suppose we have come all this way in vain. Perhaps on our way back from killing Sovereign we'll remember to drop in and tell Aberanth about the anti-blight properties of your lunar magic. Farewell then, Aberanth, do enjoy your peace and quiet!"

Rake swept over to Holt and half-turned him by the shoulder to leave.

"*Wait*," Aberanth called. The battle he was fighting within himself rang in his voice. "*Anti-blight? Anti-blight?*" His voice grew even higher now. "*There is no such magic.*"

"I can show you," Holt said. He pulled on lunar motes from Ash's core and prepped them in his hand.

Aberanth screwed up his face, then relented. He bustled off to a side room and out of sight. Moments later, a series of moving roots and vines preceded the dragon's return. They dangled from the ceiling, rose from the floor, and shot out horizontally from the wall, ever moving and reshaping and never once threatening to knock anything over as they carried a sturdy iron box. The roots transported the box to Holt, and a fine vine looped up from the ground, entered the lock, and turned like a key. The box opened.

Inside lay a blighted acorn, all green and oozing. The tainted presence of the scourge touched Holt's magical senses before he smelled death.

Aberanth appeared quietly by Holt's side, his gaze fixed upon the acorn.

Holt cycled lunar motes to the tip of his finger and gently pushed them into the acorn, pleased with how adept his control was becoming. The light shone, and then the acorn was left cleansed. A few strands of silver coated the outer shell of the nut.

Aberanth's jaw dropped. He crept forward, sniffing avidly. "*The stench is gone. Completely gone! Ah, but that is but one test. I must have more data.*"

"It works so long as the power of the blight isn't too strong," Holt said. "Power levels, just like you said." But the dragon was already off.

From out of another back room, a parade of items emerged upon more moving roots.

Holt cured several mushrooms, removed the sickness from within an unhatched bird's egg, cleansed a patch of fox fur. Still Aberanth wasn't satisfied until Holt displayed the effect on items which did not have the blight at all. What he called a 'control'.

"No visible side effects," he muttered, bobbing eagerly around his grotto. In his excitement, he knocked over some vials from a worktop that smashed and spewed forth smoking blue liquid. This did not stop him. He carried on, checking on experiment after experiment, taking in great sniffs, his tail positively quivering. Then he stopped abruptly and visibly fought to curtail his enthusiasm.

Rake beamed and said quietly to Holt, "Good work," before he moved to crouch beside the brown dragon.

"Just think of all the time you'll have to study them," Rake said.

"Study?" Holt began. "Er, Rake—"

"So many long hours," Rake continued over Holt, "around the campfire or while we Cleanse and Forge."

"Study. Observe... yes..."

"A lifetime's worth of advancement in knowledge. And a chance to improve your very special elixirs at the same time," Rake added sweetly.

Aberanth growled, then snapped at the air. The effect was not so menacing coming from such a small dragon.

"Curse you, Rake," Aberanth said. *"Fine. Fine, I'll join your wretched mission. But if I get killed, I'll see you pay for it!"*

"I'm proud of you, friend," Rake said. "And who knows. A bit of excitement? Some fresh air? You might even enjoy yourself."

FIFTEEN

The Chasm

With her eyes closed and her heart steady, Talia drew upon the smoke obscuring Pyra's core. The impurities were thick and dense, making each breath out a struggle that shook her chest. Flames billowed from her shoulders in great bursts of heat as she expelled them. Another breath and another, until all sense of time slipped away.

Suddenly she was back in the grounds of the palace, waving a wooden sword without skill.

"Hold still, uncle," she demanded in a girlish voice.

Osric smiled. "Be quicker. The riders won't accept a slow girl."

She hurled herself forward, clumsy as a puppy. Osric stood still for her this time. She struck and he fell dramatically to the ground. She pointed her toy sword down at his chest.

"Do you yield?"

"Yield?" he said, half laughing. "I never yield." He grabbed her wooden sword and yanked her down with it. Next thing she knew he was tickling her, and she laughed and gasped in hysterics.

A cold wind rose. The grounds grew dark.

"Talia," her mother called from out of sight. "Get away. Get away from him."

Confused, she looked back to her uncle, who had fallen silent. His laughing face had fallen with her mother's arrival, his complexion blue-gray and shadowed. Then his features flashed between two faces. One normal and sad, the other contoured into sharp edges.

When the dragon fangs appeared, she pushed herself from him and thudded backward onto hard stone.

Talia awoke with a start. For a second, she suffered from the delirium of waking up in an unusual place. Warmth from the great brazier eased her back to reality. She sat outside her tent with Pyra, exactly where she'd been Cleansing. It was not yet dawn. The campsite was still. Pyra slept. Only the beating wings of distant emeralds carried on the air.

A nearby brazier cast motes of fire into the orbit of Pyra's core. Not wishing to waste what little time she had, Talia started Forging. Every mote would be worth its weight in gold once they descended underground. And with Pyra asleep, it was far easier for Talia to match the rate of her heart to the steady beat of the dragon bond. If only she could have sat like this for days, weeks, months, bringing her dragon's core from a bonfire up to a great inferno. Alas, time was short.

All too soon, the first blue flecks of dawn appeared east over the chasm. The campsite rustled with the murmuring of rising soldiers and auxiliaries. The smell of frying bacon and baking bread wafted her way, and yet the rancorous sweet stench of the chasm remained.

Pyra stirred. She yawned wide, displaying her razor-sharp teeth and forked tongue.

"Good morning," Talia said.

"Did you sleep at all?"

"I got enough," Talia said, not wishing Pyra to know of her nightmare.

"I feel refreshed," Pyra said. *"With luck, the trials ahead will deepen our bond and strengthen you in turn."*

"Let's think about making it through the days ahead and worry about our bond later." She stood, strapped her blade onto her back and felt a tension in her muscles. A fight would be welcome. Lacking proper training, Talia feared she would quickly grow soft. "I'll inspect the camp and return for breakfast."

Pyra rumbled in acknowledgment, then shifted to be closer to the brazier.

Talia set off, walking through the campsite toward the chasm's edge. She ought to have worn a lesser version of her crown to display who she was, but her red armor was instantly recognizable. Having already tarnished the crown that had survived for generations until she'd worn it, she wasn't in a hurry to wear another.

She moved swiftly, reaching the lines of ditches and trenches still being dug for defense. When she reached the precipice of the chasm, she stood at its edge and peered down.

The first time she had beheld it, she had been on the run with Brode and Holt, with little hope and fewer allies. She recalled the despair, the thick, putrid air, the eerie green light cutting through the fog. Yet now, under the light of dawn, with a small army at her back and over one hundred emerald dragons, the chasm did not sap the strength from her bones as it had then.

Half a mile long with steep jagged banks and dark tunnels at the bottom of the ravine, everything about the chasm was still perilous. Emeralds sat perched on rocky outcrops, guarding the opening of the largest tunnel.

Strangest of all was how still the place felt. The Elder had arrived long before her own army marched through the woods. Neither force encountered any scourge. Not a single ghoul. She supposed if Sovereign controlled the scourge here, it would make sense for him to keep his forces safe underground. But then why the earlier attack on the Warden's squadron?

All around the chasm, the Emerald Flight burst into a series of roars, communicating as drumbeats or horns would direct a human army. Perched dragons took off to be replaced by others. To her right, a supply convoy emerged between the trees. Due to the terrain being too treacherous for wagons, troops carried supplies on foot. A small emerald walked behind the convoy, moss green and glowering from side to side.

Despite the danger ahead, Talia spared a moment to marvel at what was happening. Humans and dragons were working together on a scale never before seen. If only the Order were here to witness this.

After another round of the campsite, she returned to Pyra. A haunch of steaming beef had just been delivered to her. As Pyra ate, Talia noticed how the ambient fire motes from the brazier surged toward the dragon's core. Talia took up her spot on the grass again to Forge, but then Pyra growled low, revealing teeth with bits of beef trapped between them.

Talia turned to find the Twinblades. Eadwald held a tray, Eadwulf a jug.

"Our queen," they said together.

"There really is no need for you both to take on such mundane duties," Talia said.

It made no difference what she said. The twins seemed to have taken it upon themselves to serve her in everything. Indeed, they ignored her statement and brought forth her breakfast tray and water. Bacon and bread, the staples of those who toiled in physical roles. Yet in an army camp, they were luxuries.

"Were you this attentive to the Harroways?" she asked.

"To the old head of the house, yes," Eadwald said.

"The younger did not appreciate our service as much," said Eadwulf.

Talia wondered why. Perhaps Drefan, knowing he needed to pawn the twins off to spare the family's reputation, had distanced himself from the start.

"We did attend your uncle in our youth," said Eadwald.

"He seemed to like our company," said Eadwulf.

"For a time," Eadwald added.

Talia paused with a chunk of bread halfway to her mouth. "You served my uncle? When was this?"

"In our youth," Eadwulf said. This wasn't all that helpful, not least because the twins had an ageless quality.

"To take our lessons into the field for the first time," said Eadwald. "Do you recall that first battle, brother?"

"I do, brother. The foes in that scorching land fought with a savagery like no other."

Eadwald nodded sagely. "No other. Come, brother. The Queen will wish for peace with her meal."

"Stay," Talia blurted.

Pyra snorted and snapped at the air.

"If they are going to be around, you should get used to them," Talia said across their bond.

"Brothers, please sit with me," she added.

They did and looked at her with identical blank expressions.

"Pyra still feels ill at ease around any who drank dragon blood," Talia explained. "It is an affront practiced by a cult of dragon worshipers who hunt riders in the field."

"The Shroud," Eadwald said.

"Nay, brother, the Wyrm Cloaks."

"They call themselves the Shroud," said Talia. "But riders and any who oppose them should call them Wyrm Cloaks lest their crimes be overlooked. Harroway swears that his family has nothing to hide in that regard. Is it true?"

She searched their faces for lie or discomfort, but they were unreadable.

"Your uncle supplied the dragon blood to us and our men," said Eadwald.

"This we swear," said Eadwulf. "We did not think to question him."

"Because you had served him before?"

They inclined their heads.

"From what you said, it sounds like you served with him while he led his company in Ahar?"

"The Shah hired the Gray Cloaks to combat tribes raiding along his borders," said Eadwald.

"Where the lush lands meet the desert," said Eadwulf.

Talia tore off a chunk of her bread roll. "And what was he like as a commander?"

"Efficient," said Eadwald.

"Decisive," said Eadwulf.

Talia chewed her bread, wondering how useful these questions would be. The twins did not seem the type to plumb the depths of their feelings.

"I was hoping you might tell me what he was like as a person?"

The twins looked at each other. For the first time, they seemed unsure.

"Is something wrong?"

Still looking at each other, Eadwald said, "Brother, we should not speak of a former master."

"Osric Agravain turned traitor. It is different."

Talia now forgot about her bacon and bread.

The twins nodded to each other, and then Eadwald took the lead. "When not issuing orders or in the fight, he was reserved. Quiet."

Talia thought that quite something coming from the brothers.

"To see him otherwise was rare," Eadwulf said, "until the tribal girl came."

"We rescued her from a raiding party," Eadwald said.

"They captured her from a rival tribe and made her a slave of the flesh."

Talia wasn't sure she wanted to hear more, yet she had to. "Go on."

"Your uncle cared for her," Eadwald said. "He tended her wounds from the lashing whips."

"Neither could fully understand the other," said Eadwulf. "And yet they became inseparable."

"When we returned to the city to resupply, he spent his own share of the profits to give her a comfortable home."

"But she begged to remain with him instead. And so, she returned to the frontier with us."

"My uncle fell in love with a woman of the desert tribes?" Talia asked.

The twins nodded.

Of all the things she had expected to hear, a tale of Osric finding love at the edge of the world had not been among them. She had never heard anything about this. Not from her parents, and certainly not from Osric himself. It must have been eight years ago that he led his company in Ahar. A long time for such news to be kept quiet.

"What happened to her?" Talia asked.

"News spread amongst the tribes that our company had taken her," said Eadwald.

"She was the daughter of a chief, kidnapped by their bitter rivals."

"We found ourselves trapped between two forces, with them deciding to unite against us as a common foe."

"The girl departed, returning to her father and tribe."

Talia guessed the next part. "And she convinced him to join the Gray Cloaks in battle."

Eadwald nodded. "When battle came, her tribe struck the enemy's flank—"

"And thus the day was won," said Eadwulf.

"We remained on the frontier for another two months."

"Unpaid by the Shah, but Osric paid us from his own pocket."

"All in the hope she would return."

"But neither she nor her tribe ever came back."

Despite herself, Talia felt a great sympathy for her uncle. Recent events resurfaced to blunt this compassion, yet this tale had occurred long before Sovereign. Long before the unforgivable.

"Did it seem like he truly loved her?" Talia asked.

"He changed after she left," said Eadwald.

"He became withdrawn, rarely mixing with the men," said Eadwulf.

"His temper grew short."

"His tactics more brutal."

"He had always been inclined so—" Eadwald began.

"But it became the face he wore rather than the face he hid," Eadwulf ended.

"Thank you, brothers," Talia said. "You have given me much to think about."

She dismissed them and returned to eating her food, brooding on all she had heard.

An anger just beneath the surface. Her uncle's niece, the Master of

State had noted. How fair an assessment was that? Her anger was linked to a dragon. And yet she couldn't fully shake the similarities.

When she finished eating, she forced thoughts about Osric aside. There were more pressing matters to attend to.

Adjacent to her royal pavilion was the command tent. Talia entered it to find Harroway and his hand-picked officers poring over maps. A cartographer was in the middle of sketching a new one on a long sheet of smooth parchment.

Harroway did not look pleased to see her.

"My queen," he said, bowing. The officers and soldiers saluted or bowed, their armor rattling. "We are drawing up preliminary routes of the tunnel complex, if it please you." He gestured to the work in progress. The map was largely blank, save for a handful of crossing corridors. Two of them ended with a large X, so they knew to avoid those dead ends.

"As you can see," Harroway began, "the passages are reasonably narrow, however the main tunnel seems to widen as it delves deeper underground to the east." He tapped the relevant section. Talia noted that was where the current drawing cut off.

"Is this all we know?"

"No one was willing to continue. I'm told a fire arrow was loosed down the tunnel, but they did not see it land." Harroway gave her a grave look. "The passages seem endless. It would be easy to get lost."

"I'm still going," Talia said. "We've come all this way."

He set his jaw. "I sensed as much. How will you know when your objective is accomplished?"

"The Elder says he can sense a presence down there. I should know when I find it."

"Are you able to sense this 'presence'?"

"No," she said, knowing how it must sound. "But I'm nowhere near as strong as an Elder."

"This dragon also spoke of scourge activity here at the chasm. We came expecting a fight and yet there has been nothing. I'd say whatever portion of the enemy was here is now down in the very tunnels you wish to march into."

He allowed her another opportunity to change her mind. She didn't.

"Scouts arrived last night," Harroway continued, "bearing news from the westerlands. The remnant scourge there have disappeared and were last seen heading for the western border of these woods." He let the words hang and seemed to study her reaction. "Did your Elder dragon know of that?"

"I have yet to meet with the Elder today," Talia said. "It's possible the scourge gathering to the west have not entered the range of even his detection." Harroway did not appear comforted by this. "What troubles you, Master of War?"

"I have said it before, but I must say again. I think this is a mistake. We've brought thousands of people into empty land. No doubt we've drawn the bugs in the west toward our presence in wood. If they attack us here in the confines of the trees and with the chasm hemming us in on one side, well, I can't think of worse ground to fight on."

"We have the Emerald Flight," Talia said. "If a swarm comes, you won't stand alone. We're doing this, Drefan."

"Very well," Harroway said, resigned. "In that case, I'd suggest keeping more men above ground. Most of the archers too. I can't envision they will be of use down below."

"We brought three thousand men with us. How many do you suggest I take?"

"Five hundred."

"Five— I need more."

"You don't know that, Your Majesty. I'm not trying to hinder your mission, far from it. I want it to succeed, and given we know virtually nothing about the terrain down there, a small but properly equipped force will do better than a larger one. Long spears do not seem wise, so we'll give each man a short spear, sword, and shield. That should allow strong formations while giving them a reaching weapon to deal with flayers and juggernauts."

He had evidently given it thought. This was, after all, why she had let him take the job.

"Very well," she said. "Anything else?"

Harroway clicked his fingers and one of his officers hastened over with parchment.

"An urgent message from Port Bolca," Harroway said. "It appears an imperial Skarl warship has been spotted off the northern coast."

He spoke so casually as though this information were not wild news.

"A Skarl warship? But..." Talia struggled for words. She read over the latest letter from Ealdor Odilo. The ship had sailed into Feorlen waters and raised the white dove flag. A merchant vessel had taken a message back to port, requesting permission to dock. Odilo had seen no reason to decline and sent an invitation back to the Skarls before writing this letter to her. She looked up in a daze.

"By now, Skarl officials will be on Feorlen soil for the first time since your grandfather's reign," Harroway said.

White dove, Talia thought, reassuring herself. *Peace not war. Peace not war.*

"Talia?" He looked at her expectantly. "Odilo will need a response."

"Send word to the High Council. The Skarls are to be welcomed in the palace until their old embassy can be reopened."

"I'll dispatch a platoon as an additional escort," Harroway said. "It won't do if the Skarls are killed by roaming scourge along the way. Plus, we can keep a better eye on them that way."

"Good," Talia said, distracted. *What does this mean?* She shook her head. "We don't have time to tarry. I want those five hundred men ready to enter the tunnel at first light the day after tomorrow."

She turned, but Harroway caught her arm.

"My queen," he said, dropping his voice low. "Our soldiers will do their best, but this isn't anything they've trained for. We plan and drill to defend walls, work siege equipment, fight in large defensive formations. No one ever prepared them for underground tunnels. If things go sour down there, remember that. Remember they are only human."

His concern for his soldiers touched her. "I will," she assured him.

She returned to Pyra, and together they flew east across the chasm and over the woodland until the noise of the emeralds and army were left behind. Being so large, the Elder had only found a space for himself in a wide clearing some distance from the chasm.

He stood mighty, his core a searing power on the magical landscape. The West Warden sat on his right-hand side.

Talia knelt before him. "Honored Elder. I am pleased to tell you that my people will be ready within two days, but there is a new concern. We have reports of scourge massing on the western borders of the forest. We believe it to be the bulk of the remnants of the incursion."

"To the west, you say?" said the Elder. He raised his snout and sniffed at the air. "I cannot sense them."

Even the West Warden looked at the Elder with some concern.

"I fear the darkness below interferes with my ability to sense the world. I cannot feel the enemy out there."

"How can that be possible?" Talia asked, unable to keep a drop of fear from her voice. What could interfere with the Elder's great power? She cast out with her own senses but felt only Pyra and the emeralds. Her ability to sense magic diminished while trying to penetrate layers of soil and rock. If there was something down there, and only the Elder could gain but a glimpse of it, it must be deep indeed or else guarded in some other way.

"You and your siblings created the blight. Surely you must have some ide—"

"Much is unknown about our failure," said the Elder. "Too long did we hide from it. I fear what has grown in the depths. I am sorry, I cannot offer more. Know that I understand the risk you take."

Yet we're the ones who must take it, Talia thought.

Pyra snorted. "Honored Elder, we will brave this mission. My rider and I fear nothing." She looked at Talia expectantly.

"Yes, girl. I'm not afraid."

Such a weak lie. This task chilled her. Defending the city had been overwhelming, yes, but quantifiable and known. What the Elder asked of them was chaos in its raw form. A blind stumble into the dark. She kept that fear back from Pyra, however.

"Fire brings all into light," Pyra went on. *"It will be our honor to strike this blow against the enemy."*

"Fire shall not strike alone," said the Elder. He roared then and two new emeralds entered the clearing. Two young dragons – little stronger than Ascendants by the feel of their cores. They descended to join her in bowing before the Elder, pressing their necks low to the ground.

"Rise, children of the earth," said the Elder.

The two emeralds then stood before Talia as though for inspection. Both were smaller than Pyra.

The first, an apple-green drake, shook his head and said, *"Hail, daughters of flame. It is an honor to accompany you on this errand. You may call me Turro."*

The other emerald, slight of frame and turquoise, stepped forward. *"And you may call me Ghel."* Her voice sounded surprisingly young for a dragon. Talia was sure Pyra had never sounded that young.

Pyra was unconvinced. *"They send us hatchlings,"* she said privately.

"You're little better than a hatchling compared to most dragons," Talia reminded her. *"Besides, we're going underground. We don't even know if you will fit, girl."*

Pyra gave her a look as if to say the earth would make way for her or else.

Turro might have sensed the gist of their conversation. He clawed the earth, bristled, and said, *"Do not let our age deceive you, flame wielder."*

"We will do what is expected of us should the worst happen," said Ghel, although she did not sound as sure as her words.

"Thank you, Honored Elder," Talia said. "And to you, Turro and Ghel, for facing this with us. All help is welcome. Already it has been a challenge to guide my people toward the true threat of Sovereign and the scourge. They have been worried more by our human neighbors."

"It can be hard for hatchlings to see past their next meal," said the Elder.

"There are moments," Talia continued tentatively, "where I wonder if I should have gone with Holt and Ash to aid their mission. Pyra and I might have done more good that way." She did not know why she was being so forthright with the Elder. Perhaps because speaking with a being so old and powerful made her feel like a small child, and small children can voice their failures without shame.

A deep rumble rose from the Elder's throat. Quite unexpectedly, Talia felt his power pass over her soul, checking on her bond with Pyra.

"The journey of the sons of night is theirs to make. Had I thought your place was with them, I would have sent you."

What did that mean? A horrible, squirming sensation spiraled in her stomach. Did the Life Elder not think her capable? Good enough to venture into a chasm with an army but not good enough to aid Holt?

"Honored Elder, I assure you that Pyra and I are quite powerf—"

"It is not a question of strength. Some tasks cannot be solved with fire or stone. That you jump to this conclusion only affirms my decision."

Talia's stomach backflipped. A bout of Pyra's inner flame passed across their bond so that her cheeks scalded and smoked. She winced and died a little inside for displaying weakness to the Elder.

Pyra raised herself to her full height then. Talia threw their bond open and begged her to stop, pleading through anxiety rather than clumsy words for Pyra not to do anything. It was the coronation all over again, yet it was a thousand times worse to lose composure before an Elder. Pyra's fires, however, were not easily quenched.

"Fire is the making and unmaking of all things," Pyra declared. *"As Talia and I grow stronger, nothing will stand in our way. Her detractors will bow one by one, and even Sovereign will tremble."*

The West Warden stirred. He slackened his jaws and a swirl of green power formed at his mouth. *"You will show more respect in the presence of my Elder."*

"Pyra," Talia urged. "Settle, girl."

Pyra snorted smoke but relented and bent her neck low to the ground again.

The West Warden bit at the air over her head before retreating to his place at the Elder's side. The Elder remained still throughout.

"Forgive us, Honored Elder," Talia said. "No offense was meant.

Pyra and I have both been frustrated of late. We have not had the time to train and center ourselves as we would have had in the Order." She took a deep breath. "If we do find something down there, what would you have us do?"

"The same as all things with the blight. Burn it."

Two days later, Talia stood at the bottom of the scourge chasm. A wide tunnel loomed before her like a monster's maw. Dawn light crested above the high ridge, and the sensation of the world holding its breath dragged on.

Her task force was ready. A five hundred strong battalion. Pyra stood beside her, the Twinblades behind. When the young emeralds Turro and Ghel joined them, there was nothing more for which to wait.

Talia drew her rider's blade, the steel bleeding a red glow in the pale light, and held it high. She turned to face her men and began channeling fire motes down her right arm.

"Many have wondered why we are here," she cried. "But mark this day. Remember you were a part of it. The day the living took the fight to the scourge, the very beginning of the end. When human and dragon worked together for the first time, here in Feorlen!" To round off her speech, she set her sword aflame, pushing fire into the dragon-steel. The fire plumed, and the world's held breath broke at last.

Soldiers cheered. Dragons bellowed.

Up on the ridge, Harroway and his officers saluted and raised the royal flag. The crowned swords rippled in the breeze. Trumpeters played a stirring chorus.

Talia kept the fire burning low on her sword and turned to face the darkness.

"Whatever happens, girl, we stick together."

"Until our fires burn out," Pyra said.

And with the encouragement of dragons and humans alike, Talia and Pyra marched into the depths.

SIXTEEN

The Smith

Chains were his world. Hulking black links reformed in Sovereign's core. At times, Osric felt as though he were within that cavernous hall, bound by the steel, the cold metal clamped around his throat.

During Forging, his bond with Sovereign scarcely beat. When it did, it echoed in his chest like a lone gong within the great hall. To come close to matching it with his own heart, Osric had to breathe so low and so slow that for stretches of time he did not breathe at all.

Raw mystic motes gathered into the chamber with increased intensity. The members of the Shroud generating this resource for their master had doubled in number and were relentless in their own dedication. Motes were now pulled so powerfully into Sovereign's core that building blocks of smooth stone appeared to roll in readymade. The greater his core became, the greater the pull became.

Thanks to Osric's tireless Cleansing, there was not a speck of dust nor grain of dirt clogging the orbit of the core. He had made it pristine. Despite all of this, Sovereign's core was nowhere close to its full strength. He would remain at Windshear Hold for a deal of time yet.

Besides his core, too few of the eggs had hatched. Dahaka's single donation had done little to sway the worrying trend. Nineteen they had gathered in total. Nine were cold stone, long since dead, abandoned and discarded as they had been. Seven had hatched. None since the struggling turquoise dragon had died, but a few had ailments or other weaknesses. None displayed powers, nor would they until they matured or were placed under duress. Still, if Sovereign were to have the selection of new dragons he desired, more eggs would have to be gathered. And quickly. Osric hoped the Speaker would return soon so he might embark on his mission to the Grim Gorge and seize eggs from the Mystic Flight.

One side effect of these long meditation sessions was that their bond had to be kept open for the duration. Sovereign kept his feelings and thoughts secure, yet with an open bond Osric gained glimpses of the dragon's mind here and there. For weeks now, Sovereign's thoughts had brooded upon the west, no doubt on the contingency incursion he had set in motion. Osric could not help but think the plan a desperate one, rushed and rash. Building the Feorlen invasion had taken careful years without raising suspicion from Falcaer.

Perhaps he ought to counsel caution. He understood why Sovereign felt the pressure of time, but another failed incursion would be the ruin of his power. When not lingering on the west, Sovereign's mind seemed to flit between a blur of matters, never settling for long, except for when he ruminated on the white dragon.

Today was no different until, in a jerk of focus, Sovereign's attention shifted back to Windshear, to the hatchery, and to Osric.

Osric was so deep into his Forging that sounds from the corporeal world reached him on a delay. A bang from the door. Were those footsteps? Now someone spoke beside him. Sovereign did not allow any humans a direct audience other than the riders who joined him and one special member of the Shroud.

Osric mentally brought himself back to reality and heard the tail end of a woman speaking. He opened his eyes and found her on one knee beside him, her head bowed before Sovereign.

Her hair was a stark gray, almost metallic in the way it shined. Three irregular red and knotted scars ran from her forehead to chin. Looking past the scars, there might once have been a striking woman beneath. Long ago. However, nothing youthful or naïve remained in her eyes, nor the lines and darkness around them.

Her dragonhide cloak was also gray, paled with the whites and dim blues of a gathering cloud. It reminded Osric of his own abandoned cloak.

She was the Speaker. The leader of the Shroud. Her true name was still unknown to him.

"Did you bring what we discussed?" Sovereign asked.

"Naturally, your magnificence," the Speaker said. Her voice contained a light flutter of awe to it. "I found an old smith in a town north of Salzstad. His role-name was Chandler in the service of the Bailiff's household, but it was well known he used to be a Smith, working in Drakburg."

That is quite the find, Osric thought. A blacksmith who used to work in the Order Hall of Risalia would be a master of his craft. Yet taking him seemed another strange risk. The Shroud had smiths of their own they could call upon. Kidnapping this smith and dragging him halfway across the world had all the caution of plucking a dragon egg out from Falcaer itself.

Truly, the dragon had grown bold.

And if he had gone to the trouble of procuring a blacksmith from the Order, Osric sensed it could be but for one purpose.

"You wish me to have the weapon of a rider."

"Your use as an agent in the human realms is over. Yet you are still a weapon in my service, and you will be all the deadlier wielding dragon-steel."

Osric had often heard it called Falcaer-steel before, given each rider traveled there to forge their blade when they reached the rank of Ascendant. Yet here they were in Windshear Hold, the first fortress of the riders wherein a workshop and forge sat cold.

A childish part within Osric cheered. To hold such a weapon, to wield such a weapon, had never entered his wildest dreams. There was one thing to clarify.

"I work best with axes, not a sword."

"Make what you will," Sovereign said. *"So long as you can fight other riders."*

And kill them. Osric finished the thought for him. Such steel could part dragon scales too. Did Sovereign care? He decided not to raise the issue. Sovereign wanted more eggs. He understood what that would mean, as did Osric.

Do the job and do it well.

Indeed, the timing of the Speaker's arrival was telling. Osric now thought this had been Sovereign's plan from the beginning. Such a kidnapping could not have been planned and conducted in the time since he had first suggested the raid.

"I'll defeat whoever needs to be fought."

Sovereign made a hissing laugh. *"Very good, worm."*

"I must confess, your magnificence," the Speaker chimed in as though concerned Osric had stolen her attention, "that while the old man's mind is sound, his body is not. One hand is clenched and unyielding to him. It causes him great pain."

It sounded like the man had inflamed joints, a common enough ailment in the old. This would have led to him being switched roles in the first place, from great smith to a caretaker of candles.

"He need only instruct and guide," Sovereign said. *"Osric will do the work. Alone."*

That struck Osric as wrong. What little he knew of the process suggested the dragon and rider had to work together.

"Do I not require your assistance?" Osric asked.

Sovereign snarled. *"Lesser riders might. You are stronger. And such a demeaning, interminable task I will never suffer again."* His hateful eyes bore into Osric. *"You will commit the process to memory, worm. And share that with me when it's over."*

Osric understood the implications of that instruction too. As before, he allowed it to go unsaid and inclined his head in acknowledgment. "As you bid."

Sovereign snorted smoke. *"Be gone then."*

The Speaker rose at once. "Your greatest warrior shall soon be equipped with tools worthy of your magnificence, praise be." She gave a final bow, then about-turned with a soldier's precision and made for the hatchery doors. Osric followed her. He caught her looking long-ingly back inside as the doors closed.

Osric wasted no time. "Where is the smith?"

"Follow me, General." The awe in her voice had vanished.

They began to walk.

"I do hope your actions went unnoticed," Osric said.

"Chaos is our cloak. Many fires were set. Horses frightened. Set loose. And our master arranged a small scourge swarm to distract the town, praise him," she added, rather abruptly and loudly. She faced him with a quick, twitchy move of her head, opened her mouth as if to speak, then shut it hard without a word.

Osric gave her a strained smile. He had forgotten just how erratic she was. While she marched with the uniformity of soldier, a lesson from her days as a squire in the Order and from the siege corps of the Mithran Commonwealth, all else she said or did had a nervous energy to it.

Osric might have pitied her if he didn't have to work with her. When she wanted to, when she focused, she had a vicious, cunning mind. Ruthless in service to her beloved Sovereign.

"It is well you have returned, Speaker. Many of the new faithful lack discipline and order—"

"Order?" she said, as though the term bewildered her. "No. In Sovereign's name we shall bring chaos."

"Speaker, as I stressed to you before I left for Feorlen—"

"Feorlen," she said with venom. She rounded on him, eyes wide. "You failed in Feorlen."

That caught him off guard.

"I—"

"Oh yes, Sovereign told me of your failings. You should beg for his forgiveness. He is good, praise him. He will give it when you repent."

"The incursion was lost the moment the Emerald Flight decided to fly."

"A score of my hunters, gone," the Speaker said, as though she had not heard him. "Where did they go, General? Why did only three return to me alive?"

Osric grunted. He'd forgotten about the Shroud sent to guard the chasm in the Withering Woods.

"I equipped them better than any of your followers have been before. That twenty of your trained killers could not take on two young riders at once is proof that *I* am right."

Her gaze seemed to look through him rather than at him. "Your defeats are becoming more regular of late. When Brenin warred with Risalia—"

"I suffered a betrayal in that war."

"Most unfortunate," she said with great heaving shakes of her head. "To lose the Toll Pass to such a terrible thing. Small wonder you chose to seize it again when you had the chance rather than pursue Sovereign's plans."

This again?

"That was a victory."

She pointed an accusatory finger. "For you, it was."

He tired of this. Sovereign had not accepted it the first time, nor did he to this day. He doubted he could convince the Speaker either.

"Plans change."

She started laughing. It was hideous. Unnerving. She halted in the corridor, doubled over from the fit that gripped her.

Osric shifted away. How he missed his finest Gray Cloaks. Predictable, regimented, composed soldiers.

Still bent double, the Speaker said, through choked breaths, "General, you failed to kill two Ascendants when they were right under your nose. Perhaps your reputation is unfounded—"

In an instant he hauled her to her feet, seized her by the shoulders and lifted her from the ground.

"You might be the Speaker, but you're only human."

"For now," she said dreamily.

He shook her. "Test my good nature and the Shroud will find itself in need of another leader."

"Is that a threat?"

"Yes. And if you know anything of my *reputation,* you'll know I mean it."

"I know you do, General." Her grin was far too wide. "Go ahead. In death we are all equal. And free."

Madness, Osric thought. He was about to put her down when Sovereign's presence raced across the bond in a pulse of pain. Osric's arms lowered the Speaker to the ground of their own accord.

"Now, worm, that is no way to treat a true believer."

Osric tried to move his lips, but Sovereign had complete control over him.

"Why do you rely on such lunatics?" he asked telepathically.

"I value this one's will and devotion. You will ensure no harm comes to her."

Sovereign let go.

Osric's arms fell limply to his sides as the dragon left him.

The Speaker's features returned to normal as quickly as they had been transported into mirth. Now she was all business, as crisp and composed as any Lord of the Order.

"I'm glad you understand your true position here, *General.*" She used his title mockingly. "I've brought more of his most devoted followers to bolster our strength, and while I'm here, the new faithful shall be trained. You can aid me in this. We have so much to do if we are to bring about Sovereign's vision. This world is broken. Our kind are birthed in pain, raised in pain, work in pain, and die in pain, and that's just what we do to ourselves. So much suffering. The scourge is the elegant solution. When we are gone, Sovereign will dispose of the scourge for good and the world will be at peace. There will be no suffering then."

There will be ash and dust, Osric thought. *And fat carrion crows.*

"Do you not find it maddening?" she asked. "To have nothing but an endless cycle, ever turning, never changing?"

Osric clenched his jaw, knowing he would have to answer carefully.

"It's not my role to consider the deeper questions."

The look she gave him was almost pitying. "Why join Sovereign as you did in the first place, if you did not believe?"

Because I had no choice. He held his tongue. As if the Speaker of the Wyrm Cloa—of the Shroud would take kindly to that. Because he'd left the world behind and wandered into the mountains of the Spine, seeking the Eternals, to die beside those greatest of warriors with scourge blood upon his axes. And, in his wandering, he had stumbled upon the dragon. Or the dragon had found him. It mattered not which way it had occurred. Sovereign had taken hold of him there, and that was that.

Osric served him, even if reluctantly.

The twisted bond in his chest knotted tighter, like thorns scraping on bone.

The Speaker cocked her head, the first hint back toward the madness of moments ago. "I have seen those under Sovereign's domination. You do not show those signs, Osric Agravain. I believe you are one of the faithful, and I am sure you will admit that to me before the end."

Osric released a breath, unaware he'd been holding it, and lightly thumbed the blade of his right-hand axe. "Take me to this smith. We have work to do."

The Speaker led him to the atrium of the mystic tower. A crate sat there, surrounded by five cultists, two in dragonhide, three not.

"Was this necessary?" Osric asked.

"We kept him alive. Open it," she demanded. Her followers hastened to oblige. They lifted the lid, and Osric approached. An old man lay curled up inside, the crown of his head bald and liver-spotted. Thin and frail though he was, his hands and feet were bound, and a gag had been stuffed into his mouth. A stench of filth radiated from the crate. His trousers were damp and stained.

Osric wrinkled his nose. "Fetch this man water and clean clothes at once. Bring food too, some bread and a little broth. His strength must be coaxed back into his stomach. Go." Three of the lesser cultists scurried off.

The old smith met his eyes. They were red raw and held a determination to live, yet Osric sensed no true defiance remained in them. He reached in and pulled the gag out of the man's mouth. The smith exhaled dryly and ran his tongue over his chapped lips, but even this small exertion seemed hard for him.

"Up you get now," Osric said, reaching in and lifting the old man out like a baby. He sat him down gently, cut his bonds with his axe, then cupped his face and said, "You're now a servant of Sovereign. There is no escape. Do your work well and you shall be treated well."

"Work?" He raised his gnarled hand. Swollen joints bent his fingers out of shape.

"My hands will do the work," Osric said. "You need only guide me. Your role-name was once Smith?"

He nodded.

"You served at the Order Hall of Drakburg?"

He nodded. "For forty-five good years." He had pride in that.

As he should, Osric thought.

"You will aid me in making dragon-steel."

"No ordinary forge can create such metal."

"We are at Windshear Hold, an old fortress of the riders."

"I see." The smith gulped. "It requires a rider."

"I am one." The words felt wrong leaving his mouth. He was no rider. By rights, he never should have been one, just as his niece should never have been. Perhaps the evils that had befallen them both was how the world saw fit to punish them. "Will you help me, Mr. Smith?"

"Master Smith," he corrected. "I never married."

A knot twisted in Osric's chest, though this one was not of Sovereign's making.

"We have both been married to our craft, Master Smith."

One of the cultists returned with clean clothes. The old man stripped and changed in front of them. Then he was handed one of the Shroud's mock woolen cloaks, this one a dark green. His stiff fingers slipped as he tried to fasten it.

"Allow me," the Speaker said. She clasped the cloak into place and stepped back, jubilant. "You are now one of the Shroud. In Sovereign's name, you shall bring an end to all suffering. Praise him," she said, with the clear expectation that the old man should follow.

"Praise him," the smith said. He shivered, then wrapped the cloak tighter around himself.

The other cultists returned soon after, one with water, the other with a heel of bread and a bowl of barley broth.

The smith sat on the edge of the crate. He drank a little, then ate a little. Osric broke off chunks of hard bread, softened them in the broth, and fed them to the smith on a spoon. He had tended to men under his command in worse conditions than this, though they at least had had the advantage of youth.

The Speaker stood like a statue throughout.

When a third of the broth remained, the smith clutched at his stomach. "No more."

Osric set the spoon back into the bowl. "You will regain your strength in time."

Over the dragon bond, Osric felt Sovereign's patience wane.

"The dragon we serve, he would like us to begin. Can you manage a short walk with me?"

"Carry him," the Speaker said. "Let us be underway."

Osric gave her a dark look and shook his head. Allowing the smith to stand on his own feet, to walk at his own pace – such small things mattered when all else had been taken away.

Their journey to the forges by the eastern walls was a slow one. By the northern wall, near where the blood alchemist had taken up residence, two more dragons were giving their blood. The old smith gasped and looked away. The Speaker beamed, delight glistening in her eyes.

The blood alchemist had been mixing new bloods with varied success. At least one cultist had died testing a new concoction. Their heart had exploded. Still others had displayed greater strength and speed than the usual mixture provided, even if it did lay them up for days afterward.

Champion Dahaka's fire dragon, Zahak, lay curled up in the yard. He at least seemed to feel the same as Osric and the smith did, looking upon the blood lettings with a wary eye. Coming from the Order, he and his rider may well have encountered the Shroud before in less peaceful circumstances.

Osric gritted his teeth and, like the smith, looked away. He was thankful that he had no need to drink the stuff. Even when it came to combat, he considered magic a tool for desperate times. Its nature was chaotic, unknowable, and, compared to sword or axe or bow, resistant to his will. Magic bound him to Sovereign. The dragon's mystic energy whispered to him. Chained him. When it swam in his blood, it burned like poison. Osric would sooner rely on his own body and wits than grow dependent upon a power he despised.

Eventually the old smith made it to the forges of Windshear Hold. They were the largest Osric had ever seen. A grand elongated hearth of firebricks, with a great chamber for the coal. Connected to this were two sets of bellows, one normal in function, though greater than any normal human could operate, and one uniquely designed to be blown into by a creature with immense lungs. Dragon-sized lungs.

Members of the Shroud were already there arranging tools and depositing iron, charcoal, sand, and other materials they had unearthed in the vaults.

The Speaker cocked her head and smiled again. "Sovereign thinks of all. I must take my leave. I have my flock to attend to in his name, praise him."

Osric gave her a curt nod. "Speaker."

Glad to be rid of her, he turned his attention to the smith. "Can it be done?"

The old man examined the forge with shrewd eyes. He would have been used to a fully functional and well-maintained forge at Drakburg and so this forge was likely a disappointment to him. The smith pulled his cloak in tighter, then shuffled closer to the forge, inspecting it and then each tool in turn. He set a clamp back down with a dull thud, his expression grim.

"It has lain cold for so long, and these are not the finest tools or materials."

"They are what we have. Is there anything else you require?"

"A night's rest?"

Across the dragon bond, Sovereign gave his begrudging approval.

"One night," Osric said. "And then we begin."

SEVENTEEN

Sink, Float, Lift, and Ground

Rake's polearm descended, whistling as it cut the air. Holt parried and turned the strike aside. Rake stepped back, keeping Holt outside the long reach of his weapon as he thrust like a frenzied stinger. It was all Holt could do to keep track of the orange blade, so he never saw the tail coming for his legs.

He hit the forest floor hard and groaned.

Rake stood over him. "Amazingly you're actually getting better."

An ache ran up Holt's back. "It doesn't feel like it."

Rake helped him to his feet. "You never enjoyed proper training from a young age. And that sword isn't truly yours. There is a connection between a rider and the steel they forge which cannot be mimicked."

"That's partly why I wanted to leave it at Erdra's grave."

"Nevertheless, it is better than using plain steel. You might as well bring a butter knife to fight another rider for all the good such a weapon would do."

"Talia also said my footwork was terrible."

"Terrible? No... more like shaky," Rake said, making a balancing motion with his hand.

Holt slumped his shoulders. "Will I ever be able to make a sword of my own?"

"You need a special forge for that," Rake said. "And as all such forges are located inside Order Halls, you, erm, won't be able to. But you never know what the future might hold!"

"I'll need one eventually if I'm ever going to get good. The sword won't take my magic either, which limits my options."

Rake shrugged. "So you have a few disadvantages. You'll just have to—"

"Train harder," Holt ended for him.

"Yes," Rake said, rather pleased.

"I think you're getting better," Ash said.

"Thanks Ash. A bit of encouragement is nice."

"Just you wait until I start on you, my little white friend," Rake said. The fact that Ash was larger than him seemed to be lost on Rake. "Now, just let me get my bearings." He spun around, making a great show of figuring out which way was east.

It had been like this day after day. Not only did Rake train him in the evenings like Brode had, but he had taken to attacking him at random on the march. To 'improve his awareness and readiness'. Holt half suspected it was more for Rake's own amusement.

There had been one obvious benefit so far. Given Holt had to react in a split second, it gave him no time to overthink drawing Brode's great sword from his back. His endless practice seemed to be paying off, and with this push from Rake, he was getting more proficient with each draw.

With a flourish, Rake stopped turning and pointed ahead. "Onward — wait. Where's the dragon? Aberanth?"

They found him a way back, crouched low at the base of a birch tree. At first, Holt assumed he was gathering mushrooms, for that was all the dragon seemed willing to eat. However, he had arranged several feathers by size and was glancing between them and a slab of flattened bark. Onto the bark he had burned a runic script with his powers, beautiful flowing lines Holt could not comprehend. It was a form of capturing impressions, memories, and feelings in symbols that held meaning beyond representing sound alone. Rake explained that he only half understood Aberanth's notes, but then he was only half a dragon himself.

"Aberanth," Rake said, irritated.

The little brown dragon started and looked up. "*Oh, you're finished. Good. I just found the most fascinating set of feathers. From their smell they are all from the same nest, but the colors and properties have such a marked difference I wonder if—*"

"Riveting stuff," Rake said, "but we really must get moving along. Do keep up."

Aberanth grumbled, then used his powers to bring down one of the many oversized, sturdy leaves that functioned as his luggage. The leaf unfurled and he nosed the feathers onto it – joining other curiosities he had picked up on their journey – before wrapping them up.

Aberanth had insisted on bringing what seemed half his laboratory on his back. That which he could not carry, Ash had taken on. Holt carried their gear now, over the scabbard which housed Brode's sword. He helped Aberanth by picking up one of his supply leaves too. Something tinkled inside.

"*Maybe if I'm carrying something breakable, Rake won't attack me so often,*" Holt said privately to Ash.

"*I think it might just tempt him,*" Ash said.

They journeyed on, pressing east through the Fae Forest. On occasion, Holt consulted his maps. With Rake's guidance, it seemed they were keeping close to the southern border of the forest. Oak Hall, the rider outpost in the region, lay to the northwest, and the Free City of Coedhen was built amongst the trees over one hundred miles to the north.

Their destination was the Grim Gorge, a mountainous region far to the east. This, Rake said, was where the Mystic Flight could be found for those who knew how to look.

In time they left the forest behind, passing out into open country in a place no maps named. A dead zone between the forest and the northern tip of Loch Awe.

"Why is it called a loch and not a lake?" Holt asked.

"Because the folk of the Fae Forest and of the former Free City of Freiz have a heritage even older than that of Aldunei," Rake said. "Originating long, long ago in the mists of time."

"Older than Aldunei?" Holt understood such things must have existed, but the old republic had always seemed the oldest of knowable things, whence much of the world had sprung from. And he knew little enough of Aldunei as it was. The world before that ancient city seemed shrouded and dark in his imagination, more fantasy than reality.

"You said the former Free City of Freiz. What happened to it?"

"The scourge," Rake said. It required no further explanation.

When they reached the shores of the loch, Rake waded out into the shallows until his feet were submerged beneath the cold blue waters. He took in a deep breath, then sighed long and luxuriously.

"Always feels good to cool the feet."

Ash trotted out after Rake, and Holt felt his disappointment over the bond that dipping his own toes had not brought the same pleasure as it had for Rake.

"It's just water," Holt told him. Ash took a drink of it instead.

Aberanth padded up beside Holt. *"He came from around here, I think."*

"Rake did? Back when he was human, you mean?"

Aberanth nodded. *"Back when these shores were occupied by your kind. That was before my lifetime."*

"How long have you known him for?"

"Thirty-six years and two hundred days."

How specific, Holt thought. Though he was coming to expect nothing less from the brown dragon. He was an odd sort of emerald. His color, for one thing. It made him wonder whether Aberanth might be at the edge of a type entirely out of the ordinary groupings, like Ash was.

Aberanth went to join the others in the water and took a drink from the loch as well.

Watching the three of them milling out in the calm waters, it struck Holt what a bizarre situation he found himself in. Earlier that very year, he'd been scrubbing pots in his father's kitchens. Now here he was, half a world away, in the company of two dragons and one half-dragon, each one of them curiosities.

By comparison, he was boring as dry toast. Just a regular, scrawny sixteen-year-old. He needed a good haircut now, but wild hair hardly equated to the excitement of Ash, Aberanth, or Rake. Still, he had played a part in the downfall of Silas Silverstrike, he'd faced a Scourge Queen, and he'd been given the blessing of the Life Elder. Though those things had been because of Ash, in truth. Holt was not yet remarkable, powerful, or threatening in his own right.

But I will be.

His father's voice, ever a driver of late, reminded him again: *'Help the others.'*

Rake turned them north and led them toward the tip of the loch. Some signs of the inhabitants of yesteryear dotted the landscape. Shells of buildings and even whole villages long since abandoned. And it was just as well, for the clouds gathered and burst and drenched them for a full day. They took shelter under the remnants of an old keep. The wind bit at them and water leaked from the damaged roof, but the worst was kept at bay.

Holt trained harder than ever with Rake that night. Frustrated they had been forced to halt, Rake took that out on him.

After another brutal, short exchange, Holt winced and hobbled back to his starting position. His leg throbbed from where Rake had hit him with the butt of his polearm.

"If you want us to continue our journey, best not to cripple the boy," Aberanth said.

"I may have been too enthusiastic there."

"I don't know what you're talking about," Holt said. He grunted, then brought Brode's sword up in an overhead guard. It wasn't sense that made him say it. When he sparred with Talia or Brode, he had felt them holding back. He felt this doubly so now with Rake. It only made him eager to push himself. And push himself. Until the day that Rake would not only have to give his every effort in return but find himself on the back foot.

Still, until that day, Rake's polearm hurt something fierce. Anyone watching could tell that from his gasping breaths, and Ash no doubt could feel the pain across their bond.

"Fool," Aberanth declared.

Rake smirked. "That's my kind of fool."

After another fifty rounds, Rake took pity on him and stopped. Holt returned to Ash and collapsed in a heap at his dragon's side. Ash wrapped one of his wings around him.

"Do you think I'll be ready by the time you want to attack Windshear?"

"Maybe," Rake said, unconvinced.

Holt still breathed hard. Even with an enhanced body, this hurt. "So long as I don't face another rider in a sword fight, I'll be fine." That triggered another thought in him, one he was surprised he hadn't asked before now. "How come riders train like this anyway? Aren't they training to fight ghouls and bugs? The ghouls sometimes have weapons, but they're only a little less clumsy than I am."

"True, but, as you know, riders can go rogue," Rake said. "Many did so before Silas, and many more doubtless will before the end. When a rider goes rogue, who do you think has to take them down?"

"Other riders."

Rake inclined his head.

What a grim thought. To think that all the time riders spent training was really in case they had to kill each other down the road.

"We also can't use magic all the time, I suppose," Holt said.

"A Lord can," Rake said. "I can. But in essence, you are correct. Even a Lord or Paragon may drain their dragon's core. It's worth having confidence in your own body."

Holt's own body provided him with another round of throbbing pain.

Rake frowned. "Are you cycling motes to your limbs during these sessions?"

"No... should I be?"

"Something your old mentor didn't have time to teach you, I'll warrant," Rake said. "It's a more advanced set of techniques. Ascendants can find it difficult as their mote channels have not yet matured. Cycling techniques are best mastered as a Champion, but you don't have the luxury of time."

"Right," Holt said, taking on board yet another thing he had to learn. "So, this will help me keep up with you?"

"It would help with your physicality overall without the need to infuse your body directly with magic," Rake said. "When mastered, a rider can push their bodies further without spending the magic to do so. It means keeping the motes inside the channels rather than letting them out, which works against the inherent desire for the power to escape from your human body. This won't be easy, but perhaps Aberanth could be of assistance."

Aberanth had lain curled up tight as a cat throughout the training but now raised his snout. *"You want to give my elixirs to the boy?"*

"No time like the present," Rake said. "I'm sure you have something in that bag of sweets to ground his energy flow."

"In theory. As I said back at the lab, much of this requires testing."

"Holt's willing to test it."

"I am," Holt said, perking up.

Aberanth's eyes widened. A chance for experimentation always piqued his interest. He got up and rummaged through his leaves with all the enthusiasm of a puppy with a new bone.

Rake clapped his hands. "What have you got?"

Aberanth settled over one of the leafy packs and commanded it to unfasten. Inside lay a series of vials containing an opaque, cloudy liquid.

Holt went over to pick one up.

"Should I drink it?"

"You may wish to cycle magic around your mote channels to warm up. That way you should feel if the elixir is having an effect. And stand back from us."

Holt stepped away from the group before asking, "Why?"

"As a precaution. You'll be the first subject to take it other than myself and Rake."

"Did you sort the convulsion issue?" Rake asked.

"Should have. Go on then, Holt."

Holt looked nervously to Ash. Ash sent him reassurance over the bond, and as his soul glowed warm, Holt began to pull in Ash's light. He had cycled motes before, though not for a prolonged period. When he sent magic throughout his body, it was to infuse his muscles and bones for a dramatic boost to strength and speed.

Cycling was a different beast. Pushing magic to his extremities, gathering it at his palms and the soles of his feet, then pulling it back toward the dragon bond at the center of himself became harder with each rotation. Each cycle felt like walking up an ever-steepening hill.

The magic wanted an outlet.

"How many cycles? It's getting difficult."

"As many as you can stand," Rake said. "It will be hard. You're not a being of magic. You're borrowing Ash's power. Keeping it inside you is like trying to push magic into a blade that isn't attuned to your dragon's power."

Holt continued cycling until his stomach shook from the effort to control his breath, his mote channels burned, and silver vapor leaked from his mouth. He could not cycle any longer, so he uncorked the vial and downed the liquid in one gulp.

An intense saltiness hit the back of his throat. Sea water would only have been marginally worse.

"Keep cycling," Aberanth said. *"Feel the difference in the movement of the motes."*

Holt struggled but managed to regain his rhythm. To his surprise, he found the flow of magic toward his fingers and toes easier than before. The merest nudge sufficed now, gathering so fast that the momentum of the motes also pushed others back up, making the whole process smoother. The steep hill flattened out.

"Well, he hasn't melted," Rake said, hefting his polearm. "Try moving."

Then he struck.

Holt drew, parried, retreated, stepped lightly aside, and guarded, ready to meet Rake's next thrust. He grinned. This felt good. Rake's tail swept for his legs. Holt jumped and deflected another slash at the same time. He landed on the balls of his feet. His body felt lithe, his center of gravity lowered. Balance came easy.

Yet as his attention became enthralled by the fight, his ability to maintain the cycling faltered. He lost his rhythm, and Rake knocked him to the floor.

"That felt great," Holt said. "Other than the taste, that is." The effects of the elixir were already wearing off. "How long should it last?"

"Hard to say," Aberanth said. *"It seems to vary, but generally if you maintain the cycling, the boost from the elixir should remain in place."*

"I see," Holt said, chewing it over. "So is this what you do in a fight, Rake? Cycle motes to make you stronger? Can it have any other effects?"

"One thing at a time, Master Cook. Yes, I sometimes cycle in a fight. And yes, it can have other benefits." He raised four fingers. "There are four primary techniques. What you just attempted in cycling motes to your limbs is called Grounding. This improves your physicality."

Rake dropped a finger. "The second technique involves pushing the flow of energy up to the surface of the skin, which forms a defensive layer. This is called 'Floating', and it can help repel motes that are not your own."

"Like a sort of magical armor?"

"Crude, but, in essence, yes. Be warned. Floating is an imperfect defense. It won't protect you as thoroughly as plate steel protects against blades." Rake dropped another finger. "The third is called Lifting, which brings the flow of energy to our heads to protect our minds. Mystic Lords and Paragons are known to meditate for days while Lifting to enhance their mental capacity. The fourth is Sinking, which keeps the flow of energy close to our souls and the dragon bond. When done right, it helps us draw upon greater quantities of magic from the core faster.

"The thing you must appreciate," Rake continued, "is that these techniques require immense focus, as you just discovered. Few can attend to the physical, magical, or mental nature of a battle while also maintaining such discipline over their mote channels. Suffice to say that this is not a quick fix, but another tool to consider using when it counts."

"I'm willing to learn. You know I am."

"I know," Rake said. "And this is something Ash can work on as well. Dragons have their own mote channels, after all."

"*I am ready, Master Rake,*" Ash said. He got up and braced himself as though for a spar. "*And perhaps Holt and I can offer something to help with this. One night on our travels, Holt's body shone with white lines. His mote channels became visible.*"

For once, Rake appeared lost for words. He looked between Holt and Ash and Aberanth, perhaps hoping one of them might explain. Aberanth shook his head as if he had not heard correctly.

"*Visible?*" he asked. "*What do you mean, visible?*"

Now Ash had reminded him, Holt recalled the events of the night after they confiscated the egg from the merchants. Even that felt like a long time ago now, when they had been meandering on their own.

"Ash is right," Holt said. "I could see my mote channels with my own eyes, like they were veins running under my skin. For a while it felt easier to move motes through them."

"And this just... happened one night?" Rake asked.

"No, it was after we ate together," Holt said, racking his brain for the memory. "When we had that venison I cooked in butter."

"*Butter?*" Aberanth said as if the word were absurd. "*Butter did that?*"

"No... deer is Ash's meat type, but we didn't have a chance to hunt for more after leaving Brenin. Hold on," he said, and he went searching for the recipe book. "I noted it all down in here, I'm sure."

"*Notes!*" Aberanth said, jubilant. "*Master Cook, you're a sensible fellow after all. Quickly now. Quickly.*" He hastened to extract another bark slab and bounded over to join Holt.

"Watch it," Holt said as Aberanth almost knocked him over. He flicked through to the section on deer and found the notes in his own hand, under the heading of 'sharing meals'.

"Here it is," he said, and he mumbled his notes aloud as he read. "Suspect that eating the same piece of meat caused my mote channels to become visible. Magic flow felt easier too. Light shone from my body. Need to try it again."

"Hmmph," Aberanth scoffed as though he'd never heard such amateurish notes in all his life. *"So, not because of butter?"*

"I don't think so... we tried eating more deer cooked in butter to test it, but it didn't work. That's why I thought it was due to sharing the exact same meal. That was the only thing that was different."

Aberanth screwed up his face. *"This will have to be tested."*

"We'll keep our noses peeled for more deer," Rake said. He seemed to have recovered from the revelation. "Anything that will aid your learning will be invaluable. Even by my exceptional standards, I can't expect an Ascendant to master techniques many Champions take years to perfect. We'll start slow and use Aberanth's elixirs to help you get to grips with the methods."

Holt appreciated now why Rake had been so keen to bring Aberanth on their mission. The idea of being able to repel magical attacks had an obvious use.

"So do you think these elixirs and techniques can help us defend against Sovereign?"

"If any defense exists against the mental domination you described, Lifting might be it. Emphasis on the 'might'."

"If this dragon has the power to dominate other minds, as you say," Aberanth began, *"then he is surely experienced in breaking through such barriers."*

"We don't know that," Rake said. "Truth is, there is little we know of Sovereign. It sounds like Clesh joined him willingly and Silverstrike was dragged into it. Perhaps Sovereign can dominate certain minds with ease and not others. Perhaps this is the very reason he has been so secretive. Whatever the case, it's best to be prepared."

"My work can only offer a modest boost at best," Aberanth said.

"A brief window of opportunity is all the chance we're likely to get. And it will be all I will need. While you and the rest of our soon-to-be team keep other threats at bay, I shall get in close, ward off his initial attack, and go for his throat. I wager he's so used to domination that he's forgotten how to move quickly in a fight."

"You can't know that," Holt said, throwing Rake's own words back at him. "Does your whole plan rely on something untested?"

Rake raised a scaly eyebrow. "Do you have a better plan, Holt? I'd love to hear it."

Holt, of course, did not have a better plan, so he remained silent.

"Good lad," Rake said.

Aberanth rumbled, rustled his wings, and beat his tail. He did this the way a human might clear their throat during a conversation.

"This is all well and good, but Holt is still just an Ascendant. Are you really going to bring him into such a fight?"

"You're not that much stronger than we are," Holt said, a little defensive.

"I'm not fighting anyone," Aberanth said. *"I'm worse than you are. I'm here as support. And because Rake has such a way of convincing me to do things that I wonder if he has a spot of mind control powers himself."*

"We'll work on their rank," Rake said, ignoring the insinuation. "There is time yet. For now, Holt can practice cycling until the moon comes out."

"My supplies are finite, you know," Aberanth said, returning to his open leaf sack. *"I need my lab to make more."*

All the same, he picked up another vial of the Grounding elixir between his teeth and brought it to Holt. That done, he nosed his bark to lay before him and then looked expectant. *"This time, could you please explain what you feel slowly and in detail."*

Rake smirked, then looked to Ash and beckoned. "Come here, my little white friend. Time I started training you too. It's not only Holt who gets to suffer."

Ash growled and stepped forward with pride and purpose, as though he were to be elevated in his role by a monarch.

"I am ready, Master Rake. Teach me."

EIGHTEEN

Descent

The first hour was hard. The second harder. In their third hour of delving beneath the earth, the air tightened like ill-fitting clothes. To Talia's relief, the main tunnel did not shrink. Scourge Queens were large and had to pass through to the surface one way or another. All the same, Pyra, Turro, and Ghel each crawled more than walked, keeping their wings tucked against their sides. Ghel stuck close to Pyra, following her like a duckling.

Where the tunnel did branch into smaller offshoots, Turro and Ghel would, as they put it, 'listen to the stones' to hear if enemies lay down there.

"Even your Elder's senses were clouded," Talia said. "How can you be sure of what you perceive down here?"

"*The stones do not need magic to speak to us,*" Turro said as he pressed his talon hard into the ground.

"*Feet and weight play their own notes upon rock,*" Ghel said.

Talia had little choice but to trust them. When they heard nothing, Talia led the expedition on in the hope no ambushes lay behind.

On ever deeper, following the pull of the dark presence.

Now she was beneath the earth, Talia sensed the pulsing aura of something magical out there, like the beacon of a lighthouse far out to sea. To conserve Pyra's core, Talia dimmed her blade and carried a torch like the others.

The Twinblades stalked beside her, seemingly without fear.

"How does this compare to one of my uncle's adventures?" she asked them.

The twins looked at one another before answering.

"That we cannot know," said Eadwald.

"Until the task is complete," said Eadwulf.

"Did you ever fight the scourge as a Gray Cloak?" Talia said.

"Not in our time," said Eadwald.

"We returned to serve House Harroway after the trials in the desert," Eadwulf said.

"What about the previous incursion in Feorlen?" Talia asked.

"We were but boys then," Eadwald said. "Training as simple soldiers at our fort."

"The swarm of fifteen years ago did not trouble Harroway lands," said Eadwulf.

"So your first real encounter with the scourge was within the last few months?" Talia asked.

They nodded.

Harroway was right, Talia thought. *None are prepared.*

"I'll refresh you on fighting these creatures," said Talia. "Ghouls are deadlier than they appear. They will not tire and will move quicker than you think a dead person should. Flayers have a great reach, but if you get in close, they struggle. Go for their legs. Stingers have a weak point in their pinched waists. At least down here, they must attack us at ground level. Juggernauts are an issue. Ideally you should take them down at range or use pikes or spears. The dragons and I shall attempt to draw their attention. Abominations..."

She hesitated, unsure what advice she could give two normal men to take on such creatures.

Eadwald jumped in. "Those are the giant skeletons?"

"We slew one alongside Holt Cook," said Eadwulf.

"You did?" Talia said, surprised, before remembering the twins must have been juiced up on dragon blood at the time. In response, they nodded proudly to her, and she gave them a serious look in return. "Down here, you leave them to me."

Up ahead, she saw that Turro had stopped at another crossroads.

"Halt, flame wielders," he said. He pressed one of his front talons into the rock, then moved it from side to side.

Ghel joined him, but before starting to listen to the rocks herself, she looked at Pyra eagerly. Pyra rumbled and stalked forward to join her.

"She wants to teach me how it's done," Pyra told Talia. *"In case it is a technique other dragons might learn."* Her tone made it evident that she thought this was a waste of time.

"She seems to look up to you," Talia said. *"No harm in it."*

"I suppose this is what comes of never meeting other types of dragons," Pyra said. *"She asked if the fires speak to us."*

Talia smirked. *"If only, then we'd always find good company."*

Ghel looked at Pyra imploringly and growled. Pyra put on a good show of feigning interest and pressing her own front foot into the rock.

While the dragons worked, Talia raised her fist to draw her battalion to a halt. Quietly, the order was passed back along the line with hand signals, although their marching feet and clinks of armor made more than enough noise to alert the enemy.

She went to stand in the middle of the crossroads. Five passages branched off from it, including the continuation of the main tunnel to her left, which was larger than the others. Beyond the opening of each passage was nothing but blackness. What light they cast from their torches did not penetrate far.

Talia swept ahead with her magical senses. Other than Pyra and the emeralds, there was only one other presence that used some form of magic. It felt wispy and ragged, ugly and hunched compared to a core's pristine form. The scourge, when gathered, always had a low hum of magic to them. That was in part how dragons and riders could detect them at range, and yet this was something else. Scourge and yet not scourge at the same time.

Something new. Within the dark beat this darker presence.

Most worrying was how she sensed nothing else around it. The Elder's senses had been obscured by it, so it made sense that hers were too. Surely the tunnels were not just empty?

"This way is clear, flame wielders," Turro announced. He shifted to the next tunnel.

"This one is also clear," Ghel told them. She moved on to check the fourth and final offshoot. This time Pyra did not humor her. Instead, Pyra walked toward the continuation of the main tunnel and sniffed at the air.

"Their stench is strongest this way."

Talia moved to stand beside her and noticed something strange upon the wall of the main tunnel. There were ragged and faint markings scratched into the rock. She squinted, then stepped closer to them. The lines formed something akin to the letter E, but the vertical line instead slashed down from left to right at an angle.

How strange, she thought. Perhaps some of the bugs had scraped against the wall on their way by?

As she drew back, something imperceptible shifted in the air. The hairs on the back of her neck raised; her heart jumped. The three dragons went from calm to braced and growling. The ridges along Pyra's tail flared up, as did scales on the back of her head like the hackles of a dog.

Turro lit green power. *"Scourge approach. I will attempt to seal this passage. Ghel, aid me."*

Ghel's first steps were uncertain. She stumbled, then caught herself and squeezed through to Turro's side.

Talia drew her blade and ignited it while keeping the torch in her left hand. She held both at arm's reach and turned slowly at the center of the crossroads, trying to get a sense of which direction the first bug would come from.

"Stay back," she called to the Twinblades and the rest of her men. The battalion was still safely back in the main tunnel they had come down. "Shield wall!"

Shields had barely begun interlocking when the first shriek rang out.

"Finally," Pyra cried. *"A fight!"*

The dragon bond widened. Fire swirled into Talia's soul, warming her for battle. A chorus of Pyra's rousing song followed, and then she saw them. Eyes in the darkness. They were hurtling down each branching passage.

Turro and Ghel roared with relief and staggered back. A new wall rose to block the bugs down one tunnel, yet three passages remained open. There was no time for another wall. The advancing scourge entered the visibility of their inadequate light. Flayers running. Stingers scuttling along the ceiling.

Talia ducked as the first flayer came in slicing. She cut through its legs as she rose, then stepped into a lunge and thrust her blade into a stinger's compound eye. Movement on her right. A bug passed her by. Something heavy struck the shield wall. Calls to hold then to thrust forward rang from the battalion.

Caught in the middle of the crossroads, Talia couldn't see what was happening with her troops. She dodged the swinging tails of the dragons as much as the enemy. Never stopping. Stopping was death.

Pyra howled. A line of burning pain coursed down Talia's side but nothing had hit her, only an impression of the pain crossing the bond.

She ran to Pyra, ready to break the flayer with her bare hands, but there were no enemies left to fight. They were fleeing down the main tunnel deeper underground.

Quick as that, it ended.

Talia checked on Pyra. There was a cut along the muscle of her left wing, though thankfully not into the leathery sinew required for flight.

Heavy breathing drew her attention. Ghel backed away, in danger of stumbling into Talia's troops if she wasn't careful. The dragon shook her head, yowling.

Turro rushed to her side, brought her to a halt and placed his snout on top of hers. *"Strength, sibling."*

"Their claws are so sharp," Ghel said. Her chest and front legs were bleeding from many small cuts. Pyra growled and went to her, taking Turro's place and placing her snout upon Ghel's.

"Take heart in your Elder's selection," Pyra said. *"He must have great faith in you."*

This settled Ghel. She ceased her jerking movements and breathed easier.

"Thank you, flame wielder."

"Gone soft?" Talia asked Pyra privately. Her dragon snorted and did not deign to reply.

The Twinblades appeared at Talia's side.

"That was no real attack," Eadwald said.

"A mere test of our strength," Eadwulf said.

Turro also returned to the tunnel's opening and placed his talons into the earth.

"I am hearing mixed messages," he said. *"The enemy gathers ahead but also… around. I cannot fully discern—"*

"Enough of this caution," Pyra said, stomping up and shouldering him aside. Her fires were ablaze, pain and anger at her injuries made their bond hot and race. *"The enemy has found us. The time for quiet is over. Now is the fight."*

Talia knew she should call for further thought, but Pyra's fires laced her own veins, such heat as to burn away any fear, any doubt. Talia heeded it. Her thoughts and the dragon's blurred into one. Too long had they bandied words with the old, slow humans. Too long had the scourge scum continued to poison her lands.

Talia set her blade on fire and pointed it down the corridor. "For Feorlen!"

She burst into a magically fueled sprint, trailing light and fire as she sped after the scourge.

"Yes!" Pyra cried to her, bellowing loud enough to shake loose stones upon the floor. As they charged together, relief washed through Talia. Weeks of frustration were being unleashed.

Feet thundered behind her, but Talia focused on what lay ahead. It wasn't until she saw the rows of eyes in the darkness, eyes upon eyes, that she understood how distorted her magical senses were.

She should have known better. Should have stopped, and thought, and planned.

Too late.

Pyra shot a jet of flames into the ranks of ghouls. The searing stream lit the remainder of the tunnel, and Talia caught a glimpse of a grand chamber beyond the back of the swarm. When the fire died, she lost sight of their goal.

That taste of the end only fueled the fire in the blood. Talia reached the ghouls, slashed wide on either side with her burning blade. Those first seconds passed in a bile-spilling blur. Pyra was by her side, but she registered little else. This was the domain of the scourge, yet Talia had brought their bane.

Her dragon bond burned as she pulled Pyra's fire across it, channeling the motes down her legs and stamping into the ground. Her Flamewave ability blasted outward with every step. Within a few heartbeats, the bond grew taut. It was an absurd use of magic. It was glorious. Ghouls melted before her. Flayers shrieked and skirted her.

She stamped again, and the taut bond ripped at the edges. As the fires spanned outward from her, a juggernaut muscled its way through, shrugging off the flames. Caught off guard, she was knocked to the floor.

At once, she realized just how densely packed the enemy were. And then the worse realization that she and Pyra were out this far alone.

You fool, she thought.

The juggernaut lowered its head and charged again. Before Talia could react, a green gale passed overhead; a dragon's breath which had a weight to it. The green breath slammed into the beast, crumpling its chitinous hide as though struck by a dropped boulder.

Turro the emerald emerged in the wake of this green breath, followed by Ghel. The Twinblades arrived next, panting. Eadwald kept ghouls at bay while Eadwulf offered Talia his hand.

"My queen," he called.

Talia didn't require his aid to stand, but she accepted his hand all the same.

The three dragons took up most of the space in the tunnel. When the rest of their troops caught up with them, it became a crushed confusion of limbs, of rattling howls and armor, of scales and scraping carapaces. Torches swung mad in the melee, casting trails of flame and smoke and pockets of light in which the enemy were but passing shadows.

The shrieks of the enemy came from all sides. The clang of battle rang along their entire column.

A buzzing stinger dropped in front of Talia. She parried its mandibles, spun, stepped, and cleaved through its thin waist. More launched themselves from above. Talia looked up to see fresh eyes blooming from another tunnel or ledge. Along the entire passage, more ambushes took her soldiers unawares.

Whatever order her soldiers had disintegrated.

"Turro, Ghel!" she screamed, hoping they would hear her. "Seal those passages!"

Turro extracted himself from the front line and made for one of the cavern walls.

"*Keep them off us,*" he said. A low hum of power emanated as he weaved his magic.

Ghel made her way to the opposite wall. Blood fell from the wounds at her chest and a fresh cut at the tip of her snout. Pyra went to defend Ghel while Talia took charge of Turro's defense.

Men screamed death cries all along the tunnel. Without her aid or the dragons', the back ranks of her battalion would be easy pickings for the larger bugs.

Throwing caution aside, Talia pulled as much magic across the bond as her mote channels could handle. This fight had to end fast. Pyra also drew as much fire from her core as she had space to unleash it. The bonfire ebbed away with each passing second.

Turro sealed the first overhead passage, then another. Talia spun to check on Pyra. She fought close beside Ghel as the emerald channeled earth and rock. Being the younger, Ghel worked slower than Turro. She uttered a pained roar, and her body trembled under the strain. A juggernaut bellowed like a bull and barreled into her, cutting her work short. More scourge descended from the passage Ghel had been unable to seal.

Talia ran for them.

Ahead, Pyra swung her tail into a flayer, breaking its thin frame in two against the tunnel wall. Yet more weaved in; too many, too quick and nimble for Pyra to handle alone. Their scythe-like arms slashed in a flurry around her.

Talia felt the cuts on Pyra's scales as though her own skin parted. She screamed. Their bond became white-hot, threatening to burn a hole in her chest.

She arrived by her dragon's side still screaming in pain and defiance. Her bladework had never been so quick or savage. Raising the red steel to a cauterizing heat, Talia thrust through a final juggernaut's hardened abdomen, melting its natural armor. Pyra followed up by pouring fire over the bug.

And she kept going, lashing out with her flaming breath until the smoke threatened to choke the air and her core dropped to an ember.

"Pyra, stop!" Talia cried. She grabbed her dragon by the neck and heaved with all her might to pull Pyra's snout down. "Stop, girl," Talia urged, breathless.

Somehow it was over.

Sounds of battle faded. Ragged cheers arose soon after, which descended into anguished cries of relief and horror. And too few voices at that.

What have I done? Talia asked herself. Bodies littered the corridor. Weak light from too few torches carved out the stricken features of the dead in oily shadows.

This is no place for the living to fight.

Picking over a pile of the dead, she found Ghel. The turquoise dragon twitched and spasmed. A broken arm of a flayer protruded from her stomach. Blood bubbled at her mouth as she fought for breath.

"*Turro?*" Ghel's voice was frail and laced with fear. Her eyes bulged, searching around her. "*Turro?*" Then she breathed her last and lay still. The young emerald's core winked out.

Talia stood rooted until Turro emerged from the dark. He

approached with care, then laid his snout upon her body and let loose a low, mournful wail.

"I'm sorry," Talia said. "I... I didn't see..."

Pyra drew up beside her. The hurt and guilt which rose in her dragon so sudden and swift almost brought Talia to tears. As suddenly as it came, it went, and Talia's ability to feel Pyra grew dim. Pyra had closed off their bond.

"Pyra?" Talia said hoarsely. But her dragon was already loping away, unable to face her.

Feeling dazed and her fingers numb, Talia struggled to clean then sheathe her blade before turning to navigate the carnage. One emerald had fallen, but hundreds of her people lay bleeding, crushed, or gutted. The blood of humans and scourge alike pooled so thick in places that it covered her feet. The smell was unlike anything she had suffered before, blood, yes, but also the spilled stools of the dead, the rot of scourge flesh, and the unmistakable stomach-clenching scent of charred meat. All trapped in stifled air deep underground with no relief.

It was all she could do not to retch.

Many of the survivors did, adding the contents of their stomachs to the death mix. She could not blame them. They fumbled salutes or bows to her, their eyes miles away from where they actually were. She helped men get back to their feet, offered what encouragement she could. Where injuries were within her knowledge to help, she used her powers to cauterize wounds. It taxed her bond almost to the point of fraying, but it would be worth it should a few lives be saved.

Down at the front where the two forces had first met, she found Eadwald hauling a body of a ghoul aside. He heaved on one of his fellow soldiers next, dragging the corpse a short way before dropping it. Muffled calls of "Brother!" sounded from beneath a flayer's body.

Rushing to help, Talia and Eadwald soon extracted Eadwulf. He emerged unrecognizable. Drenched in filth and shaking. Coughing and spluttering, he fell to his knees. Eadwald bent to join him, and both brothers cradled each other like children.

Seeing the Twinblades brought so low almost sapped the rest of Talia's strength.

"What have we done, Pyra?"

No answer came.

Darkness gripped her mind. Harroway and all her damned councilors had been right. This had all been a waste after all. A waste of lives, a waste of time and resources. For what? The curiosity of an Elder dragon?

She chastised herself for trying to deflect responsibility. Down here, she was in charge; the triumphs were to be hers as well as any blame. Charging in had been disastrous. Once again, she had allowed the dragon to flow into her unchecked, turning her blood and soul to fire and burning away the cool head a true leader required. In this way at least, she was different from her uncle, though it was hardly flattering. His leadership was infamously cold and calculated.

In her blind rage and arrogance, she had thought her powers the bane of the enemy when she knew full well that was not true. Light was their bane. Ash was their bane. Worst of all, she had forgotten the very thing Harroway had begged her to remember. She did not fight alongside dragon riders. And yet she had thrown her men headlong against an enemy on their own ground.

The Elder had supplied the mission, but this blood was on her hands.

If I were a Champion or Lord, it might have been different. This is what she told herself to stay strong.

Wishing some progress to have come of her dragon bond – for even a small piece of good news – Talia checked on her smoldering bridge to Pyra. Ripped edges spoke of the toll of the skirmish. Though a quick fight, it had been more brutal than even the siege at Sidastra. There too she had feared for her life and Pyra's, but not like this. Trapped on all sides like cornered mice. Unable to escape even if they had wanted to.

As the bond healed, it would likely strengthen. Yet even the sorry state of her bond made her ashamed. She had stressed to Holt the key lesson her own mentors had drilled into her. Magic in a fight had to be sparing if the bond was to last. Swordwork first and foremost. Skill over strength. And when it had come to it, from fear and anger, she'd blown through the integrity of her bond in a few blood-soaked minutes.

She had to be smarter. Control the fire within her.

She exhaled, and smoke escaped from her throat which had nothing to do with Pyra. The release brought clarity back to the situation at hand. At the end of this accursed corridor lay their goal.

Her bond with Pyra reopened.

"Pyra? Are you okay?"

"It's only a few cuts."

It felt far worse than that, but Talia didn't want to press the issue.

"Listen, girl, what happened to Ghel isn't your—"

"I know," Pyra said curtly. *"She knew the risks. Let's move on."*

"Pyra?" Talia said, reproachful.

"It's in there. I'm certain."

Talia let it slide. Pyra liked to keep moving forward, not dwell on horrors that had happened.

"We need some time to regroup first," Talia said. *"There's no telling what else is here."*

NINETEEN

Whispers

Gathering the survivors and clearing a path took a lot longer than it would have above ground. Such luxuries as daylight, fresh air and space were denied to them in the hot close dark, reeking of so much death it may never wash out.

Over half her men were dead.

There would not be enough fit survivors to carry the dead back to the surface when the time came. All new dragon riders learned that no matter what they did, they could not save everyone. That was lesson one. Given her blunders, Talia was unwilling to risk more lives and resolved to enter the chamber with only Pyra. To do that, she needed a final favor from their surviving emerald comrade. Talia searched for him, carrying one of their few remaining torches. The wood was sticky with blood. She found Turro standing vigil over Ghel's body.

"I intend to go on alone. If you are willing to step away from your flight sibling's side, I would ask you to lead the rest of my men back to the surface."

Turro breathed heavy, taking his time to answer.

"My Elder sent us here for two reasons. To seal the passageways against overwhelming threats and to see you return to the surface at any cost."

Talia looked at Ghel's body. "The cost has already been high."

Turro growled lowly. *"I will not abandon my Elder's mission. I will stay."*

"Very well," Talia said. "Keep watch over the entrance to this chamber then. Be ready to seal it at a moment's notice, even if I am on the other side."

"I shall," he said begrudgingly.

Talia thanked him, then gave orders to her surviving officers to retreat to the surface should the worst happen.

Pyra awaited her at the head of her ragged host. Before entering the chamber, she took a moment to press her head wordlessly to Pyra's snout. Via the bond, Talia felt Pyra's wounds sting. She would have told her to stay here with the others if there had been any hope Pyra would listen.

"Ready, girl?"

"Ready."

They were just about to step over the threshold when the Twinblades arrived by their side. Eadwulf's face was so caked in dried blood that his eyes appeared as two bright orbs on a black field. Though he stood tall, a slight tremor shook his empty hand. Eadwald held a torch for the pair of them.

"I do not ask you to follow me," Talia said.

"Our oath was to serve and protect Your Majesty," said Eadwald.

"That we shall do, even—" Eadwulf gasped for a breath. "Even unto death."

Talia nodded. She knew it was important to them, and no one else was brave or stupid enough to willingly join her.

"Uncle Osric was a fool to ever let you go." She beckoned them forward.

Turro took up his position by the entrance.

"Let me enter first," she said.

Talia took a deep breath, then entered the cavernous chamber. Every small sound echoed in the place. Despite being large, the air was just as foul, as though the rot were rotting.

Something squelched underfoot. She had stepped into an oily-green substance. She took another step and the slime clung to her boot, dragging at her like diseased egg white. Talia raised her torch.

The same slime covered the ground and walls, reflecting a ghost light, a dead light, a light which illuminated nothing.

From all around there came the drips and splats of falling liquid. A dollop of the slime fell in front of Talia, explaining the source of the noise.

The twins and Pyra followed her inside.

"Take to the left," Talia instructed them. "Stay close to the wall. Let's see how large this area is. Pyra, go with them just in case."

They parted. Talia kept close to the wall on her right to pick across the slimy ground. It struck her that the wall was unnaturally smooth. At intervals, more tunnels branched off from the chamber. This place had to be some important point in the network, the wheel that all the spokes fed into.

The flickering torches of the twins became small and then larger before they rendezvoused with her. They were now on the opposite side to where they started. Looking back, Talia could see the torches of the rest of her troops bobbing in the tunnel they had fought down.

"Were there more passages on your side?" Talia asked.

"Many," said Eadwald.

"We counted four," said Eadwulf.

"They must run under more of the kingdom than we realized," Talia said. As she spoke, something lumpy fell from the darkened ceiling onto Eadwulf's shoulder. It was red, sinuous, and marbled throughout with black-green veins. Eadwulf gazed at it as it fell slowly from him. He showed no sign of disgust, but given how filthy he already was, Talia supposed this latest addition made no impact.

Following where this fresh horror had fallen from, she risked looking up.

She wished she hadn't.

Great tendrils of what looked like raw, exposed muscle hung from the ceiling or clung to high spots upon the walls. Tendon, sinew, and what could have been the guts of a monstrous beast wove around stalactites and headed ominously toward the darkened center of the chamber.

Pyra took a step, and something brittle crunched.

"A piece of shell," Pyra said.

Talia bent to inspect it. Sweeping the slime aside, she saw what looked like a great shard of black glass. A shell seemed the best way to describe it, yet it was not stony like a dragon egg nor anything like a bird's. It was as thick as clay but weighed far more. When Talia tried to break it, the shell resisted far longer than she anticipated.

"This is some sort of hatchery," Pyra said.

Now Talia knew to look for them, pieces of this black shell were everywhere.

"Over here," the Twinblades called. They stood over what looked like a large piece of discarded chitin. It had wrinkled and buckled but still held the vague shape of a great pincer. Talia could think of only one bug that would fit this.

Pyra sniffed it, then withdrew. *"It looks like it belongs to a queen, though it's smaller than the pincer of the queen we fought."*

"Do you think that queen grew in here?"

Shell and shed skin. *Something* had grown in here.

"Eadwald, Eadwulf, can you manage that piece? We should take it back to the surface."

The piece was large enough that it took both twins working together to pick it up. They made for the exit tunnel and Talia was glad to see them leave, just in case.

Bracing herself, she crept toward the center of the chamber. What she found was stranger than anything so far. The raw muscle, tendons, and guts gathered in a grotesque spiral around the largest low-hanging stalactite. At its tip was a dark, gelatinous orb that might have been a lidless eye. A green glow pulsed within it. A quick check of her magical senses confirmed this was it. The thing that had led them down here.

"Let us burn it and be rid of it," Pyra said.

"Just a moment." Something about the pulsing orb allured Talia. Spoke to her. She stepped closer. The light. The light meant something. A faint whisper brushed her ears.

"What did you say, girl?"

"I didn't say anything. Talia, let's burn it and be gone."

"Burn it?" Talia said, dreamily. "Why? It's doing nothing wrong."

Her world went silent. She felt herself being pulled closer. Two more steps and she was right underneath it. She reached up—

Pyra swung her neck into her midriff, driving the wind from her lungs and knocking her over. She slammed onto the slime-drenched floor and her dragon bond asserted itself as an inferno in her chest. The damaged edges of the bond ripped further, all while a real inferno blazed to life in the chamber. Pyra bathed the orb in fire.

Screaming, shrill as an injured horse, rang in Talia's mind. Not one scream but many, hundreds, echoing over and over and over. Bits of charred muscle and gut fell smoking to the cavern floor, releasing an acrid stench. Smoke thickened the air. Were the cavern not so high, it would have been choking.

Pyra's core guttered out, completely empty. She snarled and rounded on Talia. *"What were you doing?"*

Talia realized she had been clutching her head. The screaming had ceased.

"I... I don't know. I lost myself for a moment."

"The Elder told us to burn it. Next time, don't hesitate."

Talia got back to her feet. Slime squeezed its way through every gap in her armor.

She shuddered. "I think we've spent long enough down here." She checked the magical landscape. The dark, unknown presence was gone. "We've done what we came to do."

Daylight had never been a more welcome sight. Yet fresh pillars of smoke from the campsite turned her blood cold. Talia got onto Pyra's back and they flew up to find Harroway. Across the bond, Talia felt Pyra's wings throb from her injuries.

While airborne, they observed piles of scourge bodies being heaped on the edge of the camp. Tents lay ripped or trampled into the ground. A flayer stood impaled upon a thick stake in the broken defenses of the western trench. The giant femur of an abomination protruded from a burning pile of ghouls. Many more humans were being laid down in neat rows, while emerald dragons gathered around their own dead.

Over their bond, Talia asked once again, *"What has this cost us?"*

This time, Pyra answered. *"As much as it had to."*

Talia bit her lip. At times she wished Pyra would just offer the sympathy and reassurance she craved.

Harroway hailed them outside the command tent.

His hair was slick with sweat and blood. A sweep of his blond locks had been cut away and a thick bloody bandage was wrapped around his left ear. He favored one side but otherwise seemed unharmed.

"What happened, Drefan?" Talia asked as she dismounted.

"To this?" he asked, pointing to his ear. "Damned helmet was knocked off, then a ghoul caught me as I stumbled." He winced and scrunched his face against some fresh pain, then carried on. "As for the rest, we were attacked from the west. Without warning. Our scouts must have been killed. Were it not for the emeralds we wouldn't have made it."

"Looks like the scourge fared worse in the end."

Harroway shook his head. "It was so fast. I think that great dragon was on his way, but before he arrived the scourge forces went limp, wandered off, or else turned on each another as much as on us. One moment we were dead men between the swarm and the cliff of the chasm. The next, it was over."

"That sounds like what happened when the queen was slain," Pyra said. She had broadcast her thought to Harroway as well. He looked alarmed at hearing a dragon speak to him for the first time.

"Some of the officers who fought at the city said the same thing, only the reaction from the scourge this time seemed more extreme." He then seemed to become aware of Talia's appearance. "I see you met resistance. Were you successful?"

"We were," Talia said, beyond grateful she could at least tell him that. "We burned whatever it was. Some sort of staging chamber, perhaps. I'm afraid it only raises more questions."

Talia looked at the devastation around her. She had never been under any illusion of the hard choices of rulership. Lesson one from the Order had prepared her well enough for that. Still, it was one thing to know the risk was necessary and another thing to view its aftermath.

How many more will die because I sit on the throne? How many will bleed in the Red Range should war come?

It was all she could do not to think on that outcome.

"I regret that it has come at such a high price."

Harroway grimaced. "At the least, we've ensured this incursion is truly over." He gasped again and bent over double.

Talia moved to steady him, allowing him to support himself on her shoulder. Her Master of War was as stubborn as she was about entering the fray himself. She just hoped that would not come back to haunt either of them.

As she helped him back to the command tent, every dragon at the scourge chasm began to roar, first loud, then low, slow, and sad. A long lament for their fallen.

TWENTY

Dragon-Steel

Osric stood at ease in the workshop of Windshear Hold. Given the task ahead, he wore a loose-fitting shirt rather than his hardier wool. He expected a lengthy process, and so Champion Dahaka would attend to the hatchlings alone until he was done.

The old blacksmith arrived escorted by two cultists. Osric sent them to fetch a chair and regular food and water for the smith.

"Thank you, Honored Rider." He seemed more comfortable in calling Osric that. Osric let him. It would be natural to the old man, and anything that made the process easier was welcome. "Where is your dragon?"

"He will not be joining us," Osric said as he rolled up his sleeves. "Such work is beneath him. And he is not my dragon, rather I am his servant. We are all his servants and privileged to be so."

"Of course," the smith said wisely. "But... if I may... a dragon must work the great bellows." The smith pointed to the huge, specialized set of bellows to the side of the furnace. "We must get the temperature as high as possible. Unless you are a fire rider?"

"I am not."

Worry creased the old man's face as he recalibrated.

"What rank are you?"

"I believe my rank in the Order would be that of Lord."

"A Lord?" he said, surprised. "Hmm. That is well. The process might fatigue an Ascendant alone but a Lord—"

"I assure you, Master Smith, that whatever needs to be done, I will manage it."

"Very well," the smith said, bleak-faced. He only seemed then to notice the weapons at Osric's belt. "Axes?"

"I'd sooner make a set of these than a sword."

"Also unorthodox… but there is no reason why it can't be done," he hastened to add. "Yes. Yes, it can be done. The process to fold your power into the steel remains the same. We can shape it as you please afterward. I will warn you that the creation of this metal will be arduous. It is a rite of passage for Ascendants and not easily accomplished. Though they create their weapon at Falcaer, I had experience with older riders who wished to change or reforge their weapon. Even for a Champion, the process is difficult. At every stage there can be a fatal error, ruining the steel."

"I will do anything required," Osric said. Then, recalling Sovereign's desire for him to learn the process in full, he added, "Please talk me through the method in detail."

The smith gave a determined nod then shuffled forward. "We begin, of course, by creating the steel ingot. One ingot for a great blade ought to suffice for two axe heads."

He inspected the materials and rifled with shaking hands through tools and equipment.

"All is here as requested," Osric said.

Some items had survived the centuries of abandonment deep in the vaults of Windshear. Buckets of sand, containers of broken glass, and well-sealed raw clay. Most of the metal tools had decayed to useless rust. What they now possessed had been stolen from smithies here and there, meaning little was standardized.

The smith grunted in acknowledgment, then selected a clay pot and beckoned Osric over.

"With this crucible we shall make steel of the highest purity."

He placed chunks of iron into the clay pot. Next, he directed Osric to the charcoal and instructed him to crush a piece into finer grains. Osric took a hammer to the lump and powdered it before adding it into the crucible.

"Within the heat of the forge, the charcoal shall infuse the iron with hardness, creating steel." The smith relaxed as he spoke about his work. "To aid it along, we must remove slag from the ore so that the hardness will enter more easily."

This required a small dish of fine-grain sand and a shard of glass. Osric now understood why the riders of old had kept so much of it. The smith sifted through the glass himself to find a shard of the size he wanted, then placed it into the crucible along with the iron, charcoal, and sand.

"The sand and glass will melt, bind to impurities in the metal and float the slag away."

Osric then placed a lid on the pot and sealed it with clay.

The smith then directed Osric in placing the crucible into the furnace and covering it with coal. Before they lit the fuel, the smith became desperate to impart his next instruction.

"It is imperative that the mixture gets hot enough to melt as many impurities as possible. Furnaces outside of the Order cannot achieve the temperature required to create pure steel. That is where the dragon plays their part." He looked at the great bellows again in dismay. "If you work your own set without rest, it may suffice. These are still greater than those an ordinary smith would use."

Osric looked at the bellows on the opposite side of the furnace. They did appear much larger than others he had seen, designed for a rider with increased strength and stamina.

"Just tell me what I must do. Be blunt."

"You must maintain air flow the entire time. For at least five hours. But as you'll need to make up for the loss of your dragon—"

"Extra effort for five hours," Osric finished for him. That did not seem so terrible.

He lit the hearth. Already his hands were black with soot. As the fire bloomed, he began working the great bellows, forcing in air to feed the hungering flames.

"I can see why fire riders have an advantage in this," Osric said.

"Their power over flames allows for unparalleled control. A shame in many ways that no fire rider turns their long life to the art of metalwork. They would be able to create weapons and armor unlike any other."

"Armor?" Osric said, his interest piqued.

"Oh yes, they would make astounding armor if they turned their mind to it—not of dragon-steel, of course," he added. "Fusing magic into the ore requires extreme heat and folding, a method most unsuitable for any plate armor or chainmail. Yet their control at every stage of heating makes their blades slightly superior to other riders."

Osric grunted and continued to work the bellows. This knowledge of the riders was new to him. Fire riders were considered the greatest of the original five types, ostensibly for their effectiveness against the scourge. If their swords held an edge over the others, this too must give them additional prestige. Small wonder why the most frequent leader of the Paragons was the Fire Paragon.

"I must have missed your name," the smith said.

"I never gave you it."

"My name is Emrik."

Osric sighed. Matters would be easier later if he didn't know the man's name.

"This isn't a place suited for personal details."

"It's only a name."

"When you're broken down far enough, it might be all you have left. You should guard it." Osric threw a glance to the old man, but he seemed resolute.

"I heard some of the Wyrm Clo—"

"The Shroud, Master Smith."

"I heard some of them call you 'General'."

Osric nodded. "I led a free company for many years."

"And do you guard the name of that company?"

Osric pulled on the bellows, willing the old man to cease.

"Humor an old man, General. I'm under no illusion what my fate will be."

Osric gave him a hard look and was met with eyes as strong as the steel he'd spent years forging. He did understand.

"I led the Gray Cloaks."

"Gray Cloaks?" the smith said, chewing on the name. "I think I heard a thing or two about them. They guarded the Archon of Athra for a time?"

"We did."

"And something about the war, the one before last... the Gray Cloaks fought against us on the Brenin side."

He said 'us' because he was Risalian, Osric noted. He had served the Order, but he hadn't sworn the oath.

"We did."

"You're that Agravain fellow?"

"I am."

"They say you betrayed us in the last war."

"How could I have betrayed Risalia when I fought for Feorlen?"

"I don't rightly understand that... that's just what is said. About the taverns, you know."

Osric snorted. He had coaxed some gullible Risalian officers into thinking he could be bribed into abandoning the Toll Pass and his brother in it. But then, on the day, plans had changed.

"Each man will make up his own mind," Osric said.

"I'm not sure I believe it," said the smith.

That took Osric aback, and he paused for a moment with the bellows. The smith's eyes widened in alarm, and Osric pulled hard upon the bellows again to reassure him and asked, "What brings you to that conclusion?"

"Your hand," the smith said. "I noticed the tattoo there. It is the Gunvaldr's Horns, is it not?"

"It is."

"Risalia does not hold to the old traditions of the Skarls, but we remember enough of them. Such an honor would not be bestowed on a trickster."

Osric swallowed a great lump in his throat. For years he had lived and fought in the company of the Iron Beards. He'd posed as a lesser noble of Feorlen, a fifth son of a fictitious house, not openly lying but allowing the Skarls to make their assumptions and not leaping to correct them. The smith did not need to know that.

"I saved the life of Empress Skadi," Osric said.

"That sounds like quite the tale."

It could have been. The truth was more mundane, as these things often were.

Skadi had traveled into the western empire, into territory which had fought to break away from imperial rule during their civil war. She hired the Iron Beards alongside the Boundless Sons, Death's Daughters, and the Blood Bards to escort her. Some Jarl with a grudge sent an assassin with poisons and knives. Osric took the knife meant for Skadi before finishing the killer. For that, she granted him the honor.

He'd been jubilant, even happy, for a moment then. Recognition, praise at long last for his abilities and hard work, the way admiration ought to work rather than the insincerity of court. And yet, even as the ink dried upon his skin, a hollow feeling came upon him, and so he'd left to pursue fulfillment elsewhere.

"I did my job and did it well," Osric said.

"Quite a tale, I imagine, to take you from such highs... to here." The smith spoke softly, knowing he was treading on dangerous ground, albeit safe enough in the knowledge that Osric and Sovereign still needed him until the task was done.

"Those tales don't matter," Osric said. "They are of a life lost. Not for them will I be remembered now."

"Did you choose this? Or are you being forced as well?"

Osric pulled hard upon the bellows and delivered the old man a look of such anger that he had the good sense not to ask more on the matter.

Hours later, the smith at last told him to stop.

"It should be ready now."

Osric used a great pair of tongs to draw the crucible out. The pot glowed bright yellow, radiating heat from the ingot inside.

"Good, good," the smith said. "Place it on the anvil and break the clay away."

Osric used the hammer. He struck and the clay crumbled, revealing the cylindrical ingot inside. Already it was cooling, dulling to a warm orange.

"Strike the metal," said the smith.

Osric gave it a firm, flat blow with the hammer. Nothing seemed to happen.

The smith nodded. "No sparks," he said, relieved. "It is pure." He stood back and wiped his brow. Osric did not think the sweat had anything to do with the heat of the hearth.

"What next?"

The smith needed a few more deep breaths. After composing himself, he said, "The next step is the most delicate. The nature of crucible steel makes it difficult to hammer out into a bar. It's sturdy. The metal will not bend easily, yet strength is not what is demanded. A delicate touch of the hammer will tease it out. If you can't control your strength here, you will crack it."

Osric lifted his hammer. "Just tell me when to stop, Master Smith."

An hour passed. As the ingot cooled it turned cherry red, so he returned it to the fire, removing it when the metal glowed orange again. Under the old man's careful eye, Osric beat upon the ingot, gentle as he could, holding back so that he felt as though he were only tapping it. Two hours passed. Then three. Still the hammer clanged, the metal rang, and little by little the ingot elongated out. After eight hours of heat and hammering, the smith declared it a bar ready to be flattened out for folding.

Darkness fell over Windshear. No cultists trained or collected dragon blood. Only the wind kept them company, mercifully cooling.

Osric looked at the blooming stars. "Might we do better to wait until daylight?"

"The darker the better, especially for what comes next. The color of the metal will tell me if the temperature is correct. We have come to the stage of infusing your magic into the steel. This is the longest part of the process. The metal shall be heated, stretched, and folded over and over, all while you push power into the ore and use the heat and hammer to trap it within. Forge welding could take me a month to do right. For you, it should only be a matter of days."

"I am ready."

The old man smiled. "I am told that this part becomes pleasant after a time. Something about the slow warm draw from the core and feeling close to your dragon while—"

He stopped, perhaps sensing that this would not be the case for Osric.

Osric sniffed, spun the hammer around in his hand. The bond had been comfortable enough today, though Sovereign had it closed to a sliver.

"I need to access your core."

The dark void in his soul opened a fraction more. Through the soul-window, Sovereign's black chains hung heavy in the cavernous hall.

At once the pain returned, doubly so for all the time Osric had enjoyed its absence. He felt cheated, in a way. This piece of crucible steel would have made an axe that cut like no other. Clean. Natural. Constructed only of his time and toil. And now he had to sully it with Sovereign's hateful essence.

He was under no illusion that this would be torturous.

"I am ready."

As before, it began with heat and then the hammer. It was well into the night before Osric flattened out the steel bar into a longer piece of metal. Things went quicker because the smith allowed him to unleash more of his enhanced strength.

"Stop here," the smith said. "We will make the first fold."

Under instruction, Osric returned the steel to the fire and removed it once it was red hot. The old man brought over a chisel. He grunted as his swollen fingers gripped the tool.

"Can you manage?" Osric asked.

"Allow me this first one, Honored Rider." He held the chisel halfway along the red steel. "We cut down, almost all the way. *Almost* being the operative word. Do not go through."

Osric hit the chisel once. Twice.

"Stop," the smith gasped. Osric had very nearly cut through the steel as warned. The old man dropped his chisel, then clutched his crooked hand to his chest. "Cursed thing," he spat.

"Can we continue?" Osric asked.

"We continue," the smith said through a wince of discomfort. He called for Osric to sprinkle more fine sand over the top layer of steel. This was flux, he said, and would keep the sides clean to forge back together.

Osric then hammered the steel to bend and fold back onto itself. Once the fold was tight, he sprinkled more flux onto the sides of the searing metal, and the smith brushed off the black, flakey scale which gathered there.

"Into the heat again," said the smith. "We must bring it up to forge welding temperature." As Osric resumed manning the bellows, keeping the fire hot, the smith continued. "Once hot enough, you will hammer the layers into each other. This is how the magic will eventually take hold, but not before we have folded it many times."

"How many?"

"It varies. You'll know there is progress when black, brittle soot seeps from the metal. This is the natural hardness leaving the steel. By folding repeatedly, we in fact weaken the steel at first, melting out the hardness gifted by the charcoal. It will be up to you to replace it by pushing magic into the hot ore. The magic will seep into the gaps left by the old hardness, and there, under hammer and heat, it can be trapped and fused to the iron. Thus, dragon-steel is made."

Osric kept pulling on the bellows. "And how exactly do I put the magic in?"

"With your hammer."

"How?"

The smith blinked at him. "How? I do not know how it is done. I thought you were a Lord?"

"Sovereign does not allow me access to his powers often. And I detest them."

Another dark look passed over the old man's face as though

remembering the twisted situation he found himself in. He shook his head and said, a little desperate, "Run your magic to your hand and into the hammer itself. That's what my riders used to do."

Osric clenched his jaw. While in Sovereign's service, he had never tried to infuse other materials with magic. The dragon's powers pertained to the mind, which offered no obvious interaction with objects or the natural world, unlike fire, ice, or emeralds that had an affinity for rock and earth.

He would just have to learn.

All too soon, it seemed, crusty black flakes appeared on the worked metal. The hardness was beginning to leave. On the next fold, Osric would begin infusing magic. Once more he withdrew the steel from the forge. It shone bright yellow again as though he held a miniature sun at the end of his tongs. He took it to the anvil.

Bracing himself, he pulled in magic from Sovereign's core. A black link on one of the low hanging chains shook and rose as though pulled inexorably toward him. It crumbled, and the pieces flew over the bond. The motes ran like poison through him. Unused mote channels were forced open as he directed the magic down to his right hand. A dark light gathered at his palm.

Osric screwed his face in concentration as he spread the power evenly around his hand and then pushed it into the hammer itself. What magic he pushed into the tool blew back at once in a violent rejection. Just how was he supposed to push enough onto the hammer's head so that it transferred into the steel?

"Hurry now," the smith said. "You must strike before the steel cools."

Rushed, Osric overcompensated, pushing an inordinate amount of magic into the hammer. The dark light shone on the hammer head, radiating waves of fear and hatred that sent the old smith reeling. Despite the heat of the forge, the old man shivered.

"What... what is this dragon?"

"Our doom and our salvation."

Osric struck the steel. Black sparks flew where the hammer hit.

"Easy does it," said the smith. "Allow the lightest trickle of magic to massage into the ore as you work it. Come now." He guided Osric through the welding, hammering on the bright metal, returning it to the forge, brushing away the black crust as it emerged, and hammering again until the layers became one.

He repeated this folding two more times, hammering away with minuscule amounts of mystic motes. Keeping the venom cycling through his channels became excruciating. Still, he kept going until he thought he had a rhythm. With confidence he pushed more magic onto the hammer on the sixth fold, brought the hammer down and—

A crack like a ram at the gates rent the air. Sparks erupted from the metal, yellow, red, and black. A chunk of the working steel fell to the ground.

"No..." Osric groaned.

"Ah," said the smith. "That can happen, Honored Rider. As I forewarned."

Osric took a moment to lament the failure. His shoulders slumped and he hung his head, allowing the shame and frustration to pass. Once it did, he rallied and held up the piece of steel still in his tongs.

"Can it be salvaged?"

The smith shook his head and rubbed at his bleary eyes. "I'm afraid not. The metal has warped."

"What did I do wrong?"

"Could have been several things. Either too much magic was forced in at once or too little, or indeed the heat may have dropped too low for the power to fuse properly with the iron."

Osric disposed of the now useless lump of ore and searched for another clay pot.

"Then I begin again."

"Right now?"

Osric rounded on him, frowning and flaring his nostrils.

The old man stepped back. "As you will, Honored Rider. You know the process thus far. But if I may seek your leave? I sleep less with each passing year, but I must rest eventually."

"You know how long it will take me," Osric said, setting a new crucible down and reaching for the iron. "Just ensure you return when the folding begins."

The old smith bowed, picked up a lantern, and left the open workshop.

For Osric, the night had just begun.

TWENTY-ONE

Uncertainty is Certain

After a long journey east, Rake at last declared the Grim Gorge to be in sight. He pointed to the northeast, where a series of black mountains rose sheer and sharp. Another day of traveling and they came to the mouth of the gorge. The jagged valley stretched to the north as though scratched onto the landscape, its river a razor-thin line of reflected white light, a single ray of hope in an ominous land.

They pressed on. Despite its name, the Grim Gorge was not as terrible as it sounded. The mountains were bleak, but there was plenty of life on the valley floor and hillsides. A wildness lay about the place, untouched and unaltered by human activity. Great numbers of sheep kept the grass trimmed. Holt assumed they were the Mystic Flight's own flocks. He kept glancing up, ready to see a nest on a rocky outcrop or a wedge of mystics in flight, yet the dragons were nowhere to be seen.

"My flight keeps hidden," Rake said. "None are better at creating illusions or bewildering the senses."

"So they are around us right now?" Holt asked. He twisted this way and that as though he might catch a mystic off its guard.

"Some could be," Rake said.

Holt crested out with his magic. "I can't feel cores out there. Can you Ash?"

"I sense no other cores."

"Are they veiling their cores like you, Rake?" Holt asked.

"Not like I am."

"Could you teach Ash how to veil his core?" Holt asked.

"No," Rake said, clearly enjoying himself.

"Why not?"

"Because I said so, and because it can't be done. The most wonderful thing about it is, I'm the only one who can do it."

"That's not true," Holt said. "These other mystics can. You just said so. And Osric could too. We couldn't sense any magic on him until it all came out in the throne room."

Rake mused over this. "What you sense in riders is really a feeling of their dragon's core through their bond. Put enough distance between you and Ash, I wouldn't be able to sense his power through you. If Sovereign and Osric were far enough apart, then that would have effectively hidden Sovereign's core."

"But in the throne room, Osric – or it might have been Sovereign possessing Osric – did use magic," Holt protested. "He froze us all in place just by commanding us. There was this voice in my head. If they were so far apart that we couldn't sense Sovereign's core, how could they also be close enough to pass magic across the bond?"

"Sovereign must have been in Feorlen," Ash put in.

"He wasn't in Feorlen," Rake said. "Of that much I am certain. But you have blundered into a pertinent question. How could Osric and Sovereign share magic over such a vast distance? Aberanth, do you have any thoughts?"

"There isn't a lot of data to work on," Aberanth said. *"Distance will nullify magic passing across a bond, as heat dissipates over time or space. We don't know if there is any true limit based on the power behind the magic being transferred, simply that it would require a strength of magic of incalculable magnitudes to cross the distances suggested. Thus, I can only consider three theories at present. One, Sovereign is as powerful as an Elder or perhaps more so and*

can brute force the issue. Second, Sovereign has a technique we are unaware of.
Third, their bond is somehow different and allows it."

"A real puzzle, to be sure," Rake said. "One I'm sure we'll enjoy
gnawing on. But as for your question, Holt, I'm afraid I cannot teach
Ash to veil his core. However, our next teammate is one of the finest
illusionists I know. With him around, it will be the next best thing."

Holt nodded, disappointed, but he supposed if riders could veil
themselves or their dragons, the Order would know of such techniques. Not even Silas or Clesh had been able to do that. If this friend
of Rake's was capable of it, even briefly, they would be invaluable,
given they intended to attack a fortress defended by rogue dragons,
riders, and who knew what else. Perhaps even create enough distraction and confusion to allow Rake his one chance at Sovereign? Holt
could see how this team of Rake's was coming together, although he
did not understand what part he and Ash would play in it.

Rake suddenly threw up a clenched fist to call their party to a halt.
"We might be in luck."

Holt liked the sound of that for a change. "How come?"

"Because unless my senses are mistaken, and they never are, the
Mystic Elder is heading our way."

Holt's stomach did a backflip. He ran forward to join Rake so fast
he almost fell over. "The Mystic Elder? She's close? Wha—"

"Try not to wet yourself, Master Cook," Rake said. "And try to set
your expectations in check. This isn't a good sign."

"What? Are you joking? You said you 'had to know how to look'
for the mystics. You made it seem difficult."

"Yes, this is turning out to be most convenient," Rake said, though
he sounded as flat as Holt was excited.

Ash growled happily and bounded up close to Rake as though
intending to charge into the gorge.

"Settle, Ash," Rake said. "I did say she was coming to us."

"I can smell a deer." He nosed eagerly at the air, then paced away
from the group, moving this way and that on the trail of the animal.
"Can we hunt it down?"

"*Yes, most excellent,*" Aberanth said, delighted. "*We can expand our research.*"

"This hardly seems the moment," Rake said.

Ash yowled and licked his lips. "*Why, Master Rake?*"

"Because I said so, that's why."

Ash clawed at the ground.

Holt reached out to him. "*I'm sure he's got good reasons. He'll let you go as soon as he can.*"

Aberanth sniffed too. "*All I can smell is sheep dung covering any nice mushrooms.*" He padded over to Ash and took out one of his bark notes. "*Ash, at what range does your sense of smell operate?*"

Ash turned around and looked from Aberanth to Holt. "*He is loony sometimes,*" Ash said privately.

"You can't expect him to know the exact distance," Holt said. "I couldn't tell you how far I can smell."

"*You could not tell me how far away a vulture can sniff a carcass, but I can tell you that. One mile. More depending on the wind.*"

"Ash can smell that far?"

Aberanth groaned. "*That's what I'd like to find out. There's no wind today, if you hadn't noticed, meaning Ash must be picking this up with little help. Dragons don't have an acute sense of smell by nature. We're predators of the skies. Like the hawk, our eyes are attuned to spot prey on the ground. We're not made to smell or hear animals roaming far below. That Ash can smell and hear at these distances indicates how strongly his senses have compensated for his blindness. A little magic goes a long way in these things too. If we could test this, I'd be interested in gaining any insight.*"

"*So long as I can hunt that deer,*" Ash said irritably. His frustration at having to stay put while that juicy deer roamed nearby crossed the bond. Holt's own mouth watered because of it.

"I'm a good judge of distance, in my magical senses," Rake said, without turning from his hard stare at the gorge. "When Ash goes off to hunt it, I'll see how far he travels. That should give you a rough idea. Now, will you all keep quiet while I concentrate."

Ash slumped to the earth, moaning as though wounded. His tail flicked sadly across the ground.

"Don't worry, Ash," Holt said. "We'll get it later and then you can have venison as a celebration dinner."

"I told you not to get your hopes up," Rake said. He gave Holt a pained look, the sort a parent might give a young child who asks why people die. "My Elder is only ever certain that she is uncertain, and thus you can be certain she will do nothing."

Holt raised an eyebrow. "For someone sure enough to want to fight Sovereign, you can be so pessimistic. The Life Elder must have thought there was a chance. Why else would he have sent Ash and me on our quest?"

"I cannot account for what passed through the Life Elder's mind," Rake said. "All I know is that few things worth having in this world come easily."

Dragons came into view far up the gorge, making their way toward them. Holt crested out to the furthest reaches of his magical senses, straining to get a glimpse of the Elder's power.

When she entered his range, he did a double-take. That couldn't be it? Not that core? When the Life Elder had arrived at Sidastra, his power had been painful to look upon, like staring directly at the sun. The Mystic Elder was strong without a doubt. Magnitudes beyond the strength of Clesh and the West Warden, but not as much as Holt had expected.

Ash padded up beside him. *"Maybe she is hiding her power, like Master Rake does."*

"Maybe," Holt said over their bond.

Mystics could come in almost any color, or at least, any of the five primary types. It was why Holt had assumed at first that Ash would either be a storm dragon or a mystic. Of the dragons now approaching, one was pink, another a purple so dark it seemed navy, and one teal. The largest of them was yellow, and Holt recognized the color of the Mystic Elder from the ancient memories the Life Elder had unlocked in Ash's blood.

Rake dropped to one knee. Holt followed suit. Ash and Aberanth both lowered their necks to the ground.

The Elder's companions fanned out, one landing on each side of the group. The Elder herself landed before them, touching down so softly she might have been weightless. Her every movement seemed light and floaty, as though her wings were made of feathers and her limbs made of cloud. Nor did she dwarf the other drakes as the Life Elder dwarfed his own kin. Indeed, her physical presence did not strike immediate awe into Holt. Her most remarkable feature was how her bright violet eyes clashed against the wheat-field yellow of her scales.

"Holt Cook, and Ash, Son of Night, I foresaw this meeting in my dreams." The Elder's voice had a disembodied quality to it, as though Holt were dreaming himself.

"You—you know of us already, Honored Elder?"

Predictably, before he could say any more, the other mystics started snarling and advancing toward Ash.

Without hesitation, Rake rose and leveled his polearm at the closest mystic.

"Yes, yes," he growled. "The white one is blind. My soul is cursed. And the emerald is stunted. Vile abominations one and all." He spun slow and deliberate, showing each mystic the tip of his orange blade.

Holt scrambled upright but did not draw Brode's sword, sure that the Elder would not let it come to bloodshed.

"Such fury, Rake," the Elder said.

"Always such a warm welcome, Elder," Rake said. "Call them off or you'll find yourself short three drakes."

She issued a silent command and the three mystics backed off.

Holt felt a little tension leave him. A part of him hoped to be past this prejudice, but it would follow them wherever they traveled. Until their power was such that no one would question them.

"Honored Elder," Ash said, *"the Life Elder gave me his blessing and bid I fly free amongst his kin. I beg you to offer me the same courtesy you would to any other dragon."*

"It has been countless cycles of the world since we had dealings with our cousins of the earth, of fire, of ice, and of storm. Too long. And yet short in the scheme of all things that are, that were, and that will be. It is not for me to decide

your fate, Ash, Son of Night, not while the songs are still being written. I grant you safe passage so long as you bring no ill upon my flight."

The other mystics ceased their snarling and backed off. Holt sighed in relief, and he thought he saw Aberanth relax as well. Rake smirked, twirled his polearm in one hand, then planted the butt of it in the ground. He winked at Holt, then nodded, urging him on.

Holt stepped forward before getting to one knee again. It was not merely a gesture. Before such a being, it was hard to feel anything other than humbled.

"I know why you have come, Holt Cook. My brother's guilt trails behind you like a shadow."

"Then will you join him and help undo the scourge?"

Holt gazed up into the Elder's eyes. Where her physical form lacked presence, what piece of her mind and soul he could glean from those eyes spoke of an endless depth. Ancient layers glinted upon ancient layers, indecipherable, mysterious, present, focused and yet eons away from the here and now. For a moment he feared he might step into that endless violet sea and drown.

Rather than answer him, Holt felt her presence drift over his soul bond with Ash.

Her eyes widened and glowed.

"Will you help us, Honored Elder?" Ash asked.

"The songs of fate sing in all voices. Songs of grief, of joy, of triumph and despair. No song sings louder than the others."

"I'm afraid I do not understand," Holt said.

"My Elder has one talon in the here and now and one in all the things that could be," Rake said.

"You can see glimpses of the future, Honored Elder? Can you see a future where Sovereign and the scourge are defeated?"

"No song sings louder than the others."

Ash lifted his neck from the ground. *"That's not an answer."*

Had the frustration of not hunting the deer got to him that badly? The Elder's accompanying mystics snapped their teeth at him. Yet Ash did not back down. The Elder turned her violet eyes onto him, and within seconds Ash had cowered and stepped back.

Holt rushed to his side. "Ash? Ash, what's wrong?"

He shook his head and whimpered.

"Stop it," Holt said. "Leave him alone."

The Elder drew her snout back and Ash recovered.

"*You were... you were dead on the ground,*" Ash said. "*Your heart was still. Your smell had gone to rot. Then I heard you call my name, but not like you do now. You were cruel. You hurt me. I felt us in Sovereign's presence and I... I bowed to him. And you hated me.*"

Holt gulped. "None of that is real, Ash. We're here, together. I'd never hurt you. And I know you'd never give in to Sovereign."

"*No song sings louder than the others,*" the Elder repeated.

"If you're trying to say that all those things you showed Ash are possible, then you're wrong," Holt said. He knew it in his bones. None of those things would come to pass.

The Mystic Elder turned her gaze onto Holt. The violet burned bright, and it seemed as though the infinite layers of her eyes pulled apart and pierced him. A thrum of power struck his midriff, knocking the wind from him. He felt submerged and dragged through clouded water, and then the world turned black and white.

Shadows were cast upon the ground with no regard for the sun. One shadow rose into a skinny boy holding a scrubbing brush. Beside that boy emerged a thin-framed adult wearing a cook's apron and a beard – some version of his life that might have been.

Someone grabbed him by the shoulder. Holt whirled, expecting to find Rake, but he cried out in shock. He saw himself. His eyes were missing. Blood encrusted the empty sockets and his teeth were bared in a snarl. Another Holt shoved the eyeless version aside, this one taller somehow, his teeth whiter, his hair thick and radiant. That version collapsed into the fetal position. Flesh wasted away from its bones, and it wept and shrieked for it to end.

A chill ran through the real Holt. The monochrome world went silent.

Ash lay prone before him. His wings were torn and broken beyond hope of healing. Holt's chest burned. He sought to anchor himself out of this nightmare and reached for his dragon bond, but he struggled to grasp it, just like when Ash had been a week old.

"*Boy!*" Ash called to him.

Holt ran, falling to his knees to take the dragon's head in a bear-like hug.

"*Boy,*" Ash said, as light and weak as when he had been a hatchling. Now closer, he saw the truth. The blight. Ash's scales were blackening, ooze leaked from his talons and mouth. A sweet, powerful smell of rot rose from him. "*Help me, Holt. Help me the way Brode helped Erdra.*"

A sword entered Holt's hands.

"No!" Holt's scream rang in his mind.

Then the real Ash appeared. He was whole and well, and his white scales gleamed with health.

"*Place an arm around me,*" Ash said. Holt wrapped an arm around Ash's snout, and, though he shook from the experience, he got to his feet.

Rake appeared next, as did Aberanth. Both were luminous patches of color compared to the monochrome world around them.

"A touch enthusiastic, Honored Elder?" Rake said, his distaste clear.

Color, smell, and sound returned to Holt. The Elder and her mystics appeared as if out of thin air. Holt's head spun, and he avoided meeting the Elder's eyes.

Sniffing, he asked, "Why did you show me those things?"

"*Any of those ends may yet come to pass.*"

Holt wanted to tell her no, but it had all felt too real. Something about the visions was as true as the here and now. Each one of those terrible outcomes hung like blades over his neck.

"Why won't you do something to stop them?" Holt had not been angry before, but he was now. "The Life Elder doesn't know how things will end, but he can feel the world suffering, and he knows there will only be *one end* unless – we – try." He spat the final words.

"*I misinterpreted the notes before. I thought I could act to bring the order and peace we so desired. I was wrong, Holt Cook.*"

"So... you'll do nothing?"

"Sometimes that is the safest course. Only as events draw close can the true notes be heard, and by then they are already singing. Our meeting might have happened in countless ways. These I saw. How it has unfolded only became clear as you approached the gorge this morning. Events are not easy to follow like rivers. Had I pursued another version of our meeting, I might have forced a worse end for us all. Even the smallest stone may start an avalanche, as your own actions show."

Holt plowed on with his case. He had to make it.

"The dragon who controls the scourge is called Sovereign, or at least that is what his followers call him. He has the power to dominate minds. He's a mystic. One of your own. We plan to stop him. Will you help with that at least?"

She did not deign to reply.

A sense of dread filled Holt. He sank to his knees and stared at the grass.

"Is that it?" he asked Ash. *"Have we failed already?"* Ash didn't reply, but he didn't have to. Holt could feel the dragon's own shock, shame, and sense of being lost.

What sense was there in this? Why would she do nothing?

A hand gripped his shoulder again, and this time it really was Rake. He squeezed, ever so gently.

"Up you get, Holt."

Holt did and moved mechanically to Ash's side. He leaned into his dragon, hoping that would be the end of it.

"I don't care what she says, Ash. I'd never hurt you."

"I know, boy." Ash hesitated. *"What did you see?"*

The image of Ash dying of the blight flashed before him. He pushed it away. *"Nothing I'll let happen."*

Rake yawned and made a great, exaggerated stretch. He rolled his shoulders, then smiled as though the Elder had made a tired joke at a tea party.

"Now you've finished crushing the boy's spirits, you might spare the brainpower to recall some information for me. There was a rather infamous dragon who attacked humans in these lands. Folk said the dragon turned blood red from all the lives he took. It was said the mystics put him down. Is that true, or did the mystics perchance let this dragon go?"

The Elder's tail flicked.

"We let him go."

"And the name of this dragon?"

"Thrall."

Rake nodded. "Another occasion on which you misinterpreted the notes?"

"The songs of fate shall pass as they will."

"Unless a musician should play them better," Rake said with a smile. He shrugged, then bowed theatrically low. "Well, I feel there is nothing more to discuss. Or for us to discuss and for you to evade. A pleasure as always, Honored Elder, or was it? What do the songs sing of this?"

The Mystic Elder snorted and turned her full attention upon Rake. Her eyes bloomed into their thousand variants and Holt feared Rake too would succumb to terrible visions. He didn't deserve that.

He started forward. "Rake, don't—"

He cut off as Aberanth intercepted him, blocking his path.

"Settle, Holt. Rake knows what he's doing."

"But—"

Then he saw it. Amongst the grass at Rake's feet was a small glass vial. A drop of what might have been wine still lay within.

Rake must have swallowed an elixir. A Lifting elixir.

Trust Rake to make the first test against the most powerful mystic dragon in the world.

Nothing of note unfolded to the naked eye. Rake stood stock still, concentration etched upon his face as he cycled his motes. The most dramatic action of the confrontation came from the Elder.

She leaned in.

On the magical landscape, Rake for once became discernable. Though his core remained veiled, the Elder's power broke against him like waves upon rock. Rake could be 'seen' in the negative space amid the Elder's power.

Mere moments into the clash, Rake began to struggle. His confident smile faltered. His tail became rigid, then shook. Rake held his own against an Elder for over ten whole seconds. In the end, he roared in pain and dropped to one knee.

The Elder relented and pulled back from him. *"You grow in strength, soul-cursed, but not in wisdom."* She nodded to Holt and Ash. *"My brother sent this pair to demonstrate his hope for a new future. If you are capable of learning from them too, then perhaps the notes for that vision will grow louder."*

"Before you go," Rake said, suppressing pain. "Where might I ask is—"

"He watches over the northern nests."

"That's kind of him," Rake said. "Thank you for your time, Honored Elder." Despite already being on his knees, Rake bowed forward.

Holt, Ash, and Aberanth bowed as well.

"Walk in peace, Rake," the Elder said. *"I shall be watching."*

Another wave of power emanated from the Elder and an invisible veil lifted from the valley. A rush of cores entered Holt's magical senses. Mystics appeared both to the eye and to his magic. Nests sat on the mountainside where there had been only rock and tree before. The Grim Gorge erupted with roaring dragons, though whether this was a greeting or a threat, Holt could not say.

Having revealed the truth of the valley, the Mystic Elder took off without so much as a parting word of wisdom.

Holt fought not to succumb to despair. They would still go to Windshear Hold. He and Ash would still seek the other flights. They had to move on.

Resolved, he went over to Rake. "Are you okay?"

Rake groaned and waved Holt away. He sat on the grass, taking a rare breather.

"You're crazy to try to resist an Elder's power like that," Holt said.

"Did the elixir assist you?" Aberanth asked. He had one of his bark slabs out again. *"Describe how your mote channels feel. Does anything hurt?"*

As Rake and Aberanth discussed the effects of the elixir, Holt felt drawn by his dragon bond back to the deer. It was still out there on one of the hillsides of the gorge. Ash could smell it.

He drifted over to Ash, took the gear down from his back, and hopped on. They were of one mind on this.

"We're going to hunt," Holt called. "We'll catch up."

"Let's hope this deer doesn't hear any songs of what's to come," Holt said to Ash.

"If the deer wished for things to pass as they will pass, it might stand still for us."

Holt snorted. He was still too aghast at the Mystic Elder's inaction to consider her words or what he had seen more deeply. Some cathartic release was what he wanted now.

Doing nothing was not in his blood.

TWENTY-TWO

Vengeance and Spite

Osric worked. And worked. He pulled upon the bellows without rest to make his steel, he hammered with unwavering rhythm. During his first attempt, under the smith's guidance, he had made it to six folds of the steel before his inept handling of magic broke it. On his second attempt, he made it to ten.

Nothing about infusing magic into the hammer or the steel felt natural. The hard work he could do. The strict, methodical process of creating the steel, then teasing it out into a bar, all of this chimed with the soldier in him. Even in the worst times he found solace in routine, in discipline, in knowing exactly what was expected of him and how he could achieve those expectations.

Dazzling members of court had never been his forte. That had been Godric's. Being charming and witty and playful, that had been Godric. Osric was always more articulate in the training yard.

Night turned to day, and day into night. The old smith came and went, helping how he could. Yet it was all on Osric.

On his third attempt he made it to fifteen folds. The iron fused with some magic this time. He could tell by the way the metal took on some of Sovereign's color before it cracked as he hammered on the sixteenth fold.

He drank long from a jug of water and began again.

As he worked the bellows, his mind sank into a meditative state, not dissimilar from how it felt to Cleanse or Forge, though with the benefit of not being in Sovereign's presence. His own core, so to speak, drew his unconscious attention. Deeper memories bubbled up, and he recalled a time when he had not been so well versed in the training yard. A time when Godric held the upper hand even in that arena. Godric's two years' seniority made all the difference when they were five and seven.

At that age, they wrestled. Godric could have let him win on occasion, but he never did. Godric had to win. Every. Single. Time. And so Osric lost interest in playing. Godric would make him, though, or their parents would.

'Play with your brother,' his mother would say, adding 'I'm too busy,' before she slinked into dark rooms with strange men. 'Play with your brother, boy,' his father would chide, his breath reeking of drink. 'What are you, craven? Agravains are not cravens!'

And so Osric would take his defeats. Except on those rare occasions when he managed to gain the upper hand, and then he would strike back, pounding his little fists into Godric as he pounded steel in the here and now. Beating and beating until Godric wailed, but that did not stop him.

The adults would come to break them apart. They would scream at Osric, squeezing and shaking him so hard it hurt and demanding to know what the matter was with him. With him? They were the ones who stole his victory even though they never once stopped Godric.

No one ever did, he thought darkly. *Except for me in the en—no... no... that was Sovereign. All Sovereign.*

As these thoughts roiled, he found it easier to beat magic into the steel. Sovereign's powers were hateful and bitter. Perhaps they worked better when Osric salted them with his own grievances.

He reached a new milestone. Twenty folds.

At last, the heat and effort got to him. His shirt was a ruin of sweat and smoke, so he tore it off and continued bare-chested, driving old memories into that black light upon the hammer head.

Across the dragon bond, Sovereign scolded him. *"Work faster."*

Osric gritted his teeth and carried on.

Twenty-three folds.

Sovereign's incessant demands were nothing new. His whole life had been like that. No matter what he had done, it had never been quite right or enough.

When training as a young knight, he'd been told to show courtesy to women and to defend the weak. At seventeen, Osric thought they had meant it. When Godric had struck Felice with the back of his hand, Osric had lunged to her aid. He'd dismantled his brother and heir to the throne, giving Godric a broken lip and a black eye, and he might have done worse had Felice not intervened. Her look of terror and disgust remained burnt into him.

'I was defending you,' Osric said.

'I don't want your help,' she said. 'I don't want you.'

Twenty-seven folds. Thirty.

Osric roared from the pain of the magic and, on the thirty-first fold, his fifth attempt ended in failure. More failure. The smoking red steel clanged onto the stone.

Sovereign's presence returned. *"They were right about you,"* he hissed. *"Right to push you into shadowed corners. Merely the second son. The spare. Overlooked by your peers. Spurned by women who adored the elder brother instead."*

Osric tried not to respond but couldn't resist. Something about Sovereign's presence always made it hard to resist, even when the dragon did not use his powers directly.

"I never cared. I had my duties—"

"Lies," Sovereign purred. *"You have no secrets from me."*

Osric fixated on his work. He placed another crucible into the forge, began to work the bellows.

"Godric received everything you didn't. Cruel, I know. Yes, Osric. I know what it is to be neglected and abused. A cruel world for some and not others, is it not? Such injustice. He always had love he did not deserve. While yours abandoned—"

"*Enough,*" Osric said with as much venom as he could muster. "*I have only begged you once. Do not mention her.*"

"*I will honor that, worm. There is little torment I can give beyond what you do to yourself. All those things you've done, long before me. You are my perfect servant. So willing.*"

All feeling fled Osric, save his hatred. Hatred for this dragon who bound him like a hound. Hatred for his mother, his father, and, most of all, his brother.

"*Good,*" Sovereign hissed again. "*Make your weapons of it.*"

The anguish writhed visibly beneath his skin as though worms slithered along his flesh. His right arm bulged with blackened veins. His soul knew only agony. As much as it pained him, Osric soon felt how effective it was. His hammer blows now delivered a controlled stream of mystic motes. With each attempt, he got closer to his goal.

Sun, moon, day or night, nothing registered beyond the hammer and the fire and the steel.

On his seventh attempt, he reached seventy folds before the metal snapped.

"*Perhaps you fail on purpose, worm. Do you secretly enjoy being the center of my attention? For once needed and desired.*"

Osric knew what he had to do. Imparting his own pain aided the effort, so he removed the toughened leather gloves and worked with his bare hands. His skin was tough as dragonhide, but as hours dragged into days, even his Lord's skin began to chafe and crack and bleed as he hammered and hammered and *hammered*.

And Sovereign, perhaps sensing the end in sight, kept the pressure on, not letting one single good thought enter Osric's mind. Between the hammer blows he saw flashes of his worst fears and pains. The day he left Sidastra and no one waved him off. Fellow Iron Beards dead on the tundra or loyal Gray Cloaks lying pale and cold. Kali, Jorund, Brennon – so many, too many, their ashes piling all around him.

Then, the worst memory of all.

Under a searing sun at the desert's edge, taking no water for fear of moving just once and missing her crest the top of the dunes.

Esfir? He saw her face, as radiant as the day she'd left him. All the beauty of the desolate golden waste was in her, all the warmth held within her eyes. So dark they were, they could have pulled him from across the world if only he could have seen them one more time.

She wrapped the shawl around her head as she headed off onto the sands, her hand reaching back as if willing him to follow. But he knew his duty.

What a fool he'd been not to follow.

Then it fell away and Godric lay at his feet, his chest a mess of crumpled muscles and shattered bone. Blood bubbled at his mouth, and though he was dead, he spoke.

"You are mine." Godric's corpse's lips moved, but it was Sovereign's voice. *"Mine, now and always."*

With that ringing thought, Sovereign left him, pulling back over their bond. He left Osric in desolation, as the land aches after an incursion. The pressure and stress pushed Osric to breaking point. Blood already seeped from sores on his hands, and now it seeped from him in place of sweat. His body had nothing left to give.

Blood dripped from his bare chest, onto the ground, onto the anvil, and onto the bright yellow steel to smoke and burn.

Everything Osric had went into the tenth attempt.

For seven days and seven nights, he had flown to Windshear Hold. For nine days and nine nights, he had labored to rebuild Sovereign's core. For twelve days and twelve nights, he hammered steel, freeing long-caged fears, pouring himself into the metal as he did Sovereign's magic. His own hatreds became the mortar which bound magic and iron together.

And on that tenth attempt, at one hundred folds, Osric completed his task. The true dragon-steel accepted mystic motes like a riverbed takes water.

He stood breathless as he had never been before. Starved as never before. Exhausted, deep, deep in his bones like never before. It was more than physical. His soul's strength hung by a thread. His very being had been beaten as much as the metal.

The old smith was there to witness the end of it. He approached cautiously, as though Osric were some feral dog.

"Never in all my years did I see such effort," said the smith. "There now. We must shape it into the axes you desire. After all else you have done, it will be simple."

Osric followed the smith's instructions. With so much of himself inside the metal, he found it easier to mold to his will, as though he spoke and the steel listened.

He had them now. Two perfect axes in the Skarl fashion, made for hacking through the wretched world that deserved nothing less.

"Now to temper the metal," said the smith. "I shall see about finding water."

"No," Osric said, his voice hoarse. "Not water."

He reached over the dragon bond. *"Come to me."*

Sovereign growled but said nothing.

"We loathe each other, but there is a grudging respect too. Is there not?"

Still Sovereign remained silent.

"Into this steel I have poured myself, my sweat, my blood, and your magic. Come and I shall complete this weapon in a way no rider ever could."

Sovereign would come. The challenge, the grandeur, the torture Osric had suffered to achieve it. Sovereign could recognize a triumph.

Sure enough, he felt the dragon take flight. Soon after, his great wings beat over Windshear Hold, and he landed by the workshop. The old smith whimpered and backed away at the sight of him, buffeted by the dragon's aura.

Osric wasted no words. He brought a quench tank over to Sovereign. For once, he and the dragon were of one mind. Using a single long talon, Sovereign cut a clean line across his lower chest. Dark blood welled then fell from the wound, gathering in the tank.

After heating the axe heads one final time upon the coals, Osric looked to the smith. The old man nodded. Osric raised the red-hot axes and plunged them into Sovereign's blood. Blood boiled, spit, and hissed as the metal cooled. When he removed them and the blood dripped from their beards, he felt a sense of completion hit him.

He had forged the deadliest axes that had ever been or would ever exist.

Sovereign plucked a single scale from his body and let it fall to the ground.

"Only the scale of the dragon whose power infused the metal can polish and sharpen the steel," the smith explained.

Osric met Sovereign's burning gaze. The dragon had done this before. Osric had suspected, but whatever Sovereign had once been, it mattered little. As with Osric, there was no going back.

The scale was coarse as rock. Osric polished and sharpened the axes until the dragon-steel gleamed the same dark red as the blood which had quenched it. Layers of waving lines patterned their surfaces like the age rings of trees, as gray as his old cloak. When he pushed mystic motes into the weapons, the axe heads shone from pulsing black light. He did not know what would happen to anyone struck by this infused power who did not die from the blow. It would surely be worse than death.

He tightened his grip on the handles. Raising his left axe by an inch, he dubbed it Vengeance, and the other he named Spite.

"Are you pleased, Osric?"

Osric looked into Sovereign's eyes and spoke slow.

"The assignment is complete."

"There is one final task you must perform."

Sovereign's gaze shifted toward the blacksmith.

"You know the process now?"

"I do," Osric said. He drew in a single, deep breath. Chill wind air cooled his lungs. Then he turned, and in the turn closed the gap between him and the old smith. With his right hand he brought Spite across in a single clean stroke, removing the blacksmith's head from his shoulders. It happened so fast the human would not have registered it.

"I am sorry, Emrik Smith."

He wished he had never learned the man's name.

Blood smoked from the old man's corpse and steamed upon the blade of his axe.

Spite spoke to him. It wanted more.

TWENTY-THREE

The Illusionist

The Mystic Flight left the party alone as they traveled north through the Grim Gorge. With a belly full of venison each night, Ash pulled in a healthy volume of lunar motes to his core, and Rake allowed Holt to take advantage of this by focusing on Forging. It was an ideal time while the moon was waxing.

The extra meditation did Holt good. The focus required for Forging hours on end left no room to brood over the Mystic Elder's words and visions. Rake seemed happy to forget about the encounter as well, helping Aberanth and Ash to test the range of Ash's senses of smell and hearing. Together they had confirmed that Ash could pick up on strong smells over one mile away, and almost two depending on the wind. Aberanth was also delighted to note all Ash relayed about hearing heartbeats and other bodily functions no one else could register.

After two days, they had traversed the entire gorge. The valley ended abruptly where the black mountains on either side joined each other. At this most northern point, a final collection of mystic nests sat under sheltered ridges, but a few were also built into caves at ground level. Mystics in their nests watched the group approach with wary expressions.

Rake planted his polearm into the ground and opened his arms wide.

"Eidolan?" he called.

A purple dragon emerged tentatively from a cave at ground level. Holt had never seen a dragon that looked old – the Elders were ancient, after all, and showed no sign of age – yet this one did. Where humans developed gray hair and wrinkles, this dragon's scales lacked any shine or luster, their colors faded as though scrubbed too hard in a wash. The ridges along his back and tail were yellowed like stained teeth and blunted as though smoothed by sandpaper. His wings stretched like old leather, his neck stooped, and his green eyes did not contrast as fiercely with his lavender body as the eyes of other mystics did.

"Why must you disturb an old dragon's rest?" Eidolan asked.

"I'd thought to coax you out on one last adventure," Rake said.

Eidolan croaked a laugh. *"Tempting though you make it sound, Rake, I'll pass. I have eggs to watch over. That is my charge now."*

The old dragon turned and disappeared into his cave without another word.

Rake hefted his polearm onto one shoulder. "Come on," he said, and he stalked after the dragon into his nest. Holt followed.

The cave was deeper and larger than it appeared from the outside. Scant light penetrated to the back wall, leaving Holt squinting as his eyes adjusted. Yet what he saw made him blink to check that his eyes were working.

Paintings, some covered, some not. Other artwork too including busts, small statues, ornately patterned vases, and exquisitely crafted jewelry. There were dragon eggs too, of course, four of them nestled in a bed of leaves, moss, and twigs opposite the dragon's art collection.

Eidolan moved to place his body defensively over the eggs and narrowed his eyes. *"I don't recall inviting you in."*

Rake ignored him and drifted over to the artwork. "Looking a bit drab these days, Eidolan."

Holt thought the opposite. The collection seemed spotless to him, without a hint of dust or grime on any of it. How the dragon managed to maintain it he had no idea.

"Your skill in flattery is non-existent as ever," Eidolan said. *"Unless you've brought me something beautiful, I want you to leave."*

"No gift this time, I'm afraid," Rake said. With one hand he picked up a large vase that would have taken Holt both hands to lift. Dancing bone-white naked figures were carved in relief against an inky background. "Lovely piece, this," Rake intoned. "Is it Alduneian?"

"It's only one of the finest examples of cameo glass from the Late Republic," Eidolan said as though he found the question insulting. *"Please, put it down."*

"Not going to ask me to explain myself?"

"No," Eidolan said resolutely. *"Let me be. Let me rest."*

"Please, Eidolan," Holt said. "Just hear Master Rake out. It's important."

"And who is this?" Eidolan's tired eyes trained laboriously on Holt. *"An Ascendant outside of the Order and wandering with the half-dragon. Master Rake, is it? You'll regret leaving Falcaer, boy."*

"I never joined the Order."

"Did you not?" Eidolan said, and Holt could tell that, despite himself, the old mystic was intrigued. He growled and shook his head. *"You'll regret it anyway."*

He looked back to Rake with narrowed eyes. Something passed privately between them before Rake spoke again with a strained attempt to be jovial.

"Come on, Eidolan, old friend, I need your help."

"The answer is no."

Not missing a beat, Rake said, somewhat harshly, "Fine, then tell me what you recall about a dragon named Thrall."

Holt's attention sharpened. Rake had got that name from the Mystic Elder, but he hadn't mentioned it since.

"Get out," Eidolan growled. Then he spread his wings as best he could inside and advanced at Rake and Holt, pushing them back toward the mouth of the cave.

"Do you know what I recall?" Rake said as he backstepped. "It's something from my human days. A lot has been clouded by time, but I remember every noble house in the east shivering in fear after the entire Estermont family, household, and estate were found ripped to pieces. As if a wild animal had torn at them."

Eidolan bared his teeth and drove them outside.

"I was just a lad at the time," Rake continued, as though nothing were amiss, "but the reason I remember it is because riders turned up in our lands on the trail of this mad dragon."

Having ejected them from his cave, Eidolan turned his back on them.

Rake soldiered on. "Folk who swore they saw the dragon said his scales turned crimson from all the blood. Does this spark any memories?"

Eidolan looked back over his shoulder. *"That was a long time ago. That business is over."*

"A long time? What is three hundred years to a dragon of seven hundred?"

"I'm sorry that I can't help you, Rake. But I am old and done."

"That's a shame," Rake said. He lunged forward as though to grab Eidolan by his tail, but Rake's hands passed right through the dragon as if he were made of air. Eidolan's body rippled, then the phantom image faded.

"I hate it when you do that," Rake called into the cave. "If I'm right, you'll help kill him."

No answer.

"Dragons," Rake cursed. "Proud to a fault, you are. You hear that? All of you!"

"Rake," Holt pleaded. "Stop it. We don't need a whole Wild Flight angry with us."

"Oh, they won't do anything," Rake said. "You heard their Elder. Which is precisely the problem," he called out for all the occupants of the nests to hear.

He received a series of roars in answer this time.

Ash bristled and roared back.

"A slight overreaction," Aberanth said sniffily.

"What did they say?" Holt asked.

"It's difficult to put into words," Aberanth said. *"More the feeling of it."*

"The feeling is mutual," Rake grumbled. "Wait here."

Without another word, he strode back inside the cave. There was much roaring, this time from Eidolan, but Holt remained outside as instructed.

Aberanth and Ash lounged not far away on the grass under the high sun. Forging would not be productive. It would be many hours yet until the moon arrived. The days were growing longer as they headed toward midsummer. He supposed he should Cleanse, but he would rather continue his investigations with Aberanth.

"If we have some time, shall we experiment further?"

"You read my mind," Aberanth said.

"Excellent," Ash said, hurrying over so that Holt could take their venison supply off his back. The three of them set to work. Well, Holt set up a cooking fire and Aberanth pondered aloud while Ash simply sat licking his lips.

Since they had acquired more venison, and despite eating the exact same meal across multiple tests, they had been unable to recreate Holt's visible mote channels.

"We've tried roasting the meat, boiling the meat, cooking it in your pan and every which way we can with what we have," Aberanth said. *"We must consider that there is another element to the process we're missing. Or something you might have overlooked from that first night."*

The dragon had an apothecary's heart through and through. Holt was grateful that Aberanth believed him because he was beginning to have doubts that they'd figure it out.

"Maybe the butter was important?" Holt said.

"Hmmph," Aberanth grumped. *"It's possible, but I don't think so. In my elixir work, I discovered one core ingredient and flavor profile that aided each cycling technique. Ginger for Floating. Sinking requires vinegar. Lifting is linked to wine, red wine in particular."*

Holt noted that with interest. Rake sought ways to improve his Lifting technique to combat Sovereign's mind domination. And Holt had promised to make Rake a stew one evening. Wine should be perfect in a lamb stew for a mystic dragon to push his Lifting a little further. If only he could conjure up some wine out in the wilds.

"And salt is for Grounding," Holt said. They had been using salt on each piece cooked already as an easy test, but so far that hadn't helped. What had been different about the meat he had cooked that night?

"Salt..."

Something clicked.

"Ash, can you remember if I used one of the preserved chunks of meat to cook with?" He wished he had made more careful notes.

Ash licked his lips as if this helped him to recall the meal in question. *"It was saltier than the fresh stuff but not so strong as the meat you rubbed salt all over. I remember it being a thinner steak than the others and much drier."*

"Drier?" Aberanth asked, his interest piqued.

"I must have cut that slice thinner than the others. The meat had started to go dark, but it wasn't rotting. Ash checked."

"I think this might prove to be our next line of enquiry," Aberanth said. *"Here is my new hypothesis. Dried meat has less water in it, thus intensifying its magical properties. Along with the saltiness, it's possible you made a meaty equivalent of my Grounding elixir."*

"Your elixirs don't have meat in them, do they?" Holt asked.

"Of course they don't," Aberanth said. *"Truth be told, I never thought to explore that line as I was attempting to make something universal. Perhaps there would be ways to enhance the effects for each magic type. Hmmph..."*

He became lost in thought for a moment, perhaps uncomfortable at the thought of handling meat.

Not wishing to waste any time, Holt took out one of their new venison steaks and began to cut it into thin strips before he realized their main problem.

"Turning this into jerky is easy enough," he said to Ash. "But it takes days to air dry. I'm not sure we'll be in one place for that long."

"Is 'jerky' tasty?"

Holt shrugged. "Sure." In truth, it wasn't his favorite. He was distrustful of any food that felt like it took longer to chew than to create.

Maybe I could skewer some pieces and carry them with us when we leave.

Aberanth emerged from his reverie and came over to inspect Holt's work. *"It's good you know what you're doing."*

"I am a Cook," he said as he sliced the venison. Of the ingredients Aberanth had listed – wine, salt, ginger, and vinegar – Holt only had access to salt. He rubbed some coarse flakes onto each strip of meat, then skewered them one by one. "Ideally we would leave them hanging over a wooden rack for a few days."

"This will serve as a test," Aberanth said. *"I think the key will be in removing as much of the water as we can."*

"Don't you use water in your elixirs?"

Aberanth shook his head. *"The solution is primarily a weak spirit, with a few extras and the main ingredient for the desired technique. The ratios must be exact."*

"Downing vials of liquid for a boost," Holt mused. "Reminds me of the Wyrm Cloaks and their vials of blood."

Aberanth shifted from side to side. *"That's where I got the initial idea. The solution isn't so different from their own – minus the blood, of course."*

Holt imagined what it would be like drinking one of those vials of dragon blood. A bad taste fell upon his tongue just thinking about it. He shivered and shook the feeling off.

Rake at last emerged from Eidolan's cave, looking irritable.

"What's all of this?" the half-dragon asked, casting a hand over the new experiment.

"We're making 'jerky', Master Rake." Ash seemed to enjoy the new word.

For once, Rake didn't have any clever remarks. He stalked past the group until he found the closest tree and slumped against it, muttering all the while.

Holt made to go after him, but Aberanth's growl made him reconsider.

"Leave him, Holt. Come, we could do with some food." He sniffed around, no doubt trying to pick up the scent of nearby mushrooms.

"There's a clump to the west," Ash said. *"Underneath some mossy rocks, I think."*

"I'm sure that nose of yours is right," Aberanth said. He padded off in search of his dinner.

Holt roasted venison for Ash. As the meat spat over the fire, he ground up sprigs of rosemary between two stones and sprinkled them on top. Aberanth returned from his own hunt and unfurled one of his leaves to reveal a collection of wild mushrooms. Some were fat and round, others long and spindly with yellow gills. The dragon ate one raw before Holt had a chance to say anything.

"How about I cook those for you this time?"

Aberanth growled low as though he were unsure. He had not let Holt touch his mushrooms before.

"I don't want any meat with it."

"Don't worry," Holt said. "You can do a lot with mushrooms on their own. Wish I had some butter for them though. And garlic."

Holt readied his pan over the fire and added the mushrooms when it was hot. A lack of butter wasn't the end of the world. Dry frying mushrooms could often be the best thing for them. And with a pinch of rosemary and salt? Magic all on its own. He served them up to Aberanth, who sniffed them, then ate heartily.

"This is good, Holt. Thank you."

"Removing the water without burning them is half the battle," Holt said. "A bit like making your elixirs. We're intensifying everything."

By that point, Ash's meat was ready, and Holt served it. Pleased to have two happy diners, Holt attended to his own meal. He allowed himself a portion of the venison and cooked it up with mushrooms he had set aside from Aberanth's haul. Simple but effective, and most importantly hot.

He enjoyed the afterglow of a full stomach and the soothing presence of the sun before looking around for Rake. In a rare display of despondence, the orange half-dragon still sat slumped against the same tree.

Holt got up and went to speak with him.

"Are you hungry?" he asked. "I know you said you don't eat much, but—"

"I'm fine," Rake said.

"There are plenty of sheep in the valley," Holt said. "The Elder won't mind you taking one, will she? You are still a mystic, after all. One of her own."

"I'm fine, Holt," Rake said. He wasn't terse or angry, just quiet and sure.

"I take it your friend won't join us?"

Rake gave him a withering look. Holt could translate it by now. 'Don't ask such obvious questions.'

"Can we go on without him?"

"His powers would be invaluable in getting a small team into Windshear or causing distractions," Rake said. "That and he used to live in Windshear back when it was rider headquarters."

"Eidolan was in the Order?"

"Many, many centuries ago," Rake said. "His knowledge of the fortress is second to none. I'd hoped that..." Rake began, but then he growled and waved the notion away.

"You thought he might wish to make amends for... something?"

"Something like that."

"Something to do with this Thrall you spoke of?"

Rake stared at his taloned toes.

"Sovereign is really this dragon, Thrall, isn't he?"

Without looking up, Rake said, "I think so. When you mentioned the name Sovereign, it stuck in my mind that I had heard the name before, or I thought I had. There have been rumors of a dragon who could bend the will of others to his own. Always some moniker accompanied the tales. The Wise One, The Master, The Savior, these names and more have reached me before. Always the circumstances macabre. Always death or madness involved."

Rake met Holt's eyes again. "I know you'll keep asking, so I'll tell you this. You're right. Eidolan had a part to play in the story of Thrall. I don't know the full extent of it."

"Do you think he knows something about Sovereign? Like a weakness?"

"I doubt it. I think he would tell me of that. Yet having the full story of one's enemy never hurts. Whatever part Eidolan had to play, it is his story to tell. I won't tell you gossip, which is all I have."

Holt sat on the grass with Rake. "Not wishing to act seems to be the way of mystics. I found it hard to believe that your Elder is content to do nothing."

"I noticed."

"She has plenty to make amends for. The Life Elder told us the scourge was her idea."

Rake frowned and nodded. "That explains it."

"Explains it?"

"She interfered with the songs of fate before and made a disastrous mess of things. Why should she risk doing so again?"

"But this would be trying to put things right."

"That's what the Elders thought they were doing when they made the scourge in the first place."

Holt snorted. "Right for them."

"Find me a group of humans or dragons that does not put their own needs above all else and I'll cut off my tail."

Holt sighed, then sought around for an answer. "Maybe she's afraid? Her core was not as strong as the Life Elder's."

"Yes, I noticed," Rake said. "Though her power has been diminishing for years."

"Why would that be?"

"What do mystic dragons thrive on?"

"Thoughts?" Holt said. He had never fully understood the mystics at the Crag.

"Thoughts, feelings, minds at work," Rake said. "This is only my theory, but I suspect the entire Mystic Flight has grown weak. They need thoughts to thrive, but they have been isolated for so long. Without exposure to others, their own thinking has stagnated. Thoughts from their sheep or other creatures do not compare to dragons or even humans. So, yes, my Elder may well be afraid to confront Sovereign for fear of being defeated and overthrown. But I don't think that's the whole story."

"She should know Sovereign's actions will lead to a fight in the end."

"Will they?" Rake asked. "He stated a desire to wipe out humanity, not dragons. Perhaps he will leave the Wild Flights alone."

"Perhaps," Holt admitted, "though if your neighbor's house catches fire, you help them put it out or else risk it spreading to your own."

"For a fifteen-year-old child, you're sometimes wiser than your years, Holt Cook."

Holt folded his arms. "I'm sixteen."

Rake's signature smile tugged at the corner of his lips again. "They called you a chaos bringer back home, did they not?"

"Yes," Holt said, unsure what this had to do with their current predicament.

"And it makes little sense, doesn't it? You saved them. Your actions helped them. And then they punished you anyway. Most people, most dragons for that matter, would find that so unfair they'd be angry."

"I was angry," Holt said. "And I am angry with your Elder."

"I am too," said Rake. He shifted to sit upright. "The Elders seem above everyone and everything, but they're just living, breathing beings like you and me. And I've found that all beings – whether dragon or human – find it impossible to get out of their own way. They have a set of beliefs about the world, about the people or dragons in it, about how things are and how they should be, and anything that counters those beliefs, whether it's true or whether for good, doesn't matter – they will resist it with every fiber of their being. Even to their own detriment. To change would be worse. To surrender one's beliefs is to surrender much more."

Rake clenched his fists.

"You have to surrender your entire self in that case. You must start from scratch and rebuild yourself and how you view the world. That's so *hard* to do. To voluntarily reduce oneself to ashes and then rise again. It's so hard that most choose to stand in the flames and burn."

Rake pointed his thumb over his shoulder, back toward their camp.

"You, me, Aberanth, and Ash – we're dangerous to them. We are chaos."

Holt's mouth turned rather dry. "When you put it like that, it begs the question, what's the point in trying to change things at all?"

Rake leaned forward, his cheerful expression replaced by grave wisdom. "That, my young friend, is the only thing more dangerous. To give in. An easy thing to do. In fact, it's the easiest thing of all. So, sure, give up all hope in the face of adversity. Yet know that if you surrender yourself to that dark void, you will lose your empathy and disconnect from anyone and anything you once cared about. If the world and those in it are so terrible, then why not allow the scourge to win? Why fight if nothing is worth fighting for?"

Rake lowered his voice even further.

"That is the road of Silas and Clesh. That is the road of those who don a cloak of dragonhide. That, I suspect, is the road Sovereign slipped down long ago. But you and I, Holt, we're not going to give up, are we? I haven't. Not after two hundred and fifty years. And I'm not going to let some snake like Sovereign destroy the world before I undo what happened to me. Everyone might think of us as the chaos, Holt, but we're the little bit of chaos they all need, even if they don't know it yet."

Holt pursed his lips and pulled at a clump of grass. What Rake said was right. It was the truth, albeit a hard truth. Perhaps he did have to accept that the world wasn't going to change just because it ought to. Not quickly, at any rate.

"You're right, Rake. I won't give in. Although, if I'm honest, I nearly did at Red Rock. Just before you arrived, I spoke with Ash about staying in the town for a while. We struggled on our own, traveling across Brenin. I thought we were helping people and doing the right thing, especially taking the egg from those merchants, but if Ethel hadn't saved us from Orvel then... well, we'd be lying dead on the banks of the Versand, I reckon."

"Your heart is in the right place," Rake said. "You're just inexperienced. Dare I say naïve? Taking that egg was impulsive. If it were me, I would have let the merchants carry on and followed them to discover whom they were selling to. I would have followed the chain to uncover who was at the top and what was really going on. Then I would have cut the head off the snake."

That jarred with Holt. For the first time, he felt uncomfortable in the presence of the half-dragon.

"Do you always use killing as the solution?"

"That's rich, coming from the boy who killed Clesh."

"Well, that was self-defense."

"Are you saying that outside of a life-or-death situation, you wouldn't have done it?"

Holt hesitated.

Rake pushed on. "He killed everyone in your hometown. He murdered over a dozen riders. He killed Brode."

"I know that, but... I don't know, Rake. It's one thing cutting down ghouls and scourge bugs. Killing another person or dragon is different. If it wasn't in the heat of the moment... I don't know."

"Do you think we should not kill Sovereign?"

Again, Holt hesitated. He wanted to say yes, but something about Rake's eagerness made him pause. They knew little enough of Sovereign, but by all accounts, he did deserve to die. Controlling the minds of others was abhorrent. And yet... and yet what? Holt could not riddle out this puzzle.

In the middle of a battle, sure. That happened. To deliberately travel to a location with the express intent of killing a dragon, even if that dragon was Sovereign, held a coldness to it Holt found harder to stomach.

"Your lack of reply worries me," Rake said. "Or is it Osric Agravain you are chewing over?"

Osric had not crossed Holt's thoughts for a long time. Everything they discussed about Windshear Hold revolved around taking Sovereign down, yet Osric would inevitably be in the way.

"You want to kill him too?"

Rake shrugged. "I have nothing against the man personally, but if he's aligned with Sovereign, if he's his rider, then it seems inevitable we'll have to deal with him too."

Holt could not find any other way around it. If they arrived to fight Sovereign, then Osric would be involved. They would have to kill him. And maybe he deserved it if he had worked with the dragon to betray his family and kill countless people besides.

Except he had heard Osric's plea. A part of him had called out to Holt to tell Talia that he was sorry. A small part of him remained that was not entirely corrupt.

"He's Talia's uncle. She's lost her father and brother already—"

"By Osric's own hand, if I understand correctly," Rake said. "I'd have thought that a fire rider would have burned with vengeance for that."

"She did at first," Holt said.

"Sometimes the direct path is the quickest and safest," Rake said. "Kill Sovereign, and we'll save an incalculable amount of pain. Should Osric get in the way of that, so be it. Wyrm Cloaks and other riders will get in our way. Were it not for Talia, you wouldn't hesitate."

Holt nodded, though he felt uneasy about it all the same. But he had had enough of this conversation for one day.

"How long will we wait for Eidolan?"

"We need him," Rake said, disgruntled. "So as long as it takes."

Holt left Rake to stew by his tree and ran back to Aberanth and Ash.

"Good news," he said. "We should have time to make as much jerky as we want."

TWENTY-FOUR

A Duel of Beasts

Axes in hand, Osric Agravain stalked the passes of the Grim Gorge, coming down upon the valley from the north. Sovereign had told him that the mystics kept the poorest of their nests at the northern tip of the gorge. Those eggs suspected of being close to or outright defective. Kept at a wing's length from the rest of the flight, but perfect pickings for Osric and his raiding party.

Forty of the toughest members of the Shroud supported him, armed with crossbows, spears or halberds, large vials of the numbing agent used to slow dragons, and vials of dark blood. Some even possessed a new blood mixture, which bubbled like beer inside the vial. All had been given a cloak from the hide of mystic dragons.

Osric had been offered a cloak but refused it. No cloak would he wear to battle other than his gray one. Besides, he would rather have speed. Flexibility. Only forward. All attack. He had been held back for too long. Too long had he walked the palace in Feorlen, playing a part. Too long had he sat on a hatchery floor and played nanny to hatchlings. Too long had he gone without the release that battle granted.

He was a warrior. A killer. He had forged Vengeance and Spite in blood, and they had gained a taste for it. They hungered as he hungered.

With those axes he cut a swathe through the undergrowth and hewed the woodland of the black mountains to clear a path. He kept his bond with Sovereign closed. No mystic in the valley would feel him approaching. Wild dragons in Sovereign's service roamed farther back, out of range of detection but close enough to fly into the fray once the ambush was sprung.

As they marched down a narrow pass leading into the valley proper, the first sounds of dragons reached them. Grunts and growls of conversation. They seemed more agitated than resting dragons should be. Perhaps some disagreement was taking place.

"The arrogance of the flights knows no bounds," Sovereign had said. *"They will not look for intruders outside of their magical senses. By the time they smell you, hear you, you'll be upon them."*

Osric's blood warmed. His axes drew him forward, as though sensing the fight. The Shroud had their orders. They weren't here to kill dragons but to take as many eggs as they could.

He would keep the drakes busy for them.

Holt and Ash Forged together. Over the past two days, between trying to convince Eidolan to join them, Rake schooled them in the Sinking technique. Those lessons were beginning to pay off.

Ash now cycled existing core-forged motes around his body, then pulled them back toward his soul and core. Sinking encouraged raw motes toward him, as though Ash had created a current in the magical landscape. Magic swirled thicker than ever in the orbit of the core. It made every beat of Holt's heart doubly effective at pressuring the motes into the core itself. With the benefit of time, Rake's guidance, and more venison, Ash's core had swollen these past weeks. More and more did it take the shape of the moon, its light paling from yellow to silver white.

The valley air sat still and thick. Not even a slight breeze to cool the skin. The dragons were quiet. Birds slept. To Holt, the outside world no longer existed as his whole being centered on his breathing, his heart, the warm bond, and the glowing ball of ligh—

Someone shook him.

"Get up," Rake said, short and sharp.

Holt opened his eyes, delirious as waking from a deep sleep.

"Rake, what... why—"

"Wild dragons," Rake said. "Not the mystics. I feel them to the northwest."

Aberanth stirred. *"How far out are they?"*

Rake screwed his face as he strained, pushing even his impressive limits. "Five miles, maybe more." He spoke quick and low. "The mystics won't be able to sense them. They are staying out of range. Eidolan," he ended, almost as an afterthought. Picking up his polearm, he charged off toward the nests. "Eidolan," he called before disappearing into the dark.

Clouds blocked the best of the moon and starlight. Beyond their small campfire, there was precious light for him to see by.

"He's gone up into the nests," Ash said, tracking Rake's progress.

"Can you hear or smell anything coming?" Holt asked.

Ash moved around, sniffing and keep his ears held high. *"Nothing yet."*

"Get up," Rake was shouting. "Up now, you've got some unwelcome guests on your doorstep."

"Yes, you," a grumpy female said.

"Settle down, soul-cursed," said another.

"Get up and make me shut up then," Rake cried. "Up. Up now, you lazy drakes. You have ten dragons hovering not far from here. None of them are mystics. And I doubt they just want to chat about old times."

"I sense nothing," the female dragon said.

"Eidolan, be a dear and explain it to them, will you?"

Rake suddenly landed back in Holt's view with a great thud.

"Holt, Ash," he said, dropping his voice to normal levels again and striding toward them, "put that fire out."

"I can barely see," Holt said. "If it's a fight we're having—"

"If there is a fight to be had, it's not yours." Rake reached them and stamped the fire out himself. "Aberanth, take them south, back through the valley—Ash, get over here."

Ash had wandered to the northwest, still sniffing the air.

"There might be... something."

The mystic dragons were snarling.

"Friends," Eidolan's voice cut across the displeasure, *"Rake's senses far exceed ours. If he says there are dragons out there—"*

"Not you as well," an angry male called back. *"All of you, with your broken songs, settle or leave. The Honored Elder's goodwill may yet be taken away."*

More mystics chimed in, roaring and growling.

"Ash," Rake barked. "Here. Now."

"Hold on," Holt said, still dazed from his sudden emergence from Forging. "There must be twenty-five mystics here. And you. What are ten wild dragons going to do?"

"They are too far out for me to accurately sense their power," Rake said. "For all I know they are all strong as Lords. But the time to discover that is not when they descend for a fight. Aberanth, go with them."

"Right you are, Rake." The little brown dragon hurried over with a few of his leaves upon his back. *"Quick, Holt Cook, let's be off."*

Holt had a flashback of the Battle of Midbell. Of how Brode had told him to stay back, to run or hide. If they had, then Talia, Brode, the garrison of Fort Kennet, and all Midbell would have died.

"We're not running," Holt said. "Ash and I didn't run at Sidastra. Isn't running giving up? I thought you liked a fight."

The mystics roared louder now.

Rake had to shout to be heard over the dragons. "You're right—"

"It's so hard to hear," Ash told him.

"—I do like a fight, but I like it best when it's on my terms—"

"Boy, I smell them."

Rake was still mid-flow, but Holt ducked under his arm and ran to Ash.

"What is it?"

"The dragons cannot be in his range," Aberanth said.

"Humans," Ash said to them all. *"They're here!"*

Rake groaned and clenched his fist. "Fool that I am," he said to no one in particular. "Eidolan!" he cried harder, even above all the roaring. "The eggs! Make safe the eggs!"

A fresh bellow from a mystic stood out amidst the din. Holt heard it change from anger to confusion to fear in the span of a heartbeat. Then the unmistakable thwack of a crossbow, just like in the Withering Woods. The dragon's roar turned to one of pain.

"Wyrm Cloaks," Holt said. He drew Brode's great green sword, balanced his weight, pulled in light from Ash, and started to cycle motes to Ground his limbs. Grounding himself while standing still was one thing, of course. He'd yet to face a real fight while trying it.

In what seemed no time at all, everything descended into chaos. Steel rang. More crossbows thrummed. Dragons shrieked, bayed, howled, some fighting, some beating their wings to get away. Bursts of magic in every shade of purple flew across the valley.

A deep, menacing voice cried, "Take them!"

It was a man's voice but as close to bestial as Holt had ever heard.

Holt's vision was limited. Though the cultists carried torches, they cast a grubby half-light, illuminating only roving outlines. Holt gathered light at his left palm and brightened it, but while his immediate vicinity became visible, everything in the distance became pitch black. Frustrated, Holt cut the light and kept his attention on Grounding. He would just have to get closer to the action.

Yet a dire picture took shape in his magical senses. The cores of mystics were winking out, one by one. The ambush had taken four of them unaware, and a dozen more cores blazed as the skirmish unfolded.

Rake grunted. "See if you can impress me then."

Roaring, Rake lowered his polearm and dashed off into the fray.

Heart thumping, Holt almost charged off before remembering the jerky. The thick branch with the strips of meat stood propped up near the fire. The jerky was not as bone dry as it could be, but in the circumstances, he wasn't going to be picky.

He rammed a piece into his mouth and chewed faster than ever before as his life might literally depend on it, so fast that he barely registered the intense, earthy, gamey flavor and the heavy salt. Moments after he swallowed, his cycling eased. A power entered his limbs and his body began to glow. Light emanated from his wrists and hands, the only parts of him not covered in clothes or armor. A ghost-light, weaving in spindly lines along each finger and knotting into tight balls on his palms.

Aberanth would be delighted. Their experiment had worked.

Holt raised Brode's sword in both hands. Ash appeared at his side, their will one.

"Stay back if you want, Aberanth," Holt said.

"Call us if you're in danger," said Ash.

"Come on," Holt said, charging off into the dark. Ash matched his pace. "Eidolan's cave is at ground level," he said across the bond. "Let's make sure he's okay."

"Stay close and follow me," Ash said.

Holt did, letting Ash guide them through the night.

"They aren't shouting or making much noise," Ash said. "I'm tracking their heartbeats, feet, and weapons."

Holt tried as best he could to listen for feet or weapons clanking as the Wyrm Cloaks ran, but it was no use. His human ears couldn't pick out anything so subtle over roaring dragons.

"Three ahead."

Sure enough, when they arrived outside Eidolan's cave, they found three Wyrm Cloaks at its entrance. One had a crossbow and was in the middle of reloading.

Their dragonhide cloaks gave them remarkable armor, but Holt had a rider's blade now. He charged a Lunar Shock and sent it at the crossbowman. The ball of light blew the weapon from the cultist's hands, and before he could react, Holt cut him down. Brode's large, broad sword made the dragonhide cloak as effective as common leather.

A moment later, Ash's silver-white beam connected with another cultist. The concussive power blew her clean off her feet. She screamed over the short journey, her voice cutting short when she collided with the rocky mountainside.

The third Wyrm Cloak had time to react. He withdrew a vial, larger than Aberanth's elixirs, and downed its contents in one swift, fluid move. Smoke streamed from his lips, and his eyes shone red then ice blue. Its effect went further, enlarging the man so that his cloak stretched across a broadening back and chest.

Holt intended to Shock him, but the cultist moved quicker. He thrust his spear with a viper's speed, and Holt found himself on the back foot. The cultist was well trained, stepping in such a way that he placed Holt in between himself and Ash. The dragon had no clear shot.

Taken aback, Holt faltered in his cycling technique and his Grounded limbs lost their edge as well as their glow. Rather than attempt cycling again and risk losing the fight, Holt drew in Ash's light, intending to give his body a direct, powerful boost to finish the job.

Yet out of nowhere, or so it seemed, a lithe lilac dragon emerged on the cultist's side, its jaws wide. The blood-drunk cultist turned and thrust the spear into its heart—

Or into nothing? The spear tip cut into its scales which parted like drifting smoke, and somehow the dragon was unharmed. The Wyrm Cloak stood stunned. He was also no longer safe from Ash's line of sight. Ash took his chance and blasted the cultist with a thick beam of silver light. The cultist crumpled against the mouth of the cave, his neck twisting backward.

Holt grimaced and looked away. The lilac dragon began to melt away. Deep inside the cave, a pair of green eyes blinked out at them.

"Thank you, Eidolan."

"*I can defend my own cave,*" he answered tersely. His lilac phantom dragon vanished into the wind.

Holt huffed and turned away, taking in the valley at large.

"Are there more coming?" Holt asked Ash.

Ash raised his head and sniffed. "*More are on the ridges above. Many are already fleeing.*"

"They must have grabbed eggs already. Where's Rake?"

"*Not far off. He's fine. But above us, the mystics are dying. Something up there has a heart rate that's inhuman. It breathes like an animal.*"

"Maybe it's the dragon blood," Holt said. He flexed his fingers gripping Brode's sword. Despite all his training with Rake, it just didn't feel natural in his hand. However, now was not the time to wish for a better weapon.

Holt caught a glimpse of Rake running to the higher ledges before he focused back on the valley floor.

"Shall we help another nest?"

The words had barely left his mouth when he became painfully aware of ten new cores closing in on the valley.

"Rake was right, we're in over our heads."

"*Don't tell him that,*" Ash said. "*And more Wyrm Cloaks are coming!*"

Holt lost track of the approaching dragons as he moved to intercept the new Wyrm Cloaks descending onto the valley floor. He Grounded his body, and as the white lines began to shine, he assumed the benefit from the venison jerky was still in effect, though the light was dimmer than before. It was still easier too. Well, a little easier. Trying to regulate breath and mote channel flow while moving, while battling, was far from simple.

Yet in a straight one-on-one fight, even with his opponents drinking dragon blood, Holt felt a new confidence. This part of his training with Rake was certainly yielding results. He defeated each cultist he encountered without having to draw on magic and thus preserved the stability of his bond.

If only Talia could see this.

"*Dragons,*" Ash called in alarm. "*Watch out.*"

Ten new cores entered the gorge.

"Holt? Ash?" Aberanth called from out of sight. "*It's not too late. We can still go.*"

"*We're not leaving Rake alone,*" Ash said.

"*Don't you riders follow your commander's orders?*"

"*We swore no oaths,*" Ash said.

Holt beamed at Ash and pride swelled in his chest. Their bond burned reassuringly hot.

A dragon swooped overhead. Holt readied a Lunar Shock, but the dragon passed by without paying them any mind. Its dark wings beat upward toward a nest sheltered under a rocky shelf. It hovered, then was flying again a moment later, heading back out of the valley, clutching something in its talons. One by one, each of the new cores began to depart. They were simply grabbing eggs and fleeing.

"Look out, boy."

Ash's wing enveloped Holt and pulled him back. A second later, the body of a dragon hurtled down the rock face and landed in a wing-snapping, bone-crunching crash where Holt had been standing.

He assumed it to be one of the native mystics, but its wounds were not that of Wyrm Cloak weapons. There were four enormous gashes along its side. Such deep cuts could only be the work of dragon-steel.

"The other dragons have left," Ash said.

Holt confirmed this. How many eggs had Sovereign just gained?

"There are still Wyrm Cloaks," Holt said. "We can stop them, at least."

When they caught up to the ongoing battle, they discovered the remaining cultists were in full retreat, making for a narrow pass up the mountain slope. Rake kept those still on the valley floor from leaving, and Holt was sure the battle was over.

Then a man dropped down behind Rake. It was hard to tell more than that at this distance.

Ash growled in shock. *"I think that's Osric."*

"What? Are you sure?"

"I can smell him."

Rake loosened his cloak and shrugged it away, revealing his full half-dragon body before sending a stream of orange magic toward the figure. The man raised two axes to block the attack. The light from Rake's magic was weak but enough to reveal the man's face.

Ash was right.

~

Osric ran into the valley with the first bolts. The bolts hit the unsuspecting mystic, and he struck a moment later. His axes parted scales as good steel cuts cloth. The mystic writhed and bled out into the bedding of its nest, coating the eggs in rich dark blood. Steam trailed away from the bloody edges of his weapons.

More, they told him. More.

Bloodlust had ever been under the surface. He had become a man fighting in the shield wall of the Iron Beards. There he had learned the secrets of shield and axe, and once he had proved himself, their most terrifying warriors taught him to embrace that lust. To unleash it. With his new body, the pain of Sovereign in his chest, his blood boiling, his axes keen, Osric gladly gave into it.

He bellowed a war cry, such as any dragon might howl.

"Take them!"

He could not have said how many eggs the cultists secured, but he knew how many lives he took. Five mystics fell to his axes before his own dragon allies deigned to arrive. They plucked eggs out from the pooling blood and departed.

The gorge grew grimmer. Osric tasted copper on the air.

Running along a high ridge, one mystic sent a breath of swirling violet light toward him. He raised his axes to block the attack. The dragon-steel deflected the magic, and the wild mystic was so shocked that it hastened back, slipped, and struggled to regain its footing. Osric arrived and struck two hard blows into its flank. The dragon screamed, stumbling over the edge, and Osric kicked it down the mountainside.

Unbidden, the bond with Sovereign ripped open. His soul burned as the dragon spoke to him.

"We have enough. Leave."

Sovereign left and Osric forced the bond shut. An order was an order, and leave he would. He rushed back along the ridge. Six kills. Six seemed a poor release for his fury.

Ahead he could see the trailing cloaks of the cultists flapping as they made for the exit to the pass. Cries, death screams, and clashing steel sounded below. Even through his bloodlust, that registered as wrong. No human or rider should be here.

He looked down. On the valley floor, a large creature carved its way through members of the Shroud, lashing in great strokes with a polearm. It wore a cloak of its own.

Osric leaped from his perch, descending thirty feet to the ground. That gained the creature's attention. A pair of blue eyes beneath the hood locked onto him. The creature loosened a knot at its neck and shrugged out of its black cloak. Half man, half dragon. Osric had never seen nor heard of such a beast before.

The half-dragon gathered arcane energy around one taloned hand and blasted it toward him in a stream of orange power. Though he hated to do it, Osric pulled his bond with Sovereign taut, ready if the utmost need came. The fresh burn of pain from the bond only fueled his rage further.

He raised his axes, and the dragon-steel broke the stream as a boulder breaks the winds of a storm. Flecks of the half-dragon's power sparked around him, scorching his gray wool but falling harmless against his Lord's skin. He squinted. Under such a dark night, even this dull power seemed bright.

"Rake!" a young voice called. "It's Osric!"

The half-dragon took a step back, maintaining his magical attack. Osric held his axes and pushed through. The stream was weak. Whatever this creature's affinity was, raw magical damage was not part of it.

"Aberanth, vials."

Osric advanced, slashing his way through the onset from the half-dragon. "Fight me like a true warrior," he yelled.

The creature ignored him and shouted to a comrade Osric could not see. "Yes, *vials*. Two of them. Now!"

The stream of magic dropped. Osric's path cleared, and he ran full tilt toward his target. The half-dragon struck one foot on the ground in a sort of bounce. A fresh wave of his orange power rushed out while the creature soared backward in a mighty backflip. Osric's advance was checked momentarily by the wave of magic, but it burned out quickly, more a distraction to facilitate the creature's backflip. It landed a good distance away and now reached out a taloned hand to catch two small vials out of the air.

Osric charged again. The creature raised the vials to its mouth, bit out the corks and spat them away. Did it drink dragon blood too? Osric was in range to leap when the half-dragon blasted him again, forcing Osric to slow and block the attack. A glint of glass flew out of the arcane light. Two empty vials struck his face, shattering into sharp shards which blew upward. Though harmless to him, his eyes instinctively closed against the assault, causing him to lose a heartbeat of the battle. When he opened his eyes, the half-dragon had vanished.

A movement behind him and to his right. Senses honed through battle let him know of the danger.

Osric pivoted to find a thin orange arc hurtling at him as though painted in the air. Instinct made Osric block, and there rang a shrillness of clashing metal when the arc struck his axes. It had an edge, a slash through the night for all intents and purposes. The half-dragon stood fifteen feet away, the blade of its polearm pointing to the ground as though it had sliced at the air then projected that attack forward. Whatever this thing was, it could maneuver around a battlefield incredibly well.

It faltered. Perhaps it had used up all its tricks. Though its face was half a dragon's, Osric recognized surprise. Then it did something quite unexpected.

It grinned.

"I'll give you a fight, Agravain."

It knew his name. Someone else nearby had known his name too. What was this creature? It had magic yet no core so far as he could tell. Discovering what else they knew would be the prudent course, but Spite and Vengeance called for blood, and his own blood rang with that same song. A blood song.

Osric let out a savage bellow that would have made Skarl berserkers proud and drove forward. He brought one axe down and swung the other from right to left, strokes that would have beheaded wild boars, effort that would have exhausted normal men. He struck again and again, always moving, always forward, checked his enemy's blade, swept it aside, lunged, hacked, never giving ground, only taking it.

It should have been over by now, but this half-dragon was as quick as it was large. His polearm granted him great reach. Osric despised magic, but he despised defeat more. And his new axes offered a new use of Sovereign's power.

Drawing on those black chains over such a distance ought, he thought, to be impossible. Perhaps this was why it hurt so much? However it was possible, Osric could draw on Sovereign's core, and now he cycled that power to his hands and then into the axe heads. The beards of the axes shone with a dark, bloody light, radiating the dragon's hateful aura.

Perhaps this was why the half-dragon fumbled his next steps. A slight blunder but critical. Osric snorted like a bull and brought Spite hammering down. The creature raised its polearm to block.

Osric tasted victory.

Axes are top-heavy, less nimble to wield than swords, but their momentum and power so much the greater for it. Their nature suited Osric. With Spite brimming with Sovereign's power, it clove the shaft of his enemy's polearm in two.

The half-dragon groaned and rolled aside. It threw the broken shaft away and adjusted its grip, placing its hands on the remaining wood as though wielding a two-handed greatsword. It was skilled. Osric would grant it that.

But Osric knew something else. This fight was already over. He had momentum, and a berserker with momentum could not be stopped. In three quick, efficient moves, Osric had the half-dragon where he wanted it.

He delivered an overhead blow with Vengeance that his opponent would see as an easy block. With its height advantage, the half-dragon took the bait. Then, with his right hand, Osric enjoyed the advantages of dual wielding over an enemy without a shield. Sovereign's power still pulsed, black and hateful, indistinguishable from night, at the curving tip of the axe head. Wielding the axe like a dagger, Osric thrust low, driving the tip of Spite toward his foe's leg. The half-dragon contorted itself to twist aside, but the axe blade caught the side of its thigh. A graze. Nothing more. Yet Sovereign's magic did its work.

The half-dragon stumbled. Fell. It dropped its weapon, its eyes went wide, and it choked as though its nightmares had come to life and seized its throat.

Osric stepped before the creature and readied to take its head.

A boy emerged out of the darkness. "Osric, stop!"

Osric froze mid-swing. Holt Cook was here? A white dragon appeared not far behind him, growling in agitation as Holt stepped closer.

"We know Sovereign is making you do this. Fight him. You don't have to."

Across the bond, Sovereign stirred. *"Take them. Take them now!"* His fury could have rivaled Osric's own.

"I told Talia what you told me," Holt said. "You said you were sorry." His voice cracked from anger. "Are you still sorry? Is this you, or is it Sovereign? His real name is Thrall!"

Sovereign roiled in anger. *"Dominate them."*

Despite the bloodlust, a tiny fragment of his conscience quietly but steadfastly refused. Death would be kinder.

"Thrall," Holt repeated. "And he makes slaves of others. He's sick. Fight him Osric. He's made you do all these things."

Osric lowered his axes by an inch. Sovereign roared, and his presence surged like hot tar across the bond. He took Osric's mind and raised Vengeance and Spite to do the deed himself.

The boy must have sensed the change in Osric's bond and the power now present in him. Holt raised his own hands, fool that he was. Then white light burst forth, cold and blinding, as though the moon had crashed into the valley. Holt screamed, though whether from fear or effort Osric could not say.

Sovereign thrashed in pain inside Osric's mind and slithered back. Osric regained control, but for a few crucial seconds he had been forced to stare open-eyed into that brilliant light.

He cried out and raised his arms to shield his eyes, but the light only grew more intense. Backing away, he was forced to screw his eyes shut.

Something wrapped around his leg. He kicked out hard and removed it. Then it happened again. Osric twisted so that he faced away from the light and wrenched his eyes open. Through his watery vision, he found vines and gnarled roots binding him to the earth. His axes made short work of them, but more kept coming.

"Ash? Ash? I can't see!"

The light lessened, though it was still too strong for Osric to turn.

"Rake? Get up. Get up Rake!"

Osric fought off the roots and vines as quickly as they ensnared him.

"Aberanth, he won't move! Come on, Rake. Get up! No, Ash. We can't leave him."

The light faded.

Osric sliced through the last vine. He turned, blinking through the pockets of light flashing in his vision. The half-dragon rocked on its knees, its head buried in its hands. The white dragon was trying to shepherd Holt – who had his eyes screwed shut – away, and a small brown dragon trembled behind them.

Then a new core appeared on the magical landscape.

Immense. Unfathomable. Not far away.

"You said the Elder would be far to the south," Osric said.

Sovereign did not reply but instead closed their bond firmly shut.

Osric hardly needed an instruction. He turned on his heel and bolted, as fast as his Lord's body would allow. Rather than run the longer distance up the embankment to the exit pass, he made a direct line for it, leaping high and latching onto a shelf of rock with his axes. The dragon-steel bit into the stone and, once braced, he pulled himself up.

He scrambled into one of the nests. A dead mystic lay sprawled there. One egg remained. The exit was in sight. Osric sheathed his axes, then bent and picked up the egg in one fluid motion. It weighed little in his hands, though it was larger than the others and bulbous as though swollen. Tucking it under one arm he ran, keeping his magical eye upon the progress of the Elder.

The Elder reached the valley tip and stopped, no doubt reeling at the loss of her dead.

Osric soon caught up with the cultists. Two dozen remained, and many had an egg in hand. Along with those eggs secured by their dragon allies, Osric considered their objective fulfilled. Assuming they could make it back to Windshear.

Thankfully, the Elder did not leave the gorge. She did not appear to be following.

TWENTY-FIVE

The Mission Remains

Holt held his face in his hands. His head rang as the aftershocks of his own light-induced damage wore off. He tried to open his eyes, but colors and light still burst in his vision, and everything was a blurry, watery mess.

"I've got you," Ash said. And between the comfort over the bond and knowing the Elder had come to save them, Holt began to calm and center himself.

He had meant to blind Osric temporarily. The trick had worked well enough against Orvel, but in his haste this time, Holt had been much too enthusiastic. His bond with Ash now felt worn and sore after just that one, major explosion of power.

Still, it had been effective, arguably too much so. Even shutting his eyes had not blunted the strength of it. In future he would have to face away when he did it, although ideally he wouldn't have to use it at all. The budding ability, such as it was, struck him as desperate. Shutting his eyes and losing sight of a foe was not wise.

By the time his vision cleared, Osric and the cultists were long gone. He ran to Rake's side and tried to steady the half-dragon on his shoulder, but Rake was even heavier than he looked. Holt blew out his cheeks, trying to support him. At least Rake was no longer shaking and screaming.

"Your Elder is nearly here," Holt said. "We're safe."

Even as he said it, he craned his neck to check the sky for her arrival. The moment he did so, her core disappeared.

Holt's insides melted away. What had happened to her? She couldn't have died. He checked his bond to make sure his own senses had not been cut off. Ash was there in his soul as always, and he could still feel Aberanth and other mystics in the gorge.

"She... she's gone," Holt said. "I don't know—"

"It was Eidolan," Rake croaked. He tapped Holt gently, indicating he should let go. Holt stepped away and left Rake to sit on the grass. With the battle over and no light from torches or magic, the dark curtain of night descended. Holt risked a little light on his palm to see by, keeping a careful, steady flow.

It was then he noticed that Eidolan had quietly padded closer to the group.

"You did that?" Holt asked.

Eidolan nodded. *"It took much of my strength to conjure such a phantom core."*

"Your strength could have helped us in the fight," Ash said.

"My skill is not in brute force. I helped as best I could."

Aberanth was still shaking. *"We should have tucked our tails and fled when we had the chance."*

Eidolan snorted. *"Then even more of my flight's eggs would have been stolen."*

"How many?" Rake said. They all turned to look at him, but Rake only had eyes for the cut on his thigh. Holt sensed no lingering magic in the wound, nor did it look deep. Rake gingerly poked at his injury, groaned, then sat back with a pained gasp.

Aberanth padded forward. *"Let me take a look at that."* He sniffed at the cut, then scurried off into the night.

Rake looked at the rest of the group as if they were all slow-witted. "Well, how many eggs were taken?"

"Three of mine were lost," Eidolan growled.

"What?" Holt said, aghast. "After you as good as told us to leave you alone?"

Eidolon snarled. *"I did not think humans would be so bothersome. They struck me with something which made me ill."*

"They're Wyrm Cloaks, surely you knew—"

"No such vermin roamed the world in my day, young Ascendant."

"Stop this," Rake said, breathily. He looked to Eidolan. "You shall have to come along with us now to get the eggs back."

Eidolan snorted and clawed at the ground.

Holt shared the sentiment. "You still want to go through with this? After the beating you just took? That wasn't even Sovereign, just his rider."

"Call him Thrall," Rake grunted. "You said it yourself. It reveals who and what he truly is. If nothing else, he seems eager to be known otherwise, and I don't intend to give him that satisfaction."

"Thrall, then," Holt said. "My point still stands."

Rake sniffed hard through fresh pain, then waved Holt's assertion aside. "He took me by surprise. I prepared with two Lifting elixirs and cycling to that effect, expecting an attack on my mind at any moment. Yet what the mad axe man really wanted was a brawler's battle. Next time, I won't make that mistake."

Holt eyed the broken pieces of Rake's polearm and could not summon the same confidence.

"Next time Sovereign will be there too," Holt said.

"Yes, he will," Rake said, irritably. "What's the matter with you all? The enemy has just made off with dozens of eggs. I don't think they were discerning either. There will be healthy mystic eggs in amongst the defective—"

Ash bristled, growled, and whacked his tail on the ground.

"Don't call them that," Holt said.

Rake had the grace to look ashamed.

"Sorry," he grunted. "Old habits. I only meant that Thrall just received a bounty of the sort of eggs he's looking for. Potentially many new types will hatch under his cursed wings. That isn't something we want to happen."

Aberanth returned with one of his leafy packs and brought it to Rake. From it, he produced a pungent paste. *"Rub this into the wound."*

Rake did. He clenched his jaw as he worked the paste into the cut, then he sighed. "Thank you."

The brown dragon grumbled as he packed up his kit. Holt felt guilty for Aberanth. He was no fighter. Doubtless one of the reasons he'd built his grotto deep underground was to avoid danger. Rake had dragged him out of his home with promises of fresh discoveries along the journey, and now the journey had become as perilous as the destination. Thrall knew they were together now, right here in the gorge. What if he came for them?

"Thank you for staying, Aberanth," Holt said.

Ash caught on. *"Many thanks. We would not have made it without your help."*

"Yes, well, I'd rather not repeat that particular experiment."

"The mission has not changed," Rake said. He gave them all a good hard glare, including Eidolan, before focusing on Holt. "The Elder won't help us. The Order will never listen to us. For all we know, hatchlings have already emerged from eggs prior to this. In fact, I imagine they must have. A small sign of success spurred this riskier raid. Do you want to see more like Ash fall under his influence?"

"Of course I don't."

There was also the matter of Osric. Holt had not sensed Thrall through him until the end of the fight. Did that mean Osric had come here willingly, killed those dragons willingly, and willingly tried to kill Rake too? He had not been under the same direct control Holt had witnessed in Sidastra, that much seemed certain.

Once again, Rake had been right. Holt didn't think he had reached the part of Osric which cried out for forgiveness. Perhaps that part of him had been silenced forever. Perhaps he should stop fretting over whether to kill people who so clearly deserved it. Perhaps he should toughen up.

These thoughts were strong enough to cross the bond without conscious thought. Ash's reaction was alarm and caution, but the dragon kept quiet as Rake carried on.

"Time is of the essence," Rake said, softening now. "Thrall will still be recovering from events in Feorlen. There is a chance. The best chance we'll ever get. Only we can do this."

Holt nodded. Everything Rake said made sense, yet feeling Thrall even briefly through Osric had been a stark reminder of just how powerful their foe was.

"*What do you think?*" he asked Ash privately.

"*I still trust Master Rake. He has a plan. Eidolan was part of that, and his own powers are strong. Perhaps it will work. And we still require his training.*"

That was always the clinching point. They needed Rake more than he needed them.

Other surviving mystics began to land around them. Hidden in the dark, their cores encircled them, even if they were not visible to the eye.

"*You will all leave,*" a distraught female said. "*Your ill kind has brought this chaos upon us.*"

"*Peace, Lakeshei,*" Eidolan said. "*I have my issues with Rake, but were it not for him and his companions, matters would have been far worse.*"

"*We include you in this, human lover.*" She said it with an acidity Holt had never expected.

It was his first real taste of the ancient prejudice dragons held toward humans, which had led the Elders to create the scourge in the first place. Ill-mannered, ill-tempered, and as unkind as dragons in the Order could be, they did at least enjoy friendship with humans. These wild drakes may have had no prior contact with humans. And their first experience had been a nighttime attack in which their kin were slaughtered and their eggs stolen.

"*You are not welcome here anymore,*" Lakeshei insisted. Others growled in agreement.

"*You call us friends, but you always perched alone,*" said a male mystic. "*Hoarding your human treasures. Go fly east of east or west of west. Freeze at the roof of the world or dry out in the hot sands like the rest of your kind.*"

His kind? Holt thought. *Does he mean dragons formerly part of the Order?*

"We're sorry for what happened," Holt said. "But don't take it out on Eidolan."

"Hush, child," Eidolan said, and Holt knew he spoke only to him. Injured pride laced the old dragon's voice.

"I understand your fear and anger," Eidolan said to all gathered. *"Rake thinks he knows where the eggs were taken. If we go in force, we may yet save our eggs and avenge our kin."*

"Not your eggs."

"Not your kin."

Eidolan's throat rumbled in anger. *"The Elder herself appointed me this task. I care for those eggs as if my notes were part of the flight song which created them."*

The mystics were unmoved.

"At first light, you shall all leave," Lakeshei said. *"Or we will drive you out."*

They departed. After their wing beats had faded into the distance, Rake spoke.

"I am sorry, Eidolan."

"A lifetime of battle and war, and all I wanted was some purpose so that I could live out the end of my days in peace," he said, biting down on the final word.

"So you'll come with us," Rake said. His tone was rhetorical.

A younger dragon might have huffed and growled, stomped, or struck the earth with its tail. But Eidolan did not. Eidolan looked sad and tired

"I shall come," he said, relenting. *"But not for Thrall. For the eggs."*

Despite the tragic circumstances of convincing the dragon to join their party, Holt was pleased. Ash passed his relief across their bond as well. Having another experienced dragon with them, one who had served in the Order for a long time, vastly improved their chances.

With a groan and a grunt, Rake got to his feet. He clutched his leg, swayed, but remained upright. He smiled. "Welcome to the team."

TWENTY-SIX

A Cold Proposition

Talia sat upon her throne. She wore a crown today, though not her original one. A steel band rimmed with leather and steel arches. Not something easily set on fire. Rather than robes of state, she donned her red brigandine, which had been cleaned and repaired since the tunnel.

The heat of summer beat in from the still-broken stained glass window. Glass shards in the frame cast spots of color onto the stone floor. Such heat should have been uncomfortable in full armor, but Talia found it pleasant.

Her councilors and household sat on the tiered seating below. Pyra lay spread out at ground level, more intimidating than a hundred guards. All eyes were upon the visitors who approached up the long vastness of the throne room.

The emissary party from the Skarl Empire numbered five in total, three men and two women. The men wore sleeveless tunics that fell just above their knees and soft leather boots. The women wore richly embroidered apron dresses over simpler, ankle-length linen dresses, clasped with broaches of silver or gold.

Talia thought the most remarkable thing about them was their hair. The women's hair was true gold – brighter and more precious than even the Mistress of Coin's fair locks –woven in braids thick as rope and adorned with jeweled pins and silk ribbons. Even the men wore their hair in braids, though their look was shaggier and beards dominated their faces.

Behind them stood a dozen seasoned warriors with shields on their backs and either an axe or sword at their waist. Normally, armed escorts would not be permitted into the throne room, yet Talia hoped it would display her own confidence and power that she allowed them entry.

Talia stood and spread her arms. "Welcome to Sidastra. I apologize that I could not greet you earlier, for I had scourge to deal with. I trust you have been made comfortable?"

The ambassador and leader of the party stepped forth. He wore his hair in a long fishtail braid, accentuated by the sides of his head, which had been shaved and tattooed in blue patterns.

"We have been treated most well," the ambassador said. He spoke the common language of the Aldunei belt with a thick accent which held a harsh, guttural quality and led him to stress the first syllable of each word. "Allow me to introduce myself. I am Oddvar Helsen, and on behalf of my companions and the Empress, I thank you for your hospitality."

Despite his earnest words, the man did not kneel. Nor did any of his party.

Talia glanced to the Mistress of Embassy. Though the Skarls had been absent for decades, her memory was long. Ida had warned that the Skarls took such acts of deference to heart. The ambassador would not bow because the Empress bowed to no one. To force a gesture of submission would be foolhardy for anyone who wished to see those axes remain sheathed.

"You are most welcome, Oddvar," Talia said. "Tell me, to what do we owe this honored visit from the north?"

"My Empress hopes that our peoples might become friends in the years ahead."

"And what form will this friendship take?"

"One of marriage, Your Majesty. The Empress invites you to marry one of her sons."

This caused a stir amongst Talia's court. Some, she knew, would be delighted, those who traced blood ties to original settlers of Feorlen. The other half, of Aldunei lineage, might oppose it.

Pyra snorted and laughed in her rumbling, dragonish way. Oddvar cast her a wary glance and took a step back. At least Skarl pride could recognize a dragon's power.

"Pyra means you no harm," Talia told him. "Tell me, Oddvar, many have smeared my reign, given my bond with Pyra. Am I to take this as a sign of the Empress' support?"

Oddvar's features flickered in a moment of consideration. "Her Imperial Majesty does not lend her support lightly, though she is tireless in her aid of loyal friends and family."

So no, she does not, Talia thought. *And if I don't marry her son, I'm not going to get it.*

"This offer is as surprising as it is generous, yet it is not a decision to be made without counsel."

"Yes, of course," Oddvar said. "Let us spare our tongues and ears on endless talk. The Empress is willing to remove any doubts herself in person."

"The Empress intends to come here?" Talia asked. She knew as soon as she'd said it that this would not be the case.

Oddvar's expression was one of impeccable politeness. "Your Majesty misunderstands. The Empress would be most gratified if you were to join her in the Silver Hall."

Pyra's good-natured rumble descended into a lower growl. *"Do they think to summon you like a common Novice?"* She did restrain herself though, being satisfied merely with narrowing her amber eyes at Oddvar.

She was not wrong. Beneath the civility lay a thinly veiled order. The Empress in truth was saying, 'I am the mighty, you are the weak. If you want what I offer, you will come to me.' Talia feared that going would be granting the Empress too much power, especially when she had little interest in the proposal.

"Another generous offer," Talia said, "yet I am unsure when I will have the time for such a journey. My people face many ills from the incursion." She avoided overt and public mentions of their growing troubles with Risalia and Athra. No need to make the situation so stark for the ambassador.

"A long journey perhaps," Oddvar said. "Though much shortened on the back of your mighty dragon. A rider from, how does one say the name in your tongue, the Roaring Fjord?" Talia gave him a nod of encouragement, although she doubted he really had questioned the translation. The Roaring Fjord was but one of the two Order Halls in the Empire.

"Well, this rider," Oddvar continued, "assures me it should take no more than five days as the drake flies across the Bitter Bay."

Was that eagerness she detected? Though Oddvar sought to place her on the back foot, it seemed as though the Empress very much desired Talia's presence. Perhaps she would have more bargaining power than she thought.

"My councilors and I shall discuss this matter," Talia said. "In the meantime, I would be most honored if you and your people would remain in the city as my guests."

"That we shall do," said Oddvar. He acknowledged her with the slightest nod, then gathered his people and departed.

Talia sighed and met Pyra's eye. *"You might want to fly and stretch your wings. I think this will be a long meeting."*

The five members of the High Council assembled quickly in the aftermath of Oddvar's declaration. All were present: Geoff Horndown, the Master of State, Ealdor Hubbard, the Master of Roles, Lady Ida, the Mistress of Embassy, Lady Elvina, the Mistress of Coin, and Drefan Harroway, the Master of War. Talia wished her mother were still in the city to help her navigate these most sensitive of issues, yet she had departed on her own diplomatic mission to Brenin and had not returned.

"Before wading into the quagmire, we might start with some good news," boomed the Master of State. "News from across the realm tells the same tale. The remaining scourge have gone feral. They've fled or else turned on each other, making it child's play to mop up the last dredges of the incursion."

"I'd wager that whatever Talia destroyed in that chamber set the scourge wild," Harroway said. He used her name more readily now. She'd asked them all to do so, of course, but she knew that, for him, this was a true sign of respect, rather than keeping her at a royal distance.

"Might you remind the council of what you found, exactly?" asked the Mistress of Coin.

"Some sort of orb," Talia said. "The full details of that chamber are more gruesome than I care to recount in the light of day. Pyra burned it as the Life Elder suggested we should. He confirmed that his senses cleared after we emerged from the tunnel."

"We learned something of value about the enemy," Harroway said. "I would not have done this, but I can admit when I am wrong. Talia was right to push for the mission." He stared the other councilors down, as if daring them to contradict him. None did. The older members gave begrudging nods but held their tongues.

Talia took a moment to marvel that, of all the council, she now found her strongest ally in Drefan.

"Many lives were lost," Talia said. "I can only hope that many more have been and will be spared because of it. For the longest time, the assumption has been that a queen alone controls a swarm. This orb seems to have acted in a similar capacity. The Life Elder is now using his flight to conduct a search for other locations like this."

"Why has such a thing never been detected before?" Harroway asked. "You would think the riders would have discovered this after centuries of conflict with the scourge."

The question was pertinent, and Talia had no good answer to it yet. Nothing in her training spoke of these things. Not of tunnels or chambers, save for areas of the Great Chasm, which Falcaer kept under permanent watch.

"This information seems better placed in the hands of the riders," said the Master of Roles. "That would be most proper. It is their purpose. Mayhaps it will even buy us some goodwill with Falcaer?" He directed this last question to the Mistress of Embassy.

Ida pursed her lips. "It does give us an excuse to approach Paragon Adaskar with something to offer rather than as beggars."

"I fear we will simply hand Paragon Adaskar knowledge and receive nothing in return," said the Mistress of Coin. "Let us keep this discovery to ourselves as a bartering chip. Make a fair trade of it at an opportune time."

"What are you proposing, cousin?" Harroway asked.

"The scourge will rise again, as sure as creditors demand repayments," Elvina said. "Next time, it is likely to be in another land. As Falcaer musters against the next incursion, we can sell this information—"

"No," Talia said instinctively. "Fighting the scourge should be above such things."

"Has Feorlen not earned it through blood already?" Elvina asked.

"The Order should know," Talia said. She could feel the fire rising through her again. "The riders are apart from politics. Their care is for the fight against the true enemy. It might be Adaskar agrees to rebuild the Order here if we show a willingness to cooperate and help them more than other realms."

Lady Elvina brushed her long hair behind her ear and steeled herself. "Talia, the treasury cannot afford to rebuild the Crag, nor cover the costs riders will demand while here. Especially those unused to your late brother's decree for riders to buy their wares and supplies at cost."

"Falcaer has resources," Talia said.

"Resources they gain from tithes and taxes," Elvina said. "And special donations. The bulk of which come from the Free Cities. The riders might claim to be apart from politics, but they need to eat as much as the rest of us, and it's Athra that ultimately commands those purse strings. Until this business with Athra can be settled, I assure you we'll be on our own. I urge the council not to throw away what little of value we have left."

Talia looked hard at Elvina, but she seemed resolute.

"Who else feels this way?" Talia asked.

Her High Councilors grew reticent, looking between one another to see who would be brave enough to speak. The hesitation spoke volumes. The Mistress of Coin had convinced them.

"Master of Roles," Talia said, hoping to appeal to the most traditional of the group. "You said it yourself. The riders should know."

The old man looked down, seeming to find his papery hands fascinating. "Falcaer should be told. Who are we to deny knowledge on the scourge to the world?"

"In normal circumstances I would agree," said the Mistress of Embassy. "But we're in dire times. Messages arrived only this morning from Mithras. I'm afraid they have officially joined Athra in their trade restrictions. No Feorlen ship may dock in any port of the Mithran Commonwealth without crushing fees."

This was grave. The city of Mithras held enough power in controlling the South Strait, but its seaborne territory stretched far west and east of the city, hugging the coastline to the borders of Brenin on one side and to Ahar on the other. Half the harbors of the world may well have been closed to them.

"We still await word from Coedhen," Ida said, "but the trajectory is bleak."

The Master of State grumbled. "This is grave news. Food is stretched thin enough already at high summer. Come the winter, we'll suffer shortages."

"Not to mention empty coffers," Elvina said.

"We need support," Harroway said. "It seems to me that our hopes lie in Queen Felice's ability to convince her brother to stand with us, and perhaps in this intriguing offer brought before the court today."

And here it was. They had arrived at the topic of the Skarls and of marriage.

"Do we think this a serious offer from the Empress?" Talia asked.

"The Skarls aren't known for sleight of hand," said the Mistress of Embassy. "I would take this offer at face value. The Empress will go through with it, should we accept."

We? Talia thought. *Don't I get the final say in this?*

Lady Elvina frowned, chewing over some puzzle. "For my part, I do not see how this adds up in the Empress' favor. I'd recommend caution until we know how she is counting her gold."

"The question is," Harroway said, "whether advantageous to the Empress or not, are we in a position to turn it down? Even if Brenin can be convinced to support us, that would still only make a two-strong alliance against four adversaries."

Talia noted this different appetite to risk in Harroway compared to when he had made his bid to be Master of War. 'To face down the armies of the world and triumph,' he had said with a glint in his eye. The chasm expedition seemed to have affected him in more ways than one.

"With the Skarls at our backs," Harroway continued, "Athra would think long and hard about military action. This marriage could solve all our problems at a stroke."

The Master of State tugged anxiously at his beard. "I'm not so sure. Strikes me as a double-edged sword. Athra could be warded off, yet the Skarls would hold their protection over our heads. We'd become vassals to the empire in all but name. That's not the vision your father had for this kingdom, Your Majesty."

"My father's vision was for Feorlen to be strong and recognized as such. Now we've never been weaker. His dream seems dead. Am I to choose between destruction in war or the destruction of our sovereignty?"

The Mistress of Embassy opened her mouth, then quicky closed it again.

"Is something amiss, Ida?" asked the Master of Roles.

Ida wrestled with something, then said, "No. Nothing. It's not worth consideration."

"I'll hear any other options," Talia said.

"Talia... Your Majesty, you won't..." Ida sighed somberly. "There is one possible way out of this. Fresh demands did come in, counter-signed by Archduke Conrad of Risalia and the Archon of Athra."

The heat in Talia rose a little higher, though it was from fear this time. She knew what was coming. In all honesty, she was surprised it had taken her enemies this long to raise the option. She should have let Ida remain silent.

"It's okay," she said, meeting Ida's eye. "The others have a right to know."

"Very well," Ida said. "All restrictions will be dropped and Talia recognized as the rightful ruler of Feorlen if she gives up her rider's blade and her dragon."

Talia tried reaching for Pyra across the bond, but with her so far away, Talia may as well have tried to warm her soul over a candle flame.

"Is such a thing even possible?" Harroway asked.

"There is a process," Talia said, struggling to keep her voice level. "A way to forcibly break a bond in any the Order wishes to cast out. It takes the Paragons to perform it, I'm not sure how exactly. But most would rather die," she ended in haste. "Pyra is not my pet to be disposed of. Our souls are bonded. Ripping off my arm would be less crippling. Do not ask it of me." She hated how scared she sounded, more like the girl she was than the queen she needed to be.

Now, at least, they knew. It was their right.

"If you seek a third option," Ida said, "that would avoid war and avoid prostrating Feorlen before the Skarls, this would be it."

Talia's heart turned cold. The mere thought threatened tears. And yet, and yet... would it not be the wiser route? If tens of thousands could be spared the suffering of a war, if she could avoid her people being consumed by a foreign power, would it not be the noble thing, the sign of a true leader, to make such a sacrifice? Was this where duty led her?

She did not have the strength to call for a vote on the matter, nor did she wish to force her councilors into voicing their feelings on the matter. Once said aloud, neither they nor she could ever forget it.

"I am stuck between the flayer, the juggernaut and now the abomination," Talia said. "Which one do I charge toward?" she asked rhetorically.

No one answered. Yet some matters had to be decided.

"Ready a diplomatic party to Falcaer Fortress," Talia said. "If

Adaskar will deign to enter talks on setting up an Order Hall, then we might supply him with our new intelligence."

The Mistress of Coin pursed her lips but wisely held her tongue. Talia had met her halfway on the issue.

"Master of War," Talia continued, "do what you must to shore up our defenses along the Red Range. I expect the Masters of State and Roles to aid you in whatever manner you need."

The three men inclined their heads.

"And I will prepare to travel north and meet with the Empress. Lady Ida, I will be grateful for all you can tell me of the Skarls before I leave."

"Of course, Talia."

"I'll also prepare you an escort," Harroway said.

"No. I'll go alone. I'll make the trip and back within two weeks with Pyra."

Horndown placed his giant hands gently upon the table. "I feel I must voice the obvious – what if this is some trap?"

"You heard Lady Ida," Talia said. "The Skarls aren't known for deceit or subtlety. And I am clearly of more use to the Empress as her daughter-in-law than as a hostage. Besides, while the Skarls are known to be fearsome warriors, I have yet to meet any fighter in mail who could withstand dragon fire."

She rose and, in doing so, signaled the end of the meeting.

Talia spent the following days learning of the Skarls and setting other affairs in order. Between that and Cleansing and Forging Pyra's core, she had precious time for sleep. The only good thing about a lack of sleep was a lack of dreams. And nightmares. The spectral faces and voices of her father, brother, and uncle left her alone during this busy time.

Yet they remained just beneath the surface.

One afternoon Talia moved her work outside to be with Pyra and take advantage of the summer's day. She pored over maps, some of the Skarl Empire, others of the three kingdoms of

Feorlen, Risalia, and Brenin and the Red Range which knit them together.

"We'll fly direct over the Bitter Bay," Talia said, pointing for Pyra's benefit to the sea north of Feorlen's coast. Northeast over the Red Range lay Risalia, which she would rather avoid flying over. "We can veer into the Province of Fornheim if we're in need of land before carrying on north into Skarl territory."

"How cold will it be there?" Pyra asked.

"Colder than here, but this will be the best time of year to go."

Pyra rumbled, then slumped to the ground and clawed at the earth. She had been distracted and moody of late, and though they stood only feet apart, the bond offered Talia little insight.

"What's troubling you?"

Pyra dug her claws deeper into the soil but said nothing.

"Do you want to talk about what happened in the tunnel? I know what happened to Ghel hit you hard."

Pyra snapped her teeth. *"Many die against the enemy. We know this."*

Talia frowned. Pyra had always been proud, but she'd rarely gone so far as to outright lie. She'd closed over their bond for a time in the aftermath of the fight, a process as unpleasant as the loss of the soul on the other side of it. Talia could count on one hand the number of times she had done it herself. The day she'd learned of her father's death. And then again when Leofric had passed. Sometimes she desired to grieve alone and to spare Pyra the pain.

"Must we make this journey?" Pyra asked in a rush. *"We should be fighting the true enemy. They all should be fighting the true enemy. Why do you humans play these games?"*

A tremendous question to which Talia had no satisfying answer.

"Will you actually marry this princeling?" Pyra asked.

Talia moved to crouch by her dragon's side. "If my choice is between marrying or losing you, I'd marry the first pig in a wig they put before me."

Pyra snorted. *"I will not carry him."*

"I didn't think you would," Talia said. Was this what fueled this latest mood? "I don't want this either."

"When we fly, we could… not return."

For a moment, Talia almost said yes. The thought was tempting, but a ball of guilt formed and weighed heavy in her gut.

"We knew this would be hard. All we can do is to try… to try and make it work." She reached out a hand, but the dragon shrugged her off. "Pyra—" Talia started in a hurt voice, but before she could say more, the Twinblades spoke from behind.

"Our queen," they said in unison.

"Deorwin Steward has returned to the city," Eadwald said.

"He requests an audience with you," Eadwulf said.

Deorwin? Back? Talia had assumed him dead. No one had known where he'd disappeared to after delivering the ghost orb to Leofric. She'd assumed that Osric – well, Sovereign – had hunted him down, lest he reveal the treachery at the Toll Pass. With him back, so many questions were springing to mind.

"Yes, of course," Talia said. "Bring him at once."

Some good news for a change lifted her spirits out of all proportions. And when she laid eyes on the old steward, her heart leaped into her throat. Deorwin walked with the aid of a cane, slow and in evident pain, but step by step he came to her, flanked by the twins.

Up close, it became plain that the past year had not been kind to Deorwin. His horseshoe of white hair had fallen out, leaving him bald. His plumpness had wasted too, leaving him wrinkled and thin. Darkness sunk deep beneath his eyes, yet it could not fully dispel the kindly smile she recognized.

"Your Royal Majesty," he said, stooping his neck and shoulders.

"Dear Deorwin," Talia said. "I would hug you were I not afraid of my own strength." She settled for taking his hands in hers and returning his warm smile. "Come, please sit. Eadwald, Eadwulf, fetch shade and water."

Talia drew up a chair, and they sat together in what remained of the palace gardens. She would have introduced him to Pyra, except she lay curled up with a wing over her snout. Talia left her to sulk.

"The scourge caused much damage," Deorwin said, gazing at the empty flower beds and uprooted hedgerows.

"Not half as much as what the Risalians did to you," Talia said. In the memory her father left in the ghost orb, Deorwin had been hale and hearty compared to this shell. "How did you get away? Did Osric come after you once you returned?"

"One matter at a time, Majesty," he said. And he did go through all matters, one by one, beginning with his failed attempt to flee from the Toll Pass. "I was never comfortable on a horse, even in my youth. Last year I had more strength than this, but still I fell and lost myself to the blackness. When I came to my senses, I was already in the hands of the Risalians."

"I saw my father placing the ghost orbs into lock boxes," Talia said. "I assume the Risalians found it on you."

"Along with the key."

This confirmed a suspicion that had gnawed at her. It had not come to her immediately, not in the flaming heat of Osric's betrayal and the need to defend the city, but in the quiet ruminations since.

"Did they learn what it contained?"

Deorwin's old, weary face creased further. "Not in detail. I resisted speaking of it at first until it became clear to me that the Risalians were as eager to see Osric pay for his treachery as I was. He double-crossed them that day as well, though my captors did not know the full extent of it. The margrave who made the deal with Osric did not survive. All the Risalians had were rumors of foul play. I think they considered smashing the orb at one point to see for themselves, but wiser heads prevailed. Archduke Conrad's, I think. He let your brother know I was amongst the captives and that I had valuable information for him. A price was set. An exchange made, though in secrecy given Osric was at large. After reuniting with your brother and telling him all I knew, I made for family lands in the south, to a holdout we have in the hills for times of incursion."

"How was Leofric when you last saw him?" Talia asked. "Half the court thought he had gone mad from fear or sickness."

The darkness under Deorwin's eyes seemed to sink to new depths. "His stomach still plagued him, though what pained him more was the fear, I think. Fear of the incursion. Even before I presented him with the orb, he seemed paranoid, and as well he might have been. I was... deeply troubled to see him so frail."

Talia's disappointment slid through her, cold and numbing from head to toe. What had she hoped to hear from Deorwin? That Leofric had been brimming with energy and health, almost certainly meaning that Osric had killed him too? Or this? Fragility and sickness. Anxiety and dread. Which fate for Leofric did she want to believe in?

"Go on," she said softly.

"You've seen Osric off now, and that is well," Deorwin said. "I might have remained away, but I felt a final duty to inform you of the Archduke's actions. He sent me and my evidence back to your brother to cause chaos even as the incursion brewed. Conrad wants revenge. Losing the war to a lesser power shook his image in the eyes of his margraves."

"You were right to tell me," Talia said. The information threw into question the supposed peace that would come if she broke her bond with Pyra. If Conrad's desire for revenge was strong enough, he would merely bide his time and then pounce on some fresh excuse. "It seems inevitable that I must carry on the fight my father started, though I wish it weren't so. Thank you, dear Deorwin, for all you have done. If there is anything I can do?"

"You can find your uncle and bring him to justice." A strength returned to Deorwin's voice and eyes. It left a moment later as he winced and clutched his leg.

"I intend to find him if I can," Talia said. "He might be innocent. A powerful mystic dragon used magic to ensnare his mind. For all we know, he may not even be aware of what he's done – the real Osric, that is."

"That... that is some small comfort," Deorwin said, and suddenly he was the kindly old man again, a carer and a teacher. "I taught him and your father their letters and numbers. To think one of my charges could have turned so... but then again, Osric held a dark glint in his eye that troubled me often. Too quiet he was. Too quiet and yet too prone to outburst."

"Others have mentioned this. I suppose I did not know my uncle as well as I once thought."

"You brought out the best in him, I think," Deorwin said. "Or he always put his best self forward around you. I once felt deeply sorry for him, you know."

"What for?"

He turned sheepish. "What memories do you hold of your grandparents, Your Majesty?"

"Almost none. Of my grandfather I have but a single blurred memory of running to him, yet the nature of his face eludes me. Of my grandmother I have no memory at all."

Try as she might, she could conjure nothing more of them. Her grandfather had passed when she was a toddler. And the scandal caused by her grandmother's departure was not spoken of openly. Enough scolding looks and flared tempers from her parents had taught her not to bring the subject up.

"I think you're old enough now to know," Deorwin said, as only an old guardian can talk of their charges despite their achievements. As if Talia were not a trained Ascendant with a steel crown upon her head.

"Your grandparents had their issues," he began, tentatively, fighting a lifetime of guarding intimate family secrets. "Hard to know which of them started it. He was overly fond of his drink, and your grandmother, she, well, she enjoyed the company of other men," he said rather fast, as though he were whipping his hand back from a fire.

"I've heard the rumors," Talia said. Her own father's weakness for spirits took on a darker meaning in her mind. She was doubly glad to have removed that cabinet.

"Godric was such a bright flame in their lives," Deorwin said. "They were happy then, I am sure of it. Or at least, they were not actively miserable. Then something went awry. After Osric was born, things only got worse and worse. Your grandmother paid him less attention than to Godric. Your grandfather ignored him as well, except for the occasions when the bottle fueled him."

Despite the heat of the summer's day, Talia felt a chill. The insinuation of why her grandfather might have mistreated Osric unfurled itself like a coiled serpent at the back of her mind.

"No one ever told me that," she said. "Did Leofric know?"

"If he did, he did not hear it from me. Such things were long in the past by the time you were born. I'd hoped they would remain buried there."

"Did father never do anything about it?"

"Godric was but a child himself," Deorwin said.

Talia nodded. It was hard to think of him small and powerless, and far harder to picture Osric small, and weak, and cowering.

"How did it stop?"

"Eventually your grandmother intervened. Such a row as I've never heard before or since. I took the boys from the room as they argued. The beatings stopped after that, but the rest remained the same. In truth, Godric could have been a better brother to Osric through it all and after. I tried to encourage him so, but the two were like water and oil. They would fight sometimes, once quite badly."

"You said you used to pity him," Talia said. "If it turns out this dragon controlled him fully and that he is innocent, would you pity him again?"

"I think I would," Deorwin said sadly. "Many thought him harsh, but I saw the awkward, small boy trying to hide and not knowing what to do. For years, the worst you could say of him was that he was hard and cold. Still, if rumors of his actions abroad are true, if his heart has turned black, after what he did to your father—" He ceased the hurried flow, then collected himself. "Whatever happens, Talia, please do not tell me. I'm too frail now to suffer another blow."

Talia took his hands in hers again. "I promise. I'll speak to the Master of Roles. I'd have you live out the rest of your days in peace. If you are ever in need of anything, you need only ask me."

Watery-eyed, Deorwin gave her a wan smile and then attempted to stand. He wobbled and Talia caught him. Once he had steadied himself on his cane, she let go and watched him walk slowly back to the palace, escorted by the twins.

Her first thought was to speak to Pyra about all of this, but given their spat, she left her sleeping. Pyra had told her once that many humans had been brought before her and none had satisfied. But Talia was of a strong line and Pyra sensed they would do great things together. Would Pyra regret her decision if she knew the extent of her family's distressing past?

Talia's own edifices were crumbling in her mind. Her father sounded as uncaring and cold as they all accused Osric of being. The picture now sketching of her uncle was strikingly different to the one she had held since her youth.

She could not help but wonder if it had been a chance encounter that brought Osric to Sovereign or if he had already embarked upon a darker path that led him there.

Osric had spent years serving in a war band of the Skarl Empire – the Iron Beards. He had even saved the Empress' life once, though he spoke little of it. Yet more reasons to travel north.

TWENTY-SEVEN

Black and Gold

By the time Osric returned to Windshear Hold, he had regained his composure. His axes had drunk their fill of blood, as had he. Of the forty members of the Shroud who had accompanied him, twenty-two returned. Yet the plan had worked. Between the cultists and the dragons, twenty-nine eggs had been extracted from the nests of the mystic dragons.

In a perverse sense, reaching the door in the bedrock under the western walls now felt like coming home. He yearned for his small chamber, to clean his skin, remove the sharp bristles upon his cheeks and chin, and regain a semblance of the routine he'd missed during the mission. Sovereign would not deign to come down and give him a lift, but Osric would rather make it on his own feet regardless. He climbed the long, winding servants' stairs along with the cultists, coming up into the storehouse. As the cultists began to unpack their supplies, he strode out into the yard and was met at once by the Speaker, flanked by several of her faithful followers.

"A successful mission, General." She beamed and looked at the egg Osric held in the crook of his arm. "Sovereign's new flight grows, and the cycle shall soon be broken, praise him."

"Praise him," the others chanted.

"Save your praise for those who fell in his service," Osric said. He noted that the fire dragon, Zahak, sat by a brazier in the yard alone. "Where is Champion Dahaka? I should like to speak with her."

"She is with the blood alchemist," said the Speaker. "He has asked you attend him too at your convenience."

Osric gave a curt nod, and the Speaker strode past, presumably to resume training her new recruits. He entered the spire, climbed to the highest hatchery, and placed his egg into a straw-lined crate. The neighboring yolk-yellow egg could not have been more different, being thinner and more cone-shaped.

Given seven hatchlings from the original batch were still in residence, the nests of the mystic tower quickly filled. Osric ordered that the tower of ice be reopened and prepared should more space be required.

When all the new eggs were settled and accounted for, Sovereign spoke to him.

"Bring the hatchlings to me."

The dragon left without another word. Osric was grateful that the bond and presence did not linger long enough to cause him pain. He returned to the mystic tower and ordered all cultists to leave at once and not to reenter the tower until he gave them leave to do so. When the tower was vacated, Osric went to collect the hatchlings.

Even at a young age, the dragons were intelligent. He spoke to them and gestured, and they seemed to understand him or at least intuit what he wanted. None spoke to him, though he did not know if they could speak this young.

The hatchlings followed him like ducklings. They were a strange assortment. The half gray and half green dragon still lived. One lacked a tail while another lacked an eye. Osric found the dragon that kept changing its eye color disconcerting as it also changed one eye at a time, seemingly when it pleased.

They yapped and garbled to one another in some childish language of their own. Bolder dragons bit the others playfully on their tails. Leading the troop was the pale ginger-red dragon with swollen muscles who strutted ahead of the pack with his snout high and eyes searching. He had grown the most, already as large as the greatest war hounds Osric had ever seen.

When he opened the door to Sovereign's nest, a chill fell over the group. They stopped their squawking and fell into a sullen silence. Tails and ears drooped. Even the beefy ginger dragon took a measured step back from the door. Osric gave him a push with one foot and shunted the rest in where they would not go willingly.

Sovereign cast his gaze over each dragon like a judgmental grandfather. If he spoke to them, he did not allow Osric to hear.

One by one, the hatchlings padded out before Sovereign to receive inspection. Sovereign uttered no sound until the baby with one eye took a tentative step forward. Sovereign sniffed it like the others and shut his eyes, listening for the first delicate notes of the hatchling's song. At length, Sovereign huffed in frustration and sent the dragon back to stand with the others.

Only the pale ginger showed any strength. Sovereign growled low at him, and the brawler growled back. Its cry was high and at odds with its brawny frame, yet it stood its ground and screeched out every drop of air in its lungs. A light tug played at the side of Sovereign's lips, and then at last he acknowledged Osric's presence.

"You attempted to defy me in the gorge," Sovereign said, obsessing over the memory of Osric lowering his axes by an inch.

Osric thought on it. Was that defiance?

"It was a moment's hesitation in a chaotic fight," Osric said. "Nothing more. You know I cannot defy you."

"See it is the last hesitation."

Osric inclined his head.

"Elsewise... you did well."

"Is that praise?"

"Your task was to gather eggs and you gathered many. Had I known Ash would be in the gorge, I would have tasked you differently. Alas," he added with a snarl.

"The half-dragon with them was strong. And a creature unknown to me. It had no core from what I could sense, though it used magic."

"I have no knowledge of such a creature, although stories have reached me in *the wilds and through the ears and minds of those I have possessed. A great warrior wielding an orange blade. Yet who or what is he? Has he taken Ash under his protection? And what were they doing in the valley? Riddles to ponder."*

Sovereign grumbled, and he seemed to look past Osric as he gnawed on these mysteries.

Osric looked at the world beyond the opening of the hatchery, settling on the treetops of the woodland, bright with the green of high summer. Riddles held no interest to him. Yet he relived the fight with the orange half-dragon. Holt had called the creature Rake. Holt had also called Sovereign by another name.

Thrall.

This was no shock. Sovereign could not be the dragon's true name. Even this matter Osric only considered for a brief time before pushing it from his mind. It mattered not who or what Sovereign had once been. What truly mattered to him was what else Holt had said. Until Holt had reminded him, he'd all but forgotten he'd reached out to the boy back in Sidastra. It had been like grasping onto a cliff edge with his fingertips. He'd asked for forgiveness, from Talia most of all. He remembered that now. Though not so long ago, asking for forgiveness seemed a childish thing to him now.

'Fight him Osric,' Holt had said. 'He's made you do all these things.'

The knot of pain returned to his chest and twisted. He closed his eyes, picturing Talia as she had been. Young, willful, headstrong, and unafraid as only some bolder children can be. Her eyes were as fresh and green as spring back then, and she looked at him with nothing but love and admiration. 'My little soldier', that was what he called her. Of all his family, Talia was the one he felt real kinship with, and she the one who returned that in kind.

Talia would never look at him like that again.

"What troubles you, worm?"

Osric opened his eyes. "Nothing. What are my orders?"

"Take these back to their nests," Sovereign said. *"I will spend time with them each day after you have Forged."*

The hatchlings remained quiet against the wall, some with their tails between their legs while others looked bored. Osric gathered them and led them out of Sovereign's presence.

After the labors of forging his axes and the raid on the Grim Gorge, the following days passed in a mundane fashion. Osric Cleansed and Forged Sovereign's core again, creating the very chains that bound him. Each day he led the hatchlings to Sovereign, and each day the dragon kept them longer. Despite multiple invitations, he did not visit the blood alchemist.

One day, a commotion erupted in the yard of the fortress. Sovereign informed him that a new rider had come to pledge allegiance, one who claimed to have knowledge of Holt and Ash. As with Dahaka and Zahak, Osric went to greet them.

He found a shining emerald dragon and a rider Osric took at first to be elderly. The man had a thick snowy beard but a lush mane of white hair that spoke of youthful vigor. His skin was clear and fair, and yet his eyes were old and deep and dour.

"Welcome to Windshear Hold, Champion Orvel," Osric said. This time he opened his bond to Sovereign so the new arrivals would know with whom they were dealing. "And to you, Gea."

Both bowed low before him and Osric allowed it this time, for they bowed to the dragon and not truly to him.

"Sovereign grants you an audience, Gea," Osric said. "Champion Orvel, there are other tasks he would bid of you."

"Why am I to be denied an audience?" Orvel said, visibly suppressing his anger. Osric detected a desperation buried beneath the surface as well.

"It is not our place to question," Osric said. "You're a soldier in his service now. Do you understand?"

Orvel's face turned grave. He had been doomed the moment he set foot in Windshear. He bade farewell to his dragon, then Osric brought him to assist Dahaka with the hatchlings. Some of the eggs from the mystic raid were beginning to hatch, and so the addition of another rider was welcome.

"*A bitter failure, he is,*" Sovereign pronounced of Orvel later that day.

"How so?"

"*You saw how old he is for his rank. To remain a Low Champion forever is a tragedy. Poor Gea, what is she to do? Too many dragons are attached to weak humans, siphoning our strength, and to add insult the bonds force us to care deeply about them.*"

Osric cared little for this matter. Bonds could form for the worst reasons, like his own with Sovereign. "And what of his knowledge of Holt and Ash?"

At that, Sovereign snorted black smoke and curled his talons along the floor, causing a bone-shaking screech. "*Gea reports that they overheard Holt telling their superior of a mission from the Life Elder. He seeks to unite the Wild Flights and feels Ash and the boy are the ones to do it.*"

"Is such a maneuver likely to succeed?"

Sovereign continued scraping his talon along the floor. "*It might have once.*"

Sovereign then explained the full story of Orvel and Gea's encounter with Holt. Orvel had smuggled an egg out from Sable Spire, only to be thwarted by Holt and Ash before it could enter friendly hands. They had hunted Ash and Holt down, but their superior had arrived before they could deal with them.

Osric recalled the cultists who had reported a part of this tale. More vividly, he recalled squeezing one of their throats until it cracked.

"Why have they come here? Surely they were not banished from the Order for the removal of one defective egg."

"*The fool attacked his superior on their way back to Sable Spire. Rather than face judgment, he fled. Another rider sympathetic to our cause found him fleeing east and directed him north. He was under the impression that I would aid him in his perpetual state of stasis. It pleases me greatly that he will spend his days cleaning up the muck of hatchlings.*"

"If you think him so worthless, why not kill him?"

"*I pity his dragon. Killing him in cold blood would rip her to pieces. Few can survive such a breaking. Though I would see the Order fall, I would not inflict such a fate onto any dragon."*

Osric raised his eyebrows. Sovereign had some small measure of compassion after all. For his own kind, at any rate.

"Enough talk of Orvel," Sovereign continued. *"These hatchlings. I have come to a decision on two of them."*

All the dragons were fast asleep in the hatchery with him, piled one on top of the other for warmth.

"Which ones?" Osric asked.

"The blue one with the shifting eyes, it holds no promise I can discern."

"Some power could manifest later in the dragon. Might it be worth waiting and watching?"

"It has no song," Sovereign said. *"No notes at all. No core nor power to speak of."*

Being sparing in his use of magic, Osric had not thought to feel the babies for fledgling cores. However, he felt no need to sense the dragons now for himself. Sovereign knew his business in this regard.

"And the second dragon?"

"The other I speak of holds promise. The large one." He lowered his snout over the pale ginger who lay atop the hatchling heap, pressing his weight down on his siblings rather than supporting them. *"There is a unique strength to the thrum of his notes. Each beat booms like a larger heart pumping blood to strong muscles. In time he could become a fortress breaker. I shall begin his training."*

"As you wish," Osric said. "I shall take the others back to their nests."

With a growl and some command Osric did not hear, Sovereign woke the babies. The muscled ginger snapped awake at once and clambered over his fellows. The rest awoke one by one, yawning and stretching their limbs and tails. Osric lingered on the poor navy drake with the morphing eyes. They changed from red to silver before he fully got to his feet.

Osric herded them up and was taking his first steps toward the hatchery door when Sovereign ordered, *"Stop."*

The hatchlings halted. A sense of foreboding came over Osric.

If Sovereign spoke to them again, he kept Osric out of the loop. The muscled ginger pushed his way through toward their master as if summoned. It yapped and snarled as though taunted by fresh meat just out of reach. Next, the navy dragon, head bowed, stepped out of the pack and took slow steps to stand by the ginger's side.

The remainder of the small flight looked between each other, then to Osric and back to their master. An agitation fell over the group. Some squawked, flared their ridges and rustled their tails. Then the navy dragon that lacked a core began to cower and shake. Trembling, it lowered its neck flat to the ground before Sovereign. The other hatchlings grew more disturbed, growling their high cries louder and louder, until, as if in slow motion, the muscled ginger turned and set upon its sibling with tooth and claw.

A silence fell over the hatchlings. They went rigid. For a moment, even the world outside seemed still and quiet. All that could be heard was the wet, squelching tears of hide and flesh and the slap of entrails. Blood spilled in all directions, running thick and fast, too great a volume for such a small dragon. A cloying, metallic tang filled the air, the scent richer than human blood.

The age of the executioner made the violence worse, like handing a cleaver to an infant and instructing them to execute a man. They might get there in the end, yet not on the first stroke, nor even the tenth. This was savage, undisciplined work.

When the ginger did not stop and the other hatchlings mewled low and scrambled for the door, Osric called out, "That's enough. Tell it to stop."

Sovereign puffed smoke, but a moment later the ginger ceased its butchery. It raised a bloody snout and roared, a shrill, young roar, as loud as it could.

"We will find many uses for this aspirant."

"Train your beast," Osric said.

He left, taking the other hatchlings with him. At their nest, he found Dahaka already there. She snapped to attention.

"At ease," Osric grunted. The hatchlings sloped past him, somber and diminished. "Give them an extra ration. There will be some to spare after today."

Dahaka's eyes flitted fast over the drakes. "Two are missing."

"One shall remain with him for a time. The other is dead."

Her eyes lit with fire before she smiled and nodded as though nothing were amiss. "If it is his will."

Osric made to leave.

"Master Osric, the blood alchemist requests a donation from you. I am told the initial results of the new blends are promising."

He turned slowly on his heel and looked long into her broad face. Rather than commit to an outright refusal, he gave a non-committal nod and took his leave.

Feeling the need for air and to inform the cultists they could return inside the mystic tower, Osric ventured out into the yard. The fierce winds of Windshear were low of late, gentle breaths rather than howls. It allowed the commands of the Speaker to ring loud and clear as she drilled her faithful in the ways of halberd, crossbow, and cloak.

Under the northern walls, more dragons stood by the auxiliary buildings that housed the blood alchemist's laboratory and allowed their blood to be drained. A creeping sensation ran over Osric's skin. Dragons were a force of the natural world. Black bears, great stags, northern wolves; such powers should not be caged and bled like meat for the market.

A fenced pen that once served for sheep or pigs now functioned as a testing arena for the alchemist. Two cultists wrestled now. One drank something. Soon that person swelled, as though the power of the muscled hatchling had been injected into them. While their clothes ripped, their dragonhide cloak survived, although it now struggled to cover them. They screamed, beat their chest, then twitched, spasmed, and fell shaking to the ground. White foam frothed at their mouth. 'Promising' results indeed.

Osric looked away.

"There might be success if you were to go," the charming voice told him.

Taken aback, Osric raised a hand to his temple. He had not heard the voice as often of late. Not during the mission in the gorge. Come to think of it, he had not heard it for a time even before then. Not once while he had labored over his axes that he could recall. Strange to hear it again now. If Sovereign meant for him to give blood, then he would just demand it of him.

"Why not go now? It will help further the cause."

Perhaps he had been so long in Sovereign's service that his mind was playing tricks on him, pushing him down the road it knew he must eventually walk. Whatever the case, Osric found he did not need to listen to it right now. For the first time, he listened to the voice and chose to ignore it.

A squad of the Shroud walked by on their way back inside the mystic tower. They saluted and acknowledged him with a chorus of "General."

Osric nodded and they carried on. He wondered why he bothered to keep up the pretense of that title. He commanded no coherent army anymore. The Speaker handled her faithful. They woke each morning as genuine believers in Sovereign's cause. Dahaka did too. Why else would she so willingly visit the alchemist or encourage him to do so?

Truth was, he had no real authority or will here. Sovereign commanded them all. All Osric could do was avoid and delay. No doubt Sovereign would compel him to go to that blood-soaked work-shop in time. Yet that was Sovereign's ill task to give.

Three days later, Sovereign gave him something worse.

The hatchlings lined themselves up for inspection again. The muscled ginger prowled around his lessers, issuing a low growl at the back of his throat. Two of the babies showed him defiance, others looked for safety in the stone floor.

Sovereign silenced them and ordered that they part, leaving the dragon with only one eye standing alone as though on a stage.

"I had high hopes for this one. Her ailment made me think she might follow in Ash's footsteps as a lunar. Alas, she has no power within her."

"So be it. I'll take the others away first this time."

"By all means," Sovereign said. *"Then dispose of her."*

Osric met the dragon's hateful eyes. They burned with a fresh intensity.

"For once, you might do your own foul work."

"I do not wish the mess."

"That did not matter before."

This wasn't about the baby or blood or powers at all – it was a test or, more likely, a torture. Sovereign was pushing him.

The one-eyed dragon mewled softly. Whether understanding Sovereign's words or his mere aura and intent, she trembled worse than her navy sibling had days before. A puddle of urine streamed out from under her feet.

"Better you do it than the beast," the charming voice told him. *"A quick, clean death."*

Osric thumbed one of his axes, though his eyes were fixed firmly on Sovereign.

"I have done and am prepared to do much in the course of my duties. I have sent men and women knowingly to their deaths so that others may live. I have burned towns to defeat the blight. I have removed the heads of men I once deemed friends. And under your instruction, I have murdered my own kin."

Sovereign scoffed as though amused.

"But I will not kill an infant in cold blood, whether dragon or human. It has done no harm. It can do no harm to us or your cause. You wanted these hatchlings. They're your responsibility. If you desire them dead, do it by your own talons."

"Obey," the charming voice said, yet Osric did not find it as convincing as he once had.

Still looking Sovereign in his furious eyes, he said, loudly, "I will not."

"Where has this defiance come from?" Sovereign hissed. *"The Speaker tells me you will not give your blood to her alchemist. And now this. Come now, Osric. Is this truly where you draw the line? After all you've done?"*

"Do you really care for dragons as you claim, or is this all about power?" Osric fired back. "Would you make slaves of us all, *Thrall?*"

The bond flamed open in his soul. Pain blossomed in a flower of knives. Osric clutched at his chest and groaned as Sovereign seeped into him.

"Never call me by that name."

Across the bond came a rush of images and sounds. A tall man in blood-red rider armor clenched a fist surrounded in black light and issued a command for 'Thrall' to come to him. Small and wary, he crept forward in fear and yet in longing, longing that things would go back to how they were. How they should be. And beneath that, hatred. Hate born from a deep betrayal. A love turned sour, the most bitter of all failings.

Quick as that, it ended. Sovereign departed and closed the dragon bond behind him as he fled. Yet the damage was done.

"You hated your rider," Osric said. It was a statement, not a question. In his wroth, Sovereign had let a piece of himself show. "Though you once loved him." Osric understood that contradiction well. Better than most.

The smoke Sovereign spewed from his mouth and nostrils would have been choking had the hatchery been closed. He rose onto all fours and swept his tail hard, breaking the old pens and nesting spots.

The babies backed away. Even the aggressive ginger seemed to doubt his master's next move.

"Kill the whelp," Sovereign commanded.

Osric raised his arms, knowing full well what would happen. "This time, you'll have to make me."

The bond reopened. The black chains erupted in his soul as though from a geyser, binding Osric and dragging him back, back, deep and down into the dark recesses of his own mind.

Trapped in a corner, bound in chains and with pressure being exerted on his will from all sides, Osric could not budge.

"Stay down," the voice told him, only now it was not charming. It spoke as it had at their first meeting. Osric could then only watch, as though from afar, his own body perform actions he had not willed.

His right hand drew Spite and his left lunged for the one-eyed dragon.

Small and weak, Osric fought back. He fought with all the might left in him. Every ounce of spirit. Everything.

Sovereign guided him to the opening of the hatchery, dragging the struggling hatchling along with him. It bit and scratched at him, but his Lord's skin withstood the attacks.

There, at the precipice, the hatchling was thrust to the floor so that its neck extended over the breach. A long drop descended to the rugged foundations of Windshear Hold. The hatchling squealed and kicked as Osric's right hand rose.

He fought. He fought. Yet Sovereign had turned his full mind to this, and Osric had never known anyone to resist the dragon's magic when directed so singularly. The black chains tightened their noose.

Osric's hand fell in a strong stroke. Sunlight caught the edge of the axe and glowed red. The squeals of the hatchling cut off sudden and harsh.

Sovereign's chains unwound themselves like so many snakes and the dragon left him there upon the precipice, back in control of his body. Blood smeared the head of his axe. The headless body of the baby dragon lay under his left hand.

"There will be order in my new world. All shall be brought together, as a million minds and one. But for there to be order, there must be obedience."

The charming voice returned. *"Stay down."*

Osric did. He wasn't sure how long he remained by the hatchling's body. What he wanted was to weep, not for the dragon, but for the hollow man, the puppet he had become.

When at last he rose, gathered the hatchlings, and left, they displayed more courage in facing him than Sovereign. They hissed, snapped their teeth, and roared at him, though they kept their distance.

They hate me now, he thought. *As well they should.*

A weariness came upon him as he closed the door to the nest. When Dahaka came to tell him that more eggs from the mystic raid were hatching, he followed her reluctantly to the top of the mystic tower.

"General," the guards said as he approached. The title seemed a twisted joke to him now.

"Fetch chopped meat from the kitchens," Osric told them.

He entered the hatchery with Dahaka. Torches on the wall kept the night at bay. A drake with sandy scales and a clubbed foot already moved awkwardly in its crate. A second dragon with purple scales struggled to breathe. Osric thought it would repeat the destiny of the turquoise dragon, yet after he cleared its mouth of gunk and shell, it breathed fine. The reason it had struggled was because it had no nostrils.

The last egg shook. This was the swollen one Osric had brought from the gorge. Given its nature, he expected another muscled bruiser to appear.

The shell shook, then broke suddenly from all sides at once. Two dragons emerged from the same egg. One had scales glistening gold under the firelight. The other was as dark as the shadows cast upon the walls, shimmering like oil as it moved. The whites of its eyes stood stark against its black body and surrounded dark purple pupils mottled with black.

Despite his wishes, he was partly a creature of magic now, and something about these two sang to him.

"Do you sense something here?" he asked.

Dahaka beamed. "Yes, I do. You feel it too, Master Agravain? The golden one holds such promise. Already its notes sing."

"The golden one?" Osric eyed the black dragon again, but it had curled up into a tight ball. The golden drake cooed and yapped and clawed at its crate, ready to enter the world. "Yes, this one. For its sake, Champion Dahaka, I hope you are right."

TWENTY-EIGHT

A Life to Fight For

Browbeaten by events in the valley of the Mystic Flight, Holt, Ash, Aberanth, Rake, and Eidolan made their way south in haste. Holt now considered the valley's name of the Grim Gorge to be apt.

Their destination lay far to the south and east, to lands that hugged the eastern coastline of the Stretched Sea and extended east and south again to the borders of the Searing Sands. The region of Ahar. Growing up in western Feorlen, Ahar seemed a world apart to Holt. All he knew was the name of the Order Hall that guarded it: Alamut.

"One hundred and seventy-six years ago, I aided a dragon from Alamut," Rake told them. "On her honor, she vowed to come to my aid should I call upon her."

Another one of Rake's valued favors. Then, thinking about Eidolan and his time in the Order, Holt asked, "Is she still in the Order after all this time?

"She passed thirty years after our meeting, but the vow lingers in her blood memories."

"Then who are we going to see?"

"Her granddaughter."

As before, they traveled on foot, quicker than a traveling band of humans would, yet, given Rake's injury, slower than they might have. Eidolan often took to the sky to stretch his wings, where he could be alone with his dampened spirits. Even Rake spoke less in the days following Osric's raid. The spring had left his step, and he japed less.

On occasion, Holt and Ash would join Eidolan in flight, enjoying the freedom of the white world above clouds and the endless horizon. Other times, Holt walked alongside Aberanth, who preferred walking to flying, and discussed what other benefits food-lore might bring to the emerald's work.

"I knew about the meat preferences, of course," Aberanth told him as they marched, *"but I never considered there might be additional magical properties beyond attracting more motes toward the core."*

"I'm surprised Rake hasn't discovered something like this in his time."

"Rake has been… well, Rake for so long I doubt human cooking crossed his mind."

The half-dragon strode ahead of them. He carried the top half of his broken polearm in one hand. The other half of the shaft was bundled into their equipment.

Holt lowered his voice and asked, "What happened to him?"

"That's his story to tell, if he chooses," said Aberanth. *"I do not know it all myself."*

"Do you know his name at least? His human name. I can't imagine someone named their son Rake."

Aberanth shook his head. *"Allow him such secrets as he wills. He is brash but good, and a kinder friend to me than anyone else has been."*

"He's done much for Ash and me too."

"He knows what it's like to be like us."

"Yes, he does." Holt found himself softening to Rake again. Stubborn as the half-dragon was, he was not insane. Self-preservation seemed high on his priorities, and with Ash's words in mind, he decided to wait and hear Rake's full plan to attack Thrall before reassessing.

As Rake's temperament recovered, so too did the spring in his step and the rate at which he pounced on Holt to train him. Swordwork, cycling techniques, guided Cleansing, no line of rider training escaped Holt on their journey south.

"That's better," Rake said in a self-satisfied manner after one sparring session.

Holt stayed light on his feet and kept his sword in a guard position, expecting Rake to attack again. He was Grounding, and he could maintain it during a full exchange with Rake now, even if they were brief.

Rake carried on. "But you need to be prepared to switch cycling at a moment's notice." Orange light swirled at his hand like a sunset, then shot out. Holt barely registered it, thought too long about which technique would counter it, then before he could begin Floating, Rake's magic sent him staggering. Doubled over, Holt wheezed and clutched at his belly.

"Wouldn't it be easier just to dodge the attack?" Holt asked.

"Gosh, Holt, I'd never considered that." Rake screwed up his face in mock concentration and tapped his temple. "You know what, we should avoid being hit by all things trying to hurt us. I just don't know why no one thought of this before."

"Alright, alright," Holt said, exasperated. He straightened, cricked his neck, and gave a satisfying groan of relief. Ash sat some way off with Eidolan, taking a lesson in how to Sink more effectively during a Forging session. "Can we practice Floating for a while then?"

"Yes, I think so," Rake said. "You've got the basic knack of Grounding under control. Aberanth, if you would be so kind as to give Holt an elixir to help him get started."

Aberanth dutifully produced a vial, then backed off a safe distance from the training zone and sat earnestly with his notes out. Holt held the elixir up to inspect it. The liquid was flax yellow in color and none too appealing.

"What's in this one?" Holt said, bracing himself.

"The key component is ginger," Aberanth said. *"And just the smallest pinch of turmeric, which accounts for the color."*

Holt relaxed. That didn't sound so bad. Better than salt water for sure.

Thinking about making venison jerky for Floating, Holt asked, "Is the turmeric important? Spices like that are hard to find in most of the world."

"For the elixir, it helps," Aberanth said. *"If you're wondering for the meat variant, I couldn't say. The ginger alone might suffice."*

"Good thing we're heading to Ahar then," Holt said. He took a breath, then began cycling his motes in the Floating technique. This was harder than Grounding. That method only needed him to cycle motes to and from his limbs, something he was used to doing. Floating was a delicate matter. He had to push the motes up and outward from his soul, away from his center, to run through the thinner channels running under his skin.

After a number of false starts, he kicked the ground in frustration.

"Take your time," Rake said. "You'll find your skin itches as you find the correct flow."

It took Holt a dozen more attempts to Float for several full cycles. The next time, he pulled the cork out of the vial and drank the elixir. He smacked his lips. He'd been expecting a sharp, fiery taste, but it was warm and woody.

"Did you pre-cook the ginger?" Holt asked.

"Ah, well observed," said Aberanth. *"Yes, I found that slow cooking it helped best to intensify the profile—"*

"Is it helping?" Rake cut in.

Holt Floated for a few more cycles.

"Yes, it feels much easier now."

"Good," Rake said, short and sharp. Then he blasted more orange power, which hit Holt in his side. It hurt, as though someone had taken a club to him, but unlike before, he didn't stagger back or double over.

"I still think I'd rather dodge it," Holt said, massaging his side.

Rake laughed. "There may come a time when you can't avoid it. Also, you can take a calculated risk here and there, taking a blow to close a gap or else perform your own ability. Though you're not wrong. Avoid what you can. The good news is that if you can get to grips with Floating, then its opposite technique, Sinking, should come easier."

"You said Sinking helps draw magic over the bond faster," Holt said. "Is there much use in that? Seems like a good way to fray my bond."

"There is some utility in it," Rake said. "Show me one of your Lunar Shocks."

Holt did so. He channeled power to his palm, gathered it there, then launched the ability in a compact ball of silver-white light.

"Now, how long did that take you?" Rake asked. "A few seconds?"

"Something like that," Holt said. "I wasn't counting."

"Then count."

Holt charged up another Lunar Shock and released it harmlessly through the air.

"Two seconds," Holt said. "Maybe just under three."

"A simple technique like that doesn't take long," Rake said. "Still, a second here or there can make the difference between life and death. While Sinking, power will travel across the bond easier, making abilities quicker." He scratched his scaly chin, apparently considering something. "That burst of light you made to blind Osric, what was that?"

"Bit of a desperate last resort," Holt said. "It's not an ability I've practiced or anything. It's a bit like preparing a Lunar Shock, only I blast out as much light as I can as wide as I can. I did it to Orvel back in Brenin to try and get away. It sort of worked then, so it was all I could think to do against Osric."

"*It was quite intense,*" Aberanth said. "*If I had been closer, I think I would have been dazed by it as well.*"

"From what you told me of Osric's reaction, I'd say it worked well enough," Rake said. "It's not a terrible strategy by any means, so long as you don't blind yourself doing it."

"That's been an issue so far," Holt admitted.

"Shut your eyes then," Rake offered casually. "Might be we could develop that into your Champion ability, if you find use in it."

A Champion ability. Holt's mind boggled at the thought.

"I won't become a Champion for ages yet, will I? Takes riders years to reach it... if they do."

"That's because the Order uses timid methods," Rake said. "If you're brave and willing, there are ways to *expedite* your growth."

That seemed to catch Eidolan's attention. He snorted purple smoke and paused in his training of Ash. *"Such ways also lead to a quick death."*

"A quick death can come by slipping on a flight of stairs and breaking your neck," Rake said. "Don't let such fear hold you back, Holt."

"It's not only my choice," Holt said. "Ash," he called, and then, privately, he asked, *"I'm willing if you are. We need to rank faster than the Order would allow."*

Holt expected an immediate, enthusiastic response, but Ash took his time. Yet in the end, he did answer, albeit cautiously.

"I am willing to do what it takes."

"Whatever it takes, Rake," Holt said. "We'll do it."

Eidolan growled low and returned to instructing Ash. Rake held his head high and seemed almost proud.

"So if I practice this ability," Holt went on, "and learn Sinking, then I could perform the flash of light much quicker. I could daze an opponent without making it obvious what I'm about to do?"

Rake nodded absentmindedly and spun the remaining half of his polearm around, seeming bored. "Yes, you have the idea of it. But let's get your mind off Sinking. It's a cycling method best used for Lords who don't need to fear a frayed bond. You still have basics to master," and as he said this, he launched into another attack.

After the training ended, the group ate, rested, and Holt Cleansed and Forged while Ash Sunk his own mote channels to draw lunar motes toward him. Under the moon each night, the core developed into an ever denser orb, a far cry from the pale wisps of light it had started out as.

The days passed quickly in this fashion.

They ate what they could hunt. All the herbs Holt had brought from Sidastra had long since run out. Even his supply of salt vanished under the intense use of jerky experimentation. Ash hunted one more deer on their journey, but little of it could be taken with them without salt to preserve it. Elsewise they found other game, wild roaming sheep, slender goats, and even one bison which must have wandered far from its herd.

Rake insisted on roasting his own lamb. Holt had no means left to dress up the meal so he allowed it, though he could not help but wonder if Rake cooked the meat to spare Holt's sensibilities. It was one thing for dragons to eat an animal unskinned and raw, but quite another to see a half-human being do the same.

One evening they were forced to abandon their hunt. Two emerald dragons had drawn close, Rake said. Wild dragons, roaming far for any emeralds of the Fae Forest, which made Rake suspicious. Even if they were on their side, he thought it best not to reveal themselves to any rider or dragon.

During rare moments in which Holt wasn't on the move, hunting, cooking, training, Cleansing, or Forging, he attended to his family's recipe book. He updated his notes with all he had learned about jerky, theorizing that the same could be applied to other meats. Also, he included his lessons on the cycling techniques and which ingredients from Aberanth's elixirs linked to each one.

When not adding to the book, he leafed through its pages, searching for any recipe inspired from the lands of Ahar, few as they were. The spices and rice of the east were not easily obtained on the wet, wild, western coast of Feorlen.

Yet, from these recipes, he gathered some insight into the region. He could almost smell the onion, turmeric, and cumin as he read the recipes. Working in such kitchens would be fragrant indeed. One recipe looked perfect for ice dragons.

Trout stuffed with onions, barberries, garlic, and herbs, with lots of tamarind to give the tangy taste the ice dragons liked best. The other dishes were slow-cooked meals, with the meat of the dragon's choice softened for hours in the pot.

Holt gained the impression of a people who cared about their food and who were prepared to spend a lot of time getting it right.

South and farther south they traveled. Holt added in each cycling method to his litany of exercises and sometimes practiced gathering light and expelling it in a wider, bright flash. It was far from what he would consider a proper ability, and it took him time to do it in a controlled manner. About five seconds for each flash, and five seconds was a long time in a fight.

One night, after releasing a particularly bright flash, Eidolan rumbled at him reproachfully. *"You ought to be careful, young Ascendant. We do not wish attention to be drawn to us."*

Instinctively Holt looked to the sky. It was clear, but Eidolan had a point, so Holt kept his practice to brief moments during the day.

At length, their journey brought them to the northern edge of Ahar. Here the air became drier and hotter than the world behind. After trekking across wild stretches of the abandoned east, signs of civilization returned.

Even at a distance, Holt observed these villages and towns with fascination. A pale stone, sometimes chalk white, was favored for their buildings. Their roofs were flat rather than angled and thatched. Great sheets of cloth hung suspended over the streets to cast shade. Holt would have welcomed a bit of shade.

Midsummer had come, and he worried that the heat would become too great for him if they continued much farther south.

According to his map, the Order Hall of Alamut was situated in the north of the region. The party was thus closer to Alamut than the Order Hall was to the region's capital city of Negine Sahra near the borders of the desert.

Rake brought them to a vantage point. The summer air was thick with burnt copper dust, and in the distance rose a staircase of hills with a town draped onto the slopes. Buildings stacked upon buildings, forming a waterfall of pale stone. Atop the highest hill was a walled fortress. Its towers reached for the clouds, and the unmistakable silhouettes of dragons flew above it.

Alamut.

"Can you contact your friend from here?" Holt asked.

Rake raised a finger and closed his eyes in concentration.

"If our flight has come to a halt, I should be grateful for a rest," Eidolan said.

Without waiting for confirmation, he curled up into a tight ball, brought a wing over his snout and fell asleep. Falling asleep immediately seemed to be a trait of the old dragon.

Aberanth breathed hard. His tongue lolled out of his mouth, and he positioned himself in Rake's shadow.

"What I wouldn't do to find a nice cold cave with juicy algae and mushrooms."

Holt sympathized, though the algae did not sound appealing. Poor Aberanth struggled to find food in these drier lands.

"It is done," Rake said with a flourish.

"You found her then, the granddaughter?"

"I did not think dragons had fathers and mothers as humans do," Ash said, his voice loaded with anticipation.

"Not as such," Rake said. "A collective song of a flight sings all new eggs into being. In some eggs, a verse of an ancestor can ring true." He gave Ash a sad smile. "But, before you ask, I'm afraid you're different even to that. You are unique, my little white friend. The first of your kind. Notes collided, forming a new harmony to create you, and no lineage can I hear in your song, save for that of the stars themselves."

"I... understand, Master Rake. Others have told me as much. I was wrong to forget it."

The disappointment in Ash's voice broke Holt's heart. He moved to Ash's side and ran a hand up and down the dragon's neck. "You've got us."

Ash rustled his wings and nuzzled Holt back.

Holt enjoyed the glow of the bond for a moment before concerns that had gnawed at him since entering Ahar surged to the surface.

"Rake, are you sure you can trust this dragon? Won't she have a rider? What's to stop them alerting the whole of Alamut to us?"

"Always so many questions, Holt. It's like you think I make it up as I go along."

Aberanth gave a nervous rumble of laughter.

Rake ignored him. "Farsa, the rider, is too honorable to go running to the authorities."

Holt wished he could be so sure. His opinion of dragon rider honor had taken a severe knock in recent months.

"She says it will take them three days before they can slip out," Rake said.

This shook Holt from his brooding. He squinted up at the blazing sun and raised an inadequate hand to shield his face.

"Then might we find some shelter from the heat?"

"Of course," Rake said. He smiled, ever a dangerous thing. "Once we reach our destination. Hava and Farsa will meet us in a most important location to the southwest. Oh, don't look so down – it won't be so hot there."

"Is Hava still in range for you to speak with? We could use supplies."

"If they leave Alamut with too much it will look suspicious." Rake frowned. "Do you still have some silver from Miss Agravain?"

Holt reflexively brought a hand to the coin pouch on his belt.

"I thought you might pop into a marketplace on our way," Rake said.

Holt's first thought was that he had no idea if Feorlen silver would be accepted here. His next thought was that he would stand out like a green apple in a bushel of reds.

"I can't speak their language," Holt said.

"The common tongue of the Aldunei belt is not unknown in the east," Rake said. "And there is always the universal language." Rake indicated by pointing, nodding, and shaking his head. He ceased and grinned. "Come, let us not dwell near Alamut any longer." He gave Eidolan a none too gentle kick. The old mystic awoke with a start, throwing up dust and dry earth. "Oh good, you're up," Rake said. "Come on, we're on the move again."

Turning west, the party traveled for another day. They slept late and woke early, and before the sun crested into a red dawn, they came within sight of a far-off town. Rake ensured they were within just five miles of its walls. Enough for him to scan for other cores.

"Ah," he said. "That's a problem."

"Another rider?" Holt asked.

"Some Ascendant. Might be ice."

Holt wilted at the thought of being an ice rider in this land. Then again, they could cool themselves.

"Well, with enough distance, the rider won't be able to sense Ash through me, right?"

"Correct. But between here and town isn't far enough. If you enter the town, that rider will sense him, even faintly, through you. You would act like a signal fire in the dark. And I won't have us march for miles just to put distance between the pair of you. We'll stick here, where you can easily find us again."

"So, what am I supposed to do? The other Ascendant will sense me."

"You can close your bond for a time. That will hide the core."

"You said we couldn't veil Ash's core."

"And I stand by that. This is different. You are closing the bond from your side, boarding up the window, so to speak. Nothing occurs to Ash's core."

"Brode and Talia never mentioned such a thing."

"It's… unpleasant," Rake said. "But you'll recall from our recent encounter with Agravain that we could not sense Thrall through him at first."

Holt thought back and realized this was true.

"*I sensed nothing from the man, at first,*" Aberanth confirmed.

"*Nor I,*" Eidolan said. "*I did wonder why he caused you so much trouble, Rake.*"

Holt then had a second, more alarming realization. Just like in Sidastra, the distance between Osric and Thrall that night must have been substantial. Yet when Osric had opened his bond again, Thrall's power hummed clear and bright. Not just a signal fire, but a great lighthouse. He explained this observation on the impossible distance at which Thrall seemed capable of controlling Osric to the group and ended on a dark note.

"Is Thrall truly that powerful?"

"Oh, I don't know," Rake said wryly. "Eidolon, might you shed any light on the matter?"

Eidolan growled. *"Send the Ascendant for his supplies and let us be on our way."*

"Such team spirit," Rake said. He focused on Holt again. "Now, closing a bond. It's deceptively simple."

As Rake explained what he must do, Holt's enthusiasm for this supply run plummeted. Somehow, he was to plug up his soul with thoughts and emotions contrary to those he associated with the bond. Where Ash gave him friendship, he must counter it with isolation; grief for happiness; despair for hope; hatred for love.

"Can't Eidolan cast an illusion over me or something?" Holt asked. That seemed the simpler course.

"In this case, it would not help," Eidolan said. *"My illusions will generate a low magical presence. Not enough to be detected at a distance, but at close quarters, another rider or dragon will feel the magic. They may not understand it, but the fact it is there would mark you. It is also likely to break. Arrows can pierce an illusion without breaking it, but should another conscious being touch it, it will shatter."*

So even shaking a merchant's hand to seal a purchase would break any disguise.

"Besides," Eidolon continued, *"though I might change your skin and features to match the people of these lands, imperfectly so, you cannot speak their tongue, as you say. What good would that disguise do you?"*

Resigned, Holt nodded and unstrapped Brode's sword. He left everything else of value behind too, save for the coins he would take.

Before leaving, he went to hug Ash. "I'm sorry we've got to do this."

"It's only for a short while."

Holt patted Ash one more time, then stood back and turned his concentration to Rake's instructions. His assertion that some found this process unpleasant proved to be an understatement.

Drawing on feelings of isolation came easy enough. Holt had spent many a dark evening alone in his little house at the Crag. Grief? Cradling his father's head as the life drained from his eyes. Despair? Their time in Sidastra before the battle. As Holt sank into these miserable thoughts, he dragged them down to the level of his soul. The light from Ash's core faded, blocked brick by brick as the bond closed over. Yet it did not close. He required more. What or who did he hate? He hated Thrall, but his first attempts to clog the bond with those feelings failed.

Deeper then. Hatred. True hatred.

To his surprise, his thoughts turned to Osric Agravain. The look on his face when fighting Rake had been terrible to behold. Pure desire: not the hunger of a predator, nor hunger for glory, but for the kill itself. The kill alone. That expression haunted Holt. Given the chance, Osric would have beheaded Rake and then him, Ash, and Aberanth in turn.

Osric's betrayal had nearly broken Talia as well. Only her quiet hope that he might be brought back had kept her head above water before the battle. That she might still save the last member of her family. Most damning of all was that night in Grim Gorge. Osric had not been under Thrall's direct control. And if that was the case, then he was not a man who deserved redemption. That would crush Talia. Realizing this, Holt's hatred burned brighter.

Rake was right. He needs to die.

Across the weakened bridge between them, Ash called out to him.

"You don't feel like yourself."

Ash couldn't help it. That was why Holt loved him, but this needed to be done, and in his dark state, he channeled his hatred to clog the last gaps in the bond.

With the final brick over the window to the core, the light vanished in his mind's eye. A coldness took root in his chest. His soul felt like a long-abandoned hearth. Though he was standing still, his breath came heavier and harder.

Ash moaned low and sad.

"I don't know if I can think clearly like this," Holt said.

"You'd better try," Rake said. "We don't have much choice. You're the one human amongst us, unless you suggest Aberanth stand on his hind legs and don a robe and a rather large hat."

Holt pinched the bridge of his nose hard and waved Rake down. Taking a deep breath, he set off for the town.

When he arrived at the town gates, a guard flagged him down. A foreign boy out on his own no doubt raised questions in the man's mind. The guard spoke to him in slow, overly pronounced words.

"Who are you? Why you here?"

Impressed the guard knew anything of Holt's tongue, he replied, equally slowly and clearly, "Trading." He jingled his coin pouch, then flashed some silver. Greasing an interaction with silver had its risks, but if the guard tried to seize the rest it would be to his swift detriment.

The guard narrowed his eyes and took the coins. He bit one, then smiled broadly through his thick beard.

"Yes. Go bazaar. Bazaar."

Holt passed through the gates. White and pale limestone dazzled under the early morning sun. He'd expected a reaction from Ash, but, of course, none came. The empty feeling in his chest grew in its dead weight.

Intending to be as fast as he could, Holt ducked into the shade cast by canopies of cloth and uttered a sigh of relief. One by one, doors opened down the street as the inhabitants started a new day.

Holt found a signpost. He did not recognize the words, but he found the term the guard had been so insistent on. Bazaar. He followed the directions until he reached what he judged to be the center of the town, already brimming with life.

Bakers, Weavers, Chandlers, Carpenters, Shoemakers, and Jewelers; many stalls and wares Holt recognized, even if their role-names here did not match those of his homeland. His first stop was at a cloth stall, where he pointed in earnest to a strip of white cotton and then to a silver coin in his hand. His desperation to leave and reopen the bond to Ash helped fuel his performance.

To his fortune, the owner was a portly, maternal woman. Her dark

eyes melted at the lost, sad-looking boy miming before her. She gave
him a wan smile, then reached over, took one silver from him without
registering its origin before handing him back three worn bronze
coins.

Holt wrapped the cloth around and over his head, imitating the
townsfolk. Unfortunately, the next stalls did not have such sympathetic owners.

With each minute, he felt the weight in his chest deepen into an
ache. He passed a stall with pots of spices, yet his senses felt as deadened as his soul. Little of the spice reached his nose, and even their
colors were dulled to him. Sweat gathered fast at his neck and brow.

Wishing nothing more than to return to Ash, he resorted to
handing over too much of his silver just to seal each transaction
quickly. By the time he was done, he had not a coin left to his name.

Holt headed back the way he came and froze. A young man in blue
silks with a large cobalt scabbard upon his back strutted into the
bazaar. A painful second passed in which the other Ascendant looked
right at him. Holt's stomach knotted. Then the Ascendant's gaze
passed lazily over him, an easy, casual dismissal that Holt well
remembered.

Though pleased, he was also becoming nauseous, and so he sped
out of the bazaar and back to the gates. The guards took one look at
him, hastily stepped back, and let him pass. Sickly people had no
issues when leaving a town.

To his astonishment, he made it back to the group before his
stomach heaved. He set their supplies down, collapsed into Ash's
embrace, and reopened their bond.

At once, all was well again. He breathed easy. Light returned to
him, vanquishing the dread darkness.

"That was horrible," Holt said. He sucked in another deep breath,
then sighed in relief. "Osric must be tough. I could not have fought
like he did with the bond closed."

"Not all bonds are happy and wholesome," Eidolan said. "Any connected to
that dragon may well be pleased to be rid of him."

"We gave him that chance," Holt said darkly. "He made his choice."

"We don't know for sure," Ash said. Hearing his voice again was like soothing honey on a sore throat.

"Breaking a bond is no small thing," Rake said. "Even one made in hate. If he did manage to break his bond with Thrall, the act alone might kill him."

"That would be no shame," Holt said.

Rake snorted and gave him a nod of approval.

Ash looked reproachful, but before he could say anything, Holt hastened to reveal the results of his mission. Chiefly he had bought a good supply of dry fish, either heavily salted or smoked. Sticking with nonperishable foods, he had gathered nuts, especially walnuts, as well as dried apricots, large dates, and a heavy sack of rice. Now he felt more like himself again, he felt quite excited about the rice.

"My father rarely used rice," Holt said. "Only on rare occasions when a rider visited from Ahar. I never had a chance to cook it myself."

"Well, how hard can it be?" Rake said. He picked out a plump eggplant from a pile of vegetables. "For Aberanth, I presume?" He threw it to Aberanth, who attacked it greedily.

Holt looked on in despair. "One day we'll be near an oven again and you'll let me roast that for you."

"One day, perhaps," Aberanth said. He chewed, swallowed, and spoke telepathically all at the same time. *"Were you able to restock on salt?"*

"Yes, and I got powdered ginger. I didn't think a fresh root would last. No wine or vinegar though." Aberanth had told him that vinegar was the key component in his elixirs for Sinking. "I got you some more mushrooms too," Holt added, pointing to a final sack.

"Good work," Rake said with the air of someone wishing to move things along. "Now, on we go, or we risk missing Farsa and Hava."

. . .

After another night and day of travel to the southwest, the land grew greener and the sun kinder. Hills swept before them, rolling down to the mighty river which came out of the distant north and snaked toward the sea, marking the border between the old lands ruled by Aldunei and the east.

Rake took them into the hills, and the deeper into the winding passes they went, the worse the land became. In places it dove down in sheer drops, with routes that could not be traversed by foot. While the others flew, Rake clambered about in a way no human could have managed to navigate the terrain.

Holt got the feeling of delving deeper into a maze. Down they went, until the grassland became dust and rock and trees withered to dead husks. The air remained dry, but a foul undertone carried on it, a scent Holt recognized well.

"This place was ravaged by the scourge."

"You're walking in an ancient scourge chasm," Rake said.

"And Farsa wanted to meet us here?"

"It was I who picked the spot," Rake said. "Down in the bottom-most pits of this chasm is where Hava's ancestor swore her oath to repay me. Promises made in such spots hold power."

Eidolan prowled, keeping low to the ground. *"I'd hoped never to find myself in a chasm again."*

Aberanth shivered. The damage to the land would be affecting him the most as an emerald.

"Might the enemy still be here?" asked Ash.

"I shouldn't think so," Rake said. "At least, not close to the surface."

At last, they made it to the bottom of the ravine. A segment of the rock face caught Holt's eye. The color of the stone was off, much darker and in an unnatural block compared to the varied living stone around it. A runic symbol similar to those Aberanth made on his bark slabs was etched into the stone, only it was huge, about twice the size of Rake.

"Did a dragon do this?" Holt asked.

"One of the Order," Rake said. "When they sealed this place long ago."

A cold trickle of fear crept up Holt's spine. He reached out with his magical senses, but the rock and earth blocked any presence of the scourge, if any were in fact beneath them.

"Let's get a fire started," Ash said. *"That will help."*

They made camp. Dead, dry wood was in ample supply, and soon they had a hearty fire to comfort their spirits.

Moonlight struggled to grace them down here. Ash followed glinting patches as the moon traveled across the night sky, while Holt trained in maintaining cycling techniques during combat. He Grounded his limbs as Rake pressed him in a physical confrontation. Then Rake zipped twenty feet away, called, "Float," and launched his orange power.

Holt switched his cycling, raising magic to thin channels near his skin to blunt Rake's attack. The orange light struck his side like a forceful punch. Holt held up, but he felt another bruise form for his growing collection.

"That's better," Rake called. He blur-stepped across the distance between them.

Assuming more swordplay was about to start, Holt switched to Grounding.

Rake grinned. "Good, but that will be enough for one night. My leg pains me." He placed a hand upon his injured thigh, but the fact he was using his abilities showed he was healing well. "And I have my own training to attend to."

Eidolan uncurled himself from where he dozed, stretched, and shook out his wings. *"Ready?"*

Rake cricked his neck. "Don't hold back."

A silent battle raged. Eidolan's core flared from the effort. Rake set his jaw. The only sign of discomfort was an increasing frown upon his face. After a few moments, the pair broke their tussle. Rake groaned, rolled his shoulders, and said, "Again."

While Rake trained in the Lifting technique, Holt felt hunger come upon him. A source of water ran nearby, running through the ravine from the higher hills. Holt planned to make rice.

No notes in his recipe book contained helpful tips on making it. Dragons did not eat rice. However, as Rake had remarked, how hard could it be? He scooped two fistfuls of rice into his cooking pot, added salt, and covered it with water before setting it over their fire.

As it turned out, making rice was not so simple. First, he used too little water, then he added too much. Then the bottom layer stuck to the base of the pot.

"Blight take it," he cursed as he tried to salvage his dinner. He was left with pulp rather than fluffy pieces of rice. Huffing, he stirred in flakes of smoked fish and a couple of chopped dates. *Hopefully not a disaster,* he thought as he raised a spoonful to his mouth. Alas, the texture was slimy. The smoked fish overpowering.

"*I told you that fish was nasty,*" Ash said. The dragon lay beside Holt and placed his snout upon his front talons.

Holt smacked his lips. "I've had worse." He gazed back at his gloopy rice, fish, thing and spooned it into his mouth until his bowl was clean. Setting the bowl down, he said, "Well, that's my feast. I've had it."

The phrase caught him by surprise. It brought him back to the square table in his little house, where his father would make the same declaration after eating something less than desirable.

'Fussy boys are hungry boys,' he would add whenever Holt played with his food.

Holt spent a moment reliving those meals. He shared the memory with Ash, and their bond bloomed as warm as the hearth had been. With hot food and a fire, even that squat house could feel like a palace.

"*Maybe one day,*" Ash began in private, "*when this is all over, we'll be able to live in peace like that.*"

"*Maybe,*" Holt said across the bond. "*Might be that more lunar dragons enter the world, and you could be their Elder. I could have a hut in the hills or in the woods, wherever you decide to make your home.*"

"*Or we might be in a town again, with Talia, and Pyra, and Aberanth, and*

Master Rake. Other riders too, who we could be friends with and not fear. But peace would be the best thing. And lots of food."

Holt smirked. *"Yes, lots and lots of food."*

He gave Ash a scratch along the base of his neck. Despite his eagerness to train and to fight, he had to bear in mind what it might be for. Right now, it was about survival. Yet, in time, perhaps it could be about peace. About finding a new home. Such ideas seemed like dreams from where they were, and since Holt's last dream had come at such a cost, he felt wary of wishing too strongly.

Rake and Eidolan at last parted. Rake joined Holt and Ash by the fire. Usually, he would shut his eyes and begin to Cleanse and Forge, but for once he simply sat there and warmed his great hands above the crackling flames.

Aberanth appeared next, first as a pair of great yellow eyes, then he drew closer to the fireside, bringing one of the vegetable sacks. He nosed it toward Holt.

"If it's not too much trouble to ask—"

"It would be my pleasure," Holt said. He untied the strings, revealing the mushrooms. As he waited for his pan to grow hot, a final, most unusual event occurred.

Eidolan emerged from the night and sat with the group.

Holt beamed at the old dragon but said nothing. This was a major step for the illusionist, and Holt knew the last thing he would want was a fuss to be made.

The group sat in a companionable silence, allowing Holt to tend to Aberanth's mushrooms until they were toasted to perfection. As Aberanth ate, Holt sat back down beside Ash and enjoyed the fire and quiet. It struck him how safe he felt amongst these dragons: safe from harm, of course, but from judgment as well. He had called them a family to Ash back near Alamut, but sitting here now, he felt it for real.

He hoped the addition of a proper rider would not put this harmony in jeopardy.

"Rake," Holt said. The half-dragon glanced his way. "What did you do for Hava's ancestor that made her so grateful?"

"I helped her rejoin the Order," Rake said. "Hava's ancestor was old for the Order when I met her. Four hundred years or so. She lost her rider in battle centuries prior and did not adapt well to life outside the Order. She wished to return, but given her age, she was denied. Yet she was determined and vowed to spend one month in this chasm to prove herself."

"She fought the scourge here alone?" Holt asked.

"Riders used to use chasms such as this to train," Rake said. "They did not seal them right away as they do now. But even back then, most riders would train in such a manner for a week, maybe two at most. A month was exceptional. I was drawn here on my wanderings by the scourge activity and the lone storm dragon who faced it. An Exalted Champion observed her rite of passage from afar, but they could not sense my arrival.

"When I found her, she was half-dead, but her plea and story... moved me. I entered the tunnels in secret and reduced the scourge so that she would not be overwhelmed on the surface. In the end she succeeded and was allowed to rejoin Alamut. I believe she fell during the next incursion into Ahar, but that was what she wanted. A death with honor and meaning."

"There is something I don't understand," Holt said. "Why would the riders not wish to have an older and experienced dragon? Age only makes a dragon more powerful, doesn't it? Even without a rider to Forge. The Elders are proof of this."

"The Elders are a breed apart," Rake said. "Perhaps the very magic of the world brought them into life. Dragons will die in time, but we – I mean, they – can live many times the life of a human. Take the old viper here." Rake flicked his tail to tap Eidolan. "He's like a thousand years old."

Eidolan snorted. *"I am seven hundred and six years old."*

Ash stirred. *"Do all dragons live to be such an age, Master Eidolan?"*

"Master? It's been several lifetimes since I was called Master." He grunted a laugh as though recalling better days. *"Not all of us, child. I am old even for our kind. Though for former dragons of the Order, it is hardly a blessing. To*

linger on without your human is..." He trailed off into a groan of mourning.

Ash's anxiety and fear at such thoughts swelled over their dragon bond.

"*I understand,*" Ash said.

"*No, you don't,*" Eidolan said, though not unkindly. "*Not until you have flown the skies alone for longer than you flew together; not until you reach out in the darkness, and no one is there; not until you struggle to recall their voice, their face, and all that's left is the empty space in your soul. Then you will know, child.*"

Ash's sorrow poured into Holt, forcing him to sniff and fight back tears.

"I'm sorry, Eidolan. Our first mentor, Brode, lost his dragon, and the pain for him was hard enough. To live like that as long as you have must be..." Holt struggled for words.

"*It must be unbearable,*" Ash said.

The old dragon softened. "*It is life, young one. Our true strength lies not in staving off suffering but in how we deal with it when it comes. No living thing can last forever, save the Honored Elders. With advanced age, our bodies become unable to process motes of magic we are not attuned for. The buildup becomes toxic, and we pass. Many drakes of the Order would rather remain useful. Would rather fight and die than linger on as shades of our former selves. Yet we are cast out, as though we are broken. In the end, many choose to fly to the ends of the world on one last flight.*"

"Where do they go?" Holt asked.

"*East of east, north of north, west of west, south of south.*"

"But where is that? What lands are there?"

"*I do not know, for I am still here,*" Eidolan said. "*I have not resolved to take that final journey. Nor will I, until I see my eggs returned from the clutches of that bitter, hateful snake.*"

Holt noticed Eidolan's first overt reference to seeking revenge against Thrall. There was something more than just recent events to it, but he didn't wish to push his luck with the old dragon.

"May I ask, how did your rider die?"

Eidolan's age truly showed in his features as he answered, *"Old age."*

Anticipating Holt's question, Rake said, "Riders can't fight forever. They can, when the time is right, depart... for some cold room and a bed to die in. I'd have done anything to avoid that fate."

Rake's eyes gave nothing away, yet Holt wondered if that had been the reason behind his strange transformation. Had he tried to take some of his dragon's long life into himself to spare her lingering on after the bond?

"I, for one, was glad," Eidolan said, a strength returning to his voice. *"After Gideon and I endured the Great Incursion, witnessed the chaos of the fall of Aldunei, I was glad, as was he, to enjoy peace and quiet together in his final days."*

Seven hundred and six years old, Holt thought. Eidolan's age had not truly registered with him at first. The current year was six hundred and twelve after the collapse.

"Did you return to the Mystic Flight after he passed?" Holt asked.

"I spent a long time alone," Eidolan said. *"I had another cave then, not far from Gideon's hometown in Fornheim. There I gathered my first collection, trying to fill the emptiness."*

Somehow, Eidolan's tale humbled even Rake. "I'm sorry, old friend. I meant no offense."

Eidolan inclined his head. *"No offense was taken."*

Rake gave a grunt of acknowledgment, then he turned to Holt. "Pass me one of those smoked fish. I could eat a little."

Holt tossed him a fish and the half-dragon tore into it, devouring it as quick as Ash at his hungriest.

"You know," Rake said thickly, "that's not bad."

Ash winced and gave a dramatic shiver. Then he curled up tight and drifted into sleep. Holt stayed up with Rake to Cleanse and Forge before he too took rest.

Despite the location, despite the hard road, Holt slept better that night than he had in recent memory.

When he awoke with the light, Rake and the others were already on their feet and standing expectantly.

"Our friends are here," Rake told him.

Holt rubbed his eyes and looked to the sky.

I hope they are friends.

He sensed only one core approaching them, meaning Farsa and Hava had come alone. A good start. Fresh, fierce wind arrived with the storm drake. Hava's scales shone like clean steel, and she was almost double the size of Ash.

Farsa stepped off her dragon and onto what appeared to be thin air. Then Holt heard the updrafts that kept her afloat as she gracefully stepped to the ground. He noted the frivolous use of magic. Farsa either meant to show strength before the group or else the use was trivial to her. Holt reached out to sense her dragon bond and found a howling power. Farsa had not yet reached the strength of a Lord, but she was as close as any rider he had felt. An Exalted Champion.

She drank each of them in one by one, calm, collected. As a native of Ahar, she had dark skin, dark eyes, and strong black eyebrows. Sheets of straight hair fell in black curtains past her shoulders, making her slender figure even slighter.

The long handle of her rider's blade poked above her shoulder, yet she did not wear the brigandine armor of the riders but cool silvery silks and open-toe sandals. Some of Holt's concerns eased.

She hasn't come prepared for a fight.

"You must be serious, Rake, to summon us here." The barest trace of her Ahari accent lay beneath the surface. Farsa spoke the common language of the Aldunei belt in a more sophisticated, neutral tongue than Holt could hope to.

"Deadly serious," Rake said. He inclined his head, then turned his attention to Hava. "My, my, haven't you grown."

"Let us glide straight to the business," Hava said. Like her rider, Hava's voice held an alluring quality. *"What you would have of us."*

Rake explained the mission, about Thrall, the scourge, and the dragon eggs. When he finished, Farsa and Hava exchanged a knowing look.

"You have invoked a deep blood oath," Hava said, *"and in the name of my ancestor, in this place where you aided her, we will honor that commitment."*

Farsa steepled her fingers and inclined her head.

"You believe it all?" Holt said, amazed. He had expected more resistance and accusations of madness or doom-mongering.

"The strength of the wind is in its ability to roam free and unhindered," Hava said. *"A strong wind clears the air, laying all truths bare. What Rake says ties into our own fears and doubts, even if the vision of others is clouded. These are strange times, and the storm clouds gather."*

"Long have the scourge been absent from these lands," Farsa said. "That alone is unusual, yet few in Alamut are concerned. Despite the peace, news of the incursion into Feorlen took too long to reach us here. Falcaer has been silent since, other than to issue warrants for the arrest of a blind white dragon and his young rider." Her steel gaze trained on Holt and then Ash in turn. "When the head of our Order is more concerned about the whereabouts of a hatchling and a boy rather than the scourge, stolen eggs, or missing riders, then a black fog has settled over us all. Paragon Adaskar is of my people. He dishonors Ahar and the riders by allowing such fog to blind him."

"Have eggs also been taken from nests of Alamut?" Eidolan asked.

"One was taken," Farsa said. "We may not have noticed the loss of one egg, but a hatching was close at hand and all eggs were counted for the matriarch to inspect. A Novice under my tutelage confided in me that he witnessed our Exalted Fire Champion, Dahaka, enter our hatchery even though she had no duties there. Dahaka has since gone missing. We were close once, as Novices and Ascendants. If she has gone rogue, I feel honor-bound to bring her back or else prevent her causing chaos."

Her conviction could not be questioned. Rake's warning that riders trained to fight other riders had been brought to grim life.

"I'm glad you understand our need," Rake said. "There is also a need for secrecy. How soon can you depart Alamut without arousing suspicion?"

"We are due to depart for another Order Hall for a seasonal rotation in three weeks' time."

Three weeks?! Holt thought. In that time, many of Thrall's stolen eggs may hatch.

"We have favors of our own to call upon from our Flight Commander," Farsa continued. "I can have our destination changed to Oak Hall."

"Three weeks," Rake said, chewing on the words. "So be it. We shall rendezvous with you here."

"Forgive my ignorance, Master Rake," Hava said. *"But would it not be prudent to meet you closer to the target? In that time, more allies could be brought to the cause."*

Rake flashed a smile and raised an open arm to the party as though presenting them in a royal court. "What you see is what you shall get."

Holt tried to stand taller and straighter, for all the impressiveness this would add.

For the first time, doubt flickered across Farsa's face like a swift shadow. In a second it had gone, and she was steel again.

"Are there no others you might call upon?"

"There are drakes of fire, storm, and ice that I might convince to join us, as well as a rider or two in Fornheim and the Skarl Empire. Yet they are too far away to be of assistance. Three weeks here will prove more fruitful to the team at hand."

Farsa took them all in again, one by one. Hava did the same. Her large eyes were as changeable as the rolling sky.

Holt wondered if they would urge caution, call Rake insane, or else suggest they gather more forces regardless of the delay. A stunted emerald no more powerful than an experienced Ascendant, an old, tired mystic, and Holt and Ash with all their rough edges weren't intimidating without Rake at their side. Five Lords of the Order may well have hesitated at such a mission, never mind this ragged team Rake had cobbled together.

"That won't be a problem, will it?" Rake asked.

Hava rumbled in amusement. *"I've long known this day would come. Of late I sensed the winds changing, blowing hard to the north. We shall assist you, Rake. To whatever end. Consider our debt repaid."*

"There is *one* matter," Farsa said. "While there is honor in facing a great challenge, there is little in bringing a sheep into the lion's den.

In good conscience, I cannot condone bringing your students to their certain death."

Ash growled. *"Master Hava, Master Farsa, your words about the open winds were wise. But Holt and I have faced great danger before, and we would see the evil that is Thrall ended."*

"We do not protest at your age, your origins, or your affliction," said Hava. *"Be humble and less defensive. You are yet young, your song and core must mature. To bear a load you cannot yet lift will only crush you both."*

Holt opened his mouth to speak, but Rake cut across him.

"You need not worry about Holt and Ash. By the time you are ready to join us, they won't be such a concern."

Farsa's gaze slid to Holt for an intense moment, then back to Rake. "This area was marked unsafe even for Low Champions."

"I'm well aware," Rake said. He smiled and clapped his hands. "I think that concludes matters. Farewell for now, young Farsa and Hava. I look forward to fighting alongside you."

Hava pressed her neck low to the ground. *"And we you, Master Rake."*

Farsa steepled her fingers again and bowed low. They left in a rush of wind that somehow did not unsettle Farsa's long hair.

As soon as they were out of the ravine, Holt asked the burning question.

"What do you mean we won't be a concern?"

Rake strode to the ravine wall bearing the dragon symbol. He drew upon his arcane power, the orange light swirling around both hands before pressing it into the rock. The rune flickered to life, pulsing with Rake's magic.

The rock parted, revealing a tunnel delving into blackness.

Holt's stomach knotted. Insufferably, Rake flashed one of his mischievous smiles.

"Master Cook, by the time Farsa returns, you'll either be a Champion or you'll be dead. It's one or the other."

TWENTY-NINE

Survival

___

Holt hoisted his pack onto his back and followed Ash into the tunnel. A looming passage appeared to disappear down endlessly. He turned back, hoping Rake would laugh and tell him it was a bad joke, but the half-dragon looked serious at the cave's entrance.

"The two of you are on your own," Rake said.

A million questions raced through Holt's mind. How could this be done?

"We're not ready," Holt said.

"You said you would do whatever it takes. This is it. Your bond is as ready as any Ascendant I've known. What you need is a good, hard push."

"You said combat alone wasn't enough."

"I did, but I also said the Order provide a cowardly safety net. You'll be glad to know I don't. Once I seal this door, that's it. Don't dream of returning until you've ranked up. And don't be too long about it. Three weeks and we're gone."

Ash made a fearful rumble. Holt took a desperate step forward.

"Rake, wait—"

"I shall give you one final bit of advice. Though your bond is strong, you will not succeed until you have complete trust and reliance on each other."

Orange light shone again. Silently, the rock wall reformed, and Rake, Eidolan, and Aberanth disappeared. Darkness rushed to engulf them. Whether it was the rock or the magic of the seal, Holt could not sense Aberanth or Eidolan's cores.

Ash howled, a deafening noise in the confined space. Then a dreadful quiet descended, smothering them like a black cloak. Only their quick and frightened breaths broke the stillness.

Don't panic, Holt thought. *Don't panic...*

It didn't work. His heart quickened as though Thrall had come upon them. He reached for Ash, both across the bond and physically, groping in the darkness for him. Fear helped grow a bond – that had been one of Brode's first lessons. Genuine fear could not be mimicked in training. As Holt embraced Ash, he thought the fear in that moment ought to be enough to rank them to Champion there and then. Their bond burned white hot but cooled rapidly.

"He really means it," Holt said. His chest tightened. He'd known Rake was eccentric, overconfident, and hardly one to conform. Yet this seemed extreme. Talia had been right to be concerned.

"How are we to find moonlight down here?" Ash said.

"How are we to eat and live?" Holt replied.

He unslung his equipment. This he had been forced to pack sloppily as Rake half dragged him toward the tunnel. Holt drew lunar motes to his palm to cast a pale light to inspect his supplies. He had scavenged some firewood, enough for two small fires. A sorry amount. On top of that, they had little water. Suddenly, his bags of rice seemed worthless.

Food, never mind lunar motes, would be their chief concern down here.

"He's cracked," Holt said. "Aberanth was right. This is just madness."

"It is chaos," Ash said, sounding calmer than how he truly felt across the bond. *"We must make what order we can out of it."*

"Well, our food will have to stretch scarily thin. Did he plan this all along? I could have bought much more." Holt ceased and drew a final deep breath. Spiraling would do no good. Ash was right. They would figure things out. No other choice lay before them.

"We've got the dry fish, nuts, dried fruits, and rice. Unless we can find another source of meat, the fish will have to be reserved for you."

"I don't imagine any creatures we find down here will be good to eat."

Holt started repacking and tying his kit together, including his cooking pot and sleeping roll. As rushed as he'd been, he'd had the sense to take out the recipe book and give it to Aberanth for safe-keeping.

"Well, we won't discover anything by staying here." He hoisted his pack, then drew out Brode's sword and risked a little more light on his left hand. There was only one way ahead, and that was down.

They set off.

Holt took the lead. Ash crept behind, whacking his tail periodically against the stone. Though Ash was weedy and small compared to other dragons, the fact he could tread through the tunnel did not sit well in Holt's fears. When the scourge had carved through the rock and earth, they made the passage large enough for their hulking juggernauts, tall flayers, and great stingers. He supposed he should be grateful that the tunnels were too small for a queen to have moved through them.

Under the hills and surrounded by stone, the air grew chill. For now, he hoped this feeling was only a reaction to the sudden loss of Ahar's hot sun.

At an intersection of three passages, they paused. Ash sniffed each one, then reported back.

"The passage leading to our right has a foul hint of the scourge to it. Straight ahead, the air is damper. To our left, the air smells the best of all three, though that is saying little."

"The one that smells damp sounds good. Could be there's water that way."

Before heading down that tunnel, an idea struck Holt.

"Hold on. We should try to figure out a way to remember which way we've come, so we can find our way back out again."

"I do not know how Aberanth makes his marks."

Holt nodded, then looked at Brode's sword. Its tip was beyond sharp, broad, and strong. He returned to the tunnel they had just walked down and began scoring a line into the rock. The screech of the metal was terrible, the sound of a thousand tormented spirits. He cut an arrow pointing back up the slope, and over it he tried to carve a crude 'S' for 'start.' He quickly found attempting curved lines to be foolish and no use, so he changed tack and cut an 'H' for 'home'.

"My ears will ring for days and days if you keep doing that."

"Better than us getting lost."

They entered the tunnel straight ahead of them. Before they took another branching passage, he cut an arrow pointing back the way they had come, adding another 'H' as a marker.

Down and down they went until the low ceiling of the tunnel opened and they emerged into an underground cave. Water slapped and tapped somewhere in the gloom, its droplets falling from on high. Holt risked a greater amount of light and held his hand aloft.

They had discovered a limestone cave with a dark lake. Across the lake, a steady trickle of water descended as though a miniature waterfall. Beauty glistened in the form of clear crystals which shone as Holt's light touched them.

Perhaps the scourge had delved this way and found they could dig no more. Either through long neglect from the enemy or because they had been driven deeper underground, the lake and cave held no presence of the scourge.

Ash padded over to the water's edge and took a tentative lick from its onyx surface.

"It's fresh and cold."

"That's good," Holt said in relief. He approached the water and cast his light onto it, dispelling the inky blackness to reveal clear teal waters and the creatures swimming within. "Ash, there are fish in there."

Even as he said it, how they might acquire the fish wasn't obvious to him. Holt had no idea if dragons could swim. He certainly couldn't, and even if they had a rod and bait, he didn't know the first thing about fishing. Aside from these fish, there was moss, algae, and even patches of spindly mushrooms with ghost-white flesh.

"Aberanth would have liked it down here, though I'm not sure those mushrooms look wholesome."

A tremor ran through the dragon bond. The first gentle shake from Holt's use of magic. Heeding the warning, Holt dimmed the light on his hand and the night of the cave came clinging back on all sides. He took in a deep breath and noted how cold the air was compared to the tunnels above.

Still, for want of a better location, this might serve as a temporary base.

"We should double back and investigate that tunnel with the fresher air. Might be we'll find somewhere better to make our camp."

Conscious of Ash's core, Holt dropped his light down so he could see his next step but no more. On their way back, Holt cut arrows into the passage walls, marking these with an 'L'. Reaching the tunnel with the fresher air, they found it wound upward. When he came to what seemed the top of this incline, Ash called for him to stop.

"What's wrong?" Holt asked.

"Nothing, it's good. I can hear lunar notes, they sing faintly to me. Above."

"Maybe night has fallen?"

Holt could not have guessed how long they had been underground already.

Ash suddenly pressed on ahead with renewed vigor, brushing past Holt. Taken aback, Holt followed. Up they went now. The temperature rose a little, and then, at the far end of a narrow passageway, a second source of light appeared. A wispy beam of pale silver found its way into the tunnel from an opening in the rock. Ash tucked his wings in tight against his body and wiggled and squeezed his way down the final stretch to reach the moonlight. Lunar motes flitted into the orbit of his core, though they were painfully few compared to being out under the open night sky.

Holt blew out his cheeks in relief. "Rake could not have known this was here. We're lucky."

Other than the sliver of moonlight, this passage was a dead end.

Half gouged stone suggested the original burrowers had given up halfway through.

Reasoning they were close to the outside, Holt reached out with his magical senses, hoping to gain a glimpse of Aberanth's or Eidolan's core. Yet the rock dulled his reach, and he could sense nothing through the narrow slit through which the moonlight shone. Had they traveled for miles? He did not believe so, but truthfully, he had lost his sense of time and direction hours back. They had entered late in the morning, and though finding water, possible food for Ash, and even this tiny source of moonlight were all victories, it meant one of their precious days had already been spent.

Holt stopped the flow of motes to his palm. Save for where the moonlight struck directly, he could see nothing at all. He unslung his pack and took a rest on the tunnel floor.

First, he checked on Ash's core. Their bond was strong and efficient enough to hold up well under his use of dim light. Only a wafer slice of the core had diminished. While somewhat comforting, things would alter fast once they came upon scourge. Or scourge upon them.

"Let's spend some time topping up your core."

Holt did so, finding every raw mote he Forged many times harder than usual. Ash, for his part, concentrated on Sinking to draw the sparse motes toward his core. Alas, not long into their session, this weak supply of lunar motes dried to a trickle and then stopped altogether. Holt opened his eyes to find the pale strip of moonlight missing. All was blackness.

"Must be passing clouds."

He allowed some time to pass, hoping the moonlight would return. When it did not, he found he could make no further excuses. He knew what was expected of them both, and putting off the true trial any longer would hardly increase their slim odds.

Ash, who must have sensed his trepidation, said, *"Master Rake will not leave us here to die."*

"I'm not sure. If we believe he'll save us then we might as well sit by the lake and wait. I just wish we had more supplies. More warning—"

He stopped himself. Doubtless the very lack of preparation was all part of such an extreme form of training. Complaints would do no good, though he indulged in one final muttering.

"Not much advice he gave us either. I already completely trust and rely on you."

"If Master Rake told us so, then there must be a reason."

"I suppose. I did become an Ascendant after our first major flight through danger."

"We have no other choice."

Holt could not argue with that. He got to his feet and hoisted his pack again.

"Ready to fight some scourge?"

"Always."

First, they retraced their steps back to that main intersection. On their way, Holt carved arrows and 'M's for 'moon' into the walls. In theory, they could now navigate between the moonlit tunnel, the lake, the entrance to the whole complex, and the start of the descent into the scourge-infested depths.

Before descending, Holt ventured back to the lakeside and laid down his pack and supplies. Here it would not be thieved unless the fish grew legs and quick fingers.

Their first excursion deeper below seemed to take an age, both due to Holt carving his arrows and as a result of any new noise or smell to halt their cautionary steps. Then, all at once, the enemy sprang forth from dark crevices.

Ghouls attacked though their uncanny speed was checked by the confines of the tunnel. Holt met them with light and sword. Ash used tooth and claw. Quick as that the ghouls fell, so fast that the dragon bond had barely grown warm.

Down they went. And down. Until the pockets of ghouls became great gangs, and other long-suffering creatures of the deep came crawling. Great swollen moles with green eyes and bile dripping from their bucked teeth. Many vethrax, those insects which had been the forefathers of the scourge, scuttled underfoot and away from Holt and Ash as their light blazed.

Their bond grew hot. Ash's core drained.

Some final ghouls shambled toward them, and just as Holt readied to take them on, a monstrous worm erupted from the wall. It struck at the head of the feckless ghoul that had strayed into its path and clamped black teeth into its torso. Holt's empty stomach turned. He screamed, half from shock and half in disgust, before releasing a fully charged Lunar Shock at the worm's undulating body.

The Lunar Shock punched a hole straight through the worm. Its long body flopped down from its den in the earth, sagging against the wall. The ghoul remained unmoving in its jaws.

Holt took a step back but did not lower the light on his hand. Down here, it was the only thing that kept him sane. Foul blood lay thick on the ground, and the air was full of the shrieking of ghouls and warped creatures alike.

Deeper they went, the underground world growing hotter and closer, although that might have been his dragon bond, his battled muscles and beating blood.

Ash's core was now dangerously low and their bond strained.

Holt backed away slowly from the next passage, unwilling to turn his back lest some fresh horror appear from the dark. Step by careful step, he walked back to Ash. On his way, he could not help but be mindful of all the ghouls lying, to all accounts, dead. A thought occurred to him that the tunnels might become impossible to pass if enough scourge corpses piled up, but they had little choice but to deal with it. They could not burn them. If it came to it, they would have to shift them by force.

For now, they retreated up the winding, sometimes steep passageways, until they arrived back where they had started.

Holt extinguished his light. Now it was over, and all sense and smell of the scourge were far beneath him, he breathed out a shuddering breath and sagged over, clutching his hands to his knees.

"Our bond burns," Ash said. "We did well for our first attempt."

"We did, but how many more trips will we need? Ghouls are easy prey when they don't have the space to swarm around us, but I don't fancy exploring much further."

"Let's rest now and plan."

Holt nodded and straightened. Food or moonlight? Both were vital and, given the lengths between the lake and their solitary spot for moonlight, also time-consuming. It might not even be nighttime anymore. Who could say how long they had been down here?

Every part of him desired to leave this place. He could not foresee how they would manage for three weeks living like this, never mind growing their bond to Champion in that time.

For now, Holt chose food.

THIRTY

The Boar of the Silver Hall

Their journey north passed without event. While flying over the vast Bitter Bay, they did not stray far from the sight of land. After passing the coastline of Risalia, Talia eased, and thereafter they took more breaks. The Province of Fornheim was like a thorn growing southwest from the Spine mountains, acting as a buffer between Risalia and the Skarl Empire. Fornheim's coastline was short, and so they traveled its length and over the border into the empire in a single long day.

The further north they traveled, the more primal the land became, as though the world had started here and all places to the south were its distant offspring. The woods were dark and guarded, the rivers ice blue and quick flowing, the mountain peaks rose rough and worn like the rusted teeth of an ancient saw. The summer air remained as fresh as early spring in the south.

They flew close to the Spine, maintaining a steady course north until they flew over a region marked by five long rivers running westward from the mountains. Upon reaching the third such river, they turned west and followed it toward the Skarl capital of Smidgar.

When Talia had traveled to Falcaer Fortress to forge her sword, she had passed by the city of Athra and been in awe. Where that great city appeared unfathomable for the precision of its concentric circular walls and vastness upon the flat lands, Smidgar's grandeur lay in opposite qualities. Rocky, uneven land was connected by a webbed network of rope bridges and stairs hewn from the living rock. Gray and black stones formed its outer and inner walls, filling in the gaps left exposed by the rising land. From above they seemed a maze of stone hedgerows. At Smidgar, there were fewer towers than at Sidastra, yet each one stood as a marvel, rising many times the height of a common watchtower, thick like old oaks of granite and hollowed like honeycomb for ballistae, scorpions, catapults, and archers to do their work.

"*These are a strong people,*" Pyra said. "*Their feet are planted well into the earth.*"

Great horns blew to announce their arrival as they flew over the maze of walls.

"*There's the Silver Hall,*" Talia said. "*Ahead on the rise, do you see it?*"

Pyra did, and she made for it. The hall was in fact a long hall and got its name from its smooth, blue-gray stone which, under the cold sun, reflected a shine that could well be mistaken as silver.

Their descent drew a gathering, and by the time Pyra touched down before the doors of the imperial seat, dozens of honor guards had assembled to meet them. These were the Housecarls, elite bodyguards to the imperial family. Each warrior's face was hidden behind a dark iron helm. At least a quarter of their number were stout shieldmaidens, judging from their height and build, though they too wore the same heavy helmets. They clanged axes against shields and chanted a grunting, low humming tune.

Talia dismounted and the warriors parted. An older man dressed in soft clothes approached her. Here in the north, even in summer, his sleeves remained long, and thick white wrappings wove over his trousers from ankle to knee, ending just below the skirt of his tunic.

He spoke in the Skarl language. Talia caught a word here and there, but few still spoke it in Feorlen, and due to political wrangling over the centuries, the official language of the realm came from Aldunei. Leofric had learned Skarl, but Talia had skipped her lessons in favor of the sword, assuming she would never need to negotiate with the Skarls in their own tongue. A choice, in hindsight, she regretted.

The old man took in her blank expression, raised his eyebrows, and switched languages with ease.

"We have been expecting a purple dragon with a rider of flaming hair," the man said. "Declare yourself."

"I am Talia Agravain, Queen of Feorlen, here at the behest of Her Imperial Majesty."

Pyra declared herself with a roar followed by a jet of flames she shot high into the air. The honor guard did not so much as squeak or give an inch.

"A fierce people indeed," Pyra said.

The emissary smiled wide. "Welcome to the Silver Hall, Talia Queen. And to your dragon. We have comfortable nesting areas where she might take rest. The keepers there know how to tend to the needs of drakes. For yourself, please, follow."

Talia followed the old man into the Silver Hall. He took her to an antechamber where the furniture was carved from stone and lacked cushioning. She opted to stand as she waited. Being left here in a stone room with little pomp was not in itself a snub. Oddvar had assured her that the Skarls found ceremony dreary and obscuring, which strained their relations with other realms in which intentions were often hidden behind layers of kind words, meaningless gestures, and false promises.

Oddvar also confirmed that the Empress had three sons. Leif, the eldest and heir, Fynn, the middle son, and Aren, the youngest. Aren was closest to her own age at nineteen, whereas Fynn was already twenty-five. Of Leif and Aren she had heard nothing but praise of their valor, their skill in arms, their leadership, and how all loved them, Aren most of all. Of Fynn, Oddvar had only said that 'he is a troubled man, melancholy in spirit and lacking resilience.'

A scuffle of activity sounded outside the antechamber. The door opened and a woman stepped into the room without guards or announcement. It was obvious that she needed no herald. Her green tunic was richly woven and embroidered with a silver boar's head across the chest. Her golden hair had faded to straw and in places turned gray, yet it was braided such that the gray wove deftly, creating a pattern of its own. Broad of shoulder and neck and with iron in her eyes, Talia guessed she had once been a shield-maiden. Age bestowed a face as weathered and hard as her lands, making it impossible to believe she had ever been a young girl and had not always been as dominating as a rugged mountain.

Talia straightened and met the Empress in the eye.

"I am told you do not know our tongue?"

"Regrettably not, Your Imperial Majesty," Talia said. She allowed the Empress her title, though did not bow or curtsey. Striking this balance would be delicate work. Talia needed to maintain herself as a strong, independent queen, and yet no good would come of giving the Empress cause for offense or too strong an invitation to become her overlord.

"I hope this tongue does not trouble Your Majesty," Talia continued.

The Empress did not answer that. Her gaze drifted up to the steel crown atop Talia's head, and then she smiled.

"I thought all in the south had gone soft. Else why would they think jewels and sparkling stones should make them rulers?"

"I burned the old crown," Talia said, omitting the fact it had been by accident.

"Did you?" The Empress asked in a flat voice. "I trust Oddvar explained to you my wishes?"

"He did."

"And you have come. Do I take it you accept my offer?"

"I am here to discuss it," Talia said. "What queen would I be if I made such a decision rashly?"

"A desperate one, I should think." The Empress gave her a sly smile. "Very well, we shall discuss all matters, but we shall do so tonight. There shall be a feast. Heavy talk is best done with a heavy belly and ale. My old men with the weak arms will take you to your chambers and see to your every need."

She left without so much as a farewell. The aforementioned old men with the weak arms showed Talia to her rooms. Here at least the furnishings were more hospitable, and the floor was covered in soft furs.

With little else to do, she reached out to Pyra.

"Are you being treated well?"

"I am told I will receive a spiced ox tonight while you feast."

"That is luxurious," said Talia. To her surprise, she yawned. The trip had been long. *"I think I shall try to sleep a little."*

"May your dreams be sweet," Pyra said.

But they were not.

After drifting off, Talia found herself in a featureless room, a shadow room of vague proportions and flickering edges. Her father was there, and her mother, her brother, even Deorwin, council members, and many other faceless people besides. They were jeering at someone on the ground. It was a child in body, though it held her uncle's adult face. The faceless crowd began to kick and beat him. Talia called for them to stop, but it was as if they could not hear her.

Her father stepped up next, clubbing the child Osric with a mace. Her mother stamped on him. Deorwin hesitated, then he too kicked down. Talia beseeched them to stop – why were they doing this? – but when they handed her a club, she grasped it eagerly and beat with the same enthusiasm. Osric took the punishment in silence which made the crack of his bones all the worse. Talia's final blow split his skull, spilling no blood but releasing Sovereign's deep voice in anguish. The others looked at her disgusted, as though they were innocent, and then began to walk away.

She woke from her nightmare in a cold sweat. Luckily, she had not singed any of the bedding. Over the dragon bond, she received pleasurable beats from Pyra, distracted by eating a meal.

Talia poured herself some water and drank deeply. Without her gambeson and brigandine on, the chill of the chamber nipped at her. She shuddered, although she could not be certain it was entirely from the cold. Would these dreams ever fade?

An unexpected sound reached her. Music, though it was far removed from Pyra's dragon song. She drifted without thought across her room as though drawn to the notes. Closer to the door she heard it more clearly, and though she had never heard the song before, a part of her had known it her whole life. The strings were plucked by gentle fingers, and here and there a windblown note fluttered hauntingly over the rest.

It made her profoundly sad to hear the music, and yet not in such a way that she wished to close her ears to it. Its quiet beauty spoke to her like an old friend who knew her every care and woe.

"Can you hear that, girl?" Talia asked across her bond, yet Pyra seemed to have shrunk away, not closing the bond but slinking back as though afraid. *"It's beautiful. Listen."*

Pyra said nothing. Talia felt nothing from her. That made her truly sad in a way the music never could.

The notes quietened, seeming to move off. Without thinking, Talia left her room and turned left then right down the hallway, as though she might catch the musician in the act. She saw only the Housecarls but thought the music came from her left. Talia chased the music down a corridor or two, ever just out of reach of it, until the House-carls got terse with her and an old steward came puffing with arms flapping to beg her to return to her chambers.

Blushing and feeling foolish, Talia did so. After closing her door shut, she pressed her ear against the wood, gingerly so, like a child eavesdropping on forbidden matters. She did not know how long she waited to hear it again, but just as she was on the verge of giving up and going back to sleep, it came. She slumped against the door, happy and sad all at once to hear the song even if its nature eluded her.

Some hours later she awoke, still sat against the door. A stiffness clenched her lower back, but she felt better rested than she had in weeks.

Later that evening, Talia attended the feast wearing her red armor and her steel crown. Her blade remained in her chambers. No weapons were permitted inside the Silver Hall, save those of the Housecarls. Talia was brought to a seat on the Empress' right-hand side after a flurry of introductions to the imperial court. She struggled to keep their names in her head. This high table and its tall seats were also carved from stone, cut in sharp, rigid lines and oversized in every sense. Unlike the stone furniture in the antechamber, these were at least cushioned.

Feeling all eyes upon her, Talia silently removed the cushion from the stone chair before she sat down. Though uncomfortable, her enhanced body would not suffer so badly while sitting on the hard stone. It had the desired effect of drawing low mutterings from the court. These mutterings ceased at once when the Empress also removed her cushion before sitting down.

Without so much as a word to Talia, the Empress commanded that the doors to the hall be opened. A long column of guests marched in, carrying pots, platters, deep dishes, or casks, making their way around the edge of the hall toward the high table. Music arose, and two female singers sang in the Skarl language.

Oddvar had informed her that the Empress' sons would not sit at the high table with their mother and the court. Without official positions, they were expected to sit alongside the jarls of the land – who were equivalent to ealdors in Feorlen – and 'earn their meal like anyone else'. Whatever that meant. All the same, she expected to be introduced to them soon and so scanned the approaching guests for any who held resemblance to the Empress.

Each group of guests halted before the Empress, unveiling their contribution to the feast before she waved them on. There seemed to be little hierarchy to the guests outside of those at the high table. They took their dishes and casks and sat as they pleased. Soon, guests were roving around with their bowls in hand.

One man slammed his bowl down before a group who had brought a trencher of buttered turnips. A member of the group jumped to his feet in answer. Talia thought it would come to blows, then the men arm-wrestled. The challenger lost, yet the defender laughed, slapped him on the back and provided him with a dollop of turnips using a wooden spoon.

Not long after this, another contender approached the turnips, bowl at the ready. He was a giant of a man with corded biceps barely restrained by ornate leather straps.

"Leif, my eldest," said the Empress suddenly, pointing to the huge man.

Predictably, the defender of the turnips lost the arm wrestle to Leif, and so the heir to the Skarl Empire earned a greater portion than his failed predecessor had.

Neither Ambassador Oddvar nor the Mistress of Embassy had told her of this custom, likely because those at the high table remained seated and composed while all in the hall brought them food in tribute. Talia quickly lost sight of Leif in the crowd as dishes of stews, slabs of fish and meat, hot flatbread, steaming greens and vegetables, and sticky fruit slavered in honey were brought before her.

Yet around the room, the guests seemed in a constant state of negotiation or game to share their food. Not all exchanges were conducted through arm wrestling. Some splayed their fingers upon the table and stabbed down between each finger with a fork at rhythmic speed. Others played this game with a knife, and the level of danger correlated with the portion of food earned. Others juggled axes, ate and blew fire, or else attempted to drain a foot-sized horn of ale in a single draught.

The women took part as well, although many employed their own tricks or games. They danced, braided hair into more elaborate knots, or traded fragrant dried herbs or flowers. Some were content to offer a kiss to earn their slice of pork.

Musicians played throughout the hall, but their induvial strings or windblown notes were indistinguishable above the clamor of talk, singing, and the increasingly raucous laughter.

A slender bard appeared from the crowd to play for the high table. He played a panpipe, the high whistling notes of which stood out to Talia even through the din of the feast.

Then a flash of movement drew her attention. A young man attempted to somersault, landed poorly, and fell face-first into a great dish of peas. Talia laughed along with most of the Silver Hall.

The Empress gave a booming hoot of delight. Recovering, she said,

"Aren, my youngest." Aren emerged red-faced and laughing wildly. Peas remained lodged in the short sharp hairs of his maturing beard. Like Leif, Aren too was well muscled but more in proportion to his frame. One half of his forehead was covered in a tattoo, though what it was Talia could not discern at this distance.

The Empress raised her drinking horn to him and declared that the folly had earned all in the hall a refill from her own cask. The Skarls rejoiced, cheered, and clashed horns and mugs together. More ale sloshed to the floor than was drunk and the revelry carried on.

Talia's drinking horn was refilled for the toast, and she drank of it, and each time it was generously refilled she drank again. The ale was good, much better than sweet wine, and the fire in her veins burned the alcohol away before it had a chance to affect her. Yet the energy in the Silver Hall was such that Talia found herself drunk on the occasion. For the first time in a long time, she felt herself having fun.

"You should see this, girl. It's wild. You'd like it."

The feast was well underway, and a huge salmon lay stripped to the bone on the high table when the Empress finally spoke to her again. "You see, my people are much used to negotiation. I am sure we will come to a fine agreement." Despite drinking heartily since the feast began, the Empress seemed as lucid as she had been that morning. "How does a Skarl feast compare to a Feorlen one?"

"Favorably," Talia said. "My only regret is that I did not have a chance to earn my own dinner." The Empress gave her an approving look. "When might we begin our discussions?"

"What is the haste?" asked the Empress. "First, there must be dancing!" Then, in a sudden move, she stood and raised her hands.

At once, as though through a magic of her own, all in the hall fell silent. She announced something in the Skarl language, and afterward the guests moved the tables to the sides of the hall, leaving an open space around the central pit fires.

Music restarted and then couples emerged to dance. Even members of the high table joined in.

Prince Leif emerged hulking from the crowd and seemed to be

heading right for Talia. She braced herself. How to refuse him without causing offense? She could not show any signs of favoritism this soon.

"Leif," the Empress roared. This diverted the giant. "Come and ask your mother to dance first, you ungrateful lump."

Leif's thick brows knotted together.

Talia wondered if he did not understand what his mother had said. The Empress had spoken more for Talia's benefit, it seemed. While she puzzled over this, Leif and his mother moved to the dance floor. The Housecarls shadowed her, keeping to the edges of the hall.

Despite the merriment, Talia could not shake the feeling she was being tested at all points or else led into a false sense of security. Her joy from earlier in the evening faded as her guard went back up.

"You seem tense for such a jolly occasion."

Talia dragged her attention away from the Empress and Leif and to the panpipe-playing bard standing before her. His cloth was plain and of poor make. She frowned. Who did he think he was to speak to her so candidly?

"Might I play you a song, my lady of fire?"

"I thank you, but not at this time," she said, allowing him the benefit of the doubt. "I do not think I would even hear it above the noise," she added by way of courtesy.

She looked away, trying to find the Empress again.

Several dances later, the music fell and the crowd parted, but the Empress and other members of the imperial court did not return to the high table. A poet bobbed and bowed before the Empress and began to recite a long verse. Talia did not understand it, but as no one else was sitting, she got up and moved to mill about at the back of the crowd. A few of the Housecarls moved with her, keeping Talia in their sights.

The poet seemed to be a court favorite. The audience gasped, whooped, and laughed in a well-practiced fashion, and the Empress had the look of a cat with a bowl of cream.

"Would you like to know what he's saying?" came a voice to her right. It was the panpipe bard again. He was an unusual sort amongst this crowd. Being no taller than Talia, he was small compared to most of the men. His dark blond hair was neither long nor braided but pulled back and tied in a knot at the back of his head. His beard was short but well-kept and neat, and he wore an easy smile. A simple piece of twine held the panpipe around his neck.

"Do you know who I am?" Talia asked.

"You are the guest of Her Imperial Majesty, a fire rider judging by your armor, and from the south given you know little of our tongue. Your skin is too fair to have grown up in Ahar or Mithras, your voice contains nothing of the faeness of the forests of Coedhen. A crown you wear, though no such crown as I've ever heard of, but the horse lords of Athra wear hay on their heads, not steel. The Archduke of Risalia is alive and well, and so it is Brenin or Feorlen you call home, and perhaps it is both? The only question is, are you a rider or a queen?"

If only she knew how to answer that herself.

"You're very well informed for a bard."

"My lady of flames, any bard who wishes to earn a bowl at feasts must be as well informed as the highest of councilors. Yet while they would squirrel away such knowledge, we bards have a higher duty, that is, to share news good and ill alike through song and make all richer for it. News of our lands has not ventured far south in many a long year. I fear you are at a disadvantage to your host. Will you not hear of what this poet says?"

The reciting poet threw his arms dramatically wide at that moment. He cursed, clenched a fist, and cast it high as though commanding the heavens.

Talia considered the bard again. He was too shrewd for someone with such poor cloth, yet his offer sounded harmless enough. If she gained something useful, so much the better. If not, she would not be worse off.

"Tell me."

The bard dropped his voice. "This tale recounts the saga of our empress. Skadi is the daughter of the former emperor, Thazi. During his reign, the western jarls rose in civil war. The leader of the rebels, Jarl Ivar the Faithless, invited the Emperor and the Jarls to a great council, where the Emperor was murdered in cold blood. Skadi's eldest brother marched to war. She asked to go with him. He refused, and he did not return. Her second brother marched to war after him. Skadi begged to go with him. He too refused her, and he did not return. With no one left to stop her, Skadi vowed vengeance. She took up her father's helmet, axe, shield, and sword and marched to war herself. Those loyal flocked to her banner and pushed the rebels back into the west.

"When she brought her army to the gates of Jarl Ivar's city, the coward sought to appease her through surrender and an offer of a husband to seal a peace. Skadi could even pick of his own grandsons herself. Skadi agreed for the good of the Empire, yet Ivar the Faithless had one last trick to try. He made a condition that Skadi could only choose of his grandsons by looking at their feet."

As if on cue, the poet made an exclamation, then pointed to his own feet.

"Skadi was a young girl," the bard went on, "and so Ivar thought her head easily swayed by the thought of a tall, strong husband. He expected her to choose the man with the largest feet, a strong warrior. That grandson he was closest to and so hoped to influence her reign through him. Skadi chose the man with the smallest, for she knew that some men are bred for war and others born to wisdom, and she would have a husband who was wise to help her rule."

The poet ended along with the bard's explanation. The Skarls erupted into clapping, hooting, and stamping their feet in appreciation.

"Did that really happen?" Talia asked.

The bard shrugged. "This is what the poet says. I have heard it told differently."

Talia was about to ask when the revelry of the feast picked up again. Music screeched to life. It came on so sudden and so loud that she gasped and briefly placed a hand over her ear.

"You do not like our music?" the bard asked.

Talia could feel her mother's horrified gaze from across the world for her lapse in etiquette.

"Oh no, I do," she hastened to say. "I was only taken by surprise. I heard something I liked in the Silver Hall today, though it was much softer than this feasting music. Something beautiful." She could think of no reason to tell him this, except that it was true and she hoped a genuine comment would smooth over any insult.

The bard looked surprised, though in a pleasant sort of way.

A gap in the crowd parted in haste as the Empress strode through. She caught Talia's eye.

"Ah, there you are. Our bellies are heavy, and so now comes the talk."

Empress Skadi carried on right past her, clearly meaning for Talia to follow.

Talia intended to wish the bard farewell and to thank him for his translation, yet when she turned, he had gone. She spared a second or two to look for him, but it was as if he had vanished. Turning her mind to more important matters, she followed Skadi.

The Empress led her away from the festivities to a private room of the Silver Hall. It was dark, warm from an open fire pit, and decorated with many pelts. The Housecarls followed in force and lined the corridor, but Skadi closed the door to them, leaving the two rulers alone.

"You have spirit, child," Skadi announced. Her tone had become all brusque business. "I'd even say you are bold, but you are also a fool for coming alone."

Talia grasped a tendril of fire from Pyra's core and kept it within her, as an archer might hold a drawn bow.

"Is that a threat?"

"Not to your person, girl. I know fine well I'd be roasted to cinders before my Housecarls could so much as open the door. But to come without advisors or translators—"

"Time was of the essence," Talia said.

"Hence I called you bold. But stupid. Do you know what I announced earlier this evening to the highest jarls of my empire?"

Talia shook her head.

"I announced that you would be taking my son's hand in marriage, bringing our lost lands and kin back into the imperial fold."

"Then it's you that has been bold, Skadi. If I refuse you, you'll look a fool in front of your court."

"But you won't refuse. And even on the off chance that your dragon's flames have turned your brain to smoke, I shall still bring Feorlen back into the fold. Its very name is of our own tongue. Do you know what it means?"

"Far off land." Talia might not know the language of the Skarls, but she knew the history of her own kingdom. "Named by the Skarls who settled it. But the Empire lost it hundreds of years ago. Why care now?"

Skadi moved to warm her hands over the fire. "My empire has looked inward long enough. We were weak, and now we're strong again."

No doubt years of civil war had weakened the empire, yet Talia found this present war-mongering infuriating.

"One large incursion could wipe you out. All of us out. Save your strength for the true threat. If you want a fight, join me in an alliance against the true enemy." She hesitated. How much could she divulge without the Empress getting lost or calling her mad like all the others? "A powerful mystic has taken hold of the scourge and means to end us."

To her credit, the Empress did not so much as blink. "The scourge has always acted as if to end us. What's the difference now?"

Talia considered. In the end, ultimately things were the same. The scourge had to be stopped. The difference now, she supposed, was there was hope of an end.

"An Elder dragon supports those willing to fight the scourge. I worked alongside him and his Emerald Flight to purge the last of the swarm from Feorlen. New dragon types are emerging, ones with great power against the blight. Our enemy thrives on our division. If we all stood against him, he would not have a hope of success."

"Ah, I understand now," said the Empress. "You would raise your banner and have the whole world fall under your leadership."

"What?" Talia asked, caught off guard. "No, well, if it was against the scourge and Sovereign, then—"

"A rider becoming monarch was something every ruler and govern-
ment with half their wits always feared. It's too much power in one
pair of hands. Now we shall determine the wolves from the sheep. The
sheep shall flock to your side, thinking you can protect them. The
wolves will pounce in challenge."

Talia's fires grew hotter. The Empress had called her a fool, but
anyone who relegated the threat of the scourge was more of a fool.
That anger flared into orange flames around her hands and laced her
next words.

"Then the wolves will pounce into the dragon's jaws."

"Brave words from a young, lone dragon," the Empress tittered.
"Tell me, do you think me a sheep, or a wolf?"

Talia's heart thundered. "Neither. The wolves are already circling,
and we know you're no sheep. You are the hawk. You observe the
animals below and then descend."

Her thunderous heartbeat must have crossed the bond to worry
Pyra.

"*Strength, Talia,*" Pyra told her. Her fires burned away some of
Talia's nerves. "*No dragon negotiates with their prey. This one roars mightier
than she'll swipe. If she desired to take what she wanted by force, then she would
have already.*"

There was wisdom in this. The Mistress of Embassy had stressed
how blunt and straightforward the Skarls were in their dealings, but
things might have changed during Skadi's reign. That saga of her rise
to power spoke of a subtler mind.

Talia blew out a deep breath and took a step closer to the fire,
closer than a normal human ought to go.

"If you wanted my kingdom, why not simply invade it? The Skarls
are known for their love of battle."

"Why buy your land with ten thousand lives when I might buy it
with one son?"

"Which son do you intend?"

"Leif."

"You know I cannot accept that."

Marrying the direct heir would inevitably unite the crowns, and

Feorlen would be subsumed into the Empire. Her Ealdors would be deeply divided on this at best and openly revolt at worst. Yet, underneath all of this, Talia was stuck. Either she sacrificed her bond with Pyra, or she sacrificed some of her kingdom's independence.

"I can be understanding," said the Empress. "Aren, then," she offered, the name readily springing to her lips. "A good boy. Strong and loyal."

"He is the one who fell face-first into a bowl of peas?"

"It made you laugh, did it not?" The Empress' voice betrayed a maternal defensiveness. "Do not underestimate the power of laughter in a marriage, girl. You'd miss it sorely if it were absent. I did."

"I shall bear that in mind."

"A handsome boy," Skadi added. "As you saw."

Talia tried to conjure Aren's face, but the finer details were blurry. She could not recall what he had tattooed on one side of his forehead, if she had even been able to see it clearly in the first place.

"A brief glance at a face is hardly a meeting."

The Empress scoffed. "I chose my husband looking at less."

"What about your other son, Fynn?"

Skadi's confidence faltered for a moment.

"You do not want Fynn," she said, as though ashamed to admit he existed. "His heart is too soft." She huffed and seemed to collect herself. "You shall have Aren. You are of an age. You will be happy."

"I hope so," Talia said rigidly. Her fires cooled. She could feel an accord was about to be reached. "I will also need a formalized treaty that Aren asserts no claim to Feorlen and that rulership of the realm will be determined through my line. That will ease concerns at home."

Such a thing would be a meaningless piece of parchment, in truth. No scrap of paper had ever halted a determined army, but it would make the Skarls all the more traitorous if they broke it. Regardless, the Skarls would still enjoy a great deal of influence over her so long as the threats from Risalia and Athra remained.

The Empress took a while to answer. "It shall be done." She raised a finger before Talia could voice her gratitude. "I have a final condition of my own. Brenin. I require certainty that King Roland will join us should it come to war."

"I am sure my uncle would not abandon me."

"No, you are not," said the Empress. "Else you would not have sent your mother to plead with him."

Talia gritted her teeth. One thing was clear from this visit. The Skarl spy network was efficient.

"Think of it as the dowry from your side of the family," said the Empress. "You get my support, and I get assurances that my armies do not stand alone. Wars cost. I told you I'd rather pay with one son than with ten thousand lives. The Empire can face the world alone, but I do not like those odds. If Brenin were to stand with us both, the scales would tip such that this Athran coalition will become nervous. They will bark but not bite."

Talia stepped around the fire pit and offered the Empress her hand. She only wished that she could be more certain that her uncle would call his banners to defend her and her oath-breaking.

"It seems we have reached an agreement."

Skadi took her hand. "I shall send Aren to your lands. You can get to know and love him then."

Talia forced herself to look pleased at that, then turned to leave.

"I was sorry to hear about your uncle," Skadi said.

Talia stopped and turned back. "It has been painful for all involved."

"Are the rumors I have heard true? He betrayed your family?"

Talia thought this concern might be genuine. Osric had saved the Empress' life, it was said, though not even he had spoken of it, and he had rarely mentioned his service in the Empire.

"They are true to a point. Though he may not have been acting in his own mind."

"Magic?" Skadi said icily, as though it were a dirty word.

"We think so," Talia said, although who the 'we' were in this she did not know. She alone seemed to cling onto the hopes of mind control.

"He seemed stern to me. Not likely to fall under some spell... but then who is to say what was underneath. Lethal though. The only foreigner in two hundred years to earn the honor of Gunvaldr's Horns."

"A fair reward for saving your life."

Skadi shook her head. "Ah, but, no, you do not understand its significance. Many men saved me during the war. Some paid with their lives for it and others not, but none earned the Horns. They are given only to a remarkable show of, ah, there is no true word in your tongue to describe it, a sort of ruthless, unyielding skill. Osric did not just save my life, he defeated three drugar warriors who took out every other man there that day. Drugars are trained to undertake kill missions they aren't expected to survive. Osric defeated them as calmly as though he were in the training yard. I wanted to make him a Housecarl, but in receiving his honors his identity came out, and I could not have a member of another royal house be by my side night and day. He earned great honor elsewhere, I hear."

And infamy, Talia thought. What a strange life her uncle had led. Always moving. From the Skarl Empire to the edge of the Searing Sands. An effective way to run from his role back home or perhaps to hunt, though to hunt for what she could not say.

Knowing some response was expected of her, she said, "None doubt his skills. I like to imagine I inherited a piece of them."

Skadi studied her with a stern expression. "You have his bearing," she said. "Safe journey, Talia Agravain. I do so look forward to bringing our two peoples close together again."

THIRTY-ONE

A Trail of Bile and Blood

Holt's concern that scourge bodies would pile up in the tunnels proved unfounded. When they returned to the descent and the hunt, they found no corpses from the day before. Given the trails of blood, bile, and slime, it looked like they had been dragged off. Even the body of the pale dread worm had been sheared clean from the wall; its remaining half was stuck fast in the earth, presumably unreachable by whatever hands had taken the rest.

Alarmed by this, Holt and Ash debated what might have occurred. Holt feared that the ghouls and bugs had reanimated and risen again. Together they concluded this could not be the case. Neither Brode, Talia, nor Rake had ever mentioned this, nor did Ash's blood memories hold any such information.

Fresh corpses of the living were burned to prevent the blight raising them. A blighted creature, once killed again, remained down – a second death was final.

Despite their deductions, they were still left with the question of who or what had removed the bodies. The only clues lay in the bits of flesh, chitin, hide, and tooth which dotted the passageway.

Grim and ominous as such a trail made, it gave Holt and Ash a route to follow, making the decision to take this or that passageway easy. Following it, they encountered more scourge, and on and on it went, leading them ever deeper.

Days passed in this cycle. The moon did not always shine in their Forging tunnel, and so the exact passage of time was hard to track. It also cut into the time they could otherwise be fighting. Still, without brief glimpses of the sun, Holt reckoned he would go mad. On those occasions, he took what sleep he could.

On each of their excursions they pressed deeper, encountering ghouls, dread worms, and other mutant burrowing creatures. On what Holt guessed to be their sixth day, they encountered the first of the larger bugs – two flayers – and afterward those greater enemies became more numerous. The dark casters of the scourge, ghouls with foul magics of their own, had been few, which Holt was grateful for. So far, they had encountered no abominations.

On the eleventh day, they fought their way through a juggernaut and emerged into a cavernous tunnel, the ceiling of which they could not see. The pressure of the sticky hot air lifted from their heads.

Holt cast his light each way but found no end. Sensing no immediate danger, he stepped out into what he thought would be the middle of the passage, yet still his lunar power could not reveal the opposite wall. He flared his light until he had to squint, and only then did he glimpse the full width of the place.

"This is more than large enough for a queen." His voice sounded dry and hoarse.

"The trail grows cold," Ash said. "The scent is weaker here and runs both left and right."

Holt checked the ground and found it so caked in grime that a clear trail was impossible to discern. Feeling drained, he stopped the flow of light, letting the darkness become total again. Ash's core was low, and they could delve no further today.

"These tunnels must run under all of Ahar."

"All under the world," Holt said, speaking telepathically again, not least to save drawing more attention to their presence. This grand tunnel placed the smaller passages into a more terrifying context. He and Ash had been fighting down the country lanes leading to the great highway. On the surface, grander roads connected mighty cities and kingdoms. What did they connect to down here?

"Holt, get back!"

In the total dark, Holt could see nothing. He just managed to stumble back to Ash's side.

"We must hide."

They scarpered back to the passage they had come from.

"Ash, what's wrong?"

"Something approaches down the tunnel."

Holt stood still as the rock around them, and before long, he too heard the echoes of stamping feet. A buzz of wings sounded from far to their right, approaching fast.

"I think they are carriers," Ash said. *"Carriers flying and walking too. Those walking tread heavy. Their backs must contain a full load of ghouls."*

"Why would they be moving ghouls around? Unless they are preparing for some attack."

"Hold your breath," Ash said. *"They draw close."*

Holt drew a breath and held it. The buzz of the carrier wings peaked as they passed. The walking carriers pounded by after, a silent convoy save for their clacking mouths and a wet sloshing noise coming from under their carapaces.

Not until the sound of their travel had passed out of Holt's hearing did Ash tell him to breathe easy again.

"Let's fall back for today," Ash said.

Holt could not agree more. He hoped it would be nighttime when they reached their Forging tunnel.

Given the toil of recent days, Holt felt progress in the bond. Its edges had seared and expanded outward at a pace like their early days together. Efficiency was their main issue. Though they had made small gains, the increase was not substantial enough to keep them in combat for exponentially more time. And each time they ran dry on power, they had to retreat, wait for the moon, Forge, and then return. The petty volume of lunar motes available made things harder still. With such limited raw motes, Holt had to make every hammer blow of heart and soul count, and Ash had to Sink with increased skill. Holt took some consolation in knowing that if they survived, their ability to recover Ash's core after a fight would be much improved for their efforts.

All the same, they only managed to restore Ash's core to full once. On all other occasions, they were forced to return to the deep with less power than the day before.

Mercifully, on this evening of the eleventh day, the moon shone in the Forging tunnel. Holt was about to get to work when Ash groaned in pain.

"What's wrong?" Holt asked.

"My wing. It hurts."

With raw motes to draw upon, Holt cast a light and found a tear in the folds of Ash's left wing. Wounds inflicted by teeth. The cuts were not severe, but they were rotting the area around them black and green.

"The blight is in it," Holt said.

"I feel it," Ash said. He growled low in his throat as Holt concentrated and pushed his lunar power to the area. His wing flashed silver-white and the blight was expelled, leaving the usual silver and purple bruising behind. Holt still carried similar marks on his leg where a blighted hound had bitten him.

"I'm surprised it's taken this long for your wings to get injured," Holt said. Dragons were not made for cramped spaces. Ash had to tuck his wings in as tight as he could, stoop his body, and lower his snout just to move. Where his hide was steel, his wings were only leather. Forced to cover most of his body with his wings, Ash was thus more vulnerable than he would be on the surface, where he would have the space to spread his wings, fly, and fight as dragons should. "Maybe if we fight in that huge tunnel, you'll have it easier."

"It will be too easy to get surrounded in there. I fear that great road, especially the thought of where those carriers were heading."

"So do I, but we only have that choice. Push on. Fight harder."

His stomach clenched from hunger, but with Ash's core diminished there would be no more battles until they recovered.

They got to work, Cleansing and Forging. The sliver of moonlight was thinner than ever that night. Knowing it would make things even harder, Holt attempted to Sink his own channels to encourage every scrap of lunar power toward them while Forging at the same time. Rake had gone through the basics and Ash shared his instruction from Eidolan, though doubtless he was far from proficient in the cycling technique.

He settled into an easy flow, pushing magic on a normal cycle around his broad channels then pulling them back to his center and holding them for as long as he could before cycling them again. Starting Sinking was easy enough. Magic seemed to want to do one of two things: either escape his mortal body or else circle around the vicinity of his soul bond, the way blood will flow to the warmest part of a body.

Yet attempting both Forging and Sinking together was problematic. Rake had not allowed Holt to take any of Aberanth's elixirs underground. No aids or shortcuts had been permitted. Holt dearly wished for a Sinking elixir now as he tried to hold his motes around the bond while simultaneously matching his heart to its beat to Forge.

For brief snippets of time, he managed it, and the Sinking helped. A greater number of lunar motes drifted into him, and so he could pass them over to Ash. Whether it was worth the extra effort was another question.

Eventually he realized that not even the palest of light shone through his eyelids. Still Sinking, Holt opened his eyes to find the moonlight gone. More passing clouds, most likely.

When the light did not return, Holt ceased Sinking, allowing his channels to return to a steady state. No sooner had he done this than the moonlight reappeared, sudden, near instantaneously, as if it had always been there, just invisible to him. The passing clouds must have been moving extremely fast.

Typical, Holt thought. He blinked and rubbed at his tired eyes. Despite this, the night was not yet over, and so Holt and Ash did not stop until the dawn came, which was early at this time of summer. Then they slept. Holt fell to sleep right there on the cave floor without any danger of tossing or turning.

Ash nosed him awake some time later. Bleary eyed, Holt noted the golden hue of the daylight streaming in from the crack in the rock. Midday.

The dragon bond had cooled overnight. Again, he swore its edges had thickened and expanded, revealing a wider scene of Ash's core and the inky night sky. He had no doubt that if they continued like this, they would advance to Champion.

What he doubted was whether they would be successful within three months of doing this, never mind a mere three weeks. The midpoint of their deadline had already passed, and his food would not last the remaining days, let alone his will.

They returned to the lake cave, where Holt kept their supplies. During the second day of this 'training', he had calculated how he might stretch out his meager supplies. With wood for just two small fires, he opted to cook two large batches of rice which could then be cooled and eaten over the subsequent days. Now he was down to his last rice ball.

Holt unwrapped the final compact ball and placed it without pleasure into his dry mouth. Despite the rice beginning to turn, he chewed thoroughly and swallowed it.

"*You need more,*" Ash said.

The pain in Ash's voice hurt more than the ache in Holt's empty stomach.

"*There is no more. The dry fish, fruit, and nuts will have to see me to the end.*"

He checked on those supplies, laying them out in their clean cloth wrappings. It seemed a paltry amount now he looked at them. He thought there had been more.

A sudden surge of despair rose from his gut, but he forced it back down. He could only press onward. And, for now, Ash needed to eat.

Holt walked to the water's edge and got to his knees. The lake was a still black mirror before him. With effort, he concentrated the light swirling around his palm toward his fingertip. A berry-sized orb of light pulsed there. He hung this just above the surface of the water. Dark shapes moved beneath, then rose, coming toward the light. Holt plunged his right hand into the ice water, gasped from the cold, yet managed to lock his fingers around a fish.

This cavefish looked as alien to him as the dread worms and other pale creatures they had come across. It had no visible eyes, and its scales were wafer-thin and colorless. A wide mouth gaped red and toothless. Eerie to behold and entirely unappealing.

He threw it to Ash, who scooped the wriggling fish up into his jaws. Its bitter taste crossed the dragon bond, but Ash had not complained since the first catch. Holt had debated whether the fish would be poisonous, but he had never known dragons to suffer from food the way humans could. Dragons could eat raw chicken without issue, after all. Thankfully, nothing ill befell Ash from the cold, slimy meal, save for the bad taste in his mouth.

Holt caught a second fish for Ash and then braced himself to return to the depths. First, he cleaned Brode's sword. He dared not dip it into the lake to clean it for fear of sullying those waters. Some days ago, he had discovered that casting an intense lunar light up and down the metal would scour it clean of scourge filth. He did this now, though he was forced to shut his eyes from the bright light. Having been in the dark for so long, even light from his own magic caused his eyes to ache at times.

While not a perfect polish, it was better than nothing. A rider's blade would not dull under the effects of such uncleanliness, but riders maintained their weapons well and Holt felt it imperative to do the same, just as he maintained Ash's core.

He warmed his body by practicing sword guards, stances, and other forms both Brode and Rake had taught him. The dragon-steel felt heavy in his hand for the first time. Though enhanced, his body was still only an Ascendant's. How long could it go without sufficient food and rest?

To spare both his eyes and their magic, Holt walked in the dark as they made their way down the now familiar route to hunt for scourge. He kept close beside Ash, often with one hand on the dragon. On occasion, he stumbled or caught his foot in a crevice.

At first, these things hadn't bothered him and he had recovered at once with his agility. Each fumble now angered him. Each small stumble seemed a damning failure. They left him seething, and dark thoughts roiled, looking for something or someone to blame. Namely himself.

"What if I can't do this?"

"Allow me to carry more of the burden," Ash said. *"My strength does not wane as fast as yours."*

"You can't do it for me. We have to fight together. We have to get stronger. I have to get stronger."

"This weight should not all be upon your back, boy. It is our bond that must grow, that is between the two of us."

But Holt's dark mood cast Ash's words aside.

"No, it's down to me. I have to get stronger. I have to kill him."

"Him? Do you mean Thrall?"

No. He had not meant the dragon.

"Yes," Holt said, evasive. *"Yes, we have to kill Thrall."*

"You meant Osric again, didn't you?"

"Same difference at this point."

"I don't like this side of you," Ash said. *"You never spoke like this before. You always wanted to grow in strength to help, not to kill."*

"If we kill Thrall or Osric or both then that WILL help people."

Ash snarled and drew to a halt.

"What are you doing?" Holt croaked aloud. His throat felt as though sand and dust caked it. "We have to keep moving. We can't waste a second."

"I think you should rest and eat more."

"I've told you, the food won't last. I can't eat more today, and we don't have the luxury of rest."

"This will not be worth it if you change."

"I'm not—what do you mean? I don't understand, Ash." His head began to pound. Holt pinched the bridge of his nose hard. "We've got to. Rake's right. It will be up to us to stop Thrall and Osric."

"It's up to Master Rake, Eidolan, Aberanth, and Masters Hava and Farsa. We could linger back. We don't have to fight."

"Are you saying we should give up?"

"To spare you, yes."

Holt hung his head. "Even assuming Rake will let us out of here having failed, can you really sit idle while Rake and others fight? That's not honorable. We didn't let Talia and Pyra fight alone."

"I hate what's happening to you," Ash said. *"It's this place. It's you pushing yourself too hard. Always too hard. It's Master Rake whispering in your ear."*

"Rake is trying to help us. You heard the Mystic Elder, you heard what that rider Orvel said – we're on our own and we're hunted. We've been naïve until now. We could have saved that egg, and everyone in Dinan, and my father if we were better. Stronger. We must get stronger. Then we can see off anyone who tries to hurt us or stop any of Thrall's servants that we find. We go on," he ended harshly and strode off, pulling light to his palm. The silver brightness burned his eyes before he blinked, squinted, and adjusted.

They had arrived back at the great scourge highway.

"Stop," Ash said. He didn't sound angry, just desperate and hurt. A stroke of guilt and shame cooled Holt. He stopped, but he did not turn around. *"Please just listen to me. You're pushing yourself so hard, but I think we need to fight smarter instead of harder."*

Now they were back in the great tunnel, Holt returned to speaking telepathically. *"What more can I do?"*

"Not, more, Holt. Less. Less magic, at least."

"But I need the light to see and fight."

"I know, but it strains our bond too fast. My core drains, and then we must retreat. If we're going to manage this, we'll need to fight for longer. Which means you need to use less magic."

Maybe it was his hunger, or maybe it was the heat of the argument, but Holt's mind went blank. He did not know what to do.

"In this dark, I'm blind too."

"Then trust and rely on me," Ash said.

"I do. You know I do."

"No, you don't. Not truly. You love me, and I love you, but you still act like you have to protect me all the time. Even back in Brenin I tried to tell you this, so listen again now. You don't have to be the one who defends us. It's only natural

that you do. I was so small and frail, and you feared what would happen to us both. Things are different now. Hear through me, as I see the world through your eyes when we fly. And do what Master Brode and Talia always wanted – use your sword, conserve your magic."

Even through the malaise of creeping despair, Holt saw the sense in this. Sense-sharing could place a terrible strain on the bond, but not if they stayed close together. As Holt had no intention of leaving Ash's side down here, perhaps it could work.

He extinguished his light, stepped quietly back to Ash, and felt gently around for the dragon's snout. Ash pressed his head into Holt's.

"Is that what Rake meant?" Holt whispered. "When he had us run through the woods, is this what he tried to get us to do?"

The question answered itself. Of course it was. Rake, for all his bravado, always had some plan.

"I'll try," Holt affirmed.

He found blending his senses with Ash much harder than usual. Perhaps because Holt had fewer senses of his own to share in the first place. The highway seemed to him a black and silent place. Yet he had the warm, clammy air on his skin and the stone beneath his feet. And though he could not hear the scourge right now, their stench was ever-present in the sticky air.

"My eyes for your eyes."

"Your skin for my skin."

"My world for your world," they said together.

The scourge stink swelled in Holt's nose, a near choking toxin compared to just moments ago. The air pressed down harder than ever. And in the echoing distance he heard chinks of moving stone, soft wet footsteps, and rattling he could not discern the nature of.

Ash tapped his tail, soft and light in truth, but to their ears it rang high and clear. Its noise echoed off the rock and distant cavern walls, bombarding Holt in a torrent of information, second hand through Ash, that he could not comprehend. His sense of his surroundings was murky, but that was a lot better than nonexistent.

He tried walking but stopped after five steps.

"This will take a lot of getting used to."

"You will learn faster than you think," Ash said. *"I learned how to use your eyes when necessity demanded."*

"That you did. Okay, now, for want of a better idea, let's head in the direction those carriers went. There's got to be something out there or at least more scourge."

They walked for what might have been half a mile. It seemed easier now, compared to back in the Fae Forest, for Holt to really listen. Without sight as a distraction, and with Ash's help, he heard clearer than ever before.

Ash guided Holt's attention to where sound morphed at branching passageways and how he could tell by that change which tunnels led up and which led down. None held a strong smell of the scourge, so they followed their noses until the shrieks of the enemy sounded shrill and near and it would not have taken Ash for Holt to hear them.

Battle came. Ghouls poured from three passageways, as did a howling flayer. With his hearing increased, the flayer's cry sounded ear-splitting to Holt and drowned all other sounds. He could not separate one from the other, and his precarious picture of the world shattered.

"Hold steady," Ash instructed.

Every fiber in Holt's body wanted to draw on lunar power, to press down a Consecration and charge a Shock. But no, he had to let go. He had to rely on Ash.

Their bond warmed, anticipating the fight.

Yet when the bugs reached them, Holt could not make any decisive move in the cacophony. The enemy sounded both near and far, and upon all sides. Feet stamped, and a flayer's scythe blade whistled through the air—

Ash knocked Holt aside, out of the flayer's path, then attacked it himself. On his back, Holt found it close to impossible to resist the urge to call upon his light.

Around him in the utter dark, Ash swiped, snarled, crunched through chitin, and beat his tail. Holt struggled upright and gripped his sword uselessly before him.

Through the din, some keen part of him thought an enemy was charging toward him.

"Thrust forward."

Holt thrust without question. He struck flesh and bone, and the ghoul gargled as it died. The dragon bond blazed to life in his chest, a warmth that could have seen him through the worst of winter. Not since Ash had been a hatchling had it burned like this.

In the dark, Holt smiled. If they were careful, if he could learn to navigate the world as Ash did, they might just make it.

THIRTY-TWO

A Quiet Monster

Osric awoke before dawn. Rather than rise to do his exercises he lay there, staring up at the cold, dark ceiling. When at last he moved, his body felt stiff. It could not be from physical aching. This weariness lay deeper. Bristles itched his face, but he was not inclined to remove them. His spirit as well as his routine were broken.

A ray of dawn light fell upon his gray cloak. Draped over its stand, it looked as though it sat upon the shoulders of a ghost. Mocking him. Spite and Vengeance hung quietly on the wall, no longer thirsting for blood.

He shook his head. The axes spoke to him? What a foolish notion. The only voice he heard was Sovereign's.

Osric dressed and ventured down to the mess, hoping for an early breakfast alone. He must have lain in bed longer than he realized for many cultists already sat hunched over bowls of boiled oats. Champion Dahaka sat at the head table with the Speaker.

Osric collected half a dozen boiled eggs, bread, and a thick wedge of blood pudding. He moved to the head table and took a seat at the opposite end from where Dahaka and the Speaker sat. Eating methodically, he mentally went over the daily chores ahead of him. Cleanse,

Forge, tend to the hatchlings. With luck, Sovereign would not decide the fate of another dragon today.

His thoughts were interrupted by Orvel. The Low Champion set his food aside as he sat down.

"Master Agravain, may I speak with you?"

"What is it?" Osric grunted.

Orvel cast a wary glance over to the Speaker and Dahaka, then dropped his voice. "Might we speak in private?"

"Private? There is no such thing here. Not even inside our own minds. Speak here or hold your tongue."

Orvel licked his lips and leaned in. "I have been encouraged to visit this so-called blood alchemist. I am wary of it. As you have also shown a reluctance to attend him, I thought you might—"

He cut off as the Speaker and Dahaka moved closer to them.

The two women stared Orvel down.

"Is something amiss?" the Speaker asked.

Orvel looked at Osric imploringly.

"I am sorry, truly, that you think I can help you," Osric said.

"But you haven't gone," Orvel said, near hissing the words.

Dahaka placed her arms fully upon the table. Her forearms were laid bare, as were the still healing cuts from where she had given her blood. "What frightens you?" she asked. "This pain is but trivial suffering compared to all else we have been through."

The Speaker nodded knowingly.

Osric found the glint in Dahaka's eye disturbing. She had grown more radical with each day in the Speaker's company.

"It seems unnatural," Orvel said. "And its use? These Wyrm Cloa —" He caught himself and raised his hands. "I mean, the Shroud... well, I have fought them before. Did you not, Dahaka?"

"I still believed the lies of the Order back then," Dahaka said. "That we could find victory in the endless fight. That all life mattered – all except, it turns out, our own families. Why should their lives matter less than strangers'? What are oaths but thin shields to cower behind and assuage blame? A few make the decisions for the many, discarding some, preserving others, and for what? For those left to linger in pain and toil until their backs break or bodies crumble. What use is it? In the end, all we ever do is delay the inevitable."

Her words were salt into Osric's latest wound. His avoidance of the alchemist was only a delay, in the end. Fighting Sovereign's will was the same as fighting the scourge. You might delay death's victory, but it could never be defeated.

"Only Sovereign can end the cycle," Dahaka concluded. "The reckoning of dragons shall come, and we who stand with him will be protected. We must do all we can to assist him."

"Master Agravain," Orvel beseeched him. "You don't believe these ravings. I hear it in your voice, see it in your eyes."

The Speaker opened her mouth, but Osric interrupted.

"Life is pain, Champion Orvel. Brutal. Endless. Why fight to preserve suffering?" The Speaker then looked at him expectantly and Osric obliged her. He stood and looked her in the eye. "I've long fought against this truth and long fought against Sovereign, out of pride perhaps. But I knew the truth of his cause before we even met. The Speaker knew that of me, and she was right."

The Speaker's face grew radiant. "I knew you were faithful, General."

Osric returned his attention to Orvel. He sat slouched over his cooling breakfast. It seemed his age had caught up with him.

"Do not resist what is inevitable," Osric said.

With that in mind, he departed from the mess hall and made his way to the blood alchemist's workshop. Stepping inside, Osric was met with the overwhelming smell of iron. A slaughterhouse would have been less pungent. Several cauldrons' worth of hot, bubbling blood steamed against a far wall. Workbenches were laden with half-filled vials, clamps, bushels of dried herbs, and jars of clouded liquids and animal parts.

A figure clothed head to toe in dark overalls stood bent over a pestle and mortar. A squelch sounded with each pound of the pestle. The alchemist's face was hidden behind an enclosed mask with a long beak nose. Darkened glasses hid his eyes. He might have been mistaken for a vulture.

"Welcome, General." The alchemist's voice was deep, hoarse, and muffled behind his mask.

"Let's get this over with," Osric said.

The alchemist motioned to a door. Osric passed through the main workshop and into a side room. Incense burned, letting off a pleasant, sweet smoke, as did bowls of dried flowers and herbs. All noise of the yard of Windshear Hold, from the bustle of people and dragons to the wind itself, fell into nothingness here. Candlelight cast the space in a soft, warm glow and a cushioned chair sat at the center of the room with two small tables on either side of it. Not a drop of blood could be seen or smelled.

The door shut behind him.

"Please, sit," the alchemist said.

Osric did. "This is far from what I expected."

"It has become clear to me that blood willingly given contains more potency than when extracted by force or after life passes. For centuries, the art of blood mixing has been passed down through the faithful, yet always we relied on blood taken from dragons released from their bondage. However, under Sovereign's magnificence, we have dragons willing to give of their life force. The blood is richer, untainted by fear or battle, and hot with life rather than the coldness of death. As my work has progressed to accepting donations from riders, the same I assumed would hold true. A comfortable setting will help produce the best results." The alchemist produced a brass cup from a dark corner of the room. "Which hand do you favor?"

"My right," Osric said. All he'd achieved had been with that hand. Every feat of strength, forging his axes, even the deaths – those that mattered at any rate. He'd killed Godric with that hand.

The alchemist set the cup down on his left-hand side, exited to a side room, and then returned carrying a tray holding a bowl of steaming water, clean linens, and a long instrument topped with a glass orb.

"Are you relaxed, General?" he added, without any sense of urgency.

Osric shifted on the chair. "As I'll ever be."

In truth, he thought he could only be relaxed in such a situation given his power and his experience. This dark figure with the nightmarish visage and distorted voice, the gloom, the smoke, and the smells, it could all too easily have been a fever dream.

The alchemist began by heating the glass orb in the bowl of water, then brought it to Osric's skin. The area grew red under the warmth.

"Would you be accommodating and make the incision with your weapon?" the alchemist asked. "My lancets cannot pierce your skin."

Osric drew out Spite for the job. He carefully made a cut. Blood welled, more than he had expected, and ran into the brass cup beneath his arm.

"Why my blood?" Osric asked. "Champion Dahaka has given hers."

"I've suspected the addition of rider blood might bind with a dragon's, creating a more stable serum. Dahaka is an Exalted Champion, and so, while powerful, she is still not yet a Lord. I wish to test if there is a difference there. So many new possibilities might be explored."

"Meaning you'll need more blood later," Osric said.

"If he wills it." The alchemist withdrew the brass bowl and began applying pressure to Osric's arm with the linens. "Hold these in place, General."

Osric did, and when the blood clotted, he tied a crude bandage and made for the door.

"Until next time," the alchemist said.

Having surrendered himself so utterly, Osric retired to his quarters that night as though he had suffered a decisive defeat on the field of battle. The next day he awoke late in the morning. The day after that, he did not wake at all.

Such a draining malaise as this had sapped him only once before. That had been when he gave up on Esfir returning to him over the dunes. At least then his Gray Cloaks had surrounded him and, through their spirit and his need to stay strong for them, he'd found the strength to break free from the malady.

Sovereign cared not. He spent most of his time with the hatchlings, judging them one by one and beginning his training of a chosen few.

One night, Osric stood at ease outside the topmost hatchery of the mystic tower. He'd been waiting for a while. Even in his darkest moods he could not help but be early to his tasks. At last, Orvel exited carrying bloody buckets.

"I trust they ate well?" Osric asked.

"All but the little black one. Nothing I did could coax it out."

Osric nodded. If the dragon proved too weak for Sovereign, then it would also be taken care of.

Expecting Orvel to step aside, Osric was surprised to find him still standing before the door. The emerald rider looked darkly into his empty meat buckets.

"Is something amiss, Champion Orvel?"

"Had I known a servant's life waited for me, I never would have—"

"Do you wish to finish that thought?"

Orvel seemed to recall who he was speaking to. He straightened and said, "Not at all, Master Agravain. I misspoke."

"We are all servants of Sovereign and are privileged to be so. When the new world comes, we shall be fortunate to witness it."

Orvel wisely said nothing. He gave a curt nod and stalked off.

Osric watched him go. He would never be a true believer. A few bad decisions mixed well with bitterness and resentment at a lack of progression and a lack of respect had led to hatred for the Order. If he had worked harder, done better, he would not be here. He might have died in the conflicts to come, but he could have held his head high and proud.

A doubt gnawed at Osric. *He's not so different from you,* a small voice said, this one not the charming voice but his own.

As Orvel rounded a corner out of sight, Osric's judgment turned to pity. The fallen rider was a lot like himself, in truth. Not so long ago, Osric would never have admitted that, taking too much pride in his drive, training, prowess, and abilities. Strange how much could change in so little time.

In the end, it mattered not. Dragon, human, even scourge, they were all for dust sooner or later.

Osric entered the hatchery, feeling the instant drop in temperature. It was at least a still night and dry. The crates which housed the eggs had been discarded, and now the hatchlings lay close to two lit braziers in various states of languidness or sleep. He counted four, including the golden dragon. The oily black one must have been hiding again.

Osric took up a seat on the simple stool at the center of the hatchery. A heavy pail of raw mutton remained. Orvel must have neglected to take it with him. The man was sloppy. Small wonder he had only advanced to Low Champion despite his advanced age.

Something moved. Osric snapped his gaze to the dark corners of the room, where the shadows shifted.

"Come on out," he called to the gloom. "You are due your rations." If the black dragon moved at all, it did so in silence.

A snuffling came from his right. The sandy dragon hobbled up to him, dragging its clubbed foot.

Unless this one displays something special, it won't survive judgment either.

Drawing level with him, the sandy drake sniffed expectantly at the mutton.

Osric shooed it away. "You've had your portion. You're dismissed."

Even if the dragons did not understand his words, they understood his tone. The sandy drake gave a low cry, then loped off to lie by the fire. Once it fell back to sleep, Osric was left alone. Just the way he preferred. The pain in his chest was never so severe when he was alone, and quiet, and still. Only his right hand flexed at times, yet what it grasped for now he could not say.

For his axe? A fight? A way out?

He tried to sit in a meditative state and allow the night to pass by swiftly. Yet his mind would not leave him alone. The gnawing thought about Orvel's similarity to himself kept nibbling away at him, joined by the words of the Cook boy.

'He's made you do all these things.'

Holt may well envision it an easy thing to resist. He seemed idealistic. Someone who thought their own fortunes could be achieved by everyone else if only they tried. If only they did the right thing.

If Osric had been able to break free, he would have done it long ago. His attempt to throw Sovereign off recently proved the futility of it. Even throwing everything he possessed at the dragon had not worked. He should have known in the moment it would not work. The real test had been back at the Toll Pass. He'd failed to resist Sovereign's demands to kill his own brother. Instead, he'd crossed a line he could never walk back over.

Yet the dragon had called that a failure. A failure for Osric, but also for him. Sovereign cared only for Sovereign. The Speaker had pushed this same reasoning too.

Osric did not understand it. He had been ordered to take control of Feorlen and to facilitate the defeat of his homeland. Killing Godric and taking his place had to be done. And he had been *forced* to do it.

Another quick movement in the shadows. Osric saw the tip of a black tail slink in and out of sight. "Come on out," he said, this time softly, lost as he was in his own dark wrangling.

The Toll Pass had been a failure. Why? With distance, and time, and the warm fire and the dark shadows of the hatchery, Osric struggled to conjure the justification for his actions. Away from the battle of the Pass, away from the trumpets, the drums, the boom of siege engines and the biting steel, it was hard to recall his reasoning in the moment.

The plan only demanded that Osric be in control of the levers of power for a time. In hindsight, that did not require Godric's death, only his temporary incapacity or incarceration. His reckless brother had made that easy by trapping himself in the Toll Pass. The Risalians would have captured Godric, along with the fortress. During a wartime crisis, Osric would have been offered the regency, allowing Sovereign to begin his invasion earlier.

Instead, Osric killed Godric and won the Toll Pass in a storm of glory. Rather than be made regent, Osric had been dubbed the kingdom's hero while his nephew had been crowned king.

That had delayed Sovereign's plan.

Was that the failure? Surely only in hindsight was it a failure? Holt and Ash and the Emerald Flight could never have been accounted for. No Wild Flight had ever helped in an incursion before en masse. It was unjust to blame Osric for that. Failure indeed. If Sovereign wished differently, he should have given him different orders.

He did, that small voice said. Here in the dark, his conscience asserted itself.

Osric's right hand trembled. He fought it still and laid it out upon his knee. It had shaken like this after he'd crushed Godric's chest. He'd hidden behind lies, but his tears had been real. Those he recalled clearly. The tears had fallen until he feared they would never stop, and he had not shed another since. Not when he forged Spite and Vengeance. Not even when his nephew died. Neither he nor Sovereign had made any designs on Leofric's death. As Master of War, Osric had held all the control he required. Killing Leofric would only have risked drawing attention, but his sickly nephew's heart had burst of its own accord. Still, seeing him lying there white as bone, Osric had felt little. Under Sovereign's sway, his heart must have grown numb. Yet if that were the case, why had he not felt numb over Godric?

Stop hiding behind the dragon, the small voice told him. *Stop using him as your excuse.*

Sovereign had instructed him to take control in Sidastra. All else at the Toll Pass had been of his own making. All of it.

A shudder ran through him.

I do hope it was worth it, his conscience asked of him. *Your moment. Love and praise at long last. Was it worth it?*

"Yes," he said alone to the dark. For a moment, it had been worth it.

His greatest victory. Felice's grief a sick justice. The Ealdors of Feorlen, the High Councilors, and everyone at court beaming and applauding and telling him how fortunate they were to have him. The stoic look of sheer devotion and admiration from Talia, his little soldier.

All worth it. Just for a moment.

How had he let himself fall so far? It had been a quiet thing over the years, and it was terrible now to admit it. Where had jealousy and bitterness led him but to this dismal end, working toward bringing the ruin of all things? Just like Orvel, only so much worse.

If he had been stronger, he would have fought Sovereign when they'd first met and told him no, never, he would not be party to such evil. But he hadn't. In just the same way he'd chosen to kill Godric, a part of him had chosen to follow Sovereign. Even the Speaker, twisted as her mind was, saw the truth of that.

It was worse, much worse after Esfir left, his small voice said soothingly, as though worried it had pushed him too far.

No, he told himself in return. It would be the height of cowardice to lay the blame for his actions at her feet. She had left bravely, to save him and his men. Since then, he had strode along the path to Sovereign's malice, but he had taken his first small steps on that road before her. Burning a town rather than saving it. Leaving prisoners to starve in the wastes. Removing that traitor's head with a seething stroke of his axe.

His brother's blood upon his hands.

No, Osric told himself, stern now. *No more hiding or running from who I am. What I am.*

A clarity came to his mind, clearing a lifetime's worth of black fog. He had poured much of his hatred into his axes. With that poison removed from him, perhaps that was how he had found the strength to speak back against the charming voice.

At last, he was willing to accept the truth. Earlier, when he'd claimed to seek an end to life and to suffering, as the Speaker claimed, it had been a half-truth. A part of him wished to see life end, but not to spare the suffering. No, he sought things to end because he had suffered. In the quiet corners of his mind, something monstrous had been taking shape his whole life. He had been lost long before Sovereign had found him.

In the flickering shadows, Osric felt a tear run down his cheek.

Feet padded on the floor.

Osric sniffed, then jerked to the source of the noise, panicked that someone had seen him so vulnerable. What he found was the little black dragon, its head appearing seamlessly from the dark as though materializing from the shadows. By contrast, the whites of its eyes shone bright as snow under the sun. Its purple pupils were large, deep, and heartbreaking, looking to Osric as though hoping for something he was unable to give.

Osric remained silent. The dragon continued gazing at him with wide eyes, then sniffed and took another cautious step. And then another.

Osric placed a hand into the cold, slimy bucket and pulled out a chunk of mutton.

The dragon crept closer, keeping so low that its belly scraped along the stone. One of its fellow hatchlings growled in its sleep. The black dragon froze, snapped its head to face its sibling, then half-turned, clearly intending to run away.

"Don't," Osric said. "Running won't make you stronger." He didn't know why he bothered. The runt of the litter wouldn't survive Sovereign's ruthless selection.

"Come and eat." He tossed the meat to land on the floor between them.

The dragon's big eyes looked to the food, to Osric, and back to the food. Its forked tongue slithered out to taste the air. That did the trick. In a sudden burst of speed, it slid along the floor, tail swishing as it zoomed toward the food. It tore at the mutton, gulping it down in three big bites.

Osric threw it some more meat. The dragon ate that too, and then its attention returned to Osric himself. It crept closer. Before he realized what was happening, the little black dragon slinked up within reach of his hand. Its tongue flicked out, tasting the meat on his skin. It licked his hand clean, and then it pushed its snout into his palm and rubbed its head along his hand.

So small. So frail.

He brought his hand back, intending to stroke the dragon on the other side. The movement spooked it and it retreated to its gloomy corner, disappearing into the shadows with hardly a sound, as though its talons were made of wool.

"Probably for the best, young one."

Osric slumped upon his stool. Silence returned to the hatchery. Just as he got comfortable with it, two eyes appeared in the corner of the room. Snow white, with desperately large pupils. Eyes that stared back at him throughout the rest of his watch.

THIRTY-THREE

New Threats

On the return journey from Smidgar, Talia felt in higher spirits. Time spent traveling with Pyra had gone a long way to reviving their bond. Looking back, Talia found it scary how used to being apart from her dragon she had become. And though the decision to accept the marriage offer from the Empress came at a personal cost, that cost would not have to be paid until some indeterminate time in the future. As such, she could keep it at arm's length for now. More importantly, it was a better outcome than the other options. A crushing war or having to break her bond with Pyra. While the marriage alliance hinged on her uncle in Brenin finally declaring support for her rule, she assumed his support would come easily, especially if she could now promise the backing of the Skarls.

She should have known by now that things would not be so simple.

Not long after re-entering Feorlen air space at the northern-most point of the Red Range, Talia and Pyra were met by a squadron of emerald dragons. They led her to meet the Elder who awaited her at the edge of a wood not far from Fort Dittan, the same border fort Drefan Harroway had fought tooth and nail to defend during the war.

Even at a distance, the Elder felt diminished. Before, his power had blazed blinding as the sun, impossible to know and impossible to look upon for long. It still blazed, but now she could get to grips with it. No being other than another Elder could have hoped to match him before, yet all the Paragons of Order combined might now have had a shot.

Ultimately, he was a wild dragon without a rider to expedite the recovery of his core. Should he continue to spend his power, it would take long to recover.

When they landed before him, Talia was struck by the heady smell of pollen and rich grass. Birds twittered in the bushes and in their nests amidst the full-bloomed trees, blissfully unaware of whatever ill news the Elder was about to bestow. A sick feeling washed over her from her gut. Why else would the Elder come to seek her directly? She braced herself for this as she dismounted and got to one knee before the dragon.

"You wished to see us, Honored Elder?"

"I have sensed another dark presence below the earth," the Elder said without preamble. *"It beats loud at the southern end of this mountain range."*

"Another chamber?" Talia said. "What does this mean?"

"The presence of the scourge grows daily in the lands you call Brenin," said the Elder. *"Another incursion is in its early stages."*

An incursion into Brenin? Talia thought in horror. *This soon?*

Her stomach knotted. Across the bond, she felt Pyra growl with anticipation. A clean fight and an obvious opponent suited her over politics. Yet Talia's shoulders groaned under the new weight.

"Do not despair," Pyra said, broadcasting the thought for the Elder's benefit as well. *"This might help you. These human squabbles must be set aside in the face of the scourge."*

"Will they be?" asked the Elder.

Talia breathed hard. Her mind raced with the information. "Actually, it may make things worse."

Increased scourge activity would explain why her uncle remained quiet and undecided. He could hardly declare his support for her while his lands entered the chaos of an incursion. If Talia marched to assist him, they would both emerge weaker and be riper fruit for the

Risalian and Athran coalition to pluck. If she did nothing, her uncle would not be able to declare his support for her, meaning no Skarl marriage, meaning Feorlen would be left out in the cold.

Just like that, her path forward was stolen from her.

Talia cycled her fires, keeping them within her body. Through some effort, she found her voice.

"If we're right about these deep chambers, then another queen might be growing. If we find it, we can stop the incursion before it ever reaches boiling point."

"That is precisely the problem," the Elder said. *"Though I feel the chamber's presence, we cannot find an entry point. By the time a new chasm erupts, the incursion will be at full strength."*

"Then what am I to do?" Talia asked. "I cannot defend my borders and fight another incursion at the same time. My armies are weary and stretched thin. Honored Elder, if the Emerald Flight would aid my uncle as you aided me, that would be of great comfort to me."

"A group of my emeralds encountered trouble with riders from the dark tower in the swamp."

"Sable Spire," Talia said aloud. She had never visited that rider hall.

"They demanded we leave their lands as per the Pact."

"You broke it to help me."

"I will not drive my emeralds against hostile riders. Such needless violence would benefit only Sovereign and the scourge."

For a moment, Talia considered it would be the most cathartic thing of all if the whole damned Order just ceased to exist. Holt had it right, tossing the rules aside and doing things just as they had to be, not as they ought to be.

Thankfully, the moment passed.

"Honored Elder," she began, tentative as a lamb taking its first steps. "I cannot fight on every front. If you cannot enter Brenin, would you consent to defend my lands in the north should Risalia strike against me?"

She knew as soon as the words left her mouth that they were a mistake. The Elder growled, the first such growl of anger she had heard him make. His eyes spun into a darker shade of green.

"Never ask me such a thing again, daughter of fire." The disappointment in his voice was a palpable force all on its own.

Talia bathed in shame, but she was lost as to what she should do.

Pyra thrashed her tail, leaving a patch of burnt grass wherever it struck. *"Life Elder, you bring only burdens to my rider. She carries too much already."*

The Elder's eyes returned to a softer green, a deeper, sadder shade like distant hills under twilight.

"I am aware, young one. Know she does not bear them alone. Against your human adversaries, I can do nothing, but against the scourge my flight stands with you. Even if my kin and I cannot cross into Brenin, no ghoul will cross into your lands unchecked. Return to your city and take counsel as you see best. I shall continue searching for an entrance we can use."

The Life Elder and his squadron of emeralds departed.

Talia remained still on one knee. Once the Elder was well out of earshot, Talia let loose her fear, her frustration, and her anger. She screamed, a howl part-fueled by dragon fire. Pyra joined her, howling so loud it scattered all the twittering birds up in their fine nests. Talia screamed until her lungs emptied of air and she fell forward onto the ground and clenched her fists into the soil. Three heaving sighs of relief assuaged a modicum of stress. She ripped clumps of the earth free as she rose, then got back onto Pyra's back.

"Home, girl," she said.

The first thing Talia did upon arriving in the city was summon the council. Full of anxious energy, she hurried through the palace and arrived long before anyone else. Too slowly, much too slowly it seemed to her, the High Councilors came one by one, shepherding stewards, scribes, and other servants along with them.

Harroway was the first to enter, with three young military men like himself. The Mistress of Embassy arrived next, followed closely by Talia's mother. It was a mark of Talia's state of stress that she did not immediately think to embrace her own mother. Her stretched mind caught up to this and she did so, throwing her arms around Felice's neck.

"I only just returned myself," said Felice.

Talia pulled back and saw the bad news in her mother's eyes. "Save it for the council."

At last, all were assembled. Talia wasted no time. She told them of her discussion with Empress Skadi and her agreement to marry one of her sons. Her mother, the Mistress of Embassy, and the Master of Roles looked grave but resigned to the news. Their hearts and families were inclined toward the east and the lineage of Aldunei. The Master of State held a neutral expression. The cousins Lady Elvina and Drefan Harroway sported small smiles. Though their lineage hailed from the original Skarl settlers, she knew neither would be overjoyed at the prospect of a possible imperial overlord. Or perhaps their enthusiasm was blunted by the failure to secure Talia's marriage into their own family. Whatever the case, it was done.

She then divulged to them the news of the scourge rising in Brenin and the new chamber location sensed by the Life Elder.

Geoff Horndown, Master of State, recovered first among the councilors.

"Well, the marriage alliance is what we expected. Let us weather any storms that come from that when they arrive and not before. Our focus now must be on Brenin." He looked at Felice and Lady Ida.

Talia nodded to her mother. "I trust you spoke to Uncle Roland?"

Felice stood to address the council. Many in the room inclined their head out of ingrained respect from her time as queen.

"Councilors, I am afraid my brother's court is in disarray. Word of our troubles reached him too late. Osric's work to undermine us was efficient in that regard. Now scourge activity rises in his own lands. Many of his nobles lock themselves down in their forts. Travel by land grows treacherous. He will have to issue the summons soon and prepare for a siege against his own capital. Even traveling by ship as I did will grow perilous when navigating the Versand. What's more, the riders from Sable Spire have been sluggish in their response. Only one Champion was present in the city to help with preparations and scourge rise from the morass in greater numbers with each passing week."

"This is ill-timed in the extreme," said Harroway. "We have confirmation of Risalian troops mobilizing at their forts close to the northern Red Range. If we march to aid Brenin, there is every chance Risalia will strike."

"Without their backers in Athra doing the same?" asked the Master of State.

"We'll be stretched so thin and weak they won't need aid to ensure victory," Harroway said.

"Coedhen has also officially declared against us," said the Mistress of Embassy. The reaction to this might have been a collective shrug. What was one more piece of bad news, especially one so expected?

The old Master of Roles sighed hard and shook his head. "Time was that a scourge rising would dispel any other conflicts. Improper – most improper."

"I couldn't agree more," Talia said. "Were it that I could force these fools to walk in the dark of a scourge tunnel, their pettiness might be dispelled."

She decided to move on. It did not help her own conscience to dwell on the fact that Feorlen's woes were chiefly the result of her being on the throne. "Mother, will King Roland support us if the incursion in his lands can be dealt with swiftly?"

"Difficult to say. Before the scourge rising became his chief concern, his nobles were divided. The coalition placed trade restrictions on Brenin as well, trying to force my brother's hand to join them. If he did declare for us, it could split his own kingdom. Enough might be swayed if Roland can convince them there is something in it for them other than defending his niece, a niece who by all accounts should not be in power in the first place."

"What's his price?" asked the Mistress of Coin.

"A removal of tariffs for Brenin goods," Felice said. "And land. The Toll Pass at least."

A part of Talia considered that the Toll Pass was worth giving up just to be rid of the wretched place. A part of her thought about leveling the fortress there and blocking up the pass for good measure. So much of the traffic between the three kingdoms of Feorlen, Risalia, and Brenin passed through it that whichever kingdom held it gained tremendous power over trade and, of course, the money which flowed through it. It was also the source of eternal disagreement.

Her uncle Roland had gone to war with Risalia over its ownership years ago and lost. Her own father had gone to war to seize it and prove he and his little kingdom were strong. He had died. Now Talia held it.

"We cannot do this," said Lady Elvina. "We'll need the revenue from the Pass if we are to recover."

"Currently there is no trade," said the Master of State. "So what are we actually losing?"

"Only every life and drop of blood spent to take it," said the Master of Roles. He tapped one of the massive tomes he always carried with him. "I can tell you the numbers. I can tell you their names."

"I too would hate to see Godric's legacy lost," Felice said. "But if Brenin controls the Pass, then Risalia cannot invade through it."

"Ealdors, the fortress was severely damaged during the war," said Harroway. "The place will be hard to defend, and that's where the hammer will fall hardest. I say it's a liability."

The council descended into a heated discussion.

Talia regretted asking their opinions on the matter. As it became clear things were going nowhere, she blazed fire around a clenched fist and slammed it onto the table. This time, a crack split the wood and ran through the tabletop like forked lightning.

Silence fell.

Talia extinguished her hand and said slowly, "This talk on what we will and will not give up is moot. Unless the incursion in Brenin can be dealt with soon, none of it will matter. Our only hope is that the Life Elder and his flight can find the entrance to this new chamber under the Red Range."

"Does the Queen seek another expedition underground?" asked the Master of State.

The Master of Roles' hand fell flat upon his book. "The last one cost us much, Your Majesty."

Given Talia's recent outburst, the fact the old man still spoke his mind showed a strength Talia could not help but admire. His words also sent a painful pang of guilt through her. She recalled the river of blood underfoot, the death stench so thick she thought she might never smell clean again, the looks of horror captured in the gaping mouths of the fallen. All of it magnified by Ghel's twitching body and her high, frightened voice. It was one thing to see a frail human but another to see a dragon brought so low. Across her bond, she felt Pyra writhe uncomfortably at the memory.

"I allowed the fire to take over me," Talia said. "Those losses were my fault. I was reckless. I was wrong. I won't let it happen again."

"And what if an entrance cannot be found?" Harroway asked her. "What shall we do then?"

"Falcaer," Talia said, as though everything depended on it. Which it just might. "Please tell me there has been good news from there at least, Lady Ida."

The Mistress of Embassy looked older than ever. "All efforts to make contact with the riders have been rebuffed."

"Very well," Talia said, drawing herself back from the table. She knew what she had to do. She had known it since discussing matters with Pyra on their way back from the Life Elder. "I will go to Falcaer myself and beg Adaskar to summon the whole Order to put down the Brenin incursion quickly."

"No," Harroway said. He stood and leaned over the table as though he meant to grab and restrain her. "Talia, if you willingly enter Falcaer, you may never come out."

"Adaskar wouldn't harm a queen," Talia said, sounding surer than she felt. "It would be breaking the very rules he is angry at me for breaking. Besides, if he *really* wanted to arrest me, a team of Lords or just one Paragon could have flown to Sidastra and there would have been nothing we could do about it."

In considering it, Talia supposed she had even more reason to be thankful to the Life Elder and his flight. Their presence might have warded off just such an attempt.

"If," Talia began, injecting as much confidence as she could, "if Adaskar can see reason, if the whole Order is mobilized, then they'll descend on the scourge in Brenin with such force there won't even be a single scuttering vethrax left. The world seems poised on the brink of war, and such wars are always negative for the Order. Everyone is weakened, making the scourge a greater threat. Falcaer's resources would be at risk were a war to drag on. And even if Adaskar won't listen to me on that, he should at least know about these underground roads and chambers. That alone is reason enough to go, and he can't ignore me if I turn up in person."

The council chewed on this for some time. Talia knew she had them, yet her mother rose, her expression stricken with maternal worry.

"Paragon Adaskar would not harm a queen, but he will punish a rider. I would not lose you. Not you too." Her small plea, made so publicly, nearly broke Talia's heart. She drew on her fire to strengthen her resolve. She had to go.

"We don't have any other choice," Talia said.

Harroway groaned, ground his fist into the table, then looked her in the eye.

"We need to know, what's the worst case if Adaskar should arrest you?"

Talia gulped. "The worst case... he'll gather his fellow Paragons and break my bond with Pyra. That's the *worst case*," she added in a strained voice. "Awful for me. Yet that too would solve all our problems, wouldn't it? So the worst case isn't really so bad – at least, not for everyone else."

That brought a final and terrible silence to the chamber.

Talia glanced to each of her councilors in turn, then to the other faces around the room. Her people. All of them saved and then placed in peril because of her. She tried to determine who among them secretly hoped the Paragons would break her bond. Many, she guessed. If Talia were stronger, she might have considered it herself.

"Move as many of our forces as you dare to the southern mountains and the border with Brenin," Talia said. "If the emeralds can find a way in, we must be ready."

The High Council departed. Talia lingered for a time, then made her way down to the palace armory. Inside the vast treasure trove of armaments and armor hung the jagged gray blade of Silas Silverstrike. When Silas lived, the dragon-steel of the Lightning Lord seemed to hold a permanent spark power. Now the metal looked dull, a true lifeless gray, somehow lesser than the plain steel surrounding it.

Talia took it down and held it in her arms as if it were a corpse. Of all the weapons of all the riders who fell in the incursion, Silas Silverstrike's was the only one not worthy to hang in the halls of Falcaer. It belonged on the Rogues Row, to mark his treachery. One day, Talia would collect the others from the Crag and find where Silas had ambushed Denna and the others in the wild.

Regardless of where Silas' sword deserved to hang, she did not want it in her city any longer.

THIRTY-FOUR

Echoes in the Dark

"Behind you," Ash said.

But Holt already sensed the flayer there. He heard its feet, its bladed arms, its rattling breath. Moreover, he knew where it stood and where it intended to strike. It was not that he could picture it in his mind as if he saw it with his eyes, more that his instincts had learned to calculate without sight. Without conscious thought, he turned and struck upward with such force that he hewed the flayer's arm in two. He pressed forward, ducking under its flailing limb, and ended it without a drop of lunar light.

Yet as soon as he dispatched this last foe, he collapsed to his knees, not from wounds but from exhaustion. The dragon bond raged in his chest. His soul ached as muscles ache after a day of hard toil. The edges of the bond had strengthened under that heat and pressure, the way good steel is made. And perhaps because they had now spent such a prolonged time sense-sharing, he felt Ash in his heart like never before. Also, Ash's core shone brighter than ever in his mind's eye and brimmed with power even after so long in combat.

Still, exhaustion came upon him. Both in body from pitiful meals and in spirit from the strain of the burning bond. His limbs shook and his grip became slack on the hilt of Brode's sword.

"We must go back," Holt said telepathically. *"I must rest."*

Ash let out a mournful growl. *"We are close now. The carriers journey down the descent at the very end of this highway."*

"Exactly. I'll need all my strength to face whatever lies down there, if I can summon any more to spare."

They began to walk back up the highway. Holt hated this part the most, hated how exposed they were. Having always relied on his eyes, he hadn't appreciated what more he could understand or learn about his surroundings. In many ways, he knew more than he had before. However, he lacked finesse in his fighting. He doubted whether he would be able to face a trained swordsman in a fair fight this way. With his patchy skills, that would not have been advisable even in the best of circumstances.

Back by the icy lake, Holt cut off the sense-sharing. With it off, he felt deaf and dumb in the dark. He reignited a cold light upon his hand and winced as his eyes adjusted. A tremor ran through him, though whether from the cold or some deeper exhaustion he could not say. The lakeside was always cold, but compared to the muggy depths it felt like winter.

Holt brought out the last of his meager supplies. He reckoned this was the eighteenth day. Three days remained, if they were lucky. Yet Holt had but one half ration left. Indeed, looking on it now, it might be a quarter. Less than a handful of walnuts, three dates, and half of a small, salted fish.

No more.

He sat for a moment and breathed slow. Despite the cold of the cave, his body felt sticky and hot. Sweat clung to every inch of him. A fierce itch came upon him. His clothes felt at once confining and oppressive. He tore them off, gasping as the chill air kissed his skin. Grime from weeks of battle caked his skin in a thick layer of dust and dirt and blood.

At the lake's edge, he scooped up water to wash himself as best he could. Since becoming an Ascendant, he rarely felt pain in his muscles and bones, yet he felt it now. Deep pain. His stomach and sides were tender to touch. Just washing was difficult. One patch of dirt refused to budge, and he kept scooping up water and scrubbing himself before realizing it was a great bruise. Was that one freshly made or a memento of his training with Rake? As a result of his starvation diet and endless fighting, his body had shed remnant pockets of youthful fat and smoothed out into hardened, sinewy muscle. Elsewise he was pale as milk from lack of sunlight and food.

Groaning, he pulled his crusty clothes back on, then caught two fish for Ash.

If this was to be their final push, he was as ready as he was going to be.

Sense-sharing again, Holt and Ash descended. He could now walk confidently behind Ash without fear of tripping or missing a step. All sounded quiet in the tunnels. Even when they stepped out into the highway, things were quiet for a full mile.

Then they both froze. Heavy feet pounded the passage behind them.

Ta-tum. Ta-tum. Ta-tum.

The sound drew rapidly closer. Behind the footfalls, Holt heard the lightest zip and buzz of wings.

"Carriers," he said. *"We need to get off the road."*

"There aren't any passages nearby. The closest are behind, and those are too far."

The buzzing of those carriers grew. They were close at hand.

"We'll have to fight them," Holt said. *"If they are carrying ghouls, we'll be surrounded and overwhelmed fast. We'll need to use magic."*

"Hold until it's too late for them to react," Ash said.

They held. And held. The carriers' wings filled the highway. Sense-sharing with Ash, Holt sensed a fat-bodied bug dive suddenly down, heading right for him. Their baleful deep cries rent the air. Quick and focused, Holt pulled on Ash's core and sent a concentrated Lunar Shock at the enemy. To his left, Ash unleashed a thick beam of silver-white light.

The deep cries of the carriers turned to shocked squeals as the lunar power ripped through them. Lunar light carried on, up, up, and up into the endless heights of the tunnel, revealing more carriers and the stingers escorting them.

Both struck carriers fell with smoking wounds to crash onto the stone floor. As the light above winked out, Holt's vision plunged back into darkness. He drew Brode's sword – even blind he could draw it with ease now – and began cycling his motes to Ground his body. Ahead, the carriers coming on foot began to charge. From above, the stingers swooped down.

Ash poured forth light against their foes. The shine became blinding. Holt shut his eyes against it. Through the confusion, he stopped sense-sharing to get to grips with battling by light again.

His eyes pained him, but he opened them and took aim at the approaching dark shadows. He fired Shock after Shock before sending the motes to his feet and stamping down his greatest Consecration yet.

White light webbed the floor for thirty feet in all directions, marking the kill zone. Ash's core shrunk with each beat of the battle, yet the bond held as they laid waste to the convoy.

When it ended, Holt assumed it was too soon. Dozens upon dozens of ghouls had surely survived the carrier's death and would soon crawl out from the back carapaces. When nothing happened and no ghoul cried or snarled, he stepped cautiously behind one of the carriers.

Still with light around his palm, he found the carrier had indeed been carrying ghouls, though not ones that were alive in their first death. Dead ghouls. Broken limbs of ghouls, and even wings of stingers and chopped heads and bodies of flayers. Other corpses of small creatures there were too, rotting rodents, voles, and even birds.

The bloody trails ending within the highway at last made sense.

"They are hauling the bodies somewhere," Holt said. He regretted opening his mouth at once, for the putrid smell of the scourge carcasses rose thick and hot.

"*Why would they do that?*" Ash asked.

"*We'll find out if we keep going,*" Holt said, speaking across the bond again. The bond's edges held well. Despite their victory, Holt's heart sank at the sight of Ash's lowly core.

"We used too much magic," Holt said. *"It was only clumsy carriers and a few stingers in the end."*

"We could not have known. It was right to be cautious."

"I think we'd better double back and Forge one last time."

"Do we have time?"

Holt bit his lip. In truth, they did not. *"I think you'll be the one who gets us through this, so I'd rather you had all the strength I can give you. Let's be quick as we can."*

Their luck held – moonlight shone in the Forging tunnel. They stayed until the motes dried up with the dawn. Ash's core shone as a white orb, pure and radiant in Holt's mind, yet Holt's own strength faded.

It was the nineteenth day of their trial, and he had no more food. Not a single nut or flake of fish. By the cave lake, even in the coldest of silver light, Holt's eyes fought against him. His body wished to close them and drift off into a deep, restful sleep. Sheer willpower, or more likely fear, forced them open. The will to carry on and the fear that if he shut them, he may not wake from this toil.

His stomach ached with a hunger unlike any he had suffered. Not during the leanest winter at the Crag had he eaten so little, never mind while expending so much energy.

After catching another meal for Ash, his starving mind turned in perilous thought to those pale, eye-less fish. Fish might be eaten raw, even by humans. He'd heard tales of that from the Skarl lands. The recipe book might have helped him, and a pang ran through him that if he expired down here, it would not be with his father's book in his possession. At least it would be safe with Aberanth in his lab. For now, whether with a recipe or no, his need was desperate.

Holt caught another fish, and once it died upon the stones, he took his cooking knife and cut away its thin scales and carved out a chunk of its translucent flesh. He brought it to his mouth.

"*Holt—*" Ash began, but he found no more words. His worry crossed the bond, and Holt understood.

"It's just one bite," Holt said, then he placed the meat into his mouth. Slimy, freezing cold, chewy, and bitter as defeat. He forced himself to swallow. His stomach gurgled and roiled.

Holt dropped his knife and staggered onto his knees, bending over double as he clutched at his midriff. Then he heaved and retched the vile fish from his guts. It steamed and stank on the cave floor, and his vision swam into darkness.

So used to blackness, Holt did not know whether he dreamed or lay awake. A fever-chill rocked him. He tossed and turned. Yet through this void, the white light of Ash's core gleamed like a winter's moon, and he felt the bond beat once. A hard beat, a gong to ring across the world and drag him back from the depths.

Holt awoke, gasping and shuddering. He felt around in the dark and found Ash's hide on all sides. A wing covered him like a blanket, but that had not stopped the chill of the underground world piercing deep into him. Those icy fingers caressed the very marrow of his bones.

All that kept him going was the thought that, if he died, then Ash would suffer, as Eidolan had suffered for centuries. He could not let that happen. Unconscious of summoning the words, the old folk song which gave hope in times of the scourge came to him, of lands far across the Sunset Sea where even dragons cannot fly, there was a place, the song claimed, where the living did not die. Where dreams would come to life.

He shuddered.

"Are you sure you wish to press on?"

Holt had to consider it for some time. Yet, at length, he set his jaw and said grimly, *"Yes."*

"Then we shall."

Heat and comfort passed over from Ash, and Holt drew in a little of the dragon's light to stiffen his resolve and body.

"While I have you here," Ash began tentatively, *"I wish to finish the argument we started days ago."*

Holt cast his mind back through the haze of battle and darkness. "About Osric? About Rake?" His voice was but a whisper, but Ash would hear him. "This isn't the time."

"It is exactly the time," Ash said, and his voice grew in confidence. *"Our bond needs to be stronger and truer, yet something holds us back. This has formed a wall between us."*

"I'm not sure what there's left to say. If we make it to Windshear Hold, Osric will try to kill us. Shouldn't we fight back?"

"That's not what I meant, and you know it. It's one thing to kill in a battle, in defense of ourselves or others. But Rake sees the kill as the solution. I'm not sure he cares about the eggs Thrall has. And now you forget the eggs too, as if they are unimportant."

"If we go to save the eggs then we'll end up fighting. We'll have to kill or be killed. Isn't framing it as saving the eggs just an excuse? A way to make it more palatable? Rake's words might be harsh, but the truth can be harsh."

"You're angry just talking about it. This isn't you. We don't have to become like Rake."

"I thought you looked up to him?"

"I do, but we know something terrible happened to Master Rake and his dragon. Something went wrong. He might call us fools or naïve, but I think we'd be more foolish to follow his lead without thought."

These words struck Holt hard. Through his hunger and frustration, he searched for his true feelings. Before these awful tunnels, before Rake and before their mission, he had vowed to become stronger, though for reasons he had started to forget.

'Help the others.'

His father's ragged voice resurfaced. A plea to help, not to destroy. As Holt had saved Ash, as he hoped to gather allies to face Thrall and the scourge, the strength he sought was not to bring suffering but to end it. The difference was subtle but genuine. His doubts about Rake sharpened, and Holt found himself standing apart from the half-dragon's will.

"You're right, Ash," he said, and his voice regained some of its strength. "Of course you're right. I have not been myself. Rake can do things his way, and we can do things our way."

"*Our way,*" Ash said, and as he pressed his snout into Holt's forehead their bond blazed with fresh fire, burning away a last fog from its edges. The flames in Holt's chest granted him a last reserve of strength, banishing the cold from his bones.

He stood. Many of his joints popped or cracked as he stretched and twisted. Then he set about final preparations, drinking the last water from his skins and refilling them from the lake. It was only then that he noticed he had done all this in darkness, without even sense-sharing with Ash.

I've become a creature of the night, he thought. Promising though it was to 'see' in the dark without Ash, sense-sharing would still be needed for the fights ahead. In fact, in many ways, having working eyes was a disadvantage to him. Any light pained him, even through closed eyelids, as had happened in the fight with those carriers. He needed to block out the light completely.

Everything fell into place for him.

"I need to borrow your blindfold."

He found Ash and felt for the knot in the material at the back of the dragon's head. Taking the blindfold to one side, he lit his palm just enough so he could see while he worked. Even under such forgiving light, the black cloth was in sore need of a deep clean and perhaps of being replaced altogether. Ash had not grown much since he'd bound his eyes, but he had grown enough to stretch and fray the material. A new blindfold would have to be found eventually, even if Holt felt loath to do so. This cloth had come from Brode's own traveling cloak. It seemed callous just to throw it away.

For now, Holt cut off a section of it for his own use. He wrapped it around his head, bringing the black cloth down over his eyes before tying it at the back. The bandanna worked. Light would be less of a concern. The gut instinct he had come to rely upon in these caves told him this was right. This was the answer.

He lifted the bandanna, just enough to uncover his eyes. Before wrapping the blindfold back over Ash, Holt took a moment to gaze into those frost-blue eyes. He had missed them. A part of him wished to keep them visible, but the blindfold was important to Ash. He had asked for it after the ill-treatment of the West Warden and his emeralds – to bear his blindness as a badge of honor, and that meant far more than Holt being able to see a pair of eyes, even if they did transport him back to a damp floor and a tiny white dragon curled up in his lap.

He secured Ash's blindfold and, just like the first time, Ash suddenly seemed much older and more intimidating for it.

"We'll make quite the pair wearing these," Holt said.

Ash rumbled happily. *"I like it."*

Power swelled over the bond, and Ash's dragon song rang loud and clear in Holt's mind. Its flute-like notes rose in tempo. No longer sadness in the night but the joy of a wolf hunting in the dark. And underlying all of it was a deeper power, ringing out like the ethereal echoes of a key-harp. Music to awake a dormant primal longing and leave the spine tingling.

"Are you ready?" Holt asked.

"As we'll ever be."

Holt smiled. "I'll make a small change to the wording of our technique, I think. This feels more fitting." He cleared his throat, lowered his new bandanna, and began, "My ears, for your ears."

And with this acknowledgment, Holt swore his hearing through the connection to Ash became clearer for it. He could make out each drop of water as it plinked down the far cave wall. No longer did he struggle to determine where Ash was in the dark, as though he were an extension of his own body. He did not, after all, need to feel his nose to know it was there.

With nothing left to do but to descend on one final excursion, they took the familiar passages down. This time they met resistance before even arriving at the highway and fought their way through to discover scourge carrying off the dead bodies of the carriers, stingers, and corpses of the ghouls from their last encounter.

They caught the enemy unaware and encumbered by their burdens and so slaughtered them, yet others had since passed down the great highway. This meant the trail ran fresh for miles. They followed the scent and echoing sounds to the end of the highway and stood at the brink of a tunnel that plunged into the earth.

Ash led the way, taking the first downward step. At its bottom, the tunnel leveled out again, and at its end Holt felt a dark presence. He lifted his bandanna in case there was anything worth seeing and found a green light pulsing in the distance. Amid the green light moved shadowed silhouettes of the enemy.

They approached swiftly in the dark until they drew to the threshold of the cavern. The source of the green light lay at the heart of a chamber. A dark orb sat atop what Holt first took to be a plinth. Yet when he looked closer, he noticed the plinth was not stone but a stalk of living muscle and tendon, raw and exposed yet dried and hardened as though dead, or close to it. What light the orb cast was low so that a green mist seemed to hang in the air. Much like the highway, the top of this cavern could not be discerned. The smell was the same sickly sweet of decay they had grown used to.

To their left, scourge worked as though nothing were amiss. In single-minded fashion, a carrier took flight, hovered over what looked like a black shell basin, raised its back carapace, then tilted itself so that its load fell into the basin. Corpses splashed into a smoking substance, and as the buzzing of the carrier settled, the bubbling of whatever lay in the basin gurgled louder.

Other ghouls walked up to the basin and dumped their offerings at its base. A single abomination – a hulking skeleton animated by dark magic – lifted organic matter from the pile and dropped it into the vat.

Bizarre as the place was, it held even more grotesque oddities. The same raw, rope-like muscles ran along the ground, connecting the bubbling vat to the orb at the center.

As they were sense-sharing, Ash could see the whole thing through Holt's eyes.

"What are they doing?"

"Can't be anything good," Holt said. *"Can you feel the power coming from that orb?"*

"*Yes, but nothing else. Those scourge are right before us, yet I can't sense them.*"

Holt checked his own senses. Ash was right. "*That's strange. It's like the orb is so strong it's overriding them.*"

"*The scourge have acted strangely during our whole trial,*" Ash said. "*They're docile even now. When have we ever been able to be this close without rousing them?*"

"*Let's not complain. Maybe we can take the orb back to the surface even if we miss the deadline. Aberanth will want to study it, I'm sure.*"

Even as they spoke, the vat hissed and spat out a green slime. Then the chords of muscle connecting the vat to the orb began to undulate and a bulge began to push through the tubes, as though the strands were so many snakes passing mice through their bodies.

Though he faced unheard-of horrors, Holt did not feel afraid. His dragon bond still thrummed with a closeness to banish all fear and doubt. He could sense Ash's courage and the dragon his, and where one began and the other ended had become difficult to tell, especially while sense-sharing.

Wordlessly, the notion passed between them to enter the chamber. They came upon the ghouls like wrathful shadows in the gloom. The carrier fled. The abomination howled in defiance and lumbered to meet them. It swung its massive bone club, but Ash caught this between his jaws and pulled, starting a tug of war that kept the skeleton still. Holt recalled taking on an abomination at Sidastra and how much magic he'd needed to draw upon to allow a normal sword to cut through the creature's great leg. Holt Grounded his limbs, his weapon now a thick rider's blade, and cut the abomination's leg. When it collapsed he severed it clean in two at its waist.

With that, the chamber was clear.

"*If we're taking that orb, do it quick,*" Ash said.

Holt understood. Through Ash, he discerned that more scourge lined the passages leading away from the chamber on all sides. There were eight branching tunnels in total, including the one they had arrived from. A hum of click-clacking mandibles and pincers, a soft swish of bladed arms, gargled mutterings, the soft feet of ghouls, and the bullish snorts of juggernauts.

Holt made his way to the center of the chamber. Layers of muscles and tendon wove up like a staircase of exposed intestines, twisting and overlapping until they formed the stalk upon which the orb sat. Holt stepped onto one of the coiling strands and found it tough and able to hold his weight. Disturbed, he made his way up to the orb. As he drew close, he noticed the orb was part translucent, something like an eye, though lacking an iris or pupil.

The orb's low light flickered faster as though a quickening pulse. Holt reached for it. Someone whispered to him. He twisted around, but, of course, no one was there. Ash stood below with his ears pricked.

Movement sounded in the many branching passageways.

Now or never.

He gripped the orb and pulled. It did not budge. And yet, at the same time, he heard a cry of fury in his mind, one voice in a many-layered echo that distorted to a shrill scream and then ended.

Ash growled and stamped his feet and tail. *"They're coming."*

Holt would not have needed sense-sharing to hear them now. The scourge thundered toward the chamber. Even below and above, rumbles in the rock spoke of many running feet.

"Climb up to me," Holt said.

Ash scrambled up the grotesque stairway and stood with Holt on the high ground. They turned to face each passage in turn, trying to gauge which one the enemy would arrive from first, but it was too close to tell. Scourge poured into the chamber on all sides and did not wait to form ranks or judge the threat but carried on with speed to the base of the tendon stairs.

Holt's first instinct was to lay a Consecration. He stamped, but the lunar lines radiating from him attacked the scourge flesh they stood upon and burned out in seconds.

Below, many ghouls slipped or lost their footing in their haste, but many more climbed over them.

This would be too much for them. They needed some way to hit more enemies at once. Holt had no true ability which did that, but he did have his blinding light. He'd used it before in panic and it had backfired against him. Yet now he had all he needed to take full advantage of it.

Holt closed his eyes and lowered his bandanna. As his sight plunged into darkness, his hearing compensated with help from Ash. Scourge rushed to reach them, their bones creaking and cracking as they moved, scrambling over one another in their haste. Holt raised his left hand high overhead and pulled on Ash's core, drawing in its light with abandon.

Unlike with a Shock, he did not concentrate it into a compact, spinning ball of power, yet rather let it grow to a bubble ready to burst. He held on for as long as he dared. One-fifth of the core flowed into him and he sent it blazing up his arm, yelling from the effort as he held on long enough to make it count. Five seconds, and then the scourge were so close he had no choice but to let the bubble burst.

It did so in a silent, white, blinding explosion. At least, that was how Holt imagined it. He saw nothing of it, but he heard and felt the reaction of the scourge around him. Their wails of pain near deafened his sensitive ears, yet many of the bugs and ghouls fell, stumbled, or else ran into each other in their newfound blindness.

And while the enemy became gripped by chaos, Holt could 'see' as well as ever.

Keeping his body Grounded, he charged down set to work with Brode's blade. Ash followed. Together they carved through the disoriented scourge like a pair of wraiths.

As their foes began to recover, Holt charged another flash, bounded into a cluster of scourge, raised his hand, and unleashed the blinding silver-white explosion.

Just under half of the core was now drained. Another use of power like that and Holt would push over his limit as an Ascendant, which would fray the bond. However, while the connecting bridge of their souls shook with a taut tension, it remained sturdier than other times Holt had drawn upon so much. Far, far stronger.

Instinct told him that if he pushed it now, the bond would hold.

The fire in his chest was fuel to him. Holt readied another blinding explosion. The bond's edges swelled outward, then stabilized, strong as steel. Holt gained a newfound clarity and understanding of Ash's core and the orb of light shimmered, morphing into a true moon, now almost a perfect half-moon against a dusky night flanked by glistening stars.

"*Keep going!*" Ash called to him.

Holt pulled on more power, going past his Ascendant's limit of half the dragon's core, and set off another explosion of light. The shadow of the moon spread, leaving a visible crescent of silver, and yet the bond held firm.

Holt Cook had become a Champion.

Refreshed and revived, Holt's hunger fled. He did not feel stronger or more agile of body, but the sensory information he received from Ash grew clearer and less confusing. Each staggering step of the flayer he pursued, each grasping ghoul came to him with clarity.

Another explosion of light of the same power would drain too much of the core. Even a Champion had to be mindful not to use more than three-quarters of their dragon's core in too short a time. Yet now fighting on solid stone again, Holt pulled light and channeled the power to both his feet. He jumped high and laid a Consecration as he landed.

With the enemy disorientated from the flash, slowed and burning from the Consecration, Holt and Ash moved free and swift in the frenzy. The remaining scourge were decimated. With a final dexterous side-step and a plunging thrust of his sword through a juggernaut's neck, the battle for the chamber ended.

With his eyes closed and his bandanna lowered, Holt ascended to the green orb. He knew its scream had summoned the scourge to its defense, even if he could not explain how. Still relying on his hearing, he cut the stalk of muscles and caught the orb as it fell. It was gelatinous to the touch, and some strands of the raw muscle and tendon slapped loosely onto Holt's arm as he gripped it. He did not know if the eerie green light still pulsed, yet the dark presence of the orb beat one last time and then winked out. The chamber became a desolate place then, with Ash as the only magical being Holt could sense. He descended, sheathed Brode's sword, then brought Ash's snout down to press against his chest.

"We did it, boy," Ash said.

"That we did. Champions." He gave a breathy laugh. "It's all thanks to you, Ash. I'd never have managed it if you hadn't the courage to tell me I was wrong."

"We, did it," Ash affirmed.

Holt smiled and stroked Ash's nose. "What do you make of this thing then?" He held up the curious scourge orb. Ash sniffed it, shook his head in disgust, then backed off.

"Aberanth may know more. We should not linger here."

They left the chamber at once and, sensing no scourge, raced without caution of noise back up the great highway. Holt returned to the banks of the black lake one last time to retrieve his things before, at last, they ascended the tunnel which Holt had marked with an 'H' weeks ago.

When they reached the entrance, he thumped his fist on the stone seal over and over, hoping Rake was still on the other side to answer. To his relief, the rock parted in a sucking gush of air. Through the gap, the cores of Aberanth and Eidolan reappeared. The old illusionist had recovered a deal of his strength. Rake remained shrouded and ill-defined.

"Master Cook." Rake's voice sounded from just outside. "Or, I should say, Champion Holt. Three weeks, almost to the hour." He chuckled in delight. "I told you they'd make it, Aberanth."

"I did not agree to any wager," Aberanth said wearily.

"Is your head injured?" Eidolan asked.

Holt had to think on that for a moment. Then he realized that he still had his bandanna lowered and eyes closed. Holt canceled sense-sharing with Ash and raised the cloth covering his eyes. Golden sunlight streamed onto Holt's face through a round window in the stone seal. It was so bright, so harsh, that he had to shut his eyes against it and raise his hand.

"Not used to this," he said through a pained grunt. Carefully he opened his eyes again, blinking hard against the light until he could make out the grinning face of Rake through the window in the rock. Something the half-dragon had just said rang like an alarm bell in his mind.

"You bet on whether Ash and I would die?"

"Not in the slightest," Rake said. "I said you *would* make it, and that's why Aberanth owes me ten gold pieces."

"*I said no such thing,*" Aberanth insisted, but Rake ignored him, grinning his wolfish grin.

"*You have no use for gold, Rake,*" Eidolan said. As he spoke, the remainder of the stone seal slid away like hot oil retreating to the edges of a frying pan. Holt and Ash could leave. His first step out of that tunnel felt like waking from a long nightmare.

"You two are so dull at times," Rake said. "Fine, Aberanth. You owe me a cask of your best tonic."

"*Hmmph, I'll make you something alright,*" Aberanth said.

Holt laughed. Seeing them all, he had a strong desire to embrace each of them in turn, followed by a need to pummel Rake into the earth for forcing them into that ordeal.

As though sensing his mind, Rake smirked and said, "I think a 'thank you' is in order?"

Ash snorted and stalked out into the daylight.

"What?" Rake said, indignant. "You survived, didn't you? You even ranked up, though I knew you could, of course."

"You knew we could or knew that we *would*?" Holt asked.

Rake tapped his nose but did not answer.

Despite himself, Holt laughed again. Right now, he had only joy and relief in his heart. But then, in the light of day again, the strains of his body hounded him once more.

"Please tell me you have something for us to eat?"

THIRTY-FIVE

An Apple That Tastes Like A Lemon

The day Farsa and Hava were supposed to meet them came and went. Hoping they were only delayed, Rake allowed the party to relocate out of the ravine and move up into the surrounding green hills. A more pleasant location for Holt and Ash to recuperate, yet close enough that Rake would sense Hava the moment she flew within range.

After leaving the scourge tunnels, Holt slept, ate, then slept some more. Ash had pulled through in a better condition and insisted on going off on a hunt for some 'proper food.' He and Rake set off, and when Holt awoke late one morning, he found a deer and a rather happy Ash.

Later that day, Holt rose and ate a little of the venison so as not to overwhelm his stomach. He then set about cutting strips of meat to make jerky – if Farsa and Hava showed up before they were ready, that was a risk he was prepared to take. They had salt to create Grounding food and powdered ginger he'd bought from the bazaar to create a Floating aid.

Ash had already regaled the group about their time underground but, while he worked, Holt explained how learning to hear through sense-sharing with Ash advanced their bond.

"Fascinating," Aberanth said. "*The extended use of sharing senses seems to have created something of a second link. I wonder if other rider pairs could benefit from such a thing?"* He noted something down on his bark.

"I wouldn't think so," Eidolan said. He had been most enraptured by the discussion. *"I recall trying this technique with Gideon. The results were confusing and blurry. Pure chaos. How you younglings manage it I do not know."*

"They each provide something the other cannot," Rake said. He raised his scaly brows and ridges dramatically as though expecting applause. When none came, he scoffed and said, "Ash learned to rely on Holt from the day he hatched. The next logical step would be to have Holt learn to rely on Ash in turn, in complete trust and confidence, even letting go of his own senses and control to do so. Something unique to their special circumstances."

"But you knew that's what we had to do, right?" Holt said. He dabbed another strip of meat into the ginger and draped it over the dry branch he'd propped up as a makeshift rack. "That's why you had us follow you through the forest in the dark."

"Knew? No. Though I strongly suspected," Rake said. "Turning a weakness into a strength might be a hard road to walk at first, but you'll go further than jostling with others down the crowded path."

Holt bent to carve another portion of venison. "I presume there's some reason you didn't simply tell us what to do?"

"That's right, so why don't you have a stab at figuring it out?"

Holt frowned and pulled his next slab of venison away from the carcass. As he cut the meat into thin slices, he considered Rake's issues with the Order. He found their methods of training to be timid, too safe and hand-holding.

"Well," Holt began, "you need true fear in combat if it is to have any substantial effect on a bond. The same must hold for any other method of growing closer together. If you had just told us what to do, we would not have benefitted from figuring it out and learning together."

"Correct in one," Rake said. "You see, you don't need to ask me as many questions as you think."

"It was still a risk," Eidolan said. *"The road less traveled may turn out to*

be a shortcut, but it could also lead to a broken neck. Sometimes, the proven path is the surest, if slower."

Rake rolled his eyes. "The boy is a Champion now, isn't he? The Order might have gained a dozen more Lords if they trained like I did."

Eidolan gave Rake a sharp look. *"There are times when the untested path leads to a bottomless pit. I would not wish for Holt and Ash to suffer your fate."*

Rake's face contorted. For a moment, Holt thought Rake would burst into anger, and then just as quickly it seemed he would burst into tears.

"Don't fear," Rake said flatly. "I won't let that happen again. I'm quite invested in these two."

Ash rustled his wings and spoke. *"For someone who claims to desire our assistance one day, you took a great gamble on our lives. It nearly killed Holt."*

"You as well?" Rake said. "If you had both died, so be it. We're all going to die. Dragons too, even if it takes us a long time to wither. I've asked many powers in this world to aid me to no avail. If you and Holt could not handle such a trial, then you could never have aided me, nor survived the road we've all committed to travel. And now, if you all will stop berating my methods, we might discuss how you will best develop this flash ability now you're a Champion, Holt."

Holt stopped mid cut. He put his knife down and fully focused on Rake. "It takes me about five seconds to unleash it in a deliberate, offensive technique. Each time it drained about one-fifth of Ash's core's strength. But that should improve as I continue training the method and get my mote channels experienced in handling it."

Holt understood that riders chose their abilities as much as the abilities manifested within them. Once a technique was favored, it could be trained and made increasingly efficient, requiring less power to achieve the same effect, thus taxing the bond less while becoming more powerful. As Holt continued to grow Ash's core, the raw cost of the ability would also shrink relative to the size of Ash's pool of magic. A Lunar Shock now barely registered on either the core or bond compared to the first time.

"Seems like you have a good grip on things," Rake said. "Yet I sense an issue?"

"Not really," Holt said. "Only that five seconds is quite a long time in a fight."

"It is, but you'll find more advanced techniques require time, even if Lords make it all seem instant and easy. If you're in a pinch, you could always Sink your channels, of course."

Holt nodded.

"Darn useful if you ask me," Rake went on. "Rendering a foe blind while still being able to 'see' yourself. Besides this, as a Champion, your mote channels will grow more robust and your command over them will improve. Your natural resistance to magic will also increase as your human body drifts closer to being a magical one. We'll add in Sinking to our training now, should you require it."

"As you say, *Master Rake*." Holt pressed his hands together as Farsa had done and made an exaggerated bow.

"Don't go getting a high opinion of yourself," Rake said. "You're the lowest of Low Champions, and the trials ahead of you will make you beg to return to that tunnel. A gnat from the Crag looking to make a journey to Ahar would have less distance to manage." He sniffed heartily and looked over to where Aberanth stalked in circles around the scourge orb. "You've gone quiet, Aberanth. Is something amiss?"

The little brown dragon huffed, puffed, and looked upon the orb as though it had done him great insult. *"I'm not sure what to make of it. Judging by the connective tissue, I'd say this is some foul mix of dense musculature and bowels to carry and absorb nutrients. That seems reasonable given all Holt and Ash have described of this vat, which I assumed held some acid. But... hmmph."* He growled in frustration and raised a thin vine from the earth to prod at the orb. Nothing happened. *"Some energy radiates from it, something I cannot determine."*

"Give it here," Rake said. Aberanth lifted the orb with his vines and dropped it onto Rake's open palm. Rake gazed into the orb for a moment, then he winced, snarled, and dropped it.

Holt dove and caught the orb an inch from the ground.

Aberanth's eyes popped with excitement. *"What did you sense?"*

Rake rolled his shoulders and shook his head as though dazed. "The very faintest whispers of mystic motes. Raw. And crooked."

Back on his feet, Holt stared at the dark green orb in his hands. Where before it had resembled a gelatinous, pupilless eye, it had since hardened on the outside, and the interior had turned to a crusted gloop like dried porridge. Try as he might, he could sense nothing at all from the orb, not a wisp of power. Whatever Rake had felt had to be faint indeed, and yet it had caused such an adverse reaction in him. Holt hastened to place the orb back on the ground. Anything that caused Rake to wince as though burned could not be good for his health.

"What do you mean by crooked?" Aberanth asked. *"Be specific, please."*

"I'm afraid I can't," Rake said. "I don't rightly know what I felt in it." Rake's features showed a rare flicker of fear. His tail curled up into itself and the flaring blue ridges on his head drooped. He frowned, then said, "It was a thought within a thought within a thought."

The implications of Rake even sensing mystic motes from the orb caught up to Holt. "You mean, this thing can think?"

"I'm not sure," Rake said. He moved to crouch over the orb, though he kept some distance from it.

Eidolan padded over and sniffed furtively at the air around it. He too growled and sped backward like a scalded cat.

"You feel it too?" Rake asked.

"I can barely make sense of it. The echoes are faint, fainter than a whisper across long memory. And yet the feel of them…" He shuddered rather than utter it.

"Holt and I sensed no foulness upon it beyond the scourge itself," Ash said.

"Even if you were a mystic," Rake said, "you would not be able to sense such subtle motes at your age. These are ancient and stale, yet fresh and screaming, and yet neither all at once. I can't describe it other than it's simply… wrong. An ice dragon would know what I mean if they were to come across ice motes that were flaming hot, or a storm dragon who discovered motes of air that were solid."

"Like biting into an apple that tastes like a lemon?" Holt offered.

"If the lemon was also salted and overly sweet at the same time," Rake said. He grunted, then in a blur of speed he brought his orange blade to hang over the orb as though he were its executioner. The morning sun shone off the glassy dragon-steel. "I've half a mind to skewer the thing, burn it, then bury it ten feet deep."

"*No, no, no,*" Aberanth fussed, and he stood over the orb. "*This represents a chance to learn more of the enemy than has been done in many lifetimes. I must study this thing back at my laboratory.*"

"What do you think, Eidolan?" Holt asked. "You've lived longer than all of us combined. The Order must have delved as deep before now."

"*When riders did raid such deep passages, it was long before Gideon and I came into the maturity of our powers. When they did, the riders went alone. Ash is weedy for our kind and still young. Only a hatchling would be able to walk under the earth, and the Order was not like to send hatchlings into the slaughter.*"

"*There were large tunnels too, Master Eidolan,*" Ash said. "*Great enough that you and I and Hava included could have flown down them.*"

"*I do not doubt your tale,*" Eidolan said. "*Their vile queens must maneuver to the surface somehow. For my part, I never ventured deeply into these underground roads. When setting out officially from the Order, riders would not, after all, remain trapped as you two did. In my time, especially prior to the collapse of Aldunei, the numbers of scourge below the crust of the soil were immense. Their aggression as ferocious as a cornered dragon. Your tales make it sound as though the scourge you found were docile, lacking the driving will of old.*"

"Curious indeed," Rake said. "One would think that if Thrall has taken hold of the scourge, then they would have a clear drive."

"Perhaps he keeps them docile until he needs them," Holt said.

"Entirely possible," Rake said. "Scourge activity was low across the world years prior to the recent incursion into Feorlen. If I were Thrall, I'd keep my forces hidden underground rather than allow the scourge to roam far and wide as they used to. And yet this orb reacted to your touch? Almost like it sounded some sort of alarm to nearby scourge."

"There was a horrific scream," Holt said, "but it was in my mind and when it ended, the surrounding scourge surged into the chamber. It's too much of a coincidence."

"*And those that came were suddenly more aggressive,*" Ash added. "*Much more like the enemies we faced in Feorlen.*"

"Docile until compelled to act," Rake pondered. "It makes some sense. Yet the bugs and ghouls were deliberately gathering corpses and who knows what else to feed into this great vat, which raises a question. Is that what the scourge would do by their own twisted nature, or has Thrall changed their habits and created this orb in the process?" Rake reached out to the orb again with a single long finger and brushed it with the tip of his talon nail. Once again, he winced and recoiled his hand. "Something tells me this is not wholly the work of the dragon."

"*Thrall's notes are in that discord,*" Eidolan said.

Rake frowned. "You're sure?"

Eidolan gave him a grave look. "*I'll never forget the hateful, bitter notes of that dragon's song. They lie within that orb, even in some small fashion.*"

"*Then we have a working hypothesis, I think,*" Aberanth said in a hurry. "*That the scourge, in this region at least, have been left to their own devices. That this orb represents some way in which commands can be passed to them. Thrall is currently focused elsewhere, hence their idle nature. When Holt touched the orb, that alerted him, and so all remaining scourge in the area converged to attack.*"

"*You were lucky to have cleared out most of the enemy in the weeks prior to discovering that chamber,*" Eidolan said. "*If the enemy now fears a secret has been discovered, I suspect greater guard will be placed on others. Such expeditions will not be so easy in the future.*"

"I don't have any burning desire to do it again," Holt said. "If we can help it."

Ash raised his head and stretched his neck to its full height. Holt assumed he was about to agree with him, but then the dragon's ears picked up.

"*I hear a dragon coming from the south.*"

Rake hefted the remainder of his polearm and moved to stand with Ash. "Hava and Farsa ought to approach from the east."

"Perhaps they reached the ravine by a different route," Holt said. As Rake and Ash fell into silence, Holt returned to slicing and seasoning his venison. He checked on the jerky he had laid out the day before. Each piece had gone dark but still had some moisture in it. They needed two days at least to fully dry.

Rake broke the quiet of the group. "Where are they, Ash?"

"I lost them. The dragon hasn't roared again. I can't hear wings too high and too far."

Rake frowned and looked skyward. Clouds grayed out the world and granted cover for anything flying above them. Rake's senses were prodigious, but he could not sweep all the air.

An unease fell over Holt, and he too searched the skies for signs of an approaching dragon. Eidolan and Aberanth did the same.

"There, in the west," Aberanth said. The group turned. Nothing was out there. *"It dropped below the clouds for moment. I swear."*

"It's not them," Rake said. He then did something very strange. Rake got down on all fours. "Eidolan, cover me and Ash."

At once, Eidolan's core flared. A shimmer fell over Rake, the air waving as though he were in a heat haze, then faded. When it passed, Rake appeared to have changed. No longer a half-dragon crouched on his hands and knees, but a normal dragon with orange scales and blue ridges along his back and tail.

Ash also shimmered and changed, yet not so dramatically. His scales merely darkened in places, graying out some of his snow-white scales enough to pass him off as a storm drake.

Eidolan braced himself as he strained with his magic. *"Save me some effort, Holt, and take off Ash's blindfold."*

Holt untied the black cloth from around Ash's eyes.

"They are close now," Rake said. Yet while Rake spoke, the illusion of him did not move its lips. "It is a storm rider but not Farsa."

"They'll know we're here when they sense the cores," Holt said.

Even as he spoke, the storm rider and dragon descended from the clouds. They were close enough now for Holt to sense them – middling High Champions in power – and to discern that the scales of the dragon were a grim gray, almost as dark as Clesh's had been.

Without roar or menace or any sign they would engage, the pair made one long, sweeping pass and then turned sharply to the west.

As the storm rider shrank to a dark speck in the distance, Rake got back to his feet. The illusion shattered as he rose. He gripped the shaft of his weapon tight with both hands, and his blue eyes tracked the passing rider as though he had the ability to leap into the air and catch him.

Rake took a step—

"No," Holt said. He ran to block Rake's path. Ash followed right behind him.

Rake looked stern. "We don't know who sent that rider. Let me find out."

"You can't catch them."

"I could try," Rake said. He pointed to the distant rider. "For all we know, Thrall sent them. Seems unlikely that another rider would just happen to show up two days after you took that orb."

"And what if they're from the Order?"

Rake shrugged. "Then I'll let them go. We'll be moving on soon enough. With luck, I'll convince them to forget they saw us at all."

"*How exactly?*" asked Ash.

Rake thumbed his orange blade. "I can be very convincing."

Holt looked grave faced at Ash. He did not like the situation one bit. Yet Rake had a point. If the rider was an agent of Thrall—

"*Stay, Rake,*" Eidolan said. "*You cannot catch them, and we need you here to signal Hava when she arrives. As you say, we will be moving on. Let Thrall think we're in the south for all the good it will do him.*"

"They might have seen nothing," Holt added. "Eidolan's illusions looked pretty convincing on their own."

"Let us hope for that," Rake said. He scowled. "Maybe making you a Champion was an error. You're getting defiant. I like that in people, just not when they are defiant to me."

"We break rules, remember," Holt said.

Rake inclined his head, said no more on the matter, and stomped off.

Ash stepped close and lowered his snout down to Holt's eye level. *"I'm pleased you jumped in to stop him,"* he said privately.

"We're lucky that we're moving on soon," Holt said. *"If we weren't... well, it's no matter. Come here while I put your blindfold back on."*

Given they had been spotted, Holt hoped Farsa would arrive soon. However, it wasn't until late into the next day that Farsa and Hava flew into the range of Rake's telepathy. Holt was tending to his jerky – the first batch of which had dried out nicely – when the storm rider and dragon touched down.

Farsa wore her brigandine now, the outer leather layer wrought in the customary dark gray of her magic type. The studs binding the steel plates to the leather glinted silver under the clear sky, and Hava's steel-like scales reflected intense patches of white light.

"You're late," Rake said.

Farsa jumped from Hava. When her feet hit the earth, she pressed her hands together and descended into a deep but genuine bow.

"A thousand pardons, Master Rake," Farsa said. "We were met with scrutiny upon return from our meeting. Much has been amiss, and my Flight Commander pressed me hard. I do not think he believed my answers in full, but he knows my honor. If he cannot trust me, I fear he will have lost faith in the entire Order. Alas, I had to petition him many times to change my posting to Oak Hall, leading to more attention than I would have liked. Word will reach the enemy that I am due in the north if he cares for such knowledge. If we wish to maintain the ruse, I will have to travel to Oak Hall before our mission."

"The movements of individual riders can't be that important to him," Holt said.

"You'd be surprised how well the riders are tracked," Rake said. "At least senior ones. The Lords especially. A lot of people are concerned with knowing where they are. And it would be a simple matter for a servant at Alamut to have been taken in by the Wyrm Cloaks, never mind the riders that may have turned."

"The Shah of Ahar has his agents at the fortress as well," Farsa said. "As the kings in the western realms have agents in their Order

Halls, and as the Archon of Athra has spies at Falcaer. In any case, the air at Alamut has grown thick with tension. Riders I once called brothers and sisters have turned inward, keeping to themselves. Conversations are whispered rather than had out in the mess hall. Trouble brews. I took what precautions I could, providing five different days and times for my departure to various riders and servants."

"We also took a winding path," Hava said. *"High on the winds, letting them guide us where they may for a time, and checking regularly if we were followed."*

"And were you?" Rake asked.

"Thankfully not," said Hava. *"Though few in the Order could hope to catch us once I command the winds to bear us swiftly."*

"That's well," Rake said. "For we had an unwelcome visitor."

He told them of the other storm from the day before.

"No other storm rider at Alamut is of that rank," Farsa said. "Nor do I recognize the coloring of the dragon."

"Does the Order still keep a watch over this chasm?" Rake said.

Farsa shook her head in a slow, solemn movement.

"That was my fear," Rake said. "Too much to hope that a long-ranging patrol from Falcaer or Squall Rock had coincidentally come to check on a dormant area. I should have hunted them down after all. Yet if you can command the winds to speed you so, you might hunt this pair down for us."

Hava growled low in her throat. *"We shall not. We can't jump to conclusions, and whether friend or foe, chasing this rider down would only reveal our presence here, which we've been tireless in trying to hide. I wish no more complications than necessary, Rake, and no innocent blood upon my talons."*

"There is no honor in such a hasty chase," Farsa said. "Let the sure, quick strike be our aim rather than careless swipes. It has been to our fortune then that we arrived late. With luck, no one in the enemy's service will know we stand with you. Your plan may still proceed."

That was true, Holt thought. Thrall knew of the rest of the team from the raid on the mystic nests. The addition of Farsa and Hava still remained concealed from him if the storm rider's precautions had been effective.

It was then that Holt felt Farsa and Hava brush over his bond with Ash.

"I trust Ash and I will no longer besmirch your honor?" Holt asked.

"You have grown your bond in such a short space of time," Hava said, and though she repressed it in her voice, Holt could tell she was impressed. *"Yet the youngling's core remains small. Be mindful not to let your rank outpace you. There is danger in advancing too quickly."*

"Do you accept us joining this mission or not?" Holt asked again.

Hava puffed pale smoke.

"However you achieved this feat, however fresh and low powered, you are a Champion," Farsa said. "Though the difference between Low and Exalted might be the span of the world, I am still yet a Champion and not a Lord. Join if you will, Holt Cook."

Ash roared with pride, and Hava relented and roared alongside him.

Rake clapped his hands and rubbed them together. "Glad you four are getting along, but then I only recruit the best and brightest. Now the time for talk is over. We've got a long journey ahead of us, and Thrall's head won't cut itself off."

THIRTY-SIX

Falcaer Fortress

As the drake flies, a journey from Sidastra to Falcaer Fortress would be shorter than to Smidgar. However, Talia and Pyra took a longer route, flying southeast and hugging the coasts of Feorlen and then Brenin before arriving at the westernmost coastal territory of the Mithran Commonwealth. From there they turned north, making straight for Falcaer.

This region had once been the beating heartland of the ancient Aldunei Republic before the Great Chasm gouged into them. Lying ever in the shadowed presence of that dreadful place, these lands between the ruins of Aldunei and the coast of the Stretched Sea lay largely abandoned. Falcaer Fortress had been built into the ruins of the old city to watch over the ever-active chasm.

On her first trip to Falcaer, Talia had noticed that the skies above Aldunei were always darker than the world around it. High summer meant little here, and today was no different. Buildings stood half crumbled across the landscape like a rash. Larger ruins stood too, with towering columns supporting roofs no longer there. And ever visible was the Great Chasm itself, or more precisely the western, jagged tip of it. From above, its sheer dark drop looked as though a long arrow with a barbed tip had lodged into the ancient city. Its size was hard for her to wrap her mind around. Merely this narrow tail end of the Great Chasm was larger than the entire chasm in the Withering Woods.

Falcaer Fortress was not a fortress in the common sense of the word. Three ancient legionary forts on the northwestern outskirts of the city had been combined into one enormous complex. It appeared as a giant rectangle from above, with simple walls and four gates enclosing rows of barracks for the legions they had once housed. The strength of Falcaer lay not in the thickness of its walls or towers – for there were none – nor in the size of its garrison. Its strength now lay in the number of dragon riders who dwelt here.

Many of the barrack houses had been gutted and turned into dragon nests. Other sites had been torn down and replaced with housing in the early Athran fashion, or the Mithran style, or whoever happened to have donated money to construct them. Layer upon layer of the six-hundred-year history of Falcaer made it uniquely its own, belonging to no one culture or time.

A great smithy housed the forges of the Order's artisan smith, where Ascendants toiled to create their dragon-steel weapons. Work-shops manned by those skilled in their roles kept daily life at Falcaer running smoothly, and it was here where mystic riders and their dragons produced ghost orbs to sell to the world.

Talia and Pyra's arrival hardly went unnoticed. Soon, no less than four High Champions were escorting them to the Paragons' Sanctum at the heart of the fort. Even this place stood on the bones of a palatial republican villa and had wide colonnaded courtyards, though the luster of the stone had weathered with time. Steam issued from large bathhouses at the back of the sanctum.

As they made their descent, Talia noticed that one of their escorts was none other than Sigfrid, one of the riders who had arrived in Feorlen shortly after the incursion. He had not believed a word of her or Holt's story. She also found it strange how still and quiet Falcaer felt. The dragons lay curled in their nests, the training grounds empty.

They touched down in the courtyard of the sanctum. Between the columns stood the same gnarled, twisted posts as had stood at the entrance to the Crag. Their balls of light pulsed a dark orange today.

Talia did not know what exactly that said about the mood of the dragons here, but it was clearly not happy.

She had expected to feel on display, with gawking riders judging her on every side, yet the courtyard and the walkways above it were empty.

"Something is amiss," Talia said privately to Pyra.

"I was prepared for the dragons to lash out the moment I came in range, but so far they've been silent."

Sigfrid and the other Champions dismounted. Talia did the same, wary of their hard, judgmental gazes. One of them kept a hand at his shoulder, ready to draw his blade at the slightest provocation.

Maybe this wasn't such a good idea.

Pyra snarled at them, and some of that courage crossed to Talia and bolstered her.

"They judge us, yet we have done more to fight the scourge of late," Pyra said.

That was true. Talia scratched her dragon's neck. *"I'll try to keep that in mind."*

"We meet again, Ascendant," Sigfrid said. Having been to the far north, she now recognized his Skarl accent. "Is it wisdom or folly that brings you to Falcaer?" His eyes drifted to the steel crown on her brow. "Hmm, I think folly."

"I'm here to meet with the revered Paragons," Talia said. "If they would honor me with a meeting." She took out the wrapped scabbard. "Please inform the revered Paragons that I've brought Silverstrike's blade as a gesture of goodwill and that I have valuable new intelligence on the scourge."

"Wait here," Sigfrid said. His companions had nothing to say. Only daggers in their eyes. While Sigfrid entered the sanctum, they remained to guard her. This standoff held until Sigfrid returned to the courtyard.

"Paragons Adaskar and Eso are currently dealing with another willful rider. They will see you after. You shall wait with us in the meantime, and Pyra will be escorted to one of the nests. She has had a long journey."

The other dragons growled at Pyra, urging her to follow.

"Go on," Talia said, patting her down. "You deserve a rest."

Once the dragons had departed, Sigfrid extended a hand. "And if you will be so kind as to hand over Silverstrike's sword, I shall take it to the Smith."

"No," Talia said, clutching the sword closer. "I'd see the last journey of the sword through myself."

Sigfrid looked torn between the need to chastise a lowly Ascendant and the restraint required for Talia's ill-defined status.

"Walk softly then, Ascendant," he said, chewing on every word. "All eyes in Falcaer are upon you."

The great forges of Falcaer were sweltering. A team of young smiths hammered away at their work, paying Talia little mind as she strode by. She found the Artisan Smith working on what Talia took to be a helmet, though it was exceptionally long, and only once she was close did she realize it was a chaffron, a helmet for a horse. The Artisan Smith was a short, nut-brown man with a sinewy body. He lacked the packed muscle of other smiths, but his every stroke fell with a strength as though he were a rider himself. He set the chaffron on the anvil but kept his tongs and hammer in hand like two weapons.

"Who is this girl?" he said. "A blade she bares on her back already, so she is not a new Ascendant." He spoke as though to himself and as if no one else could hear him. While crafting her blade, Talia had come to think nothing of it. "Ah," the Smith exclaimed, his eyes locking onto the sheathe in Talia's hands. "She brings one back with her. Bring it here, bring it here," he added, hastening to a workbench, still wielding his hammer and tongs.

Talia unsheathed the sword and laid it on the workbench. The Smith placed his tools down with care and removed his thick leather gloves with the air of a physician preparing for delicate surgery. He then bent low over Silas' sword, running his fingers along the flat of the blade as though playing a set of strings only he could see.

"A storm sword, of course," he said to himself. He flicked the metal with a finger and bent his ear over it as if listening for a heartbeat. Next, he tapped it with his hammer in the same fashion before finally gripping the hilt, even though he could not hope to lift it. "Yes," he said as though he'd come to some great revelation, "attuned for lightning. Its wielder reached the rank of Lord. Gray-blue was its color in life. Five and a half days it took to create, if I'm not mistaken – a difficult one. Ambitious, driven."

Talia had forgotten just how eerie his insights were. The Smith would not even have been born when Silas had forged his blade. After reaching his conclusions, he gazed up to the riders, and his demeanor became somber and professional. "This was the sword of Silas Silverstrike. Strong he was. A shame that he died."

"He died a traitor," Talia said. "He aided the scourge and killed many riders."

All the blacksmith had to say to her accusation was, "I see." He gazed at the steel as though looking for answers, then back to Talia. "And who are you to bring me it?"

"Don't you recall me?" Talia asked. "I forged my blade under your guidance not two years ago."

He met her gaze with a frown. Talia drew her weapon and placed it next to Silas', and the Smith repeated his examination on her sword.

"Fire, of course, and young. Still tuned to an Ascendant. Three days and two hours it took to craft. Quick learning. Keen, yes, but torn, unsure, guarded." He looked to her now as though greeting an old friend. "The sword of Talia Agravain. I remember."

"There are other weapons still in Feorlen," Talia said. "When I have time, I will gather and send them to you as well."

"So many?" the Smith said, sounding sad. "Ah, but, yes, an incursion. Great swarms. Riders dead. They should be brought to me sooner than late. Such weapons deserve to be set to rest. More noble work than to hammer such crude pieces as these," he said, casting the chaffron a contemptuous look.

Talia spotted other pieces of horse armor around the forge in various states of progress. Crinets to defend their necks and cruppers for their flanks, each gilded in a different color and etched with black, white, or even golden words and patterns. They were masterpieces in the making and no doubt cost a small fortune. This commission smelled of the horse lords of Athra, and the reality of the Order had never seemed so stark.

"They are beautiful," Talia said.

"Steel is ugly," said the Smith. "It rusts and wears. It is mortal. Dragon-steel," he added lovingly, "now that is eternal."

"Not even dragons live forever," Talia said, but the Smith either didn't hear her or else he dismissed the point.

"If only more use could be made of our steel," he went on, "the world would be a glistening, beautiful place."

Talia felt a pang for the Smith. His gift was all the more curious given he was not a rider himself and could not bear the weight of the weapons he guided into creation any more than he could smelt the metal himself. Dragon-steel, once forged, was too heavy for a non-rider to lift. Its magical properties could only be enjoyed by the rider whose dragon's motes were bound to the iron. Though powerful, beyond weaponry it held little use. A process grimly suited to the riders.

Talia picked her own sword off the tabletop and sheathed it with a loud snap.

The Smith seemed to stare right through her. "They say she is a chaos bringer, and yet she brought back the storm sword. Why break one rule and not another? A tool made for two jobs is expert at neither. A hammer cannot cut, and a chisel cannot flatten."

He looked forlornly over his masterwork horse armor and then seemed to notice the plain steel crown upon her brow for the first time, giving it a disapproving look as though it were a dent in an otherwise perfect breastplate. "Ugly," he said with a sigh and shake of his head.

Talia instinctively raised a hand to touch her crown, somehow feeling a greater judgment from the Smith than from any rider.

"Silas gave into the chaos of the scourge," she said. "Let that be on the plaque beneath this sword with the other rogues. Let it be a warning."

"Such a shame," said the Artisan Smith. He took out a clean leather apron and laid it over the gray sword. Then he seemed to forget Talia was there and returned to work on the chaffron he thought so crude.

Talia left to return to the sanctum. Sigfrid and the three other Champions were waiting for her outside the forges. They fell in around her on all sides and escorted her to the very doors of the Paragons' inner sanctum.

Emblazoned on the doors in gold was a pentagon circled by a coiling dragon, the symbol of the dragon riders. These doors and walls were defended by the magic of the Paragons so that no sound escaped the inner chamber.

Before long, the doors to the inner sanctum opened and a woman in pale blue brigandine stormed out into the corridor. A High Champion of great power. Her blonde hair was long, braided, and streaked through with white, and though she did not look older than late thirties, she was likely far older than that. It did not take her armor to know her magic type, for her expression was ice cold. She marched off without so much as a glance at Talia and the Champions escorting her.

Sigfrid tutted. "Too much willfulness these days." His companions grunted in agreement, and then he motioned for Talia to enter. "Be respectful, yes? Paragon Adaskar does not enjoy tall tales as much as I do."

Talia gave him a look to rival the ice Champion's and then entered the inner sanctum. The heavy doors shut behind her of their own accord, producing a resounding, solid thud. A sensation of being trapped came upon her.

The inner sanctum was a pentagon, each corner of which was dedicated to one Paragon. Three of the corners lay dormant. The plant life in the emerald corner was dry and brown. Without the cold touch of the Ice Paragon, water ran freely in her space. No electricity crackled between the orbs in the Storm Paragon's corner, nor did wind blow.

Only two Paragons were currently in residence. Lurid, violet light floated in long lazy strands around a man in indigo robes. Lord Eso, Paragon of Mystics, did not seem altogether present. The whites of his eyes were somehow too big. He did not blink, and his gaze was fixed somewhere high above Talia's head. Also, Eso muttered to himself, low, deep, and quick and as though no one else was there. Unlike the Artisan Smith, Eso's mumblings were garbled and coherent only to himself, if they were at all.

And directly ahead of her, in prime position between all the others, stood Lord Adaskar, Paragon of Fire. Though neither notably tall nor short, Adaskar stood with an unmatched bearing. His eyes were like burning rubies, matching the color of his silk tunic patterned in flaming lines of black and gold. All else about him was dark and foreboding. Hailing from the region of Ahar, his skin was dark olive, his eyebrows strong, his nose stronger. Long strands of onyx hair swept back from his head like trailing smoke.

There were no chairs for the Paragons. They were never to be seen at rest. Eso stood on the marble floor, and Adaskar stood barefoot on a bed of smoldering coals.

Adaskar's burning eyes fell upon her, as did his power. Talia gasped as though winded. His aura swept over her, checking her bond and judging her.

"Step forth."

Talia approached the center of the room and struggled to make a choice to kneel or not. As a rider, she would have dropped down at once. Her legs screamed at her to bend. Yet as queen she should stand, even to a Paragon, and Talia needed him to treat her as a queen. With an effort, she remained on her feet, though she had to fight to keep herself upright and her back straight.

"Paragon Adaskar, I thank you for this audience." She turned to address Eso. "Paragon Eso, I thank you as well."

Eso did not look at her. His gaze remained lost in the half distance, though he spoke and said, "Songs begin yet are ended too soon. Others remain trapped in stone."

"I'm sorry?" Talia said.

"Paragon Eso has entered one of his trances," Adaskar said. His voice crackled like the fire coursing through him. "What brings you so boldly back to Falcaer?"

"Duty," Talia said, "as Queen of Feorlen and as a rider."

"You cannot be both."

Talia steeled her courage. "An incursion is in its early stages in Brenin."

"I am well aware."

"Of course," Talia said. She gulped, then carried on. "I have come to request, no, beg of you, to lead the riders in a full flight to secure the kingdom."

"Your uncle's kingdom."

For a while, the only sound was the crackling of the hot coals and Eso's incoherent murmurings.

"Such a measure is one of last resort," Adaskar said. "It has not been needed for nigh on sixty years. I cannot deplete the rest of the world of its riders to spare your uncle a few months of hardship. The rising in his lands bears no marks of a world-level threat."

"I do not ask only for my uncle's sake but to spare a much larger war."

"I do not follow." His voice could have broken stone.

"I'm sure you are aware of my predicament. Risalia and Athra have formed a coalition against me. I am sure they mean to go to war. However, if the incursion can be destroyed with haste, then I hope to secure my uncle's support, which will gain the Skarls. No one will risk such an uncertain conflict then. There will be peace."

"Peace?" Adaskar said in a threatening manner. Smoke escaped from his lips. "You are audacious, Talia Agravain. It pains me that Denna was so wrong to trust you."

"You will not fly to Brenin's aid?" Talia asked.

"Not in the manner you request."

"Then you doom the west to war."

"No," Adaskar growled. "You did that yourself."

"Fate conspired to give me the worst of choices. I could either leave my home to burn in civil war or else step into the breach."

His flaming eyes burned even fiercer. "Chaos in one kingdom is more desirable than chaos across many. Much will burn because of you."

"I do not seek war," Talia said, her voice rising at the accusation. "There is no need for any realm to fear me on the throne. I know the true enemy. I would use my position only to fight the scourge. Risalia is bitter and uses me as an excuse. Athra sniffs plunder or else irrationally fears I would seek to supplant them. They could just as easily set this aside. Rather than watch the fires rage, you could do something to help put them out. It's in the Order's best interests that there be no war."

"Our neutrality is sacrosanct."

"Neutrality? Or Athran gold?"

Adaskar blew fresh smoke, then stepped off the coals. Steam rose from each step he took on the cold marble floor. As he approached, Talia took an instinctive step back.

"You are such a child," Adaskar said. Every word lanced from him with a searing heat. "You break the laws of our Order and the balance of the world and cry foul when there are consequences. You assume what I, leader of the dragon riders, should do? That I should send your former brothers and sisters to help you avoid a fate of your own making? Yes, we rely on Athran gold. As we rely on the goodwill of all realms. I cannot display a favorite. I must consider my actions in terms of generations, not in days or even years. This Order existed long before the fall of Aldunei and it must endure even if every empire falls, every border is redrawn, and all tongues alter beyond recognition. You come here pleading for my intervention without a thought that I had already done so." He drew out these last words as he stepped right in front of her, coming within an inch. His hot breath smelled of soot and ash.

Talia's body quaked as his power radiated in blazing waves. It was all she could do to remain standing.

"I don't know what you're talking about," she said in a low voice.

"You are not the first to come begging. I shall grant you that much. The Archduke and the Archon beseeched me to fly to Sidastra and remove you myself. I told them, as I tell you, that I will not interfere in such a manner. But you're not wrong. I would see war avoided if I could. I told them to give you a way out. A way to satisfy all parties."

"To break my bond with Pyra..."

"It has been your only option."

Talia feared he was right.

Paragon Eso moaned then. He shook his hands at some unseen horror, crouching and whining as though beset by apparitions.

"Is he okay?" Talia asked.

Adaskar breathed like a bull. "It is none of your concern."

Eso recovered a moment later and gave a small shudder. "Twin stars," he said to no one in particular. "One light, one dark, yet their souls do not reflect their cores."

"Talia," Adaskar said with menace. She looked at him and saw that, past the anger, a weariness had taken root. "To know it was a fire rider who brought this shame unto the Order is of great personal pain to me."

"I brought shame?" Talia said, incredulous. "What about Silverstrike? He murdered everyone at the Crag. He would have killed everyone in Feorlen if I hadn't stopped him."

"Those matters are still under investigation."

"There could be others like him," Talia plowed on. "Others who have gone over to Sovereign. You might have known all this if you had not rejected my emissaries."

Adaskar stepped lightly again, moving in a circle around her.

"This name of Sovereign has reached my ears. First from the reports of Champions Sigfrid and Maria, repeating your tales. And once again through Champion Ethel." He stopped pacing behind her, forcing Talia to turn. "She ran into your servant friend."

At once, all thoughts of Brenin, Risalia, crowns and wars went.

"Holt? Ash? When? Where?"

"In Brenin, months ago, but they were sighted again recently in the east. A white dragon with a Champion rider."

"Champion?" Talia said. Her jaw went slack. How could that be possible?

"Rapid advancement, assuming it is your role-breaking friend," Adaskar said. "The storm rider who spotted them said illusion magic was at work, but he saw the white dragon before the mystic scrambled to disguise them. The rider also reported an orange drake who did not have a core at all."

Rake. It had to be Rake. Holt must have found him, and his guidance had pushed him to Champion. Had she been wrong about the half-dragon?

"What are their plans?" Adaskar asked, studying her reaction.

"I don't know anything," she said genuinely. "Since Holt left Feorlen, I haven't heard from him. But whatever they're doing, you should leave them to it. They are good-hearted. It's riders like Silas you ought to worry about. Come to Feorlen with me, Lord Adaskar. Meet the Life Elder yourself. He can convince you of these things if I cannot."

"Wild Flights. Chaos bringers. Rogues. Nothing is as it should be. We are not what we once were." As he spoke, his gaze drifted from Talia to linger for a moment on the enclave of the ice paragon. "I will put things back together again. We must have order."

Across the sanctum, Paragon Eso gasped as though he had come to a deep revelation. "North she went and north she stays, upon her return all shall change."

Adaskar snapped his attention to his fellow Paragon. "Peace, Eso."

Eso's mutterings quietened until he fell silent.

A sense of unease fell over Talia. For all the power of Adaskar, he appeared to be alone in his fight to maintain and run the Order. Small wonder, with all she knew to be occurring in the world, that he found himself suddenly wrong-footed. Where were the Paragons of Earth, Storm, and Ice? How many riders were under Sovereign's sway? Having Holt out there gave him a clear anomaly to hunt and destroy. He was wrong, but she knew she had no hope of convincing him of that.

"When the riders of Sable Spire do respond to the incursion," Talia began, "there is something they should know."

She told him of the chamber she had found under the Withering Woods and what occurred when Pyra burned the strange structure within it. When she finished, Adaskar gave her a hard, imploring stare.

"Such a thing has not been done in centuries, and for good reason."

For the second time in this meeting, Talia's mind reeled from shock. "You knew of these chambers and tunnels?"

"I know nothing of any chambers."

Talia hoped against hope that she might be onto something, that on this, at least, Adaskar would listen. "Will you tell the riders of Sable Spire this? The Life Elder has located a second chamber. It might be controlling the swarm entering Bren—"

"Enough," he said, fury blazing in his voice. "You were lucky once. The scourge rises like the tide. Try to stop it and you'll drown. In ages past, greater riders than you lost their minds in the attempt." He gathered his power again, and this time Talia quaked under it. She backed off but he advanced, and smoke billowed from him unchecked. "Your status might protect you, but if you open up passages that the scourge may use to reach the surface, then you will force my hand. Keep those chasms sealed, Talia."

Talia found she had backed almost all the way to the door.

"I'm not the enemy," she told him, appalled to hear her voice shake so much before the Paragon of Fire. "Nor are Holt and Ash. Their magic can fight the scourge like no other. I know how terrifying change can be, but change is coming whether we wish it or not. We'll need it, if only a little. Or else the scourge will never be stopped."

"Or else the scourge will never be stopped," Adaskar repeated in a final, biting tone. "You sound like every rider ever to go rogue. Submit to breaking your bond or get out and face your fate."

"Then I shall face it. With Pyra. Together."

She left the inner sanctum, and the world outside the chamber felt bitter cold. She barged past her would-be guards, and this time Sigfrid did not try to come after her. Tears of fury and doubt streamed down her face.

"He wouldn't listen," Talia said when she reunited with Pyra. "Not to any of it." She wanted to scream. She wanted to burn something to cinders. She wanted at least one thing not to spiral into chaos and one reason why she should stay the course and not submit to the Paragons. None came to her. She slumped into Pyra.

They were out in one of the training fields, alone save for the watchful eyes of some sparring Ascendants at the far end of the grounds.

"Nothing is working, girl. I can't... I can't do this. Adaskar's right, I made everything worse. And now there's no way out. Either we fight a war we can't win, or we... we—"

"*I am not breaking our bond.*"

"If we don't, thousands will die. What good is there in that? What does that make us if we allow it? And when we're not traveling, I don't have the time to be with you like we used to. We were struggling anyway."

"*Look at me,*" Pyra said. She lowered her head, and Talia stepped back to gaze into her brilliant amber eyes. "*That Master Adaskar will not help or listen only proves the Order is broken. Holt and Ash were right.*"

"Yes, they were." She sniffed. "Damn them."

"*While I waited for you, I spoke with Strang. His rider is Ethel. He said they met Holt in Brenin.*"

"Adaskar told me."

"*Did he tell you that Strang and Ethel stopped another rider of Sable Spire from killing them? A Champion called Orvel.*"

"He left that out."

"*Strang told me all of it. He was furious. They were summoned to Falcaer for questioning, but Orvel and his dragon Gea fled. Despite remaining loyal, Ethel and Strang have been treated like rogues for letting Holt go. They are to remain here at Falcaer rather than return to Brenin to help with the fighting.*"

Talia recalled the blonde woman storming out of the inner sanctum. That must have been Ethel.

"*Strang told me Ethel is Feorlen-born and that they knew Brode and Erdra. Ethel was fond of Brode, Strang said. Holt had his remains and his sword. That's why she let him go.*"

"Sounds like Ethel has some common sense," Talia said. She ought not to judge the others too harshly. How were they to know? They had

not been through what she had. Months back, before the last winter
had ended, she had been just like the rest of them.

"Holt's a Champion now," she added, half in a trance, as though
this information was unimportant.

Pyra rumbled. *"Adaskar told you this? How can he be sure?"*

"A patrol in the east spotted a white dragon with a Champion
bond. How many white dragons are there?" She bit her lip, her mind
conjuring images of Holt smiling and shrugging nonchalantly as
though mocking her. "How did they do it?" she added with a bite.

"East..." Pyra said, her words dragging out into a pulse of daring
across their bond. Talia understood.

"We can't go and find them," she whispered, as though to voice
the very notion aloud was insane. And then the madness lodged in her
and started to crystalize.

Two choices faced her. Fight a war she could not win or break her
bond. But there existed a third option. Flee. Fly into the wilds, find
Holt and Ash and Rake, and go truly rogue. Adaskar considered her
just that as it was.

She banished the thought. It would be the coward's choice. She
would sooner break her bond than scarper, and Pyra would rather die
than flee with her tail between her legs. There would be consequences
for taking the throne, and they would have to face them.

Still, the desire to find Holt remained, to find the comfort of a
friend, one who always seemed to find the good in matters. Bizarrely,
things had made more sense back when they had been facing an incursion on their own. Moreover, she could find out how he had made it to
Champion, which would help her advance as well. All of that was
important. Yes, important; it would not be fleeing her situation.

It was poor logic. She should return to Feorlen sooner rather than
later, but if they could learn anything on how to advance, that would
be worth its weight in dragon-steel.

"I hope you're rested, girl," Talia said, her voice still low. "If we're
going to do this, we can't stop until we find them."

THIRTY-SEVEN

All Or Nothing

The team moved north. Their journey to Windshear at the most northern point of the Fae Forest would be a long one, in large part due to Rake. His leg had healed well while Holt and Ash had been in the scourge tunnels, yet as fast as the half-dragon could run, he could not do it forever.

They were also waylaid by the increased presence of wild dragons and even a rider or two where before there had been none in these empty lands. The wild dragons were mostly emeralds, though a fire drake flew close one morning. Rake detected them all, meaning they could stay out of range until the dragon or rider passed. It seemed too much to hope that this increased activity was due to anything other than themselves. Falcaer, Thrall, and maybe the Life Elder might be trying to track them. None could be trusted.

While Rake bristled with each delay, Holt did not mind the wait. Every additional day to him and Ash was precious in gaining as much experience and power as they could. With four cycling techniques, a new ability to hone, swordcraft, and the never-ending tasks of Cleansing and Forging, he had plenty to get on with. Months ago, he believed he had gained an appreciation of how hard rider life truly was, but he'd been a blind child even then.

If anyone cared to ask him now, he would have admitted that his life as a Cook's son and future apprentice had been notably easier. There were fewer pressures for one, far fewer expectations, and his life and the life of his dragon were not forever under threat. It had been dull, at times, but safe. He'd never appreciated the value of it being safe. He'd worked hard, of course – so many people did. They broke their backs performing their roles and took pride in their work. Yet others didn't or else brewed resentment to this, that, or the other. Edgar Smith had resented the riders, and many had agreed with that sentiment. On occasion, Holt had shared in those feelings, when he thought himself trapped and every rider free.

Well, he'd learned that was not true either.

Edgar Smith had been wrong, and Holt had been wrong. There were great riders who cared deeply and worked tirelessly. And there were riders who turned to evil or else to some other pettiness like Orvel. Rider or not, they were all people, and all were capable of greatness or malevolence in their own way.

With Ash as his conscience, Holt hoped he would never stray onto a path that might lead him to the same ends as Osric or even Rake. It would have been easy to do so. Without Ash, he would have veered off in such a direction already.

Their conversation by the freezing lake weighed on Holt's mind as they moved north, away from the baking sun and onto more bearable grassy plains.

Training his new ability – which he had named Flare – proved difficult, both due to the amount of magic needed to practice it and for its potential to draw a lot of attention to their location at night. As such, he did so sparingly.

During one cycling session with Rake, Holt switched to Sinking to see how much faster he might be able to produce a Flare in a tight situation. His rudimentary grasp of the technique demanded a great deal of effort and only shaved the time needed to prepare a Flare from five to three seconds. He grumbled at that.

Rake shrugged. "It's like I said, Sinking is a Lord's privilege. For Low and High Champions, the results are not worth the effort, at least so far as combat is concerned. As we're preparing for a fight, we'll refocus on Grounding and Floating the closer we get to Windshear."

"What about Lifting?" Holt asked. "We've barely practiced that and we're going to fight a dragon with mind control powers."

Eidolan laughed harshly. *"Lifting won't help you. Lifting won't help any of us, save maybe Rake."*

"Maybe Rake?" Holt said. "His whole plan revolves around it."

"Not my whole plan," Rake said. "But take Eidolan's advice to heart. You're not strong enough to have a hope of blocking Thrall's attack if he goes for you. Farsa might withstand it for a moment or two."

Farsa, who had been sitting quietly with her legs crossed meditating, emerged at that. "It would be prudent to share your thoughts on the battle to come, Master Rake." Rake stroked his chin, and Farsa's steely expression became sharper. "You do have a plan?"

"Of course he does," Holt said. Rake's eyes widened, which made Holt hesitate. "You do, don't you? You had one for Ash and me to advance."

"Did I?" Rake said sardonically. No one laughed. Humor was unwelcome on this particular subject. A tense air gathered around the group, and Rake no doubt sensed this, for he relented. "The ruins of the Free City of Freiz are not far. I had *planned,*" he said irritably, "for us to take shelter there and feed ourselves from the Loch. We can discuss these matters there."

He got up with that and started running north again.

The team reached the ruins of the once proud Free City late in the afternoon. An orange sun sank lazily in the western sky, the first real indication that the world was drifting toward autumn.

On the outskirts of the old city, the once well cobbled streets had become overrun with earth and untamed grass. Wild goats roamed the ruins, leaping from building to crumbling building, little fearing dragons until today. Ash, Eidolan, and Hava caught a goat each and brought another back for Holt and Farsa. Rake announced a distaste for their meat and so left and returned some time later with water dripping from him and several fish gripped in his taloned hand. Aberanth struggled foraging for plants, so for once he ate a little of the fish Rake caught.

While the dragons ate and Holt prepared his and Farsa's meal, Rake busied himself gathering small rocks and other detritus and stacked them up in a shape that began to look like a pentagon. At each corner he stacked crumbled stone and bits of old timber to elevate those points and then scratched some markings here and there into the earth with his long nails. These markings included the arrows of a compass to show which way north would be. The whole structure was big enough for him to stand inside and move around.

Holt was just about to tuck into a haunch of goat when Rake cleared his throat.

"Gather round all," he said as though speaking to a group of wide-eyed children. He stood in the middle of his construction, looking satisfied with himself. "Behold, the fortress of Windshear."

Holt looked down at the collection of rubble. He didn't know what to say. Other than the general shape, he couldn't discern much.

"It's not quite finished," Rake admitted. "I'll need Eidolan to fill in a few blanks for me. There are a few things I can't cobble together from bits of stone. For one, the fortress is built high atop a rugged mountainside, almost a plateau of rock in truth. There is no front gate, nor any way to access the fortress through its walls. You fly in, or, unless I'm mistaken, there is a narrow set of stairs built under the fortress accessible from a small door at ground level. Though I am not sure of its location."

Eidolan carefully approached the miniature Windshear on its western side and roughly scratched at the earth. *"It's on this side, under the wall connecting the ice and mystic towers. Though it's closer to the ice tower. The stairs are built inside the rocky foundations of the fortress. It was the servants' stairs, though anyone who was not a rider had to climb them, whether prince or cobbler."*

"Thank you kindly," Rake said. In a fluid move, he leaped over the western wall of his model fortress and wrote 'door' in the earth Eidolan had marked. If only it would be so easy to get over the walls of the real Windshear.

"So," Rake continued, "no way in or out save by flying or climbing one narrow and lengthy set of stairs. Let's get the obvious out of the way. We can't take the stairs. It's much too easy to get trapped or for the defenders to hold, and in any case, the dragons can hardly take them."

He pointed to the tottering stack of pebbles and rubble in the southwestern corner of the fortress. He had carved 'mystic' into the ground there.

"Thrall is in the mystic tower," Rake said. "He was there when I last scouted the area, and I don't see why he would leave it. The beauty of my idea is it can work no matter which tower he's gotten cozy in. What we need to do is get inside, get down to the base level hatchery where he's resting, and kill him." He said it entirely matter of factly, as though the mission to assault Windshear Hold was as routine as planting a crop of turnips.

"We'll have to be fast and coordinated," Rake said. "We'll fly with all speed toward the upper levels of the mystic tower. Hava can aid us with that."

"How will you fly?" Holt asked.

"On Eidolan's' back," Rake said. He winked at the illusionist. "Don't worry, old friend, I've lost some weight on our adventure."

Eidolan scoffed. If flying was required – and it seemed the only way they could all get inside the fortress – then Eidolan would have to carry Rake.

Still speaking to Eidolan, Rake went on. "Your part will be in this early stage. We'll need as many phantom drakes as you can muster to mask our approach. Keep them up even after we enter the tower. The more of Thrall's allies you can draw off, the better.

"Our aim is to enter one of the mid-level hatcheries. There should be one large enough for Eidolan and Ash to fit inside. Once inside, Farsa can create a strong barrier of air to block anyone from entering behind us."

Farsa gave a single nod.

"Hava, you'll need to remain outside, but stay close. With luck the enemy will go after the phantoms, but if they come for you, lead them on a merry chase."

"Unless the Storm Elder himself is present, I'll lead them in as many circles as needed."

"Good," Rake said, no doubt pleased there had been no objections so far. "While Farsa covers our backs and Eidolan projects his phantoms, the rest of us will secure the hatchery. Ash, I'll need you to put your ears to work and tell us how many enemies are inside the mystic tower and where they are."

"I'll do my best," Ash said.

"Holt, Aberanth," Rake said, turning to face them, "once we have our bearings, we three will leave the hatchery and work our way down the spire. I'll need you both to bar and then hold the main door of the tower as long as you can."

A shock of early adrenaline raced down Holt's spine just at the thought of it. He would be apart from Ash, which would make his new sense-sharing technique impossible. It would come down to his own swordplay, though he supposed he could still cast a Flare to blind opponents.

Aberanth fidgeted. Fighting was not his forte.

"I'll feel better knowing you're with me," Holt said to the brown dragon.

Aberanth made a noise which threatened sickness. *"Let's just hope the door is sturdy."*

"The doors swing in from the outside," Eidolan said. *"If you can seal them and bar them with your powers, they should hold against all but a strong rider."*

Without giving time for a debate, Rake asked them, "Got it?"

"Yes," Holt said hurriedly.

Aberanth nodded.

"Good," Rake said. "You won't have to hold the tower for long. While we're securing the tower, Hava I need you to block Thrall's hatchery."

"Can you be sure I can hold him?" Hava asked.

"No," Rake said curtly. "But if the slithering wyrm decides to flee then we'll have put ourselves in a perilous position for nothing. No half measures. Use as much power as you can to try and keep him trapped in there."

Hava hummed, and Rake carried on.

"As Hava blocks Thrall's escape and Holt and Aberanth bar the tower, Farsa will drop her own barrier and head down the spire to join us. Ash, Eidolan, you will go defend Hava."

"That's not going to work," Holt said. "Ash can't fly without me."

"I can fall out of a hatchery and hover," Ash said. *"Though I won't be much use beyond that."*

"Just do what you can," Rake said. "This whole thing needs to happen within minutes or else we're doomed. Once the dragons are in position and Farsa has rendezvoused with me outside the hatchery, we'll all attack at once. Farsa will enter with me, and the three dragons will fly in on their side. Pincer him. He might dominate one of you, but it won't matter. I'll have prepped Lifting and gathered all my power to Blink across the hatchery and cut Thrall's throat in a single heartbeat." He thrust his weapon forward in a strong, clean blow. "Once Thrall's dead, his forces will scatter. Most will panic knowing their leader is gone, others will flee because they were under his mind control in the first place. Unless there are dozens of riders there devoted to his cause, we can take whoever remains."

Rake ended and gave them all a hard stare. His plan was simple in many ways yet mad in its ambition, though he conveyed it with such easy confidence that Holt almost missed the maddening elements.

Luckily, Farsa was present.

"It's a fine enough plan, assuming absolutely nothing goes awry and we don't face overwhelming defenses within the mystic tower. What of our exit strategy?"

Rake's tail flicked and knocked over a section of the model Windshear's wall.

"Our exit strategy," Rake said, as though unsure what that meant, "is to kill the insane evil dragon."

"Meaning you do not have one," said Farsa.

"An all or nothing approach," said Eidolan.

"Worked for the kid," Rake said, nodding to Holt. He scowled again. "Of course this is all or nothing. If we fail, then Thrall wins, but if we don't take the chance now, he wins regardless. The Crag was wiped out. One Lord at least turned and is already dead. Farsa speaks of discord inside the Order, which will only get worse if Thrall continues to place wedges between the riders. He tried to be too clever in Feorlen, working subtly to avoid raising the ire of Falcaer, and it almost worked. Next time he is unlikely to hold back, and there may not be enough riders left opposed to him to fight back. We can't gather more allies. Many won't listen, and a small team like ours has a better chance of taking him by surprise. Before the season changes, all the eggs he took from the Mystic Flight will hatch, meaning there's a chance he'll leave. We can't wait. It's now or never," Rake ended on a firm note.

The group were silent. Holt cast a wary eye around and found each member's face attempting to mask their doubts. Only Farsa remained unmoved, except she sat so still as to be unnatural. Even her long hair did not move in the breeze. Holt did not yet know her well, but he reckoned this was a dangerous sign for her, like a wild cat going still as stone before pouncing.

"You are sure," she asked, "beyond doubt that this dragon, Thrall, is controlling the scourge?"

To everyone's surprise, it was Eidolan who answered. *"I had room to doubt, young Champion, but after Holt and Ash brought back that piece of the scourge from the darkest depths, I am now sure. I sensed Thrall's song within it."*

"You've had dealings with this dragon before?" Farsa asked.

"To my regret," Eidolan said. Now he had publicly admitted it, he could not avoid the topic. *"I do not know his whole tale, only a small part of it. He was a dragon in the Order, and when his rider died, he came eastward searching for his wild brethren. In those days, only a small number of mystics lived in the Grim Gorge, though it was not called that back then. Humans lived in the southern part of the valley. Thrall came but was shunned like so many dragons from the Order are. I knew what that was like, and I felt a pain in his severed bond that spoke of cruelty. Not all riders are kind. Yet he was too much in grief, or so I thought, to take a friendly voice seriously, not with so many scornful ones about him. Rather than heed me, he sought to prove to our kindred that he*

held no love for humans. Thrall descended upon a human estate not far from the valley. He killed almost all of them."

"The Estermonts," Rake said. "I was only a small boy then, but I well remember the shock which ran through all the east. All of Freiz was up in arms." He looked around the ruins of that city, and for a moment Rake became lost in sad memory.

"Even after this, I... pitied him," Eidolan said. *"His actions were not of a dragon in his right mind, or so I hoped. I pitied him,"* he repeated, as though this would absolve him. *"And that made me beg our Elder to shelter him and try to help him through it."*

"A dragon attacked a human settlement?" Farsa said. Her voice was high and cutting, and she seemed surprised for the first time.

"The Order would not have allowed that to go unpunished," Hava said. *"Thrall must have known that."*

"They came," Eidolan said. *"An armed force from Freiz supported by three riders came looking for the 'mad dragon'. A group of us went with Thrall to meet them, including a Warden of my flight. I believed a part of Thrall did wish to settle, heal, and atone – but another part of him had grown hateful. Time with the flight may not have been the best course for him..."* His story trailed off there for a long moment, and Holt wondered what secrets Eidolan guarded now.

He had a hunch. That Thrall had learned of the true nature of the scourge, the Elders, and the dark past between dragons and humans now long shrouded by time. And if he had had an abusive rider, as Eidolan hinted at, then like as not, Thrall would see no redeeming qualities in humans. Nor, by extension, in riders either.

"Thrall attacked?" Holt offered.

"Not at first," said Eidolan. *"At first he tried to convince the other dragons of the Order to abandon their riders and join him in the wild. One was swayed. Another seemed unsure. The third rejected him. But now the riders were split, and a fight seemed imminent. I tried again to reason with Thrall, but he wouldn't have it. The Warden intervened, desperate to avoid a war between the flight and Falcaer, but with so much roaring and stamping, the human troops panicked. They fired their scorpion bolts and mortally wounded the Warden. The wild mystics went savage. The two remaining riders attacked, making straight*

for Thrall. He threw the full might of his powers at one pair. I don't think Thrall had ever unleashed everything at once like that. He crushed the will of both rider and dragon so completely that mystic energy poured from their broken minds and crossed to Thrall, swelling his core. I felt it. It was grotesque, as though Thrall ate of the dragon's flesh. Then the violence we feared came. Humans and dragons and riders went to war in the valley. Only the arrival of the Mystic Elder and the Mystic Paragon from Falcaer brought peace. Rather than face judgment, Thrall fled, but he took others with him, wild mystics and even the dragon from the order who had gone over to him, with his rider going unhappily as well. And that's... that's all I know."

Another stunned, contemplative silence fell over the group.

Rake rallied first. "Given all Holt and Ash have told us about events in Feorlen and all the strange happenings with the scourge and the riders, Thrall would appear to be the master behind these events. Yes, Farsa, Thrall has found a way to control the scourge. How, I could not say. Yet it's clear he must be stopped."

"I only wished to ensure we were not entering this danger without certainty," Farsa said.

"I think we have it," Rake said. He smiled broadly, for it must have seemed as though the discussion was over. "Does anyone not understand their role in the plan?"

"He didn't once mention the eggs," Ash said across their bond.

Eidolon must have thought much the same as Ash, for he said, "The eggs, Rake. What of the eggs?"

Rake gave him a quizzical look, then hastened to say, "I don't understand. We kill Thrall, we by extension save the eggs."

Holt couldn't fault the logic, yet given all that had passed between him and Ash by the lakeside, he decided to speak up on the matter.

"What if we can't kill Thrall? It might be worth having a backup plan to rescue some of the eggs in case—"

"In case what?" Rake interrupted. "In case Thrall allows us to root around his tower and carry off some of his plunder? If Thrall isn't dead within minutes, we're done anyway. Best we could do in such a short time is destroy the remaining eggs and kill the poor hatchlings before retreating."

"We're not going to do that," Ash said, and Holt had rarely heard him so sure of anything.

"Ash, I know why you're repulsed by that idea," Rake said, "but you're not thinking clearly. What's better for the world? What's better for those hatchlings? If it's a choice between Thrall raising them to some evil or death at our hands, which way would you have it?"

"I'd have neither," Ash said.

Rake growled and swept his orange blade through a section of his model fortress. "You're letting your empathy get the better of you."

"Brode used to tell us that," Holt said.

Rake scoffed. "Then he became a wise man, even if he learned the hard way. Staying to defend a doomed town alone was not wise."

"I think it was brave," Holt said.

Rake rolled his eyes. "It makes a good song for bards and little else. So Red Rock limped on. Brode was a rider. He could have done so much more over a longer service with his dragon than committing to a suicide mission."

"And how is this mission much better than that?" Holt said. His temper rose now. Rake's belligerence was nothing new, but attacking Brode felt personal. It felt cheap. Perhaps this was the true Rake, without the wit and japes he often hid behind. "Folk could call what you propose brave or stupid. Which is it, Rake?"

Rake clenched his free fist, growled half a dragon and half a man, then ran his hand down over his snout. "I know this is a long shot," he said, calmer now. "I doubt I could have convinced anyone to come who didn't owe me. But you all do. Aberanth, all your work reliant on the supplies I procure for you. Eidolan, a lifetime's worth of treasures saved and carried across the world. Farsa, Hava, a blood oath long overdue. And Holt and Ash, you two owe me your lives."

Holt exhaled hard, feeling defeated. He and Ash did owe Rake their lives, possibly many times over. Such things mattered.

"So, we're just here because we all feel forced?" Holt asked softly. "Not because we think Rake is right or, heck, just because it's the right thing to do?"

And not, he thought grimly, *because of mutual respect or any sort of friendship.*

A squirming, cold ball of false hope unraveled inside him. Save for Farsa and Hava, this was a group of outcasts who he had thought to call a new family. Perhaps not. The sting of this fresh wound crossed the bond and made Ash bare his teeth.

"Has everyone lost their voices?" Ash said.

"I am here to rescue mystic eggs and hatchlings," Eidolan said. *"My history with my flight is troubled, as you now know. When I returned to them, I took on a role as egg keeper to repay my debts and find my new place. I cannot return to them empty-handed."*

Farsa steepled her fingers. "I would know whether my former sister, Dahaka, has turned rogue, and so avenge the honor of Alamut."

"And if there was a way out?" Holt asked. "Or another way?"

"We agreed to fulfill the oath," Hava said. *"We agreed to whatever end."*

Aberanth rumbled and rustled, then he stood and stretched his wings and tail so he took up the maximum space he could. The same move from Hava would have been impressive. For Aberanth, it looked like a puppy trying to stare down a mastiff.

"I came to learn. Not all things can be deduced inside my grotto. But I am wary of battle, and so I would choose not to fly to Windshear if I had the choice."

Rake shook his head, then sniffed the air loudly and very dramatically. "Fear. You all reek of it." He narrowed his eyes, then twisted his neck suddenly to the southwest, raised his blade, and gripped the broken shaft hard. A moment later, he exhaled in surprise and relaxed. "We shall continue our discussion later. We have a visitor."

Holt drew Brode's blade and turned sharply southwest. The copper sky shimmered behind clumps of wooly cloud, but he saw no dragon.

"Is it that storm rider again?"

"A fire rider, actually," said Rake. "Miss Agravain has found us."

THIRTY-EIGHT

Reunion

A purple dragon descended from the gathering night. It puffed a bout of flames, then tucked its wings and tilted sharply down. Holt could hardly believe his eyes. Even when he sensed a Fire Ascendant, he still did not believe it.

Talia and Pyra were here. But how? And why?

Farsa reached for the hilt of her sword. "You know this pair?"

"Yes," Holt, Ash and Rake all said together.

Holt's initial thought that something must be terribly wrong vanished the moment the two of them touched down. He found himself running to meet them, Ash bounding along just behind him.

Talia jumped down. She wore red brigandine over a black gambeson, and a steel crown sat upon her head. Yet, rather than looking pleased to see him, she had a fiery expression and stormed toward him, pointing an accusatory finger.

"Talia—" Holt began, but she cut him off.

"You are a Champion," she said, half impressed and half livid. "How?"

"It's good to see you too." Then, remembering who she was now, he bowed. "Your Majesty."

"Oh don't," she huffed.

Holt rose out of his bow and beamed at her. She cooled and grinned back, then they embraced. A tension left the air at that, and when they parted, Ash muscled his way in to nuzzle Talia, nearly knocking her over in the process.

"Hello, Ash," she said, half-laughing as she fought to remain upright under his assault of affection. Holt weaved around them to go to Pyra. Her usual aura of discouraging physical contact remained but she lowered her head for him, allowing him to lightly stroke her snout.

"Hello, little one," she said. "It gladdens me to find you both well."

"Same," Holt said. He allowed Ash to greet Pyra and went back to speak with Talia. Before he could get a word in, Rake appeared by their side and placed a great hand on Talia's shoulder.

"Were you followed?" he asked.

"Not that I'm aware of," Talia said. "We flew fast and without rest." Dark bags hung under her eyes.

Rake grunted, then half-turned to call back to the others. "Hava, do a sweep of the area before night falls."

The air around Hava seemed to suck in a great breath before she leaped and surged off quick as an arrow.

"Are you hungry?" Holt asked.

Talia grimaced and placed a hand on her stomach. "Starving, actually."

"We've got food," Holt said. "I'll put some on the spit for you. Pyra, there are goats in the ruins." Pyra licked her lips and kicked off on a hunt.

Holt brought Talia to their campsite. She looked inquisitively at Rake's model fortress with its one broken wall, then seemed to decide she didn't have the energy to enquire.

Holt found his abandoned dinner. The meat had grown tepid, the grease congealing. He ate it anyway and prepped a fresh haunch of the goat for Talia.

"So this is the other thorn in Adaskar's side?" Farsa said, giving Talia an inquisitorial stare.

Talia seemed to notice Farsa for the first time. "Well met, Champion. Do I assume rightly that you serve at Alamut?"

"You do."

"And what do they say about Talia Agravain in Alamut?"

"They say you are an oath breaker and a chaos bringer," Farsa said. "They say you will get all that you deserve for your lust for power."

Holt braced himself for Talia's outburst. Yet none came. Holt knew something was truly wrong then.

"They say you set your crown on fire at your coronation," Farsa went on, and Holt felt she was pushing Talia now. It didn't seem like her. Farsa was out here with a band of chaos bringers and renegades; did she really care that much about Talia's actions too?

"They also say you slew Silas Silverstrike," Farsa continued, and now she sounded impressed.

"I did."

Farsa's steel face was unmoving. "That's exceptional, even if his dragon had already perished. You must be skilled." Before Talia could respond, Farsa went on. "Some are calling you the Fire Queen, the Red Queen." She extended a hand. "It is an honor to meet you, Red Queen."

Taken aback, Talia took Farsa's hand and shook it. "It's an honor to meet you as well…"

"Farsa," the storm rider supplied.

"You don't care that I broke my oath?" Talia asked. "Most of Falcaer curses my name, as does half of Alamut by the sounds of it."

"That still leaves the other half either quietly in support or at least undecided," Farsa said. "I joined the Order to battle the scourge. You led the fight against an incursion as a seventeen-year-old Ascendant. I think you should be called a hero for that. As for your throne, you were offered it. You did not seize it. All riders seek power of a sort. To my mind, the more important question is how they do it, and for what ends they desire it."

Talia was lost for words. Holt turned the goat on the spit, and Rake made the rest of the introductions. Talia smiled and answered everyone politely, though her mind was clearly elsewhere. After meeting Aberanth and Eidolan, Talia sat by the fire and rubbed her hands over the flames. The fire bloomed, hotter and healthier than a fire its size ought to.

"That's better," she said. "My hands were frozen after such a long flight."

Holt didn't press her for more information until her meal was ready and she'd taken the first reviving bites. Her color improved after just a few mouthfuls, then she attacked the meat with a dragon-like ferocity, impeded only by having to work around the bone. She finished, sighed in relief, wiped her mouth of the juices, then placed her hands back over the fire.

Holt felt it safe now to ask the pressing question. "What's wrong?"

She gave him a sideways glance, then fixed her eyes on the crackling flames. "What's not wrong?"

Without taking her eyes from the fire, she took the steel crown off her head and dropped it to the earth. Then she proceeded to tell him everything that had happened since he'd left Sidastra. The story spilled out of her in a deluge. Ash, Aberanth, Eidolan, Farsa, and Rake most of all listened intently, allowing Talia to tell her tale in full. Pyra returned midway through the telling but sat quietly with her meal outside the immediate light of the fire. Night fell over the ruined city of Freiz, and the wind dropped precipitously as though it held its breath as it listened to the Queen of Feorlen recount her mounting problems.

"And so, we came to find you," she ended on a low note.

"I'm sorry," Holt blurted out, feeling impotent in the face of Talia's crisis. "I wish we could help, but I'm not sure what we can do."

"We just thought, well more *I hoped*, that we might learn how to advance as you have," Talia said. "I didn't believe Adaskar at first, but it's really true."

"Did Adaskar mention anything about the rider who spotted us?" Rake asked.

"No," Talia said, puzzled. "He just said that Holt and Ash had been sighted. Why?"

"We thought the rider might have been sent by Thrall," said Holt.

"Thrall?"

"That's Sovereign's true name," Holt explained.

"Sovereign sent the rider?" Talia said in alarm. "But does that mean Adaskar is—"

"I shouldn't think so," Rake said. "More like the rider is a good double agent."

"Things weren't right at Falcaer," Talia said.

"Trust between brothers and sisters is breaking down," Farsa said.

Talia nodded slowly, then looked around at them all. "Brenin will suffer for it, and then my own people," she added bleakly. "Pyra and I also thought we could ask for your help. Would you come back west with us?"

"I thought we were banished," Ash said.

"You still are," Talia said, sheepishly. "Come and help, and I'm sure I can have the banishment revoked."

"Tempting though I'm sure it sounds, I'm afraid we can't," Rake said in a tone that would brook no argument.

"We have a time-sensitive mission," Holt said. He then told her about his and Ash's travels since leaving Feorlen and the details of their mission to kill Thrall. Talia bit her lip, and when he told her of meeting Osric in the gorge and the fight he'd had with Rake, she seemed to retreat to that brooding place inside.

"You could join us?" Rake offered. There was no sarcasm. He meant it.

For a moment, Holt thought she would say yes. Pyra growled, but if she said anything it passed privately between her and Talia.

"I can't," Talia said at last.

"Your enemies take umbrage with you being a queen," Rake said. "Just leave. Then they will have nothing to bleat over."

"No," Talia said, rather quick. "No. I broke one oath, I won't break another. It's my responsibility to fix."

"A shame," Rake intoned. "Although gratifying nonetheless to know the Queen of Feorlen still owes me a favor."

She narrowed her eyes. "I offered you my uncle's help if you came to Sidastra to help us. You didn't."

"I sent Brode to the Life Elder, and that brought his whole flight to your aid. Magnificent though I am, a whole flight surpasses what I could contribute alone."

"Have it your way," Talia said. "I probably won't be queen long enough for you to come and collect your favor. Truthfully, there would be no point in you coming back west unless we can find a way into this second chamber."

"This chamber sounds like it has much in common with the one Holt and Ash discovered," said Aberanth. He had two of his bark slabs in front of him. *"The orbs at the center, the large gut-like organs. Holt's chamber had a working vat of acid to break down dead organic material. And Talia's chamber had evidence that a queen grew inside it."*

"Incubation chambers," Eidolan said. *"We long discussed the prospect of such places in the Order of old, though few ever had the courage to delve so deep. Those that did rarely returned, and those who did make it back were never the same. Their minds were broken from whatever they found."*

"Adaskar mentioned something to that effect," Talia said. She shook her head, and the fire flared from her irritation. "I can't believe the Order has knowledge of this and does nothing. That there is danger should hardly stop us. If Thrall is growing a new queen under the Red Range, then we have to kill it before it's ready."

"All the more reason to come with us," Rake said. "You're closer to Windshear than to Sidastra now. Help us kill Thrall, and this all goes away."

"No," Holt said, louder than he intended. "It won't all go away. The scourge will still exist even if Thrall no longer controls them. Talia should destroy this new queen."

Pyra snarled and stamped closer to the group. Her swishing tail struck a wall of the model fortress, scattering rock and pebbles. *"If we knew how to find the entrance, we wouldn't have gone to Falcaer in the first place."*

"But the solution is simple," Aberanth said. Everyone looked at him, and the little brown emerald rolled his eyes. *"Hmmph, dullards. These scourge roads are plainly connected. The tunnels Rake sent Holt and Ash down—"*

"Shoved, more like it," said Ash.

"I prefer nudged," Rake said.

"That place," Aberanth soldiered on, *"used to be kept open by the riders of Alamut to train in. Seems to me that if you find similar training locations used by the riders of Sable Spire or the Crag, then you'd have your way in."*

For the first time since arriving, Talia smiled. A light not of the fire lent new life to her green eyes. She got up as though she intended to run off west and pursue the plan at once.

"Yes," she said, more to herself than to the group. "Records at the Crag burned, but there must be some way to find the locations. If even one rider from Sable Spire could—"

She stopped, gripped it seemed by a thought too daring to voice aloud. Facing Pyra, Holt guessed something passed between them, something which made Pyra rumble and beat her wings with a tense, excited energy.

"And if we do find a way in," Talia said, speaking aloud again, "then we might even be able to help your mission."

"How do you intend to do that?" Eidolan asked.

"Not directly, of course," Talia said, "but if Thrall is focusing his efforts into this new incursion, then killing the queen early will surely draw his attention. Maybe he'll expend a lot of power trying to control things from afar. If nothing else, it should distract him and give you all a better chance attacking him at Windshear."

Aberanth perked up at that suggestion. Eidolan rumbled happily. Farsa was unmoved, and Rake stroked his chin.

"We can't wait forever," Rake said. "It would take you too long to ready such an expedition."

"Maybe, and maybe not," Talia said. "I instructed my Master of War to move men and supplies to the southern Red Range and to the border with Brenin. I won't be starting from scratch. The emeralds will help again. They know how important this is."

"When?" Rake asked bluntly.

Talia pressed her lips together, and her eyes glazed as she did some quick calculations. "The first day of autumn."

Holt set to working out their own deadline too, but Rake got there first.

"Not soon enough," Rake said.

"I can't promise anything sooner," Talia said. "That's us going flat out and assuming I find the opening in days, not weeks."

"We shall request that the Honored Elder send you drakes," Pyra said.

But Rake shook his head. "That would take too long. Besides, the more powerful our force, the more likely we are to be detected. There is no way the Life Elder could sneak up on Thrall, same as if we had a score of riders. Our advantage is in speed and being weak enough to move unnoticed whilst just strong enough to maybe – just maybe – succeed. The first day of autumn is too close to when those mystic eggs will all hatch for my liking. There is no guarantee Thrall will linger in the fortress after that."

"He might," Holt said. "It's a fortress, and he's recovering. Why not stay?"

"Because the longer he stays, the longer he risks being exposed," Rake said. "Wherever he hid before, nobody found him, or escaped at any rate. At Windshear, he's stationary, known. Wyrm Cloaks must be coming and going, as are his wild dragon allies and some of his riders. Eventually, even the stubborn Order will notice something. He might stay, Holt, you're right. He might stay for a week or two to judge the hatchlings, he might stay for months. I can't say for sure. So I'm working with what we know for certain. Those eggs are on a timer. They should all hatch before summer ends, and each hour we dawdle preparing ourselves after that is time in which he might leave, and we'll miss our best chance at killing him. Not to mention that if Talia's distraction is too good, he might well fly off entirely—" Rake sucked in a breath through his teeth, but the damage had been done.

Thrall might leave Windshear if Talia's distraction worked too well. Holt seized on that.

"We could save the eggs and hatchlings then," he said brightly. "If he leaves in a panic, there's no way he spends time gathering them up."

"We've had this argument already," Rake said, mashing his words through gritted teeth. "The objective is Thrall's ugly head rolling down the mountainside."

"But that's a million in one chance," Holt said. "And we didn't have Talia to distract Thrall before. This seems like a win-win to me. Either Thrall is distracted on the day, making our chances all the better. Or he leaves, and we can then easily save more hatchlings than we could have with him there."

"No," Rake said harshly, suppressing a shake of rage. He didn't seem able to summon a more effective counter-argument.

"It won't be a shock to hear that I am in favor of a distraction," said Eidolan the illusionist.

"This would seem to increase our odds by a significant margin," said Aberanth.

Rake turned his hopes on Farsa. A decision did not come as easily to her, but at last she spoke. "I do not fear death or defeat, there can be honor in such things. But I do fear this dragon taking hold of Hava's mind or my own and forcing us to do his bidding. That would bring great shame."

In desperation, Rake turned to Pyra. "Pyra," he purred, "you are fire made flesh. You scorned those emeralds outside the Withering Woods and roared to them that notes from the Fire Elder's own song ring within you. Surely you cannot condone this caution?"

Pyra snorted smoke, stamped, then snorted more smoke and parted her teeth so that flames burst in a black-red cloud. Her amber eyes burned like two summer sunsets. Rake looked triumphant, sure he had won over at least Pyra, and yet Talia went to Pyra's side and placed a hand at her chest. Pyra's growling descended to a rumbling, and her wings drooped.

"She's in pain," Ash told Holt. *"She is torn."*

Talia stroked Pyra and must have spoken to her privately, though she made soothing noises. And Pyra relaxed. She hushed and wrapped a wing around Talia.

"When we marched into the chasm in the Withering Woods," Talia began, "we let the fire overrule our sense. That rage is useful when you're supported by fellow riders and merely need to obliterate the enemy. But it's not helpful for a leader. We both let the fire drive us, and it was foolish. Too many died. I need to be better as a queen, and I won't get better if I don't learn from my own failings." She looked hard at Holt. "There are only so many risks you can take until your luck runs out."

Holt set his jaw. A part of him knew she was right. And a part of him knew Rake was right.

"What do you think?" he asked Ash across their bond, though he knew what to expect. Ash would want to save the hatchlings above all.

"The Life Elder tasked us with seeking out his siblings and gathering the flights to defeat the scourge once and for all. We can't do that if we're dead."

Holt nodded, then met Rake's judging eyes. "I say we wait for Talia's distraction."

Rake's expression turned frigid. "Cowards," he spat. "And to think I thought you had what it takes." Never had more disappointment been crushed into so few words. He planted his orange blade hard into the ground, causing the splinted shaft of the polearm to tremble, then he spread his open palms as though to beg. "If we did this, we would save the world. I thought you would all have risked everything for that."

He turned and marched off into the darkness off Freiz, leaving his weapon stuck fast in the earth.

Pyra growled from shame, but Talia held her own. "Let him sulk, Pyra," she said, though her voice shook a little. "It's all of us against one. We've made the right choice."

The wind rushed from all sides then, and Hava returned.

"You were skilled or fortunate, young embers," Hava said. *"No dragon or rider is out there."* The storm dragon seemed to take in the mood of the group then. *"What has happened? Where is Master Rake?"*

"I shall tell her," Farsa said, and she moved off with Hava to speak privately.

Aberanth fidgeted and rustled his wings. *"What have we done?"*

"We stood as one and did not allow Rake to manipulate us to a quick death," Eidolan said. He puffed pale violet smoke as though that settled the matter. *"Will you stay the night, daughters of fire?"*

"We'll have to leave right away if we're to have a chance of making this work," Talia said.

Holt looked earnestly to Talia. He would much rather she stayed at least one night, but he also knew that was selfish.

"Do you have the strength, Pyra?" Holt asked, one last hopeful attempt for a genuine reason.

"I'll find the strength," Pyra said.

"I'm sorry, Holt," Talia said.

He smiled wanly. "It's what needs to be done."

Things suddenly got awkward then.

"Come, Aberanth," Eidolan grumbled. *"Let them say their goodbyes."* The pair of them slid into the night, leaving Talia, Holt, Pyra, and Ash alone.

Talia opened her mouth, hesitated, then closed it. Holt found himself lost for words. There was too much to talk about and nowhere near enough time. Talia was to be married. That sent a fresh pang through him which he could not fully fathom. He'd be lying to himself to deny he hadn't wondered what might have been if Talia hadn't taken the crown, if she'd left everything to roam in the wilds with him, searching for Elder dragons. Such things were as deep a fantasy as a cook dreaming of becoming a dragon rider. They had been through a lot together, but a few battles did not forge an unbreakable bond, hence the awkwardness of this very parting.

Talia made to speak again, and this time she managed it.

"How did my uncle seem, when you fought him?"

"Uhm," Holt said, caught off guard by the question. He summoned the memory of Osric's ravenous, battle-drunk face and considered what he should tell her carefully. Then he resolved for the cold hard truth. "He seemed to be acting in his own mind and he was completely bloodthirsty."

"I see," Talia said.

"But we don't really understand how Thrall's powers work," Holt said. "He did reach out to me in Sidastra. A part of him was still in there, and that wasn't so long ago."

"And he hesitated," Ash said. *"Holt pleaded with him in the gorge, and*

Osric hesitated. He lowered his axes, just for a second, and then Thrall's presence raged inside him. He still might be saved..." yet even Ash trailed off in saying it.

"Maybe," Talia said. "Though the more I learn about my uncle, the more I fear everything he's done is two parts Osric and only one part Sovereign—I mean, Thrall," she corrected, sounding weary again. "When you reach Windshear, you'll have to fight him. Or Rake will, at least."

It was not a question but a matter of fact.

"He will," Holt admitted. They both knew how that fight might end.

A grimness settled into Talia. "The worst parts of my uncle are in me too. The anger. The rage. The pride. The need to prove ourselves. I think that's partly why Pyra bonded with me."

Pyra rumbled reproachfully. *"Amongst many other things."*

"All the same," Talia said, "I'd give much to know he could be redeemed, but if he's too far gone, then I understand what must be done." She ended on a hard note, and Holt felt that, despite her words, she would take it terribly hard if Osric did perish. A third member of her family she would have failed to save.

"Okay," Holt said. He swallowed hard. Such a grim discussion. Talia showing up should have been an occasion for celebration. In the end, he said the only thing he could think of, the same words he had spoken at their last parting. "It would be better if you could come with us."

She smiled. "It would be better if you could come back."

"Goodbye, Pyra," he said.

"Farewell again, little one. Fight well."

Ash padded over to them both, allowing Talia to hug him around the neck and then receive a bite of affection from Pyra. He nipped her back, and then the dragons pressed their heads together.

Feeling a lump forming in his throat, Holt turned, not wishing Talia to see his hurt.

"Wait," she said.

Holt turned, and his heart jolted from how hard it thumped.

"Yes?"

"You didn't answer my first question! How are you a Champion already?"

"Oh, that."

"Yes, that," Talia said, half-laughing. "It's rather important. Yet again, you two did something incredible. I don't have anyone to train me now, so if there is anything you can share—"

"We went through torture and sheer terror and back." He spoke more mechanically now. "Three weeks in the dark underground. Three weeks of fighting and Forging, with little rest and even less to eat. We pushed ourselves through me learning how to hear as Ash hears."

He lowered his bandanna to demonstrate. He raised it a moment later and saw the disappointment on her face. She could not take such a risk, nor could she and Pyra rely on sense-sharing, which worked uniquely well for him and Ash.

"But that's just how we did it," he added cheerfully. "Rake's advice is probably good for all. You need to reach a state of total trust in each other. For me, that meant giving up being our defender and guide and trusting in Ash to do the same for me."

Talia looked at Pyra and placed a hand on her dragon. "That's it? I already do trust Pyra completely."

"That's what I thought," Holt said. He shrugged. "There must be something. You'll have to figure that out between you."

Poor Talia looked overwhelmed. She had too much to handle as it was. He would have taken some of that burden from her if he could.

"Thanks for the advice, pot boy."

"You're welcome—" He almost said 'princess' then caught himself and said, "Red Queen."

Talia got onto Pyra's back. "Red Queen," she said to herself. "I do like that. Goodbye, Holt. And good luck."

Holt watched them go, vanishing into the dark of the night. Ash came to his side.

"Are you okay, boy?"

"I'm fine." He rubbed the dragon's neck. "Come on. Rake might be angry with us, but that doesn't mean we should skip training."

THIRTY-NINE

Cold Winds

Life at Windshear trudged on. The Speaker drilled the faithful, Sovereign judged the hatchlings, and the Blood Alchemist brewed his concoctions. Having secured the blood of riders, and Osric's own, the alchemist had unveiled his success to the Shroud one summer's night. Now when cultists drank of the blood – a mix of different dragon types, human and rider – their bodies swelled with functional engorged muscle and grew to accommodate it.

The issue lay in reverting back to normal. That was a slow-going and painful process, sometimes requiring days of bed rest, yet most eventually survived. The Speaker could not have been happier. Osric was pleased too, if only to the extent that future operations would be made easier.

Orvel and Dahaka continued to attend to the hatchlings. There were over a dozen now, and the mystic tower was as lively as if the old Order had returned. To make space, Osric sent eggs that were yet to hatch or be confirmed as lifeless stone to the ice tower, allowing more of the hatchlings to live together.

Elsewise, Osric sat cross-legged in the great hatchery and continued to work on Sovereign's core. Countless pillars stretched off to the dark horizon in the black chain hall, seeming more like prison bars to Osric than columns of hard stone.

His work was made more difficult with the presence of Sovereign's favored hatchlings. They growled, roared, gargled, and yapped under the dragon's tutelage. They wrestled with one another, though none willingly faced the ginger bruiser. With his natural bulk and aggression, none of the other hatchlings stood a chance, and the bruiser never let them win.

Yet that was Sovereign in a nutshell. The dragon only understood and recognized power.

"The smaller ones will be more willing if they think there is a chance they can win," Osric told Sovereign one day.

"Your brother did not let you win," Sovereign said. "And it made you strong."

"It made me resentful," Osric said. "And later, I killed him. Do you want your new dragons to hate each other?"

Sovereign did not answer, and as Osric watched the babies struggle against one another, he reckoned Sovereign did want it this way. If they fought each other, they would not fight or unite against him. Sovereign held a strange balance of beliefs. He would not kill a rider, if he could help it, for the sake of its dragon, yet he would push his chosen hatchlings to fight each other for dominance.

As though sensing Osric's train of thought, Sovereign said, "The largest one benefits from being physically active. His core strengthens as he uses his body, which in turn makes his body stronger."

The muscled ginger snorted and roared, as though to taunt the next challenger.

"So long as he does not kill the others in the process," Osric said.

The hatchling with the golden scales – the twin of the little black dragon – roared in answer to the bruiser and stepped forward as the next contender. The muscled ginger, more than double the younger hatchling in size, stalked around the golden drake with a quiet confidence. Yet when the brawl began, the golden dragon held its own. It lost in the end, but it fought longer than the others.

"That one shows great promise," Sovereign said eagerly.

There were three dragons that Sovereign kept close to him now. The bruiser and the golden drake along with one truly unique sea-green dragon. This one lacked wing sockets, yet its webbed feet suggested it was built for a different means of travel. The ridges down its back were thinner and more angular, and there were segments of layered, open scales along its sides that Osric took to be a form of gills. A dragon that could rule the rivers or even take to the open seas would be invaluable to Sovereign.

Osric closed his eyes to continue Forging when Sovereign demanded, *"Fetch the others."*

Osric stood. "The usual?"

"Yes," Sovereign hissed. *"And any others I have not yet inspected."*

Osric dutifully made his way up and down the mystic tower, collecting the hatchlings in question. There were three Sovereign inspected regularly yet struggled to decide on.

First on the list was the sandy hatchling with the clubbed foot who lived in the topmost hatchery. Osric entered and looked for him. He hobbled out to him at once, hopeful for food.

"Sovereign wants to see you," he said. The sandy hatchling's eyes went wide and it yapped with excitement. It gave the other hatchlings a sweeping look of superiority, yet they were asleep, save for the little black dragon. Its deep purple eyes also widened, though this seemed more out of alarm, as though afraid to be summoned.

So far it had avoided judgment, slipping into dark corners at night or early morning and so evading the likes of Orvel, who was less diligent in his duties. And while in darkness, the dragon became impossible to extract.

Yet with the current position of the sun, most of the hatchery was illuminated. Currently the black dragon was bathed in sunlight. Osric took half a step, intending to take it with him. Sovereign would want to know of its potential as much as any other. It squeaked in fright as he approached and shot toward the pen of its golden twin, where a short wooden post cast a sliver of shadow across the floor. Osric finished his stride and the black dragon wriggled into the shadow.

Osric halted. He ran his hand down his face as though his eyes deceived him. When he looked again, the black dragon was still nowhere to be seen. And yet from within the thin shadow on the floor, two startling eyes stared back at him: pearl white opals with dark purple hearts. The eyes seemed to ask him, *why?* Before Osric could make a move, the eyes vanished. All that remained was an unnatural bulge within the shadow, something easily missed unless you knew exactly where to look.

Osric turned and ushered the sandy dragon to follow. The black dragon evidently held some unique power, yet so long as it hid, he could not reach it. A part of him wrestled with the notion to return and drag the poor creature out, which was what he should do. Yet the quiet part of him that had spoken so soft and yet so true in that very same hatchery guided him otherwise.

With the clubbed-footed sandy dragon at his heels, Osric descended through the mystic tower, collecting the other aspirants. In a mid-level hatchery rested a stout drake with rust-colored scales and rusty, permanently bloodshot eyes. Such eyes gave the impression that the hatchling had just finished crying, yet the dead nature of its blank stare suggested something more sinister at work. The third dragon was amethyst in color and its scales held a crystalline quality. It had no tail.

He brought six hatchlings into Sovereign's lair, led them to the feet of the great dragon and kneeled, and the babies took his lead to press their necks low in reverence. Sovereign, however, had his back to them. A sleek gray dragon hovered outside the opening of the hatchery.

It took some time for the wild dragon to relay its report. Osric's knee would have ached by now were he not enhanced. The babies kept their necks low but could not quite stop their hind legs or tails from fidgeting from boredom. Eventually the storm dragon turned sharply and flew off, and Sovereign labored to turn his great body. He stamped impatiently and seemed taken aback when he found Osric and the hatchlings before him.

"Are there no others?" Sovereign asked.

"None," Osric said. The lie came so naturally and so readily that he almost believed it himself. When had he last knowingly lied to the dragon?

Sovereign exhaled cold smoke, said, *"Very well,"* then got to work inspecting the hatchlings. His chosen three stood at the back of the hatchery, looking down their snouts at their fellows. Osric rose and trudged to his meditation spot, brooding over how very much like humans these young dragons were. Malleable as soft clay. Sovereign would make of those three whatever he desired.

Osric could only half focus on Forging now. Sovereign was less patient than usual with the hatchlings, growling louder and scraping his talons to a horrendous pitch across the floor. Before he was finished with them, one of his loyal ice dragons appeared outside the hatchery. Two such messages in a day was unusual. Small matters were attended to via telepathy at a distance, but to come face to face with Sovereign meant news of an extreme nature.

After this ice drake left, Sovereign turned around so fast he struck the wall with his tail. Dust shifted from the stones overheard. That had not been intentional. Sovereign was agitated, distracted.

"Is something amiss?" Osric asked.

Sovereign rounded on him, as though Osric had interrupted a deep thought. *"Things are accelerating. We will have to leave soon. Once the war begins."*

"War?" Osric said sharply. "What war?"

Curse the dragon, he thought, and this time no charming voice replied reproachfully. *Curse the dragon,* he thought again. Sovereign claimed to respect his experience as a general, but only when it suited him. Only once all the pieces were already in play.

"The ice dragons have been recalled to the utter north," Sovereign said, more to himself than to Osric, then he added harshly, *"You will instruct Zahak and Gea to fly additional patrols to replace them."*

Zahak and Gea would not relish such basic duties. Nor would they, even flying around the clock, be enough to replace four ice dragons. For all Sovereign's strengths, a cool head was not one of them.

"I understand you're in need of haste," Osric said. "But you will have time yet. The wild strike oft goes astray."

"There is so much to keep a grasp of," Sovereign admitted, for once letting his voice betray the strain of the many puppets on his many long strings.

"Let me help you," Osric said. "What war is about to begin?"

"The only one that matters, in which even your experience will mean little."

A war not of steel and men, Osric assumed. What Osric lacked was knowledge of magic. A war between dragons then? Between those who would support Sovereign and those who would not? Perhaps, but Sovereign would avoid that if he could.

The riders. They were all that still stood between Sovereign and victory. Did he think it time to take on the whole Order? Each Paragon was said to be worth several Lords or more. Sovereign had his rogues and turncloaks, but were they enough?

Things were accelerating. There were so many things for him to keep in his grip.

"What of the contingency plan for Feorlen and the west?"

"It grows," Sovereign growled. *"The Life Elder and his emeralds scurry over the region. The bugs and ghouls spill out into Brenin, not Feorlen as I'd hoped, but in truth this is well. The Elder cannot intervene in Brenin without crossing the riders. Much will depend on whether they involve themselves directly and on whether the Order opposes them. Still, the west is but a distraction now."* He snarled deep bouts of anger in his throat. The supplicant hatchlings backed off from him.

Osric worked through Sovereign's scant information, trying to assess the situation as well as he could. The previous swarm had taken years to nurture and carefully assemble without drawing the attention of the riders. Moving too quickly in that arena would mean a swarm easily crushed or the opposite, one so large and hastily thrown together that he would struggle to direct its intentions.

Yet a second incursion was now to be a mere distraction. A fog he conjured to obscure his true war. The Feorlen incursion was supposed to destroy that small kingdom and raise a swarm from its dead such as had not been since the Great Chasm broke Aldunei in two. The Order would have gathered its full might to combat such a swarm, and though the losses would be brutal, they would contain the incursion eventually. The plan had not been to destroy the riders utterly but to mortally wound them for the killing blow.

Assaulting Falcaer head-on, with the majority of its Lords and even two Paragons still in place, would end in defeat unless Sovereign went himself. Though the dragon had grown bolder, flying to Falcaer in his current state with his current followers seemed like lunacy to Osric. As a hasty incursion in the west would not draw the full attention of Falcaer, Osric ruled out an attack on rider headquarters.

Dragons then? One of the Wild Flights seemed the most likely target. The emeralds worked against him. What of these ice dragons and their recall to the north? Only one being could hold such sway over all dragons bound to ice.

"Does the Ice Elder work against us?" Osric asked.

More smoke trailed out from Sovereign's nostrils in a thin, steady stream. *"That is yet to be seen."*

Many strings indeed did the puppet master pull. All the more reason Osric reckoned he would drive on regardless of the appropriate preparations.

"You will only be allowed one more chance," Osric said. "You have time yet. Do not rush into an early defeat."

"Time slips away from us," Sovereign said. *"Your assertion that Holt and Ash could not become a threat due to lack of training has proved false. They were seen in the borderlands of Ahar and Mithras. They are already Champions."*

"That cannot be possible," Osric said. "The boy only became an Ascendant when he crash-landed in Sidastra." It had taken Osric far longer, several dreadful long and painful years, even under the duress and forced domination of Sovereign, to grow their hateful bond together. "You're sure? One of your riders just happened to spot them?" Osric asked, incredulous.

"I sent the rider. I felt a… disturbance there." Sovereign offered nothing more on the matter.

"Whether gaining power or not, they can't be a threat to all of your scourge alone unless they were Paragons. They seem a minor issue on the grand scale. And you'll have a hard time converting or killing them so long as that half-dragon is with them."

"There were others too. A mystic working illusions. A lowly emerald."

Osric frowned deeply, knitting his heavy brows into a solid line. Sovereign was allowing himself to be distracted by this little band.

"If you'll take my advice," Osric said, "leave this place. You've lingered here long enough. The longer you and the Shroud remain, the higher the chance you'll be detected. Likely you already have been."

"This fortress fears no human army," Sovereign said. *"I have enough agents at Falcaer to know if the Order discovers us, and no flight could travel in force undetected."*

"I've given you my counsel," Osric said.

"I'll consider it."

The next evening, Osric found himself drawn back to the hatchery of the twin dragons. He had no duty to, yet he came anyway to sit on a squat stool in the dark. It was the quiet, he told himself. That was why he felt drawn back. A place to think. Calmness. He found the pain of his bond less severe while he sat here. The tightness of the black chains loosened around his soul, allowing his spirit to breathe.

Yet if it was the quiet he valued, why not one of the other hatcheries? Why not his own chambers? And why did his heart skip a beat whenever the little black dragon crawled out of the darkness?

He tossed it a chunk of pork. The black dragon threw wary glances from side to side before darting toward the meat. It chewed rapidly, eyes still roving around in search of threats. Osric smiled. It gulped, focused on him again and took another small step. Such delicate steps. Its sharp, little features were almost dainty. He extended his palm to the hatchling but otherwise sat still as stone.

She rubbed her snout into his hand.

She? What made him think that? A mere gut feeling was all.

"Hello," he croaked in the gloom.

She pulled back in a sudden jerk, keeping low to the ground as though he'd raised one of his axes.

"Sorry," he said in a hushed whisper. It struck him as a rather foolish thing to do. Why apologize to it? To her?

Silence then. Complete stillness was what she wanted. He barely breathed to achieve it, and then, sure enough, she crept back. Against his better judgment, Osric dropped another piece of pork at her feet.

He really ought to take her down to Sovereign. If he decided to leave Windshear, then he would take his chosen few with him, but the fate of the remaining eggs and hatchlings was unclear. A whim of his mood on the day, though it would make sense for his followers to bring them along in time.

Osric would advise that, of course, but it would be safest for her to be chosen. She had control over shadows, maybe even darkness itself. Even if not powerful, it would be useful. Surely, she would be picked. Then she may at least live.

He dared not contemplate what would happen if she was not.

Talia – Falcaer Fortress

"Land right in the middle of the training field," Talia told Pyra as they dove. *"Most of the lower ranks will be drilling in swordcraft at this time of the morning."*

"Whatever you tell them, I'll spread the message to the dragons," Pyra said. Their bond grew hot in anticipation. For the first time in a long time, Talia felt at one with Pyra, and her dragon song rang clearly in her mind. Powerful, booming horns; each note strong, eager, and full of pride.

As before, several Champions rose to escort them, but Pyra ignored their instructions this time. As she'd predicted, there were riders out training in a large field between two barrack houses. Groups clashed with swords, and smaller groups trained in maces and a few even in spears.

Rather than head for open ground, Pyra made for the largest collection of riders, the Ascendants. They scattered just in time before Pyra touched down. She roared, arched her neck and belched a jet of flames as high as she could maintain. Thirty feet, forty, fifty feet the flames lashed.

Riders shouted at her from above and on the ground. She breathed hard, and with Farsa's words close to her heart, she pushed the storm of dissenting voices aside. Half of Alamut either supported her or were undecided. Farsa considered she was a hero, not a villain. If even some fraction of Falcaer felt the same, she had to find out.

"Novices, Ascendants, Champions, Lords of Falcaer," she cried, trying her best to mimic the easy confidence of Empress Skadi. "Hear me. I am Talia Agravain, Queen of Feorlen. No doubt many of you hate me and think me an oath breaker and a chaos bringer. Well, I am those things. I accepted the throne which was my brother's and my father's before me. I killed Silas Silverstrike, the Hero of Athra."

More shouting at her. Insults and cries of disbelief, yet not from all, she could see that. Some stood grim-faced and listened to her. She spoke to them now.

"But Silas was a traitor who slaughtered our brothers and sisters and the Crag. He aided the scourge and its new master. A dragon of great power who used to fly in our very Order."

The Champions landed around her. One by one, the riders hit the ground hard while their dragons closed in above.

"I think you all deserve the truth," Talia yelled harder than ever. "Sidastra does not stand today because of me alone. A serving boy fought beside me along with his dragon that he saved from death; a blind dragon with power drawn from the moon, whose light is more effective against the scourge than fire. And the Emerald Flight, wild dragons in their hundreds, came as well. If not for them, Feorlen would have been overrun. A great swarm would have swept east, and many of you would be dying now to defeat it."

The Champions drew their swords and closed in. Pyra roared once more, rearing back, but Talia clung on.

"Let her speak," someone called.

"We want to hear," another cried.

The Champions hesitated. It was all Talia needed to press on.

"I am the light that guides through the dark," she called, repeating those parts of the rider oath that still made sense to her. "I am the shelter in the storm. I am the first strike and the last shield. No life will be beneath my aid. When death comes, I will make it wait. I shall halt the blight and defeat the scourge, in this rising, and the next, and for all to come. *Defeat the scourge,*" she cried even harder. "What good is order if it's so rigid we cannot move, so tight we cannot breathe? I'd break my oath a thousand times over if it meant defeating the scourge. How many of you would do the same?"

The response was not enthusiastic, but she had brought them to a silence. Half might have seethed in fury, but the other half were gripped.

"Things are changing," she said. "Things are changing because they must. An Elder dragon works with me now. We have a new way to take the fight back to the scourge, rather than only defend our ground. Scourge roads run deep under the earth, to chambers where their queens grow, and dark magics keep the swarms in check. I would use my strength as a queen to lead the fight into these depths, to attack our enemy rather than sit idle and wait for the next rising. Any who would join me are welcome to come to the southern Red Range. There we seek entry to the tunnels below to destroy the incursion threatening Brenin before it truly begins!"

She drew her red blade and set it ablaze, and in a sudden burst of inspiration, and with Pyra's dragon song ringing hard between her ears, she brought magic to her head, only this time she used the steel upon her brow as a guide. Flames burst, flickering in a low heat, yet nonetheless ringing her head in a crown of fire. Alas, the plain steel was a poor conduit, and the flames died moments later.

The silence which greeted her was as harsh as it was barren. No one cheered, though no one protested either. Riders at last ripped their gaze from her to look anxiously between each other. Then, across Falcaer, dragons bellowed and roared.

"*They are arguing,*" Pyra said.

"*Time to go then.*"

And with another deafening cry and bout of flames, Pyra took off. The dragons guarding them overhead parted without a fight. Talia did not look back.

FORTY

An Uplifting Meal

With the parameters of the mission changed, Rake's team gained more time. Yet Rake himself took a step back from decisions now. Surly and downhearted, he acquiesced as the group agreed to make a detour to Aberanth's grotto on their way north. It was not the most direct route, but it held many appealing advantages and it seemed foolish not to use the delay wisely to make additional preparations.

So it was that they approached the southern border of the Fae Forest, reentering the trees not so far from where Rake had led Holt, Ash, and Aberanth out of the woods months ago. Before crossing into the forest's boundaries, Farsa announced she would take her leave.

"Our lengthy journey from Alamut to Oak Hall will already have been noted when we arrive. If we wait until after the mission, we'll suffer questioning for sure."

Rake waved them off without so much as a grunt of protest.

"Are you sure you'll be able to rejoin us?" Holt asked. He did not like the thought of going to Windshear without the Exalted Champion

"We will," Hava assured him. "Even if we have to flee in the dead of night. Even if it has consequences on our return. We gave our oath, and it shall be fulfilled."

Using the air alone, Farsa drifted up and onto Hava's back. "Until we meet again."

And, just like that, their group was reduced to five again.

"Should have headed north at once," Rake grumbled, but that was the only grumble he gave that day.

Later that evening, under the utter pitch black of the roof of the forest, Ash smelled a deer.

Holt looked back upon their troubles hunting deer and smiled fondly as though recalling the blunderings of a much younger version of himself. It had been only a matter of months since their days wandering on the borders of Brenin, but the time since had been almost as eventful as their hasty flight across Feorlen. Holt and Ash had certainly learned more in that time with Rake as their guide than they had under Brode. And putting part of that learning to work, Holt shared his senses with Ash and lowered his bandanna.

Now he too heard the deer. Its hooves lightly brushed over root and undergrowth, and as they drew closer, he swore he could hear its heart beating. He could smell it even from afar, its wild, earthy musk, and the oils on its thick hair. Through the dark, Holt crept closer, closer than Ash could dare to between the trees, and when he made his move, the deer could not escape his Grounded Champion's body. They preserved most of the meat for the days prior to the mission and to make more jerky at Aberanth's grotto.

Returning to Aberanth's laboratory with its firefly lights, luminous roots and security underground felt like a homecoming. While here they could feel safe and be comfortable. Eidolan and Ash remained above ground, while Rake, Holt, and Aberanth descended and emerged as required.

Aberanth was happier than Holt had seen him on the whole journey. Back in his grotto, with all his equipment and supplies and as many fresh mushrooms as he could stomach. His first act was to take the scourge orb into a back room.

"*For tests,*" he declared, before digging out casks of his homebrewed wine and vinegar used in the creation of his elixirs. Holt hauled these back to the surface, where he set to work creating jerky with these new ingredients, cutting dozens of fine strips of meat to hang and dry. On some he rubbed salt for Grounding, powdered ginger into others for Floating, dipped others in wine for Lifting, and drowned some in vinegar for Sinking.

Aberanth also offered Holt the chance to clean the clothes he had worn in the scourge tunnels. Holt took the opportunity to throw his bandanna and Ash's blindfold into the wash basin. Barefoot and wearing only his spare loose-fitting linen shirt and trousers, he spent the better part of a morning with his sleeves rolled up and his arms deep in a tub of hot water mixed with a cleansing lye.

For a time, he felt transported back to the wash basin in his father's kitchens – the grease floating in the water, the coarse feeling of the scrub brush pushing against copper and iron. He would make a brilliant pot boy now, he thought. He would be able to stand all day without getting aches in his back or neck. There had been satisfaction in seeing the sparkling dishes at the end of it, as there was in seeing his clothes made new again. Removing the filth was the best he could do. Most soaps Holt knew of were made from animal fats, and so Aberanth had none. To clean his mail coat, he rubbed the links with sand to scour the metal of grime and rust.

He hung the clothes outside to dry and then returned below with his belt to discuss an idea with Aberanth. If he was going to make use of elixirs and the jerky in combat, he needed easy access to them. To do that, he needed to be able to carry them on his person and easily grab whatever he needed without fiddling with pouches. Holt's skills in sewing were rudimentary but Aberanth's tools and supplies were thankfully extensive, and even when wielding a knife with his vines, his skill at making small incisions could rival that of any physician.

Together they worked on Holt's belt until it contained holsters for elixir vials and small openings in the leather for jerky to be placed in and secured with twine. It wasn't a perfect solution, Holt knew. He worried that too much jostling would cause vials and meat to fall loose, and yanking pieces of jerky out from a tight bundle sometimes ripped the meat or else caused the whole lot to fall. Not to mention that an enemy might smash the elixirs in a fight. But, for now, it was the best they could do.

Holt tied on his modified belt and returned to the surface equipped with a Floating elixir and a piece of gingered jerky. Wearing only his shirt and trousers, he had a notion to test the effects of stacking all the magical defenses he could while lacking any other form of protection.

Holt Floated his flow of motes, bringing them to the surface of his body to create a second magical skin. He slipped the Floating elixir out of his belt and drank it, enjoying the warm woodiness of the ginger. Cycling became instantly easier. Next, he shimmied out the piece of ginger-infused jerky. Dry and supremely chewy, the ginger overpowered the subtle venison and produced a greater fire at the back of his throat than its elixir counterpart. He coughed, half choking from the spice and dryness of the food, but he got it down. Cycling energy eased further so that Holt increased the volume of motes he cycled without interrupting the steady rhythm of the technique. His mote channels glowed, visible even in daylight, given Floating focused the energy on his outer body.

Holt just had time to notice this when Rake launched one of his magical attacks. Holt braced, the orange light hit him full in the torso, and yet he held. No staggering, not even a wobble, and the pain was dulled to a soft slap.

Rake followed up with a burst of power, a deeper shade almost ochre in color. Holt crossed his arms in front of himself as a poor shield, and when the light struck, this time it was a hammer blow that took him clean off his feet. On his back, staring up at the specks of light through the heavy canopy, Holt spluttered and the air left his chest. His rhythm of Floating stalled, then crumbled.

Rake appeared a moment later to offer him a hand.

Holt took his hand and got to his feet. "What was the need for that second attack?"

"To see just how strong the defense was, of course. I put a fair kick into that second one. It was no timid training move. A worthy discovery, this food of yours."

"I'd make you some if we had any lamb."

Rake gripped his shoulder and seemed to want to say something important. Instead, he grunted again and said, "I wouldn't have time for that." Then he stalked off to brood between the trees.

Aberanth emerged later that day with Rake's now fully repaired polearm between his teeth. Its wood was darker now and shone from the hardening treatment Aberanth had given it. For the first time since the ruins of Freiz, Rake genuinely smiled. He held his repaired weapon lightly for balance, placing two fingers just below where the hilt of the orange rider's blade fused into the wood. It did not so much as wobble. Still smiling, Rake twirled the blade, then spent some happy minutes testing it in every conceivable guard and form.

"You've made it longer," he observed.

I thought you could benefit from a greater reach," Aberanth said.

"Thank you," Rake said, and he meant it. He planted the butt of the polearm into the ground, and the tip of the orange blade now stood an impressive three feet above his already mighty seven-foot stature.

"That will help you go for Thrall's throat," Holt said.

Rake pressed his scaly brows together. "If he's there," he jibed. Then he kicked up his polearm and readied it for a fight. "Draw your sword, Holt Cook. You won't be idle, even here."

That evening, as the light died and Holt throbbed from a fierce training session, he allowed himself the luxury of preparing a slow-cooked meal. Without wandering too far from the grotto, he found thyme, garlic, and luckily a few wild onions. Aberanth kindly donated some of his mushrooms to the cause. Holt marveled at these; they were huge, thick, flat discs in shape and the yellow of thick cream. Even raw, their taste was immaculate, meaty, and velvety, as though the mushrooms had grown in a bed of butter-soaked soil. These he added to his cooking pot along with his foraged goods and diced venison.

Leaving it to brown, he turned to the wine. He sniffed it. A fire laced his nostrils and he coughed. The alcohol content must have been higher than normal, but most of that would burn off in the cooking. He poured in a generous helping to cover the venison and stirred it gently until the bulk of the wine had reduced to a thick syrup, and then he lifted the pot higher above the flames to let it simmer.

Both Ash and Eidolan lay dozing. Rake sat on a tree stump. His blue gaze seemed to look at everything and nothing at the same time.

Holt Cleansed Ash's core, stopping occasionally to stir the stew. Its meaty, wine-rich aroma began to fill the clearing above Aberanth's grotto, strong enough to bring even the emerald dragon up from his laboratory, nose first and sniffing.

"It's nearly done," Holt said. He scooped out a piece of meat to check it. The venison melted in his mouth. Dinner made, he offered a little to Eidolon and Aberanth to taste. Eidolan politely declined. Aberanth asked for a mushroom-only portion. Holt woke Ash last and gave him a full bowl. His small traveling pot could not hope to cook a portion large enough to satisfy a dragon, but Ash would relish every drop.

Finally, he dished up two final portions and took a bowl to Rake.

"A peace offering," he said as he handed it over. Rake took it in silence. "I know it's not lamb, but it'll be filling. And who knows, all that wine might help with your Lifting later, or something," he ended lamely.

After the first spoonful, Rake grunted and said, "Thank you, Holt. This is the best meal anyone has made me since... well, I can't remember."

Holt sat with him and ate his own stew. Though biased, he had to admit it was good. It had been ages since he'd had the time for such cooking, never mind the luxury of time to enjoy it. Across the glade, Ash licked his bowl clean. The dragon's delight at the venison flowed as hot as the food over their bond, and Holt tasted the stew doubly as Ash's pleasure melted into his own.

Rake finished and set his bowl down. Holt did the same.

"I'm sorry things changed," Holt said.

"No you're not," Rake said. "You got your way. Don't apologize for that. Wait until we see the results of it, and then tell me you're sorry."

"Talia made a good case."

Rake sighed. It seemed like he readied himself for an argument, but then he shook his head. "Please say you didn't do this all because it was her idea? I know you're soft on our Red Queen."

"I'm not," Holt said, far too fast.

"That can never be, you know."

Holt looked down, staring hard at the dregs in his bowl. "I know."

"It's not because of who she is," Rake said, speaking slow. "But of who you are."

"I'm aware I'm not high born, Rake."

"Not that," Rake said, sounding irritable now. "Holt, most people work their roles, marry, have children and try to lead a normal life. For most, that unwavering routine and that unwavering certainty – of where they are going and what they will be doing – provides so much security in their psyches that they believe it to be happiness. That's not you. I know that because that's not me. We few, *we unlucky few*, are too single-minded and exceptional for that. Our eyes are fixated on the mountaintops, are they not? Perhaps you might have been normal like that once, but not now. You couldn't have that sort of life with anyone, never mind a queen. You just... wouldn't be there for them and all the mundane obligations of their daily life."

"Master Rake," Ash said softly. *"Do you regret joining the Order?"*

Rake huffed and snapped his attention in Ash's direction as though startled. "Curse your ears, Ash," he said, and then he added in a croaked voice, "No. No I don't regret joining. That's the point. I could never have lived a normal life."

"Even if it might have been a happy one?" Holt asked.

"We have our bonds," Rake said. "That's a joy reserved only for a few." He leaned forward, planted his elbows on his knees, brought his hands together to form an arch and rested his chin upon them. "I wouldn't trade in my time with Elya for anything. And I won't be able to find a way to bring her back if Thrall destroys everything."

When he finished, a silence gripped the glade, interrupted only by the pop and crackle of the fire.

"There will be another day," Holt said at last. "Even if this doesn't work, we'll find him again." He stood and collected the bowls. "I am sorry, Rake. Maybe I'm not as exceptional as you thought."

"You're not," Rake said, terse. He growled low and turned his back on the group.

"He doesn't mean it," Ash said privately.

"No, he means it," Holt said.

Weary now, he collected the other dishes and took them down into Aberanth's grotto to wash up. When he finished, he returned to the surface to find Rake shrouded by the night and wearing his great cloak with the hood up. Holt ignored him and went to sit beside Ash, leaning into his dragon and feeling entirely not in the mood to Cleanse or Forge.

He lay there, giving himself a rare rest with a belly full of rich, warm food. He drifted to sleep but did not have a restful night. He tossed and turned and seemed permanently gripped in a state of half-sleep yet was unable to wake up.

In the cold blue light of early morning, he woke to a dull headache, a rare thing with his enhanced body. The dragons still slept, yet Rake no longer sat perched on his tree stump. In fact, there was no sign of Rake anywhere, nor did he reappear late into the morning or throughout the whole of the day.

Rake had gone.

FORTY-ONE

Three Chances

In a military camp at the southern end of the Red Range, only a day's march from the border with Brenin, Talia found herself once again with Harroway and his officers poring over maps. They conducted their work in an open pavilion, giving the men a chance to escape the late summer heat. While they sipped cool water taken from mountain streams, Talia drank cup after cup of spiced nairn root tea.

Raising the cup to her lips, she discovered to her dismay that it was empty. She blinked and rubbed fiercely at her eyes. The yellow face of the sun blazed painful light. Pyra slept, but Talia forced herself to remain awake. Each day ticked closer to the first day of autumn and she felt the need to act press upon her. She rubbed her eyes again, then squinted at the maps. Their neat thin lines and small text were beginning to blur together, mountains to forests and forests to seas. Wooden dragons, markers usually used for riders, stood scattered across Feorlen.

Two of Harroway's officers hastened to his side and entered a hurried, murmured conversation.

"Our queen," the Twinblades said.

Talia was delighted to find they had brought another steaming pot of tea and a small bowl of slender green chilies. "Thank you," she said, offering her cup for them to fill. She popped a whole chili into her mouth, and something about its fire bolstered her own. Her blood burned with a pleasant low heat and a tension left her mote channels.

Harroway's expression grew grave. He dismissed his two officers, then faced Talia.

"Would you like the ill news or the good?"

"I'll take the good," Talia said.

"We can eliminate one more location." He picked up a wooden dragon that stood within the Red Range itself. "We suspected it to be inaccessible by foot, the old reports suggested so. Supplies were taken as far as they could, but the riders themselves had to finish the journey somewhere high into the hills."

Their information was imperfect and rushed, cobbled together from old supply requisitions in the ledgers of past Masters of Coin and State. Talia had returned to Sidastra to demand the information and flown back with chests heavy with aging yellow papers and fraying parchment. The difficulty partly lay in the records not being clear for what purpose the riders made their demands, only that they had made them, and referring on occasion to villages and towns that no longer existed. And even once the area had been fathomed, each had to be scouted to check it was viable for a small army to march into.

They had now whittled their options down to three.

"Pyra and I can check this one," she said, indicating the location farthest from their camp. "By the time we return, horsemen should have made it back from the other two."

"You ought to rest a little," Harroway said. "Even a rider cannot go forever. When did you last sleep?"

Talia considered. Sometime just before they had returned to Falcaer. Five days ago, or thereabouts. She may also have dozed on Pyra's back, as dangerous as that had been.

"I managed to fight at Sidastra on little sleep." His look of concern was mortifying. Her fingers twitched treacherously, evidence of frailty and an excess of nairn root that she could not hide. Yet whether due to tiredness or a crumbling sense of pride, she let it wash over her. "What's the ill news?"

"Three new divisions of Risalian infantry have amassed outside of the Toll Pass."

Talia allowed this news to wash over her as well. It almost did not matter now. All that mattered was finding an entrance to this new chamber. Without that, without destroying the queen within, things would fall apart faster than she could grasp at the strings. In response to Harroway's news, she merely grunted an acknowledgment and took another fortifying gulp of tea.

"I can't remain here much longer," Harroway said.

"I know."

Before she could say more, a commotion of voices erupted at the edge of the pavilion. It turned out to be Ambassador Oddvar at the head of a party of Skarls. For a moment, Talia did not understand why he was here, then she saw who Oddvar fussed over.

Prince Aren, standing tall, broad, and strong.

With a small army to prepare, a chasm to open, and a Scourge Queen to kill, this was the last thing Talia wanted to deal with. Despite her insistence to Oddvar that the Skarls remain in Sidastra, it seemed her husband-to-be would not be satisfied with that.

"Let them in," Talia said wearily. "Let's get it over with," she added under her breath.

Harroway moved around the table to her side. "This is hardly the time," he said, equally low.

"What can I do? Lock them up?" She thrust her nairn root tea under his nose. "Have a sip if you're tired."

He eyed the goblet in disdain. "I should rather remain upright," he said, and indeed he cleared his throat and drew himself up, straight and true like the perfect soldier. No doubt he wished to make a good impression on the future king consort.

The Skarls approached, Prince Aren strutting at the head of his entourage of Housecarls and a cluster of beautiful serving girls. Oddvar trailed just behind him. She almost did not recognize Aren. His hair was dark for his family, and both his beard and braided tail of hair were shorter than the older men. He moved with a bullish confidence, his lips pressed together hard and his gaze single-minded.

Despite herself, Talia was impressed. Not just any young man could have marched so brazenly toward her. When he drew up before her, she discerned that the tattoo on one half of his forehead was a boar's head, surrounded by a web of lines that might have been many overlapping hour glasses.

"My Aldenei... is... ungood," he said with tortuous effort.

"My Skarl is also poor," Talia said.

Ambassador Oddvar came blustering up to Aren's side. "Forgive His Imperial Highness. I shall translate for him."

Barely allowing Oddvar a moment's breath, Aren burst into a speech as though rehearsed. Oddvar spoke over him, translating on the fly.

"I was filled with sorrow when you left the Silver Hall so soon, my queen. I would have danced with you until your legs grew weary."

"I assure you, your legs would have grown tired first," Talia said.

Oddvar translated. Aren made a stilted laugh, though it seemed nervous rather than forced. There was something in his eyes that screamed of youth, and though he was older than her at nineteen years old, Talia sensed she was speaking with a much younger soul.

"I am flattered that you have traveled so far and so quickly," she said, and Oddvar babbled a hasty translation. "But these lands are not safe, Prince Aren. The scourge rise across the border and may emerge here soon. You should return to the city, where you'll be safe."

A few seconds later, Oddvar finished translating and Aren exclaimed in evident disagreement.

"I would fight at your side and so win your heart. Strength can only love strength."

"What strength do you think can impress me?"

"There is talk of a scourge tunnel and battles with horrors in the deep places. Riders must brave these things. Soldiers must suffer these things. I choose to go with you. Allow me to wield my axe and sword in your name."

Talia looked imploringly to Oddvar. "You must convince him otherwise. Would the Empress be happy to know of this?"

"I have tried," Oddvar said. "But the Prince insists, and I have no power over him. To refuse would give great insult."

Talia bit her lip. She did not imagine Skadi would be happy to hear of her son's death in aid of Talia's brash plans.

Aren turned to his entourage, spoke low, and snapped his fingers. One of the maidens hurried forward, carrying a large bunch of purple flowers. Aren seized them as though grabbing an enemy by the throat and spun to present them to Talia. No two flowers of the bunch were of the same family of plants. One looked akin to a thistle, yet it was purple of stem as well as petal. He raised the bunch in a rush, and a hand fell on his arm to stay him.

Eadwulf's grip on the Skarl prince seemed firm. The twins had reappeared at her side, swift and silent as two shadows.

Aren grunted something but Talia did not need to wait for Oddvar's translation.

"It's just flowers, Eadwulf," she said gently. "If they sting me, I'll burn them."

The Twinblades drew back. Prince Aren seemed most put out that his moment had been stolen from him, but he proceeded, raising the flowers and gently tapping her face with them. First one cheek and then the other, as though knighting her. The Skarl maidens gushed in cries of joy, batted their eyelids, and beamed, seemingly delighted by this display. A few were plainly jealous.

"The Prince selected these himself on our journey from Smidgar," Oddvar said, as proud as if Aren were his own son. "It is a mark of deep affection, Your Majesty."

Aren lowered the flowers and Talia intuited that she was to take them. She did, feeling awkward and unsure what to do now the bunch was in her hand.

Aren spoke softly now, and Oddvar translated. "I am told that riders grow closer to their dragon through battle. It is my desire that we shall grow a bond in this way, as warriors. Together, unstoppable."

Talia searched those bright eyes. *Just a boy*, she thought. Had he even faced the scourge before or only heard the tales sung in the Silver Hall? She held his gaze, though she spoke to Oddvar.

"If he gets himself killed, the marriage and alliance will be in jeopardy. I can't risk that."

"Then I suggest you do your utmost to ensure he does not die, Your Majesty."

Talia's heat rose and the steel crown grew hot.

"Does the Prince not have guards of his own?" Harroway asked.

"A dozen Housecarls are with him," said Oddvar.

"Then I'll add a dozen more from my own household," said Harroway.

"And two of the finest warriors in Feorlen," Talia added. "Eadwald, Eadwulf." The twins came forward in synchronized steps. "He could ask for no finer guards, save a rider."

Oddvar explained and Aren looked appalled. He babbled in quick Skarl.

"The Prince asks for no special treatment," Oddvar said.

"The Prince will take this protection or he will not come at all," said Talia.

Aren bristled, his ego wounded. Likely the Skarls were unhappy to have Feorlens placed at their side, able to report what was happening as much as keep them safe. Yet Aren had the sense to relent. His acceptance of these terms was brusque and far removed from the charm he'd displayed to her with the flowers. When the Skarls departed along with the Twinblades, Talia realized she still held the bunch.

She sniffed them, enjoying their heavy aroma and the break from the smoke, sweat, and heat of camp life. Their petals reminded her of Pyra's scales.

"Send out riders, Drefan," she said. "We must find a way into this chamber."

She and Pyra journeyed to the furthest of the three entry sites, but despite searching high and low and enlisting the aid of the Emerald Flight, they could find no runic seal. Nature itself must have buried the place long ago. Another site down. With two to go, Talia began to fear that neither of them would work either. By the time they returned to camp it was the middle of the night, and there was nothing she could now do to keep her eyes open.

In her dreams, her fear became real. A chasm broke wide in Brenin. Uncle Roland's capital burned. Risalians poured over the border, marching in perfect black-uniformed columns. Her people burned, screamed for her, asked her why it had to be this way.

Her councilors pointed accusatory fingers. Pyra lay on a field of corpses with ballista bolts in her belly. A hole grew in Talia's chest where the fire used to be, now ice cold. Empty. A shrill scream rang from a green orb in the dark.

Talia raged and cried but no one would hear her until a blistering hot hand forced her to turn. Paragon Adaskar looked weary but stern and told her that these were the consequences of her own selfish actions.

"Did you think taking the crown could undo your father's and brother's deaths?"

When she could not answer, he pushed her away into the arms of her uncle. Sobbing, she dropped to the ground. Osric let her heaving breaths come to a shuddering halt, then offered her a silent hand. She took it, and he led her off into the night.

When Talia woke it was with a gasp. No light seeped in from the tent fold. It was still the middle of the night.

"How long was I out?" she asked Pyra.

"Barely two hours."

Talia clutched at her head. The pain confirmed the lack of sleep.

"Stay in bed," Pyra said.

"I can't, girl." Cold sweat clung to her. She shivered. What she wanted was warmth.

Talia dressed lightly, forgoing the trouble of fastening on her brigandine, and left her tent. The camp was eerily quiet, with no wind nor sound save the rustle of mail from a patrolling soldier or the heavy flicker of naked flames.

Two servants of the palace hastened to her. She bid them fetch her hot water, no tea this time, and fuel for three braziers. She then went to Pyra, arranged the braziers in a triangle around the dragon, and lit them. Steam rose from a jug of water placed beside her, and the first drink felt hot and cleansing.

She crossed her legs on the grass and attempted to clear her thoughts. Dense smoke obscured Pyra's core. Talia began to Cleanse. Yet try as she might, she could not focus her own mind on the task. A choking haze of clouded thought plagued her. The hot water could not wash her mind clean. Each rattling breath she blew shook those fears and doubts and anxieties from one to the next.

Skadi loomed over her while her sons in the guise of crooked imps danced at their mother's feet. "It seems you are the sheep now," Skadi scorned.

"*Talia,*" Pyra's voice brought her back. "*You slipped off to sleep again.*"

Talia gulped a breath and opened her eyes. She was still sitting on the ground. The only difference was that Pyra had shuffled closer.

"I'm sorry," she said groggily. "I'll get back to work."

"*I thought your nightmares had ended?*"

"You knew about those?"

"*Sometimes, when you sleep, a feeling of panic and pain comes from you. But that hasn't happened in a while.*"

"They did stop, briefly."

"*What happens in them?*"

"Lots of things," Talia said. "Confusing things. They're just bad dreams, Pyra. No need to worry."

She rumbled. "*I should worry. I want to worry.*"

"Worry is our mind tormenting us. It does us no good."

"*Holt's words have lain heavy on my heart since we parted,*" Pyra said. "*We have total trust in battle. We trust in each other's capabilities. That was Holt and Ash's problem. Ours lie off the battlefield, in our worries.*"

"What are you saying, girl?" Talia said, speaking telepathically. "*That you want to talk openly about things now? You hate weakness.*"

Pyra huffed and rustled her wings. "*Most dragons do,*" she said defensively. "*But you should never have felt you could not speak with me.*"

"That's not fair," Talia said. "*You could not stand to feel it when my father died, when Leofric died, when Brode died, even when Ghel fell in the—*"

"*It hurt,*" Pyra said, sounding oddly young and frightened for the first time since, well, Talia could not remember when. "*You were in such pain, and even the echo of that pain across our bond was unbearable. It hurt all the more knowing how much you suffered and that there was nothing I could do. Fire should not feel pain. Fire causes it.*"

"*I'm not a fire dragon. I was only human before we bonded.*"

"*Looking back, I do not think I fully understood what that meant until I felt your fears. Blood memories are very... selective.*"

"*Do you wish I was stronger?*"

"*Sometimes,*" Pyra admitted. "*Do you wish that I was... more like Ash?*"

"*I want you to be you,*" Talia said. "*At any rate, ice dragons are known to have cold hearts. You feel, girl, you're just... too ashamed to show it.*"

"*I told you that I was drawn to you because I sensed we would do great things. I wanted to remain in the Order, I wanted a rider to build a powerful core, I wanted to destroy scourge, become a legend in the song of the Fire Flight. I saw only the battle and glory. I did not understand what a bond with a human would truly mean. You have changed me, Talia.*"

"And you me," Talia said aloud. "The dragon flows into the human, after all. Soldiers rely on one another. Riders will trust each other in a battle too. I'd like to think we're more than just sisters in arms, Pyra. Aren't we friends?"

Pyra lowered her head so that the tip of her snout lay in Talia's lap. "*We're family.*"

Talia stroked Pyra's snout, and the beat of their bond settled into a steady rhythm. Some of Talia's jumbled thoughts smoothed out, still there yet not as loud as before. After some time, she returned to Cleansing, and it felt easier now.

Hours later came the dawn. Despite her aching head and eyes, despite the weight bearing down upon her, Talia felt remarkably at ease. Far calmer than when she had awoken from her nightmares. A pale blue sky blotched with pink hung over the world. Pyra snored peacefully, and her dragon song reflected that with notes of a softly plucked lute.

Then came a haunting, whistling note. Pyra's song did not have such notes, and then Talia realized the music registered in her ears rather than through the bond. She stood. Her legs shook from fatigue. The music drifted in from outside the pavilion, ethereal and quiet in its beauty. She'd only heard such notes once before in the corridors of the Silver Hall, a ballad known to her deeper than her conscious mind could conjure, something on the distant edge of memory. Talia walked toward it half in a dream, passing stirring guards and servants.

The music moved and Talia followed its sound, yet ever the musician remained elusive at the edge of sight. Near the eastern perimeter, she saw him. A distant figure with a lute. He had a feather cap upon his head. No sooner had she glimpsed him than he sprang away and down an embankment, still playing all the while. Talia followed, leaving the camp and coming to the bank of a swift-flowing stream. The bard stood, eyes closed, with a lute sheathed on his back like a rider's blade. The haunting melody came from the panpipe around his neck.

Somehow, Talia was not shocked to see the bard from the feast in the Silver Hall. The feathered cap hid his knot of hair, yet the neat beard remained the same, and his clothes were just as poor – a tattered shirt under a rough-spun coat and worn cloak. He played a final long and somber note at her arrival.

"My Queen of Fire, your beauty does not burn so bright this morning."

Talia was sure she looked gray, her eyes raw and her skin puffy.

"Were you playing that same song in the Silver Hall?"

"I might have been," he said. "A few others know this song, though Prince Fynn, he likes the way I play it best."

"Prince Fynn? I'm afraid I never got a chance to meet him."

The bard shrugged. "They say he is poor company."

"And why is that? His own mother said much the same."

As the bard considered, he played a few notes on his pipe. "I know only that the song you heard relates to him."

"Would you play it again for me?" Somehow, she did not feel foolish in asking.

"Alas," he said, with disappointment bordering on the dramatic.

"That you overheard my playing cannot be helped, but in my homeland, it is forbidden to sing or play or speak poetry to a maiden."

"You Skarls have strange customs."

"Not so strange, I think. It is known that songs can seduce and
bind a maiden, for in them lies power."

"It's only words and music."

"I am told that a dragon's magic is a form of song. My sad song
brought you here, did it not?" He twisted on the straps of his lute,
pulling it around to his front, ready to play. "What does a fire song
sound like, I wonder?" He played several strong chords, then ceased
abruptly and gave a dismissive wave of his hand. "No, nothing so
crude as that."

He experimented a little more. Abashed, Talia stepped to the
stream and splashed cold water onto her face.

"You told me at the feast that any bard worth their dinner knows
much more than they should."

He doffed his feather cap to her.

"You must have been around my camp for some time now," she
said. "Tell me, what is said of me?"

"I've heard talk that the Red Queen is mad. I've heard men say that
the Red Queen will get them all killed. I've heard much, as I always
do. The truth is hard to know, but much like creating a new song, you
know it's right when you hear it."

Talia was unsure what she'd wanted to hear. She could not say why
she remained here, only that there was something tranquil about the
sound of running water and an aloofness to the bard she found calming. Everyone else revealed themselves to her almost at once; they
made demands of her, needed her, sought to use or destroy her, but
the bard seemed content to be reserved.

"And what is said of Prince Aren in his homeland?"

The bard plucked his strings again before answering. "You recall
that tale you heard in the Silver Hall? About Empress Skadi and how
she chose her husband."

"By looking at their feet," Talia said, wondering where this was going. "She chose the man with the smallest feet, taking him to be smarter."

"A charitable interpretation," he said with a wicked grin. "I know a truer version of this tale. Skadi chose the smallest man because she thought him easier to control. He was."

"Prince Aren has rather large feet."

"As is his need for his mother's approval," said the bard. "Or so they say in Smidgar."

"So they say," Talia echoed. She studied his eyes. There was no lie in him, yet some half-truth shrouded him still. His assessment of Aren was at least in line with Talia's own impression. Given how keen the Empress was to push Aren onto her and how her youngest son was the maternal crack in her otherwise granite armor. For all intents and purposes, marrying Aren would be marrying Skadi herself. She had no choice, but it was good to know what she would be getting into.

"You have many cares, Red Queen."

"More than some," Talia said. "Less than others."

He smiled at that. "You might write a good song with such to and fro. If it's of any comfort, I have also heard that Prince Aren will give you his heart."

"Because he's told to?"

"Yes," the bard admitted, "but he is serious in his duty, and so he will. He travels with maidens, but they are only for show. Beneath the coarse black hair, he is a romantic at heart. Why, he has even vowed to ink a dragon onto his head to join the boar when you are wed. He will be devoted, no doubt, in his own way. Is this what you want?"

The comfortable ground Talia had been upon wobbled. "I don't want—" she began, then managed to control herself. Anything she said to this bard could be in lyrics and moving between the lips of her soldiers and the Skarls alike by dusk. Nothing could be allowed to undermine the marriage alliance, least of all her mouthing off to this perfect stranger. If any song were to be sung, she'd rather it be a different one.

"What I want," she started carefully, "is that there be no war, that all humanity come together to face the scourge, and that we might have a world free of the blight."

"Spoken like any leader hiding their true desires."

She frowned. "You're impertinent, bard."

"Ah," he said, playing soothing notes, "I seem to have struck a chord."

"Fine," Talia said, sourly. "Before I was a queen, I was a dragon rider. No matter what anyone says I am now, I am still bonded to my dragon. And while I am, what I want is to be with her, to train with her, to grow with her, as any dragon rider should. Anyone who wishes to marry me should know that."

The bard ceased playing and gave her an appraising look. Talia wondered if he'd heard his truth, then his gaze drifted up over her head. Talia turned to follow his gaze and saw the Twinblades atop the embankment, looking down at her.

"Our queen," they called, then they negotiated the slope to join her.

"You were missed at breakfast," Eadwald said.

"There was concern for you," said Eadwulf.

"I can take care of myself," Talia said, both irked and impressed at how hard it was to shake them. "You should not have left your place by Prince Aren's side."

"You are our queen," they said, as though this satisfied.

"Right now, little is more important to the survival of Feorlen than this alliance," Talia said. She threw the bard a look, wary that he was still present, and chose her words with care. "Prince Aren has bravely chosen to join our expedition and fight by my side. He must be defended at all costs. Do you understand?"

"We do," said the twins.

"Very well," Talia said, "but this cannot be the only reason you have sought me?"

"The Master of War has need of you," they said.

Talia glanced back for the bard before leaving but he had vanished again, just like he had in the Silver Hall.

Back at the command tent, there was a bustle of activity. Servants, officers, and soldiers alike were bringing packed goods out of Harroway's tent. Drefan himself was assisting with the packing, making ready his own clothes, armor and bedding out of engrained habit. He asked everyone to leave, and Talia bid the Twinblades return to Aren.

Once they were alone, Harroway told her the bad news. A contingent of Athran's elite cavalry had now joined the massing Risalian infantry. Worse, Turro the emerald brought word from one of the remaining two tunnel locations. Unfortunately, this place would not do either for it was in a small gully, and Turro sensed a sheer drop of over fifty feet below the seal. Stingers and carriers might have crawled or flown up from it in ages past, but it was no place to march an army toward.

That left only one location.

"We should pack up and march at once," Talia told Harroway.

"And if it isn't suitable either?" he asked.

"Then I'll be out of time to help Holt and Ash," she said. "But otherwise, all I can do is keep searching the records. There could be other locations."

Harroway looked doubtful. "We combed that material thoroughly, going back three hundred years."

"Giving up isn't an option. Even if I must wait for a new chasm to erupt in Brenin itself or here, the queen has to be dealt with. The alternative is—" She stopped. She couldn't say it.

"War is coming," Harroway said. "Faster than we thought. I understand that the notion of turning your power onto fellow humans must be disturbing."

Talia could not meet him square in the eye. "I don't know if I could do that."

Harroway's lips became a severe line. At length, he said, "I must head north. I'll be of little help above ground this time, there are no scourge nearby. And should Risalia—"

"There is no need to explain, Drefan. I would much rather my Master of War helmed the defense of the realm. Go, though I am sorry to see you leave. I've grown fond of your company."

"The company of a prince ought to make up for the loss."

"Skarls," Talia scoffed. "Perhaps I should have married you, Drefan. It would have been easier."

"Truth is, I was rather relieved that notion fell through," Harroway said. He looked down, suddenly fascinated with his toes. "It would, of course, have been advantageous to our family, but not for me on a—on a *personal* level."

"You could always have refused."

"Refuse?" Harroway said, incredulous. "My family would have roasted me alive. Only a fool would turn down such an opportunity. But things have worked out for the best, I think, at least in that regard. It would have been a loveless affair." He hesitated then added, "I'm not *interested* in you in that way."

To her surprise, Talia blushed and pushed her hair back behind her ear. "Naturally. Our age gap—"

"I'm not interested in any woman in *that* way."

"Oh," Talia said, taken aback. "Oh," she said again, rather stupidly. She nodded. "No one told me of your… preferences."

"Few know," he said, looking at his toes again. "Not even Cousin Elvina. Very traditional."

"How could you know I'm not as well?"

He found the courage to raise his head and look her in the eye again. "You don't seem a stickler for the norms. Oath breaker."

She might have been, not so long ago. Since then, too much had happened to care about something so intimate. The taboo on the issue had more to do with encouraging marriages and keeping the birthrate high in the face of the scourge. She hoped no one would think less of him for it, yet all the same it would be better to keep it a secret.

A thought struck her. "This is why you so doggedly fought against investigations into your house? Into you? I suppose getting rid of the twins was for the same reason?"

"You've seen how they cling at you like limpets," he said. "Sneaking off quietly for a private meeting would be impossible. They track you down like bloodhounds."

Well, that was true enough.

"And you value your privacy," Talia said, repeating what he'd told her months ago. "You could have told me, Drefan."

"I didn't know you then."

"Well, I'm honored that you trust me enough to share this now."

He gave her a small smile. "It appears I do."

"Even after I've been selfish?" Talia said. "If I submitted to the Paragons, this could all be over. Instead, it seems I'm dragging us back into a war... one we cannot win." She wanted to go on, but it was so hard to admit her fears. Then again, how would she ever grow as close to Pyra as she needed to advance if she could not even admit what was so plain to another person?

"Can I trust you in return, Drefan?"

"Of course," he said, and he took her hand in his and squeezed.

"I'm afraid I've made a huge mistake," she said. "I worry about that all the time. I fear I can't do this and that we'll all suffer for my decision. I'm so overwhelmed I can barely sleep, and when I do, nightmares haunt me. All that keeps me going is the next clear objective. I liked that about being a rider. A simple goal. A fight with an end point."

"Your choice may well end us all," he admitted. "But you know that. I thought you had made the wrong choice too. I wanted to be Master of War because I thought you needed to be reined in. A part of me hoped that your expedition would fail or else prove disastrous and so no such thing would have to be endured again. I was wrong. The council was wrong to banish Holt and his dragon. I believe in your goal now, Talia. Taking the fight directly to the scourge, rather than cower and wait and die as we always have. Defenders of a fort can only last if the assault is at some point broken. If the rest of the world are too stubborn to see that, if they crush us and push Feorlen into the Sunset Sea, then maybe the scourge deserves to win."

Talia hugged him before she realized what she was doing. Her strength nearly toppled him, but she kept the pair of them upright. She sniffed, and with her face planted in the crook of his shoulder she said, "Thank you."

He patted her back gingerly. "I'm sorry for my stunt at your coronation. It was the only move I saw for myself at the time."

"You're forgiven," Talia said. She parted from him. "Now go keep our home safe."

"And you keep Prince Aren safe. At least he's pleasant to look at." Then he snapped his feet together, placed his hands behind his back and bowed low. "My queen," he said solemnly.

Talia left him to his packing but spared no time in ordering the division to break camp and be ready to march for as long as the light still held. This they did, and they had barely traveled one league when the West Warden flew into telepathy range. With the aid of human scouts, they'd found the final location.

A ravine far easier to access than the chasm in the Withering Woods, with the seal of the riders clear on the rock face for those with the power to see it. A viable entry point. Her second expedition could go ahead.

FORTY-TWO

The Dragon's Den

Rake pulled his heavy cloak about himself, securing it at the nape of his neck and drawing up the hood. Vials of elixirs clinked as he adjusted it, secured in the layered lining and pockets of the cloak.

From between the trees, he looked at the fortress of Windshear, imposing even in its ruined state. Thick walls loomed hundreds of feet above him on an impenetrable bed of stone. The storm tower at the southeastern corner of the fortress rose so high he had to crane his neck to see the top of it. To his right, the sheer base of the mountainside rose sharply upward to dwarf the eastern wall of the fortress.

In the old days, the riders kept a vast no man's land between the bedrock and the edge of the Fae Forest. Yet now the forest ran wild and unchecked save for a space under the western wall, making it obvious where the door to the servants' stair must be.

Rake, however, would not be taking the stairs.

A dragon passed above, gliding to the south. Some emerald of low power. Well, low compared to him, though the fewer dragons of any sort at Windshear the better. Ten drakes had supported the raid on the mystic nests, yet only five remained. Two riders were inside the fortress as well – both Champions, one Low and one closer to Farsa in power. Whoever they were, they might prove bothersome. Although if this was Dahaka, Rake had the notion to kill her too while he was inside. Farsa and Hava might learn then to act, and if they never forgave him for it, so be it.

The whole venture had been flawed from the start. Always he had worked alone, and for good reason. Better and easier this way. In the end, all he had was his own strength, cunning, and wits. He'd gotten Elya and himself into this mess and only he could get them out of it.

A painful beat issued from his soul. Rake placed a hand over his chest.

I did not give up on the boy, Rake thought.

The pain beat for a second time, more insistent. His fingers clenched, and his sharp talon nails broke the surface of his scales.

He's the one who gave up. On me and himself. Ash did too.

For a moment, Rake swore he heard a rasping cry from the depths of his cursed soul, although the wind had also just picked up in a howl.

We'll find some other way, he promised his dragon. Another twist of pain, and then Elya left him alone. Rake gasped. A dribble of blood ran from where he'd dug into his own scales. These soul pains had been there from the beginning, yet he could no longer deceive himself that they were the same as before. In recent years they had grown worse and showed no sign of easing. He chalked the most recent bouts up to the stress of what lay before him. Elya had always been anxious before a mission. Once Thrall was dead, he would have time to recenter.

Tonight. He should have done this months ago.

Leaving the tree line, Rake ran for the mountainside east of Windshear. He placed the shaft of his polearm between his teeth and locked his jaw in place.

Then he began to climb.

To call the mountainside treacherous would be like calling Thrall a minor inconvenience. The wind ripped through the narrow causeway between mountain and fortress, attacking him the whole way up as though enchanted to sweep interlopers away. Yet grasp by grasp, and with a constant drive from his legs, he made it to the overhang.

This shelf of rock protruded like a nose. Its upper side would work as a platform from which to make his next move, but on either side the mountain smoothed out as though polished, leaving no hand or foothold to approach. Only the underside was navigable, and so Rake carried on until he hung parallel to the ground. His tail worked doubly hard to enable him to keep his balance until, with relief, his grasping hand found the edge of the overhang and he pulled himself up.

The easy part was over.

He stood now upon a ledge high above the eastern wall of Windshear. Peering down, the ramparts looked like toy blocks. Very old and battered blocks. Time had eaten away at the walls. At two points, the tops of the ramparts were connected only by wooden planks. No one patrolled them. All activity in Windshear seemed clustered on the western side of the fortress, between the mystic and ice towers. There tiny torches and braziers flickered, barely staying lit under the relentless wind of the region.

Having got his bearings, he readied himself for the second, more dangerous part. The first, of course, would be attacking Thrall.

Rake began by Grounding his body. Tonight, the wind pushed in hard from the north, and over the distance he would be falling that could well nudge him off course. Everything had to be exact, and so he adjusted accordingly and turned toward the storm tower at the northeastern corner of Windshear. Failure would mean ending his long life as a splat of scales and bones. Not even an Elder dragon would survive such a fall.

Even Rake knew when an idea was mad. Flying in would have been so much simpler and elegant, and he'd enjoyed envisioning the brazenness of storming into Thrall's tower.

Oh well, he thought. *Needs must.*

Rake leaped. The distance between the ledge and the wall was too great to make in a conventional jump. He relied now on the trajectory of his fall, his estimation of the power of the wind, and a healthy sprinkling of luck. As he fell, the force of the wind shifted his direction so that he was blown backward toward the rampart rather than away from the parapet entirely. Landing this way would still shatter virtually every bone in his body, and his legs for certain.

He readied himself to Blink. Elya's affinity with mystic energy had always given him an edge when maneuvering around a battlefield. This technique was something he could never fully explain. All instinct and some raw connection to the arcane. His old master had called it a teleport, yet it was not quite so miraculous. Rake would be propelled in the direction he faced with body and vision, meaning forward and only forward, until he reached an obstacle. Blink into something solid, say, for example, a giant wall of an ancient dragon rider fortress, and the wall would win. Even hitting something much smaller, such as a mad axeman named Osric, and the impact would damage Rake as much as whoever he hit. Blink was nonetheless lethal in battle. If timed carefully, directed surgically, he could close distances, zip behind a foe in a flash, feint with ease, or else make a tactical retreat. Such a technique taxed the body greatly, however, even with his large, well-matured mote channels. After using it, he could not Blink again for at least thirty seconds.

Which meant, of course, as he fell toward the gray stone rampart, if he mistimed his Blink even by a hair, he'd either die instantly or fall to his doom, unable to Blink again.

The wind howled. His cloak flapped around his feet, and his tail, so useful for climbing, trailed out as dead weight behind him. The top of the wall rushed up to meet him.

Rake crested the parapet. His feet were moments away from crunching into the stone when he twisted left to face along the straight stretch of the wall and Blinked.

The world behind him seemed to clamp down hard, compressing and pinching his whole body as though it were the pincer of an emperor crab. Rake shot forward, just over twenty feet in an instant, his momentum changed. He flung his hands out, intending to roll, and threw up a hasty Barrier, spinning a buffer shield of mystic energy which cushioned the impact. His hands touched the cold stone and he rolled forward.

Even with all these measures, the roll was messy, sending him head over tail several times before he skidded to a stop. Sprawled out, it took every fiber of his being to resist the urge to groan. He clambered upright, picked up his fallen polearm, and checked for anyone coming. So far, so good. No one could have expected an intruder on the eastern wall by foot. The trouble now was that the mystic tower was as far away as possible. All of Windshear lay between him and the tower and thus Thrall.

Rake could sense him. His power had recovered by an order of magnitude that should have been impossible, yet more terrifying was how much of his core's boundaries were still to be filled. Were it a deep bathtub, then Osric had managed to refill it with several cups of water. At full strength, Thrall would rival an Elder's power.

Rake could not wrap his mind around it. Such power in a comparatively young dragon could not be possible. The Elders were a breed apart, their songs pieces from the music of creation. If only things were different. Rake could have learned so much from him.

Remaining outside any longer seemed a needless risk. Rake channeled mystic energy to the soles of his feet. This made running more awkward, like running with plump pillows lashed to his feet, but it muffled his footsteps.

Quick as he could, he dashed down the wall, heading for the emerald tower. The disrepair of the wall became clearer as he ran. Deeply entrenched vines covered segments of the wall from base to top, their roots eating deep into the mortar. Not far from the door to the emerald tower, Rake's foot gave way beneath him. A section of the stone crumbled, beginning a small cascade which ended in a boulder crashing down into the forges below.

So much for muffling his steps.

Cursing, Rake canceled the muffling effect and sprinted for the door. He entered the emerald tower, taking great pains not to allow it to slam shut behind him. But the damage was done. Two cores for two dragons were heading to the southeastern corner of the fortress. At least with the tower abandoned he could move through it unrestricted, heading for the southern wall connecting to the mystic tower.

He halted with a hand upon the door. The dragons were circling, but whether they were right outside or up at the roof, Rake could not say. Tracking the movement of dragons via their cores was accurate on a broad scale, but at the micro level it was a poor way to know where an enemy was. The magical senses failed to detect important elements such as the layout of a fortress.

All of this meant that Rake had no true idea of what he would find on the other side of the door. Yet he had to move. Wyrm Cloaks would doubtless head over to inspect the damage of the debris and then climb up to check on the wall itself.

The dragons outside the tower were fire and storm. No need to protect his mind then. Rake Floated his mote channels, creating a flawless second skin to ward against hasty magic. He drank a Floating elixir for good measure and almost spat from the taste. He hated ginger.

Rake opened the door. A dark storm dragon hovered directly over-head. For a moment they locked eyes, then Rake ran. The dragon roared and bolts of lightning rained upon the wall. With his magical defenses at peak capacity and the drake being lowly enough, Rake let two bolts hit him. They stung like giant bees but rebounded off his defenses. More stone crunched and crashed behind him.

Rake ran, making the most of each second of the storm dragon's shock. No muffling now, he just pumped his legs as fast as they could go. Every core in Windshear suddenly bloomed to life, including Thrall's.

The fire drake soared in on his right. Still running, Rake raised a Barrier on that side, absorbing the brunt of the flames. He was two-thirds of the way along the southern wall when the storm drake and now a mystic added fresh attacks to their fiery comrade's.

Knowing his weak Barrier was about to give out, Rake stopped, turned to face the three dragons, and pulled on a greater volume of motes to strengthen the ability. He spun his polearm in a wide circle in front of him, a motion which aided the speed of his swirling mystic power, reinforcing the shield. Such a shield could block the power of a Lightning Lord like Clesh, but it slowed him almost to a crawl.

Maintaining his Barrier as best he could, Rake inched backward toward the mystic tower. Under the barrage, holes ripped open in his Barrier and sparks of his enemies' power jumped through the gaps to sting him. Two more drakes would soon be upon him. Ideally, he would have been closer to the mystic tower, but he was out of time.

Diverting motes to his legs, Rake kicked back from where he stood. As his foot bounced on the stone, orange power blew out from him – a diverting blast which would have staggered nearby foes – but the full effect of his Disengage ability launched him back in a far-reaching backflip. The flames, arcane power, and lightning of the three wild dragons blasted onto the stone where he'd been standing a moment before.

Rake landed, turned elegantly, and Blinked the remaining distance to the tower's door. Lowering his shoulder, he smashed through it and made for the descending flight of stairs. Heat licked the back of his head, but the fire dragon belched its power in vain. Inside, he was at least protected from the wild dragons.

The stairs wrapped around the tower at its edges, forming a steady incline. Rake raced down, his great strides forcing him to leap multiple steps at a time, heedless of what lay behind him. Cultists most like, and what threat were they? One jumped out of his way, and Rake did not waste the time to kill him.

His attention was on Lifting his mote channels and trying to gauge where the riders were. All activity was centering beneath him, inside Thrall's hatchery. All they had to do was slow him down. Delay him, slow him, come at him from all sides and overwhelm him.

Having to cross the whole fortress had allowed this. Striking into the tower quickly would have prevented a coherent response.

The stairs leveled out as he reached the second floor. Around the bend, he found the great doors to the largest of the hatcheries. And attempting to block the door were three cultists with violet cloaks stretched over hulking bodies. Rake snarled in disgust. He'd never seen three uglier faces in all his life. Their eyes were beady, stupid things wedged into hog-like faces. They bellowed loud enough to compensate and charged at him.

Unfortunately, the three of them were not in a nice neat line. Had they been, then a single sweeping Soul Blade could have cut them all down. As it was, Rake funneled magic down the shaft of his polearm to gather upon his blade until it shone as though coated with oil. The closest Wyrm Cloak was still well out of reach but Rake thrust forward as if to spear him anyway. Across the distance, a projection of his attack appeared as a hardened orange spear tip which drove into the unsuspecting cultist's chest.

One down.

Rake's glassy blade smoked from the ability, and he had no hope of performing it again before the other two closed the distance. Neither seemed aware that their comrade had fallen. Rake stepped to meet them, thrusting forward for real this time, but the first brute dodged then grabbed onto the shaft of the weapon. The cultist yanked, and Rake found himself fighting a brief tug of war. The second brute, rather than try to attack him outright, seized the shaft of the polearm as well. Were they truly stupid or just ill-trained? What caught him off guard was just how ferociously strong they were. They heaved with dragon-like strength, pulling Rake's polearm out of his grasp and him inexorably forward.

Rake stumbled. A meaty fist connected with his jaw. A second slammed into his kidney. Most unsportingly, a heavy foot slammed onto his tail. Rake howled at that, looked for his weapon, and found it flung out of easy reach. Fine. He'd do it with his fists, then. The brutes had taken him by surprise, but they had not anticipated one thing.

Rake had claws.

He slashed. Blood flew. Narrowly he missed a face, then found his arms pinned from behind. The other pounded a fist into his stomach, then made a clumsy movement toward the fallen polearm. Rake swept his head back against the cultist holding him. A nose cracked, then Rake tripped the brute using his tail.

The bleeding cultist returned brandishing Rake's own polearm, though it was clear he did not know how to wield one. Rake dodged then raced in close to repay the cultist in kind, driving his claws into the swine's stomach. He ripped his way free. Guts sloshed wetly to the floor. The cultist bent over double, dying, and Rake helped him on his way by seizing his head and smashing the ugly pig face against his knee.

He snatched the polearm out of the dead man's grip, turned lithely and threw it like a javelin. It pierced the third cultist right through the dragonhide cloak, through muscle and bone like a ballista bolt, driving him back against the wall where the orange blade buried itself into the wall.

Growling, Rake leaped over and withdrew his weapon. The Wyrm Cloak slumped to the floor. All three were dead, but they had done their duty. Though the fight had been brief, they had slowed him down. Worse, they had interrupted his Lifting. Countless cultists were approaching from above and below now. With no time to spare, Rake cycled his energy up to his mind and swallowed no fewer than four Lifting elixirs.

Blood and magic rushed to his head, and for a moment he feared he would become too dizzy to fight. Colors flashed in his vision, his tail swung out of his control, he endured a sickening sensation of being disembodied and leaving his scales behind. A violent shake of his head ended in a piercing crack, as though the vertebrae at the base of his skull had snapped into place. The dizziness vanished, but the multiplicative Lifting effect remained.

Rake wrenched open the hatchery door.

His assessment of what he would find inside had not been far wrong. Closest to him was the Low Emerald Champion with a leaf-shaped green blade and a white beard hiding his face. Behind him, his verdant dragon. Next the Exalted Fire Champion. Dark hair, dark skin, dark eyes, she was clearly from Ahar. Dahaka then, and the dragon red as burning coals must be Zahak. Osric stood at the far end of the hatchery near the opening to the night beyond.

And to Thrall. The mighty mystic had retreated outside the hatchery, sending his servants in to deal with Rake. Had others come with him, stuck to his plan, Hava and Farsa could have trapped Thrall inside. Were magical senses more accurate, Rake might have known his target hovered just outside and so he would have run up the tower rather than down and launched himself from some higher nest above.

So be it, he thought again. With so much magic pulsing around his head, his mind worked quicker than ever, crunching through his limited options. He had a core which was really two cores overlapping, not as strong as two but greater than one. A core which he had nurtured into a lake of power over centuries. All of which he was prepared to spend.

A route to victory took shape. He let his cloak fall away. It would only drag him down.

Rake set to work.

He began with the Low Champion, hitting him with a strong stream of raw mystic power. The emerald rider deflected it with his blade, but it drove him aside, and Rake charged forward. The rider's dragon unleashed no magic against him. Their affinity must have been in living things, not earth and rock. A small stroke of good luck then, for the emerald resorted to leaping at him, jaws wide like a viper. Rake slid under the dragon and raised a Barrier. The emerald's spiked tail struck the Barrier but could not break through. Letting magic flow throughout his body for strength and agility, Rake flicked himself up onto his feet and was running before the emerald could turn.

Thrall's attack against his mind arrived at that moment like a payload from a trebuchet. Not only was the dragon formidable in the raw power of his telepathic assault, but he shaped that power into key surgical strikes, as an assassin slips a knife between rib bones. Rake's defenses trembled but held.

Dahaka moved in. Before she got too close, Rake unleashed a flurry of Soul Blades against her. Hardened arcane energy appeared, slicing through the air before her, forcing her to pivot, block, and otherwise avoid them. Rake passed her by.

Zahak breathed fire toward him. Rake threw up a Barrier, yelling from the effort as his core drained to maintain it. The effort to ward off Thrall while dealing with his underlings was as intense a test as he'd ever faced. Knowing Dahaka would be close, and the emeralds right behind her, Rake powered forward, his Barrier wilting under Zahak's heat.

His speed brought him to Zahak's unguarded body and Rake could have skewered him, but that would waste precious seconds. He intended to jump, but then something screaming hot lashed around his foot. Rake roared. A fiery whip issued from Dahaka's left hand, its forked tongue wrapped around his leg. She used that to pull herself in a magic-induced leap toward him, sword ready to guard against more of his Soul Blades.

Things almost unraveled right there. They may well have done had Thrall's mental assault not ceased. Hidden behind Zahak's body, Rake had broken line of sight with the self-proclaimed Sovereign. Was that enough? However it had come about, the respite from Thrall's attack gave Rake a chance.

He readied energy at his feet, and as Dahaka landed he let the power go, kicking back into a Disengage. The blast wave staggered Dahaka, and the backflip took him up over Zahak's back. His snout missed the tip of Zahak's longest bone ridge by a hair.

Rake landed in a crouch, turned, and sprang back toward his charge. Thrall's mental attack resumed at once, confirming that line of sight was important.

Osric stood between him and Thrall, his head lowered like a bull. Black light pulsed around the axe blades. Rake did not relish the thought of suffering from those madness-inducing cuts, nor of even engaging the man in a fight. He was too good. Fortunately, he was near the opening of the hatchery now. Thrall beat his wings heavily, far from the edge. Rather than get bogged down fighting Osric, Rake kicked off the floor as hard as he could, launching himself high again.

Below, Osric bent his knees, perhaps intending to jump and clash with him in the air. Rake gave him no chance. First, he drew back his arm, ready for a strong thrust with his polearm. Then he emptied the majority of his core into the most powerful Blink he had ever dared.

The technique usually propelled him twenty yards forward. This was taxing enough on his mote channels and body. To propel himself further by even a few yards cost him exponentially more magic and left his body unable to handle another Blink for even longer relative to the distance. Rake had perfected the art of the short burst use of the ability, yet as his world focused on Thrall, as his mind buffeted under the dragon's renewed assault, Rake threw almost everything he had into his great gamble.

Two hundred yards it took him, over Osric's head, over the precipice of the hatchery, over the jagged rock far below, through the clear cold night to emerge in mid-air in front of Thrall. In that instant of emergence, it seemed the world had frozen and he hung stationary in the air. The shock in Thrall's eyes alone was worth it.

Rake rammed his polearm toward the dragon. In those last moments, Thrall's besieging powers penetrated a weak point in his Lifting defenses, much as his Barrier had cracked under the onslaught upon the wall. Thrall's presence surged into his mind, but he spent his last free will into aiming the thrust of his arm, sure it was now too late for Thrall's influence to matter. Yet already he was falling through the air, skewing his aim. A firm nudge from within him, not of his own making, pushed his arm off course by a fraction.

The orange blade flashed in the starlight, then parted Thrall's black-blood scales and sunk in. Deep. Blood gushed down the shaft, spraying Rake in the face.

All sense of triumph turned to ice within him. The wound was in the wrong place. Rake had meant to take Thrall in his neck but had struck into the thicker hide just above the leg joint. A serious wound, but not a fatal one.

Thrall bellowed in pain and beat his wings to back away. The dragon's presence left Rake's mind, and Rake, sapped of all strength and knowing he'd failed, lost his grip on his weapon. He fell, hurtling down to the bedrock of Windshear.

His soul felt hollow and empty.

I'm sorry, Elya. I tried.

Talons wrapped around him. He felt weightless as though he were in water and then he began to rise, back up toward the mystic tower. Thrall's roars of pain were a reminder of his failure.

So close. He'd come so close.

The wild dragons carrying Rake deposited him on the hatchery floor. His soul beat feeble as a new Novice. Half-conscious, he rolled over to see Osric pull the polearm free from Thrall's chest.

"I will break you." The dragon's voice rang in his mind

Rake's head slumped onto the stone. He blacked out.

FORTY-THREE

A Fading Illusion

A day came and went without Rake. Holt wasn't too worried at first. Rake's flair for the dramatic could surely stretch to making them fear he had abandoned them. He filled his time with training, aiding Aberanth with chores in the lab, and finalizing his own notes in the recipe book.

To those pages he added lines of his trials in the scourge tunnels with Ash, of their sense-sharing and its multiple benefits, and updated his technique list to include Flare. After another night and day went by, his new batch of jerky was ready, allowing him to test and confirm that both the vinegary pieces for Sinking and the wine-soaked pieces for Lifting worked as well. He updated the jerky section, and altogether Holt's additions now filled four new pages of the recipe book.

Yet after three days without any sign of Rake, the remaining members of the team could no longer hope he would return.

"He's gone to Windshear alone," Eidolan concluded. They were all in the glade outside Aberanth's grotto: Holt, Ash, Aberanth, and Eidolan. The seven-strong party was reduced now to four.

"But he needed all of us for good reasons," Holt said. "Even Rake couldn't hope to do it on his own, otherwise he'd have tried it by now."

"Mad fool," Aberanth piped up. *"No concern for odds at all."*

"Can he even get into the fortress?" Holt asked.

"He must have a way," Eidolan said. *"Or else he would have stayed."*

Doubt shot up Holt's spine. He bit his lip, ran his hands through his wild hair.

Ash rumbled. *"We could not have known he would act this rashly."*

"No, we couldn't," Holt said. "But it doesn't change the fact that without Rake, any version of the plan just got a whole lot more impossible." He began pacing, now the sole human amongst three dragons. "Maybe we were wrong."

"It was not weakness to voice concerns," Eidolan said. *"Greater riders have fallen on less dangerous ventures. Recklessness is not bravery. I fear the dragon side of him is all but dominant now, and dragons with that much pride are a danger unto themselves. Were he under my wing in the Order I'd have told him long ago to be less petulant. But Rake has... issues."*

"I'm not sure I understand," Holt said. "You mean his own dragon is taking over his mind?"

"No, far from it. I did not know Rake as a human, or his dragon Elya, but the way he used to speak of her gave an impression of a kind and patient soul. As a human I have no doubt he was inclined to behave like this, but being half a dragon has brought it out all the stronger. He wasn't as bad as this in the early days."

"I thought you did not know him then?" Ash asked.

"Not as a human," said Eidolan. *"He came to me already in his hybrid body. Rake found me in a cave I used to call home in Fornheim. Gideon's will instructed his heirs to give the art we gathered together to me. They brought it to my cave, where I hid in my grief, but that seemed to spark a rumor that I was a wild dragon who would grant favors if brought tribute. One day an old Potter brought me a bowl. She had spun it in a dark clay I'd never seen before, patterned using only her fingertip at the wheel. I desired it, and so I granted her wish. She wanted to be young and beautiful again, to enjoy the attention of men and feel the envy of other women, even if only for a short time."*

"Granting wishes?" Aberanth asked dubiously. *"Did she know all you could give her was the illusion?"*

"I do not think they grasped what I did, only that I did it," said Eidolan. *"I*

explained the limitations. I could make the Potter as beautiful as in the bloom of youth—"

"But she could never be touched or else the illusion would break," Holt said.

"Quite so," Eidolan said. *"When I was a hatchling, I sulked over these impediments on my powers, but with age I see them as necessary. No magic should be capable of doing what the Potter wished, and yet she and many others still wished for it, if only to enjoy the experience for a time. After her the rumor grew and spread, and over time more humans came to me with requests and art."*

"You're a strange dragon," Aberanth said, which Holt thought a bit rich coming from him. *"Were these treasures so important to you that you were happy with humans traipsing all over the place? No privacy."*

"I liked that I could bring happiness to them," Eidolan said. *"Even if briefly. And the art I valued both for its beauty and its inspiration for my own work. Conjuring an illusion is far easier with proper inspiration, and Gideon helped accrue a deep well of that for me while he was alive. Without him, what did I have but the art and the work?"*

"Hmmph," Aberanth intoned. *"That I can understand."*

Eidolan rumbled solemnly and carried on. *"In time I felt a desire to rejoin my flight, and you know how well that turned out. By the time I returned to my little cave it was with a heavy heart. Knowledge of the wish-granting dragon had passed into a legend of the area. Yet Rake turned up one day, an orange half-dragon bringing me a ring with the largest amethyst I'd ever seen."*

"What did he want?"

"He wished to be human again," Eidolan said. *"Not to undo what happened to him, of course. Unlike the humans, Rake understood my limitations perfectly."*

"And you made him look human again?" Ash asked.

"For a time," Eidolan said.

"Rake's family was from the east, from near Freiz, I thought," Holt said. "And your cave was in Fornheim? Can you really create illusions across such a distance?"

"If it is my sole focus to do so," Eidolan said. *"Making Rake look like his old self was also not too difficult. Far easier to make something look as it has been than to make it something it cannot be, or will never be.*

"I don't see the utility in it," Aberanth said. *"Why would Rake do this?"*

"Wouldn't you wish to see your family, especially after suffering trauma?"

Aberanth shifted around awkwardly, tail swishing through the tall grass. Holt didn't imagine Aberanth had ever felt compelled to return to his flight, not after being banished. Holt understood that well enough. Eidolan quickly realized his indiscretion, for he approached Aberanth and lowered his snout for the emerald to touch.

"I am sorry, child," Eidolan said. *"Forgive me, I forgot to whom I spoke."*

Aberanth hesitated, then raised his much smaller snout to touch Eidolan's own.

"Did it work?" Ash asked. *"Making Rake look human again?"*

"Naturally," Eidolan said with a form of professional pride. *"Multiple times, across the years. Yet one by one his family passed. His mother and father died, then his brothers and sisters. His nieces and nephews grew old, and their children had children, and in time I think the relations grew so distant that Rake no longer cared. Generations went by while he lingered longer than even a rider could. I judged that the human side of him faded with each visit. The illusion itself became harder to conjure. And then he stopped asking for my help."*

As Eidolan concluded his tale, Holt's ire toward Rake softened. He had never really stopped to consider how lonely his existence must have been. All he'd seen was the power and bravado; he'd never once considered his struggles. Even after learning that lesson in getting to know Talia, he'd forgotten to apply it to Rake as well. Maybe Rake was right to be disappointed in him. Still, charging off to Windshear alone was all on him.

"Master Rake has suffered," Ash began, *"but so have we all. That does not mean he is right."*

"I didn't say he was," Eidolan said. *"He's walked a long road. Yet a hatchling who flies into the fire to make the Elders rescue him is not to be encouraged."*

"How did you come to owe Rake a favor?" Holt asked. "All of us owe him, but it sounds like he paid you fairly for your illusions."

"As my hoard of treasures grew, so did the boldness of certain humans. Increasingly I had to defend myself from thieves seeking to take it from me. Rake helped me flee the area, fighting off a mob that came to my cave. I lost much of

my collection, but were it not for Rake I'd have lost it all, and probably my life as well."

Holt nodded, and then, rather suddenly, words spilled out of him.

"We should head north anyway." He'd made up his mind, though he'd known this would be the only worthy course to take. "When we reach Windshear, we'll find either Thrall or Rake—" he almost didn't say it, "—dead. We can't help him now, but if Talia's plan works, Thrall may still leave, and there's a chance we could save an egg or two."

"Masters Hava and Farsa do not know what's happened," Ash added. *"We should go to meet them at least."*

Aberanth scoffed. *"Poor results either way if you ask me. Either we bury Rake, or we find him insufferably triumphant and will have to kill him ourselves."* He spoke in good humor, although Holt could not quite summon the laughter.

"So we go then," Holt said, trying to sound commanding and decisive.

"We've come too far not to try," Ash said.

Eidolan growled low and nodded. *"Agreed."*

They all looked at Aberanth. Under their collective gaze, he swiftly caved. *"Oh, yes, very well. Very well,"* he added, trying to sound wearied and resigned, though Holt knew he was just nervous. *"Come with me below, Holt. There is something you should see before we head off."*

Curious, Holt followed the little brown emerald down the firefly tunnel and into his grotto. The beech tree at the heart of the lab pulsed from root to branch in warm yellow light today. The usual odors of sterilizing alcohol were mixed with wafts of wine, tangy vinegar, and ginger from where a batch of elixirs brewed.

"This way," Aberanth said, trotting off into a back room. Holt followed. He entered a smaller, darker chamber and stepped carefully lest he ruin some experiment.

"I'll add some light."

A low blue light rose slowly from branching white roots in one of the walls, revealing a stone table with the scourge orb upon it. Only the orb was now in pieces; some were razor-thin, others in chunks, others knobby as though dipped in a corrosive substance. Aberanth's bark notes lay scattered about, but Holt could not understand a single rune.

"Looks foul," Holt observed.

"*I've dissected the orb as well as the stem,*" Aberanth said in a tone like a kitchenhand counting off stock in the larder. "*It's scourge, of course, but we knew that. I have a dye which helps discern flesh akin to the vethrax, that part of them which finds light abhorrent. I'd hoped to find evidence of how the scourge protects itself from light in the lining of the muscle fibers or the lid of the orb, but I don't think it has any. Why would it? It was never meant to leave that chamber. A shame.*"

"Right," Holt said, wondering with increased worry just what ominous thing Aberanth had actually found. He hadn't asked Holt to come down just to tell him that.

"*I've confirmed it's partly a brain,*" Aberanth said, rather matter of fact.

"A brain? So it could think."

"*Partly a brain,*" Aberanth stressed. "*Just one part, actually. Its structure is representative of the... well, hmmph, of the area of a dragon's mind that allows us to communicate via thoughts.*"

Holt's mouth went dry. He looked upon the neatly carved orb and slimy muscles and experienced the sadly familiar sensation of a spider creeping up his spine on legs of ice.

"What does that mean?"

"*I'm not sure,*" Aberanth said. "*Perhaps Thrall has created these orbs to better communicate with his new minions. They might act as mini brains for him to leap from, which could explain how his powers extend over great distances. But I don't think that's the whole story.*"

"Why?" Holt asked in trepidation.

"*Because while the brain tissue is close to a dragon's structure, it's not wholly dragon. There are human elements in there too.*"

"Human?" Holt said in alarm.

"*The scourge has corrupted and risen humans beyond count in its time. It would not be absurd to think it may have... learned something of your kind.*"

"You're sure about this?"

"I triple checked. All my notes, all my learning."

"And you know what dragon and human brains… are like?"

Aberanth squirmed. *"Holt, I wasn't exiled from the Emerald Flight for my love of mushrooms. Nor even for investigating the world… to a point."*

It came to Holt, quick and disturbing. "You cut open dragons and humans to study them?" He was surprised just how disgusted he sounded.

Aberanth rumbled low and backed away. *"Never living ones,"* he pleaded.

"Still, you… you burn bodies, Aberanth. Else the blight gets into them."

"Well, I do—I did! Once I was finished. Please, Holt, I learned so much. My work could do so much, I know it could, but it's this reaction which prevents my kind from learning. Your human physicians perform surgery on living people."

"To amputate blight-infected limbs, to take arrow shards out of people's guts, to—" Holt said, but then he found the power to stop and center himself. Aberanth meant no harm. His elixirs were incredible, and he deserved better from Holt than revulsion.

"Rake brought you some of these… bodies, didn't he?"

"Yes," Aberanth admitted.

"He didn't… he didn't kill anyone to acquire them, did he?"

"No," Aberanth said, firm. And then, with the slightest hesitation, he said, *"I'm ninety-nine percent sure he did not kill anyone."*

"Okay," Holt said, slowly. "Okay," he repeated, reassuring himself. "Well, this matter of the orb is disturbing, but I'm not sure if I can be of any help to you figuring it all out."

"I just had to tell someone," Aberanth said. *"And I thought you and Ash at least should know."*

"You'd rather Eidolan didn't find out about your methods," Holt said.

Aberanth nodded.

"Okay," Holt said for the third time. He looked at the oozy pieces of the orb once more, recalling the green light that had pulsed in it and the howling it had made when he'd touched it. Had that been Thrall's howl of anger at him finding it?

His worries turned to Talia and Pyra who were deliberately trying to find another one of these chambers, which would, in theory, contain an orb of its own. And he wondered if that was such a good idea after all.

FORTY-FOUR

Rogues

The runic symbol of the Order's magic was far larger than she'd imagined. Even approaching at a distance, she could see it clearly on the ravine wall.

"If you are ready, daughters of fire, I shall break the seal." The Life Elder's presence behind her was vast and reassuring.

"We're ready," Talia said.

The Elder's power struck the rock face. The runic seal pulsed green, and then the wall began to peel away from itself, revealing an endless dark tunnel. Pyra groaned and raked her talons across the earth. No scourge came forth, only stale air, yet it was evident at a glance that this passageway was too low for dragons to move down.

"We must find another way," Pyra said.

Talia gulped and shook her head. "There's no time. And there might be no other way." She turned and instinctively dropped to her knee when facing the Elder. "Honored, Elder, do you sense the dark presence within?"

"I do, child, stronger than ever. Never in my long years have I felt such power from the scourge as I do now."

Pyra beat a path to stand before the mouth of the tunnel. *"I won't let you fight alone."*

"I don't have a choice," Talia said. A door of ice slammed shut in her chest. She could no longer feel Pyra.

"That is how you will feel fighting without me," Pyra said. *"I won't have you die alone in the dark."*

"Stop this," Talia said, alarmed by how afraid she sounded. Pyra reopened their bond, and the fire returned to Talia's chest. She gasped as though emerging from water.

"Honored Elder," Pyra said, prostrating herself before the great dragon. *"Will you not stop her?"*

"What is this fear, daughter of fire?" the Elder said. *"I thought you and your rider feared nothing."*

"I can't lose her," Pyra said. *"I beg of you, Honored Elder. Seal the tunnel once more."*

"If this is to be Talia's fight, then it is her decision to make."

Pyra moaned. She knew fine well that Talia would not – could not – turn away. Despair crossed their bond, unlike anything Talia had felt from her dragon before; Pyra who was fire and wroth made flesh. Neither tried to hide it from the other.

The breeze changed, picking up to a chill wind from the north.

Talia wrapped her arms around herself as the cold both pressed from without and sapped from within. She felt the Elder's gaze upon her. His eyes phased from a bright summer's green to a swirl of brown, yellow, and red. The first day of autumn had truly come.

"I will fulfill the mission."

Lost for an answer, Pyra snorted, roared, and took flight, heading south to their new encampment. Distance rather than direct intervention numbed the fear between them now.

"I'm sorry you had to witness that, Honored Elder," Talia said.

But the Elder was no longer looking at her. He lifted his snout high and sniffed at the air. *"Did you feel that?"*

"I cannot sense the chamber from here."

"No," he said, sounding distracted for the first time. *"A chill."*

The season was changing, yet he knew that.

"I must go," he said. And without any word of encouragement, he took off, heading north over the peaks of the Red Range. The Elder

had barely left Talia's sight when the West Warden reached out to her.

"My orders are to remain with you, youngling." She sensed him heading down from the hills, with a score of emeralds in tow. *"My squadron and I are at your service."*

Talia felt bolstered by this, not because the Warden or his dragons could help her underground, but because the change in his demeanor was a sure sign of growing respect, if grudgingly given. She knew she was on the right path, even if it loomed dark and perilous before her.

"Watch the tunnel and have drakes watch the border," she said, for they were mere hours from the border with Brenin here and who knew what might cross it – scourge, riders, or even her uncle's troops turned to the Athran cause. *"And if one of your emeralds would be so kind as to give me a lift back to camp, I would appreciate it."*

She felt the Warden bristle at the request, yet she received a reply.

"I shall assist you," came the voice of Turro. He landed in the ravine beside her in short order. Turro's apple green scales had darkened since their expedition, as had his eyes. Talia got onto his back, and despite her enhanced body, despite her experience of riding, being on the back of another dragon felt rough and uncomfortable compared to Pyra.

"Thank you, Turro. I know it is no small matter to carry a human."

"The pride of younger drakes is not so great. It is my honor to carry the Red Bane of the Scourge." They took off, flying low over the ravine then out over their encampment. Turro swooped low where instructed and Talia leaped from his back to land amidst her startled officers.

She gave the order. Her forces were to assemble at the mouth of the ravine, six hundred strong this time. Many were veterans of the first expedition, which took her aback. She'd made it clear that those who had served on the first assault were to be offered the chance to refuse the second mission. After they'd gone through such horror, she thought it only fair. Yet well over two hundred were here again, almost all the survivors from the Withering Woods, forming an experienced backbone for her forces.

Striding through the camp, men armed themselves to face death itself, and she did not take their willingness to fight lightly. They were allowing her the chance to prove she could learn. A second grave mistake and she would not be granted that luxury again.

She had no intention of this. Lessons from the first expedition had been implemented. Short of full plate, each soldier was as well defended as they could be, with heavy helms, reinforced pauldrons, chainmail, leather, and greaves. Their shields were broad. Short swords hung from their hips and spears were in their grip. Professional soldiers, each one trained for the role of facing the scourge from birth. All of them veterans of Sidastra, and some even of the incursion of Talia's infancy. Bulking the ranks were no fewer than fifty knights – sons of richer families selected to face the scourge and who could afford a full harness of plate, a horse, and a squire to aid them. Many of them would once have been Squires of the Order, those who had failed the rigors of induction or to bond with a dragon, yet who had sworn to battle the scourge nonetheless.

The Skarls readied themselves as well. Each Housecarl accompanying Prince Aren stood in their war glory, faces hidden behind heavy helms and – with the exception of the shield-maidens – heavier beards. Upon their arms glistened bands of silver and iron, and even polished chitin taken from stingers or juggernauts. The Twinblades stood on either side of Aren, who seemed to be trying his best not to acknowledge them. Even amongst so many formidable warriors as the Housecarls, the twins still stood out, partly from the crimson garb Talia had provided them with but also from their severe expressions. Aren towered over them all. He gave her a wolfish grin but she walked on, not wishing to get bogged down in ingenuine words of comfort or affection.

Drums beat. Horns blew. Officers barked commands. If the bard remained in her camp, his music was lost in the din. High above, the circling emeralds roared in encouragement. The cookfires burned low. The field hospital was prepared. With each stride she took, her army took one step closer to battle.

She found Pyra in the heart of the camp, surrounded by many

burning braziers. Pyra got up and stomped toward her, knocking a brazier aside in her haste and spilling hot coals to the ground.

"I'm sorry," Pyra said.

Talia pressed into Pyra's chest and tried to throw an arm up around her neck, but the dragon must have grown and she could no longer manage it.

"You're afraid," Talia said. "It's normal."

"What have you done to me, human?" Pyra said, though she wrapped her neck around Talia and squeezed her in close. The beat of their bond returned in earnest, thumping hard with the drums and the horns and booming voices. *"In case this is the last we see of each other—"*

"Don't say that."

"In case it is," Pyra insisted, *"let us go for one last flight. I would have that be our parting memory."*

And so they flew, joining the emeralds to spiral and dive and weave in their dance upon the autumn winds. No matter the danger, a flight of joy could dispel any dark cloud. How cruel it was then that she sensed a Champion coming in fast from the east. Two, three, four more of them, and some ten Ascendants as well.

Adaskar must have decided to arrest her after all.

The Warden reached out to her. *"Whatever happens, we cannot intervene to protect you."*

"We understand," Talia told him. Pyra pivoted in the air to head east and meet their fate. Better to meet with the riders away from her troops. Ahead, they spotted the inbound riders, dragons of all colors and sizes, their wings beating fast as though the Storm Paragon willed them on.

Talia and Pyra did not fly alone. Turro fell in beside them.

"We cannot intervene," he repeated, *"but we can make it appear as though we might."*

Two more emeralds then fell in around Pyra, and Talia sensed two more were on their way. The force Adaskar had sent was strong, but the Warden's distant presence and the emeralds flying in an honor guard around her might just scare them away.

Yet when the leader – a pale ice dragon – drew in close, it made for the ground rather than meet them in the air. A sign that they were to talk.

"That is Strang," Pyra said. That meant his rider must be Ethel. The rider who had saved Holt and Ash and then let them go.

Talia and Pyra touched down, and she recognized the Ice Champion who had stormed out of the Paragons' inner sanctum.

Pyra roared, her joy lifting Talia's own spirits.

The other riders touched down some way off.

Ethel dismounted, unstrapped her sword, and threw it to the ground.

"We heard your speech, Talia Agravain," Ethel said, and it was evident from her voice she was a native of Feorlen. "We liked what you had to say. I'm sorry we could not bring more."

Talia felt lost for words. One moment she had been staring down the task alone, and now more than a dozen riders were here. Her dragon bond blazed with fresh life. Pyra's hope was euphoric, and Talia could not help but beam as happy as the day she'd first bonded with the dragon.

"You have nothing to be sorry for," Talia said. "It's more than I dared hope for."

FORTY-FIVE

Rhythm and Bones

"Are you ready?" Rake asked. Elya gazed back at him, her eyes wide and startlingly blue. She seemed especially magnificent today, beautiful and fierce. Her orange scales radiated a sense of calm warmth like a hazy sun setting over untouched sand.

She cocked her head, seeming sad. He didn't understand. Their bond was pure, strong as dragon-steel. He was prepared to take the next step. They had worked day and night for decades for this. Of all the rider pairings, they could manage it.

"Are you ready?"

This time, when he asked, he reached out a hand to touch her snout. Two things struck him as wrong. His hand was human, with pale skin and short nails rather than talons. The second was that Elya was cold to the touch. There was no life in her. Something beat weakly in his chest. That was wrong too because his bond always thrummed with life, unwavering in its rhythm as his love for his dragon was unwavering and hers for him.

"Elya? Please talk to me."

But all he felt was the faint, tap, tap, tap in his chest, as though his heart was hollow.

Rake started and found himself in darkness. The ache from his soul and core hit him a moment later, and he knew assuredly he was awake. Dreams, however nightmarish and cruel, never hurt as real life did. He smelled nothing but his own sweat and a dampness in the surrounding stone. A chill lay in the air, despite the time of year. He crested forth with one hand and found a bar set into the stone, then another, and another. A small portcullis.

The bars would be dragon-steel, sturdy even after long centuries of neglect. Rake had seen such cells at Falcaer, dug deep underground and walled in on all sides by stone. Should the rider in question be an emerald with an affinity for rock and earth, then the cell would be secured with metal walls and further safeguarded with surrounding water akin to a moat. Rake, of course, held no such power over the earth. A standard cell would do for him.

A door opened above, letting in a dim light from the top of a short ramp leading up from the portcullis. Rake still lay on the ground and so strained to look up through the bars. Osric Agravain stood silhouetted in the doorway.

"Can you eat bread?" Osric asked.

"Bread?" Rake croaked. He could not recall the last time he'd eaten bread. "I don't know." Groggy and barely awake, Rake closed his eyes for a moment. All was dark again when he opened them. He crested one hand between the bars and found chunks of stale bread and a tankard. Grasping his rations with feeble fingers, Rake pulled them through the gaps. At full strength he ate rarely, yet if he were to recover properly, he would have to eat what they deigned to provide him.

He drank first. The water was lukewarm and tasted unclean. The bread crumbled with all the pleasure of chalk in his mouth. It did not taste terrible, however, and so perhaps he could eat bread and had only stopped due to the difficulty in acquiring it.

Yet within the hour his stomach burst into excruciating pain. He cried out, alarmed to feel his belly swell. The pain in his gut forced him to double over. With a wrenching effort, he crawled into a corner and heaved. A vile smell overpowered the stale air, and he passed out again.

When he woke, the dim light had returned. Rake shuffled to the portcullis and grasped onto the bars for support. At the top of the short ramp, Osric again stood in the doorway.

"No bread then."

Rake tried to speak but produced a hacking cough from his dry throat, dislodging a piece of dried vomit.

"You must be more dragon than human," Osric continued. "Ordinarily I would not offer meat to prisoners over my own men, and we have many hatchlings to feed. But Sovereign wants you alive." He hefted a large pail and shook it. Bones rattled within. "Tell me your name, and I'll throw this down."

"Call me Rake," he said hoarsely.

Osric kept his word and emptied the bucket onto the ramp, and the contents rolled down to the gate. Mutton legs and other animal bones with loose scraps of meat and gristle. Osric left, closing the door.

In the dark, Rake fumbled for the bones. He started with the scraps of mutton. Lamb would do him good. After he'd sucked the meat from the bones, he cracked them open and ate the marrow. He'd been reduced to the actions of a half-starved dog. Humiliated, Rake sat with his back against the wall, facing the darkness. The tension and pain in his stomach eased, and he groaned in relief.

His core still starved, however. Not one scrap of mystic energy reached him down here. This was, of course, the intention of such cells. All riders gained some small measure of alignment with the magic of their dragon, often discovering how much they relied on its presence when suddenly they lacked it, like a growing alcoholic stripped of drink.

The cells were bitter cold for fire riders, yet the floors could be heated to force an ice rider to sweat. No breeze or strong wind blew for storm riders, no living plant or soil for emeralds. For mystics, the forced distance from other living beings and their thoughts was an easy torture. For Rake, this would be doubly worse, seeing as he held his own core.

Not that he had much of a core left. He had entirely forgotten what life felt like without a well of magic inside him. It was dim, empty, much like his soul felt now.

Elya, are you there?

A painful series of heartbeats passed without any form of reply. And then Rake received a feeble tap within his soul.

I'm going to get us out of here. Do you hear me? Elya?

He woke with a start sometime later, unsure when he had drifted off. His assertion to Elya that he would get them out seemed laughable in his current predicament. However, the first day of autumn grew ever closer. Even if Holt and the others had abandoned the mission, Talia would, with luck, still succeed in her plan. If she could draw Thrall off, then Windshear would be disrupted. If there were a time for escape, it would be then. Ironic, really, that now he should hope for Thrall to leave.

A lock clunked. The cell door opened, letting in a few rays of light. Rake blinked as his eyes adjusted. He moved to the portcullis to meet with Osric. Agravain nodded to himself, as though pleased to find Rake was strong enough to stand.

"Things will go easier if you don't resist," Osric said. "Believe me."

Rake sensed no obvious trace of Thrall's presence in him. "He does not have to control you, does he?"

"As I say, it will be easier if you don't resist."

"I'm not a mindless soldier. I can decide my own fate."

"Then you made a foolish decision in coming here." Osric slid his axes out from his belt. "The wild dragons first noticed you at the emerald tower. How did you get inside?" He spoke with a wounded sense of professionalism.

"Doesn't matter how I did it," Rake said. "No one else can repeat it. Your precious master is safe."

"He shall be your master too. You'll be his prized possession, his greatest warrior. You almost succeeded, after all. I didn't think anyone capable of that."

"Do you wish I had?" Rake asked. Looking up at an awkward angle, it was hard to read Osric's face, but Rake liked to think he saw a twitch. "I met your niece not long ago," he added, inspired to provoke

Osric and see if it led to anything. "She didn't ask about you, nor did she care to hear we'd fought. When I kill you, I don't think she'll shed a tear."

Nothing. Osric's face remained inscrutable.

"You're not going to kill me," Osric said. He disappeared, and shortly after, gears squeaked to life. Metal scratched against stone as the portcullis lifted.

Rake considered his options. Do nothing and became a pawn of Thrall. Fight back, though only delay the inevitable. Fight harder, perhaps enough so that Thrall would kill him rather than dominate him. Elya, he knew, would rather die as well.

Rake leaped up the ramp, claws at the ready. Osric stepped away from the winch mechanism and dodged Rake in an almost lazy fashion. He sighed, then kicked the back of Rake's knee. Rake crumpled. He fell badly and his arms refused to support his weight. Osric's heavy boot slammed into his side and stamped on his back. A rib broke. Rake's next breath came with great pain.

"Your core must be all but dry," Osric said, speaking in the same level tone as though nothing had happened. Rake wheezed. "Get up," Osric said. "Follow me on your feet or I'll tie a rope around your neck and drag you."

Rake stood. His chest ached double now with his broken bone. Fighting would not be an option then. He had no concept of his own weakness. He'd been too strong for too long.

He followed Osric out of the prison block, finding himself in the northwest corner of Windshear, close to the ice tower. As they trudged across the inner yard to the mystic tower, they passed a storage house built against the western wall. The servants' stairs emerged in that building. Though he would be met at the bottom by the riders or wild dragons, it seemed like his only real point of escape, should he get a chance.

His return to the great hatchery on the second floor of the mystic tower was as far from daring as it could get. Osric kicked hard at the back of his legs again, forcing him to drop and prostrate himself before Thrall.

The scales on Thrall's lower chest had been cauterized to seal the wound. Rake grimaced. It was a reminder of how close he had come and yet a stark sign of failure.

"Look at me, Rake."

Rake slowly raised his head to meet the oak, blood-worn eyes. Thrall seemed eager, the same way Aberanth looked when discovering a new puzzle, or Eidolan a fine piece of art. Wondering if Thrall's powers required eye contact, Rake closed them.

"That doesn't stop me."

Rake dredged up the last vestiges of his core and began Lifting the motes. At this point, a shield of paper would have offered more protection. Thrall shattered his defenses with a mere flick of his power and pierced into Rake's mind. Now he only had his will left to resist the dragon. Fortunately, Rake had always been stubborn and determined.

"Lie down," said a charming voice, though it sounded shaky and unsure of itself.

Rake refused.

Thrall's presence moved awkwardly through him, fumbling, as though this were the first time the dragon had attempted such a domination. He growled low in this throat.

"Your mind is unlike any I have experienced before."

He retreated, and Rake gasped in relief.

"Not making things difficult for you, am I?"

"You have power, that's undeniable," Thrall said. *"How is it I have never encountered you before? Are you young?"*

"Younger than you, older than most."

"Osric believes you are more dragon than human. I'm not so sure. Tell me, how did you come to take such a form?"

Rake frowned. If Thrall was asking for information, he must have struggled to seize his mind. Whatever the reason for that, it gave Rake a chance to drag this out.

"I'm not going to talk," Rake said, "so if you're going to dominate me or torture me, you'd better get on with it."

"If you insist."

That first meeting carried on in a silent war for control. Thrall's presence invaded then dug in like an occupying force while Rake scrambled to resist, striking back at every point he could. In the end, Thrall left him and Rake dropped to all fours, breathing hard.

"You insult all dragons in this abominable form," Thrall said. *"How did this happen?"*

"How did what happen?" Rake said. "I've always been this way."

Thrall placed a warning talon to his throat.

Rake chuckled, though his pain distorted the laughter. "You think that frightens me?"

"How did this happen to you?" Thrall asked again.

Rake considered. "Deep in the mountains of the Spine, where the Eternals roam, lies the tomb of the first rider. When I tried to take its treasure, a curse fell upon me."

Thrall grunted in annoyance and attacked. When it was over, Rake rasped for breath, every heave a sufferance from his broken rib. In his magical senses, he felt Thrall's core pulse like a quickened heartbeat. Could he really be putting up that much of a fight, or was Thrall's strength much less than he'd assumed? Controlling the scourge must take its pound of flesh, he supposed.

Whatever the case, Rake was escorted back to his cell. The next time he was brought before Thrall the dragon penetrated deeper into his mind. Rake continued to resist where he could. Information on Holt and Ash seemed of the highest interest to the dragon, allowing Rake to obscure such things as the location of Aberanth's grotto and the identities of Farsa and Hava.

In truth, Rake could do nothing more than surrender ground one inch at a time. By letting Thrall sweep easily into certain pathways, it allowed Rake to cling onto more precious things.

"How did this happen to you?"

Rake's head lolled, and drool ran from his mouth. Blood tinted the spittle, stark red amidst the dry straw on the hatchery floor. Some flecked his own hand, his orange scales faded in color to pale old wood.

"I'm too curious for my own good," Rake answered, still looking at the blood on the floor. "In the Order I always wondered how the eggs were sung into being. I crested out to add my powers to the flight song and got caught in the crossfire."

"Do you think yourself amusing?"

"Less than some," Rake whispered. "More than most."

"I will master the pathways of your monstrous mind. I will find what I seek."

"I'd like to see you... try," Rake said, bracing for another round.

Yet his will grew brittle. Over the sessions, Thrall pulled memories from the depths. Countless nights sleeping out under the stars, sheltering in cold caves from rainstorms, wintering in the Jade Jungle, and trekking snow-capped mountains in summer. All of them alone. Searching for an answer that was nowhere to be found.

He dropped to his knees before his Elder, then to the others one after another. All turned him away. In a guise cast on him by Eidolan he visited his hometown, his old estate, unable to hold anyone lest the illusion break. Family members passed by until he no longer recognized them. Then he walked those streets without anyone knowing who or what he was, just for the longing to walk them again. He fought scourge there too, in the crammed streets, in the very grounds of his family's home. Yet he alone could not save it from falling along with all of Freiz.

Thrall searched clumsily as though grasping for a single grain in a sack of wheat. A moment of the fateful day was unearthed, and Rake stood with Elya by a stone altar made by the first men to cross the endless, eastern grass sea. Legend spoke of these sites as the earliest in which dragons and humans made contact. Rake saw significance in that.

"Are you ready?" Rake asked. Elya gazed back at him, her eyes wide and startlingly blue. A low burning sun set her orange body ablaze with a warmth he could have melted in. His excitement was palpable, yet she cocked her head, seeming sad.

He did not understand why.

"Are you ready?" he asked, insistent now.

"No," Rake said, weeping inside as he fought Thrall. *"Get away from her."*

Thrall left. The hatchery, Rake's empty core, and his exhausted hybrid body came rushing back to him. Once again, he fell to all fours, and for the first time he wished for it all to be over. For the first time, he considered giving in.

"How did this happen to you?" Thrall asked. There was an air of finality to his voice. He knew Rake was ready to succumb.

Rake swallowed hard, drew in a shuddering breath, but could not summon a misdirection this time. "It was a mistake," he rasped. "A terrible mistake."

"You and Osric aren't so different," Thrall said. "You lie to yourself."

Another long night passed in his cell. Rake gnawed his bones and scraps of meat, then sat with his back to a wall. His healing rib prevented him from lying down. He shivered in the dark and pulled his knees up to his chest and wrapped his arms around them. The latest session with Thrall had unnerved him. Perhaps he would be broken sooner than he thought. Unable to sleep, he brooded on some way to fight back. All magic had its limitations.

Though mystic dragons relied on the thoughts of others, few stopped to consider the nature of the minds which produced them. In Rake's estimation, the brain was distinct from the mind, the brain being machinery that the mind made use of. Whether dragon or human, this held. Thrall could wrest control of the mechanisms of the brain. He could convince his victim to take the action he wished, but he could not truly alter a conscious mind.

Meaning, he could force someone to say that the sun was really the moon, that day was night, and have them change their behavior accordingly, but that person need not genuinely believe the lies. They would be acting under duress.

This in truth made Thrall's powers crude. Blunt, effective, and dangerous, but crude. He only had as much control as he had power to wield. It was a mark of his cunning that he chose to sway many through manipulation, by giving others a cause to follow and by being selective in who he chose to dominate.

These musings alas provided Rake with no practical means to thwart Thrall's attacks. There was, however, a common pattern to them. Aberanth's findings showed that the brains of both humans and dragons were divided into two parts, left and right. In every single session, Thrall went for the left side and largely ignored the right. Rake could only guess at why that was the case. For all he knew, it was out of habit.

The torture continued. Another day spent in a silent battle of wills resulted in that same painful memory of Elya by the stone altar. This time when he emerged, Rake spat blood.

"Why resist?" Thrall asked.

"Why indeed." A copper taste refilled his mouth and he spat again. "Fighting you is like fighting the scourge. Might be pointless in the long run, but there isn't any other choice but to fight."

"Your condition," Thrall said, sounding disgusted, *"it occurred when you attempted to push past the boundaries of Lord."* It was a statement, not a question.

So, Thrall knew about such things.

"What of it?"

"You look like a dragon, you eat like a dragon, but your heart is all human. Jealous of dragon power and driven to any lengths to take it for your own."

"I was a rider," Rake said, proud. "I loved my dragon. We were partners. Equals."

"You stole of her power," Thrall said, angry now. *"You stole her life."*

The tapping in Rake's chest quickened.

I'm not listening to him, he let Elya know.

"Was your rider mean to you?" Rake asked Thrall in mock concern. "Did the big bad dragon get a telling off from his little human?"

"He turned my own magic against me," Thrall said, and for once a tremor ran through his voice.

Rake struggled to imagine it. A rider of ruthless ambition and zero empathy crushing his own dragon's spirit. What would the benefit have been? To force Thrall into missions or tasks rather than negotiate and compromise as all other riders must? To force the dragon to Sink day and night to draw motes to his core? To somehow force a bond to grow?

For the first time, he felt a pinch of pity for Thrall. "What your rider did sounds abhorrent. But that's not most riders. That wasn't me. How many of your fellow dragons at Falcaer loved their humans?"

Thrall did not answer.

Rake winced from a fresh lance of pain in his soul, then carried on. "I could never have hurt her."

"*I killed my rider,*" Thrall said, his voice deadened. "*He too desired to break the boundaries of Lord. And as he tried, he lost his grip on my mind. I took my chance.*"

What a terrible fate. Rake could hardly conceive of the mental state needed to kill one's soul-bonded partner. Killing his own rider likely warped Thrall's soul worse than anything his rider did to him, and that would be saying a lot. He envisioned Thrall now as a frightened young drake, cowering in a corner of his mind before an unhinged and abusive rider. Few would have thought such a thing possible. Dragons were too strong, were they not?

To think that the woes of the world could trace their roots back to one ruthless, cruel rider. A nameless, forgotten man now turned to dust, but his legacy lived on.

Thrall evidently thought Rake to be a kindred spirit to his rider. That reignited the fight in him. Rake burned with anger again, which raged over his pain.

"You think Elya did something to sabotage me? I am not your rider. Something went wrong in the transference. A technical error." He found the strength to stand and clench his fists in defiance.

Thrall lowered his head to pierce Rake with his hateful stare. "*I wondered if there was some lesson to be learned from you. I'd see no rider achieve what you sought. But now I know what you really are, leech. I'm going to enjoy breaking you piece by piece.*"

The tapping in his soul ceased. Rake's heart skipped a beat in fright.

Elya? Elya!

Yet before he could hear her reply, Thrall was in his head again. Rake retreated deep inside himself, rallied, and then launched his counterattack. He was weaker now than ever before. The rhythm of his soul did not return.

Even in the centuries of his half-life, he had never been truly alone. Elya had been with him, or a part of her at any rate. Yet now the silence was total. Crushing. The pain vanished, which was worse somehow. He had become unfeeling. He tasted true loneliness for the first time and, worse, his first bitter drops of hopelessness.

FORTY-SIX

Windshear Hold

It was the penultimate day of summer. Eidolan led Holt, Ash, and Aberanth to the lands surrounding Windshear. Holt glimpsed the fortress through the canopy, but none of them risked flying above the tree line. They kept their distance to avoid magical detection, finding a glade to the south in the rough area Farsa and Hava had agreed to meet in.

Though still in the Fae Forest, this northern section of the wood felt less claustrophobic than around Aberanth's grotto. The air was fresher and bright moss grew instead of stodgy fungi. Already the summer heat faded here, and the first cool tendrils of the changing season swept by. Wind howled seemingly in all directions.

With little else to do until Farsa and Hava arrived, Holt checked and adjusted his supply belt for the dozenth time. He closed his eyes, running a quick hand around the vials and reciting what each one was under his breath. He knew their placement by heart now. Four of each elixir, sixteen vials in total and the accompanying jerky.

He wore his cleaned clothes, leathers, dark boots, and chainmail jerkin. Brode's sword now felt natural upon his back, and he drew it with the same ease as Talia drew hers. He practiced lowering and raising his bandanna in fluid, smooth motions. Together, he and Ash had practiced melding senses without the crutch of the focusing words. Their time in the scourge caves had propelled them forward in that regard. Ideally, Holt hoped to reach the point where sense-sharing became as simple as closing and reopening their eyes.

Yet no amount of preparation could dislodge the haunting fact of Rake's absence.

"*He must be dead*," Holt said privately to Ash. "*If he wasn't, he'd have come back.*"

Ash did not try to convince him otherwise. He pawed at the soil in low spirits, and then with a strange burst of energy he got up and began ferreting around on the forest floor. He picked up a fallen branch, brought it to the center of the glade and dropped it.

"What are you doing?" Holt asked. "We have firewood."

"*We should mark out the fortress again to go over the plan,*" Ash said. Almost mechanically, Holt joined Ash in hunting for building materials. There were no ruins to harvest stone from here, so they made the towers out of dead logs or dug grooves to place thick branches upright into the ground.

"*How does it look?*" Ash asked.

"See for yourself," Holt said. The strong earthiness of the forest made it a simple matter to sense-share. Once done, he stepped around the model fort to examine it from different angles for Ash's benefit.

"*Master Rake's was better,*" Ash said. He cut the sense-sharing off from his side. Holt realized he hadn't thought about Rake while doing the task and reckoned that was in part why Ash had suggested they do it. Somehow, he felt better having done even this small thing.

"Thanks, Ash."

A knowing warmth glowed in their bond, and then they set to work Cleansing and Forging before Farsa arrived. Yet the Storm Champion did not come, and the first day of autumn arrived. Holt woke that next morning to find a single red leaf upon the ground, the first flake of the avalanche that would follow.

After breaking their fast on a light meal of dried meat, Ash lifted his ears. "*A dragon and rider approach on foot from the south.*"

Holt relaxed. It had to be Farsa and Hava, for Thrall's followers would have flown openly toward the fortress. Sure enough, the core of an Exalted Storm Champion entered his magical detection. Hava's size made navigating the forest difficult, and she reached the glade only by squeezing through a pair of trees, causing the branches to shake and leaves to fall in her wake. Her steel-like scales lacked some of their luster, and she looked thoroughly disgruntled.

Farsa followed close behind her, looking immaculate as ever. She swept her gaze over the group and frowned. "Where is Master Rake?"

Eidolan, the senior and de facto leader of the group, informed them of Rake's departure.

"And now we have reunited with you," he concluded, *"I relinquish command in favor of a current rider. How would you have us proceed?"*

Farsa shared a hard glance with her dragon. For a moment, Holt thought they might take flight right there and then and head back to Oak Hall. If Rake was dead, then they had no obligation to fulfill. Would her desire to find out the truth about Dahaka be enough to make them stay?

Aberanth had a hopeful glint in his eye. Farsa leaving would put a stop to any attempt to storm the fortress. Eidolan's expression was stony. Perhaps his mind turned even now to his old cave out west and a third lonely exile.

"This throws much into doubt," Farsa said. "We must attempt to gain intelligence on what we face. Alas, Master Rake was perfect for such reconnaissance, but I shall do it." She turned to Hava and placed a hand lightly on her dragon's snout, the most tender exchange Holt had seen the pair make. A moment later, Farsa dropped her hand heavily to her side, and her dark skin seemed to drain of color.

"She's closed over their bond," Ash said.

Holt winced at the mere memory of doing that back in Ahar and was glad Farsa was the one willing to do it now.

"I shan't be long," Farsa said. She strode off to the north.

Another wary and anxious wait was endured. Holt found himself checking and rechecking the vials at his belt and adjusting Brode's scabbard countless times.

At length, Hava sprang up and stretched out her tail and her wings as far as the trees would allow.

"What's wrong?" Holt asked. "Is Farsa in danger?"

"Farsa is fine," Hava said. *"It's Master Rake. He's alive and he's made contact with her."*

Holt's jaw dropped. His heart swelled. He could hardly believe it. "He did?"

Ash imitated Hava, although he could fully stretch his limbs and flap his wings. Aberanth and Eidolan were speechless.

Moments later, Farsa came bursting back into the glade. The first thing she did was carry on running to Hava's side and place a hand on the dragon's snout again. A subdued reunion, but the gray tinge to her skin vanished as she reopened their bond.

"He's alive," Farsa said. "He reached out to me just as I stepped within his range. Thrall has taken him prisoner."

"How can we be sure Rake is acting of his own free will?" Eidolan said.

"Do any enemies come for us?" Aberanth asked.

"I hear no one coming," Ash said.

"No cores," Farsa said.

"Then we might safely deduce Rake is still in his own mind," said Aberanth. *"Else his contact with Farsa would even now bring Thrall or his servants out to find us."*

"It could still be a trap," Eidolan said.

"I don't think so," Holt said. "Thrall wants Ash, and if he can't have us, he wants us dead so we can't become a threat to his scourge. I don't think he'd risk giving us a chance to turn around and leave. Not when we're so close to him."

"It's still a risk," Eidolan said. *"Better to wait and see if your friend's plan works and draws Thrall off."*

"We may not have time for that," Farsa said. "Rake is alive but deathly weak. Thrall could break him at any moment."

"We must rescue him," Hava said. Her blood debt would not allow for anything less.

"I agree," Holt said, without so much as thinking it through.

"Me too," Ash said.

Eidolan grumbled. *"We spoke out against Rake's madness with good reason. Don't throw that all away now."*

"This is different," Holt said. "Before, waiting was about reducing the risk so we might save more eggs. Now waiting means certain death or worse for Rake. Ash and I owe him our lives. You owe him too, Eidolan."

Eidolan bristled and seemed ready to argue further, but Aberanth drew everyone's attention. He stood on his hind legs, stretched to his full height, and flapped his wings hard. He stopped abruptly as soon as everyone fell silent, clawing at the ground twice before mustering up his courage.

"As a young drake, I assumed I would be cast out for my size and strength," he said. *"But not so. It was my mind that led me into trouble, hmmph, my mind that would not slow down."*

He threw a nervous look at Eidolan and Hava. Holt bit his lip on the dragon's behalf and scrambled to think of something to say should either of the senior dragons question the nature of Aberanth's work. Thankfully, they did not, and Aberanth carried on.

"When the East Warden chased me from the flight, none of my kin flew to my aid or even once came looking for me. Hmmph." He snuffled. The memory clearly still stung. *"Only Rake ever came to find me. He is… he is my friend. He is the only friend I've ever had. And I won't live with the shame of not going to help my friend,"* he ended, somewhat lamely, and yet Holt found it as stirring as though the Life Elder himself had spoken.

Eidolan wilted under Aberanth's declaration. *"Very well. Let's rescue the fool."*

"We shall need a new plan," Farsa said. "Rake is being held in the rogue cells. Eidolan, I trust you know where those are?"

"They are close to the ice tower at the western wall," Eidolan said.

"We can mark it on our new model," Holt said. He pointed to his construct of twigs and branches.

"Oh, that's what that is," Farsa said. She squinted, then drew her long silvery blade. "Very well, so roughly here," she said, cutting a small 'x' into the ground. "Rake said he is in his cell during the night and early morning. Elsewise he is in Thrall's company. I see no sense in striking into the mystic tower as planned. We needed Rake at full strength for that. Our best hope now is to get Rake out before Thrall has a chance to react."

She cut a small square into the ground just outside the model's western wall. "This is the entrance by foot?" she asked Eidolan. The illusionist nodded. Farsa moved to the opposite side of the fortress, to the eastern twig wall. "Rake was also at pains to stress how damaged parts of the eastern walls were. Vines, he kept saying."

"I can't bring an entire wall down," Aberanth said. *"There would be no benefit in that even if I could."*

"Even breaking a large chunk would make a useful distraction," Farsa said. "Position yourself to the east and be ready for when we call for it. Eidolan, have your distractions ready as well. Hava will then fly into the second-floor hatchery and extract Rake from there." She paused to gain confirmation from the dragons.

"Who will rescue Rake?" Holt asked.

"I will," said Farsa, as though this were obvious. "We'll need someone to reach him on the inside. I'll take the stairs with my bond concealed. With Hava at a distance, I should not be detected."

"What are Ash and I to do?"

"You can enter the ice tower with Hava and deal with any Wyrm Cloaks there."

Holt nodded but felt this was a role designed to keep them out of harm's way.

"How do you intend to cross the yard and enter the prison building?" Eidolan asked.

"A clogged bond removes magic but not the strength in my body," Farsa said. "Speed will be our ally here. As with the old plan, we'll succeed quickly or not at all."

"Thrall will surely be heightened to intrusion after Rake got in," Aberanth said.

"Where do the stairs come out?" Holt asked.

"We've marked that," Farsa said.

"No, I mean what sort of building, what is its function? Does it come up into a larder, perhaps?"

"Not directly," Eidolan said. *"It comes up to a general storehouse, whence supplies are taken to each tower."*

"Taken how? By more passages underground? Servants are to go unseen, and this is an ancient place. I can't imagine the old riders would have wanted to see servants moving around if they could help it."

"You're not wrong," Eidolan said.

"And the kitchens. Are they somewhere central, or does each tower have its own?"

"Each tower had its own kitchens."

"Where is your mind going, Holt?" Farsa asked.

His mind pieced something daring together. He explained, watching Aberanth's eyes pop and Farsa's brow knit into a bold line from how hard she frowned. There were questions, calls for him to reconsider, yet in the end, they agreed to his plan.

The team made their final preparations. Aberanth took his leave, using his parting words to hope that Talia's plan would indeed bear fruit and Thrall would leave before nightfall. With leafy packages strapped to his back, he set off east, giving the fortress a wide berth to avoid detection. Eidolan's illusions would be his signal to attack the eastern walls.

Holt and the others went in the opposite direction, getting as close to the ice tower as they dared while still being well hidden in the wood. On the way, Eidolan noted the position of the servants' door. Thrall's minions had made it easy to spot, given they had cleared an area of the wood around the entrance.

Unfortunately, Aberanth's hopes did not come to pass. The first day of autumn wore on until the sun began to wane, and yet no sign came that Thrall bestirred himself. No dragon nor rider left the fortress.

Holt could not help his attention wandering west to Talia and Pyra.

"I'm worried about them," he confided privately to Ash.

"Me too," Ash said. *"But they have their mission and we have ours. Let's focus on the night ahead."*

Almost as though she could hear their conversation, Farsa arrived by Holt's side just then and extended her hand. "It's time, Holt."

He unbuckled Brode's sword and handed it to her. Without its weight upon his back, he felt exposed, almost naked. Something of his unease must have shown in his face.

"Are you certain you want to do this?" Farsa asked.

"If it works, no one will question why I'm going over to the prison. It's the servants' stair, a larder, and a kitchen. Meaning no offense, but you would not fade into the background easily. Your whole bearing radiates—" he was going to say superiority but stopped himself. "It will feel natural for me," he said instead.

"It's imperative to keep your bond blocked," Farsa said. Her tone was in no way patronizing, and Holt had the distinct impression she was speaking to him as she would any other rider. "If you falter, even for a moment, then all of Windshear will know you're there."

"I can do this," Holt insisted.

"Holt won't fail," Ash said.

"If we're ready," Eidolan butted in, *"I shall place the illusion over him."*

Farsa nodded and stepped back with Brode's sword in her hand.

Eidolan closed his eyes and rumbled deep in his throat. The air around Holt shimmered and then a weak blue dragonhide cloak appeared over his body. To Holt the phantom cloak seemed semi-transparent, and he was able to look right through it if he wanted to, yet to the outside it would look the part. Its hood was drawn to help conceal his face but also to cover his bandanna. Eidolan knew his craft.

"Its magic is low enough to go undetected until you get close to a rider or dragon," Eidolan said. *"Best replace it with a real one before then."*

"I know," Holt said, rather sharp, but this was more from nerves. They had been over the details half a hundred times, or so it felt. He ran a hand over the vials and pieces of jerky at his belt, reassuring himself one final time. This time his fingers brushed over the hilt of his regular sword which he had unearthed to provide some measure of defense. To feign a Wyrm Cloak returning from some mission might look strange if he was unarmed.

With nothing left to do, he went to Ash and they pressed head to snout as Holt stroked Ash's face. "Stick close to Hava. I'll be with you again soon."

"Good luck, boy."

Holt squeezed his dragon and in his mind's eye drank in the beauty of the core. Its moon was full and silver, bright with power, well Cleansed and Forged since leaving the scourge tunnels. Now, he had to endure the hideous experience of closing the bond over.

Loneliness for friendship; sorrow for joy; despondency for optimism; loathing for love.

Back in Ahar, Holt had thought of Osric to generate the hatred needed. That had been blazing, ill-defined, and more influenced by Rake than his own feelings. Holt did not desire to kill him now, though he would if it came to it. His was a colder fury now, a fury based in Osric not resisting Thrall, in not being better, in giving in and allowing so much evil to happen.

The process felt all the worse for being so counter to his being, so instinctually and fundamentally wrong. He understood now how aghast his father became when ordered to change a dish to satisfy someone's tastes, even if that meant ruining the meal. Through force of will, he packed mud over a beautiful thing. The moon vanished. Holt shivered, and his chest rose and fell heavily. He groaned, as did Ash, but they both pushed through the pain.

"I'll see you on the inside," Holt said, then he quickly turned and marched for the forest's edge before he lost his nerve.

The journey felt long, walking alone in the gathering dark. At least in the clear land before the western wall he enjoyed the presence of the moon peeking out between thick clouds. A red dragon flew laps around the outer wall but paid Holt no mind.

With each step he hoped to hear Rake's voice. He was in range; Farsa had been farther away when he had contacted her. And with each step without hearing from Rake, Holt's nerve strained further. All he could do was keep marching forward, not too quick and not too slow. Nothing to draw attention to him.

Somehow, he made it to the base of the jagged bedrock of the fortress. Weaving around the sheer dark stone, he was well hidden from any watchful eyes up on the wall.

The servants' stair was guarded by a simple, sturdy door. No grand gate or causeway. Such things would have required space, and space could bring armies with equipment. It was a door begrudgingly built into the rock, serving those humans who were lesser and without the privilege of a dragon. The only other opening was little more than an arrow slit for a guard to look out from.

A voice called out to Holt through that narrow gap. "Halt, brother."

Holt drew up before the door.

"What is your purpose? None of the faithful are to travel alone."

"Please, brother," Holt said, beginning the tale he'd rehearsed. "I have traveled so far. My comrades and I were sent to Fornheim in search of eggs, but we were attacked by riders there. I barely escaped. I have... I have failed Sovereign. Please, allow me to report my failure and beg for forgiveness."

"Fornheim?" The darkness shifted from behind the slit as the cultist moved off, perhaps to confer with another guard. Holt strained his hearing, trying to discern how many guards were behind the door. Two he could handle. But what if a dozen sat behind it?

Worried the cultists were taking too much time to think, Holt dropped to his knees and raised his hands like a beggar.

"Oh, please, brothers, sisters," he sobbed. "I hear his voice even now. Won't you help me? A scrap of bread or sip of water?" His voice went hoarse, though it was not all performance. The icy emptiness in his chest already ached. Cold sweat beaded on his brow and neck, and his eyes felt as though he'd rubbed them raw. "If his forgiveness cannot be earned," he said, "then I am ready to accept my fate."

The low voices dropped, and the original guard returned. "Sovereign has been known to forgive those who have served him well," he said, although nothing in his voice suggested this was anything more than hollow words spoken to a dead man. "Praise him," the guard ended.

"Yes, praise him, praise him," Holt ended, as though tasting redemption.

The door opened by a crack. A young man with a hooked nose and heavy brow stepped out with a waterskin. He did not even wear a cloak of dragonhide. Holt stood, took the water, and drank heartily.

"Thank you," Holt said, wiping his chin of dripping water. The hooked-nosed man ushered him inside to where three low burning torches lit a dank passageway. It turned out that four cultists were guarding the door, but only two of them wore cloaks.

The nothingness in his chest sent a dizzying wave through him. Holt fought to keep focused. Four cultists in a confined space could prove an issue. He might be best getting up the stairs as quick as possible and taking the cloak from a lone guard higher up. Then again, there was no guarantee that he would find a sole cultist up in the actual fortress.

Before he could make up his mind, the door squeaked closed.

A gentle hand fell upon his shoulder. "Fear not, brother," said the hooked-nosed cultist. "In death we are all equal and free."

A weight plunged through Holt. In the dim light it was not immediately clear that the phantom cloak began to flicker. Holt struck fast before it died, throwing the man behind him sideways against the wall. As the illusion died, the other three cultists cried out in shock and scrambled for weapons.

Holt drew his sword. This simple piece of steel felt flimsy in his hand now, more a toy than a weapon. Its reduced reach caused him to miscalculate two of his strokes, enabling the two cultists to form a front against him. Holt slashed, but the pair raised their cloaks and the scales checked the blade.

Holt took one step back and breathed hard. The dead weight in his chest made his every movement feel heavy and labored, even if they were still fast compared to the humans.

The two with cloaks advanced. One took out a vial. Holt thrust this toy-like sword for the exposed hand. This time he struck true, causing the man to howl and drop the vial. His opponents changed tactic. All three charged him at once, throwing him to the ground.

The fight descended into a brawl of fists and hard kicks. Holt fought inexpertly, but through virtue of being able to kick harder, punch harder, and take more than his fair share of blows, he emerged victorious from the heap. Head ringing, he staggered upright and retrieved his fallen sword.

A whimper sounded from behind him. Holt whirled, having forgotten about the first guard. The hooked-nosed man with no cloak stood with a vial of dark red blood in one hand. He trembled, though Holt did not think it was fear of himself but of the vial of blood.

Holt snatched the vial from his grip and smashed it upon the floor. The young man ceased trembling and got to his knees, begging as Holt had pretended to beg. Rake would have killed him. Holt had likely just killed three of his fellows or else crushed half their bones. Yet the whimpers and shaking gave Holt pause. This one was no threat; he'd even been kind, in his own way. Holt knocked the man out cold instead.

He took a moment to support himself against the wall, ensuring his bond with Ash was still blocked, then checked the supplies at his belt. Three elixirs had smashed: one each of Sinking, Grounding, and Floating. *Just great*, he thought, picking up a strip of fallen jerky from the pile of bodies. He sniffed it. The wine was potent, so he shoved it back in with the Floating meat.

Next, he bent to pillage a green cloak. He would have felt sick putting it on had he not already felt so terrible. He fastened it at the front to help conceal his belt and drew up the hood. At least there would be no low hum of magic from the illusion to draw attention to him now.

Finally, Holt grabbed an open-top crate with waterskins and assorted supplies for the guards. This additional piece of his hasty disguise taken, he made for the stairs. Already his muscles ached as though gripped by fever, and he had not even started the climb. As he took his first steps, Rake's voice entered his head.

"Holt?" he said, faintly.

"I'm coming," Holt replied in his head. *"Hava should be just within range of you. Tell her I'm in."*

"Holt..." Rake sounded so weak it was frightening.

"Hold on," Holt urged, groaning as his body protested under the strain of the blocked bond and the steep stairs. Resting stations were built at intervals, though they weren't manned.

"There are five wild dragons," Rake told him.

"Farsa told us," Holt tried to tell him.

"Two storms, and one each of fire, mystic, and emerald. No ice."

"Rake, listen to me. Tell the others I'm in."

"He's so strong," Rake said, and Holt began to worry that Rake could not hear his replies.

"Rake, are you still there?"

No reply came, but then it hadn't exactly been a conversation. Fearing for Rake, Holt powered on up the never-ending stairs.

~

Osric

After dragging Rake back to his cell, Osric returned to the mystic tower to gather the favored hatchlings and bring them before Sovereign. Five had been selected now, and they assembled before their master in the great hatchery.

There was the strong ginger bruiser; the sea-green drake with webbed feet and no wings; the rust hatchling with blood-worn eyes; the amethyst dragon with the crystalline scales and no tail; and the golden one, who bore no obvious physical defects and was of a normal size and build. Of the five, the golden dragon seemed to understand this and held itself with a bearing Osric could only describe as noble.

Osric stood at ease, awaiting his orders. Sovereign was on his feet, shuffling around the hatchery in lieu of having room to prowl. A restlessness had come over Sovereign, and his eyes seemed far away.

"Is there anything else you would ask of me?" Osric said.

Sovereign snorted and gave him a sharp look. *"Stay."* His snout twitched and then he turned, facing southwest toward the Fae Forest and far into the night.

At length, the door to the hatchery opened and the Speaker entered. The scars on her face were half-veiled by the shadows tonight, though the mad glint in her eye could never fully be darkened. Her smile was crooked, and she did not meet Osric's eye as she approached.

"You should not be here," he said. Should she bond with one of the dragons by chance, it would have serious implications.

She ignored him and stalked past to drop to one knee. "Your magnificence, I have instructed the Shroud to make preparations. Supplies are being gathered for your chosen aspirants as we speak."

"Food for the hatchlings?" Osric said. "You intend to leave."

"You are capable of good counsel," Sovereign said. *"I have decided it is time. The prisoner will break tomorrow, I'm sure of it. He can join us then."*

"Is it worth straining your power to take him?" Osric asked. Sovereign still faced west. Something or someone clearly drew his mind. And he did not reply.

A few moments of silence passed, and then the Speaker rose abruptly.

"I shall see it done, your magnificence."

The moment she left, a silent, snake-like shudder ran up Sovereign's long neck. His oaken eyes fell upon Osric in a deadened stare.

"Tell me what is wrong so I might assist you," Osric said. "Is it the scourge? The riders? Wild Flights?"

Sovereign made to speak, but at the last moment he closed his eyes as an unmistakable flicker of pain creased his face. It had to be something to do with the scourge, Osric thought. What else could strain his focus so much?

"Only five," Sovereign said, and he must have meant the hatchlings. *"After all this time and effort, I had hoped for more."*

"Better an elite force than a rabble," Osric said. "All the hatchlings have been brought before you. You have chosen the best."

"All of them?"

Osric's heart seized. "Of course," he said. The lie came so easily that he almost fooled himself. The shadow dragon, twin of the golden drake, no doubt skulked in the corner of her hatchery even now. Despite telling himself over and over that he ought to bring her before Sovereign, he'd never been able to bring himself to do it.

"What would you have us do with the others in your absence?" Osric asked.

"Dispose of them."

"If a garrison remains to hold the keep then a few might—"

"None can stay." Sovereign winced through some fresh pain and closed his eyes. He growled, then snapped his jaw as though the air insulted him. The five hatchlings squawked and yapped then, rustling their wings and slapping their short tails off the stone.

"I have called the Champions to us," Sovereign said. *"You will stay with me until they arrive."*

Holt

After a hard climb that left his enhanced lungs clawing for air, Holt reached the top of the servants' stairs. Another small, sturdy, unassuming door stood between him and the fortress beyond. He pressed his ear against it and heard a bustle of activity within the storehouse. Holt took the time to collect himself. His desire to reach Rake soon had to be tempered with him playing a role.

When ready, he pushed on the door. Even knowing it would open, he was amazed that it actually did from the outside. That was the power of riders, he supposed. What human could threaten them in their fastness of rock, so high it might as well have been built upon the clouds? A scourge force big enough to threaten them would never reach this point undetected, and only ghouls would be able to fit inside the stairwell. Hardly a threat at a choke point such as this. So it was that Holt entered Windshear Hold.

Several non-cloaked cultists glanced his way as he entered, took in his cloak and his crate, then returned to their tasks without a second thought. Holt moved purposefully to the trap door on his right.

The passage was narrow and lit by candlelight. It led him to a cold larder far larger than the Crag's, though only a fraction of it was in use. Open barrels and hanging meats clustered around a step ladder at the heart of the cellar. Bubbling water and the smell of boiled cabbage drifted down with a half-light from another trap door.

"All the hatchlings?" a tired voice asked.

"Just those ones Sovereign favors best," said another.

"How come? We just sorted their food—"

"Don't ask questions. Just do it."

A non-cloaked cultist – a kitchenhand as far as Holt was concerned – descended the step ladder. Holt kept to the shadows, unsure how best to proceed. It was hard to think clearly when his head pounded relentlessly.

The kitchenhand unhooked a haunch of pork and returned up the ladder, leaving the trap door open. He must have intended to return for more.

Quickly and quietly, Holt emptied the crate of its waterskins and breadcrumbs and pilfered two hanging legs of lamb which he placed in the crate instead. Along with his throbbing head, his stomach roiled. A powerful need to retch swept over him, but he gulped it back down. He could not bring himself to vomit inside a larder.

Footsteps rang, approaching the larder. Holt scurried back to the shadows. The same disheveled kitchenhand wearing a stained apron returned. Holt wondered whether these non-cloaked people were true followers of Thrall or unfortunate victims forced into service.

The servant left, shutting the cellar door behind him. Holt sighed in relief and made his way back into the passage leading to the storehouse. After the first bend in the tunnel, he could no longer suppress his gut and so allowed himself to retch against a wall. After that, he felt marginally better, though the sweat was beginning to make his shirt feel sodden.

Just a little longer, he thought.

Back in the storehouse, only one servant remained, and she was too preoccupied with stacking crates of blood vials to notice him.

He stepped out of the storehouse and into the yard of Windshear Hold. The moon was a shard of silver tonight. The distant side of the vast fortress was shrouded by night. Despite the time, the yard was surprisingly busy. Groups of cultists walked with heads bowed against the wind, and two wild dragons rested close to the mystic tower. The others and the riders he could not discern without his magical senses, and he appreciated how reliant he was on his sixth sense now it was gone.

To his left and straight ahead, the ice tower rose like a black obelisk. Not far from its base was a low windowless building. The prison. Holt made for it. It seemed the best he could do. Stride out with purpose and hide in plain sight. He kept his strides even, however, the right sort of speed. To stop would be to draw more attention. He was supposed to be here – he kept that thought in his head. He was doing some mundane duty. He was to be invisible.

Alas, he was not far from the prison when heavy movement and a snarl caused him to stop. A dragon crept toward him, sniffing the air hungrily. Its coloring was hard to make out, but if it was this enamored by the raw legs of lamb it could only be a mystic.

Holt froze. It was both the correct response of a servant and also of genuine panic.

"Honored dragon," Holt said, his throat bone dry. "This food is intended for the prisoner."

The mystic snarled and slithered out its forked tongue to taste the air.

"What is the meaning of this?" A woman hastened to them, wearing red brigandine. Her broad dark face could not hide the fact she hailed from Ahar. Could this be Dahaka?

Holt gulped. "Honored Rider, I am fortunate for your arrival. This food I carry is for the prisoner."

"The prisoner?" she said, confused. "He has been fed on bones and scraps. Who gave you this order?"

"Lord Agravain," Holt said, and then, recalling the words of the cultist at the gate and Osric's link to Thrall, he added, "I am honored to carry out his will, and of Sovereign. Praise him."

"Praise him," Dahaka said, though she said so slowly. She shooed the mystic drake away. "Leave before I have Zahak discipline you." The mystic rumbled low in its throat but evidently did not have the power to challenge a rider. It sloped off, and Dahaka stared toward the mystic tower for a painfully long moment. Holt thought she might be communicating with her dragon or indeed Thrall himself. Then the moment passed and she dismissed him with a terse, "On your way."

Holt bowed his head and said, "My humble thanks, Honored Rider." He didn't want to overdo it, not knowing exactly how the Wyrm Cloaks might speak to a rider, but Dahaka had swept off before he'd risen from his bow.

Legs trembling, Holt forced himself to keep moving. To his great fortune, Dahaka had accosted him close to the prison so that the guard had witnessed the incident. This cultist wore a cloak of dark blue scales.

"I'd feel more comfortable if General Agravain were still the one to deal with the prisoner," the Wyrm Cloak said, in an accent reminiscent of Brode's Athran upbringing. "Not natural what that thing is. Stolen the dignity of a dragon, I reckon. Sovereign will undo it, praise him."

"Praise him," Holt said in a low voice. And with that supplication to Thrall, to Sovereign, Holt was allowed inside.

It wasn't a large complex, little more than a long corridor with five grim doors. Holt opened the first one and found a short ramp leading down to a cell dug out from the living rock, just as Eidolan had described. A portcullis barred the cell. Behind it, scored by shadows from the bars, lay an orange tail.

"Rake," Holt hissed. "It's me."

Rake seemed to almost flop out of the shadows. He gripped the bars for support and dragged himself half-upright. Holt threw a glance back to the entrance of the building, then stepped down to the bars.

"Eat these," he said, passing the lamb through. "I know you can have it raw. Just eat it, okay." Rake took the meat and tore into it without hesitation. "Are you able to reach out to Eidolan?"

"Yes," Rake said. Blood from the lamb ran down his chin.

"Tell Eidolan it's time. He and Aberanth will give us cover to reach the ice tower." He pulled out a Grounding elixir. "Drink this."

Rake took the vial and drained it along with a strip of lamb he tore from the bone. Still chewing, Rake said, "You look awful."

Holt felt almost giddy with relief. Rake was still Rake.

"I'm blocking my bond," Holt said. "Threw up once already. I can't hold it much longer. Are the others coming?"

Rake nodded. "You must have really missed me to endure that. Get me out of here, Holt."

Holt backtracked and found five ancient pulley and winch mechanisms with heavy chains. Only one chain was pulled taut to the ceiling.

Holt grasped the winch with both hands and began to crank. The resistance was incredible, and for a moment he did not think he could do it without reopening his bond. Yet the chains shook, then a sharp screech rang as the portcullis began to rise.

Luckily for Holt, the noise of the portcullis was covered by roaring outside. Shouts followed, nothing Holt could make out, but he assumed Eidolan's distractions were taking effect. He cranked the shaft, the chain wound around the trunk of the winch, and sweat poured down his face. Rake emerged, stumbling through the doorway of his cell. He clutched his chest and leaned against the wall for support.

The door to the prison was thrown open then and the guard burst in. He might have been about to ask what was taking Holt so long. He might have wished to warn him that the fortress was under attack. Holt never found out. Seeing Rake out of his cell, the guard cried out and raised his blue cloak, for all the good it would do it. Rake seized him bodily and threw him hard against the far wall, turning the man into a skin bag of broken bones. The crunch and snap were terrible.

"Don't look at me like that," Rake said, wincing and clutching his chest on one side. "You'll spill more blood before the night is over."

"I don't have an issue with killing," Holt said. "I just don't enjoy it." He let go of the winch. The portcullis screamed closed, but the time for quiet had passed.

Holt reopened his bond to Ash. The relief was delirious. Ash's warmth flooded his body, and Holt felt human again. Information from his sixth sense flooded in. Thrall's power stood as a giant among children. And he was on the move, leaving the rough area of the mystic tower.

It was so hard to process that Holt didn't register Ash's words at first.

"No," Ash wailed. "Holt, we weren't ready."

"What?" Holt asked dumbly. His magical senses began to catch up. Ash, Eidolan, and Hava were at the edge of his detection. They weren't yet inside the fortress, nor were Eidolan's illusions.

"What have you done?" Rake said.

A booming roar seemed to shake the entirety of Windshear Hold.

Osric

Sovereign's distracted mood grew worse. His every word was terse. The hatchlings wailed, voicing the tension Osric felt. Even with the bond closed over, something of the dragon's thoughts echoed between them, rising and falling in a staccato rhythm.

Champion Orvel arrived, looking wary and confused by the summons. Other than to defend him against Rake, Sovereign had never requested his presence. Osric maintained a stony expression and met the Low Champion with narrowed eyes.

Champion Dahaka came next, and though more enthused to be in

Sovereign's presence, she too bore a wary expression. She came to a halt on Osric's right. To his left, Orvel shifted closer.

Osric remained at ease, suppressing an instinctual twitch to draw his axes.

At last, the Speaker returned. She stepped forth before the three riders and dropped to one knee, closest of them all to Sovereign. The dragon visibly fought to return his attention to the hatchery and lowered his snout over the Speaker's head as if to hear her whisper. Whatever discussion they had took place privately. When next Sovereign spoke, it was to Osric that he directed his thoughts.

"You have lied to me."

"That is not possible." He noticed then, really noticed, the lack of pain in his chest. The dragon bond had been closed over often of late. Occupied with interrogating Rake, Sovereign had left Osric alone for longer stretches of time. Even his routine of Cleansing and Forging had fallen by the wayside. Alas, all things, whether good or ill, must end, and so Osric expected Sovereign to rip open their bond and seize the truth from his mind.

Instead, with his gaze still fixed on Osric, Sovereign said, *"Speaker?"*

"The black dragon is in the highest nest, your magnificence. Just as the Champions said."

Both Orvel and Dahaka refused to look at him.

"The moment the youngling saw me, it seemed to reduce to oil and merged with the shadows," the Speaker continued. "Forgive this failing."

"There is nothing to forgive, dear Speaker," Sovereign said. *"You have been loyal."* A pressure grew in the air then, or so Osric felt. It pressed upon him, coiling at his chest and throat, as though Sovereign's black chains had become real. *"Of all the troubles I foresaw from you, Osric, betrayal was not one. A soldier through and through. You did not even consider such a possibility in your own men."*

Osric had not. When with the Iron Beards, he had seen ties form between comrades as strong as any between rider and dragon. He'd been an ill-fitting cog in their machinery, but he'd hoped his Gray

Cloaks could become that for him. A new family. He should have known better on that front as well. Family was no guarantee of safety.

A Risalian within their ranks had betrayed the company, costing Osric the Toll Pass in the war between Brenin and Risalia. Osric had taken the man's head, and with it the sense of brotherhood he'd felt for all of them. That blow had sent him on his journey to the Spine. To Sovereign.

"Nothing to say?" Sovereign asked. He screwed his eyes shut through some new strain and struck his tail off the wall. When he reopened his eyes, they shone with his dark power. *"Having you make those axes was an error. You've been defiant and will only grow more so. Perhaps you've outlived your usefulness."*

"You need me," Osric said. He wasn't afraid for himself. If Sovereign killed him, so be it. For Sovereign, the sudden loss of a bond, even theirs, must surely lead to some torment. He needed a rider to efficiently Cleanse his core. What Osric feared was what Sovereign would make him do before killing him.

Even as this fear blossomed, the dragon bond reopened. Sovereign's presence ventured across like probing tentacles, more effortful than usual. Osric tried to gauge what drew the majority of his mind but saw nothing but black corridors with the occasional pocket of fleeting amber and green light.

"You shall not move," the charming voice said, and Osric agreed with it. He had no intention of moving anyway.

"Leave, dear Speaker," Sovereign said. *"Leave tonight and take what faithful you can with you. You are too precious."*

Hunger bloomed in the Speaker's eyes. Whether today or a week or a month from now, Sovereign would cast Osric aside, leaving the position open to one more loyal. She prostrated herself one last time before sweeping out of the hatchery.

"Orvel," Sovereign near spat the name, *"go and retrieve this black hatchling."*

Orvel looked relieved to be leaving and cast Osric a final sympathetic glance before departing. Osric tried to move. His feet twitched, but he remained rooted to the spot.

He wondered how it would end. After being forced to kill the hatchling, would Sovereign have Dahaka take off his head? Whatever happened, he hoped for the chance to grip his axes as he passed. Dying with a weapon in hand would be more honorable.

Just then, Dahaka and Sovereign exclaimed in shock. Osric felt it a moment later. A new presence within the boundaries of the fortress. A Champion, fresh and rough around the edges, yet something of its essence put him in mind of deep night and distant starlight.

Sovereign bellowed, though it was with joy. His thoughts ran wild, spilling over to Osric in an unchecked torrent. The boy was here. He'd come right into his talons. Take him, take them. The girl in the west mattered little compared to this. Rake his. Ash his. The world his. A million minds and one. Ours. The chosen must be safe. Loyal drakes must come.

Something ran underneath the deluge from Sovereign. A reverberation of sorts, not an echo but more of a counter-current, distorted and at odds with Sovereign's own will. Osric could make no sense of it. He clutched at his head, willing whatever it was to end.

Three wild dragons hovered outside the hatchery. With their arrival, Sovereign backed out and left. The hatchlings scurried forward like pups frightened by the departure of their master, and the wild drakes flew in to guard them. Each one gathered power at their mouths, their eyes fixed on Osric.

There was no need for it. Sovereign's chains held him firmly in place. He only wanted to obey. Thoughts continued to spill across the dragon bond in confusion. Inside Holt's mind. He would have him. Resistance? A portion of the boy was sealed off. What was this?

The flow ceased abruptly. It was so sudden and silent that Sovereign might have died. Then horror raced, a panic unlike anything Osric had felt from the dragon before.

A booming command rang out.

"Destroy the eggs and the spares. Leave none for the enemy."

∾

Holt

Thrall's roar shook his bones. Holt knew his blunder had killed them all. He'd revealed himself to Thrall. He'd been so sure the commotion outside had been Eidolan's distractions.

"We have to run," he said in a high voice. It wouldn't work, but it was all they could try. Holt tore for the exit and Rake lumbered after him. Outside, Windshear was in a state of thunderous activity. Dragons flew to the mystic tower, while cultists bolted across the yard or else seemed stunned into a catatonic state.

Above a great dragon loomed, then descended sharply into the yard. Thrall struck the ground, his scales a seething red of black blood, his eyes shining with the same black light Osric had imbued into his axes. His presence so close drowned all else; where the other dragons were now, he could not tell. Even Ash paled for a moment under the pressure exerted by Thrall.

Rake placed a gentle hand on Holt's shoulder. *"Focus on one clear, powerful thought,"* Rake said telepathically. *"Something he cannot break. And trust me."*

Thrall advanced. *"You do not disappoint, Holt Cook. Before I seize you, know you have my thanks. Great powers will rise because of your discovery, and I shall lead them in shaping the world anew."*

Holt did not even have a chance to open his mouth. Thrall's presence raced into his mind, more complete than when he'd tried from afar in Sidastra. The sweet voice urged him to be still, and Holt found no reason to argue against it. He went rigid.

Holt – the part of him that was still himself – shriveled almost to nothing. One thought. Rake had said to cling onto one unbreakable thought.

Naturally, he first turned to Ash, and yet, grim as it was to conceive, his bond with Ash was not unbreakable. Bonds could break, even if it took death. Both could linger on after the other passed. They each required something even deeper than the bond to root them.

'Help the others.'

His father's dying wish. Holt's wish. Even before Ash, he'd hated seeing suffering he was unable to relieve. Even were Ash to die, Holt would continue to help where he could. Even a dragon-less rider had strength and he would put his to use, not sit in an Order Hall in quiet grief. He would help. He was a defender, not a killer. No matter what Rake desired of them.

'Help the others.'

These words were unbreakable. Holt used them as his shield. The charming voice whispered instructions, though it was not so convincing now. And then, without any reason why, the voice cut off mid-sentence. Holt could no longer feel Thrall's presence. Nor could he feel half of his body. His vision on his right side went dark, he no longer felt his right arm, hand, or leg. Yet vision on his left side remained, and he retained weak control of that side of his body as though learning how to move for the first time.

Some invisible yet solid force in his mind kept Thrall at bay. Holt could not push against it, as though he were hemmed in by a wall.

Rake's hand squeezed Holt's left shoulder, the side he could still feel. Rake. Somehow, Rake was doing this. Yet surely it was all for naught. Already, Thrall's power besieged the defense, and Holt had no way to buttress it against the assault.

In the physical world, Thrall backed off, snarling at something unseen. He roared, and it was in unmistakable panic. The wall inside Holt's mind crumbled. Rather than confronting Thrall's full power, he found the dragon's presence already leaving. And in the hastiness of Thrall's retreat, Holt gained a glimpse of the horror that suddenly gripped the dragon.

A dark chamber. A tunnel of green and amber light. Scourge corpses. Slime and blood. A rider stood before him. Crimson was her armor and her hair fell like golden flames. Talia. It had to be Talia, yet that was all he saw.

Thrall left him. Holt rushed back into full control of his own faculties, his head spinning from the intrusion.

Several things happened at once.

Thrall issued a thunderous roar and kicked off into the air. A host of new cores popped into existence somewhere beyond the western wall. Rake yanked him to one side and grunted, "Run."

Holt faced the base of the ice tower. He started to run. The green dragonhide cloak he wore trailed in the wind. Rake followed with agonizing heaving breaths. No sooner had they begun to run than dozens of drakes flew over the western wall.

Eidolan's phantoms were vaguely shaped, yet under the cover of night they sufficed. A mixture of emeralds, which made the attacking force appear somewhat plausible. Two collided and passed right through one another, but in the brewing chaos such things were easily missed.

Thrall's wings beat heavily. He was already beyond the northern wall, rising into the night. Wild dragons followed in their master's wake, carrying small hatchlings in their talons. Inside the fortress, his forces scattered. Wyrm Cloaks ran in every direction, and dragons took flight before the ghostly emeralds.

Trying to track the cores became impossible, like trying to hear a lone voice in a crowd. The one he could feel was Ash's, and he was coming.

"Holt? Holt! He's leaving."

"Youngling," Hava's voice cut through. *"Make for the ice tower."*

Holt ran, as did Rake. No notion to fight entered his mind.

There came a crack from across the yard so great that the mountainside might have split. Crashing stone ended in a clang loud enough to wake the dead.

More chaos. Wyrm Cloaks peeled off, no doubt running to the eastern wall, where surely some attacking force had broken through.

Holt's world condensed to the door of the ice tower. They were going to make it after all.

That was when his world became fire. Flames fell in a stream of blazing red from above, landing between them and the tower.

"Halt, beast!"

Rake fell, sudden and hard as though his legs had gone out from under him. Holt pivoted back around. A forked barb of fire from a long whip gripped Rake's shin.

Dahaka advanced with her rippling red blade drawn in one hand and the whip in the other. Rake was down. Fire swirled ever closer, encircling them, trapping them. Dahaka raised her sword. Holt had seen Talia cast lethal jets of flame from her own sword as an Ascendant and did not like the look of Dahaka's blade charging with magic.

Hastily he took a bite of ginger-infused jerky, washed it down with a woody elixir and Floated his mote channels. His skin shone silver under the dual benefit of both potion and food, and as the roaring fire raced toward him like a ballista bolt, he raised the dragonhide cloak.

The scales were of some poor emerald, not fully flame resistant, but they bore the brunt of the attack. Dahaka's Exalted Champion fire burned a small hole through the cloak and then a lashing tendril struck him. Pain lanced at his side. It felt like grasping a hot pan handle with his bare skin. Holt screamed and twisted aside yet met only the wall of flames, a wall which wound ever tighter around him.

Just then, a fierce gale blew hard from the west. The flames were flattened under its power and Hava shot overhead a moment later. Her scales, bright as steel, shone from both fire and moonlight. While she carried on into the broader chaos of the yard, Farsa descended to the ground, cushioning her landing with a strategic use of air. Wordlessly, Farsa threw Brode's sword Holt's way. He snatched the scabbard out of the air, drew the blade, and dropped the sheath. If he survived, he'd find it later.

"Surrender your blade, sister," Farsa called, her voice hard.

Dahaka did not surrender. She screamed some curse in her native tongue, then the two Exalted Champions clashed. Wind and fire roared. The entire yard of Windshear quickly became an arena for their duel.

Eidolan came over the wall next, with Ash flying jerkily close behind him.

"*Change of plans,*" Eidolan said. He touched down, a little shaky from concentrating on his army of illusions.

Ash landed badly behind him. Holt sensed his disorientation and anxiety from the solo flight, a feeling he now knew well from learning to walk blind in the tunnels.

"Boy, you're hurt," Ash said.

Holt only then remembered the searing at his side. He shrugged out of the cloak and looked at his injury. Half his shirt was singed black. A fist-sized patch of his skin was raised red, blistered and dry. He wished he had worn his leather and mail. He wished his body's burgeoning resistance to magic had been allowed more time to develop.

"I'm sorry," Holt said, his eyes streaming from the burning pain. "I messed up."

"Now's not the time," Ash said. *"We should get Rake out of here."*

"No," Rake gasped. He leaned on Eidolan's proffered neck for support and got to his feet. "Thrall's gone. If anything worthwhile will come of this, now's our chance."

Savage screeching cut over him. Hava flew above the battling riders, twisting and turning, fighting off two dragons at once: one the red of burning coals, the other a verdant green Holt swore he recognized.

"Get on my back, Rake," Eidolan said.

Rake pointed to the mystic tower. "He's ordered the remaining hatchlings be destroyed. Can't you feel it?"

Holt's magical senses were still overwhelmed, though most of the genuine cores were indeed clustered around the mystic tower. Many fledgling cores with dim or flickering power, and even as he observed them, one was snuffed out. Then another.

The cultists were still in disarray. Many fled toward the storehouse above the servants' stair. Within the mystic tower there was at least one other Champion, though they were of a lower rank. There was still one great danger unaccounted for.

"Osric might still be in there," Holt said.

"We must try," Ash urged. A need to do this for all those like himself passed over their bond. Holt agreed without the need for words. They melded their senses. Holt jumped onto Ash's back and they took off, giving the warring dragons a wide berth as they made for a hatchery halfway up the mystic tower.

Ash hurtled into a slaughter. Two surviving hatchlings cowered before hulking, swollen cultists. At the doorway stood three Wyrm Cloaks with crossbows. They fired at once and, being impossible to miss at close quarters, all three bolts sank into Ash's hide.

"*Poison,*" Ash said. Light gathered at his mouth, but just before he launched his beam, he staggered sideways. The beam missed the crossbowmen and splintered the door instead.

Holt leaped down as Ash stumbled. He could deal with the brutes first and save the hatchlings or attack the crossbowmen and spare Ash further harm. Though it pained him, it was an easy choice. Holt sped through the crossbowmen, taking the trio down one by one with ease.

He then Grounded his mote channels and made for the great brutes. They were much too fast for such large creatures, reminding him of scourge abominations, wielding long halberds as though they weighed nothing.

To Holt's dismay, the brutes seemed unconcerned by his presence and entirely fixated with the desire to kill the hatchlings. One brute swung its halberd so hard it cut a little pink dragon clean in two. Ash roared with fury and found a burst of strength through the numbing agent to pounce to the brute's side and drive it to the floor under tooth and talon.

The second brute made for the last hatchling. It was brown, a true oak brown, not merely muddy like Aberanth. Foolishly in his haste, the cultist turned his back to Holt, making him easy prey. After dealing with the brute, Holt checked on the brown hatchling. As it seemed unharmed, Holt ran to Ash's side and pulled the poisoned bolts out.

"Should have remembered that."

"*No way to avoid it fighting them,*" Ash said. His movements were sluggish, and his feet no longer seemed capable of supporting his weight.

The surviving hatchling wailed. Holt tried to calm it, but it kept backing away. Something or someone behind Holt drew its attention. Its eyes went wide, then it scurried around Holt, heading for the door.

Heading for a man in green brigandine Holt could hardly believe was here.

Orvel, the same Orvel who had tried to kill them in Brenin, stepped into the hatchery. The hatchling scampered up to Orvel, then slid in behind his legs. It must have known Orvel. Must have thought it would be safe with him.

"Don't," Holt cried, but too late. With a blank expression on his face, Orvel turned in a fluid motion and his dragon-steel blade took off the hatchling's head.

Ash tried to bellow but the roar gargled in his numbed throat.

Holt screamed well enough for them both, "Blight take you!"

If Holt was surprised to see him, Orvel was doubly so in return. "How are you... I thought the Order must have—"

He cut off and looked at Ash, squirming under the effect of the numbing agent. He smiled and raised his leaf-like sword.

"Once again, your dragon is weak, and you are nothing without him. Ethel won't save you this time."

While he spoke, Holt wasted no time. He wolfed a strip of salted jerky and downed a Grounding elixir. Silver veins marbled his muscles and he eased into a more confident pose, enjoying the lithe strength and speed waiting to be unleashed.

He ran through his odds. Ash was all but out of the fight. Holt would have to go sword to sword here. Orvel's powers required living soil and plants much like Aberanth, so, magically speaking, Holt had the advantage.

His sense-sharing with Ash was still in effect. Holt closed his eyes and lowered his bandanna. As his hearing increased to compensate, he tracked Orvel's blade as it cut the air. Holt danced aside from those first strikes, prioritizing building a strong Flare in his left hand. A split second before he unleashed the light, Orvel turned. It was a slight movement, but Holt registered the shuffle of feet and the change in direction of Orvel's sword.

The result was that Holt's Flare had little effect. A heartbeat later, Orvel turned back and renewed his advance. Holt's strategy seemed suddenly useless. Scourge were unthinking, dim-witted opponents. They did not consider what a glowing ball of light might mean, and as it took Holt five seconds to build a Flare, his intentions were well signaled.

"You were only an Ascendant before," Orvel said, his voice dripping with bitterness. From the sound of it, he would take pleasure in the kill.

Holt could not claim he did anything but hold his own. When the chance arose, he drank his last Grounding elixir and managed to maintain the cycle of energy to his limbs. This kept him in the fight, but he could not gain the advantage. Orvel at last put him on the back foot.

Holt needed a Flare to work. He needed to blind Orvel, even just for a second. His problem was the length of time needed to ready the ability.

Holt switched from Grounding to Sinking. His skill in this cycling method was far from ideal, but any edge could mean life or death. He pulled on light from Ash's core, and with energy swirling close around his bond, the power needed for a Flare flowed quicker than before. Holt raised his hand, picturing the white light exploding in Orvel's face. Orvel still predicted the move, though not quite fast enough this time. He half-turned as the light exploded. Groaning, Orvel ducked away, putting distance between them to recover.

Holt took that chance to drink one of the black elixirs. Vinegar burst upon his tongue. The energy flow around the bond picked up in pace. Orvel hesitated, coming to a halt. Holt used the available seconds to ram a sour piece of jerky into his mouth. The mote channels around the bond gripped with a new strength, as though squeezing the magic through from Ash.

"What is this?" Orvel called. A touch of fear lay beneath his voice.

Holt did not detect anything unusual. A light might have been pulsing at his sternum, which would be visible through his thin shirt. Perhaps, though it seemed an odd thing for Orvel to be shaken by. More frustrating was that Orvel had not advanced again like Holt had assumed he would and remained half-turned, ready to face away from the light. Holt did not have many chances left.

Flares still consumed a good portion of Ash's core. In the scourge chamber, the ability drained almost twenty percent of the core. Since then, Holt had Forged the core to new heights, practiced the ability, and trained his mote channels to be more efficient in it. Producing a Flare now cost him less magic. Even so, he could maybe produce a Flare five times before fraying their bond when fresh. Almost half of Ash's moon already lay in shadow. He could do two more Flares at best, and then his bond would fray.

Holt had to force the issue or change tactics. He lifted his bandanna and opened his eyes, hoping this might trick Orvel into thinking he'd given up on trying to blind him.

A darkness lay heavy over the hatchery. For a moment, Holt wondered if he'd opened his eyes at all, but then a grimy firelight from low braziers reached him. All the same, Orvel and even Ash were obscured by a black miasma. In contrast, Ash's core shone brightly from an increased volume of lunar motes. That made little sense. There was only a slim waxing moon this night, and they were currently half inside a building.

Orvel backed out of the dark fog, and the further away from Holt he moved, the more visible he became. It was then Holt understood. His super-charged Sinking – boosted by potions and jerky – not only centered his own power but also drew lunar motes, lunar light, toward him, into him. As he lacked a core, the motes spilled over his bond to Ash. Holt was sucking in the moonlight. He was creating the darkness.

"*Start Sinking,*" he told Ash, and he threw a piece of Sinking jerky over to help.

Orvel swept his sword in broad strokes and stepped carefully to the edges of the hatchery. Yet the area not engulfed by darkness was diminishing fast. With Ash's help, the scant moonlight reaching the hatchery was pulled toward them both with such force that the blackness became pitch and complete, as thorough as any underground tunnel. Braziers stood as inadequate islands, and otherwise the only light came from the fires raging below in the yard.

Still Sinking, Holt lowered his bandanna again and stepped with confidence through the darkness. He heard, faintly through Ash, the thumping of Orvel's heart.

"I might not be strong without Ash," Holt said. "But that's the point, Orvel. If you care only for your own personal power, you'll gain little. It's a partnership. A bond of equals."

Orvel came at him blind, his strokes wild and exaggerated. Holt parried with ease, forced him back, checked the green blade again, and ended with a strong slash at Orvel's midriff. Brode's sword parted the leather and steel plates of the brigandine. With his more sensitive ears, the breaking of the steel sounded shrill, and the squelch of cut flesh held a whimpering quality to it. Metal clanged against stone, then slipped with a clatter into the night. Orvel gasped, a sharp intake of breath as though he were surprised.

His heart fell silent.

The roar of agony from a dragon below could not be described as anything other than heartbreaking. A sound to challenge whether any good could happen again. If there could be pain such as this, then it was cruel to be alive and court the risk of such tragedy.

Holt felt flat. Not deadened from apathy but from accomplishing a deeply unpleasant task.

He ceased Sinking his mote channels and Ash followed suit. Raising his bandanna, Holt readjusted to the pale moonlight of the hatchery and the fires burning below. Orvel was nowhere to be seen. The lack of the sound of a body collapsing should have made this obvious, but Holt hadn't realized he had fallen back over the edge. Orvel's final journey had been made in silence.

He peered over the edge. Here at the precipice, Holt stood over a world on fire. Heavy smoke billowed at the mercy of the winds. Gea was nowhere to be seen. Hava, free of the emerald, turned her full attention to the fire dragon Zahak. She hurtled through the night, too fast to be caught. Surrounded by the wind of Windshear, she was in her element.

The last time Holt had stood at the edge of a hatchery had been with Ash's egg. He'd held it over the gray waves and found he hadn't had the strength to let go. It seemed the world had irreversibly changed since then.

He drew back and ran to Ash.

"I'm fine," Ash growled. *"The hatchlings. Go to them."*

Holt turned his attention back to the fledgling cores within the tower. A handful still flickered, and he assumed they were higher up the tower. Over their bond, Ash willed him on.

'Go', the feeling seemed to say. *'Save at least one of them.'*

Holt's heart almost broke right there again. With Brode's blade in hand, he left the hatchery and took the stairs up the mystic tower.

Osric

Sovereign's command was an endlessly tolling bell. *"Destroy the eggs and the spares."* Sovereign had taken his chosen five. The rest held no meaning to him, and so they held no meaning to Osric. None of them. Once done, he would deal with Holt Cook and Rake once and for all.

Yet despite the charming voice's insistence, Osric found himself passing hatchery after hatchery, leaving those nests to others. He passed Orvel on the stairs and continued to climb until he came to the top of the tower.

The door was open. Members of the Shroud had made it here before him. The sandy, clubbed-footed dragon had fought well. A red-cloaked woman lay in a pool of blood.

"Kill them all," the charming voice insisted.

Osric searched for the black dragon. He found her big eyes looking out in horror from a dark corner. A cultist with a halberd closed in on her.

Osric threw the man aside. "She deserves a better death than from the likes of you."

He advanced slowly, gazing into those purple eyes floating as though on black clouds. Osric drew Vengeance. He drew Spite. He stopped. His desire was to follow his orders, for he was a good soldier, obedient and efficient. Why, then, had he stopped?

No more, his own small voice suggested.

"Do it," the charming voice said, stern now.

Not her, the small voice said, growing stronger.

"Obey me, scum," Sovereign said, his voice reaching across the rapidly growing distance between them. The chains seized Osric, yet the links seemed taut and shaky. Brittle iron rather than unbreakable dragon-steel.

In his current fury, Thrall had abandoned subtle nudging, and Osric found himself moving forward involuntarily. His right arm raised itself high. The beard of Spite glinted with a savage dark light.

The black dragon squealed. She cried out to him, so small and so fearful.

Through it all, one peculiar thought occurred to Osric. Sovereign was not raising both axes. His left arm hung loose at his side. Osric could feel the wood of the handle against his palm. He could move it. He flipped the axe around in his hand so that the beard of the blade pointed up. And as Thrall brought Spite down to kill the black dragon, Osric, of his own free will, brought Vengeance up hard toward his right hand. His writing hand, his fighting hand. The hand that had killed his brother.

Osric severed it at the wrist.

The black chains shattered. Thrall bellowed, and then, as though skidding to a cliff edge, he tried to dig in but with all the success tooth and talon would have upon rock, inexorably falling to his doom. His presence left Osric. The knot of thorns in his chest imploded. He fell hard to his knees, blood spurted from the stump, his skin turned chalk white and clammy. His mote channels, darkened, died, then broke down. Black sweat oozed from him. No, not sweat, the last of Thrall's poison.

The pain was such that he did not feel it at all. His whole being was emptiness. Broken beyond repair. Dead. Already dead. What final vestiges of him remained were the last gasps of a husk.

From the shadows, a black snout emerged as though forming from slick oil. She no longer seemed frightened but sad, then something behind Osric drew her attention and, for the first time, she bared her teeth.

The Wyrm Cloaks were still in the hatchery. They would kill her, and his efforts would have been in vain. He could not let that happen.

'Do the job and do it well.'

He was a soldier. Soldiers killed, but they also protected. He had known that once, fought for that. If he were to die here, then let it be in defense one last time. He'd taken his own life to save the hatchling, but the task was not complete.

'Do the job and do it well.'

Osric rose onto one foot. Then the other. He turned, the world still silent to him. The sandy dragon lay dead, its tongue hanging from its mouth. The Wyrm Cloaks now charged for the black hatchling. Osric still held Vengeance tight in his left hand. His throat throbbed with a scream he could not hear as he cut them down. First one, then two, then three, then four, until blood drenched his axe and arm. He killed them all.

He saved her.

Osric collapsed. His vision swam. The black dragon hurried out to him, crying her small soft cry and nudging him with her wet snout.

"*Look at me*," he said, the thought no more than a whisper. She seemed to understand him and lowered herself, so her great dark eyes met his. Now he understood why he found them so captivating. The last pair of eyes to affect him like this had been Esfir's.

A swell of love rose within him. Where such a store of it had been locked away, he did not know, but now it washed through him like a cold salve. Love cleaned the wound in his soul and, still holding the dragon's gaze, he managed to tell her, "*Stay*."

A kernel of warmth bloomed in his chest, and then the world went dark.

～

Holt

. . .

He took the stairs as fast as his Champion's body permitted. Yet he knew he had failed. Spectacularly failed. Only a lone core remained. This one. He had to save this one. He'd promised Ash, and he'd promised himself.

He skidded to a stop before the open hatchery. Death reigned here. Cultists and infant dragons alike. To his astonishment, Osric Agravain lay sprawled upon the ground. Blood seeped from a severed wrist, and his skin was as pale as Ash's scales.

This struck Holt dumb.

"Osric's dead," he told Ash. Ash shared his uncertainty over how to feel, but before either could think it through, a shadow across Osric's chest wriggled. The shadow morphed, becoming a dragon, a small oily black hatchling. The sole survivor of the night. It bared its teeth at him and wailed, placing its body over Osric's own.

"I'm here to help you."

The black dragon either did not understand him or, more likely, did not trust him. He dropped Brode's sword, then showed the hatchling his palms.

"I'm not going to hurt you."

The black dragon continued its barrage of feeble roars and would not move from Osric's side, though it seemed too terrified to do anything more. Holt crouched low and approached slowly, offering it his hand to inspect.

The hatchling's roars dropped to a growl. It sniffed his hand then gagged, as though choking on something foul. Yet it ceased growling at him. Instead, it crept to Osric's stump, cooed lowly, and licked at his wound.

"Don't," Holt said, dismayed. It was only then his mind caught up to reality. Osric's wound still bled, which meant his heart still beat, which meant he was alive. Barely. Holt knelt at Osric's side, feeling judged by the stare of the little black dragon. 'Do something,' it seemed to implore him.

"He's alive, Ash. He's not dead. I need Aberanth. Tell him to fly to the highest hatchery and bring his pastes."

Holt elevated Osric's injured arm. He unbuckled his belt, letting vials and jerky fall to the floor, then wrapped it around Osric's upper arm and tied it tight. He knew to do that much.

"You want to save Osric?" Aberanth asked him.

"Yes... no... I don't know," Holt said.

"I'm flying up now."

"What are you doing?" Rake sounded livid.

"Stopping a man bleed to death."

Rake ranted on but Holt ignored him, searching the hatchery for evidence of what happened. It looked like all the other hatcheries. Dead hatchlings. Cracked eggs. Cultist bodies from where the dragons had fought back. Many cultists had gaping wounds through their cloaks that could only have been made by dragon-steel wielded with unnatural strength.

Osric had killed them. This mere fact could only mean one thing.

Aberanth arrived in the hatchery with two of his leafy bundles between his talons. The little black dragon yowled at him the moment he landed.

"Take the hatchling to one side," Aberanth said.

Holt tried to move the baby but it snapped at him, squirmed free of his grip, and went back to Osric.

"We're trying to help him," Holt said. The hatchling settled a little, though it looked on at the proceedings with wide eyes and continued to issue small mewls.

Aberanth inspected the wound. *"It really ought to be cauterized."*

"I take it Dahaka did not surrender herself?"

"She's dead," Aberanth said dully. *"As is Zahak. Farsa and Hava won."*

Holt nodded, dimly aware now of the absence of the Exalted Champion in his magical senses. Farsa and Hava were there but felt different than before.

"The brazier in the corner," Aberanth said. *"The coals can heat a piece of metal. Not dragon-steel, it won't be hot enough for that."*

One of the Wyrm Cloaks had a dagger tucked into their belt. Holt took it. Aberanth also told him to pour one of his Floating elixirs over the blade to clean the steel. That done, Holt placed the dagger into the brazier. The steel gave off a sizzle of heat when he removed it. Holt gently pressed it into Osric's wound, and now the sizzle was grotesque in both sound and smell.

"That will do," Aberanth told him. He opened one of his leaves, then nosed out the jar of healing paste. Holt needed no instruction. He applied it thickly and the mixture bubbled as it worked. As it cooled, Aberanth produced clean cloth from one of his leaves, and Holt wrapped up Osric's stump.

With Osric out of immediate danger, Holt's own charred skin asserted itself. He peeled away the remains of his shirt from the site of Dahaka's fire and winced as he looked upon the blistered flesh. Aberanth sniffed, scoffed, then urged him to apply the paste. Holt rubbed it in. It reeked of a bitter herb he could not place, but its cooling effect was as much of a relief as reopening his bond to Ash had been.

Heavy footsteps and a rhythmic clunk of wood sounded from the corridor outside. Rake limped into the hatchery, out of breath, using the shaft of a halberd as a walking stick.

"A cruel thing to do," Rake grunted. "To save a man only to kill him later."

Holt retrieved Brode's sword from the floor and held it warily. "We can't kill him in cold blood."

"I can," Rake said. He limped closer. The black dragon must have sensed the danger in Rake for it sprang into action, roaring its sad little roar and placing itself between him and Osric.

"Think, Rake," Holt pleaded. "Those Wyrm Cloaks would have offered him no fight. Osric must have cut his own hand off. He can't be under Thrall's influence anymore."

"I sense none of Thrall's power in him," Aberanth said.

"Meaning nothing," Rake said. "We didn't sense Thrall through him before, but he was there. We couldn't kill the dragon, but this is the next best thing." He advanced, halberd raised. The black dragon roared louder, but Rake brought his weapon down.

Holt moved fast and blocked the blow.

Rake snarled. "Are you going to fight me, Holt?"

"No, but I will stop you." They parted. "You're injured. Your core is spent."

"I had enough to save your mind from Thrall," Rake said. "Now step aside."

"No," Holt said firmly.

"Master Rake, stop this," Ash pleaded.

Aberanth too stepped in between Rake and his patient.

"You as well?" Rake said with scorn. "Killing Osric removes Thrall's rider. It weakens him."

"If you kill him," Holt began, "Ash and I will abandon you. If you want help undoing what happened to you and Elya, you won't get it from us."

"Keeping Talia's uncle alive won't change a thing between you."

"I know, Rake," Holt said, shouting now. "I know. This isn't about me, or you, or Talia, or even him," he added, pointing to Osric. "It's about not murdering a man in cold blood. He's—" Holt froze. He'd felt it then. A pulsing beat from Osric. A dragon bond. "It can't be Thrall, it's too—"

"Weak," Rake finished. His grip on the halberd slackened.

All eyes turned to the little black dragon.

"It feels like..." Holt began, searching for the words.

"Like our bond did just after I hatched," Ash said.

"Yes," Holt said, his voice hoarse now.

"As fresh as a Novice bond can be," Rake said.

"If you kill Osric then you'll surely kill the hatchling along with him," Ash said.

"Can we know for certain he's rid of Thrall?" Rake asked. "What's one hatchling to be sure?"

"Ash was just one hatchling," Holt said. He tightened his grip on Brode's blade, ready and prepared to use it now. "I won't let you do it."

Rake sighed and the fight went out of him. He slumped his shoulders and let go of the halberd. It clattered to the floor. The black dragon stopped its squalling. Holt assumed this was due to the end of the argument, but then he noticed Osric blinking through heavy lids. He opened them to narrow slits of vision.

"Look who's the prisoner now," Rake sneered.

FORTY-SEVEN

The Deep

Progress under the mountains was slow but steady. What scourge they encountered were few, sporadic, and easily rebuffed. Above ground the Emerald Flight, along with the dragons of the Order come to join her, patrolled the hills, checking for wayward scourge. It seemed too easy. Then again, Talia had come better prepared this time, advanced cautiously, and had the added advantage of five seasoned Champions and ten fellow Ascendants alongside her. Though their magic was limited, each was worth scores of men, bolstering her front ranks into a deadly force.

"Are you still with me?" Talia asked Pyra.

"We're here," Pyra said, though she sounded muffled as the bond struggled to penetrate the layers of solid rock between them. General telepathy with other dragons on the surface was now impossible. *"Can you sense the chamber?"*

Talia strained her magical senses, looking beyond the riders around her and cresting out through the dark. On the previous occasion, the presence of the scourge orb felt like fallen bark compared to the mature oak of a dragon's core. Now, with the distance from Pyra limiting her and the orb still deeper underground, the best she could say was that 'something' was there.

"Is this what you felt the last time?" Ethel asked. She'd tied her blonde hair back into a long ponytail.

Talia nodded. She raised her torch to get a read on the other riders. Their expressions were grim.

"If they had doubts," Ethel said, "then they've been dispelled."

They carried on, and as they descended deeper, Talia felt Pyra's presence drop to the merest flicker. Before the distance became too great, Pyra offered a fiery blast of support, a torrent at the source, yet by the time it reached Talia it was reduced to a spray of water at the end of the waterfall. Another step and Talia lost her dragon completely.

Loss through distance was not so severe as a closed bond, and a world away again from a broken one. All the same, a pain stabbed around her heart.

Talia halted, pressing a hand to her chest. Cold waters seemed to flow through her veins, or perhaps they were only returning to the temperature of a normal human. She blew a shuddering breath, feeling a chill in the tunnel for the first time.

Other riders stumbled and leaned against the tunnel walls, more dropped to one knee with a fist pressed into the stone. Fire went out from the hand of one Ascendant. For a moment all of them stared vacantly into the dark, as though feeling mortality for the first time in years.

Beside her, Ethel moaned as though ill. "I was not prepared for that. Does the tunnel feel hot to you?"

"Feels cold," Talia said.

Ethel breathed hard and pulled at the collar of her gambeson. "I have not felt apart from Strang in fifty years."

"You have a strong bond with him," Talia said. "I'm sure he's suffering from your absence as well."

She thought of Pyra in pain and had to push it aside to carry on.

A few officers, including the Twinblades with Aren between them, came out from the front ranks.

"Our queen," the twins said. "Are you well?"

Aren cast the sickly riders a wary expression and muttered something in Skarl.

"We can no longer communicate with our dragons," Talia said. "It's unpleasant, but we'll adjust."

A number of Housecarls stomped out to their Prince, throwing dark looks toward the Twinblades. They tried to encourage Aren back, but he shrugged them off with stern words, then looked fiercely to Talia and planted his feet in a firm manner.

"We think he's been trying to walk by your side," said Eadwald.

"He pushed through the ranks during the march," said Eadwulf. Neither of the twins understood Skarl, and none of the Housecarls spoke Alduneian. Talia's one hope to keep Aren's head on his shoulders lay in his guards being as keen for him to fall back as she was. Wordlessly she pointed back to the front lines, willing him to heed her. He gave a small shake of his head and took another firm step forward.

Talia did not need Pyra's fires for her anger to rise. She pushed him, well, more a gentle nudge for her, but it caused him to take a step back.

"Don't make me force you," she said, hoping her tone would convey her meaning. Aren didn't move, but he didn't take any more stubborn steps either.

Her officers followed next, voicing concern for the riders and wishing to know if the expedition would continue.

"We go on," Talia said.

A short time later the passage reached a great crossroads. The riders identified the passage where the presence of the orb felt strongest. One Mystic Ascendant highlighted strange markings upon the wall of the tunnel, three simple lines stacked evenly on top of each other. Carved into the rock, they could not have been accidental.

Talia touched the markings. She recalled the carvings in one of the passages leading to the first chamber.

"What is it?" Ethel asked, stepping in closer.

"I'm not sure, though I saw something like this before."

She had not investigated further then, for they had been

ambushed, and after events in the chamber she had wanted to get her men out as soon as possible. Yet there was some time now. Talia backtracked up the tunnel they had come down and searched the wall there. Near the mouth of that passage where it met the crossroads, she discovered another carving: two clean horizontal lines not unlike an equals sign.

It soon became clear that each correct fork in the road was marked by similar carvings as though someone had already cleared the path ahead and marked the way.

Down they went. The air grew stiff and humid. Bond or no, everyone felt the heat press in. A rancid smell drifted up as if out of a nightmare. At length, Talia and her riders came to the end of an expanding corridor, marked at its end by the most intricate series of carved lines yet. More intriguing, however, was how the carving shone with a green light.

Some form of magic, Talia assumed, and the riders approached with care. It turned out that the carving did not produce the light but reflected that of their torches and lanterns. It was of a smooth, shiny, resin material, amber in texture yet lurid green from the blight.

Almost as one, the riders pulled back.

"No ghoul or bug could have made this," Ethel said. Her hair clung to her from sweat, though her breathing was normal again.

"Has anything like this been reported before?" Talia asked.

No one answered.

Her soldiers muttered and whispered to each other. News from the front ranks passed back up the whole column.

As Ethel was the most senior of the riders, the others took their lead from her. "The enemy has been left unchecked," she told them. "Something fouler than we could imagine has grown in the depths. We must go on."

However much the discovery of the worked amber caught Talia by surprise, it was nothing compared to the shock of stepping out into the next passage. A cavernous space, an endless dark above, and good flat earth underfoot. By the time two Champions had advanced to the other side, they must have been two hundred yards away from her.

The air felt lighter here and did not reek as badly as the narrow tunnels.

If only the surface entrance had connected directly to this vast highway. Their dragons could have easily ventured down with them, with space to fly.

"Look down," Ethel said.

Even as she said it, Talia stepped on something. A bone crunched underfoot. The skull of some small creature, a squirrel perhaps, though she could not be sure. Other bones littered the ground at intervals, some with decaying flesh clinging to them and quietly festering. Patches of bloody fur or hide lay rotting as well. Yet bits and pieces of the scourge were evident too, shed chunks of chitinous exoskeleton, and between it all were trails of dried blood, bile, and other fluids of creatures from who knew how long ago.

Not so long ago, Talia thought. Enough time would have broken the flesh down and turned the fluids to dust. Dried out and grizzly though it was, it was no ancient trail.

Talia pulled Ethel to one side. "Holt and Ash described something like this from their time underground. They said that carriers took materials to a chamber to be processed. If we follow this trail, we'll find the end of the road."

Ethel said nothing but drew her sword. The other riders followed, and Talia too drew her red blade. A seventh sense, not magical but instinctual, that told her battle drew close.

The sheer width of the highway stretched their ranks perilously thin, so her soldiers collapsed into a tighter square formation. Upon all four sides shields were held outward, with the men of the second rank holding their shields over the heads of the first rank, and then the third row shielding the second. Behind them, spearmen kept their weapons aloft to ward off enemies from above, and crossbowmen kept a bolt loaded. Supplies and other equipment were taken into the middle of this moving fortress. Riders stayed outside the formation on all sides.

At a turtle's pace, or so it seemed, they progressed down the highway. Slow though it was, Talia would not have them break it. Her own desire for the fight burned low without Pyra's fires in her chest, but she'd rather lost her appetite for reckless danger. She would not charge blindly into the dark again.

The trail of bones and detritus led them in sight of a great archway. Unlike the other roughhewn passages, which were circular, as though eaten out by some great worm, this arch was sculpted, crudely, as though by child-like hands, yet deliberately. Beyond it lay a smooth descending hallway. Pockets of genuine warm amber sparkled in the ceiling alongside more of the blighted resin. A soft light bounced between all points, and such a light in the utter darkness seemed suddenly bright and painful.

Something pressed upon her heart. Her magic lay far behind her, yet she knew the chamber and orb lay down there.

"We're close," Ethel said.

That was when the first tremor ran up from the amber hallway.

Ethel sheathed her sword and spoke to the other riders. "We need fire, not steel."

The second tremor beat harder and lasted longer. A shrill cry raced to greet them.

An Earth Ascendant pressed their hand to the ground before remembering they lacked their magic to listen to the stone.

Talia spun around. Her troops were a hundred yards behind the scouting riders.

"Hold there," Talia cried, then darted back to them along with the riders. The most senior officers, Harroway's handpicked men, urged her to form a wedge and so split the oncoming tide. She agreed. As the troops reformed, those carrying ceramic jugs upon their backs came forth. These jugs contained balls of pig fat bound by thick linen. Other jugs contained oil. Talia called the riders to her.

"We don't need accuracy on these," she said, picking out one of the balls of pig fat. She dipped it lightly in oil, then set it alight with her torch. As the fire blazed up the cloth, she hurled the ball up the highway. "We just need some light to see by."

Riders should have balked at a task clearly intended for slingers. Yet these were no longer riders of the Order and this no ordinary mission. None protested as fifteen riders of Falcaer sheathed their blades and picked up pig fat. Soon, over a dozen flaming balls were soaring. She could not take credit for the idea, for it had been Harroway's, drawing inspiration from trebuchet payloads used to light up a besieging swarm. Riders were a more efficient delivery system than he could have hoped for. Half their supply was depleted within a minute, creating tiny islands of fire in the otherwise dark sea between their wedge and the amber hallway.

The shrill screams reverberated up the never-ending highway like a choir of the damned. Ghouls scrambled up from the amber hall, dimly lit by the blue fires of burning fat. Flayers came next, cutting ghouls aside in their haste to reach the wedge of shields and steel.

Talia and half of the riders stood at the tip of their formation to bolster the soldiers there at the thinnest point. There was precious time to think, never mind communicate, before the swarm thundered into them.

All the horrors of her last fight in the depths remained the same. The terror of the dark. The deafening cries of scourge and dying men. Bile and blood gushing to become slippery underfoot. Yet the panic was not the same. Their wedge held. Spears protruded at every point like a metallic hedgehog. The best-trained soldiers given the best equipment – they held.

Lacking Pyra's inner fire, Talia felt sluggish. A sweeping arm of a flayer caught the tip of her steel crown and ripped it from her head. The crown scraped her forehead and pulled strands of her hair free with it. Two riders aided her with the flayer, taking it out at its thin knees. She spared a moment to look for her crown, found it by the glint of the metal, and then a juggernaut pressed its bulk on top of it. Talia, Ethel, and the others encircled the juggernaut, making it hesitate over which way to turn before they struck at once on all sides. It fell bodily upon her crown, and with the fight raging she left it there.

A buzzing dominated the air. It took Talia a few moments to extricate herself from the fight and realize the zip of approaching wings came from behind. Without dragons or siege equipment, her men were vulnerable from above. Thwacking thumps of triggered crossbows sounded in vain. A stinger or two might fall, but she remembered vividly how the carriers at Sidastra crash-landed onto groups of soldiers, killing themselves but taking many men with them. That same tactic here would break her formation in a matter of seconds.

"Ethel," she cried, "push ahead to the tunnel." As Ethel rallied riders to her and struck forth toward the amber hallway, Talia urged the formation on. "Make for the tunnel. We must take cover."

Maintaining formation while cutting forward was slow going. The stingers and carriers would arrive long before they reached the safety of the tunnel. Crossbowmen fired blindly, but howls from the dark suggested some bolts struck true. Talia moved to the back, pulling riders to her as she went. Four stood with her, including the one who wielded a spear. All their blades dripped with black gore.

What sparse light they had could not reveal the descending stingers, and their field of flames was now being trampled by their own wedge pushing forward.

Talia braced herself yet missed the first stinger as it dove out of the blackness. It flew over her head, right into the flank of the wedge. Another dove after it. This time she leaped in time and cut a grievous wound into its bulbous body. It crashed down harmlessly into the space the formation had just vacated.

She led this desperate rearguard fight all the way to the amber hallway. One Ascendant went down under three stingers and Talia lost sight of her as the darkness swooped in. The spear-wielding rider was a powerhouse, his long reach a perfect counter to the flying scourge. Flaming balls of fat flew with little effect over Talia's head, though she appreciated that someone had the sense to dispense with them before entering the confines of the tunnel.

Somehow, they made it. Amber and green light threw the world into sharp relief. Stingers were forced to scuttle along the ground, losing balance on their unsteady legs as they scrambled over the bodies of scourge and human alike.

While they were now safe from bombardment, the column was trapped in a sloping tunnel and fighting on two fronts. Talia had no idea how Ethel and the others were faring at the bottom of the shaft.

She had no knowledge of the twins or Aren or any of the Skarls. All she could do was prevent the stingers and carriers from entering the tunnel.

Their compound eyes glistened like wet lumps of coal. Dark foam frothed at their mouths. A hundred spots of amber light sparked in them, and a hundred red swords swung as Talia kept them at bay.

She feared they were trapped and confronted by overwhelming odds. All the caution and strategizing in the world might have been in vain. This was the scourge's home territory; for once the humans were the encroachers, and their greatest warriors, the riders, lacked their main advantage down here in the deep.

Yet with a sudden chorus of shrill shrieking and clacking mandibles, the bugs retreated, fleeing over the dim embers of smoldering fat until they vanished into the dark of the highway.

Talia breathed hard and allowed herself a laugh of delirious relief as the troops began to cheer. Her fingers gripping her sword felt numb. Strips of red leather and cloth from her brigandine were torn free, but the steel plates had done their job and kept her intact.

The scourge had fled as though thoroughly routed. Ethel must have pushed into the chamber and severed the controlling orb.

Talia made her way down the slope of the amber hall, beaming along with her troops. A chant of 'Red Queen, Red Queen, Red Queen,' rose out of the victory. She passed the Skarls and was relieved to find Aren dirty-faced but unharmed and the twins still at his side.

The bottom of the ramp leveled out into an antechamber with a final archway. Ethel and the other riders stood over the corpse of an abomination and looked down in sorrow. Talia followed their gaze and found the body of a Storm Ascendant in gray brigandine lying under the giant skeleton.

"Without our magic, what are we?" one Champion asked.

"The best warriors the living still have," Ethel said. Her armor was damaged like Talia's. Her blonde hair was matted, her face stained with blood, some of it her own from a thin cut on her temple. The wound, though small, issued a black puss, and the skin around it grew dark.

"The blight," Talia said.

Ethel raised a hand to her face as though surprised by the injury. "I'm okay," she said, suppressing a shudder in her voice. "It's minor. Once I make it back to Strang, I'll fight it off."

How Talia wished Holt and Ash were with them now. A High Champion like Ethel would be fine from a minor infection, but many others would not be so lucky.

"We pushed through too hastily," another rider said.

"If you hadn't, half the army would be flattened," Talia said. She looked for evidence of the orb's destruction. "Where's the orb?"

"We haven't gone past this point," Ethel said. "One moment we were fighting to hold the tunnel and the next the ghouls and flayers fled as though their queen had fallen."

Talia's heart skipped a beat. The scourge had lured her into a trap before. What could this retreat be but another ploy?

"We've got to destroy the control orb right now," she said. "Come, riders, with me."

They stepped through the archway and into the chamber. A vat bubbled, hissed, and smoked acrid vapor. The riders fanned out with torches in hand, and a few troops gingerly followed in behind.

Talia squinted ahead, looking for some sign of the green light of the orb. With Ethel by her side, she approached the center. They reached the beginning of a mound of enormous bowels winding upward. Talia spared a moment to keep from retching. The peak of this meaty hillock was veiled in a dark cloud which was not altogether natural, like smog but thicker.

She placed a foot upon the horrible entrails. They were stiffer than she'd anticipated and could take her weight. Even as she took her first step, the dark cloud above parted in a burst of tainted light. Lurid purple and green streaked with black pulsed along the surface of the higher entrails, revealing the monstrosity above them.

The growing queen hung suspended from the ceiling. Undulating raw muscle, tendon, and tissue formed the strings of this horrifying mannequin. Its pincer was large enough to cut a man in two but still far from its full, dragon-crushing potential. Its other arm was fully grown and so seemed gangling, with spindly fingers each the size of spears. A lower body remained encased in a gelatinous, semi-transparent shell through which the early stages of leg development could be seen. Such small legs on such large a creature might have been comical, but under the circumstances it was only sinister. Its skull was half-formed, flat and ant-like, with enormous hollow eyes and a gaping mouth filled with teeth closer to a dragon's than any insect.

The eyes filled with swirling red energy, just as she'd seen in the fully grown queen at Sidastra. Talia got the impression it was looking directly at her. It opened its mouth and issued a wet, gargled sound laced with creaking bones.

She took a step back, but Ethel carried on up the mound.

A ghoul emerged at the top of the mound, under the queen and beside the orb. It began to speak, if speech is what it could be called, and though it was mangled, the ghoul had once been a person or grown from one, and so something of the words made it through.

"T-touch... iitttt."

Ethel advanced, her icicle-blue blade raised like a lancer.

Something was clearly wrong. Talia felt to do the obvious was to court blunder.

"Wait," she called to Ethel, but too late. Ethel dispatched the ghoul, and its words died in its throat. She turned on the orb. Talia started up the mound again. Just before Ethel could strike, she seized. Dropped her sword. A still, quiet moment gripped the entire chamber. Then Ethel screamed. She screamed so hard Talia feared her throat would burst, and she twitched in angular, painful movements before falling and rolling down the entrail hill.

Talia rushed for her, but a strike of black power blasted into her path. She whirled, finding the incubating queen's long-fingered hand brimming with magic. The queen was still fixated on Talia and crackled something incoherent. Was it trying to speak to her? Nearby, a ghoul Talia presumed slain staggered up onto its knees and talked to her in the same mangled speech.

Touch it – touch what? The orb?

"Nobody move," she called to the other riders.

A growling battle cry came from behind. For a moment, she thought one of their dragons had dug their way down to them, but it was Aren charging with the Twinblades, his Housecarls hot behind him. The young man had a set of lungs that did his family's sigil proud. He hurled a throwing axe toward the talking ghoul, then turned his attention to the queen.

Talia sensed the danger but could not make it to him in time. The queen hissed and sent a torrent of power toward Aren. He stood rooted and stunned, perhaps feeling the warmth of magic for the first time. Eadwald ran in front of the prince and absorbed the blast.

Talia's own shriek of fury was drowned by Eadwulf's howl. Talia ran for the fallen brother. His skin marbled from the blight – there would be no surviving this, perhaps not even if Holt had been with them.

Seething, Talia turned her fury onto Aren. "Back," she bellowed. "All of you, back." Aren looked at her, and his youth and inexperience had never been plainer. He was fierce but not yet strong. She was ready to knock him to the ground and drag him off herself, but he shrank before her. A Champion had the sense to physically shepherd them away.

Ethel was still moaning low and gasped every breath. Eadwulf dropped down to join Talia at his brother's side, hands trembling as he made to take Eadwald's hands in his. Talia seized his wrists.

"No," she said. His silent submission was awful, but she would not have them both taken by this thing.

"I am... cold, brother," Eadwald said in a high voice. Then his eyes rolled up into the back of his head, leaving only the whites shot with green veins. He went rigid, then cricked his neck in a disturbing manner.

"This – vessel – will – suffice."

The words left Eadwald's mouth, but it could not be him speaking. Each word uttered was stilted, as though the puppeteer was learning how to pull the strings.

"Thrall?" Talia asked.

"Not – the – jailor," Eadwald said. He jerked into awkward movement, trying to stand.

"Brother?" Eadwulf's voice cracked.

"Get back," Talia urged him. "Please."

Her soldiers followed her orders and retreated into the amber tunnel. Aren and the Skarls were nowhere to be seen. It was just her, the riders, Eadwulf, and Eadwald's animated body.

"We – would – speak with – thee – Agravain. We do – not have – much time."

FORTY-EIGHT

A New Order

It wasn't Thrall speaking to her. This impossible, insane thought didn't quite register. Whatever possessed Eadwald cricked his neck again, causing a horrible pop of bone.

"We have splintered – ourself," the thing said. Its words were better formed than before. "We must speak with thee in haste. He – knoweth."

Whenever the thing stopped speaking, a deathly silence reigned in the chamber. Ethel lay quiet and still in the fetal position. No one went to her side. Few moved at all, save the riders at the distant edge of the chamber taking the most delicate of steps, trying to return within earshot.

This thing had gone to great lengths to speak with her, so Talia would humor it, until she thought it safe to strike at the orb.

"What are you?"

"A thousand minds – and one."

"You're a creature of the scourge?"

"We are every creature we have tasted and every mind we have subsumed. We are the swarm, and the swarm is us."

The creature spoke strangely, and though it suggested it was not a single entity, it spoke with a clarity that surely only a unified mind could bring. Scourge Queens were thought to be the pinnacle of the scourge, but perhaps not. Was this an emperor of sorts? A queen of queens?

"Do you control the scourge?"

"We did." Though its speech had smoothed out, it still used Eadwald's mouth clumsily, pulling his lips wider than needed on almost every word. With his eyes rolled back to show only the whites, the blight spreading across his skin and now this stretching of his lips, his face had turned into a grotesquery.

Eadwulf sobbed. Tears ran from his eyes and his arms trembled in fury. Talia trusted him to keep it together.

"Does Thrall control you now?"

"He doth, though there are fleeting moments when a piece of ourself breaketh free."

"The other chamber that I found," Talia began. "Was that you or Thrall?"

"T'was us. Through this and the dragon we know of thee, Talia Agravain."

"Your minions tried to kill me and my men just now. Why attack if you wanted to speak with me?"

"We cannot be present in all places at once. Through their eyes we witnessed thine assault. Thou art not the sole human to discover us of late. Another piece of us hath been lost."

That would have been Holt and Ash's work.

"I can't say I'm sorry to hear that."

"Thou must find more of us."

"Why would I want to do that?"

"We have grown pieces of ourself abroad to control our swarm. The dragon hath seized our mind and maketh use of these to extend himself. Thou must destroy more to waste the dragon's reach."

Talia looked at the green orb. The queen still looked directly upon her with its swirling red eyes. This whole thing was as obscene as it was horrific. How she wished for Pyra to be here to burn it clean.

As best she could puzzle over what the creature meant, it seemed to be an answer to how Thrall was able to use his powers over vast distances, directing the incursion into Feorlen and now likely Brenin.

"If more chambers can be found," Talia said. "If they are destroyed, won't that harm you as well?"

Altruism would not be the creature's motivation.

"We shall lose these pieces and awareness but not forever."

"What does that mean?"

Eadwald's neck pulled back before the creature jerked it forward again to hang at an awkward angle over one shoulder.

"We shan't say."

That was hardly surprising. The creature wouldn't reveal more than it had to. Right now, it seemed to have adopted the enemy of my enemy is my friend mentality. Thrall was their common problem, so she should focus on him.

"Tell me anything else you can about Thrall. Anything that might help me stop him."

"We will not."

That did take her aback.

"Don't you want rid of him?"

For the first time, the creature seemed to consider. Eadwald's face twitched as though fighting some internal war.

"If the dragon prevaileth too soon, he will eradicate us," it said, ending in a hiss. "And yet much of his ambition aligneth with our desires."

She supposed that much was also true. The blight's purpose was to wipe out humanity, something Thrall sought as well. The dragon riders were the only real obstacle. Thrall turning riders to his cause weakened the Order. A conscious mind behind the scourge would also benefit from these actions, making its own task easier, assuming it could break free from Thrall's control in turn. Her gut clenched. Adaskar had predicted her actions would lead to chaos and disaster. And what had she done? Helped to splinter and weaken the Order further.

What to ask the creature next did not come easily. Its own goals were balanced on a knife edge. Aiding Talia and the living too much could lead to its own destruction, yet too little and Thrall would succeed.

"If Thrall destroys you, would the scourge end with you?"

It did not answer.

"If you wished to stop Thrall, why not act sooner? He nearly conquered my lands."

"We are aware," it said harshly, as though it had faced its own demise at swordpoint. "Thy victory didst weaken him. And we be stronger now than when he first came upon us—" It clammed up, and Eadwald's body twitched. With a jerk he became still as stone, and the creature regained its former bearing. "Seek other pieces of us."

"Does Thrall know I am here?"

"Yes."

"Then he'll place heavy defenses wherever these chambers are."

"Where possible we shall splinter ourself as we do now to assist thee. Thou must do this," it urged. "Thwart thine adversary."

"You are my enemy," Talia said. It made her feel sick. Destroying these chambers was necessary and right, and yet doing so seemed to be in the creature's interest. For all Talia knew, taking out the control orbs helped the creature in some way, irrelevant of Thrall. Both had to be stopped, and yet to fight Thrall was to also aid the scourge itself.

It was perverse.

"We are," it said. "But if thou wishest to vanquish the dragon, these steps must be taken."

"I'll still kill any scourge that I find."

"As we will assimilate all we find. Until the world is ours. A million minds and one." Eadwald bent double. Crooked and hunched, the creature twisted his neck to look at her with his blank white eyes and said, "Hurry. He cometh for us."

"Good," Talia said, revolted with herself and the whole situation. With nothing more to be said, she raised her red blade and took the squelching staircase to the queen and the orb. With a clean stroke, she cut the orb free from its plinth of hard muscle. No screech of pain or defiance rang this time. All light from the orb and the eyes of the queen snuffed out. Some of the riders came to join her in cutting the queen down and taking off its head.

Back on the chamber floor, Eadwulf knelt by his brother's side. Eadwald's eyes had returned, but whether the man behind them had as well, she could not say. He held his brother's gaze in silence and they clasped hands. Rasping breaths grew shorter and shorter until he breathed no more, his chest stilled, and his eyes closed mercifully over. Eadwulf wept, and his own silence was somehow worse than any cry of agony.

Ethel was back on her feet, supported by a Mystic Champion.

"So many voices," she sniffed. "I'm sorry," she added, though she said it to no one in particular.

"You have nothing to be sorry for," Talia said.

Ethel gulped and clung hard to her fellow Champion. "Strang," she said feebly. "Where is Strang?"

Talia's mind turned to Pyra. Eager to be gone, Talia and the riders took their remaining jugs of pitch oil and doused as much of the chamber as they could. Once their soldiers and the injured were safely back up the amber hallway, Talia threw down a torch and began the blaze.

It would not be enough. No fire could cleanse such a place completely.

She ascended the amber hallway and left its glow behind to rejoin her expedition. Her men picked their way across the battlefield in the highway. Eadwulf struggled to haul the body of his brother with the help of another soldier.

"Give him to me," Talia said. She took him in her arms, and Eadwulf stayed close and held a torch for them to see by.

"It should have been me," he said.

Only empty platitudes came to her lips, so Talia held her tongue.

Eadwulf stroked his brother's hair. "I am the elder. The elder should be the first to meet the end. Poor little brother."

As they trudged across the battlefield, Talia caught a glint of crooked steel jutting out from under the belly of a juggernaut. Her crown, or what was left of it, twisted and broken.

She left it there to rust.

Only when the pink light of dawn fell upon her face did Talia realize how long they had been underground. Fresh air brushed her skin, cool and soothing, while the full and unhindered connection of her dragon bond brought heat back to her blood. The reassuring beat thumped in earnest.

She set Eadwald's body down beside the rest of the fallen. She told Eadwulf she was sorry once more but that she must attend to other matters, and he softly bid that she go. Talia left him sitting by his brother's side, stroking his blond hair, its wildness tamed at last by death.

Each rider looked for their dragon on the overhanging rocks above the tunnel's entrance. Talia found Pyra up there with them, her scales beautiful under the rosy light. As wonderful as she felt, the anguished wails of two dragons for their fallen riders brought back the chill of the tunnels.

Looking into Pyra's amber eyes, Talia wanted to tell her so much, yet something unspoken passed between them, a weariness and relief in survival and the knowledge that there would be a better time and place for such unburdening.

"He has come," Pyra told her.

Talia looked along the row of perched dragons and counted their number as too many. Past Pyra and Strang, past Turro the emerald and others of his flight, there were four others – one storm, one mystic, one emerald looking wary of its wild kindred, and one fire, who stood as a behemoth at the end of the ravine.

Talia felt the power of three Lords and then of Paragon Adaskar. Her steps grew labored as though their presence physically pressed upon her. She waded through this quagmire, head held high. If he would listen to her, to all who had heard what she had, then surely all would be forgiven. Surely then things would change.

As she progressed up the ravine, she felt Pyra shadowing her along the ridge.

Adaskar's dragon, Azarin, the true power of the pair with a core comparable to the Life Elder, warmed the air around him to a heat haze. Within his aura, one felt as if they were at the edge of the Searing Sands. His scales glowed like molten steel, smoke peeled away from every beat of his wings, and golden were his eyes as well as the ridges down his back and tail.

Adaskar stood sentinel with three Lords of the Order behind him. Talia knew none of the three. With measured steps she drew up before them, but this time she felt no compulsion to bend her knee. Then she noticed that the Paragon of Fire went barefoot even outside of the Inner Sanctum. He stepped toward her, leaving burnt grass in his wake.

"I told you there would be consequences," he said in his crackling voice. "You have forced my hand. How I wish you'd had the humility to heed me."

"Paragon Adaskar, mightiest of riders, if you would but listen to what happened to us—"

"What could possibly have happened to change anything?"

"The scourge has a consciousness, a mind of its own. It spoke to me. It's how the dragon Thrall – Sovereign, as I reported him to you before – has taken control of it."

A shadow passed over Adaskar's face. "Voices in the deep. A thousand voices and one?"

Azarin's aura began to affect her then. Sweat rolled from her brow, stinging into one eye and tasting of heavy salt on her lips.

"You knew?"

"You're not the first rider to seek answers in the deep places," Adaskar said. "Even before the Fall of Aldunei. Many went mad, I told you that. The blight was in them."

"But this – this changes so much of how we think of the enemy," Talia said, though even as she said it, her voice faltered. Adaskar knew, or at least he knew of tales, half-buried and suppressed secrets for only the highest echelons of the Order.

And with that knowledge, such as it was, he had chosen to do nothing.

"What does it change?" he asked, serious as the grave. "Whatever the scourge has become, whatever grows in the darkest, unreachable depths, we cannot touch. Dragons are our power. How did you fare this day without Pyra by your side?"

It was then that Pyra found the space to land beside her. *"You see victory, Revered Paragon. Even as an Ascendant, Talia has done more to fight the scourge than many Lords."*

The three Lords behind Adaskar, veterans of a dozen incursions across the world, collectively narrowed their eyes.

Talia placed a hand on Pyra. She appreciated her support more than she could say, but she had not been there, and Talia had yet to share everything with her. The first expedition had taken the creature by surprise, she was sure. This second mission would have ended in ruin had the creature not desired to speak with her. The third, if there would be a third, would be real. Would be terrible.

Still, what choice did they have but to try?

"What would you have us do, Paragon? Do nothing? What choice is that?"

"Sometimes, nothing is the right choice. You're so eager for change without a notion of how fast things can fall apart. This world. All the living. Our Order. All order everywhere is but one poor decision from collapse. The scourge is part of the world, and we stand against it. Chaos rises, and we put it right, and there is stability in that. For over a thousand years there has been stability in that, but you would have us throw it away on a gamble."

His hand flashed in a flourish so quick she almost missed it, and then she found herself staring down the rippling, flaming blade of the Paragon of Fire.

"Talia Agravain," he said, his voice rising under heat and power. "Ascendant of Fire. Oath breaker. Chaos bringer. By the authority of the Dragon Riders of Falcaer, I hereby denounce you and sentence that your bond be broken. Submit yourself or be taken by force." His ringing voice carried all through the ravine and to the camp behind them.

Pyra bellowed but Azarin drowned her out and bore his power into hers, forcing Pyra down until she lay on her side with her belly exposed. Azarin issued a torrent of fire into the sky to seal the verdict, a beacon so great she thought Holt might have seen it too, were he to be looking to the west.

When it ended, Talia found herself on her knees, though she could not recall falling to them.

"It is over," Adaskar said. Before she could answer, he lifted his gaze and growled in a most dragon-like way. With a trembling hand, Talia gripped the hilt of her blade. She drew it an inch from the sheathe and then a cold hand fell upon hers.

"Champion Ethel," Adaskar said. "We will deal with your insolence separately. You were warned as well."

"She might be young," Ethel said. "She might have broken every oath and law and custom, but she's not wrong. We all heard this thing speak. It tried to take hold of me. We should fight it. It's what we swore to do."

The three Lords drew their weapons in unison and gathered their power. Their dragons joined them overhead. Together they could destroy Talia, Pyra, Ethel, and Strang so quickly it might as well be a single thought.

Yet others came. Still on her knees, Talia sensed them; first the other Champions who had come with Ethel, and even the Ascendants, one by one. Their dragons came next, and then Turro, several wild emeralds, and distantly, coming just within range to be felt, the West Warden. Talia thought it was the Warden's presence that at last made Adaskar hesitate. If pushed, he and the Lords could have cut through a dozen lesser riders and their dragons, bloody though that would have been. Yet to do all of that and break the Pact as well?

Talia and Pyra got back to their feet.

"Our enemy is the scourge and Thrall," Talia said. "Never should it be each other. Leave, Honored Lords, Revered Paragon. You will fight as you see fit, and we shall fight as we see fit, and any who wish to join us will be welcomed."

Paragon Adaskar sighed. It was a sad sigh, one of genuine pain and trailing smoke. "You weaken the riders. And when our Order is weak, chaos reigns. I judge countless will die because of you."

"Many have already," Talia said, then she stiffened her resolve. "And more will before the end. I can only trust that many more will be saved because of what we'll do."

Pyra roared and took a bold step forward. Azarin lowered his huge neck to shield his rider, but Pyra stayed her ground, and then Strang, Turro, and all the others roared to join her. The noise was deafening. Talia clasped her hands over her ears to no avail. Pyra and the others kept up their assault until Adaskar and his lords were well out of earshot.

At that point, the roars of defiance turned to bellows of joy. Talia ran to Pyra's side and threw herself into the hot embrace. A wing fell gently around her.

"Did we just chase off a Paragon?" Talia asked across their bond.

"With a bit of help."

"That's what I call a great thing," Talia said.

"I agree," Pyra purred.

Their bond beat climbed to a drumming rhythm and to a white heat, becoming stronger than it had been since the siege of Sidastra.

FORTY-NINE

No Victory

It took some time to get Osric to his feet. He refused to be carried, insisting on making his own way. The black dragon followed a step behind, almost within his shadow.

"I must fetch something from my chambers," Osric said.

"I don't think so," said Rake.

"Your weapon is there. He wanted it kept safe for you."

"Because he expected to break me."

"You would have," Osric said.

Rake huffed and rolled his shoulders but did not answer.

Holt felt leery about sending Osric off on his own or, worse, with only Rake. Ash sensed this turmoil.

"I'm alright, boy," he assured him. *"Go with them."*

"I'll see to Ash," Aberanth said, and he trotted off ahead of the group, small enough to walk out into the corridor and take the stairs.

Holt escorted Osric, Rake, and the black dragon – Osric's dragon, he supposed – to Osric's chambers. The polearm stood against the far wall. Rake made for it at once. Osric, on the other hand, stepped carefully toward a gray cloak draped over a tall stand. His steps were light, timid, reverent. His remaining hand trembled. When his fingers touched the cloth, he retracted them as if stung. Osric's dragon cooed at him. He looked upon the drake and strained to form a smile as though he had forgotten how. When next he reached for the cloak, he took it. One-handed, he attempted to put it on and failed.

"Here," Holt said, helping him slip his maimed arm through the sleeve.

"Thank you," he croaked.

The black dragon swished its tail and for the first time gave a rumble of contentment.

"It already loves you," Holt remarked. "I suppose you saved his life."

"Her life," Osric corrected. "And she is the one who saved me."

Rake tapped his foot by the door. "Are we ready?"

Osric nodded and they shuffled out into the stairwell. As they moved down the tower, the full events of the night were pieced together. Osric confirmed that the Wyrm Cloaks had been preparing to leave the fortress anyway and so fled under Thrall's panicked command.

"Most of the Wyrm Cloaks made for the storehouse," Rake said. "But a fair number seemed adamant about killing us. Once Aberanth joined me and Eidolan, we backed inside the ice tower to hold the doorway, but they kept trying."

"They will have been trying to destroy the eggs," Osric said. "I had some unhatched ones moved to that tower."

Holt's spirits almost rose from that news. Perhaps their efforts had not been entirely in vain.

Where Thrall and the Wyrm Cloaks would go, Osric did not know.

Down a few levels, Holt was hesitant to leave Rake and Osric alone, but Aberanth agreed to escort them down the tower. While the others took the stairs, Holt reentered the hatchery where he'd fought Orvel and sank into Ash's embrace. A low burn was in their bond, but it was in good shape considering the night's events. All the same, what they had spent magically had been in just one duel with a fellow Low Champion. The bodies of the fallen hatchlings further chipped at his enthusiasm. For all their progress, they had not been strong enough to make a difference.

They were Low Champions playing in a game of Lords.

All the same, Holt tried not to be too hard on himself. Taking down Clesh had been a lucky shot while the dragon was distracted. Fighting Orvel had been closer to a fair fight, and he'd pulled through it.

At length, they flew down into the yard. Ruins of smoldering timber, soot, and blackened stone remained. Such damage from two Exalted Champions dueling made Holt dread to consider the consequences when Lords or Paragons came to blows.

No wind blew, though outside the confines of the fortress it raged on. While the air in the yard was calm, it had the feeling of a wild dog brought to heel.

Farsa and Hava stood vigil over two bodies, one human and one dragon. Dahaka and Zahak had been arranged to look almost peaceful.

With time to consider it now, Holt understood the difference in Farsa and Hava's bond. It now shone with a permanence, no stutter, no flicker, no wavering of any kind. Farsa had become a Lord in that fight. It seemed a strange reward for killing a former friend. Far easier to have let Dahaka go. Far easier to have avoided the harrowing task by claiming they could not be the ones to do it. Holt supposed facing such trauma head-on would deepen a bond.

Holt could not summon the words, so he bowed, and Ash pressed his neck to the ground before Hava.

Farsa's expression was steely as ever. A smile tugged at the corner of her lips, but she seemed unable to commit to the gesture.

"You fought commendably, Holt Cook," Farsa said. "You have my thanks. Our victory would not have been possible without your own." She nodded toward the base of the mystic tower.

Holt turned slowly, knowing what he'd find. A bright emerald lay sobbing. Gea, he recalled. Her name was Gea. Eidolan sat by her side. Of all the group, he was best placed to have some notion of the pain she would be in.

Rake, Aberanth, Osric, and the black hatchling emerged from the mystic tower, and they beheld Gea with bleak faces.

"What will happen to her?" Ash asked.

"Whatever we decide," Rake said. "Seeing as she was recently an enemy and may well rejoin Thrall if we let her go, there is one obvious option. However, as we just decided to let this one live," he growled, nodding to Osric, "I imagine you have a different approach in mind."

"She was of the Order," Farsa said. "She should return and face judgment."

"Which will be exile," said Rake. "Which might send her straight back to Thrall."

"Then she will pay the consequences of such a choice," Hava said. *"She may choose instead to take her final flight."*

"There is a third option, of course," Rake said. "She might swear revenge and make it her life's work to hunt Holt and Ash down."

Holt had an ill feeling that was more likely than not. She had been unkind at their first meeting and now would hate them both with a bitter passion, and rightly so. He would rather have left her there, and yet he could not shake the feeling that, as he'd slain her rider, he owed her some words. Though what words they might be, he did not have a hope of knowing. The thought of saying 'sorry' had never sounded more hollow. Unable to look at the sobbing dragon anymore, he changed tack and said, "We should burn these bodies."

"What we should not do is linger," Rake said.

"Rake is right," Hava said, *"We do not have the time to burn all of the slain, but I will not leave Zahak's body for a future blight. His at least must burn, and Dahaka along with him."*

Rake acquiesced to that.

"Before we go," Holt said, speaking to Osric, "is there anything left to learn here? Some information that the Wyrm Cloaks might have left behind?"

"The Blood Alchemist's workshop did not burn," Osric said, pointing to the place. "There might be something in there, but I would not trust in hope."

On their way to the workshop, Holt retrieved the scabbard of Brode's sword and sheathed it on his back. He felt whole again with its weight there. Sadly, the Blood Alchemist's workshop lacked anything incriminating.

"I'm not surprised," Osric said. "The cult avoids detection because it lacks a trail you can follow. No records. All is kept within the minds of its members."

Rake circled the yard and returned with more bad news. "Aberanth's collapsed wall destroyed the forge. You'll have to wait a little longer, Holt."

Holt nodded. It was, genuinely, the last thing on his mind at present.

Rake carried on. "I wouldn't have relished remaining exposed here for days while you worked." He grunted, shrugged then headed back through the yard. When they reached Gea and Eidolan, Rake called out to the illusionist that it was time to go.

"*Go on,*" Eidolan said. "*I shall stay a while longer.*"

"As you will," Rake said.

Holt was ready to leave. The words he felt he had to say to Gea never materialized. Ash, however, padded over.

"What are you doing?" Holt asked.

"*There is a fourth option,*" Ash said. Eidolan looked at Ash warily as he approached. "*Do you wish to see Thrall succeed?*"

"*Youngling,*" Eidolan said sternly. "*She's in great pain. Be on your way.*"

Gea answered all the same.

"*Why not let him succeed?*" she said miserably, unable to look away from her rider's broken body. "*There's nothing left for me now.*"

"*Your rider was not beyond redemption,*" Ash said. "*He could have turned from this path, and so can you. Go back to the Order with Master Hava. Tell them of Thrall. Do not go until they listen. Make them listen. That might do more good than any of us could do alone. And if they send you away, find your Elder. He will forgive you.*"

"*Why would he do that?*" Gea asked.

"*Because the Honored Elder also has to forgive himself,*" Ash said.

Gea tore her gaze from Osric then and looked at Ash in wonder.

"*You were blessed by him. You did not lie. I hear his notes upon you now... I am... I am sorry, young one. For what we did. He was so unhappy for so long.*" Her plea was a quiet desperation, uncomfortable to hear. "*Nothing we did could... could ever—*"

She cut off, aware that Farsa and Hava approached. Gea sniffed and pressed her neck low and tucked her tail under her body.

"Honored Wind Lords, I beg of you, let his body burn. Do not let the scourge take him."

"We will add him to the pyre," Hava said.

Gea broke in relief. She sank flat to the ground, weeping, before covering her snout with one wing. Farsa picked up Orvel's blade. Dahaka's red sword already sat upon her back alongside her own.

"These blades shall be returned to Falcaer," she explained for Holt's benefit. "There they will hang on the Rogues Row, as a warning to others."

Holt wondered how Farsa would explain her own wayward behavior. If Paragon Adaskar landed here right now, they would all be treated as rogues. Maybe as a Lord, Farsa and Hava would be treated with more respect. For once, however, Holt held his questions. Now was not the time.

Eidolan eased himself away from Gea. *"This is a hollow victory,"* he said. *"To spill the blood of riders and dragons only weakens the living."* He gave a somber rumble. *"All the hatchlings were killed, you say? Save for this one,"* he added, eyes training on the little black dragon. She stepped back and hid her snout behind Osric's legs.

"You may wish to check the ice tower," Rake said. "Our 'friend' here says some eggs may yet remain."

Osric nodded. "Although by this point, they are likely stone."

Eidolan padded over to Osric, sniffing at the black dragon, but she shrank into Osric's shadow. *"So this youngling came from a mystic egg?"*

"From an egg I carried from the gorge myself," Osric said. "Twin drakes lay within. Her brother is golden."

Eidolan clawed at the ground and looked at Osric with pure loathing. *"I ought to take your head for the deaths of my fellow mystics."* Then he sighed. *"But for the sake of the hatchling, you will walk free,"* he continued, although he said these last words sourly.

As Eidolan went to investigate the ice tower, Aberanth, Ash, and Hava worked together to lift and carry Zahak's body down to the forest floor. Farsa carried Dahaka between her arms all the way down the servants' stair and Holt carried Orvel. Rake limped silent and sullen the whole way.

In a glade in the forest, they built a pyre and burned the bodies. Gea used her magic to part the earth and bury Dahaka's and Zahak's charred bones, but for her rider she chose to dig the grave with her own talons. Over Orvel's remains she raised a dome of soft, clean-smelling earth and used a deal of her remaining core to bloom a garden of white roses, white lilies, and white irises.

"Thank you," she said to them all. *"I'm glad he is resting now."*

"There is but one last thing," Hava said. She looked at Rake. The half-dragon leaned against a tree, aiming for nonchalance but unable to mask his weariness. *"May I consider my blood debt repaid?"*

Rake pushed off the tree to stand straight. He looked around them all, at Farsa and Hava, now stronger than ever, at Aberanth, who looked exhausted, at Eidolan, who had returned quietly with a single egg, and at Holt and Ash, on whom he lingered the longest.

"You saved my life," Rake said. "None of you owe me anything."

Holt and Ash shared a sense of quiet but pleasant surprise.

Rake cleared his throat with a stiff cough and said, "I suppose congratulations are also in order, Wind Lords."

Farsa steepled her fingers and inclined her head. "Thank you, Master Rake. Until we next have the honor of fighting by your side, farewell."

There was now nothing more to be done. Gea went peacefully with Farsa and Hava. Oak Hall was their destination.

"I'm glad you found at least one egg, Master Eidolan," Ash said.

The egg in question looked perfectly normal, cone-shaped and light gray.

"The others were stone," Eidolan said. *"Ash, I hope you do not think ill of me for wishing this hatchling be a true mystic. To have gone through so much only for it to suffer exile or worse for being different—"*

"I understand," Ash said.

"I once thought as they all do," Eidolan said. *"You have opened my mind and my heart, son of night. As have you, young Aberanth. May your knowledge one day be seen as a blessing."*

Aberanth gave a squirmy thanks. They were yet to discover whether Eidolan would be so understanding of certain experiments.

Rake clapped Eidolan upon his back. "May your illusions never fade."

"May your tongue never dull, friend," Eidolan said. He picked up the egg, spread his wings, then hesitated. *"Thrall is a mistake I can no longer ignore. When the time comes, you can call upon me."*

He took flight, snapping through the canopy. That left Holt, Ash, Rake, Aberanth, Osric, and his black dragon. Osric swayed where he stood. His skin held a greenish tinge not dissimilar from the blight.

"He needs somewhere to recover," Holt said.

"Fortunately for him, we know a place," Rake said. "Don't fret, Aberanth. We'll blindfold him and the youngling."

FIFTY

The Bard's Tale

It felt like an age since Talia had stood in her crimson office. With the royal blacksmith and his team of apprentices with her, it seemed as though no time had passed at all. After explaining her needs and those of the riders who had joined her, the smith stared momentarily into space, struggling no doubt to process the change.

"Can it be done?" Talia asked.

The smith cleared his throat and came around.

"I should think so, Your Majesty. If your fellow Champions are willing to assist me in the design. I would not wish to be a burden—"

"They will help," Talia assured him. "And they are not my fellows in power. I am still only an Ascendant. Should any issues arise in working with these riders, Champion Ethel will see to it."

"Of course, Majesty." He and his team left with half-sketched blueprints and instructions in hand. It would take more than an adapted forge to make an Order Hall here, but it was a start. Moreover, Talia had mentors again. Her stalled progress should begin to advance. Given the clarity with which she now saw Pyra's bonfire, she thought that advancement might come sooner than later.

Her meeting with the smith had gone quicker than she'd anticipated. She had time now before Ambassador Oddvar was to arrive, yet she found herself unable to sit at her desk. After all that had happened, returning to paper and ink seemed too passive and slow.

Drifting almost unconsciously to the window overlooking the northern palace grounds, she smiled to see Pyra swooping in flight with two former dragons of the Order. A storm dragon and a sibling of fire. Her racing thoughts lifted Talia's spirits, making her feel she too had left the restraints of the ground.

Dive. Bite your tail. Got you. Fun, fun, fun. Soar now. Faster, faster.

Talia drew herself back from the rush lest she get lost in it. It pleased her no end to see how much happier Pyra was compared to months ago.

A knock at the door. Oddvar, likely with Prince Aren in tow. There was only so long she could reasonably avoid him.

Eadwulf entered alone, looking diminished. No matter what she said, he refused to take time away from his post.

"Ambassador Oddvar, the Skarl Prince, and the Mistress of Coin are without," he announced.

Elvina? What is she doing with them?

Quite unsure what could have caused this unlikely trio, Talia thanked Eadwulf and bid them enter. In stepped Oddvar, his fishtail braid swinging wide from quick, uneven strides. A light sheen of sweat wet the shaved sides of his head, and he did not seem entirely sure what to do with his arms.

Elvina floated into the room as though upon a cloud, the movement of her feet barely perceptible under her long white gown.

Behind them were a group of Housecarls and between them the bard. He lacked his lute and his feather cap, but the panpipe still lay upon his breast. Talia flicked her gaze between the bard and Oddvar, then rolled her eyes. The bard must have unveiled something of their conversation which Prince Aren had taken the wrong way.

Well, better now than six months from now.

"What is the matter, Oddvar?"

"Ah," Oddvar began, his voice sounding dry. "Ah, Your Majesty, I am most embarrassed. Truly. Please take my assurances that the

Empress herself will hear of this and will no doubt take swift action. I would not have brought this matter to you, but I... but I—"

"The good ambassador fears you shall be brought to a fiery wroth," said the bard, "and that you will take that wroth out on him." He came swanning into her office without so much as an invitation. Oddvar made a squeak that might have been in protest, but the bard raised his fingers to his lips and made a shooshing motion. "Dear Oddvar also fears you might be so offended that you'll reject the marriage, which he is under great pressure to see through. Be easy on him. None of this is his doing." He came to a halt and inspected the spiced snacks and drinks with a wary eye.

Talia stood slack. When she came to, she looked first to Elvina, who seemed to be enjoying the situation, then back to Oddvar.

"Ambassador, whatever this bard has told you, I can assure you I can explain. I'm afraid that in my weariness I might have spoken too candidly."

Oddvar licked his lips, then found his voice again. "Your Majesty, I have the honor and privilege of introducing to you, Prince Fynn of the imperial bloodline."

Talia's jaw slackened again. She rounded on the bard, on Fynn, expecting to see a smirk there, but instead she found a sad smile, as though he regretted his deceptions.

She felt a complete idiot. His cloth even now might be poor but nothing else about him had been. His confidence in speaking to her, his mastery of her own language, his persistent interest and veiled knowledge of Skadi and Aren, it all seemed painfully clear to her now.

"Prince Fynn," she said evenly. "Had I known—"

"My Prince's actions were most unbecoming," Oddvar said in a hurry, regaining himself now the thorn had been drawn from the wound. "He made his own way to Feorlen in secret. I assure Your Majesty that nothing he has said or done comes with the sanction of Empress Skadi."

Talia only half-heard the ambassador. "What do you want?" she asked, her sense of formality melting under the situation, before looking to the Mistress of Coin with a frown. "Elvina, what is the meaning of all this?"

It was Fynn who answered. "I am aware you have a couple of outstanding issues, Red Queen. If you're willing to hear me out, I believe I have solutions."

"I had asked my own councilor to speak," Talia said tersely, giving Elvina a hard look.

"Prince Fynn came to me with some suggestions only this morning," Elvina added quickly. "I believe they could work, a way to appease your uncle Roland's need for something tangible without us needing to sacrifice any land."

It was a measure of how in need Talia was for a solution that her heart throbbed. "Speak, then," she said to Fynn, much harsher in tone than she ought to speak to a foreign prince.

"My mother requires a guarantee that your uncle in Brenin would call his banners alongside Feorlen and the Empire. Your uncle, King Roland, must satisfy his own nobles and minimize the impact of restrictions Athra might place upon them. I can help arrange a trade agreement most favorable to my people and theirs—"

Oddvar let loose a held breath and blustered into speech. "My Prince, to deal in matters of coin is unseemly." He did not seem to care that Elvina was nearby. "You are above such matters. The Empire is above such matters. Your mother—"

"Speak to me like a child once more and I shall see you sent to the western tundra in disgrace, ambassador." Fynn was neither angry nor scornful, but his voice was iron. Hearing him, Talia understood she was dealing with someone far older in spirit than Prince Aren.

"Perhaps it would be best if I spoke with Prince Fynn in private," Talia said. Elvina curtsied and left at once. Oddvar hesitated, then he too went. When the door closed, she rounded on Fynn, and still with half the room between them she said, "Why should I entertain your ideas after your deceptions?"

"You're not angry with me," he said.

Talia could feel her neck growing redder. "Am I not?"

"You let yourself be vulnerable, and now you feel played for a fool."

From the array of food, he selected an almond coated in dark spices, sniffed at it, blinked from the heat, then thought better of eating it. He clenched his fist, waggled his fingers, then opened it to show his palm. The nut had vanished.

"Parlor tricks do not impress a rider," Talia said.

"You're not a fool," Fynn said, as though nothing had interrupted him. "And that's why I am willing to help you."

"By arranging a secret trade agreement somehow only you can provide?"

"My people are very proud," he said. "Much value is placed in the warrior's arm over the clerk's abacus, but we must farm, and sew, and eat like everyone else. My mother has reasons for this marriage she did not share with you, and Aren would never share them."

"But you will?"

"I will," he said. "If you set Aren aside and marry me in his stead."

There was an uncomfortable pause. Talia did not know how to react. Laughter, weeping, rage, all seemed acceptable in their own way. At last, she managed to think.

"Your mother insisted it be Aren."

"You recall our conversation outside of your camp, yes? My mother would do anything to have her favorite son in this position. She has complete control over him."

"Why should that trouble you?"

"My mother and I have a difficult relationship. She has always considered my choices to be... unworthy ones. Suffice to say I would like to frustrate her plans and find a way out from her constant control. If I remain in the empire, I'd never be free of her."

"So my options are to marry your mother's puppet or to risk her wroth and refusal by insisting on you, all so you can rebel against her? So far I don't see what's in it for me."

"I've spent time in your inns and taverns," Fynn said. "They debate who will be stronger of will, the Empress or the Red Queen. Though if you are agreeable to Aren, as so many are, then don't let me sway you. How could I? He is every bit the man most women look for, and his talents with a sword would be useful to you, yes? I am not so tall, nor fair of face, and my talents lie in songs and words and books."

"You make a weak case for yourself, Prince Fynn."

He shrugged. "I make my case honestly. My heart belongs to one I cannot have, and so it cannot be yours. But your heart is already given to your dragon, yes, so there is no harm. I cannot aid you on the battlefield, but I can assist off of it, and some battles are won with words. I will doubtless anger my mother and that will cause you grief, but at least you will not be so easily manipulated by her. A real choice, not one forced upon you. Learn the lesson of my mother's saga and choose the smaller feet." He pointed to his toes and wiggled them beneath the soft leather of his shoes.

Talia bit her lip. Despite claiming his case was weak, it was in fact strong. Skadi might not like it, but the link between Feorlen and the Empire would still be forged.

"Would you play that music for me?" she asked.

He smiled. "Once we are wed. Or any other song you wished."

"You said it was about Fynn, about you. Did you write it?"

"I did."

"Does it relate to where your heart truly belongs?"

"It does," he said, and for the first time he sounded evasive.

Talia could almost hear the music. It still unnerved her how easily the tune had gripped her, how it stuck in her mind as easily as Pyra's own song. As though the gentle melody spoke in whispers to her, she came to understand the bard, this prince, a little better.

"I'm sorry for what happened to you," she said, not wishing to pry further than that.

"It's done now," Fynn said, and he seemed to search for something in the bowl of nuts that was not there. "Do you see merit in my proposal, or shall I find a ship across the Bitter Bay?"

"Eadwulf," she called, and the lonely twin entered. "I have a new assignment for you. To guard Prince Fynn. I will not force this of you if you do not feel ready."

Eadwulf's wide eyes looked at Fynn in a vacant stare. "My queen, I do not wish to receive special treatment—" he cut off and glanced to one side expectantly, anticipating his brother to finish the line of thought. Eadwulf swallowed hard, and, still glancing into the empty space beside him, he said, "I would much rather be occupied, and I shall perform any task you set as well as Eadwald did."

Talia went to him and gently turned his head forward to face her. "Let us hope your duties do not require that of you. Thank you, Eadwulf. Prince Fynn is to be my personal guest here in the palace. Keep him safe."

Eadwulf stiffly inclined his neck. "My queen."

"Thank you, Eadwulf. Please wait outside a while longer. Fynn will join you when we are done. And send for Lady Elvina if she does not still wait without."

That done, Talia sought out her favorite chair and dropped into it. She eyed the kettle of nairn root tea but thought better of it. She'd drunk enough of it recently that the herb might be part of her blood now. But she did allow herself a handful of the nuts.

"Sit with me, Fynn," she said. "And tell me of these solutions you have."

FIFTY-ONE

Mushroom Farming

Maimed and seeming upon the brink of exhaustion no matter how much he slept, Osric was quiet on their journey from Windshear to Aberanth's lab. When he did speak, he was polite but curt, although Ash often overheard him muttering under his breath to his dragon. Small nothings, mostly, asking how she was, was she hungry or cold. While sense-sharing with Ash one night, Holt overheard one such muted conversation and found Osric's gentleness disconcerting; it did not seem possible that one so bestial could also be so tender.

By the time they returned to the woodland above Aberanth's grotto, leaves had gathered upon the ground in copper piles. The days grew shorter, and crocuses bloomed in rich purples under the shade of tree and bush.

The grotto seemed small once Aberanth, Holt, Rake, Osric, and the black dragon had all congregated inside. Aberanth cleared an alcove to make a space for Osric to recover and fashioned a nesting area of dry moss and grass. Osric and his dragon slid inside, and both were asleep within a minute.

Back by the beech tree, Aberanth nearly bumped into displaced crates and grumbled. *"He cannot stay here forever."*

"Ash and I will stay to watch over him," Holt said. "For his dragon's sake as much as yours, if you're willing to have us stay as well?"

"I don't mind you two being here," Aberanth said. *"There is much about your magic I'd still like to investigate."*

"So you just want to study us?" Holt asked, though he did so with mock consternation.

"You also make such excellent mushrooms."

Holt raised his eyebrows.

Aberanth rumbled, then gave his customary, *"Hmmph,"* and then, with all the effort of an abashed child, said, *"I would also... appreciate the company. It can be lonely here."*

Rake, who was leaning with his back against the beech tree, cleared his throat loudly.

"What's that, Rake? You'd like to stay as well?" Aberanth asked sardonically.

"Oh, I know when I'm not wanted," Rake said. "But I'll stay anyway. I need to heal too," he added, placing a hand dramatically to his chest.

They all knew his rib had repaired by now. Rake's hybrid body granted him the benefit of healing fast like a dragon. Aberanth knew it, and Ash confirmed that Rake's chest no longer creaked each time he took a breath. They all knew it, yet they allowed Rake his pretense.

"We'll feel safer with you here," Holt said. He was relieved in truth, though he didn't want to give Rake too much satisfaction in that. Osric might still be dangerous. While he was no longer connected to Thrall, Holt thought an attack unlikely, but better safe than facing that axe head-on.

"I'll expand my mushroom production," Aberanth said brightly. *"Though it will take at least three weeks for the oyster mushrooms to grow and longer for the others."*

"I'll hunt," Rake said. "Don't fret, I'll be back before the murderous marionette wakes up."

After Rake left, Aberanth beckoned Holt to follow him. *"Come, Master Cook. You can earn your keep by assisting me."*

And so Holt underwent his first lesson in mushroom farming: how to cut the stems and prepare the right conditions for them to spawn and grow. This section of Aberanth's complex sat closer to the surface, with more ventilation tunnels to regulate the air.

As he worked, he felt Ash relaxing out on the surface. A clear sky made for a cool evening where the autumn moon hung low even before nightfall. Gently the lunar motes fell onto Ash's extended body, like soft hands soothing worn muscles.

Not long after night truly fell, Rake returned with a bounty of rabbits. Unlike the last time, Ash was content for Holt to prepare them properly. While his options were limited, a stew was always possible so long as he had time and a good pot. Aberanth directed him to wild garlic, small onions, and parsley nearby. Along with a donation of mushrooms and homemade wine, the stew was as good as Holt could hope for with campsite cooking.

As he dished up bowls for Rake and himself, Osric and his dragon crept up from underground to join them. Holt handed Osric his bowl.

"My thanks," Osric said, before settling onto the earth to eat. The black dragon crept behind Osric into his shadow, cast long from the fire. After a few spoonfuls, his face broke into something close to a warm smile. "You're an asset to your former role."

"Thank you," Holt said, a little stiff. From behind Osric's back, the shadow dragon poked out her snout. Her eyes were more oversized than Ash's had ever been. "Would you like some?" Holt asked her.

The moment she realized he spoke to her, she mewled and pulled back behind Osric again. Osric placed a spoonful of the stew onto the ground beside him. A few moments passed, then her snout emerged from the shadows to scoop up the meat. She lingered to sniff at the ground. Osric gave her his last portion, and after that she stepped out of his shadow, and though she kept herself low to the ground, she risked a lingering look at the rest of the group.

"Timid thing," Rake said. "What did you do to them?"

"To her, nothing," Osric said. "This is just her nature."

"Has she spoken to you yet?" Holt asked.

Osric shook his head but did not seem disappointed. After Thrall, a quiet companion was likely welcome, Holt thought. The hatchling began licking the bowl in Osric's lap.

"Give it here," Holt said. The hatchling squealed as he took it and Osric pulled her back.

"Do not whine," he admonished her. And she quietened.

Holt refilled the bowl, and she ate heartily from it. Rake leaned forward as she gobbled up the rabbit. Holt assumed he was trying to gauge whether the black dragon reacted well to the meat and therein discover her preference. Rabbit was not linked to any other type, so it may well be hers. Yet the dragon finished the bowl and Rake's face remained unmoved, meaning she was likely still too young for her magic to manifest.

Ash's magic had emerged swiftly for a dragon, but Brode had thought that was due to the constant stress they'd found themselves in. Ash had grown rapidly at first, but that might have stunted his future growth. The black dragon enjoyed a growth spurt in the days after leaving Windshear, but as matters calmed, so did her development. She was currently no larger than a small hound, with a slender tail as long again as her body.

Rake provided his empty bowl for Holt to eat his own dinner. As he ate, he considered they ought to carve out extra dishes and spoons if they were going to remain here for an extended time.

When the hatchling finished her meal, she did not return to Osric's shadow but stretched out and placed her snout in his lap. Heavy lids fluttered over her eyes, and she fell asleep. Osric enveloped them both with his gray cloak and stroked the top of her head with his remaining hand before making a sudden, sharp wince and clutching at his stump.

"The pain should fade in time," Aberanth told him.

"I'll take this over Thrall in my chest," Osric said. Shortly after this, he picked up his dragon and retired into the grotto.

"Is so much rest good for them?" Ash asked once they were beneath the earth.

"Lethargy comes after a point," Rake said, "but I do not think they are there yet. The dragon is healthy. Let them come around in their own time."

Holt agreed and took the opportunity to demonstrate to Rake and Aberanth the effect on moonlight when he and Ash entered an extreme state of Sinking. The mouth of Aberanth's tunnel offered the perfect place, where only a limited amount of the cold light was present in the first place, making it easier to draw all of it toward them.

"Yes, most intriguing," Rake said. "Now let the elixir and food wear off and try it without them."

They did so and found the draw of lunar motes was marginal at best.

"Well, allow me to commend both you and Aberanth on your discoveries," Rake said.

"I never thought such interactions were possible," Aberanth said. *"To draw on light to cloak yourselves in literal darkness… it's almost ironic. I like it, even if the application is limited."*

"Having niche tools is never a bad thing," Rake said. "The less often a technique is used, the less your opponents can learn from it."

They discussed when and how Holt and Ash or either one alone might make use of this excessive Sinking, and Holt went to sleep that night with his head full of notes for his recipe book. The next morning, he fleshed out another page, detailing the effects both with and without the aid of elixir and jerky. To his list of abilities, he added a new header which he named 'Cycling Abilities' and wrote a summary there like he had for Lunar Shock, Consecration and Flare. He named this new technique Eclipse.

The following days were much the same. Holt aided Aberanth in his farming, Cleansed and Forged where he could, but his regime was laid back compared to the intensity of previous months. When they lacked game from a hunt, he ate light meals of nuts and greens from Aberanth's larder and was pleased to find that his Champion's body could cope well with periods of fasting. Ash was no longer ravenous at all hours either.

Even the tension surrounding Osric and his dragon eased with the passing days. Osric requested to be put to work, and so Aberanth directed him to chores in the grotto or the glade of the woodland. He performed every task, including digging fresh latrines, without a hint of complaint. His dragon also came to trust the rest of the group, or at least trust they would not harm her. While Osric was off in the woods one night, she remained by the campfire in Holt and Ash's company.

Ash dangled his tail before her, attempting to coax her into chasing it. She seemed too wise or wary for that, though she began to stare at Ash for long stretches of time and permitted Ash once to sniff her and she him. Both dragons growled and pulled apart at that. Ash opened his mouth and flicked out his tongue as though ridding his mouth of a vile taste.

Holt and Ash were not sense-sharing, so Holt only got an impression across the bond, but to him the black dragon had a scent of aniseed, of cool earth and dark, dusty corners in neglected rooms. Not an addictive smell, perhaps, but far from unpleasant.

One night, while the others slept, Rake came to Holt and told him he would leave in the morning.

"Not for good," Rake assured him, "but we've been out of touch with the rest of the world for a long time. I'll seek out the East Warden again. With luck he'll know some news of Talia and events in the west."

Holt nodded. He was eager for news.

"I could bind him until I return," Rake suggested.

Holt gave it consideration but in the end decided against it. "He's not our prisoner."

"So be it," Rake said, and though it was a small matter, Holt appreciated that Rake did not push him on it.

The following day Holt worked alongside Osric to plant new spawn in Aberanth's expanded shroomery. Aberanth's careful labor had carved out a new shelf of space in the cave wall, about the size of two kite shields placed side by side. Holt placed thick white stems into a bed of damp soil and crushed bark. His circumstances in that moment struck him as so bizarre as to be dizzying. Back in Sidastra, Holt had dropped to his knees before Osric when he was still the Hero of

Feorlen. And now here they were, planting fungi in the cramped burrow of an exiled emerald. Both with nowhere else to go.

"There's something satisfying in growing things," Holt said by way of broaching a conversation.

Osric hummed in agreement but offered nothing more. A coarse stubble more gray than brown now covered his cheeks and chin. Weathered skin, gray hair, and his haunted eyes all made him look older than he was, although his strong frame, down to his beefy forearms, showed that the vigor of his soldier's body remained. Carefully Osric cut another slender stalk and handed it to Holt to plant. Holt parted some soil and proffered another calculated question.

"Will you name your dragon or wait for her to pick her own?"

"I did not think riders named their dragons."

"They usually don't," Holt said. "I named Ash because we bonded when he was a hatchling, like yours."

"I see," Osric said without expansion and returned to search amongst the various mushrooms for another likely specimen. Determined to draw Osric out, Holt pressed on.

"What was different between her and the others? Must have been special to make an impact even through Thrall's influence."

Osric glanced at him. "She's quiet. I prefer quiet company."

Holt had suffered through too much to feel abashed. Inspired by Rake's own forthrightness, he said, "I enjoy the quiet as much as the next person, but you've got a lot to answer for and I'm not going to give up easily."

Osric sighed as he selected a thick gilled mushroom. "There will be time enough to talk all things through. Where else will I go? For once, I have no mind for the future. No goal. No mission. Bonding with another dragon would not have been my choice, but now it's happened, I'll see she is strong enough to enter the wilds before doing anything."

"Will you return west?"

"The one thing I know for certain is that I cannot go back."

"Talia understands you were not in your right mind," Holt said.

"You know that's not true," Osric said with the firmness of a drill sergeant. "At first, perhaps I did act solely under his will, but after a time…" He trailed off, and his inexperienced left hand misjudged his next cut and so wasted the stalk. In silent fury, he put down the knife and stared hard at his boots. "After a time, he no longer has to control your every waking moment. His voice remains, but it nudges rather than commands. Thrall's real skill is knowing you better than you know yourself."

"What are you saying?"

"I'm saying that my sins are my own."

A heaviness fell over Holt's heart. He had suspected it, but he'd held onto hope. For a moment he rustled aimlessly at the soil and bark. A part of him did not wish to confirm more, but he had to.

"So those mystic dragons—"

"All me."

"King Godric, your brother—"

"Need not have died when or how he did, but I took the opportunity." Osric reported this dispassionately as though informing a subordinate of the essentials to bring them up to speed. What tremor lay in his voice was deep down, suppressed, Holt thought, but there nonetheless.

"And King Leofric?"

At this, Osric seemed taken aback, as though he'd forgotten all about his nephew. To Holt's surprise, Osric shook his head.

"Leofric did not die by my hand, not directly. Nor by Thrall's through me. There was no need to. The incursion was going as planned and, being Master of War, I had all the control I required. No, Leofric's illness and fear killed him."

"His fear of you," Holt pressed.

Osric frowned hard, a flash of the rage he was capable of. Yet he relented an instant later. "Yes. Fear of me. If only that orb of Godric's had never reached him. At least it remained for Talia to unveil me."

"If I do meet Talia again," Holt began, "I'll tell her all of this. I won't lie to her for you."

These revelations turned the atmosphere morbid. Holt's own hatred of the man had cooled since Windshear; Osric could not be exonerated, but nothing would be resolved by nursing animosity. All the same, Holt did hate to think what this news would do to Talia. As appalling as his admission was, he was also still alive, and if not wholly well then in time, with a new dragon bond, he might be. He did not deserve his new chance but did not deserve the energy to hate either.

"I understand," Osric said, and with that came an unspoken understanding to fall quiet again, as the once prince, once mercenary, once General preferred.

For the next three days, Holt honored Osric's wish. It was Aberanth who pestered him now for information. With a slab of smoothed bark between his teeth, he took to following Osric around and asking, *"Please describe everything that happened at the moment you broke your bond."*

Osric evaded each attempt until Aberanth caught him at the mouth of the grotto's tunnel and blocked his entry. The black dragon responded overzealously, launching herself at Aberanth so that the two little dragons scuffled in the tunnel. By the time Holt arrived upon the scene, Ash had already broken the pair apart.

Osric now stood at ground level outside the tunnel, his dragon braced by his side and glaring. Her tail disappeared and reappeared as it passed through his shadow.

"He's not going to give up either," Holt told him. "For a dragon or rider to bond a second time is almost unheard of, so naturally he's curious. We all are. It's the least you could do considering Aberanth's hospitality. He also saved what's left of your arm."

Osric had the grace to look ashamed. He crouched to soothe his dragon and then offered his apologies.

"What would you like to know?" he asked.

As Osric told of his final moments with Thrall, advancing upon the black dragon with axes raised, Holt was struck by the detail of remaining in control of his left side.

"I experienced something similar," Holt said. "But Rake did something to help me. He placed a barrier in my mind, I think."

Aberanth scrunched his features in confusion. *"A barrier but—oh…*

Yes, of mystic power, I suppose." He furiously carved runes into the bark. *"Tell me of that, Holt."*

"Well, it sort of cut me in half," Holt said, struggling with how to phrase the unique experience. "I lost all sensation and control on my right side. It blocked Thrall too, though I could feel his presence exerting pressure on the wall, so to speak."

"I fail to see how this is relevant to my experience," Osric said. "Rake did not place anything into my mind."

"Be that as it may," Aberanth said, *"Holt's experience may help explain your own. Did you know that human brains are in fact split in two?"*

Both Osric and Holt shook their heads.

"Two sides," Aberanth went on, *"where the left brain connects to your right-hand side, and the right brain the left. The connecting fibers between them comprise a relatively small bridge. It sounds to me as though Rake placed a block at this bridge. In his recount of Thrall's attempt to break him, Rake told me that Thrall always attacked the left side. Thrall must have been in your left brain also, and so Rake's defense allowed your consciousness to take shelter within the right hemisphere. Most fascinating! Wait there, I shall need more bark."*

Aberanth tottered off, livelier than Holt had seen him since their first meeting. His energy lifted Holt's own spirits, although Osric still looked dour.

"Aren't you pleased?" Holt asked. "It might be we've found a way to resist Thrall."

"If you think so. All would fall under him in time. Even Rake, though he won't admit it."

That's true enough, Holt thought.

"Was it painful, breaking the bond with Thrall?" Holt asked.

Osric considered. "More than I can describe, so much it numbed me. But equally it was a relief. Like lancing a boil or having hot wine poured into a wound."

"Every rider or dragon who has spoken of this says the pain of losing your partner can kill you outright."

Osric shrugged. "There was no love lost between me and Thrall. A bond formed through coercion and manipulation does not strike me as typical."

"Your bond with the shadow hatchling must have formed fast."

"I think it must have been forming, in some fashion, before breaking the first bond. But these matters of magic make me wary. What's done is done. I fear you and your inquisitive friend cannot learn anything of value. Though it worked for me, I would not recommend anyone break their bond on purpose. I would have died were it not for her."

The hatchling growled with pride and shook her tail merrily, and Osric took her out into the woods on a long walk.

When almost a week then passed without Rake's return, Holt grew worried. Even so, he was taken aback at the relief he felt when Rake reached out in thought late one afternoon. Everyone gathered above ground to greet him. Little heat was left in the autumn sun, its pale gold light reflecting in white spots off the last stubborn green leaves. Such light turned Rake's scales softer in color, a creamy orange like good hard cheese, and his ridges the blue of fresh spring water.

"They've gone," he announced without preamble.

Everyone looked at Rake in a mixture of confusion or alarm. The black dragon ogled him too, mimicking the actions of the others even if she did not fully understand.

Aberanth recovered first. *"Preposterous. You must be mistaken."*

"I don't make mistakes," Rake said. "Alright, I *rarely* make mistakes. But not on this. The East Warden has left his hidden grove and all his emeralds have followed him."

"So we wait until they return," Ash said.

"They should not have left," Aberanth said. *"They can't have left,"* he insisted again.

"I assure you they have," Rake said.

"You speak as though dragons taking flight is impossible, Aberanth," Holt said. "The Warden must have duties to attend to in the wider forest."

"They would never fly too far north and risk encountering the people of Coedhen," said Aberanth. *"Nor too far west and encroach on Oak Hall's territory. A Warden would not leave their post unless the Elder called."*

"Then the Elder must have called him," Holt said.

Aberanth squirmed and curled up into a tighter ball. *"Whatever the reason, it must be dire."*

"Cold winds from the north," Osric grunted. They all faced him, but he turned to the north, gazing at nothing through the thinning trees. His burgeoning black beard half-concealed his pursed lips as he pondered something. The black dragon pawed at him as though to encourage him. "Cold winds," he said again. "The wild ice drakes in Thrall's service left not long before Rake infiltrated the fortress. They were recalled."

"You're sure?" Rake asked.

Osric nodded.

"Do you know why?"

Osric shook his head. "Thrall did not elaborate. I'm not sure he even knew."

"Why would he know?" Aberanth asked. *"Was Thrall in contact with the Ice Elder?"*

"Not to my knowledge," Osric said. "Although as many drakes at Windshear were ice, I think there was some understanding between them. Perhaps no longer."

"It sounds as though Thrall was distracted," Aberanth noted.

"He was," Osric said. "Even before Talia drew his focus."

Holt was reminded of what he had glanced through Thrall: the chamber, the distant amber light, and Talia cloaked in shadows. Strongest of all had been the dragon's panic. He swallowed back the impulse to share this. Merely thinking about it caused him a chill that not even Ash's bond could fully dispel.

Ash's unease flew across the bond to join Holt's own. Such talk put their quest to find each Elder into grave doubt.

"Could the Ice Elder really be a threat?" he asked.

"I've had but one brief interaction with her," Rake said. "I can't say I had any desire to do so again. Her kin are known for their shrewdness, and she is the most cunning of all. This might only be a cautious move to bring her flight close until events unfold. If it's anything worse, I fear all we'll be able to do is react too late."

Rake drove the blade of his polearm into the earth so that the tall shaft stood upright. He took off his cloak, hung it from the butt of the weapon, then sat upon the bronzed leaves.

"This is a game of unknown size quickly gaining players," he went on. "The Ice Elder recalls her flight. The emeralds are summoned away for reasons unknown. My own Elder cowers, unwilling to act even when Thrall strikes directly at her dragons. Distrust grows in the halls of Falcaer, of Alamut, and likely every Order Hall from the Roaring Fjord of the Skarl Empire to Angkor by the Jade Jungle. So far as we know, Thrall maintains his grip on the scourge, and war threatens to divide the human powers. Amidst this, new magics are rising. It's a lot to take in, even for someone as brilliant as me."

"Order is breaking," Osric said. "Soon all will be consumed in chaos."

"Perhaps," Rake said, "though there is a dreadfully long way down until we reach the bottom of such black pits. Until we do, it will be hard to know how to start rising again."

"Holt and I were tasked to find the Elders," Ash said. *"Even if the Ice Elder acts suspiciously, we must go to her or else seek out the Elders of Fire and Storm."*

Aberanth gave a cautious rumble. *"I can't believe I'm admitting it, but I would heed Rake's words on this. There are too many variables right now to account for."*

"It wouldn't hurt to gather our strength," Holt said to Ash privately. *"We've been on the move constantly with barely a chance to breathe."* He dredged up the memories of the smashed eggs and dead hatchlings back at Windshear, of the frustration and guilt. *"The world grows more dangerous by the day. We're not ready to find and stir two Elders, especially now we cannot be sure the Life Elder's siblings will be on his side."*

"We should not doubt ourselves so much," Ash insisted. *"Talia's plan worked. A plan we agreed to. If Rake had not gone alone, we would not have been forced to rescue him, and so Thrall would not have reacted as he did with enemies already inside his fortress."*

Holt glanced at Rake at that, and the half-dragon seemed to sense he was being discussed.

"Things became messy," Rake said. "Had we stuck to my plan, Thrall would have died."

"*Might have died,*" Aberanth corrected.

"*We did what we felt to be right,*" Ash said.

"And it didn't work out so well this time, Ash," Holt said. Letting their hearts guide them had been enough before, but Rake was right. This time the situation had become a complete mess with an outcome none of them had foreseen. "We failed. We're as much to blame as Rake for the loss of those hatchlings, all of us. Eidolan, Farsa, and Hava too."

Rake inclined his head.

Ash grumbled and sank to the ground, a feeling of dejection crossing the dragon bond.

"*Not every experiment will yield the results you desire,*" Aberanth said. "*You must learn to accept failure as well as triumph.*"

Ash snorted white smoke and rumbled some more.

Holt went to sit at his side and spoke privately again. "*We won't win every fight.*"

"*I'm aware of that,*" Ash said.

"*Then we also need to be okay with it, as Aberanth says. If we beat ourselves up over every loss, we won't move forward. For a while I was so driven to become stronger, to never fail, that it almost led me down a dark path. You pulled me back from that.*"

Ash puffed fresh smoke, then raised a wing and wrapped it around Holt. "*It would be nice to stay here for a time. To grow stronger.*"

It wasn't quite the settled life they had envisioned together back in Ahar, but it was the best they could hope for presently. As they leaned into each other, physically and mentally, the bridge of the bond seemed to melt away, coming closer to one being.

"Aww," Rake said. "Is there anything more touching than the intensity of a young bond? Or anything more likely to bring up my dinner?" When no one rose to his bait, Rake shrugged it off and stretched out his limbs and tail. "Yes, I definitely preferred it when the two of you were deferential. Yes, Rake. How can we help, Rake? Would you like your feet rubbed, Rake? Well, you don't owe me anymore, I suppose, but it was good while it lasted."

Holt frowned, confused. "We still respect you, Rake. We're just a little less in awe."

Rake snorted.

A thought occurred to Holt. "Are you worried that Ash and I won't assist you now we saved your life in turn? You don't need a favor to call upon for that."

"So long as there is trust, there is friendship," Ash said.

"Trust is a rare currency," Osric said.

"Not between us," Holt said, looking around the group. "What do any of us have to gain from secrets now?"

Despite Holt's efforts, Rake bit his lip. "You will still help me?"

"Don't lie to us, and we will," Holt said.

"If we can, I should be honored to, Master Rake," Ash said.

Relief visibly broke across Rake's face.

"No more secrets," he affirmed. "Though I'm afraid it might be too late for me now." He clutched again at his chest. "I've always felt Elya as a beat in my soul, like the bond used to beat. It's grown fainter over the years, but during my *time* with Thrall, it ceased completely. And has yet to return."

So that was what Rake meant when he said he needed to recover, Holt thought.

"It might still return," Holt said. "Maybe you just need more time."

"Maybe," Rake said. "Yet more than ever, my hope lies in you two succeeding where I failed. If you do, I might at last understand what went wrong and how to correct it. And if you succeed, then perhaps your own power will be great enough to assist me."

"Don't exaggerate," Aberanth said. *"No rider could ever match or best an Elder's power."*

"It sounds farfetched, and I'd wager you're correct, Aberanth, but as no one has succeeded before, we just don't know. Holt, Ash," he added, serious now. "I tried to break through to a rank beyond Lord."

"You mean to become a Paragon?" Holt asked.

"Not quite," Rake said. "Paragons are still, in practice, Lords with bonds that will not fray. The Paragons are merely the greatest of the Lords, elders of the riders who have forged their dragon's cores to heights beyond what any fresh Lord could dream of. What I sought lay beyond even that."

"I've never heard of any such rider," Osric said.

"Because none have managed it," Rake said. "Thrall's rider attempted it, and that was his downfall. The great snake told me himself. It's why he was so interested in interrogating me, hopeful that I could reveal knowledge of it to him. If only I could."

"I still don't see how it's possible," Holt said. "How could a rider gain more power than full access to their dragon's core? You could keep Forging the core, but Paragons can do that."

"They can," Rake said. "But what they lack is access to a second core. Their own core. I'm talking about the rider at last becoming a being of magic as well. A core in the rider as well as the dragon. Two cores, whereby both of you might Forge each other's power. It would be more than just double your strength, and not even the Elders could know what effect that would have on your mote channels. No one can conceive of the potential."

"My own core?" Holt said in wonder.

Would such a thing really be possible?

Osric, on the other hand, seemed trapped somewhere between anxiety and disgust. "Magic is a plague," Osric said. "I say it's well that no rider has achieved what you seek. There is such a thing as too much power."

"You will feel differently about her power," Rake said, nodding to the sleeping black dragon.

Osric did not answer but pulled his cloak tighter around himself and seemed to shrink within it. Rake redoubled his attention on Holt and Ash, his voice elevating in his eagerness.

"Elya and I had a bond like no other. Not the then Paragons. Nor any of my fellow Lords. I was sure we could succeed. It almost worked. A new core gathered inside me, but then something went wrong. Our bond collapsed and dragged our souls crashing into one.

For whatever reason, I, or what was my human side, remained conscious while Elya shrank. Our cores overlap even now, their songs in discord and so hidden from prying eyes. My ability to go undetected is purely accidental. Whatever I am, it is a mistake. If you're willing to follow me, I can't promise that things will work out. There is every chance you'll end up like me. Or dead. But your bond is the purest I've felt since my own. If you cannot succeed, I fear no one can. Know that the path we'll walk is beyond all knowledge."

It was a lot to take in, to say the least. Holt stared at Rake for what felt like hours. He and Ash already had a heavy burden on their shoulders. Given the power set against them, they needed as much of their own, on their own terms, as they could get. What Rake offered sounded like just what they needed – perhaps too much power, as Osric warned. Too good to be true, in many ways, although Holt sensed no lie in Rake.

Ash listened to Rake's heart, and that confirmed it. Rake believed wholeheartedly in what he said and held nothing back.

"Well," Holt began, "we have a long way to go until we reach Lord, never mind what lies beyond."

Rake clapped his hands together, grinning broadly.

"Seems to me there's no time like the present. Let's begin."

Epilogue – Crimson Dawn

Two Months Later

Talia toiled at the forge. She drew the crucible from the oven and the clay glowed a golden yellow. The incredible temperature of the ingot inside called to her like a moth to the flame. Fresh waves of raw motes rolled into the conflagration of Pyra's core.

"This attempt will surely be the one," Pyra said.

Talia hoped so. The royal smith had never worked with dragon-steel and knew nothing of its making. Every rider with her had made it, but most had only crafted one weapon in their life. Recalling the process in every exacting detail was a work in progress.

She placed the radiant pot on the anvil and cracked the clay open with her hammer. The ingot inside already cooled, dimming to a burning orange. The moment of truth would be now. She struck the ingot with her hammer.

Sparks flew high and far, causing the blacksmith to step back.

"I am sorry, Majesty," said the smith. "There must be something we are missing."

Sparks meant the ingot was not pure. The steel had to be flawless before the forge welding.

Talia sighed, put down her tongs, and wiped the sweat from her brow. "We'll try again. Pyra, call the riders."

She had managed to place the iron, the charcoal, and the sand into another crucible by the time the riders arrived. Ethel was there along with the Fire Ascendant and Mystic Champion, who held the best recollections of their own forging.

"We're missing something," Talia told them.

It was the Fire Ascendant who recalled a shard of glass had to be added, or was it glass instead of sand? At least resources were not what they lacked. Talia tried both. Using only glass proved disastrous.

The next day she and Pyra worked the bellows again. The royal smiths had done exemplary work in adapting a forge for a dragon to assist with. Hours upon hours were spent maintaining the furnace at an exact temperature. Where generating enough heat for crucible steel was often the concern, for fire riders the issue lay in not overpowering the hearth and destroying the whole forge.

Another evening descended. Talia picked up the tongs, ready to draw another crucible from the fire. This one included both sand and a shard of glass.

Before she reached in for it, Drefan Harroway and a cohort of officers arrived.

"You're back," Talia said, a little dazed. No one had informed her.

"I insisted I come to you in person immediately," Harroway said. "All Risalian and Athran forces have pulled back from the border. I thought it safe enough to return."

A weight lifted from her shoulders.

"I much prefer it when you bear good news," Talia said. "And you're just in time to see dragon-steel in the making."

She withdrew the glowing pot from the hearth.

"*This one,*" Pyra said, so fierce as if to scare the metal into purity.

Talia cracked the clay, extracted the ingot, and struck the steel. No sparks. Not even a flicker. It was pure.

The royal smith blinked through tiredness and gazed at the ingot.

All his apprentices did the same, and Talia allowed them each to strike the cooling steel so they could test for themselves.

"Wonderful," said the smith. "The heat you both can produce... far greater than anything... just wonderful," he ended. Sparks appeared in his eyes, and Talia was pleased to see him and his apprentices so in awe.

She wondered how the Artisan Smith at Falcaer would react to her new creation. Would he think it wonderful, or would he think it unsightly?

The next morning, she returned early, ready to flatten out the ingot into a bar. She struck the metal delicately, as though teasing it. Hours rolled by.

Lady Elvina, the Mistress of Coin, came to tell her of the proposed trade that would keep Brenin and the Skarls sweet. The coast of Feorlen's western peninsula held dangerous waters. To avoid these routes, goods could be brought upriver to Sidastra and hauled overland to Port Bolca before heading safely for the Skarl Empire. Feorlen would take no fee on the goods but would benefit indirectly from the increased traffic. A long-term strategy, Elvina explained, but one she approved of. Prince Fynn, she said, had been most helpful in explaining the Empire's economic concerns. Talia was glad for that, for she found the topic confusing and trusted Elvina to trust his judgment. At least the switch to Fynn seemed to be paying off.

Hearing of things going right was a welcome change. And though creating the bar took all day, it felt soothing and meditative to focus so single-mindedly upon a repetitive task. The cherry-red heat of the ingot was pleasing to her, and the clink-tap of the hammer falls were light like the windchimes of Midbell.

With the bar made, Talia rested. Forge welding was best done in dim light so the blacksmith could help judge the temperature of the metal. Where blacksmiths might work indoors to achieve this, riders worked outside so their dragon could be close even when they were no longer required for the bellows. Talia would become a creature of the night, like Ash and Holt, until the dragon-steel was complete.

In the day, she rested. That first night she pushed to twelve folds.

Crumbs of black, brittle soot seeped from the hot metal, evidence of the natural hardness leaving the steel. Magic had to be pushed in to replace it. Naked flames swirled around her hammer as she pounded motes in and trapped them under the pressure and heat of folding. At dawn, she retired.

The second day she slept through until twilight. When she arrived in the forge, her mother, Prince Fynn, Harroway, Elvina, Ethel, various members of her household, a few Skarls, and some of her fellow riders were already present. Before Talia could even ask, her mother had curtsied to her, kissed her on each cheek and wished her a happy birthday.

"You forgot, didn't you?" Felice said.

"I had," Talia said, half-laughing, surprised at how readily she had forgotten an occasion that used to mean so much. "Your guests have cake, but the palace cook has prepared something special for you."

This something special turned out to be a dark cocoa slice spiced with red chilies.

Talia felt in two minds. She wanted to continue with the steel.

"Enjoy this night for a while," Pyra urged her. *"They will sleep eventually."*

So Talia did, and as she ate her spicy treat, the others ate sweet cake, and the wine flowed. Prince Fynn kept an unusual distance, but in time he took up his lute and offered her a song.

"This is a name day song from my homeland," he said. As he played, the Skarls edged in closer, perhaps chaperons of a sort, though a birthday song seemed not to count as wooing any present maidens.

When at last they retired and Talia bid them goodnight, she returned to her steel in high spirits. The royal smith remained to assist her, his cheeks rosy and his eyes glazed from the wine. Talia bid him rest once she was confident about judging the temperature and timing, and despite the lateness in starting, she drove to a fitting eighteen folds.

Her rest was cut short that next day. The Mistress of Embassy had need of her to meet with the Brenin ambassador. This too was a cheerful meeting. The ambassador delivered letters from her uncle Roland for both her and her mother together with news that the remaining pockets of scourge in the realm were being taken care of. Terms of an alliance were discussed. All seemed in place. No ink or wax were yet put to parchment, but that would come in time.

Talia shook the ambassador's hand and begged him to follow her down to the forge.

"Strike the steel," she said when the metal glowed hot, "I wish a piece of Brenin to be in it."

She took to this notion, and from then on had others strike the steel as well. Her victories, her defeats – all should be within it. For as much as had been achieved, daunting tasks loomed mountainous before her.

Almost all her attention and effort had gone into the immediate consequences of assuming the throne to the neglect of many issues at home. The population was still in disarray from the incursion and its aftermath, warned the Master of Roles. She took in all he had to say and then offered him the hammer. Old Hubbard could not strike hard, but he did strike firm, and by coincidence more burnt carbon crusted the edge of the steel when he did so. She wiped it clean and pressed more magic in.

Geoff Horndown, Master of State, discussed at length the ongoing reconstruction in the city and the kingdom at large. Victuals and food moving into winter would not be so dire now the threat of war was gone, though Athra's remaining restrictions may yet bite. With so many new riders and their dragons to consider, his tone was far from merry. At least when he picked up the hammer, he swung it with such enthusiasm as to almost be a rider himself.

They came one by one, all her councilors, the riders who had abandoned Falcaer for her madness, Eadwulf too, and her mother came often.

Yet no word came from Holt or Ash, nor from the drakes the West Warden sent east to investigate. Turro the emerald brought her tidings that Windshear Hold lay cold and empty, yet of Rake, Ash, or even

Thrall, there was no sign. None of the flight seemed to know when their Elder would return.

Tendrils of foreboding crept up Talia's spine, but with the need to channel fire and hammer steel, that ice was kept away from her heart. For now. Turro blew lightly on the metal as she folded for the last time that day.

She worried Osric and her night phantoms might return after speaking with Turro. To her surprise she slept well, though later, when her mother came to visit her at the forge, she could not help but ask, "Did you hate Osric?"

This time, her mother did not weasel away from the issue.

"I do not think I hated him, Talia. I found him unnerving often, and I know my friends and my handmaids did as well. But I think the person who hated Osric most of all... was Osric."

Talia chewed on this as she folded and beat the metal down. It proved harder now to meld each fold, but that only meant she was drawing close to the end.

"The Twinblades told me an interesting story," Talia said, and she explained about the desert girl who they claimed Osric had fallen in love with.

The surprise on her mother's face was genuine. "I knew nothing of this. Osric and a tribe girl?"

"The daughter of a chieftain," Talia added.

Felice fluttered through half-formed words before reaching her final thought. "It's a great shame, if true. Perhaps if I... no, none of us knew how to reach through to him back then... though perhaps we should have tried harder. I was younger than you are now when I came to court here," she added, a little defensively. "So young. So besotted with your father. I laughed and went along with all Godric said of him and did to him, for I did not like him. I heard brothers often fought but meant little by it."

They parted from that meeting somberly. Osric's fate remained unknown, and Talia accepted now that she had never truly known him, not fully, not enough to love or condemn him. If he did come back whole and himself and he could explain, then she would be his little soldier again. If not, she did not hold herself to the same account. His fate was his own, just as she created hers even now.

All of this, whether spoken, thought, or brooded in the quiet hours, she shared with Pyra. Pyra, for her part, listened well, for hours at a time.

As she neared completion, she could feel Pyra's magic slipping with ease into the metal until she could channel magic through it as readily as her own blade. Under the smith's eager eye, she worked it one final time into the shape of a thick band.

A quench tank had been prepared for her, filled with hot water instead of cold. She fed the metal into the tank and the water evaporated in a torrent of steam. Flames issued from the band as though it had been plunged into oil, a last growl before turning tame.

The dragon-steel was complete.

The dragon bond pushed its boundaries out, widening and thickening at its borders.

"I knew we could do great things," Pyra purred.

Though sore and tired from the labor, Talia beamed. She supposed they had done great things together. Killed a Lord. Fought a Scourge Queen. Worked with an Elder. Fought beside a Wild Flight. Broken their oath to save a kingdom and created a new one to save it. Defied the Paragons. Gathered riders for a new sort of Order, dragon riders who would take the fight back to the scourge. None before them had done this, and given the stakes, none would again if they failed.

Pyra picked a loose scale from her chest. Talia did not need to sharpen the metal as for a weapon, but she did rub off the grit and roughness, allowing it to shine pearl smooth. Her blade had turned out red where Pyra was purple. This band was closer to Pyra's color, though it retained a reddish hue throughout.

The dragon-steel was at last a crown.

Talia placed the crown upon her brow. A perfect fit. Though made of heavy metal, it felt more comfortable than soft fur, as though it were an extension of herself. When she set it ablaze, the flames flickered warm and reassuring, and her dragon bond changed as thoroughly as the ore inside the forge.

When she'd become an Ascendant, it had come with its pains. A body made stronger through magic was not lightly felt. This time it felt smooth, as though cords loosened at every limb. This is how it should always have felt. Part fire and part flesh.

A year ago, she'd been an Ascendant and a former princess.

Now, Talia stood a Red Queen and a Champion of Fire.

Afterword

Thank you for reading Unbound! I'm sure I said Ascendant was hard but this was even harder! Hopefully that means it is even better. If you enjoyed it, please consider leaving me a review on Amazon or Goodreads. It need not be long, only a couple of lines. Reviews are incredibly helpful to authors in getting Amazon to recommend their book to other readers.

If you'd like to read more about this world you can get a FREE novella about Brode and his mission with Silas that went so terribly wrong by signing up to my mailing list at https://www.michaelrmiller. co.uk/signup

Just pop in your email and the story will be sent to you. Once you're on my newsletter you'll also get updates on future books in the series as well as any promotions or giveaways.

If you'd like more then consider joining my Discord server to chat to me and like minded readers here https://discord.gg/C7zEJXgFSc

Once again thank you for reading Unbound!
Michael R. Miller

Acknowledgments

Few books are created in isolation. *Unbound* is no exception.

First and foremost, I am especially thankful for the developmental editing support of my friend and colleague Brook Aspden (a co-director of Portal Books and author of *Gamified*). Songs of Chaos would not be the series it is without Brook's aid in vetting ideas and acting as a sound board to help me clarify everything from the character arcs to intricate details of the magic system.

Others helped me in this regard too including Taran Matharu (author of *Summoner* and *The Chosen*), Neil Atkinson, my parents Walter and Linda Miller, and my partner Pegah Adaskar (yes that's where Paragon Adaskar got his name from!).

A special mention goes to Jonathan Smidt (author of the *Elemental Dungeon* series and *Dungeon Core Online*) for guiding me toward the research resources for all the blacksmithing in *Unbound*. Countless messages and questions helped to hone the system by which dragon-steel is made. I'm particularly proud of this piece of world building but it would not what it is without Jonathan's insights as a blacksmith.

Thank you to the copy editor for *Unbound*, Anthony Wright (author of *Caesar's Shadow*) for wading through my various messes and the difficult task of ensuring this UK author got everything correct in writing in US English. Any remaining errors are, of course, my own.

To my advanced reading team for catching the final typos and silly mistakes prior to release, and for helping to review and promote the book at launch. You guys are an integral part of the process!

Randy Vargas did an incredible job creating the cover art. His portfolio can be found on his website here https://vargasni.com/

Thanks again to Peter Kenny for his stunning narration. I still find it surreal to hear him reading these stories. I cannot imagine the voices any other way now, and they were in my head as I wrote *Unbound*.

Along with Peter, we mustn't forget the work of ID Audio and the team there for their editing and QA work on the audiobook. Everything is taken care of without me ever having to worry over this.

And, as always, thank you reader! Without you, the series wouldn't be. Without you, I would not be allowed to write about dragon riders and call it a job. Without you, I wouldn't be able to share in these cool and, hopefully, inspiring ideas. I hope Songs of Chaos has been inspiring so far, and I'm as eager as you are to see where things go next!

Best wishes to all and, remember, sometimes the world needs a little chaos....

Michael R. Miller